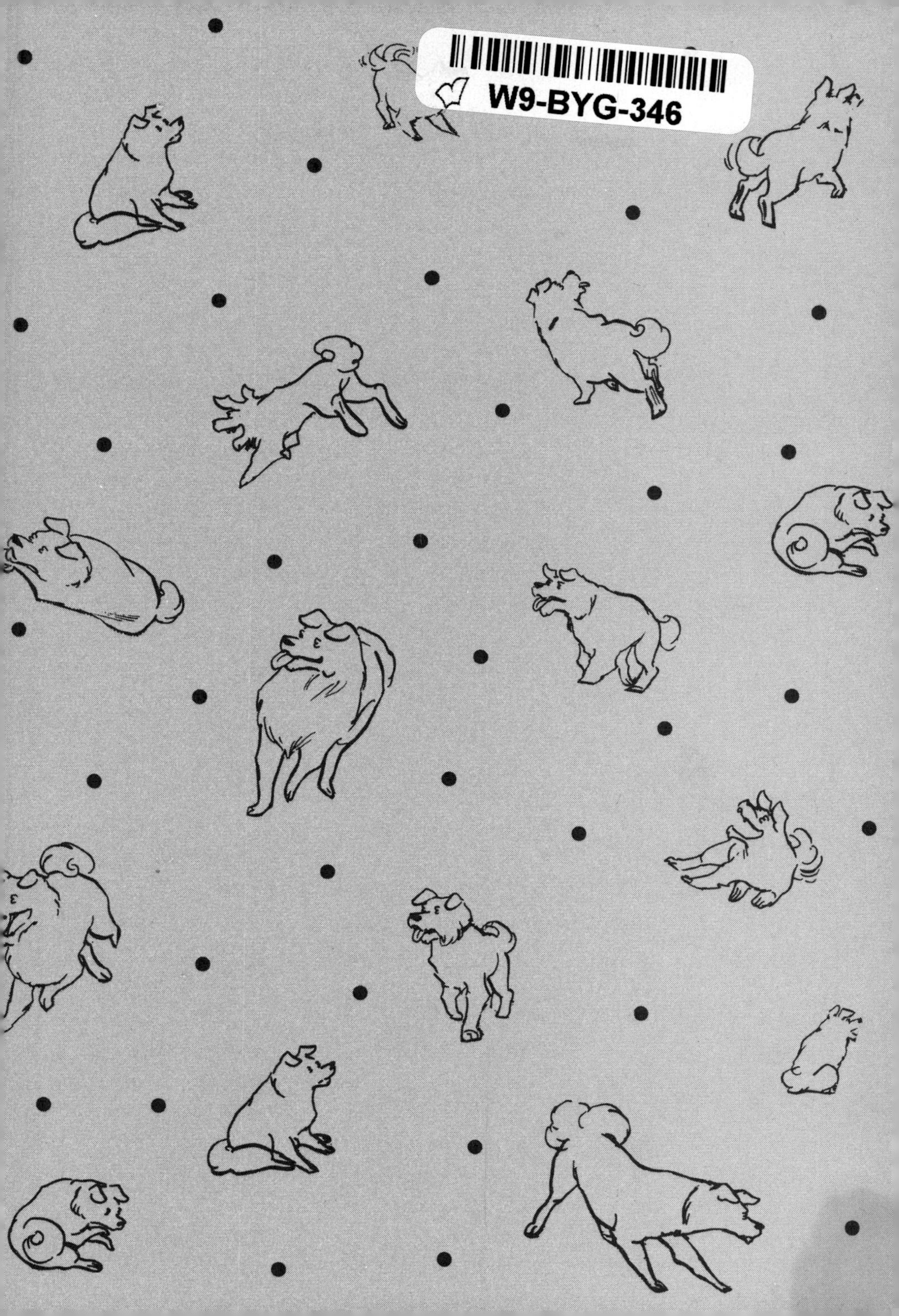

VIZ GRAPHIC NOVEL

MAISON IKKOKU™
HOME SWEET HOME

STORY AND ART BY
RUMIKO TAKAHASHI

CONTENTS

This volume contains MAISON IKKOKU PART THREE issues #1 through #6 in their entirety.

STORY AND ART BY RUMIKO TAKAHASHI

English Adaptation/Gerard Jones & Toshifumi Yoshida & Mari Morimoto
Touch-Up Art & Lettering/Wayne Truman
Cover Design/Viz Graphics
Editor/Trish Ledoux
Assistant Editors/Annette Roman & Toshifumi Yoshida

Managing Editor/Satoru Fujii
Executive Editor/Seiji Horibuchi
Publisher/Keizo Inoue

© 1995 Rumiko Takahashi/Shogakukan, Inc. MAISON IKKOKU is a trademark of Viz Communications, Inc. All rights reserved. No unauthorized reproduction allowed. The stories, characters, and incidents mentioned in this publication are entirely fictional.

Printed in Canada

Published by Viz Communications, Inc.
P.O. Box 77010 • San Francisco, CA 94107

10 9 8 7 6 5 4 3 2 1
First Printing, September 1995

Part One

The Black Widow's Bite

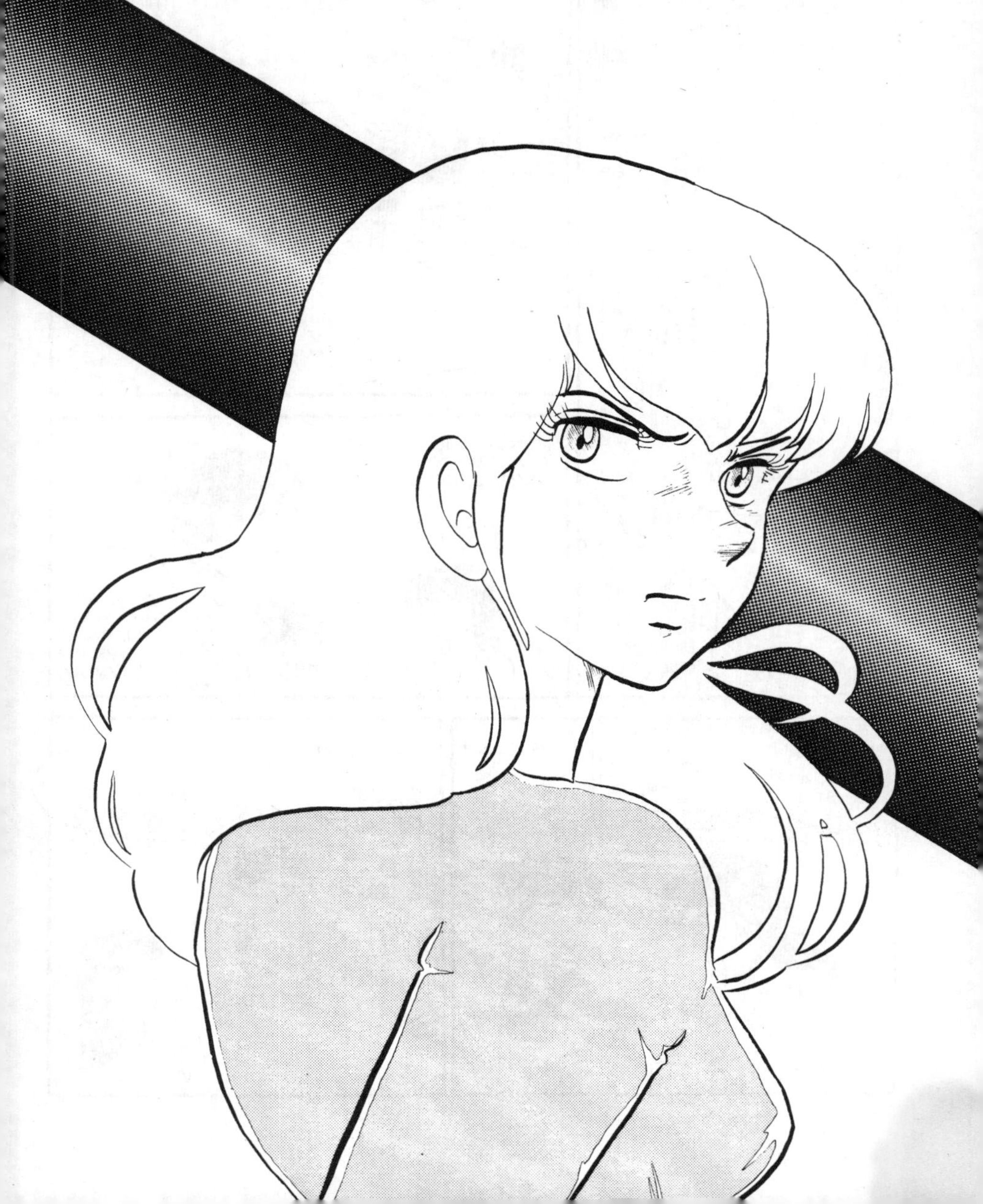

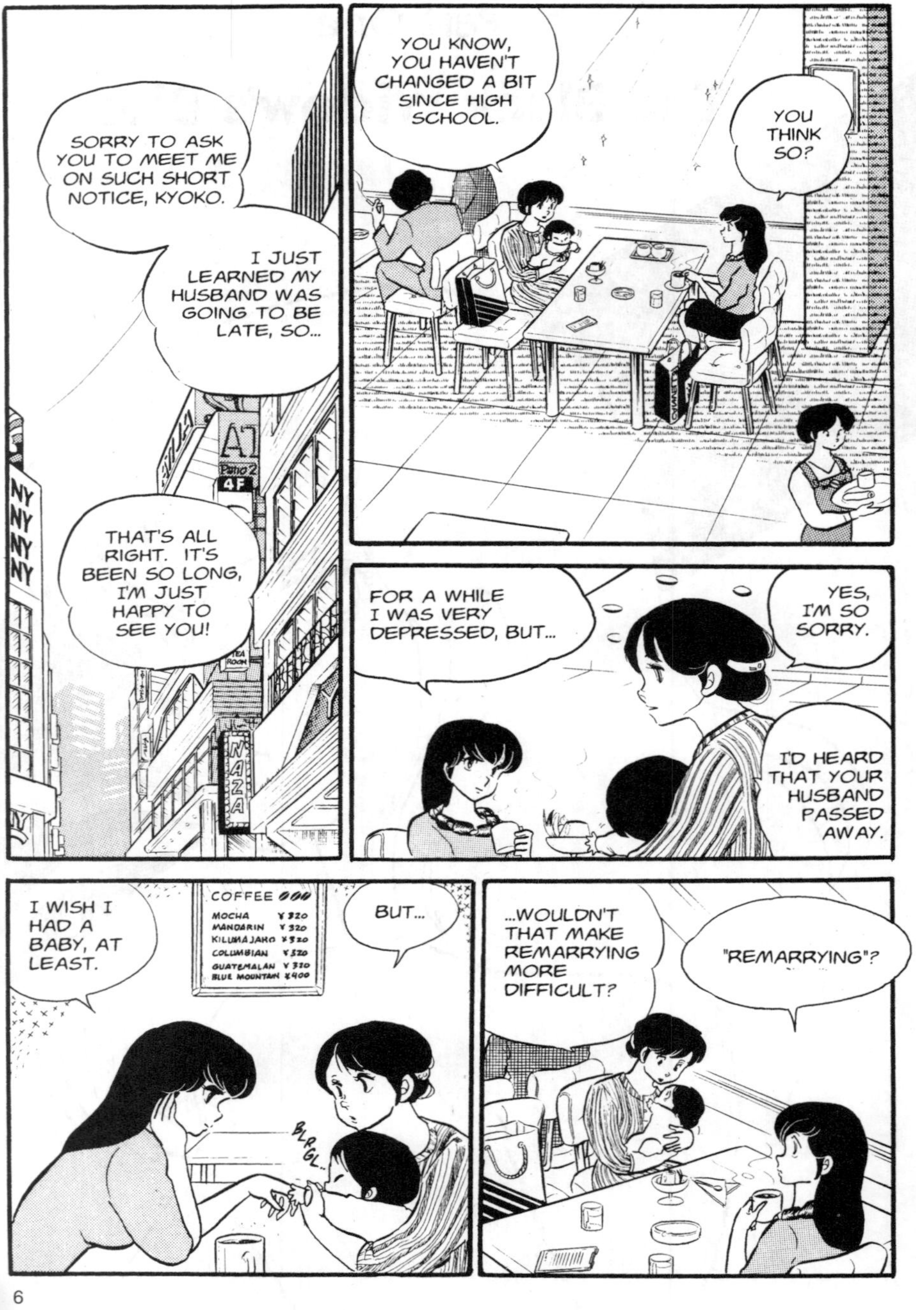
SORRY TO ASK YOU TO MEET ME ON SUCH SHORT NOTICE, KYOKO.
I JUST LEARNED MY HUSBAND WAS GOING TO BE LATE, SO...
Patio 2
4F
THAT'S ALL RIGHT. IT'S BEEN SO LONG, I'M JUST HAPPY TO SEE YOU!
TEA ROOM
NAZA
YOU KNOW, YOU HAVEN'T CHANGED A BIT SINCE HIGH SCHOOL.
YOU THINK SO?
FOR A WHILE I WAS VERY DEPRESSED, BUT...
YES, I'M SO SORRY.
I'D HEARD THAT YOUR HUSBAND PASSED AWAY.
I WISH I HAD A BABY, AT LEAST.
COFFEE
MOCHA ¥320
MANDARIN ¥320
KILIMANJARO ¥320
COLUMBIAN ¥320
GUATEMALAN ¥320
BLUE MOUNTAIN ¥400
BUT...
BLRGL...
...WOULDN'T THAT MAKE REMARRYING MORE DIFFICULT?
"REMARRYING"?

WELL, YOU DON'T PLAN ON SPENDING THE REST OF YOUR LIFE ALONE, DO YOU?

I MEAN, YOU'RE YOUNG NOW, BUT...

I SEE WHAT YOU MEAN.

YOU MUST HAVE MEN AFTER YOU, RIGHT?

WELL... I GUESS SO...

STILL, I CAN'T SEEM TO LET SOME THINGS GO.

KNOWING YOU, I'M AFRAID I'M NOT THAT SURPRISED.

YOU REALLY SHOULD START PLANNING AHEAD, THOUGH.

YES... YES... BUT...

WHAT'S GONE IS GONE. AND EVEN YOUR MEMORIES OF HIM WILL FADE SOMEDAY.

AND THERE'S NO GUARANTEE THAT THE MEN WHO ARE AFTER YOU NOW WILL WAIT, IS THERE?

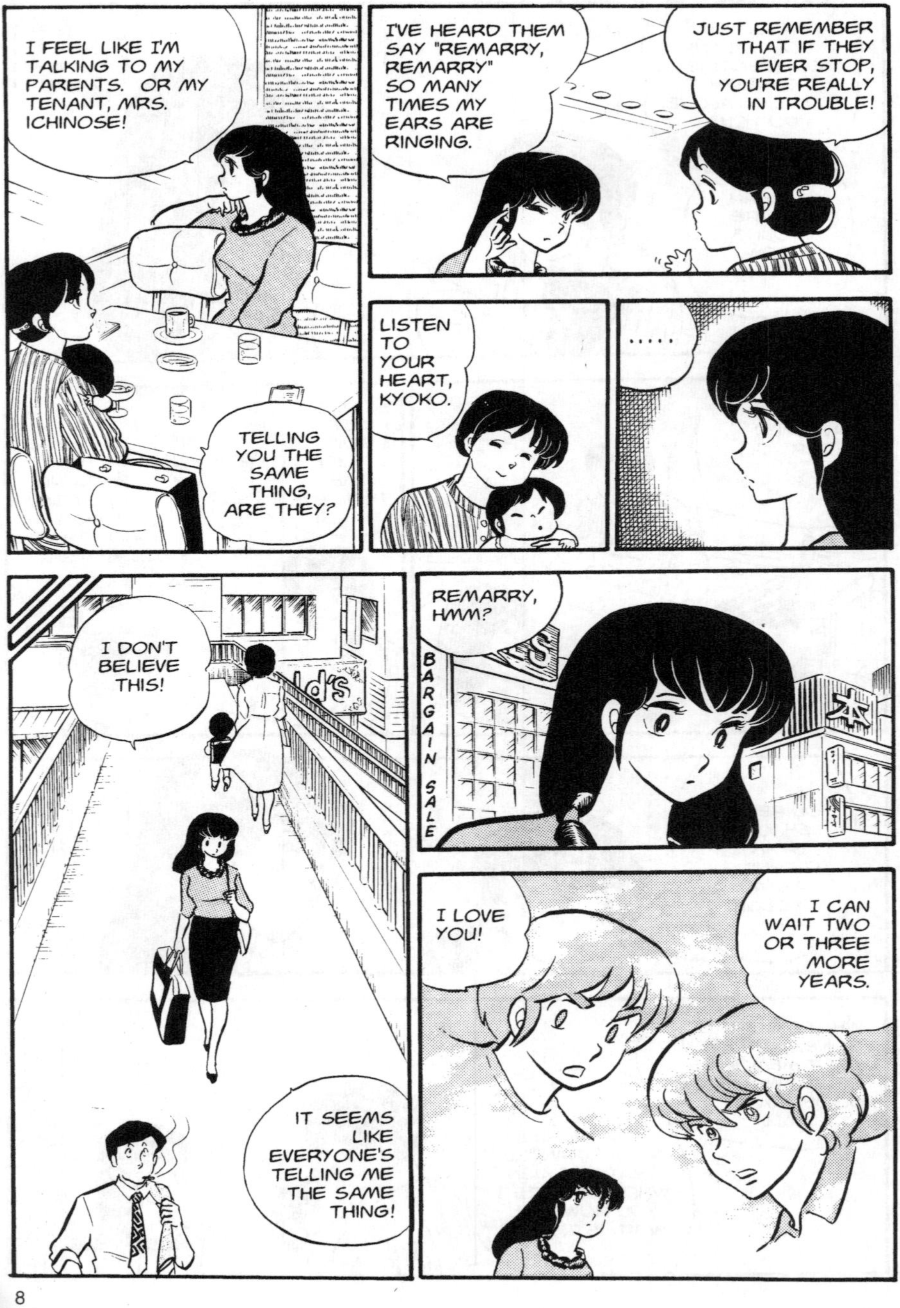
I FEEL LIKE I'M TALKING TO MY PARENTS. OR MY TENANT, MRS. ICHINOSE!
TELLING YOU THE SAME THING, ARE THEY?
I'VE HEARD THEM SAY "REMARRY, REMARRY" SO MANY TIMES MY EARS ARE RINGING.
JUST REMEMBER THAT IF THEY EVER STOP, YOU'RE REALLY IN TROUBLE!
LISTEN TO YOUR HEART, KYOKO.
.....
I DON'T BELIEVE THIS!
IT SEEMS LIKE EVERYONE'S TELLING ME THE SAME THING!
REMARRY, HMM?
BARGAIN SALE
I LOVE YOU!
I CAN WAIT TWO OR THREE MORE YEARS.

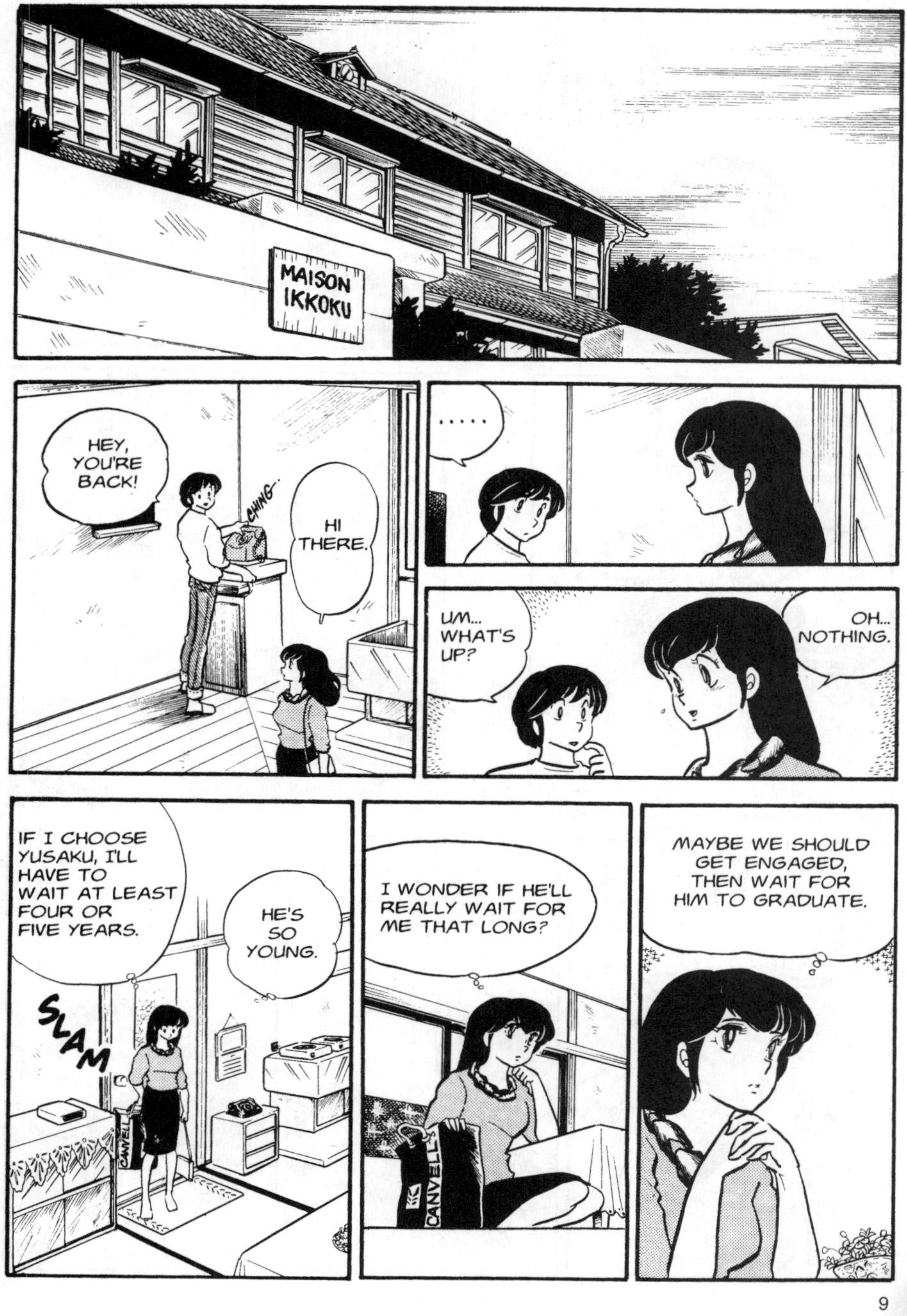
MAISON IKKOKU
HEY, YOU'RE BACK!
CHING
HI THERE.
.....
UM... WHAT'S UP?
OH... NOTHING.
IF I CHOOSE YUSAKU, I'LL HAVE TO WAIT AT LEAST FOUR OR FIVE YEARS.
HE'S SO YOUNG.
SLAM
CANVELL
I WONDER IF HE'LL REALLY WAIT FOR ME THAT LONG?
CANVELL
MAYBE WE SHOULD GET ENGAGED, THEN WAIT FOR HIM TO GRADUATE.

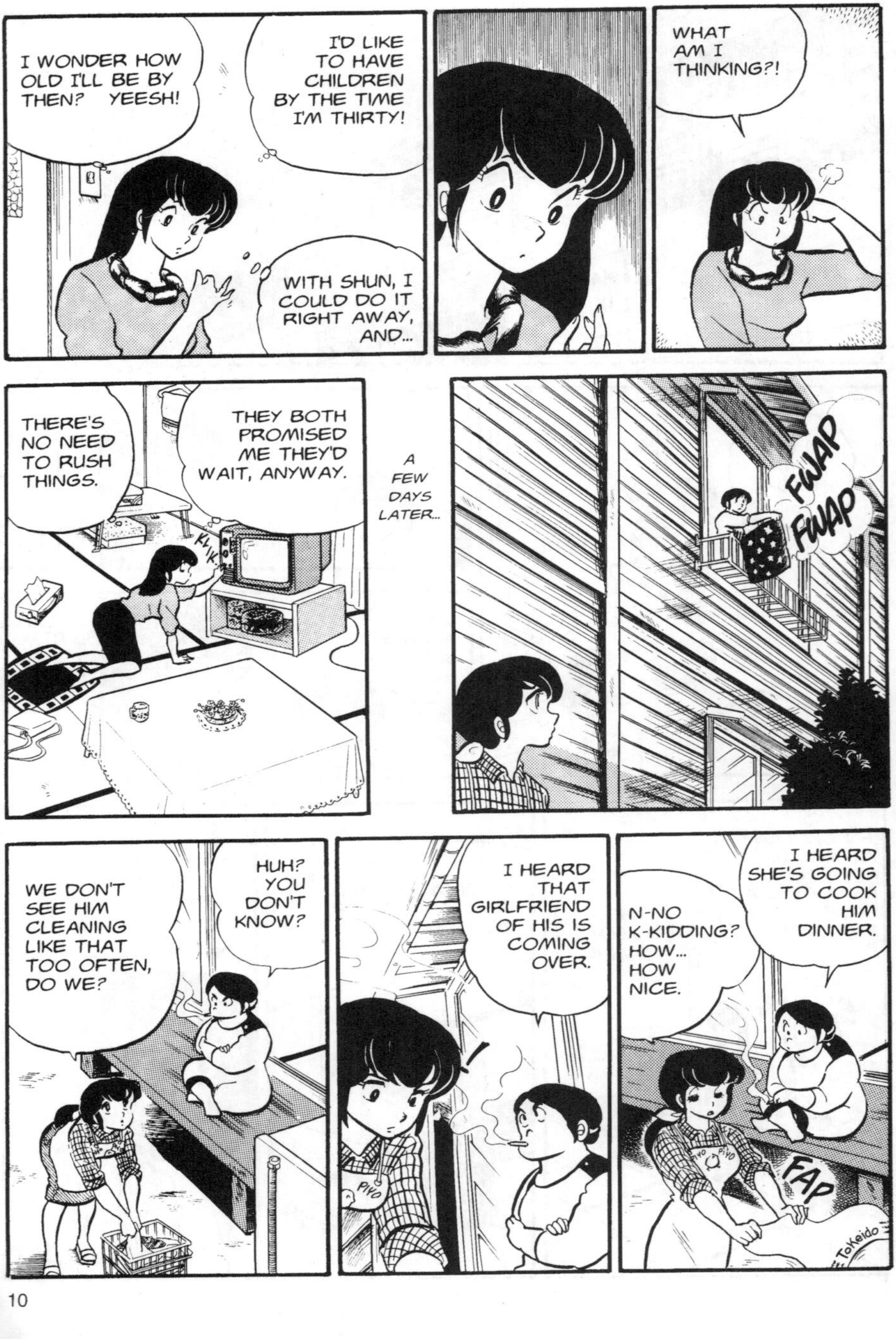
I WONDER HOW OLD I'LL BE BY THEN? YEESH!
I'D LIKE TO HAVE CHILDREN BY THE TIME I'M THIRTY!
WITH SHUN, I COULD DO IT RIGHT AWAY, AND...
WHAT AM I THINKING?!
THERE'S NO NEED TO RUSH THINGS.
THEY BOTH PROMISED ME THEY'D WAIT, ANYWAY.
KLIK
A FEW DAYS LATER...
FWAP
FWAP
WE DON'T SEE HIM CLEANING LIKE THAT TOO OFTEN, DO WE?
HUH? YOU DON'T KNOW?
I HEARD THAT GIRLFRIEND OF HIS IS COMING OVER.
PIYO
N-NO K-KIDDING? HOW... HOW NICE.
I HEARD SHE'S GOING TO COOK HIM DINNER.
PIYO PIYO
FAP

SHE EVEN OFFERED TO DO HIS LAUNDRY, BUT BELIEVE IT OR NOT...

...HE SAID HE COULD HANDLE IT!

TO THINK THAT EVEN AN UNRELIABLE KID LIKE THAT CAN FIND A GIRL TO TAKE CARE OF HIM.

WELL, HE CERTAINLY HAS A LOT OF NERVE!

HOW'S THAT?

I MEAN...BRAGGING ABOUT WHAT THIS GIRL WILL DO FOR HIM!

HE DIDN'T SAY A WORD.

. . . . .

BUT...

I CAN HEAR HIM ON THE PHONE FROM MY ROOM.

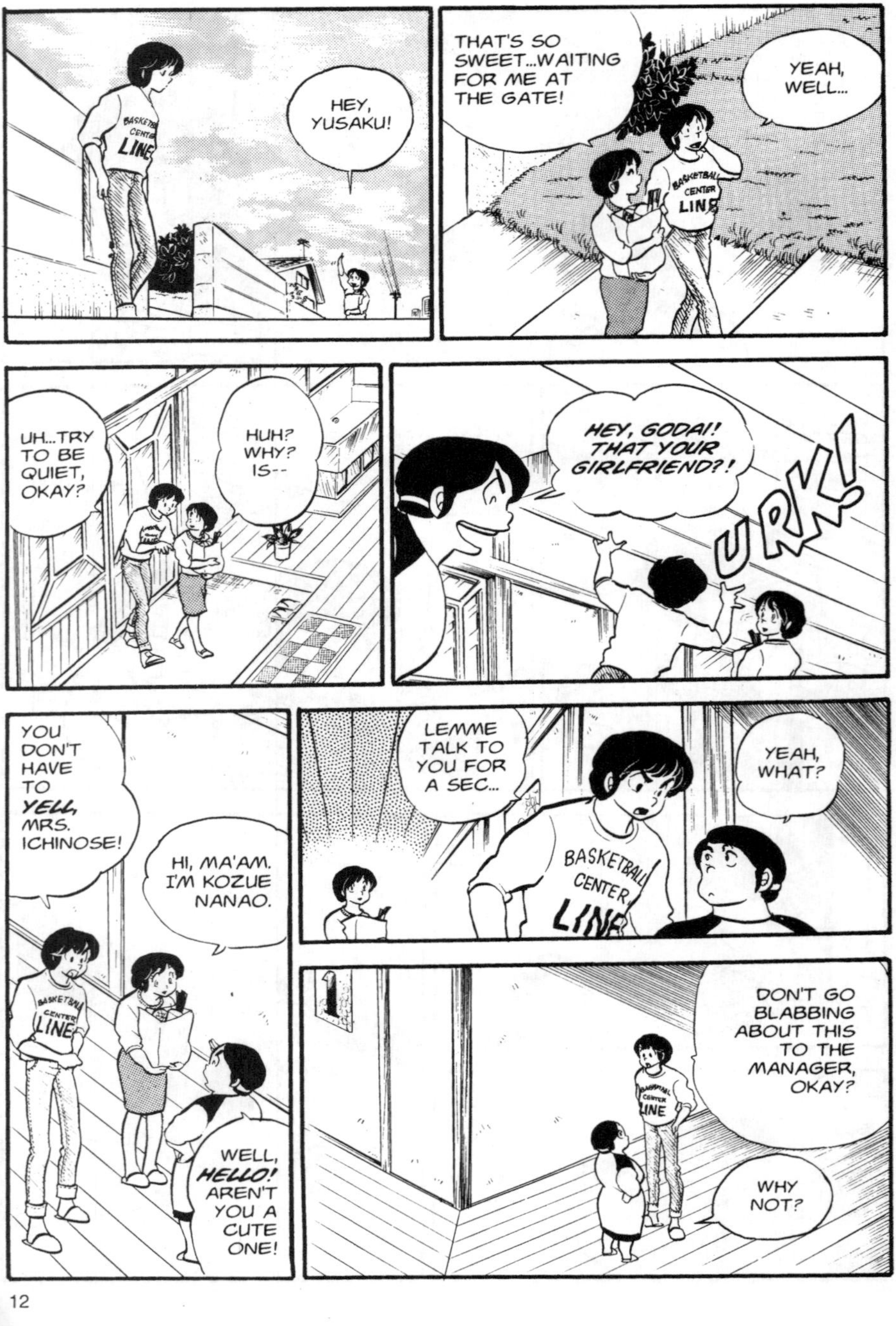
HEY, YUSAKU!
THAT'S SO SWEET...WAITING FOR ME AT THE GATE!
YEAH, WELL...
UH...TRY TO BE QUIET, OKAY?
HUH? WHY? IS--
HEY, GODAI! THAT YOUR GIRLFRIEND?!
URK!
YOU DON'T HAVE TO YELL, MRS. ICHINOSE!
HI, MA'AM. I'M KOZUE NANAO.
WELL, HELLO! AREN'T YOU A CUTE ONE!
LEMME TALK TO YOU FOR A SEC...
YEAH, WHAT?
DON'T GO BLABBING ABOUT THIS TO THE MANAGER, OKAY?
WHY NOT?

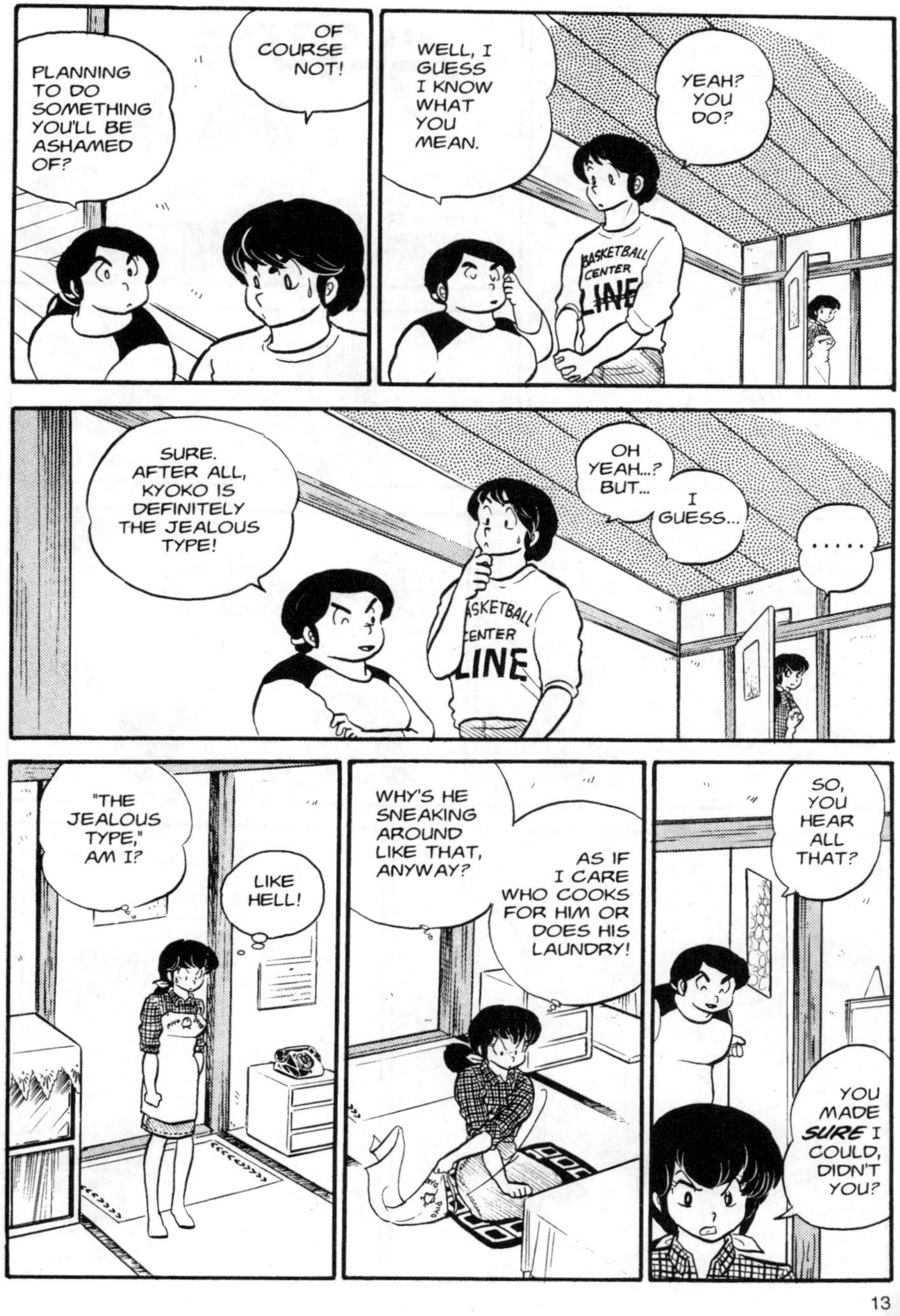
PLANNING TO DO SOMETHING YOU'LL BE ASHAMED OF?
OF COURSE NOT!
WELL, I GUESS I KNOW WHAT YOU MEAN.
YEAH? YOU DO?
BASKETBALL CENTER LINE
SURE. AFTER ALL, KYOKO IS DEFINITELY THE JEALOUS TYPE!
OH YEAH...? BUT...
I GUESS...
.....
BASKETBALL CENTER LINE
"THE JEALOUS TYPE," AM I?
LIKE HELL!
WHY'S HE SNEAKING AROUND LIKE THAT, ANYWAY?
AS IF I CARE WHO COOKS FOR HIM OR DOES HIS LAUNDRY!
SO, YOU HEAR ALL THAT?
YOU MADE SURE I COULD, DIDN'T YOU?

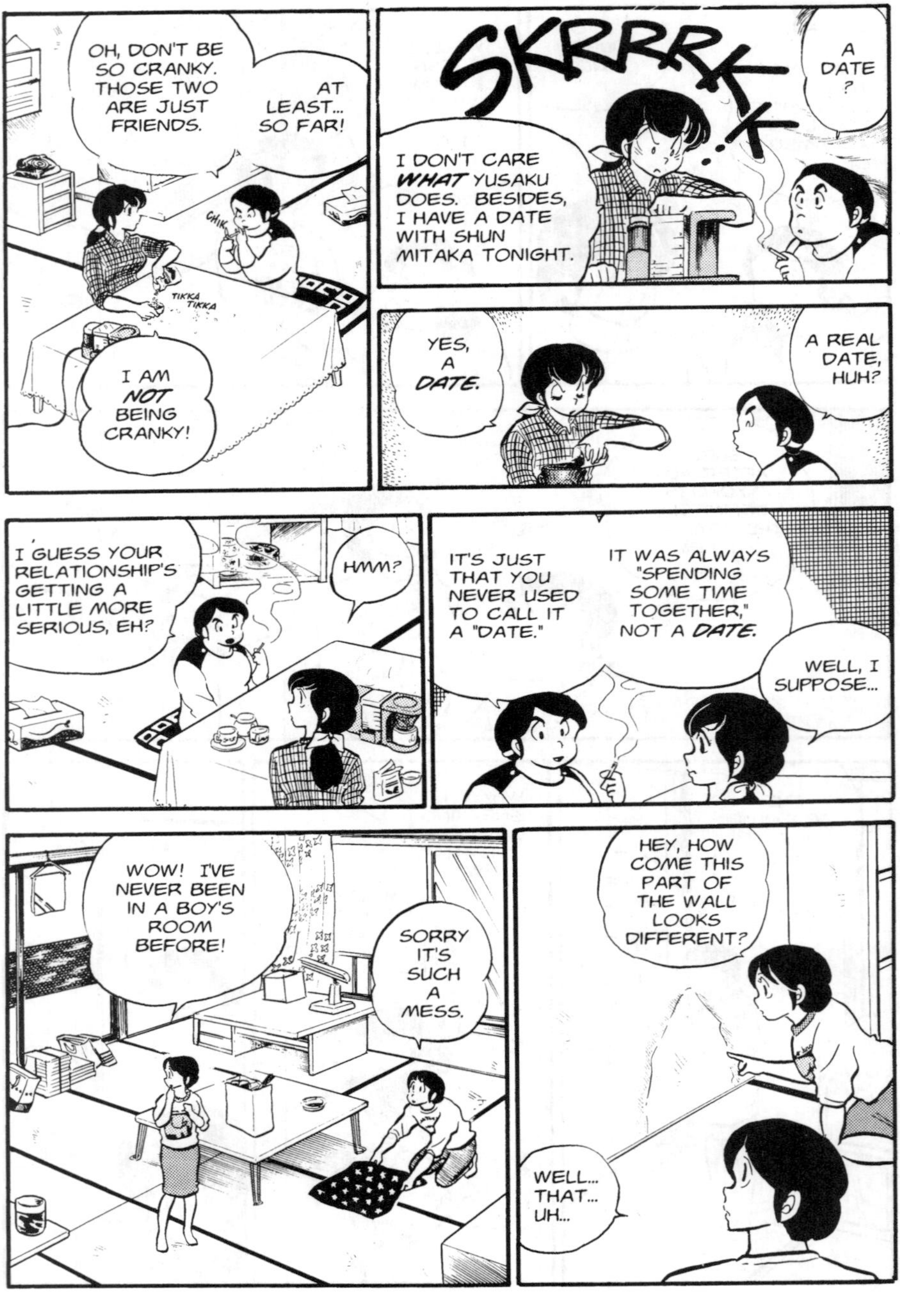
OH, DON'T BE SO CRANKY. THOSE TWO ARE JUST FRIENDS.
AT LEAST... SO FAR!
CHIK
TIKKA TIKKA
I AM NOT BEING CRANKY!
SKRRRKK
I DON'T CARE WHAT YUSAKU DOES. BESIDES, I HAVE A DATE WITH SHUN MITAKA TONIGHT.
A DATE?
YES, A DATE.
A REAL DATE, HUH?
I GUESS YOUR RELATIONSHIP'S GETTING A LITTLE MORE SERIOUS, EH?
HMM?
IT'S JUST THAT YOU NEVER USED TO CALL IT A "DATE."
IT WAS ALWAYS "SPENDING SOME TIME TOGETHER," NOT A DATE.
WELL, I SUPPOSE...
WOW! I'VE NEVER BEEN IN A BOY'S ROOM BEFORE!
SORRY IT'S SUCH A MESS.
HEY, HOW COME THIS PART OF THE WALL LOOKS DIFFERENT?
WELL... THAT... UH...

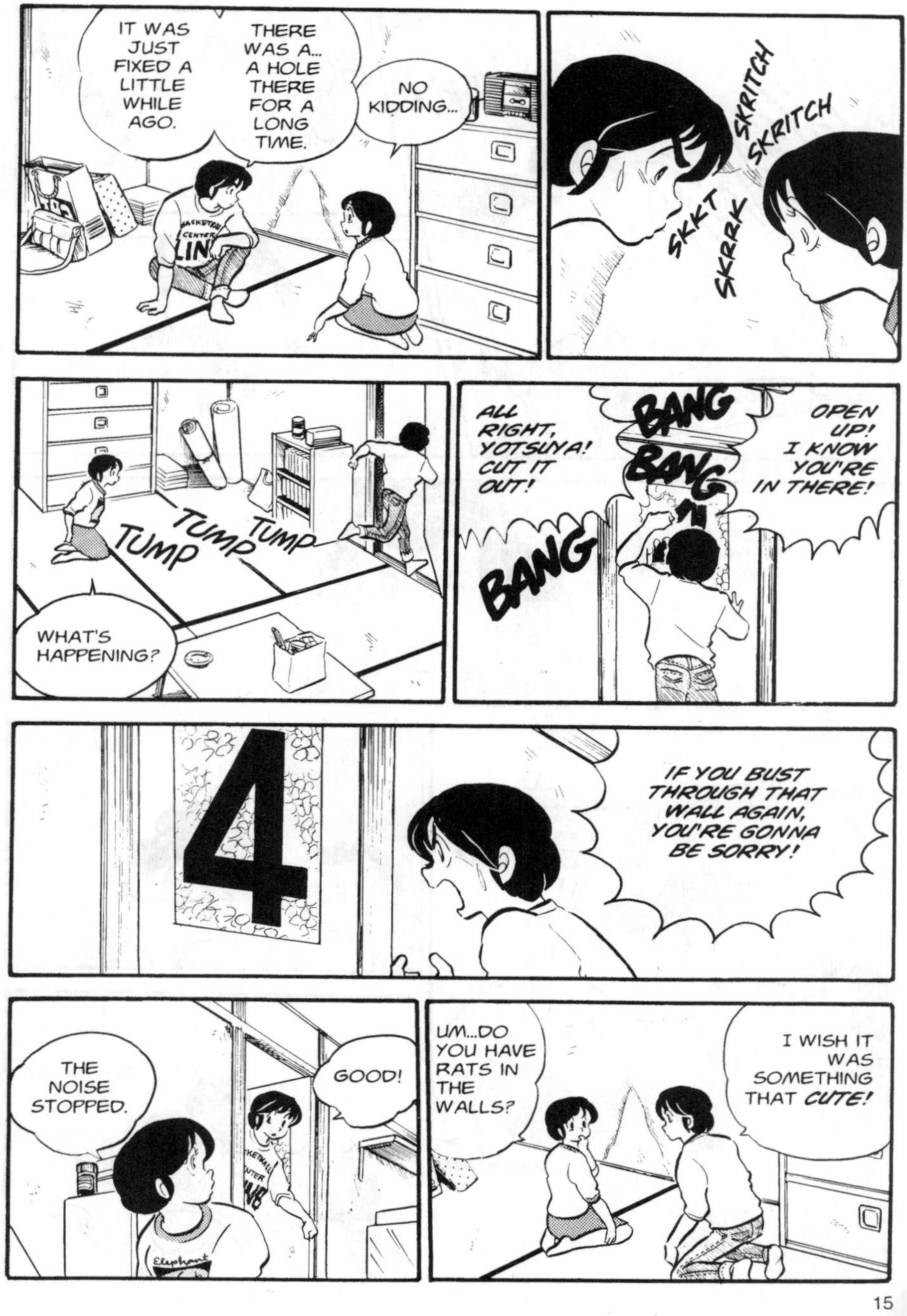

IT WAS JUST FIXED A LITTLE WHILE AGO.
THERE WAS A... A HOLE THERE FOR A LONG TIME.
NO KIDDING...
SKRITCH
SKRITCH
SKKT
SKRRK
TUMP
TUMP
WHAT'S HAPPENING?
ALL RIGHT, YOTSUYA! CUT IT OUT!
BANG
BANG
BANG
BANG
OPEN UP! I KNOW YOU'RE IN THERE!
IF YOU BUST THROUGH THAT WALL AGAIN, YOU'RE GONNA BE SORRY!
THE NOISE STOPPED.
GOOD!
UM...DO YOU HAVE RATS IN THE WALLS?
I WISH IT WAS SOMETHING THAT *CUTE!*

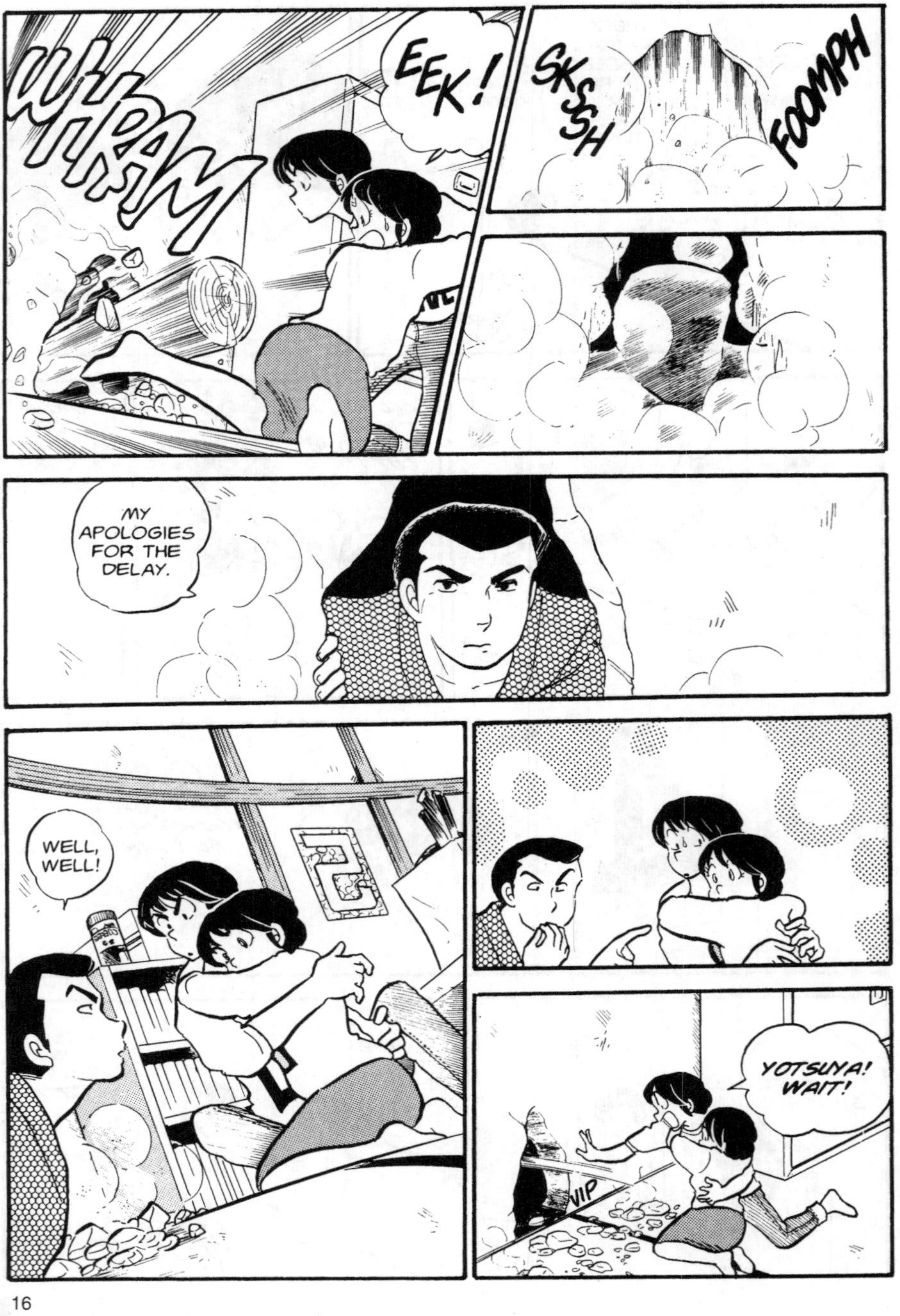
WHRAM
EEK!
SKSSH
FOOMPH
MY APOLOGIES FOR THE DELAY.
WELL, WELL!
YOTSUYA! WAIT!
VIP

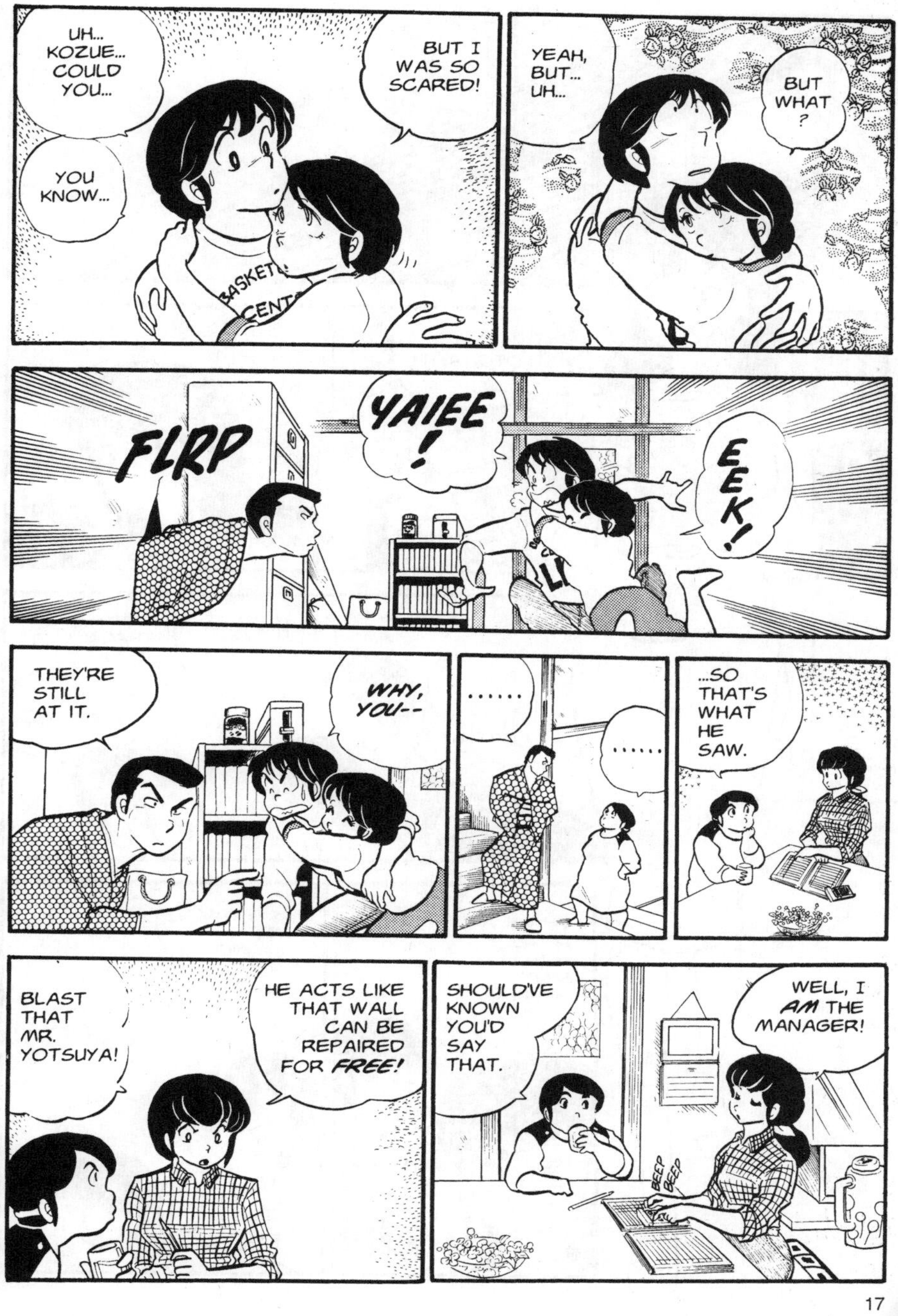
UH... KOZUE... COULD YOU...
YOU KNOW...
BUT I WAS SO SCARED!
YEAH, BUT... UH...
BUT WHAT?
FLRP
YAIEE!
EEK!
THEY'RE STILL AT IT.
WHY, YOU--
......
......
...SO THAT'S WHAT HE SAW.
BLAST THAT MR. YOTSUYA!
HE ACTS LIKE THAT WALL CAN BE REPAIRED FOR FREE!
SHOULD'VE KNOWN YOU'D SAY THAT.
WELL, I AM THE MANAGER!
BEEP BEEP

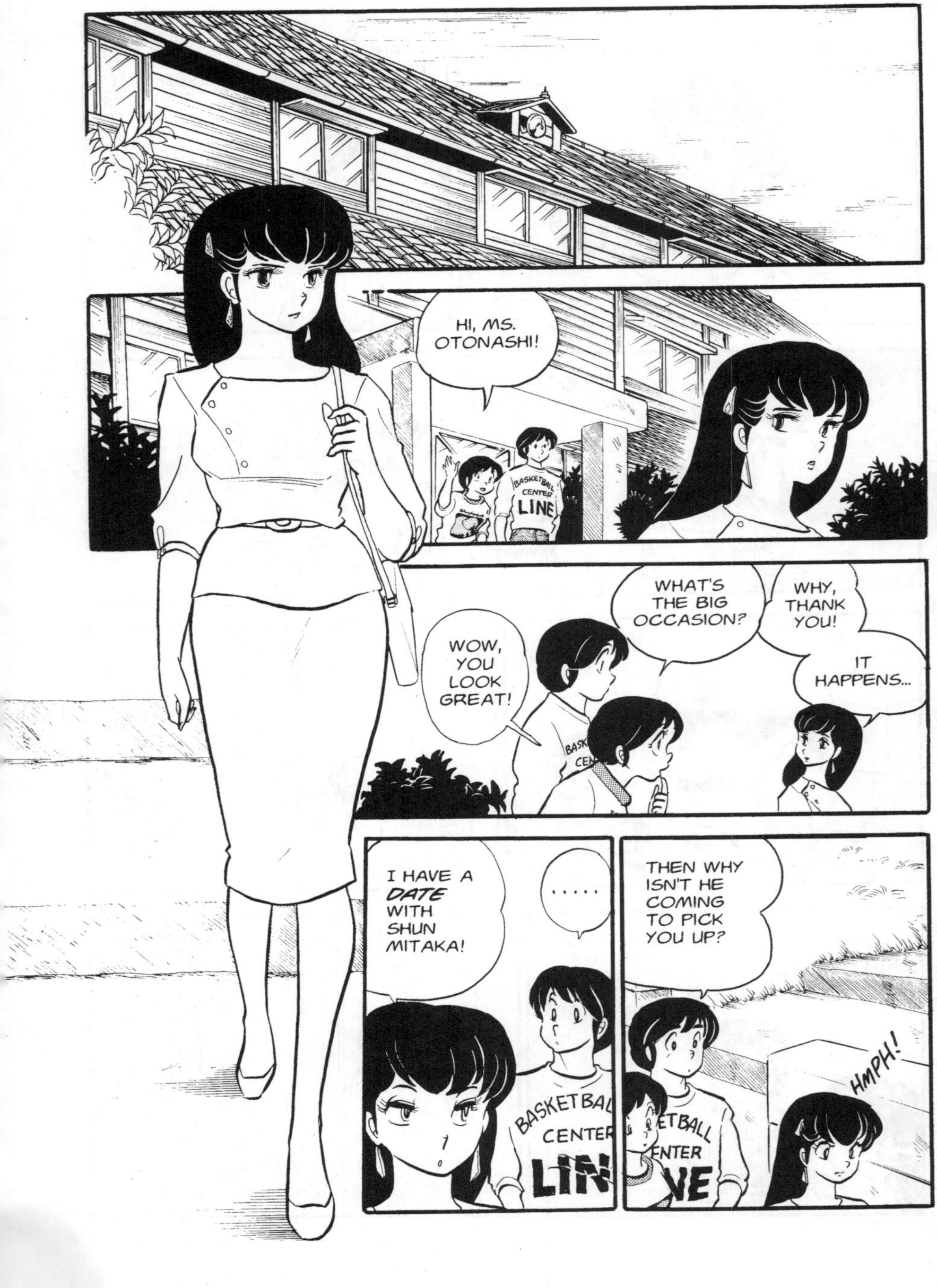
HI, MS. OTONASHI!
BASKETBALL CENTER LINE
WOW, YOU LOOK GREAT!
WHAT'S THE BIG OCCASION?
WHY, THANK YOU!
IT HAPPENS...
I HAVE A DATE WITH SHUN MITAKA!
......
THEN WHY ISN'T HE COMING TO PICK YOU UP?
HMPH!

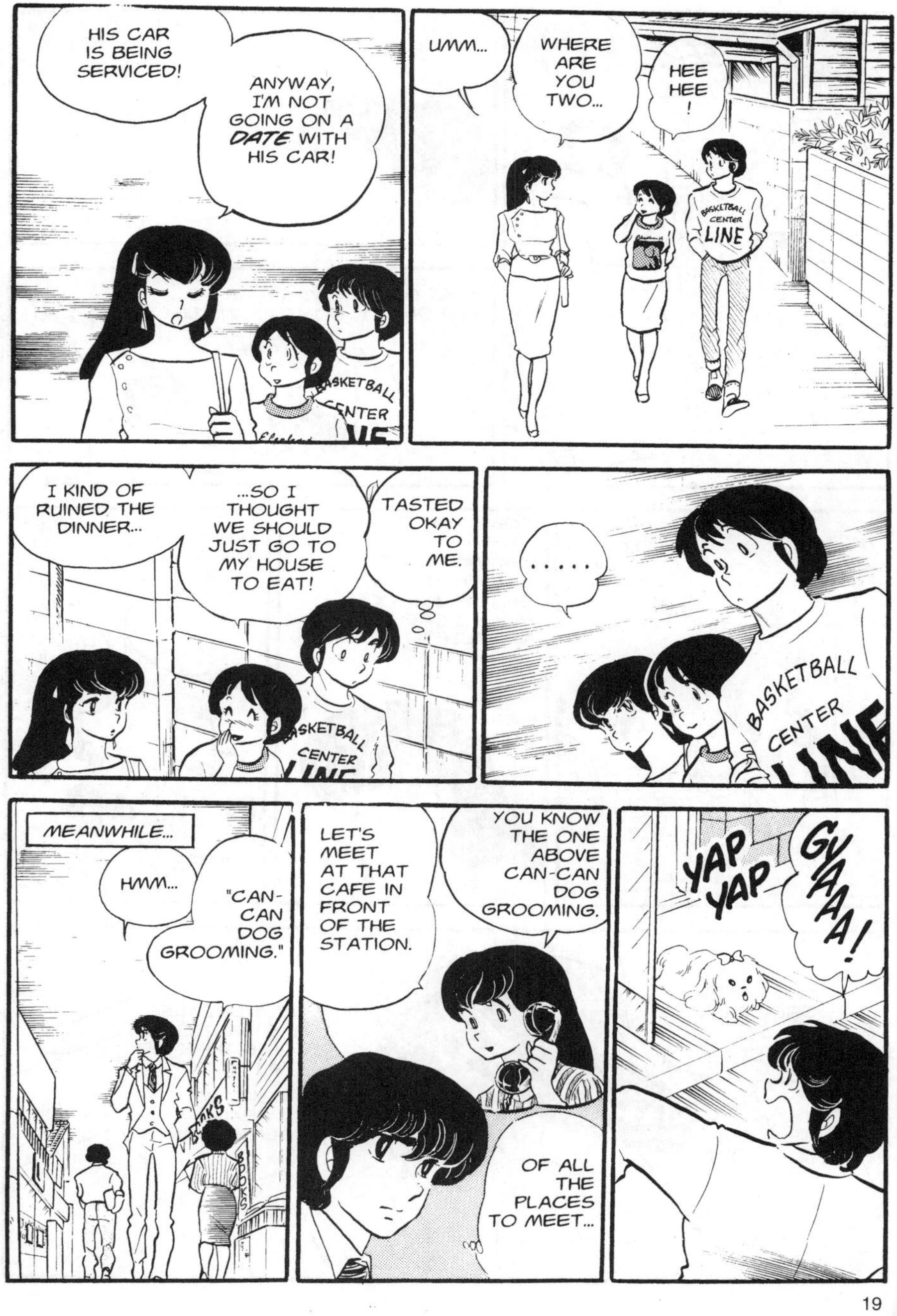
HIS CAR IS BEING SERVICED!
ANYWAY, I'M NOT GOING ON A DATE WITH HIS CAR!
UMM...
WHERE ARE YOU TWO...
HEE HEE !
BASKETBALL CENTER LINE
I KIND OF RUINED THE DINNER...
...SO I THOUGHT WE SHOULD JUST GO TO MY HOUSE TO EAT!
TASTED OKAY TO ME.
......
BASKETBALL CENTER
MEANWHILE...
HMM...
"CAN-CAN DOG GROOMING."
BOOKS
LET'S MEET AT THAT CAFE IN FRONT OF THE STATION.
YOU KNOW THE ONE ABOVE CAN-CAN DOG GROOMING.
OF ALL THE PLACES TO MEET...
YAP YAP
GYAAAA!

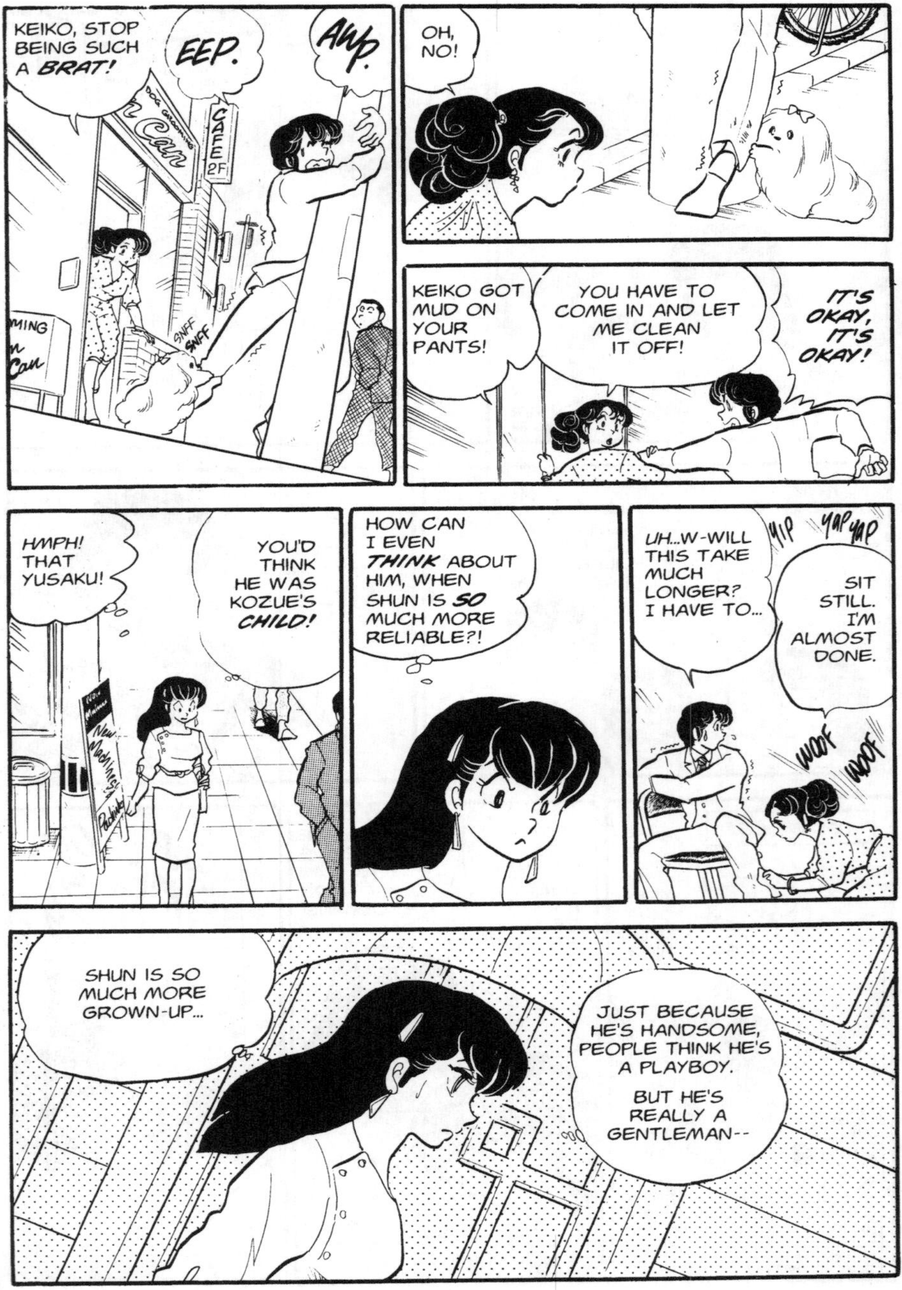
KEIKO, STOP BEING SUCH A BRAT!
EEP.
AWP.
CAFE 2F
MING
SNFF SNFF
OH, NO!
KEIKO GOT MUD ON YOUR PANTS!
YOU HAVE TO COME IN AND LET ME CLEAN IT OFF!
IT'S OKAY, IT'S OKAY!
HMPH! THAT YUSAKU!
YOU'D THINK HE WAS KOZUE'S CHILD!
New Machines!
HOW CAN I EVEN THINK ABOUT HIM, WHEN SHUN IS SO MUCH MORE RELIABLE?!
UH...W-WILL THIS TAKE MUCH LONGER? I HAVE TO...
YIP
YAP YAP
SIT STILL. I'M ALMOST DONE.
WOOF
WOOF
SHUN IS SO MUCH MORE GROWN-UP...
JUST BECAUSE HE'S HANDSOME, PEOPLE THINK HE'S A PLAYBOY.
BUT HE'S REALLY A GENTLEMAN--

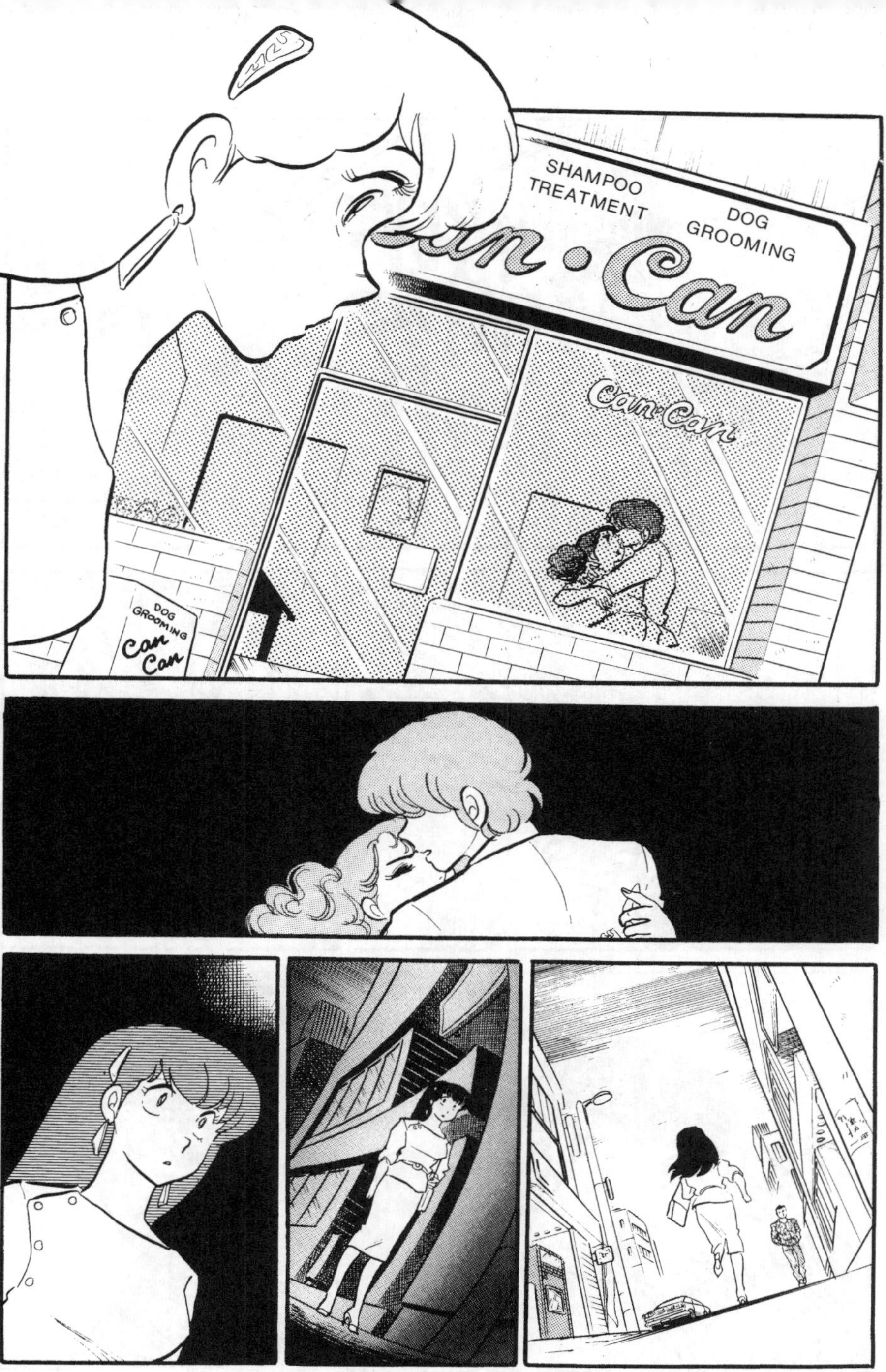
SHAMPOO
TREATMENT
DOG
GROOMING
an • Can
Can-Can
DOG
GROOMING
Can
Can

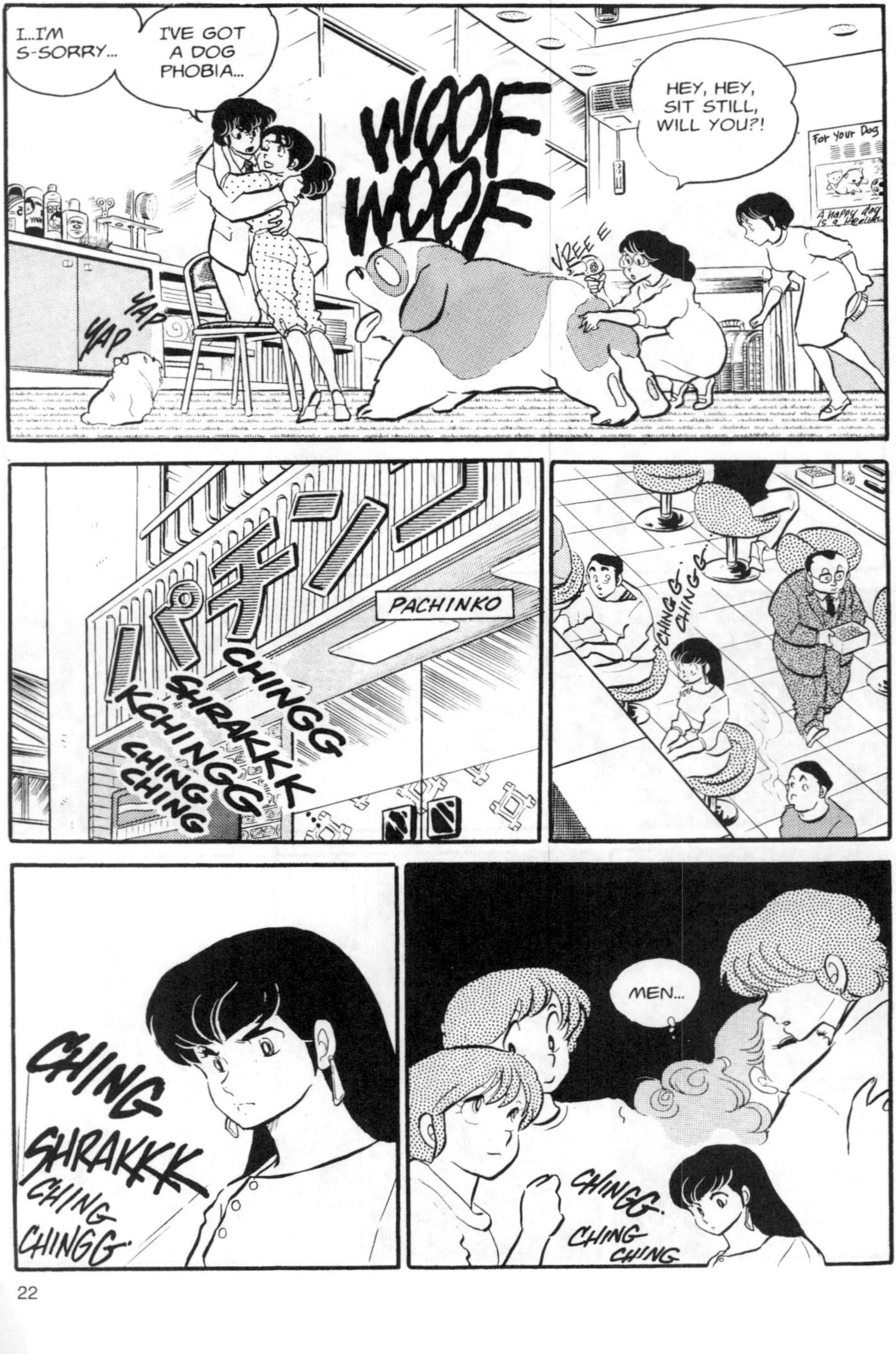
I...I'M S-SORRY...
I'VE GOT A DOG PHOBIA...
YAP YAP
WOOF WOOF
VREEE
HEY, HEY, SIT STILL, WILL YOU?!
For Your Dog
パチンコ
PACHINKO
CHINGG
SHRAKKK
KCHINGG
CHING CHING
CHINGG CHINGG
CHING
SHRAKKK
CHING
CHINGG
MEN...
CHINGG
CHING CHING
CHING

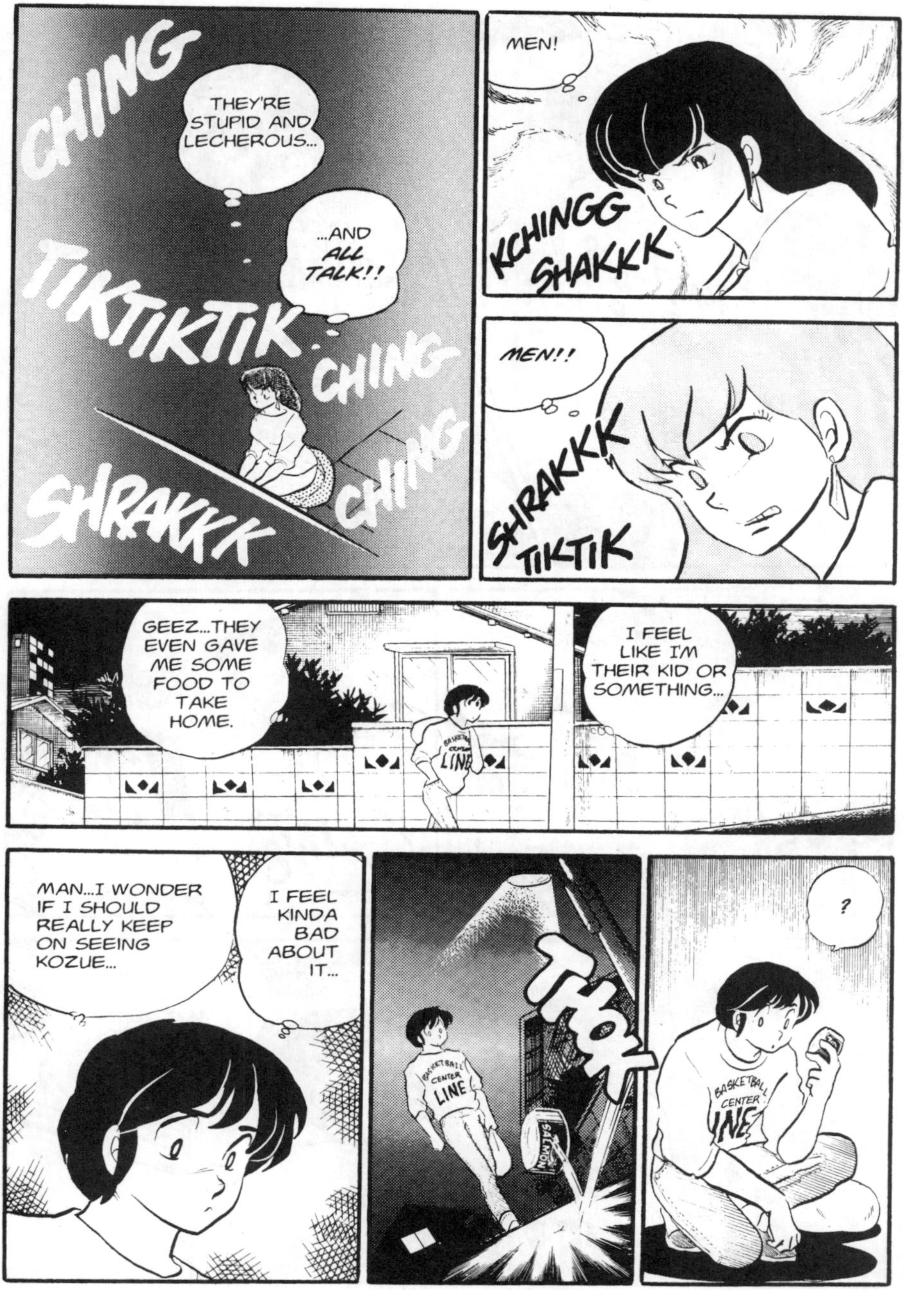
CHING
THEY'RE STUPID AND LECHEROUS...
...AND ALL TALK!!
TIKTIKTIK
CHING
CHING
CHING
SHRAKKK
MEN!
KCHINGG
SHAKKK
MEN!!
SHRAKKK
TIKTIK
GEEZ...THEY EVEN GAVE ME SOME FOOD TO TAKE HOME.
I FEEL LIKE I'M THEIR KID OR SOMETHING...
MAN...I WONDER IF I SHOULD REALLY KEEP ON SEEING KOZUE...
I FEEL KINDA BAD ABOUT IT...
THOK
SALMON
?

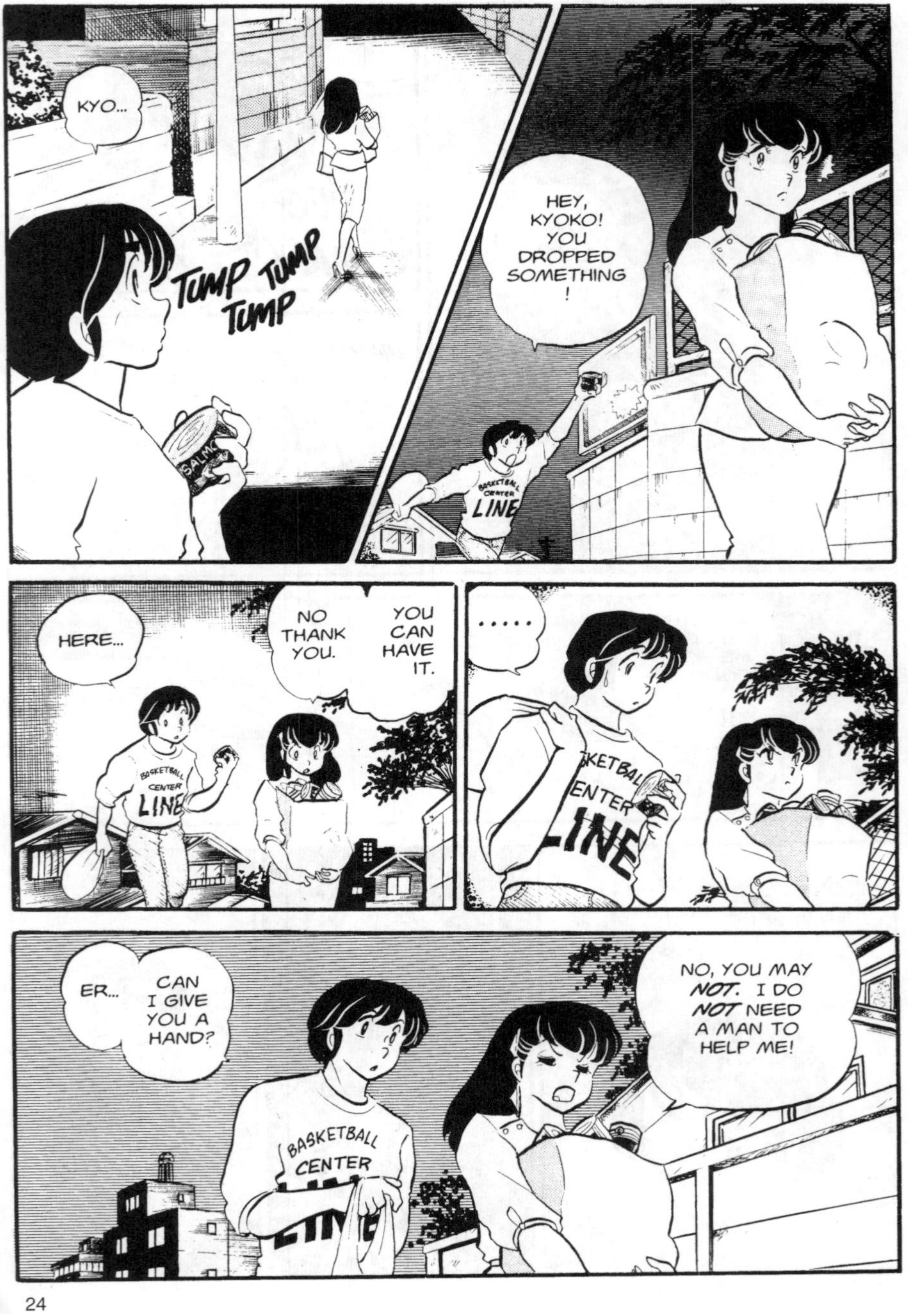

KYO...
TUMP TUMP TUMP
SALMO
HEY, KYOKO! YOU DROPPED SOMETHING!
BASKETBALL CENTER LINE
HERE...
NO THANK YOU.
YOU CAN HAVE IT.
BASKETBALL CENTER LINE
.....
BASKETBALL CENTER LINE
ER...
CAN I GIVE YOU A HAND?
NO, YOU MAY **NOT.** I DO **NOT** NEED A MAN TO HELP ME!
BASKETBALL CENTER

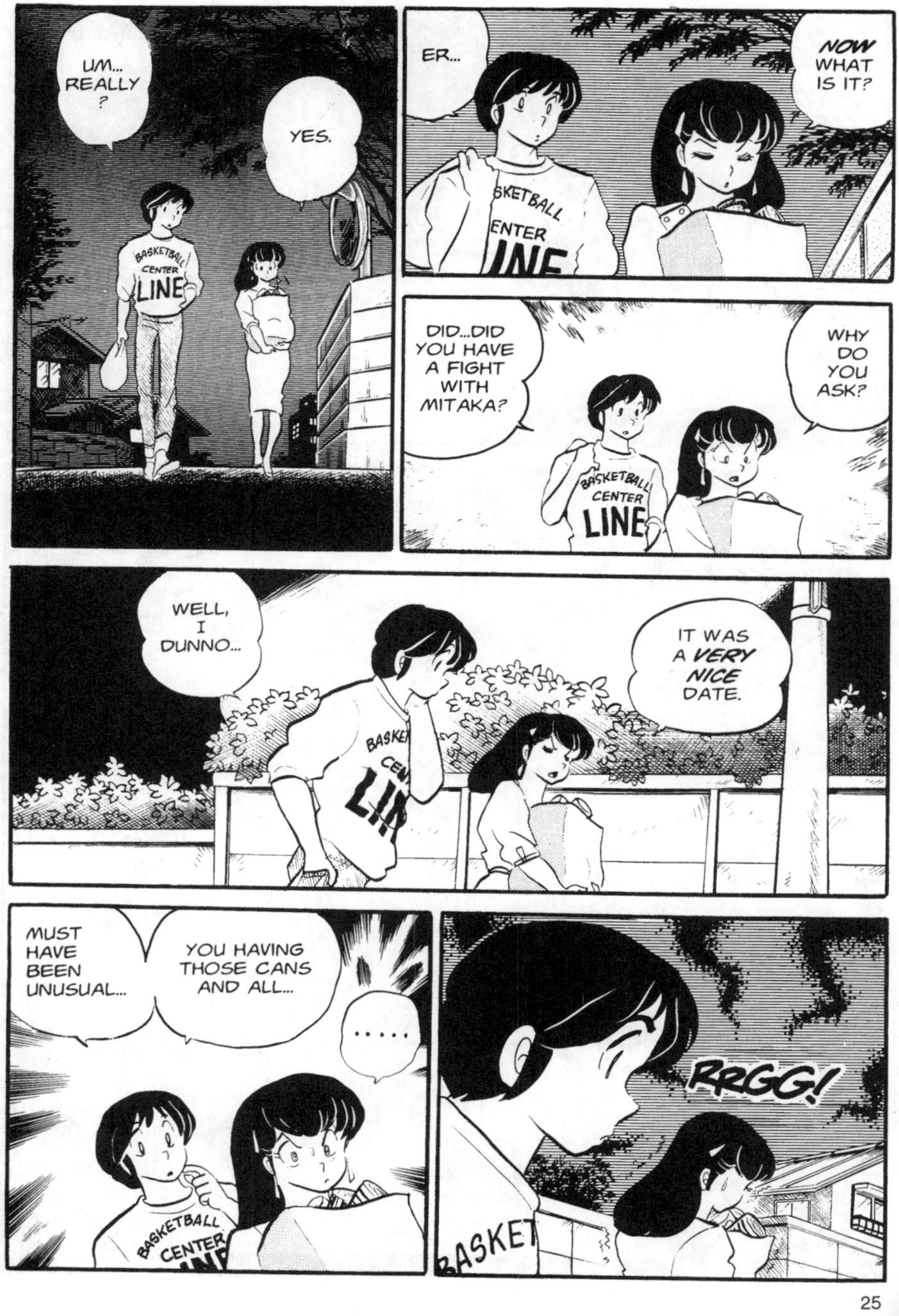
UM... REALLY ?
YES.
ER...
NOW WHAT IS IT?
DID...DID YOU HAVE A FIGHT WITH MITAKA?
WHY DO YOU ASK?
WELL, I DUNNO...
IT WAS A VERY NICE DATE.
MUST HAVE BEEN UNUSUAL...
YOU HAVING THOSE CANS AND ALL...
......
RRGG!

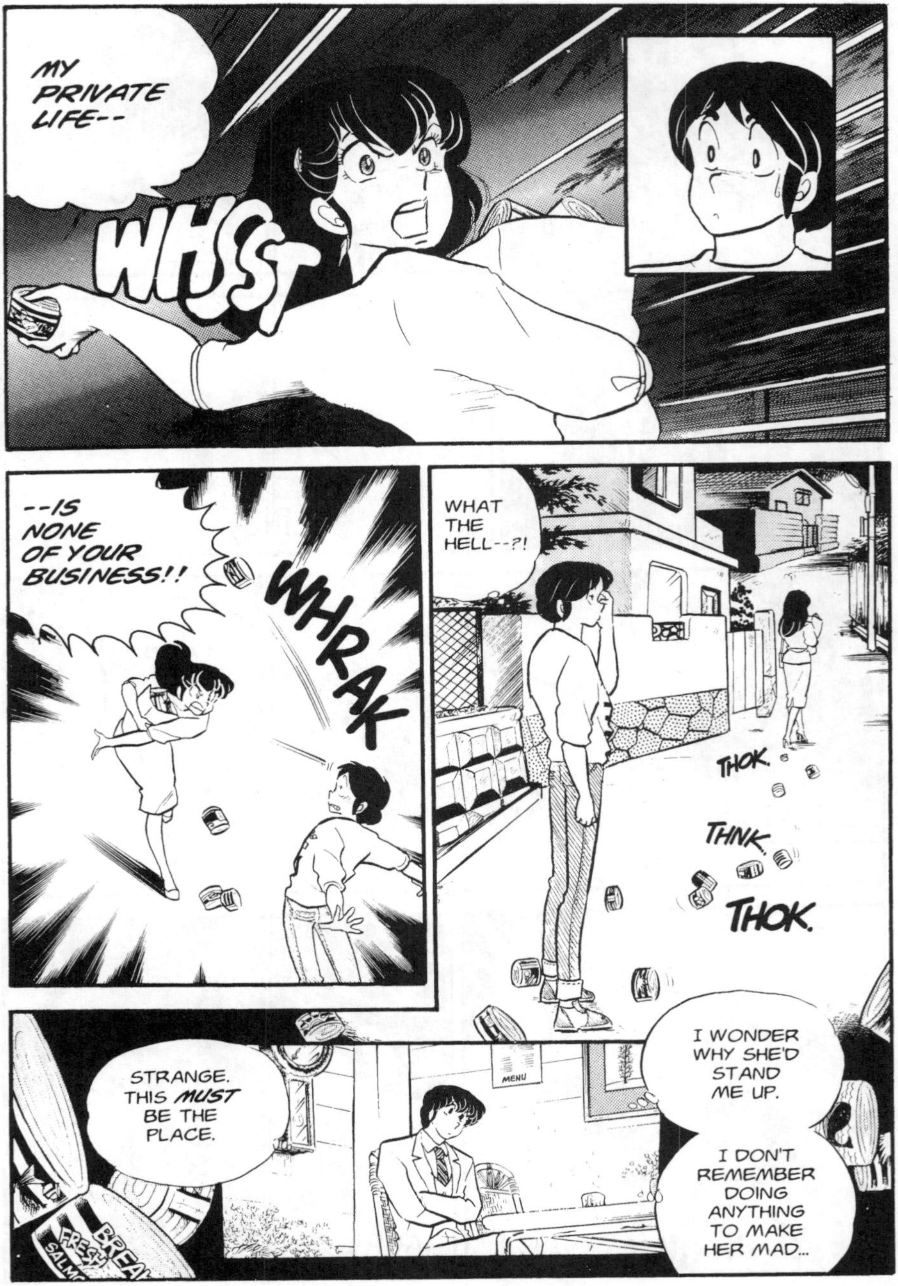
MY PRIVATE LIFE--
WHST
--IS NONE OF YOUR BUSINESS!!
WHRAK
WHAT THE HELL--?!
THOK.
THNK.
THOK.
STRANGE. THIS *MUST* BE THE PLACE.
MENU
I WONDER WHY SHE'D STAND ME UP.
I DON'T REMEMBER DOING ANYTHING TO MAKE HER MAD...

Part Two

Catch of the Day

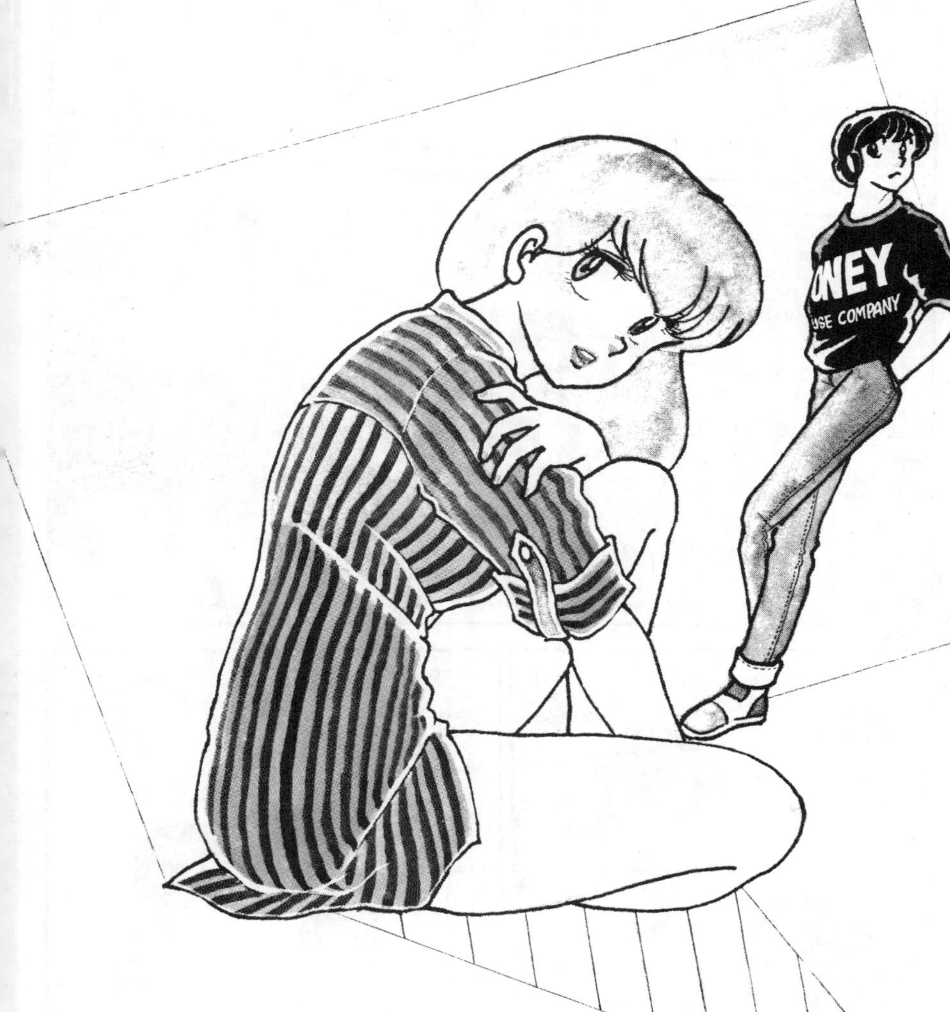

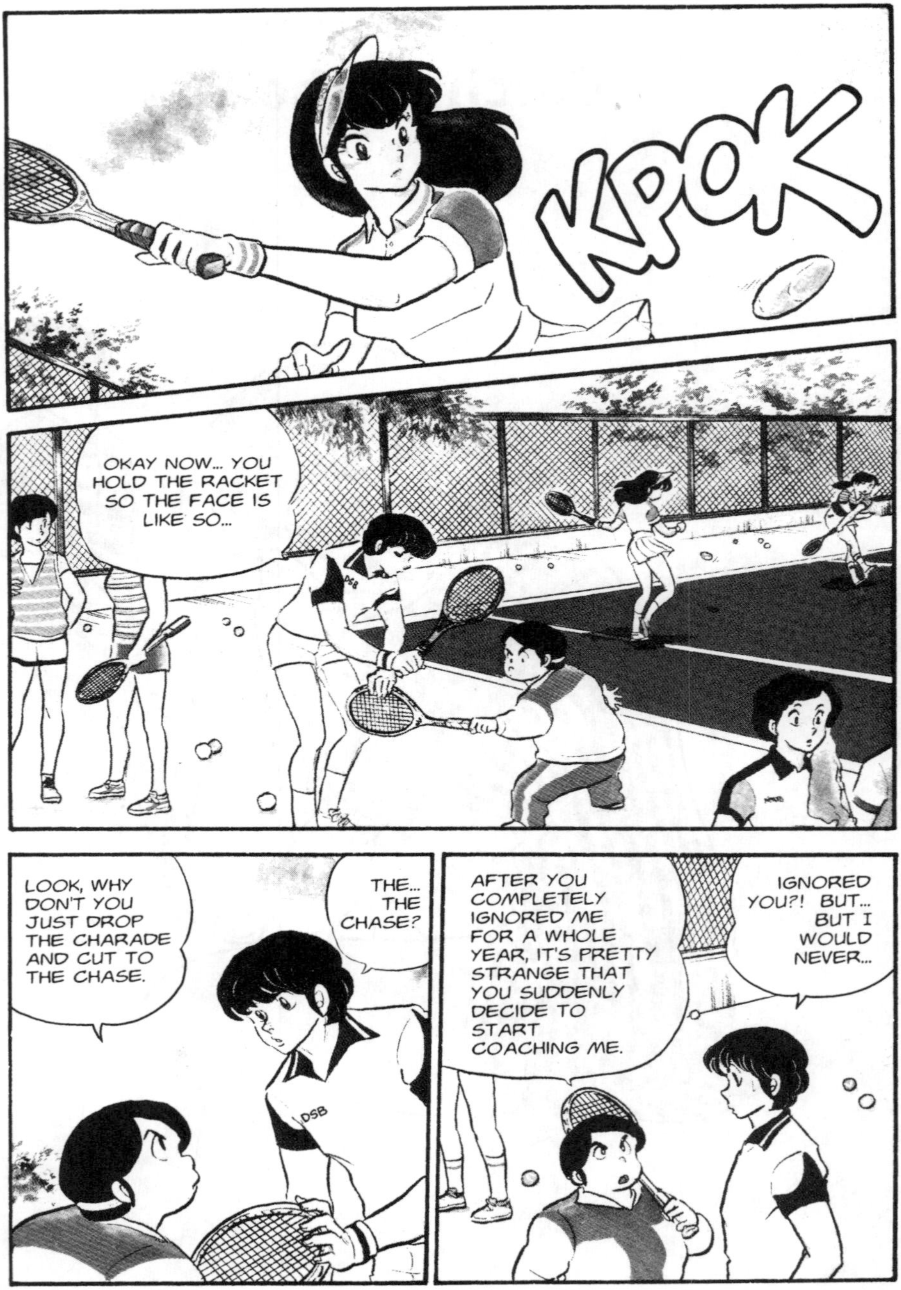
KPOK
OKAY NOW... YOU HOLD THE RACKET SO THE FACE IS LIKE SO...
LOOK, WHY DON'T YOU JUST DROP THE CHARADE AND CUT TO THE CHASE.
THE... THE CHASE?
AFTER YOU COMPLETELY IGNORED ME FOR A WHOLE YEAR, IT'S PRETTY STRANGE THAT YOU SUDDENLY DECIDE TO START COACHING ME.
IGNORED YOU?! BUT... BUT I WOULD NEVER...

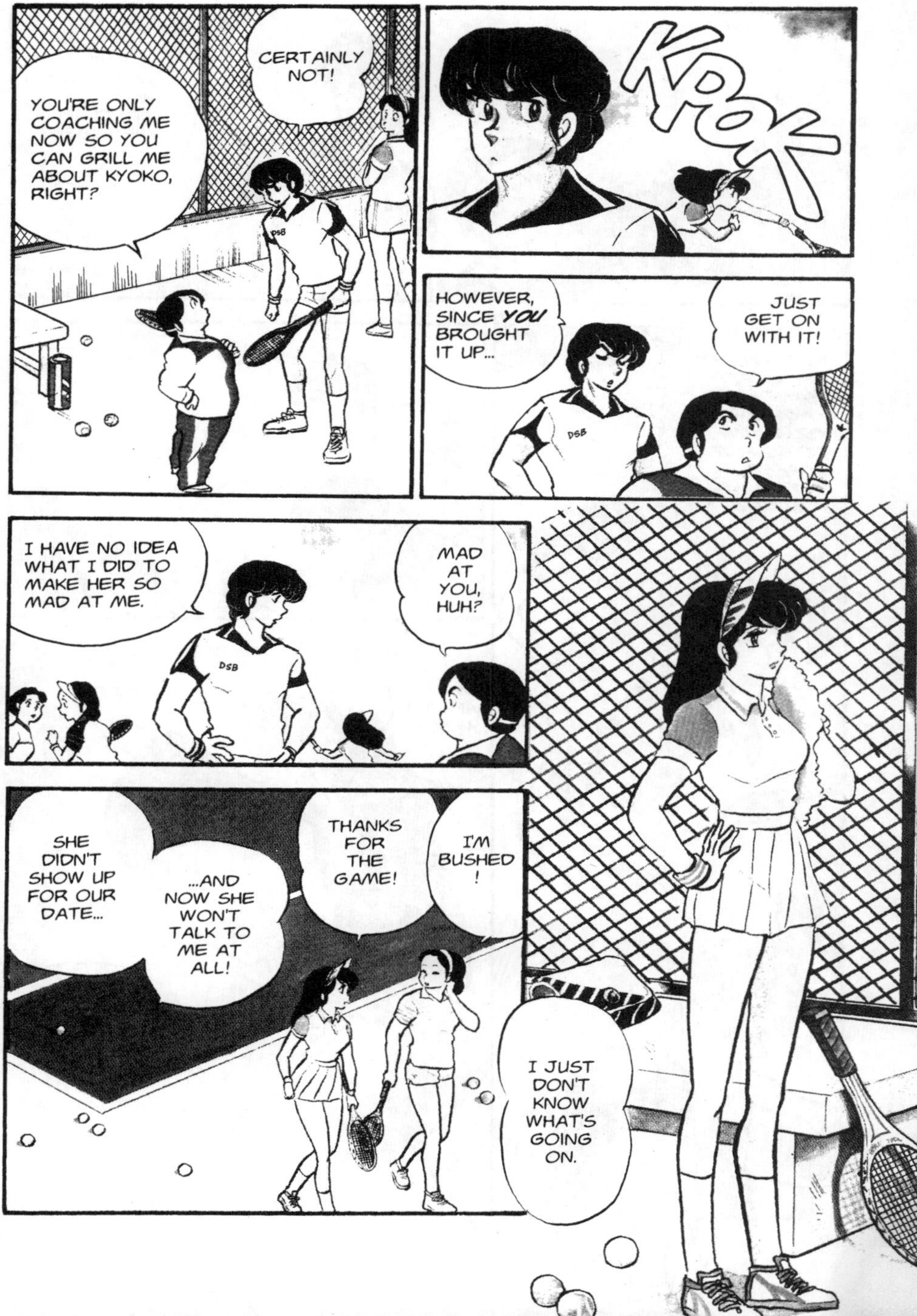
YOU'RE ONLY COACHING ME NOW SO YOU CAN GRILL ME ABOUT KYOKO, RIGHT?
CERTAINLY NOT!
KPOK
HOWEVER, SINCE YOU BROUGHT IT UP...
JUST GET ON WITH IT!
I HAVE NO IDEA WHAT I DID TO MAKE HER SO MAD AT ME.
MAD AT YOU, HUH?
SHE DIDN'T SHOW UP FOR OUR DATE...
...AND NOW SHE WON'T TALK TO ME AT ALL!
THANKS FOR THE GAME!
I'M BUSHED!
I JUST DON'T KNOW WHAT'S GOING ON.

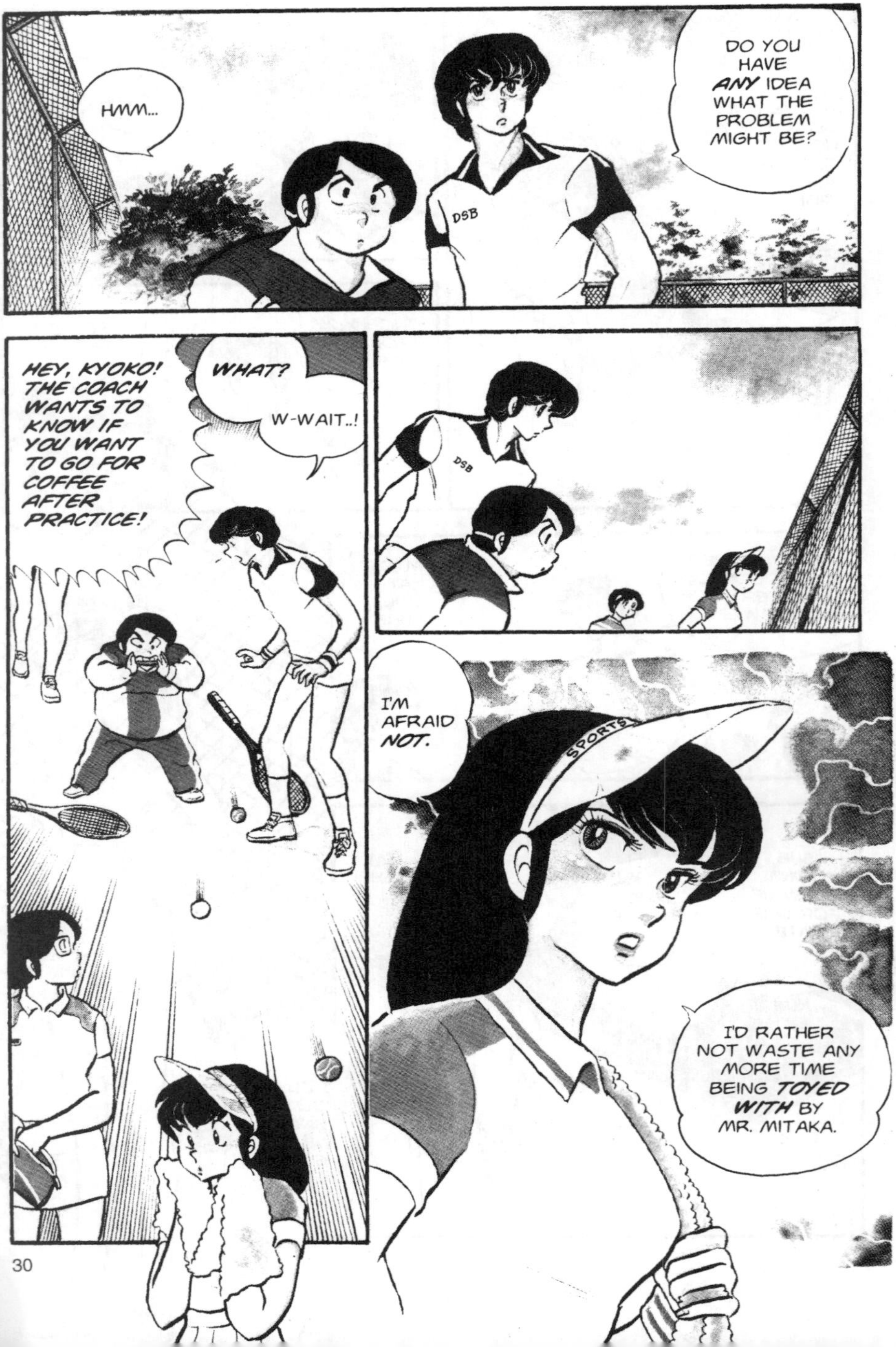
HMM...
DO YOU HAVE ANY IDEA WHAT THE PROBLEM MIGHT BE?
HEY, KYOKO! THE COACH WANTS TO KNOW IF YOU WANT TO GO FOR COFFEE AFTER PRACTICE!
WHAT?
W-WAIT..!
I'M AFRAID NOT.
I'D RATHER NOT WASTE ANY MORE TIME BEING TOYED WITH BY MR. MITAKA.

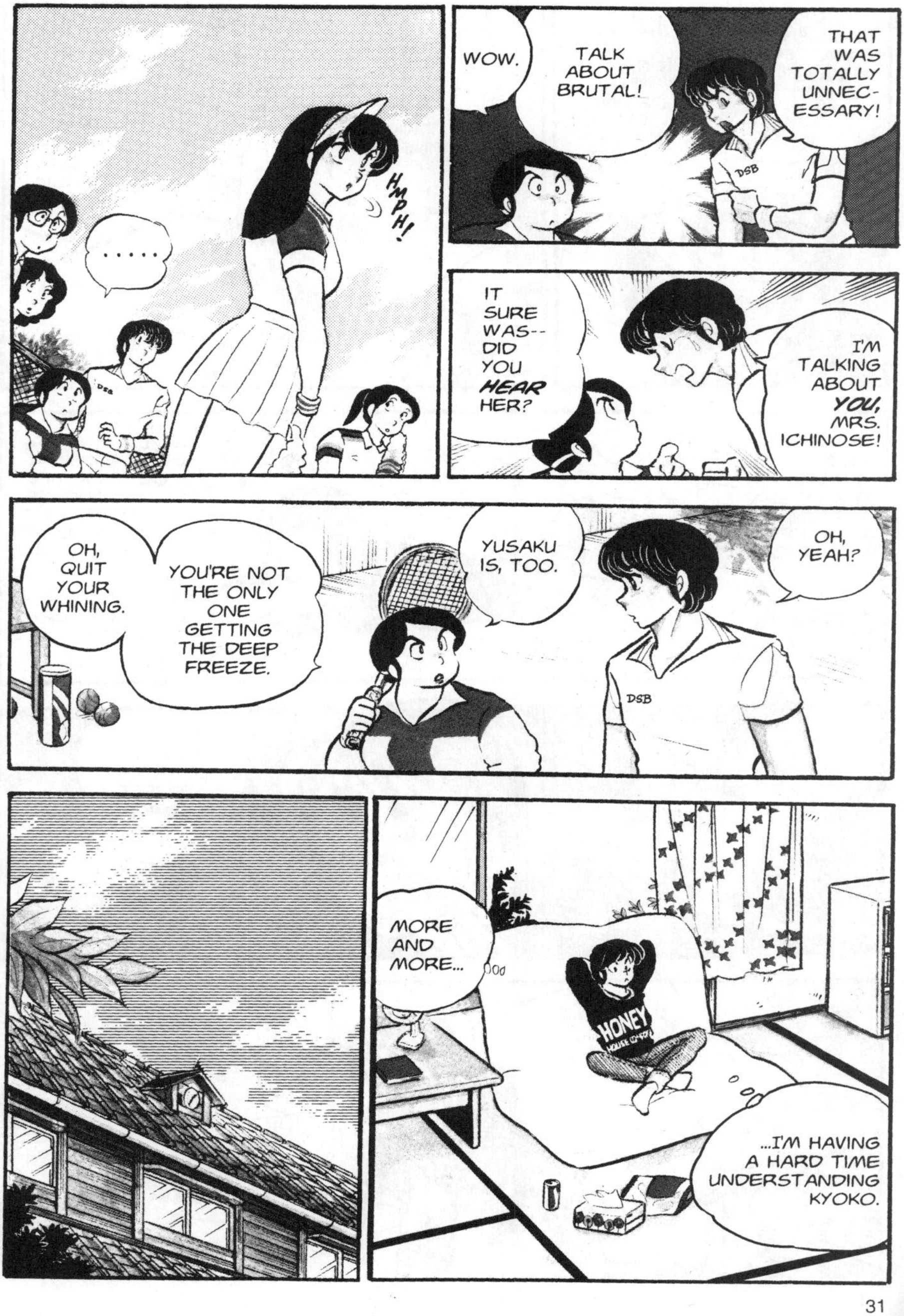
......
HMPH!
WOW.
TALK ABOUT BRUTAL!
THAT WAS TOTALLY UNNEC-ESSARY!
IT SURE WAS-- DID YOU HEAR HER?
I'M TALKING ABOUT YOU, MRS. ICHINOSE!
OH, QUIT YOUR WHINING.
YOU'RE NOT THE ONLY ONE GETTING THE DEEP FREEZE.
YUSAKU IS, TOO.
OH, YEAH?
MORE AND MORE...
...I'M HAVING A HARD TIME UNDERSTANDING KYOKO.

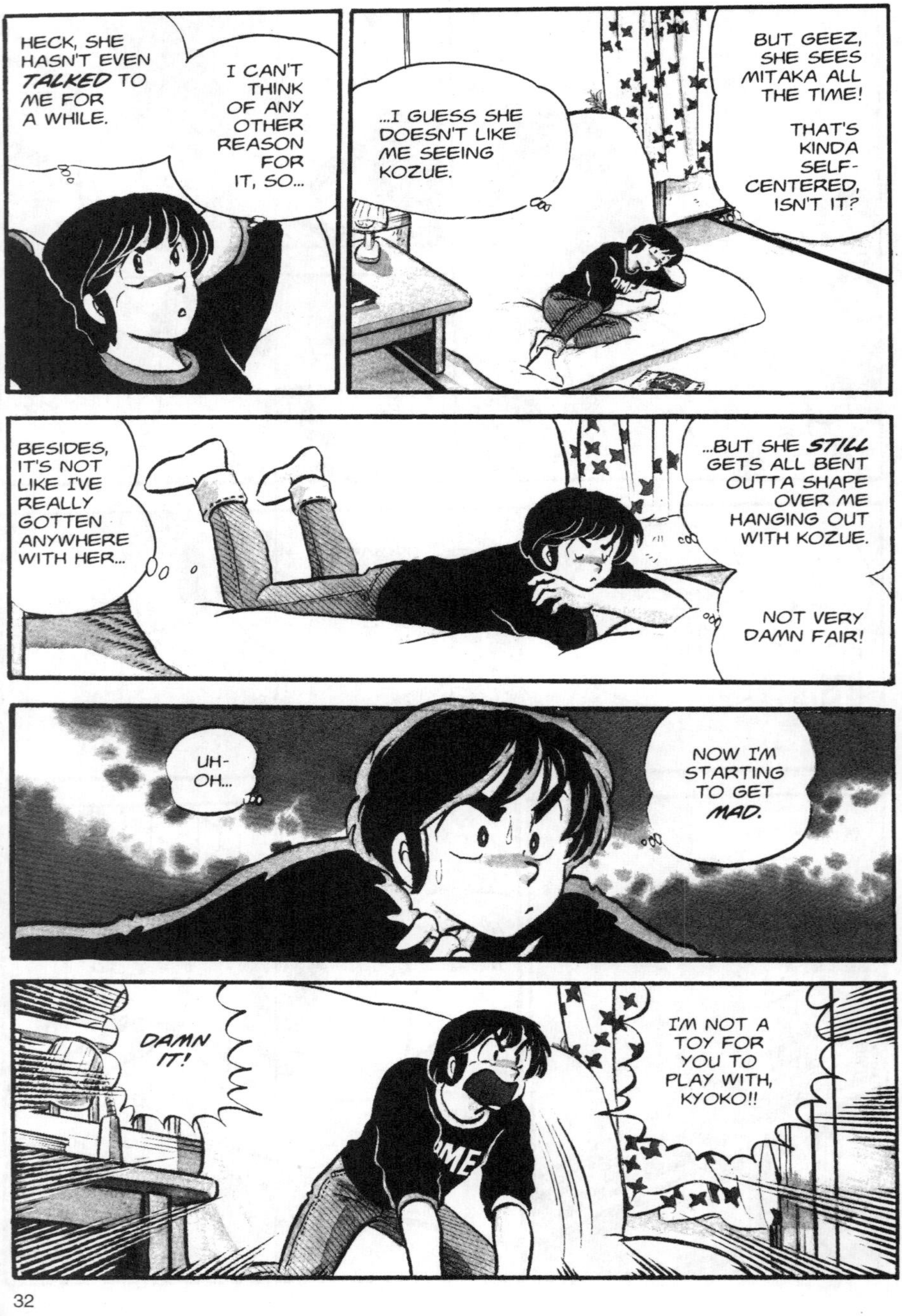
HECK, SHE HASN'T EVEN TALKED TO ME FOR A WHILE.
I CAN'T THINK OF ANY OTHER REASON FOR IT, SO...
...I GUESS SHE DOESN'T LIKE ME SEEING KOZUE.
BUT GEEZ, SHE SEES MITAKA ALL THE TIME!
THAT'S KINDA SELF-CENTERED, ISN'T IT?
BESIDES, IT'S NOT LIKE I'VE REALLY GOTTEN ANYWHERE WITH HER...
...BUT SHE STILL GETS ALL BENT OUTTA SHAPE OVER ME HANGING OUT WITH KOZUE.
NOT VERY DAMN FAIR!
UH-OH...
NOW I'M STARTING TO GET MAD.
DAMN IT!
I'M NOT A TOY FOR YOU TO PLAY WITH, KYOKO!!

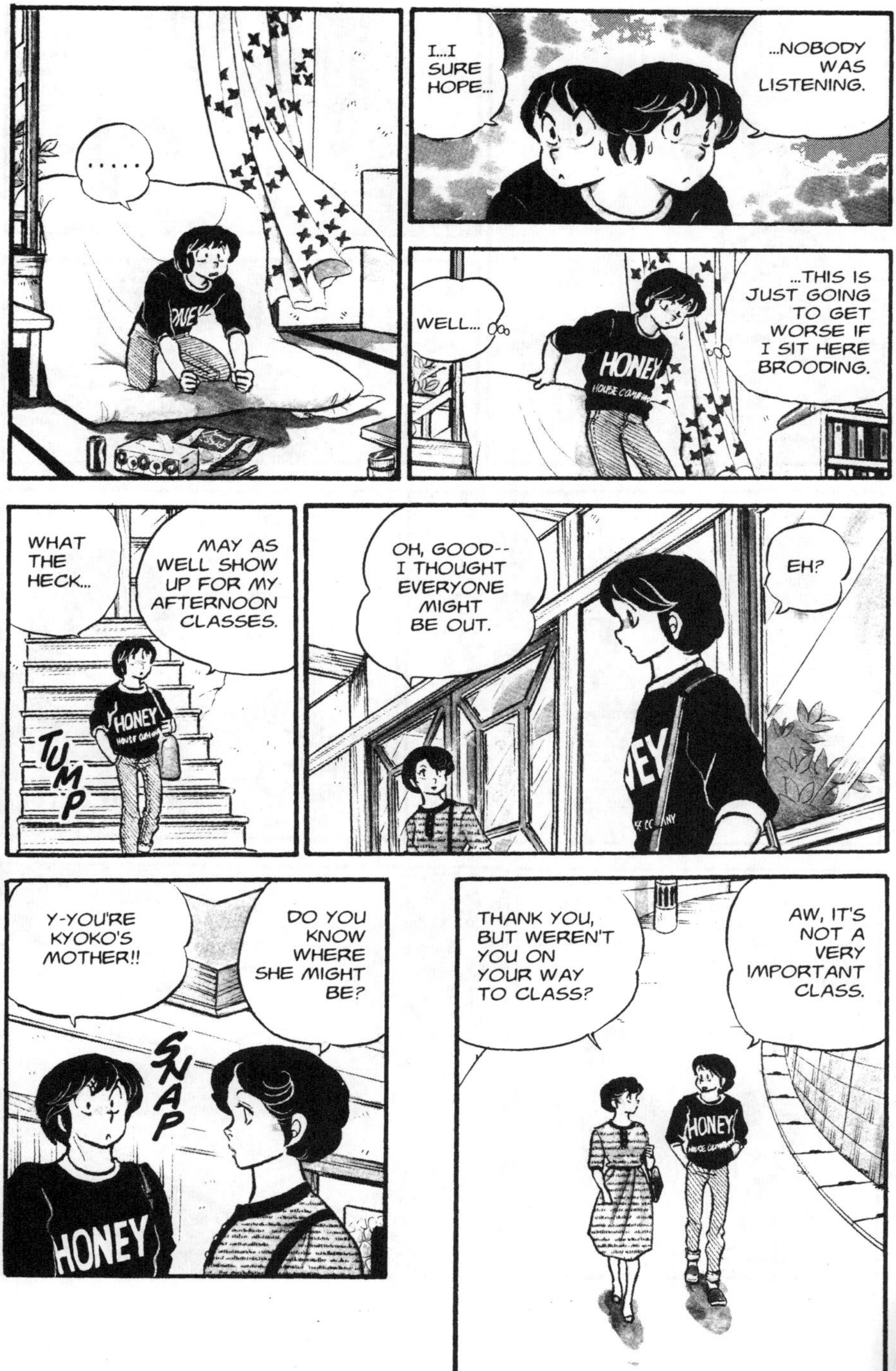
.....
I...I SURE HOPE...
...NOBODY WAS LISTENING.
WELL...
...THIS IS JUST GOING TO GET WORSE IF I SIT HERE BROODING.
WHAT THE HECK...
MAY AS WELL SHOW UP FOR MY AFTERNOON CLASSES.
TUMP
OH, GOOD-- I THOUGHT EVERYONE MIGHT BE OUT.
EH?
Y-YOU'RE KYOKO'S MOTHER!!
DO YOU KNOW WHERE SHE MIGHT BE?
SNAP
THANK YOU, BUT WEREN'T YOU ON YOUR WAY TO CLASS?
AW, IT'S NOT A VERY IMPORTANT CLASS.

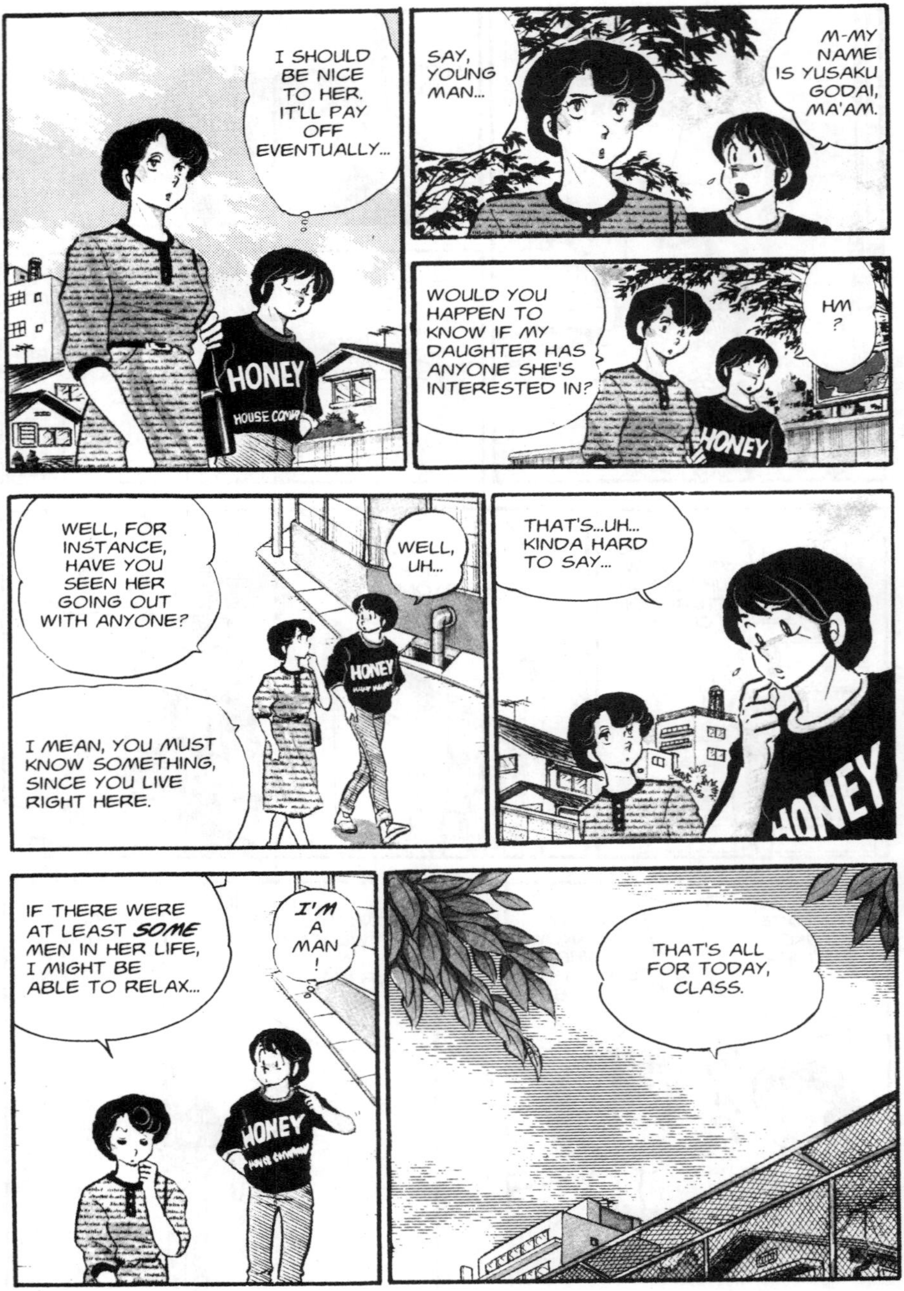
I SHOULD BE NICE TO HER. IT'LL PAY OFF EVENTUALLY...
HONEY
SAY, YOUNG MAN...
M-MY NAME IS YUSAKU GODAI, MA'AM.
WOULD YOU HAPPEN TO KNOW IF MY DAUGHTER HAS ANYONE SHE'S INTERESTED IN?
HM ?
WELL, FOR INSTANCE, HAVE YOU SEEN HER GOING OUT WITH ANYONE?
WELL, UH...
I MEAN, YOU MUST KNOW SOMETHING, SINCE YOU LIVE RIGHT HERE.
THAT'S...UH... KINDA HARD TO SAY...
IF THERE WERE AT LEAST *SOME* MEN IN HER LIFE, I MIGHT BE ABLE TO RELAX...
I'M A MAN!
THAT'S ALL FOR TODAY, CLASS.

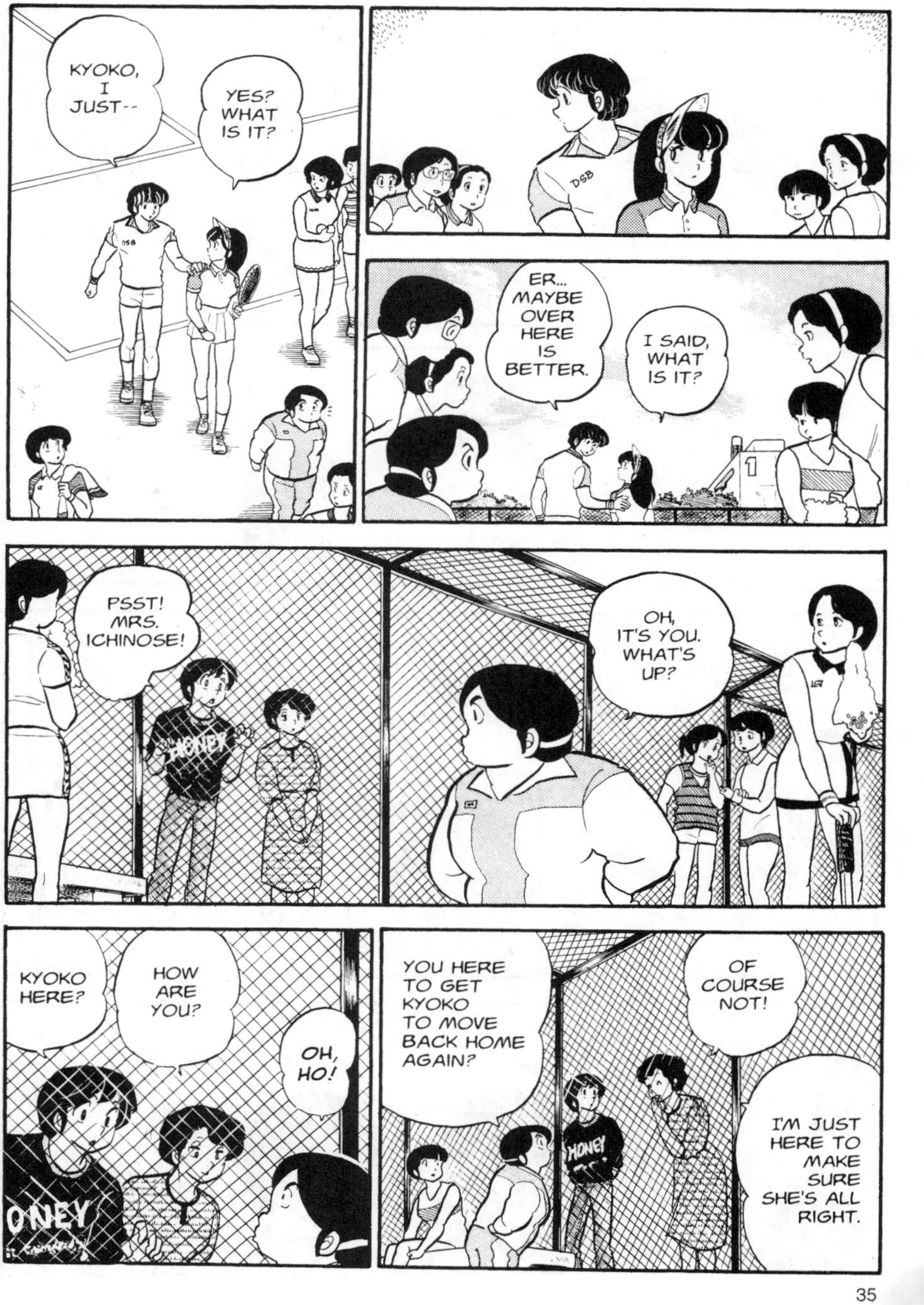
KYOKO, I JUST--
YES? WHAT IS IT?
ER... MAYBE OVER HERE IS BETTER.
I SAID, WHAT IS IT?
PSST! MRS. ICHINOSE!
OH, IT'S YOU. WHAT'S UP?
KYOKO HERE?
HOW ARE YOU?
OH, HO!
YOU HERE TO GET KYOKO TO MOVE BACK HOME AGAIN?
OF COURSE NOT!
I'M JUST HERE TO MAKE SURE SHE'S ALL RIGHT.

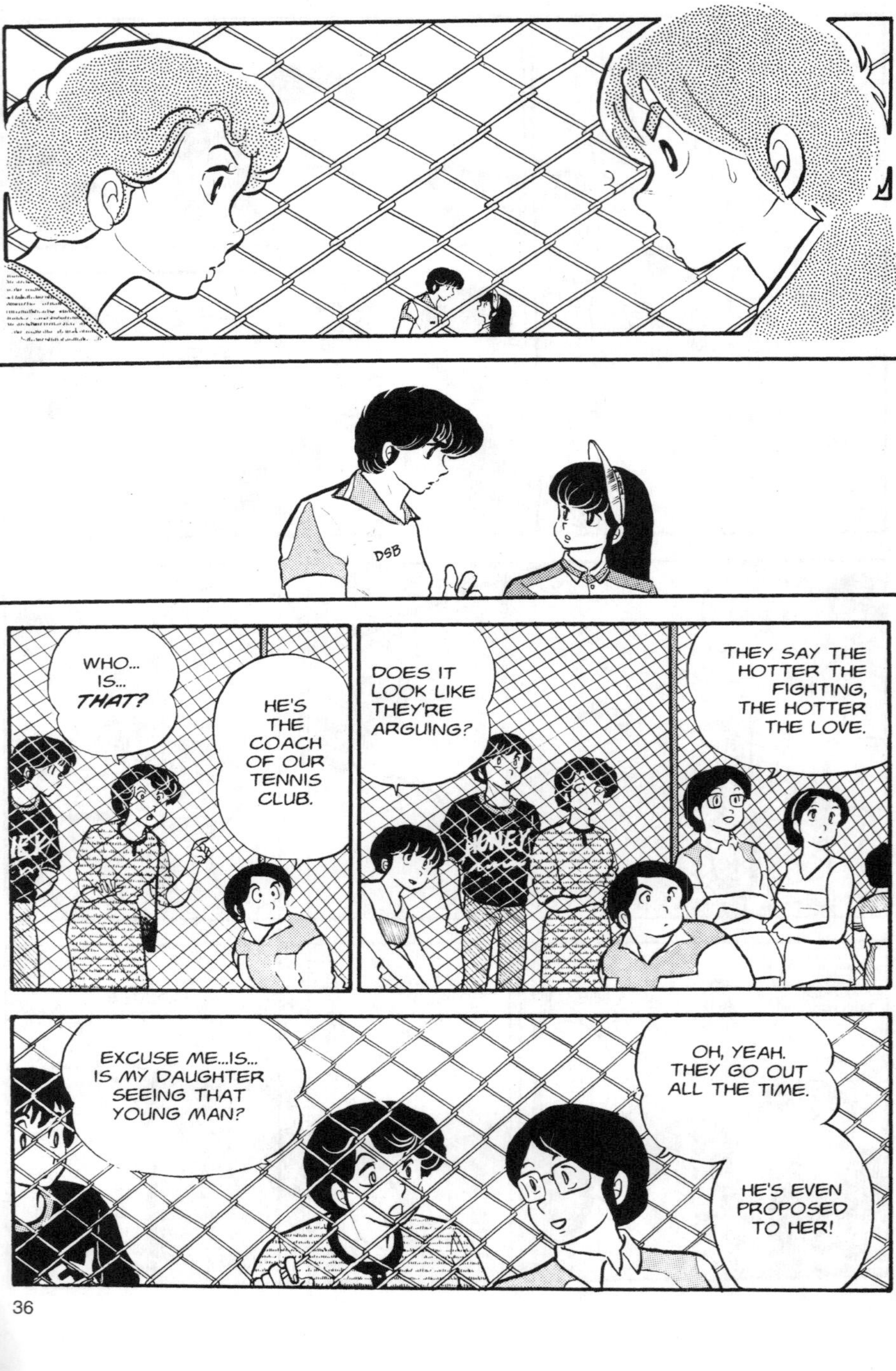
DSB
WHO... IS... *THAT?*
HE'S THE COACH OF OUR TENNIS CLUB.
DOES IT LOOK LIKE THEY'RE ARGUING?
THEY SAY THE HOTTER THE FIGHTING, THE HOTTER THE LOVE.
EXCUSE ME...IS... IS MY DAUGHTER SEEING THAT YOUNG MAN?
OH, YEAH. THEY GO OUT ALL THE TIME.
HE'S EVEN PROPOSED TO HER!

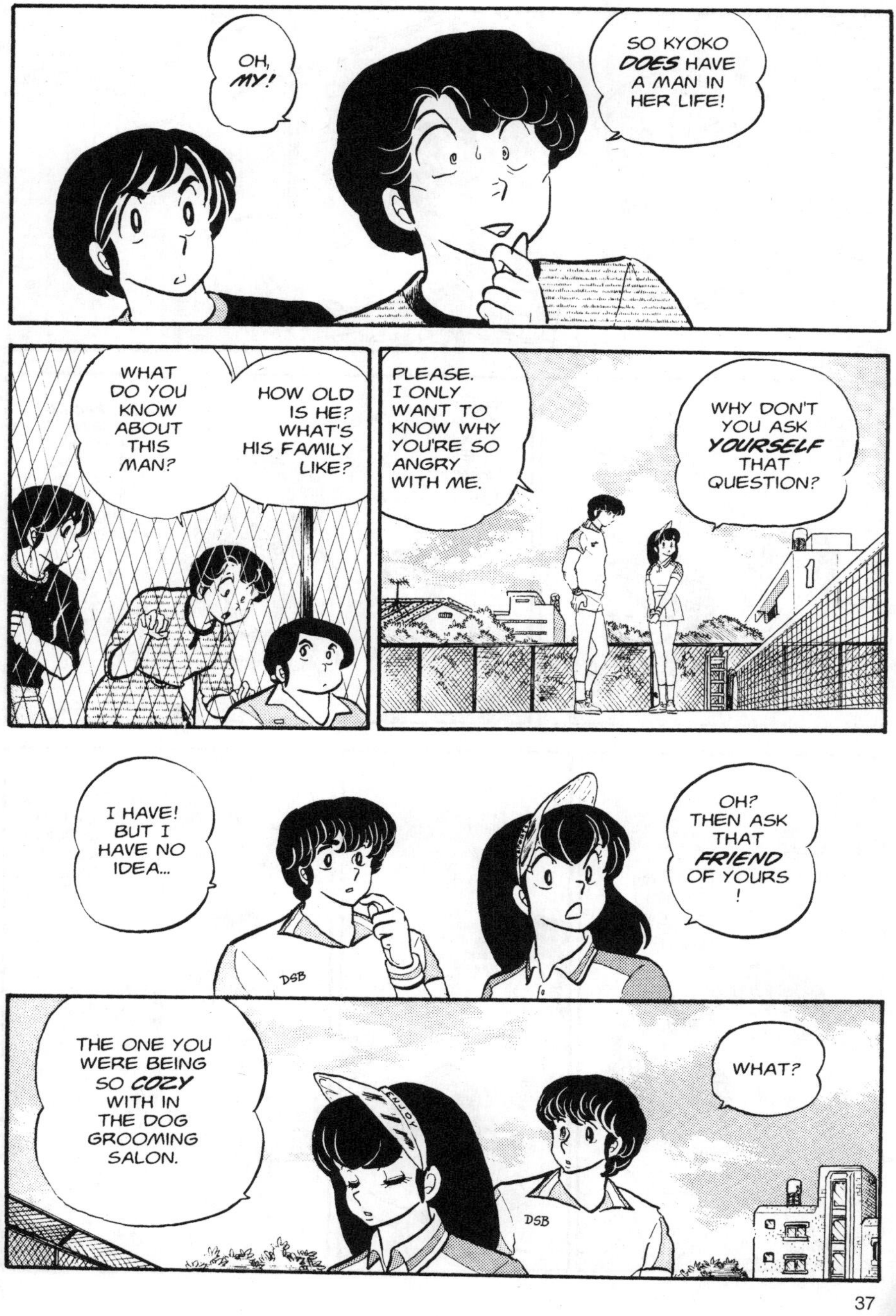
OH, MY!
SO KYOKO DOES HAVE A MAN IN HER LIFE!
WHAT DO YOU KNOW ABOUT THIS MAN?
HOW OLD IS HE? WHAT'S HIS FAMILY LIKE?
PLEASE. I ONLY WANT TO KNOW WHY YOU'RE SO ANGRY WITH ME.
WHY DON'T YOU ASK YOURSELF THAT QUESTION?
I HAVE! BUT I HAVE NO IDEA...
OH? THEN ASK THAT FRIEND OF YOURS!
THE ONE YOU WERE BEING SO COZY WITH IN THE DOG GROOMING SALON.
WHAT?

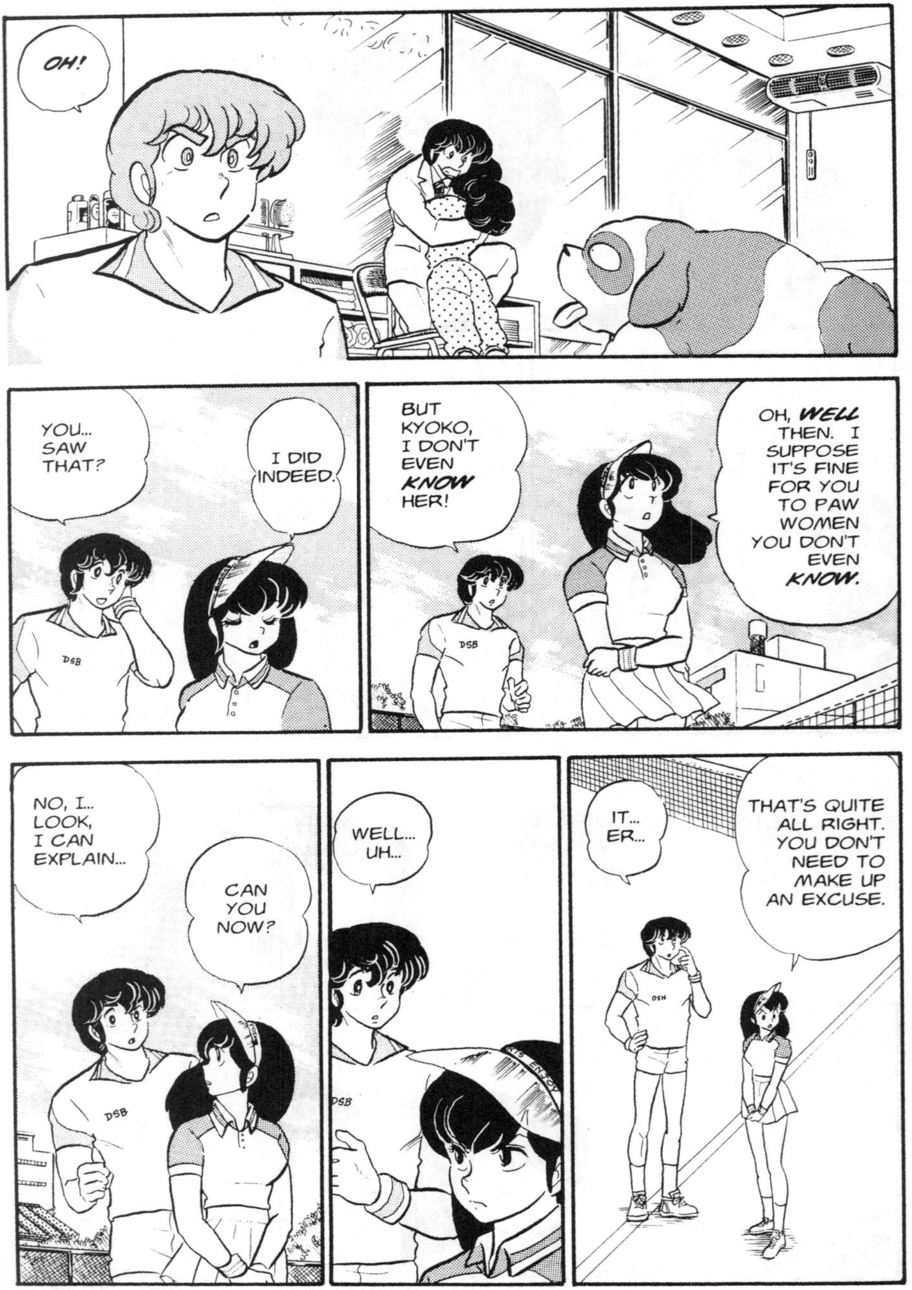
OH!
YOU... SAW THAT?
I DID INDEED.
BUT KYOKO, I DON'T EVEN KNOW HER!
OH, WELL THEN. I SUPPOSE IT'S FINE FOR YOU TO PAW WOMEN YOU DON'T EVEN KNOW.
NO, I... LOOK, I CAN EXPLAIN...
CAN YOU NOW?
WELL... UH...
IT... ER...
THAT'S QUITE ALL RIGHT. YOU DON'T NEED TO MAKE UP AN EXCUSE.

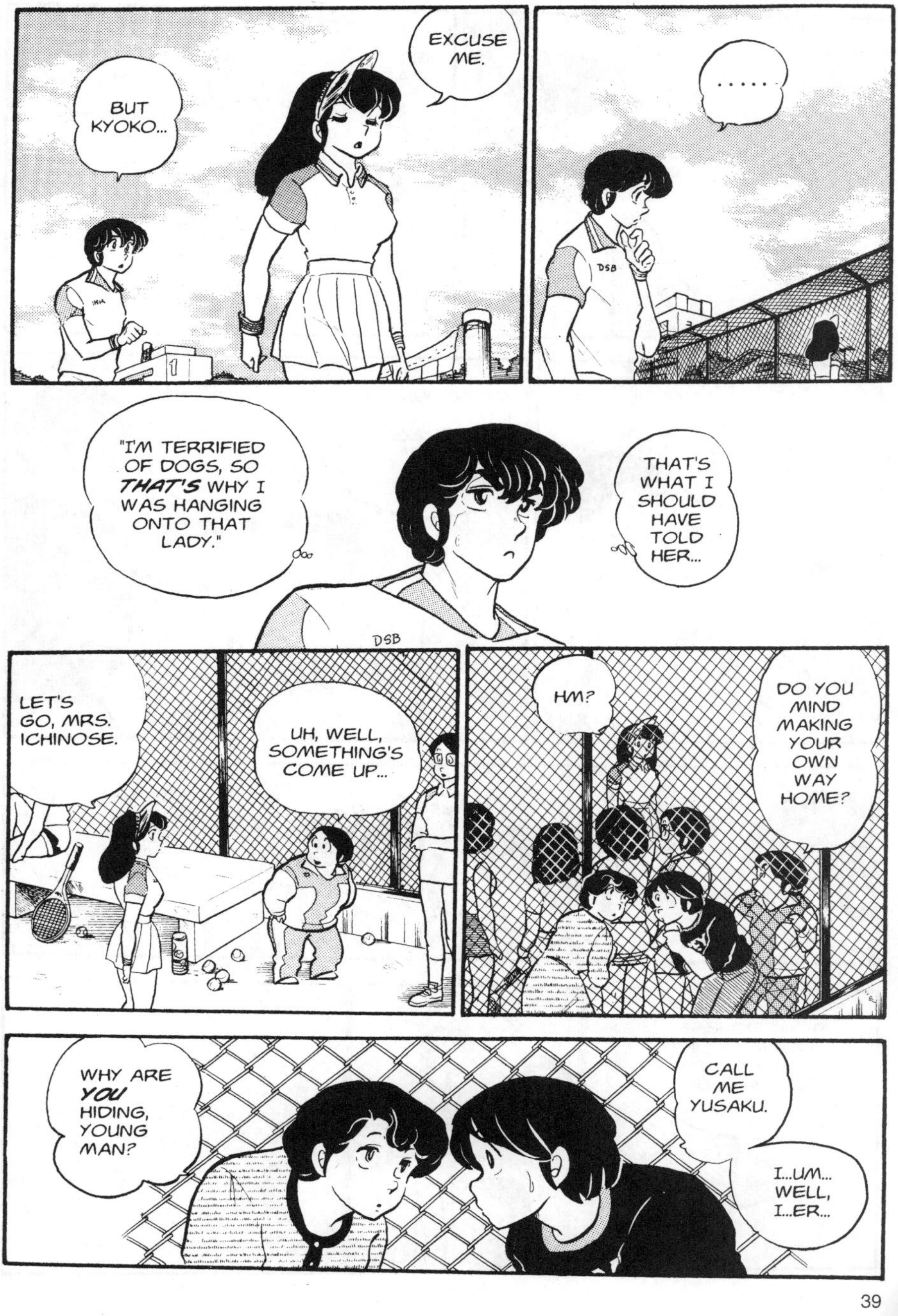
BUT KYOKO...
EXCUSE ME.
......
"I'M TERRIFIED OF DOGS, SO THAT'S WHY I WAS HANGING ONTO THAT LADY."
THAT'S WHAT I SHOULD HAVE TOLD HER...
LET'S GO, MRS. ICHINOSE.
UH, WELL, SOMETHING'S COME UP...
HM?
DO YOU MIND MAKING YOUR OWN WAY HOME?
WHY ARE YOU HIDING, YOUNG MAN?
CALL ME YUSAKU.
I...UM... WELL, I...ER...

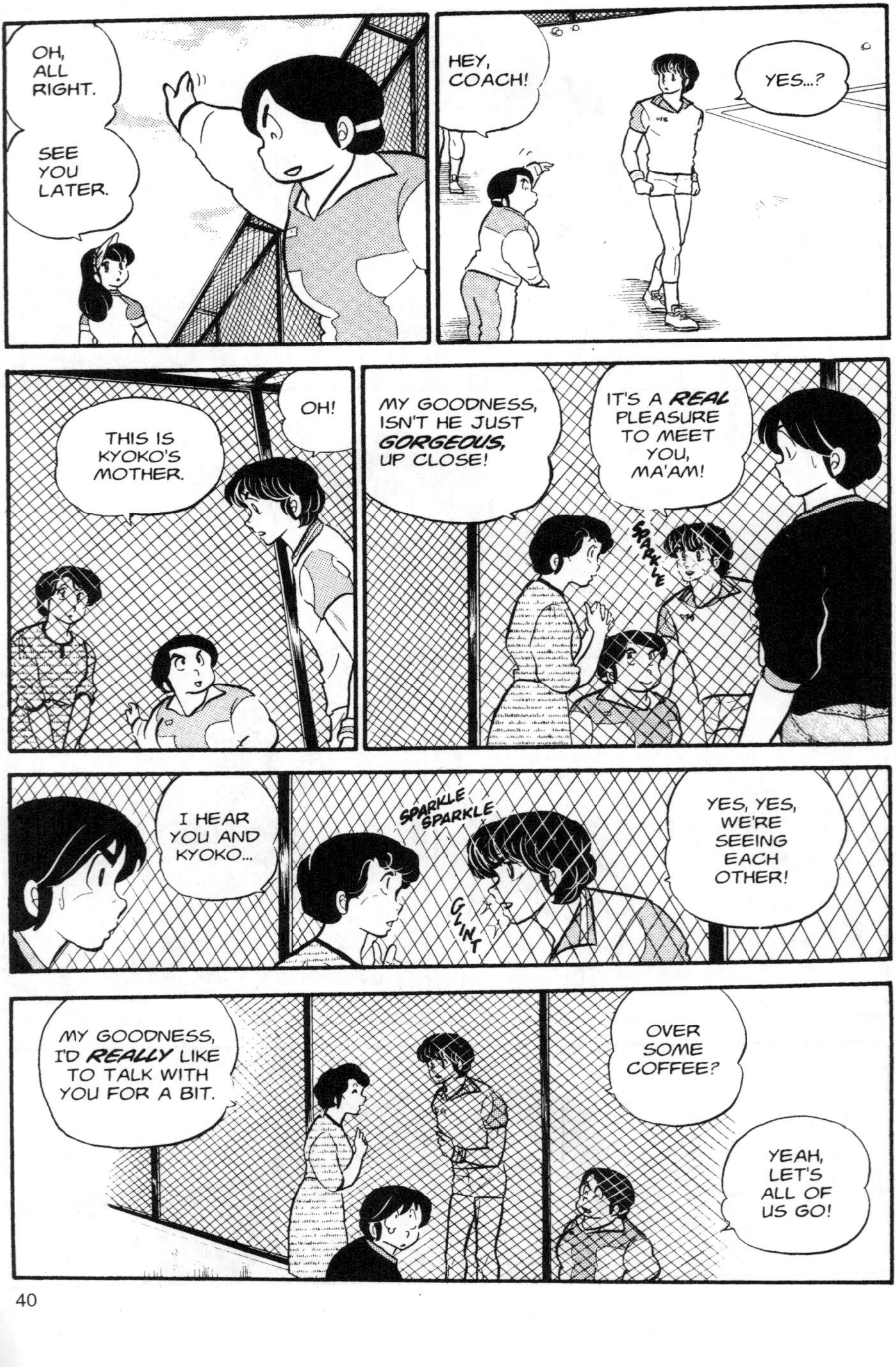
OH, ALL RIGHT.
SEE YOU LATER.
HEY, COACH!
YES...?
THIS IS KYOKO'S MOTHER.
OH!
MY GOODNESS, ISN'T HE JUST *GORGEOUS*, UP CLOSE!
IT'S A *REAL* PLEASURE TO MEET YOU, MA'AM!
SPARKLE
I HEAR YOU AND KYOKO...
SPARKLE SPARKLE
GLINT
YES, YES, WE'RE SEEING EACH OTHER!
MY GOODNESS, I'D *REALLY* LIKE TO TALK WITH YOU FOR A BIT.
OVER SOME COFFEE?
YEAH, LET'S ALL OF US GO!

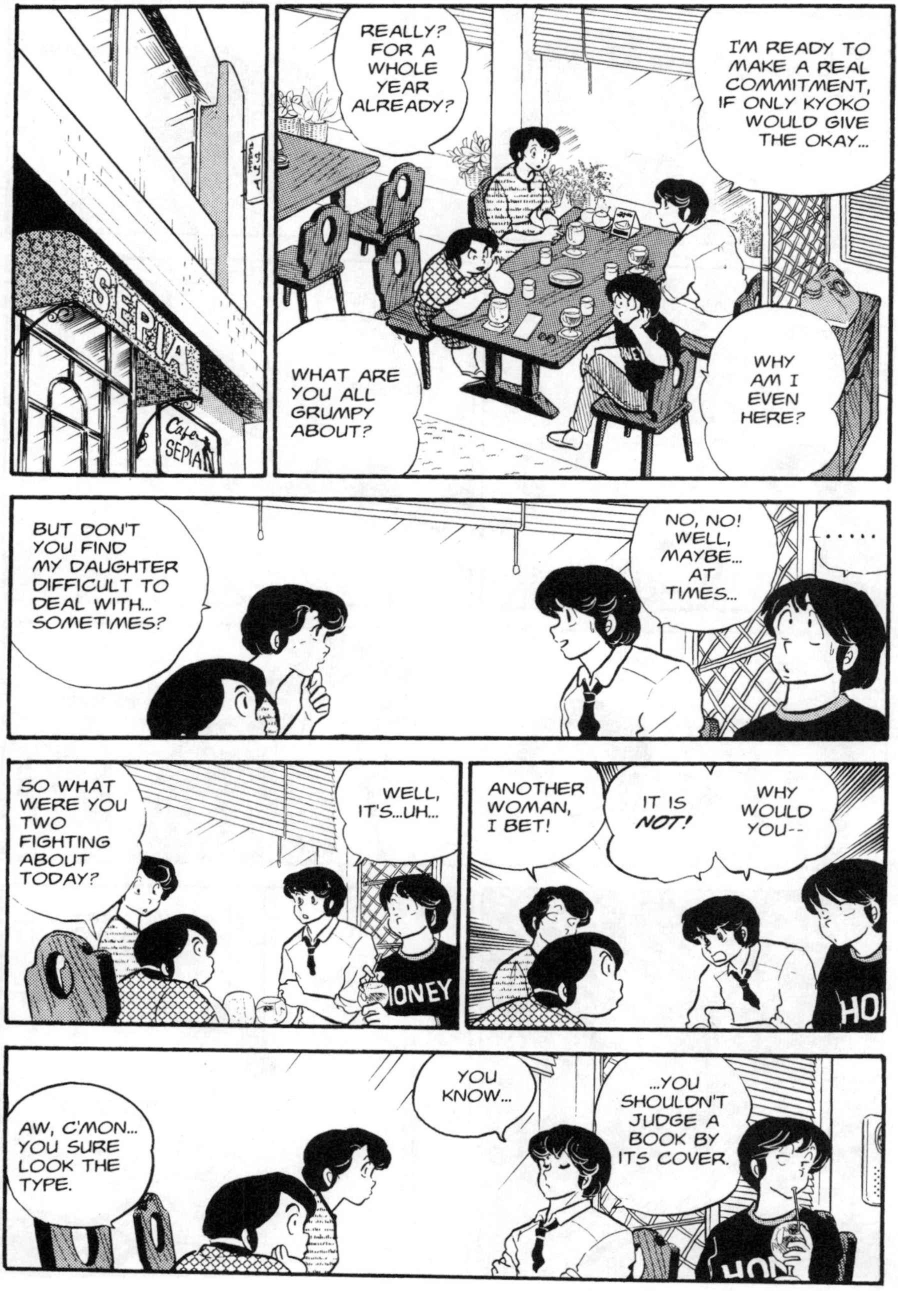
SEPIA
Cafe SEPIA
REALLY? FOR A WHOLE YEAR ALREADY?
I'M READY TO MAKE A REAL COMMITMENT, IF ONLY KYOKO WOULD GIVE THE OKAY...
WHAT ARE YOU ALL GRUMPY ABOUT?
WHY AM I EVEN HERE?
BUT DON'T YOU FIND MY DAUGHTER DIFFICULT TO DEAL WITH... SOMETIMES?
NO, NO! WELL, MAYBE... AT TIMES...
.....
SO WHAT WERE YOU TWO FIGHTING ABOUT TODAY?
WELL, IT'S...UH...
HONEY
ANOTHER WOMAN, I BET!
IT IS *NOT!*
WHY WOULD YOU--
AW, C'MON... YOU SURE LOOK THE TYPE.
YOU KNOW...
...YOU SHOULDN'T JUDGE A BOOK BY ITS COVER.

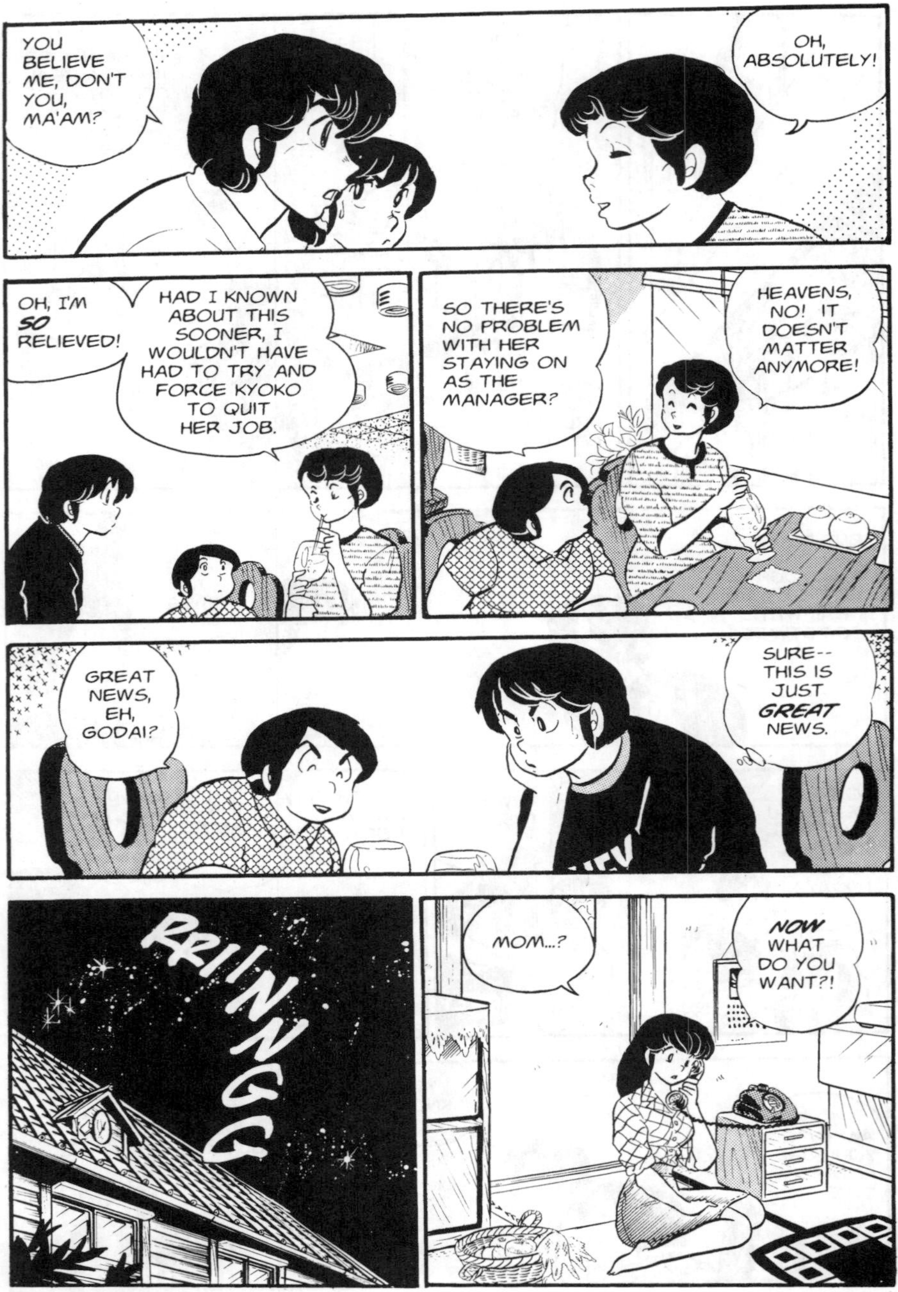
YOU BELIEVE ME, DON'T YOU, MA'AM?
OH, ABSOLUTELY!
OH, I'M *SO* RELIEVED!
HAD I KNOWN ABOUT THIS SOONER, I WOULDN'T HAVE HAD TO TRY AND FORCE KYOKO TO QUIT HER JOB.
SO THERE'S NO PROBLEM WITH HER STAYING ON AS THE MANAGER?
HEAVENS, NO! IT DOESN'T MATTER ANYMORE!
GREAT NEWS, EH, GODAI?
SURE-- THIS IS JUST ***GREAT*** NEWS.
RRIINNGG
MOM...?
NOW WHAT DO YOU WANT?!

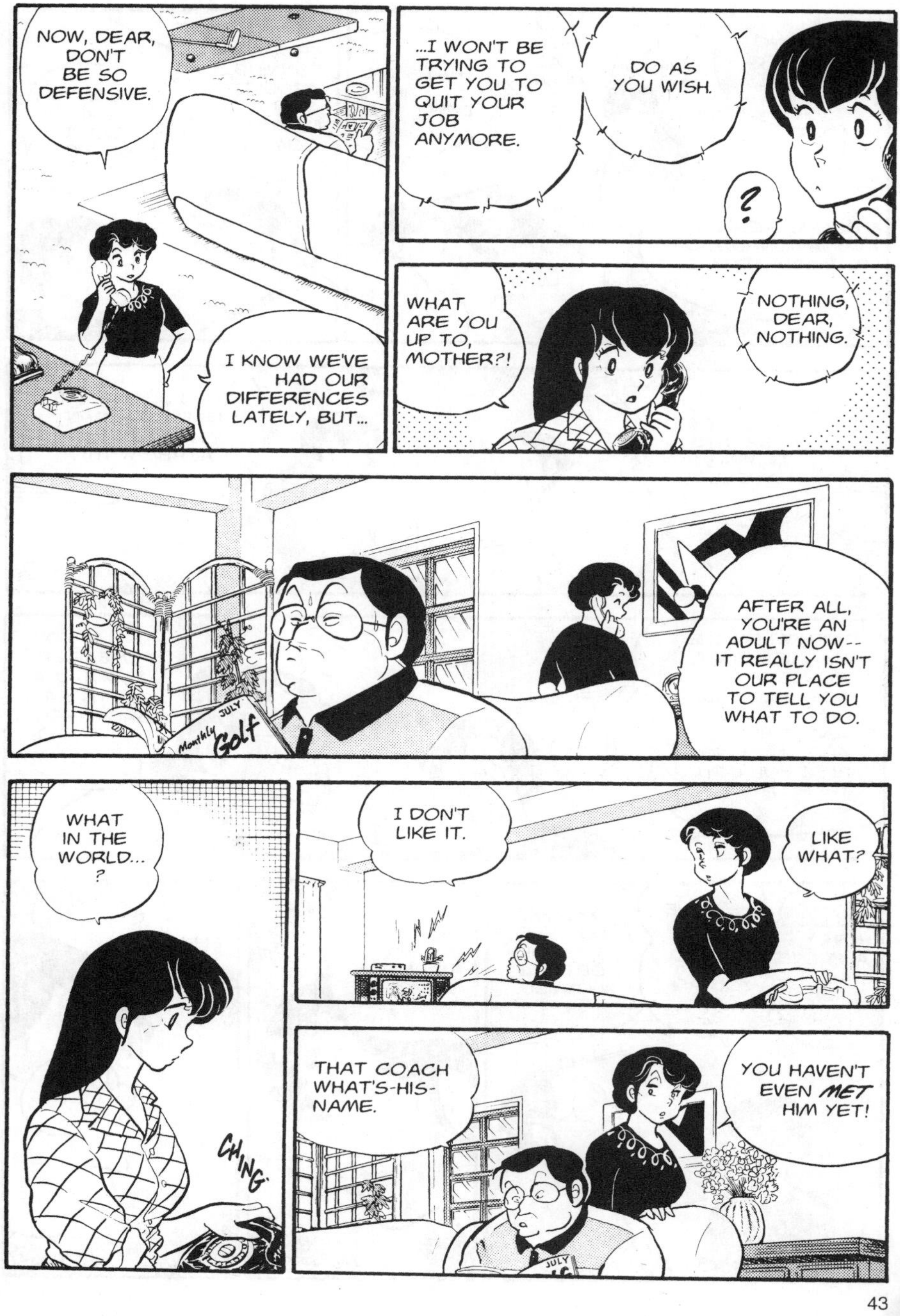
NOW, DEAR, DON'T BE SO DEFENSIVE.
I KNOW WE'VE HAD OUR DIFFERENCES LATELY, BUT...
...I WON'T BE TRYING TO GET YOU TO QUIT YOUR JOB ANYMORE.
DO AS YOU WISH.
?
WHAT ARE YOU UP TO, MOTHER?!
NOTHING, DEAR, NOTHING.
JULY
Monthly Golf
AFTER ALL, YOU'RE AN ADULT NOW-- IT REALLY ISN'T OUR PLACE TO TELL YOU WHAT TO DO.
WHAT IN THE WORLD... ?
CHING
I DON'T LIKE IT.
LIKE WHAT?
THAT COACH WHAT'S-HIS-NAME.
YOU HAVEN'T EVEN MET HIM YET!
JULY

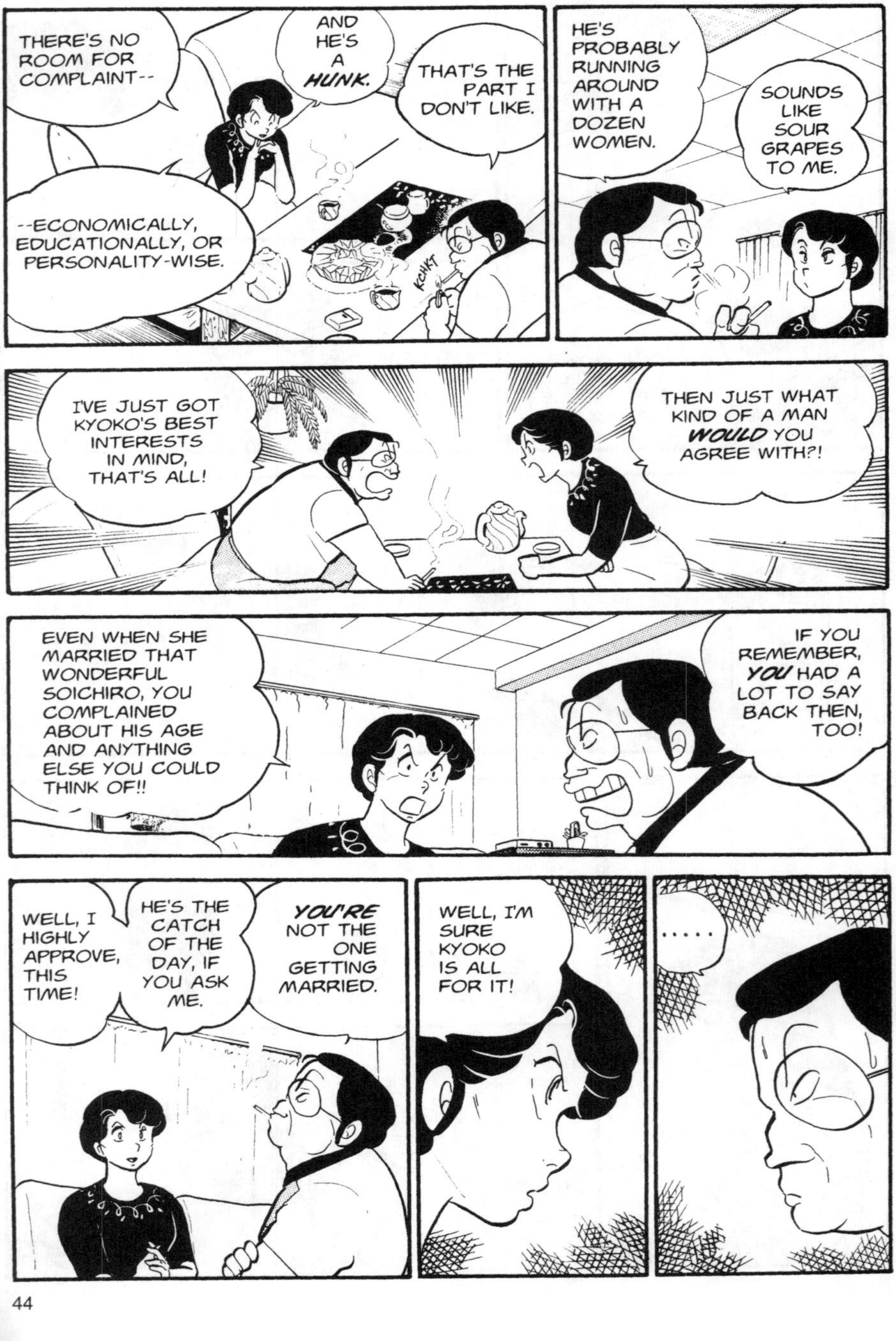
THERE'S NO ROOM FOR COMPLAINT--
AND HE'S A **HUNK.**
THAT'S THE PART I DON'T LIKE.
--ECONOMICALLY, EDUCATIONALLY, OR PERSONALITY-WISE.
KCHKT
HE'S PROBABLY RUNNING AROUND WITH A DOZEN WOMEN.
SOUNDS LIKE SOUR GRAPES TO ME.
I'VE JUST GOT KYOKO'S BEST INTERESTS IN MIND, THAT'S ALL!
THEN JUST WHAT KIND OF A MAN **WOULD** YOU AGREE WITH?!
EVEN WHEN SHE MARRIED THAT WONDERFUL SOICHIRO, YOU COMPLAINED ABOUT HIS AGE AND ANYTHING ELSE YOU COULD THINK OF!!
IF YOU REMEMBER, **YOU** HAD A LOT TO SAY BACK THEN, TOO!
WELL, I HIGHLY APPROVE, THIS TIME!
HE'S THE CATCH OF THE DAY, IF YOU ASK ME.
YOU'RE NOT THE ONE GETTING MARRIED.
WELL, I'M SURE KYOKO IS ALL FOR IT!
.....

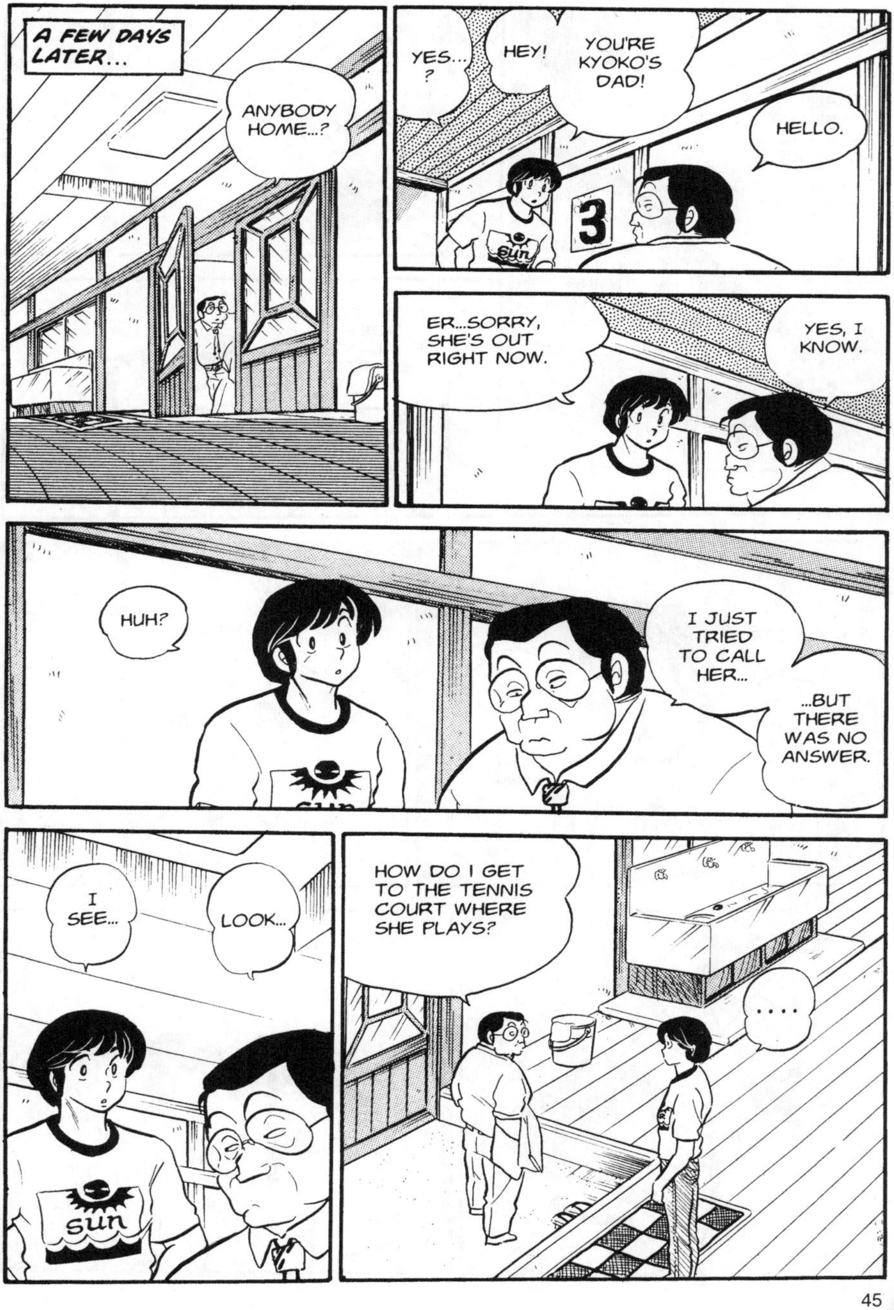
A FEW DAYS LATER...
ANYBODY HOME...?
YES...?
HEY!
YOU'RE KYOKO'S DAD!
HELLO.
ER...SORRY, SHE'S OUT RIGHT NOW.
YES, I KNOW.
HUH?
I JUST TRIED TO CALL HER...
...BUT THERE WAS NO ANSWER.
I SEE...
LOOK...
HOW DO I GET TO THE TENNIS COURT WHERE SHE PLAYS?
....

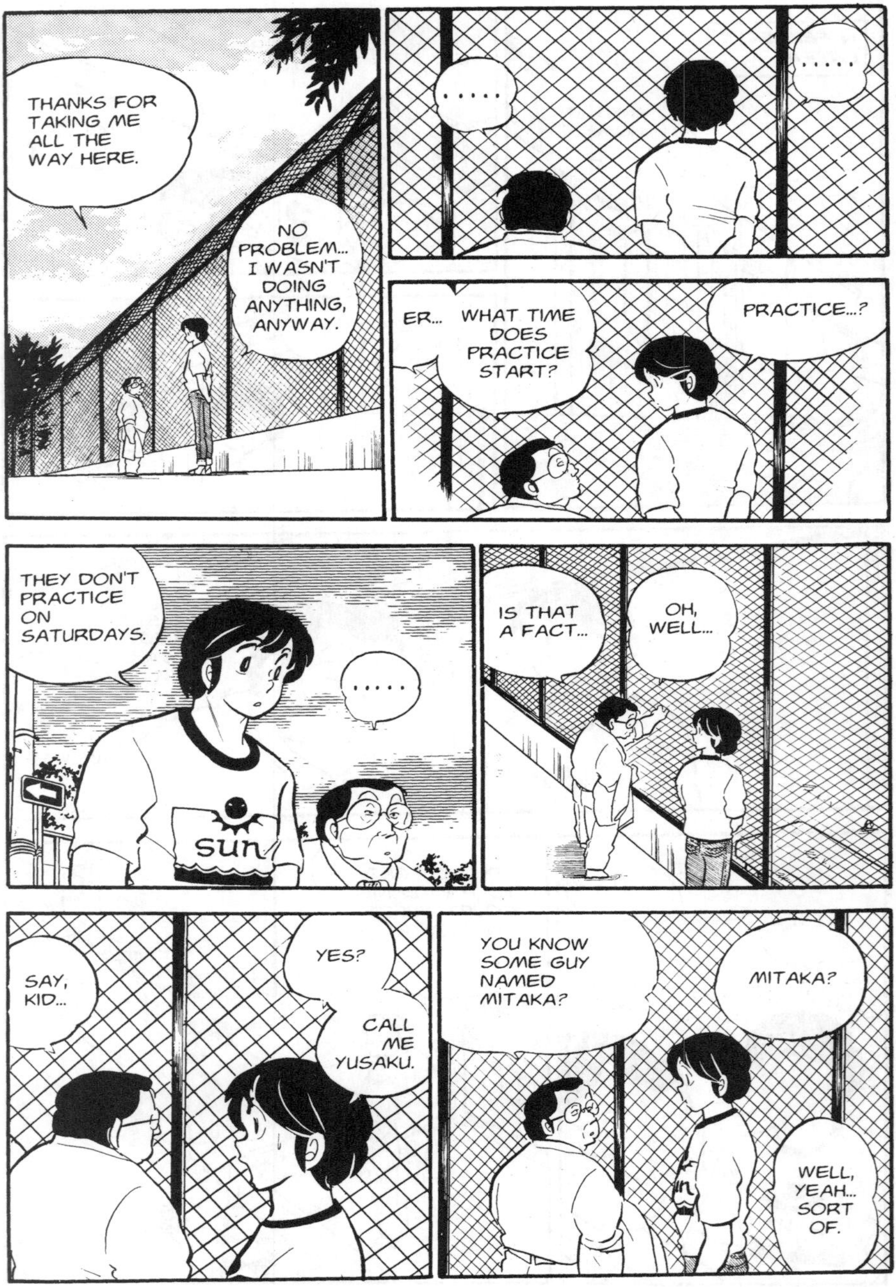
THANKS FOR TAKING ME ALL THE WAY HERE.
NO PROBLEM... I WASN'T DOING ANYTHING, ANYWAY.
......
......
ER...
WHAT TIME DOES PRACTICE START?
PRACTICE...?
THEY DON'T PRACTICE ON SATURDAYS.
......
IS THAT A FACT...
OH, WELL...
SAY, KID...
YES?
CALL ME YUSAKU.
YOU KNOW SOME GUY NAMED MITAKA?
MITAKA?
WELL, YEAH... SORT OF.

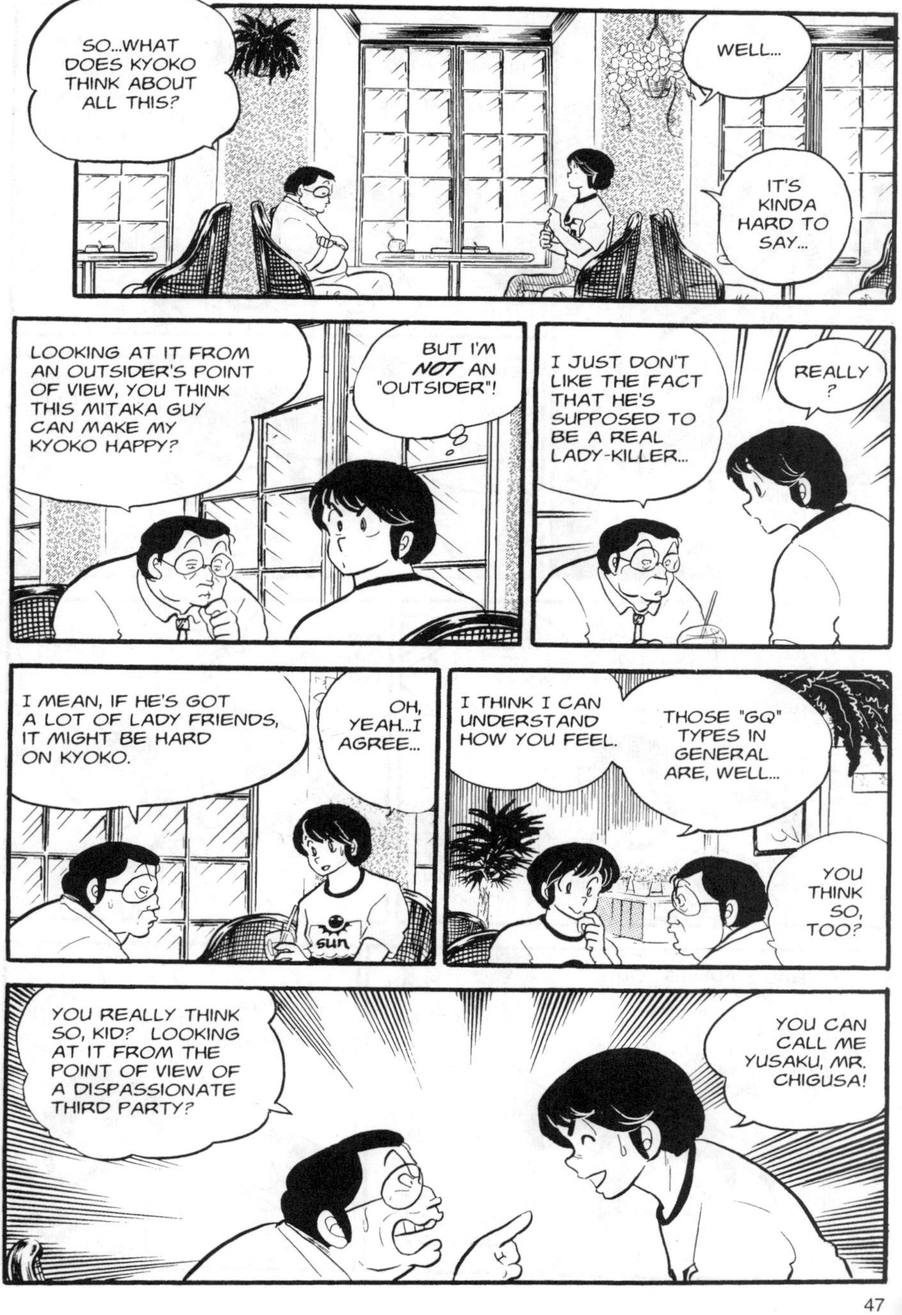
SO...WHAT DOES KYOKO THINK ABOUT ALL THIS?
WELL...
IT'S KINDA HARD TO SAY...
LOOKING AT IT FROM AN OUTSIDER'S POINT OF VIEW, YOU THINK THIS MITAKA GUY CAN MAKE MY KYOKO HAPPY?
BUT I'M *NOT* AN "OUTSIDER"!
I JUST DON'T LIKE THE FACT THAT HE'S SUPPOSED TO BE A REAL LADY-KILLER...
REALLY?
I MEAN, IF HE'S GOT A LOT OF LADY FRIENDS, IT MIGHT BE HARD ON KYOKO.
OH, YEAH...I AGREE...
SUN
I THINK I CAN UNDERSTAND HOW YOU FEEL.
THOSE "GQ" TYPES IN GENERAL ARE, WELL...
YOU THINK SO, TOO?
YOU REALLY THINK SO, KID? LOOKING AT IT FROM THE POINT OF VIEW OF A DISPASSIONATE THIRD PARTY?
YOU CAN CALL ME YUSAKU, MR. CHIGUSA!

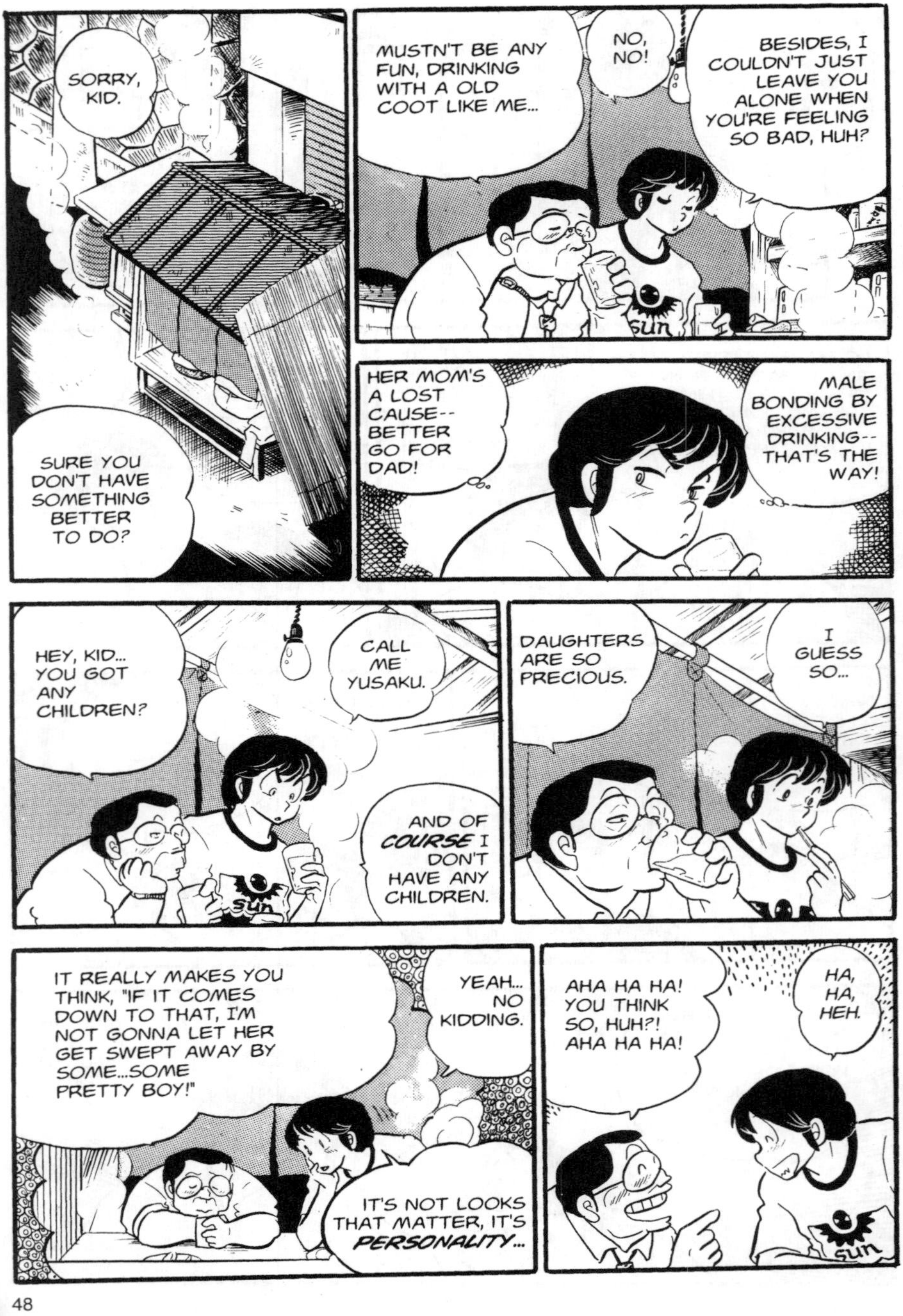

SORRY, KID.
SURE YOU DON'T HAVE SOMETHING BETTER TO DO?
MUSTN'T BE ANY FUN, DRINKING WITH A OLD COOT LIKE ME...
NO, NO!
BESIDES, I COULDN'T JUST LEAVE YOU ALONE WHEN YOU'RE FEELING SO BAD, HUH?
HER MOM'S A LOST CAUSE--BETTER GO FOR DAD!
MALE BONDING BY EXCESSIVE DRINKING--THAT'S THE WAY!
HEY, KID... YOU GOT ANY CHILDREN?
CALL ME YUSAKU.
AND OF COURSE I DON'T HAVE ANY CHILDREN.
DAUGHTERS ARE SO PRECIOUS.
I GUESS SO...
IT REALLY MAKES YOU THINK, "IF IT COMES DOWN TO THAT, I'M NOT GONNA LET HER GET SWEPT AWAY BY SOME...SOME PRETTY BOY!"
YEAH... NO KIDDING.
IT'S NOT LOOKS THAT MATTER, IT'S PERSONALITY...
AHA HA HA! YOU THINK SO, HUH?! AHA HA HA!
HA, HA, HEH.

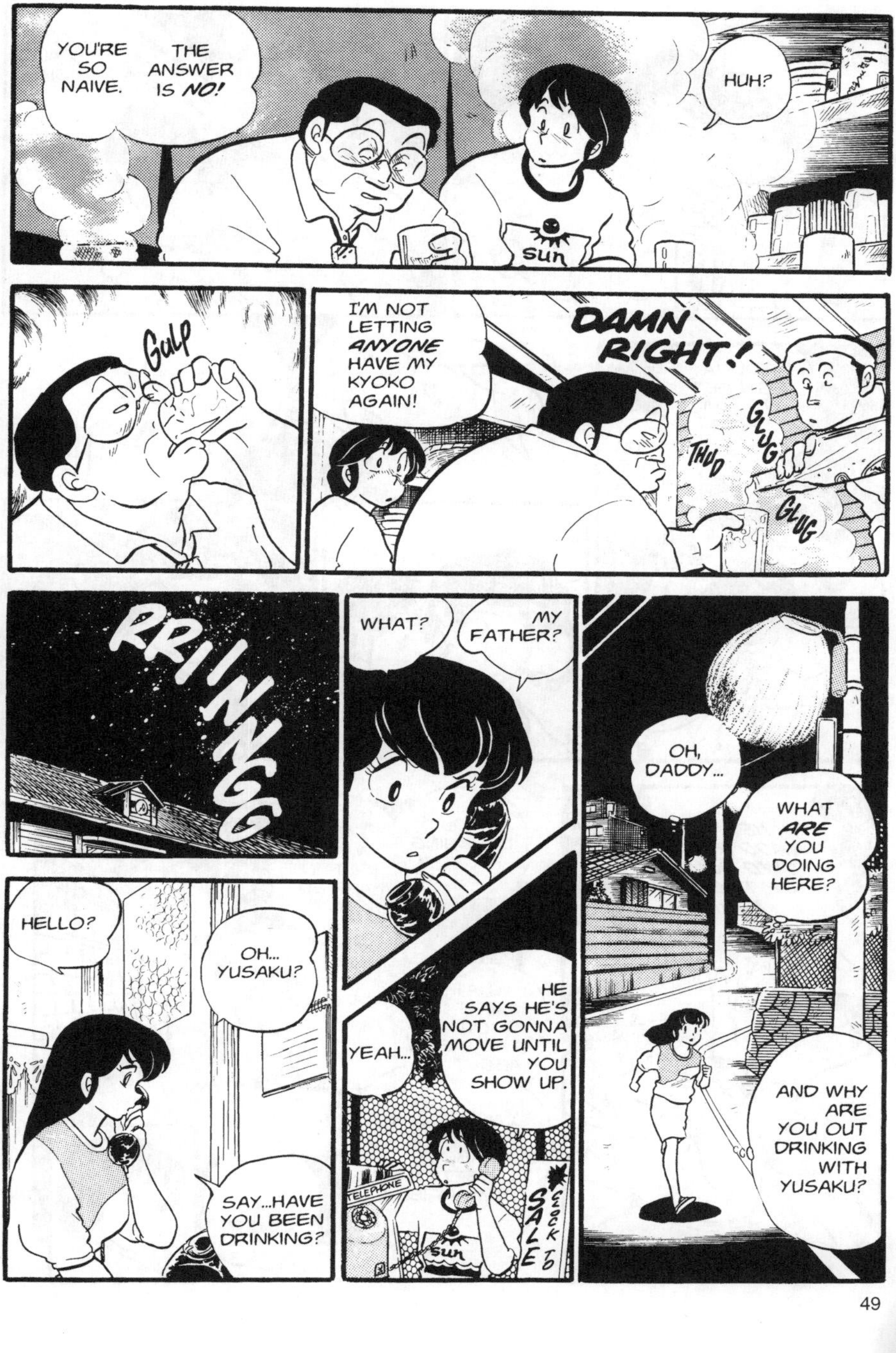
YOU'RE SO NAIVE.
THE ANSWER IS NO!
HUH?
GULP
I'M NOT LETTING ANYONE HAVE MY KYOKO AGAIN!
DAMN RIGHT!
THUD
GLUG
GLUG
RRIINNGG
HELLO?
OH... YUSAKU?
SAY...HAVE YOU BEEN DRINKING?
YEAH...
HE SAYS HE'S NOT GONNA MOVE UNTIL YOU SHOW UP.
TELEPHONE
SALE CLOCK TO
WHAT?
MY FATHER?
OH, DADDY...
WHAT ARE YOU DOING HERE?
AND WHY ARE YOU OUT DRINKING WITH YUSAKU?

YUSAKU...?

KYOKO!

COME ON, FATHER... UP YOU GO.

C'MON, IT'S ALL RIGHT.

GODDA GO'N GET KYO- ⤙HIC⤚ -KO...!

I'M RIGHT HERE.

HEY!! WADD'R YOU TWO DOIN' UP THERE, HUH?

YOU LISHENING, KYOKO?!

I DON' WAN'YA GETTIN' MARRIED 'GAIN!

WHAT *ARE* YOU TALKING ABOUT?!

I NEVER SAID ANYTHING ABOUT GETTING REMARRIED!!

DARN OL' COOT!

Part Three
Turn the Other Cheek

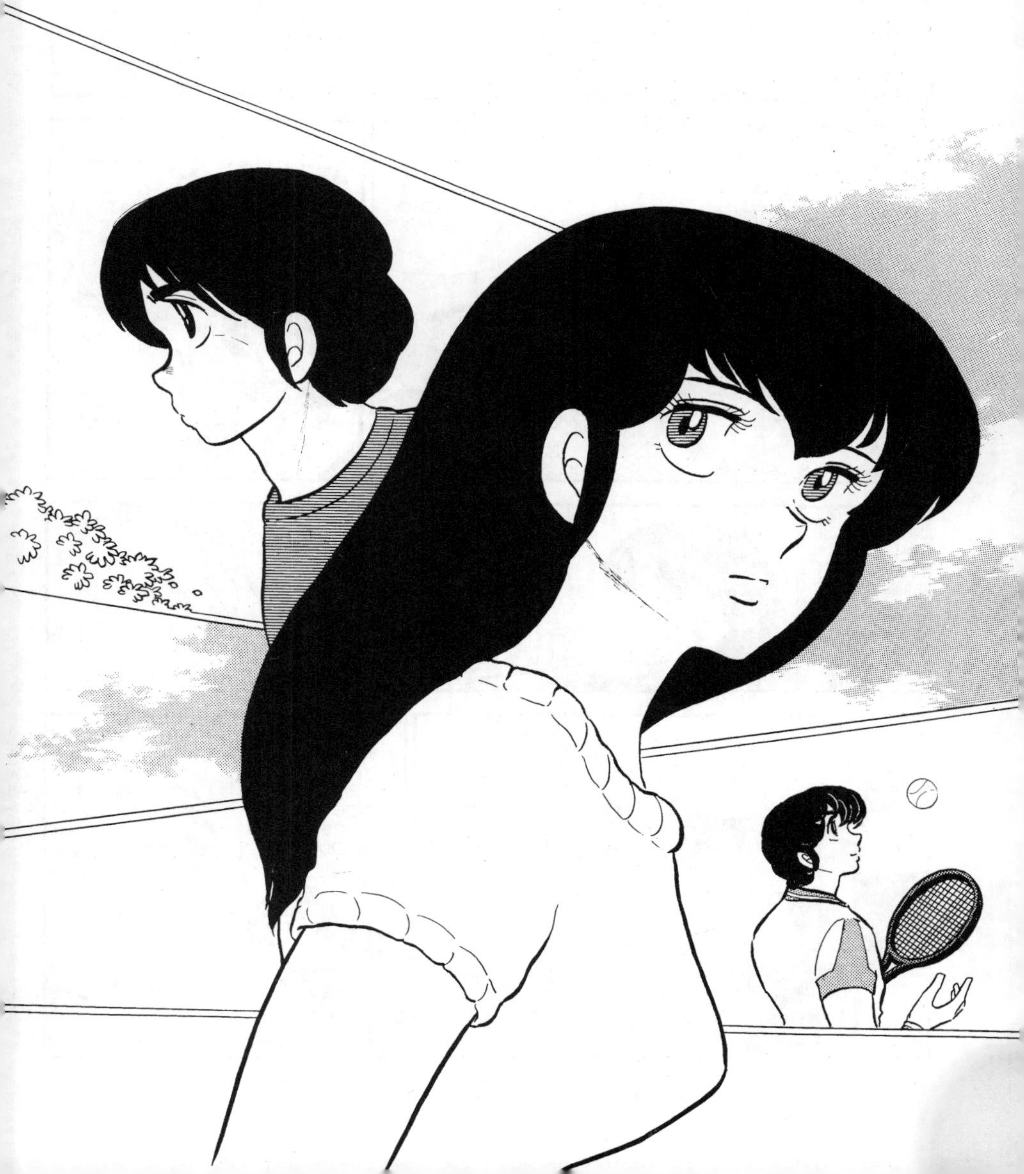

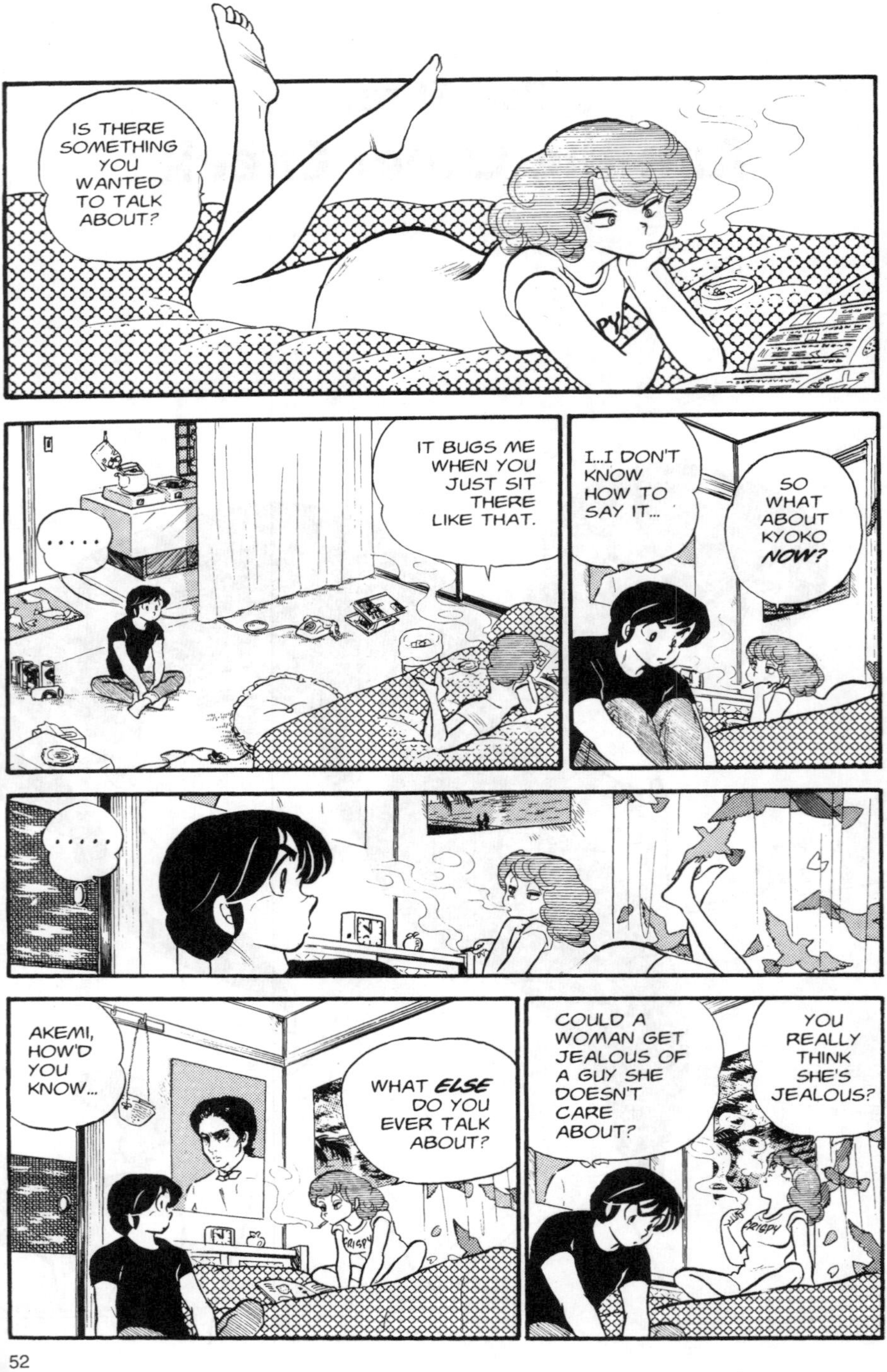
IS THERE SOMETHING YOU WANTED TO TALK ABOUT?
.....
IT BUGS ME WHEN YOU JUST SIT THERE LIKE THAT.
I...I DON'T KNOW HOW TO SAY IT...
SO WHAT ABOUT KYOKO NOW?
.....
AKEMI, HOW'D YOU KNOW...
WHAT ELSE DO YOU EVER TALK ABOUT?
COULD A WOMAN GET JEALOUS OF A GUY SHE DOESN'T CARE ABOUT?
YOU REALLY THINK SHE'S JEALOUS?

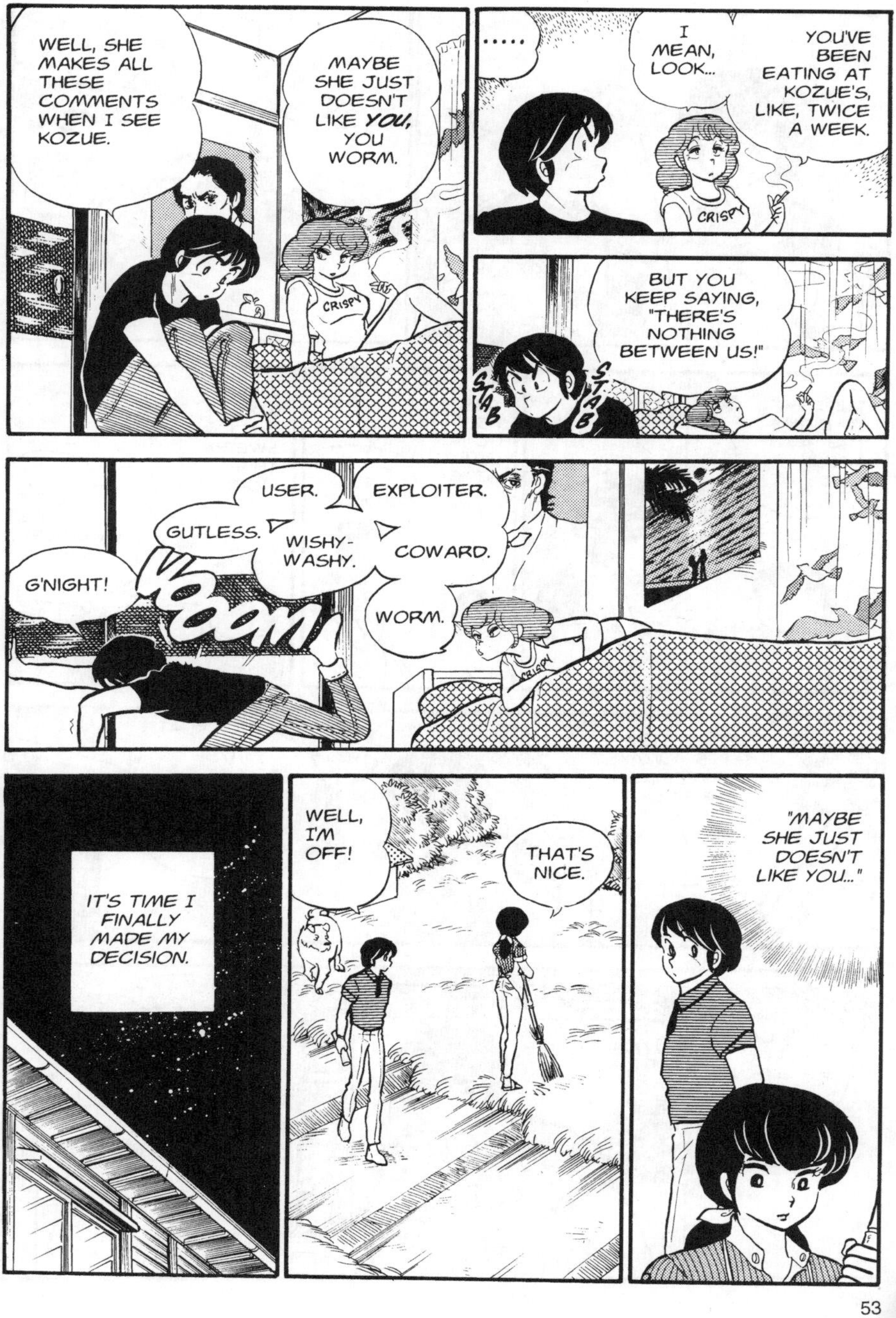
WELL, SHE MAKES ALL THESE COMMENTS WHEN I SEE KOZUE.
MAYBE SHE JUST DOESN'T LIKE *YOU,* YOU WORM.
.....
I MEAN, LOOK...
YOU'VE BEEN EATING AT KOZUE'S, LIKE, TWICE A WEEK.
CRISPY
BUT YOU KEEP SAYING, "THERE'S NOTHING BETWEEN US!"
STAB
STAB
G'NIGHT!
VOOOM
GUTLESS.
USER.
WISHY-WASHY.
EXPLOITER.
COWARD.
WORM.
IT'S TIME I FINALLY MADE MY DECISION.
WELL, I'M OFF!
THAT'S NICE.
"MAYBE SHE JUST DOESN'T LIKE YOU..."

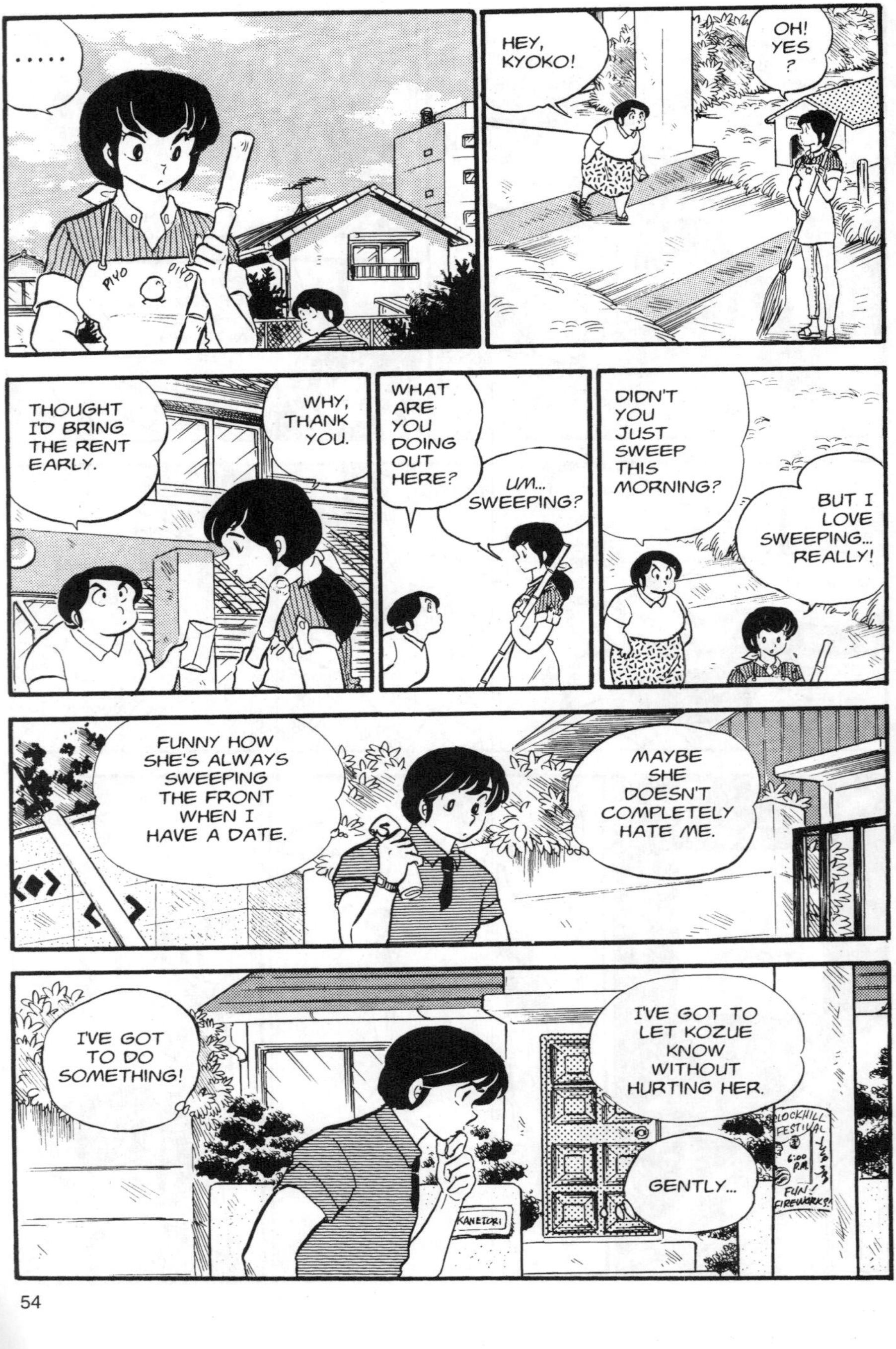
......
PIYO PIYO
HEY, KYOKO!
OH! YES ?
THOUGHT I'D BRING THE RENT EARLY.
WHY, THANK YOU.
WHAT ARE YOU DOING OUT HERE?
UM... SWEEPING?
DIDN'T YOU JUST SWEEP THIS MORNING?
BUT I LOVE SWEEPING... REALLY!
FUNNY HOW SHE'S ALWAYS SWEEPING THE FRONT WHEN I HAVE A DATE.
MAYBE SHE DOESN'T COMPLETELY HATE ME.
I'VE GOT TO DO SOMETHING!
I'VE GOT TO LET KOZUE KNOW WITHOUT HURTING HER.
LOCKHILL FESTIVAL
6:00 P.M.
FUN! FIREWORKS?!
GENTLY...
KANETORI

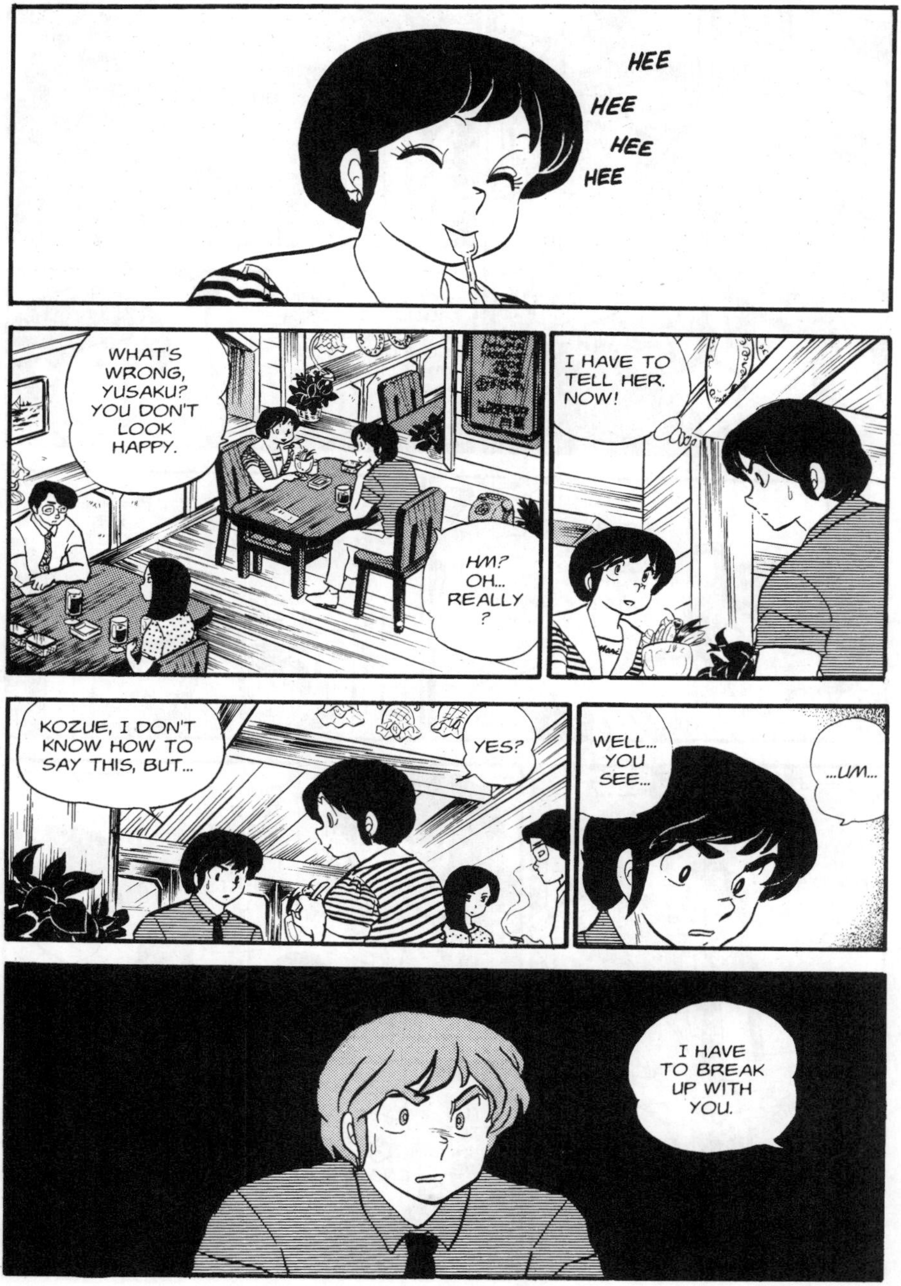
HEE
HEE
HEE
HEE
WHAT'S WRONG, YUSAKU? YOU DON'T LOOK HAPPY.
HM? OH... REALLY?
I HAVE TO TELL HER. NOW!
KOZUE, I DON'T KNOW HOW TO SAY THIS, BUT...
YES?
WELL... YOU SEE...
...UM...
I HAVE TO BREAK UP WITH YOU.

. . . . .

WH-WHAT?

BUT... WHY?

I'VE BEEN THINKING ABOUT IT FOR A WHILE NOW, BUT I COULDN'T BRING MYSELF TO HURT YOU.

BUT...BUT HOW CAN YOU DO THIS? WHY?

ANSWER ME!

I'VE TRIED TO BE EVERYTHING FOR YOU! BUT NOW YOU--

PLEASE! BE QUIET!

ANYWAY, THIS BAND'S ACT IS, LIKE, SO GROSS!

2P

2P

DO THEY REALLY BRING A PIG'S HEAD ON STAGE?

I'VE EVEN TOLD MY PARENTS ABOUT YOU! WHAT'S HAPPENED?!

THE TRUTH IS, I'VE...

...I'VE... GOTTEN ENGAGED!

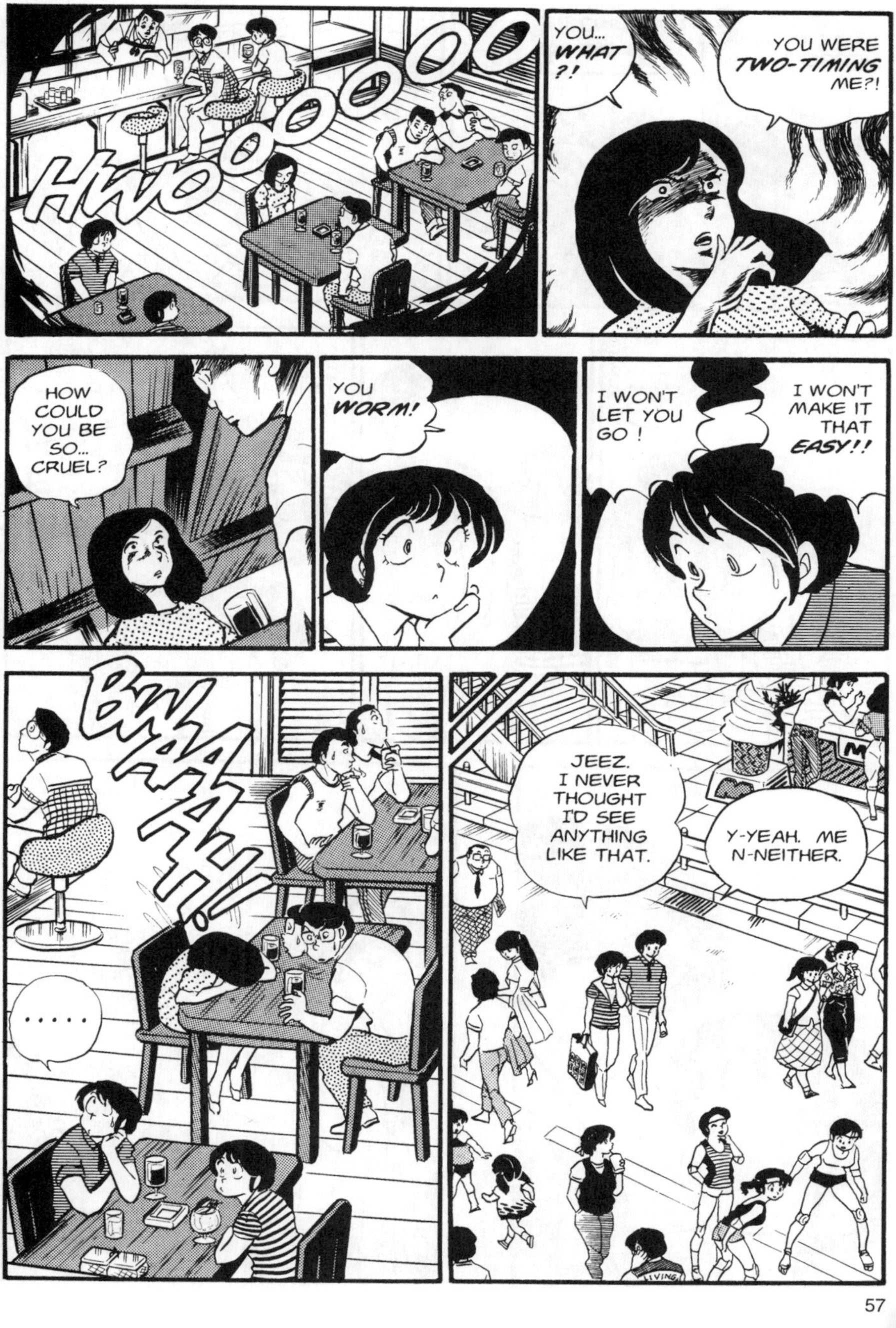
HWOOOOOOOO
YOU... WHAT ?!
YOU WERE TWO-TIMING ME?!
HOW COULD YOU BE SO... CRUEL?
YOU WORM!
I WON'T LET YOU GO !
I WON'T MAKE IT THAT EASY!!
BWAAAH!
.....
JEEZ. I NEVER THOUGHT I'D SEE ANYTHING LIKE THAT.
Y-YEAH. ME N-NEITHER.

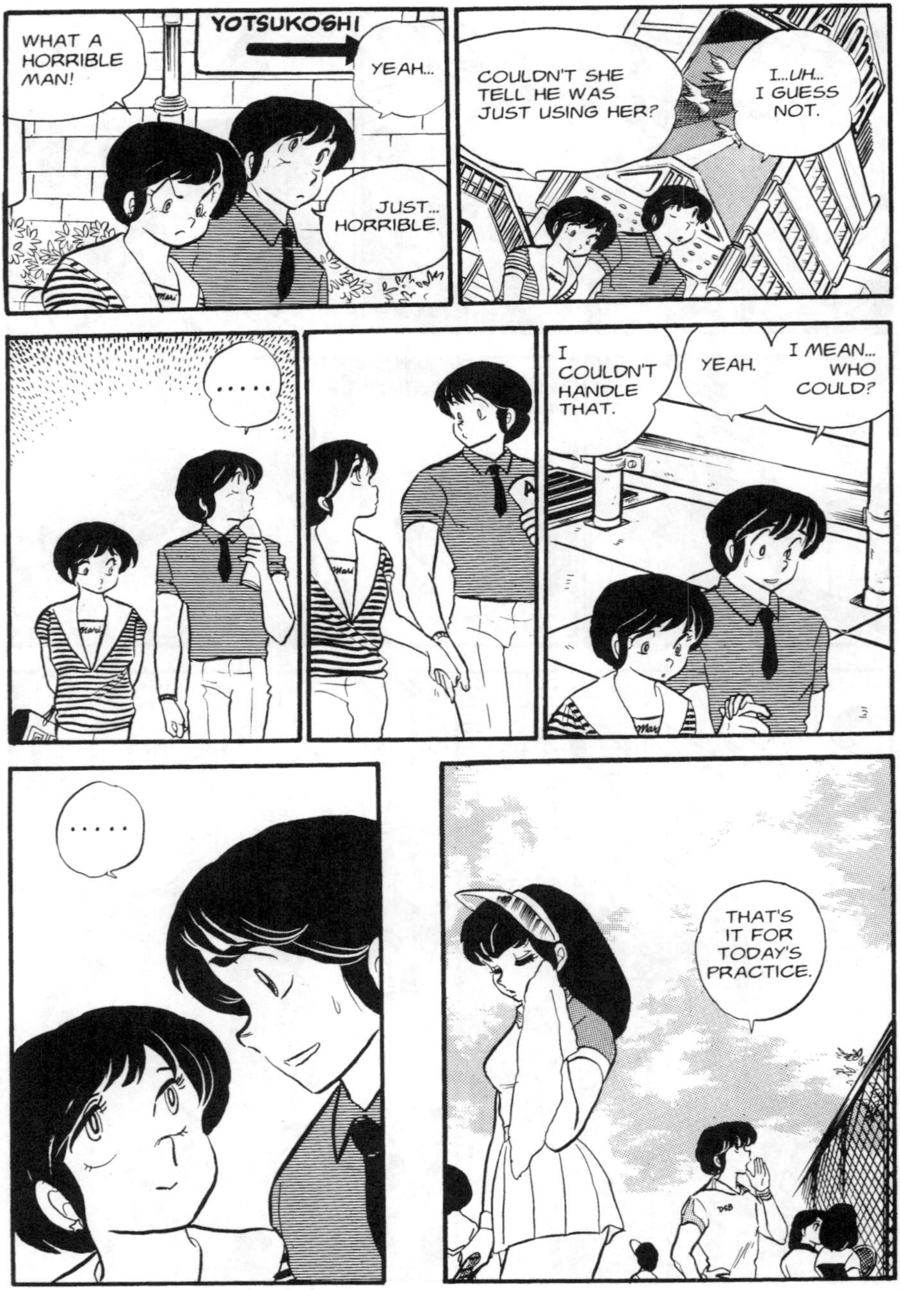
WHAT A HORRIBLE MAN!
YOTSUKOSHI
YEAH...
JUST... HORRIBLE.
COULDN'T SHE TELL HE WAS JUST USING HER?
I...UH... I GUESS NOT.
.....
I COULDN'T HANDLE THAT.
YEAH.
I MEAN... WHO COULD?
.....
THAT'S IT FOR TODAY'S PRACTICE.

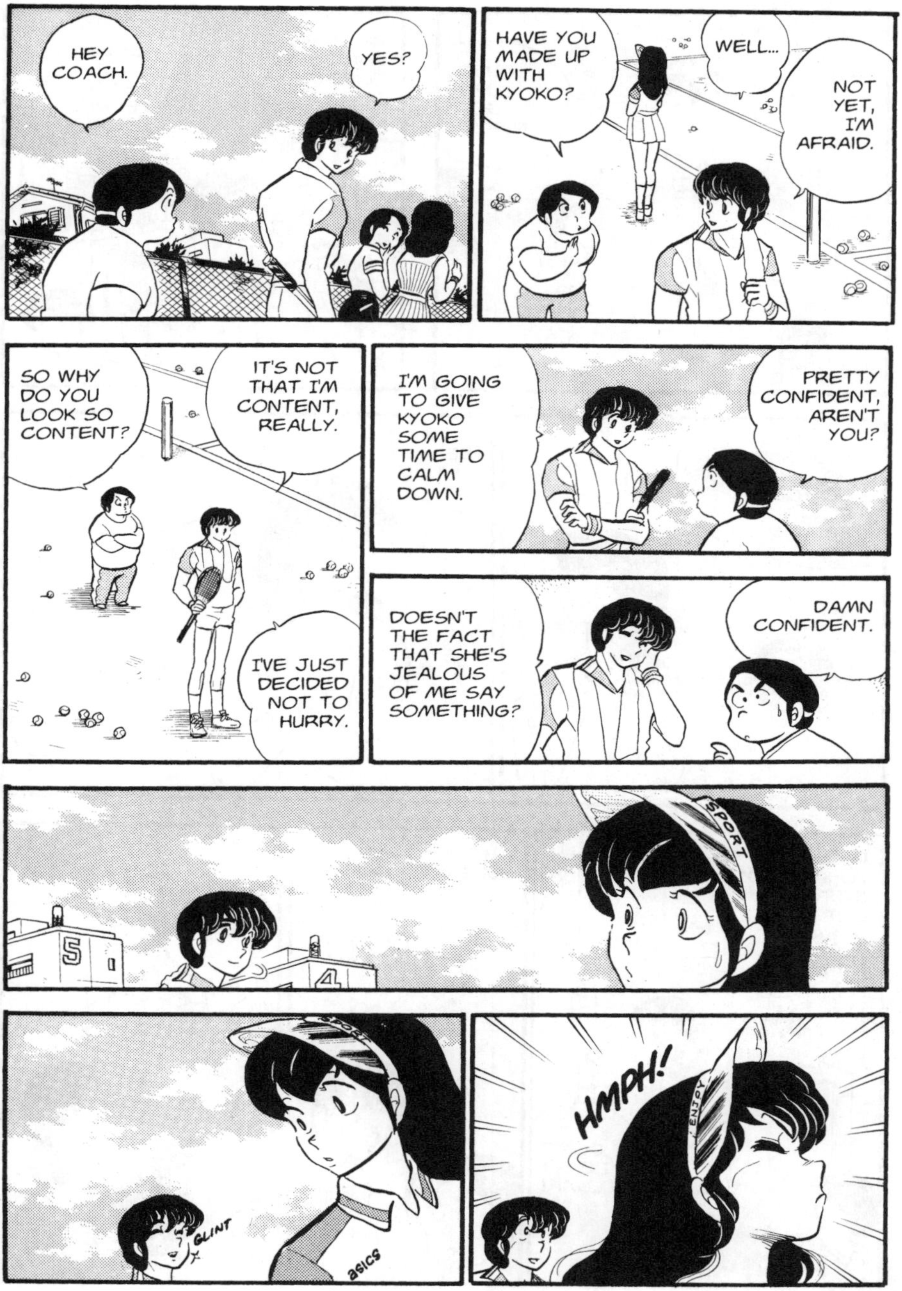
HEY COACH.
YES?
HAVE YOU MADE UP WITH KYOKO?
WELL...
NOT YET, I'M AFRAID.
SO WHY DO YOU LOOK SO CONTENT?
IT'S NOT THAT I'M CONTENT, REALLY.
I'VE JUST DECIDED NOT TO HURRY.
I'M GOING TO GIVE KYOKO SOME TIME TO CALM DOWN.
PRETTY CONFIDENT, AREN'T YOU?
DOESN'T THE FACT THAT SHE'S JEALOUS OF ME SAY SOMETHING?
DAMN CONFIDENT.
SPORT
5
4
SPORT
GLINT
asics
HMPH!
ENJOY

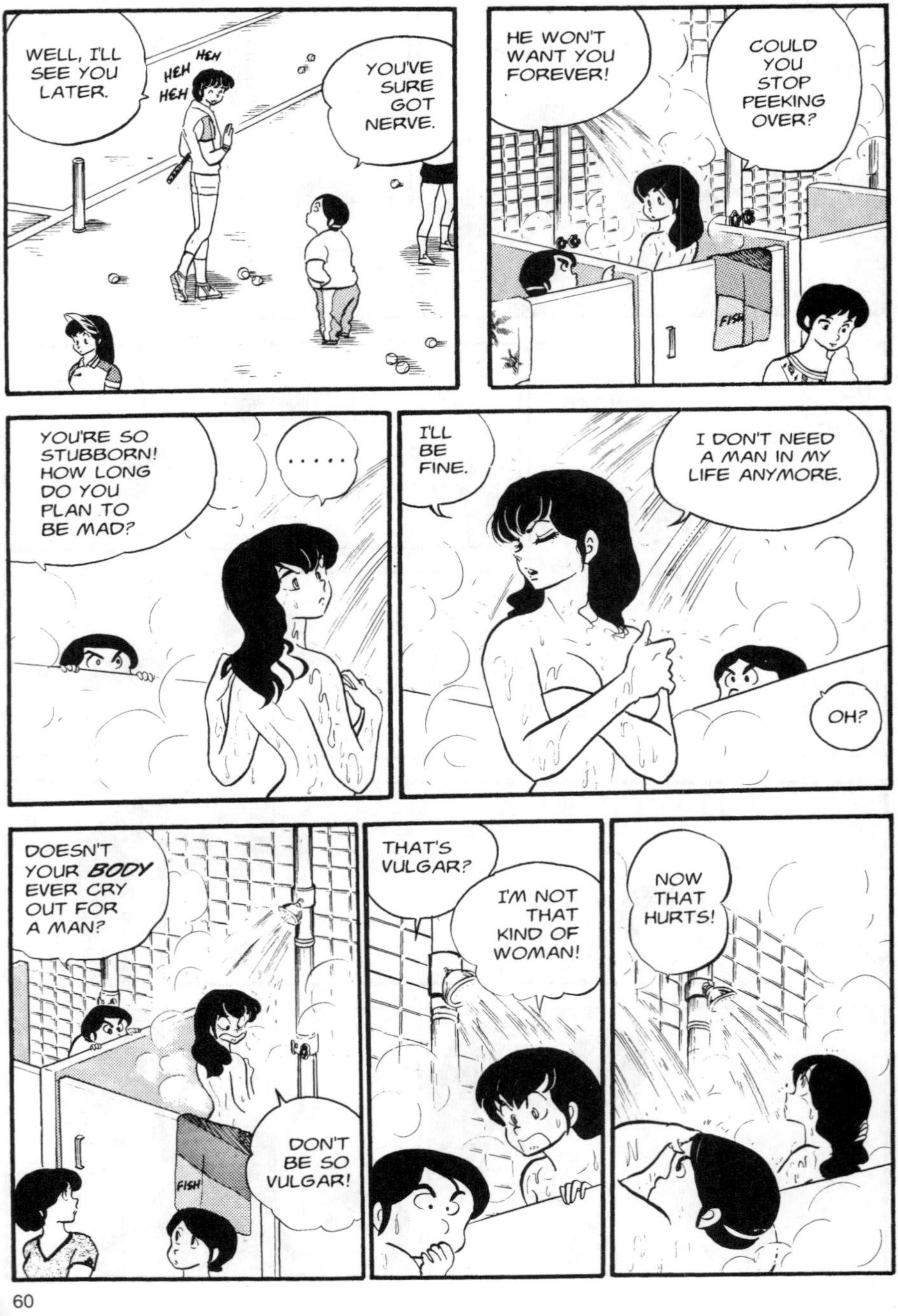
WELL, I'LL SEE YOU LATER.
HEH HEH HEH
YOU'VE SURE GOT NERVE.
HE WON'T WANT YOU FOREVER!
COULD YOU STOP PEEKING OVER?
FISH
YOU'RE SO STUBBORN! HOW LONG DO YOU PLAN TO BE MAD?
......
I'LL BE FINE.
I DON'T NEED A MAN IN MY LIFE ANYMORE.
OH?
DOESN'T YOUR *BODY* EVER CRY OUT FOR A MAN?
DON'T BE SO VULGAR!
FISH
THAT'S VULGAR?
I'M NOT THAT KIND OF WOMAN!
NOW THAT HURTS!

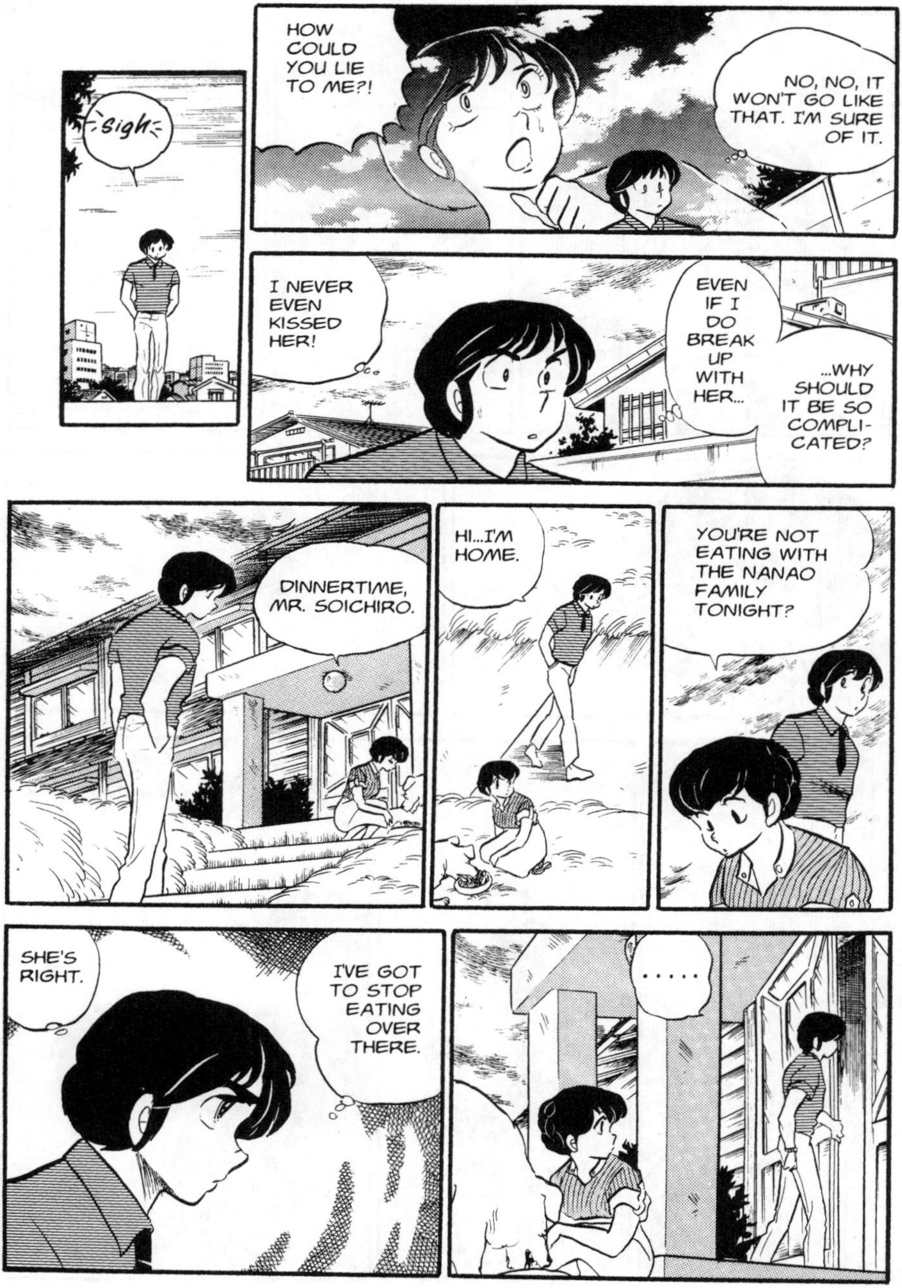
sigh
HOW COULD YOU LIE TO ME?!
NO, NO, IT WON'T GO LIKE THAT. I'M SURE OF IT.
I NEVER EVEN KISSED HER!
EVEN IF I DO BREAK UP WITH HER...
...WHY SHOULD IT BE SO COMPLI-CATED?
DINNERTIME, MR. SOICHIRO.
HI...I'M HOME.
YOU'RE NOT EATING WITH THE NANAO FAMILY TONIGHT?
SHE'S RIGHT.
I'VE GOT TO STOP EATING OVER THERE.
. . . . .

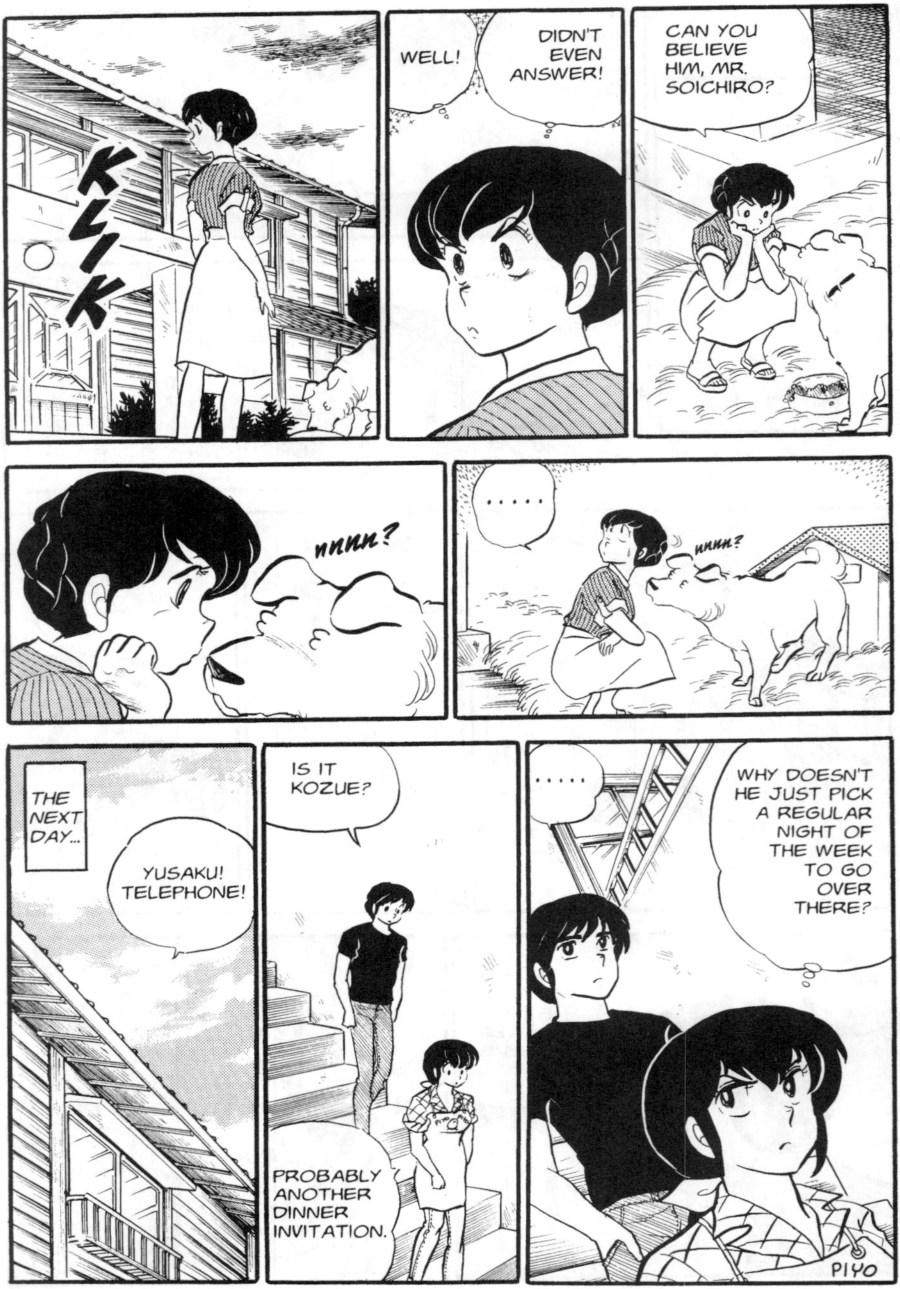
KLIK
WELL!
DIDN'T EVEN ANSWER!
CAN YOU BELIEVE HIM, MR. SOICHIRO?
nnnn?
......
nnnn?
THE NEXT DAY...
YUSAKU! TELEPHONE!
IS IT KOZUE?
PROBABLY ANOTHER DINNER INVITATION.
.....
WHY DOESN'T HE JUST PICK A REGULAR NIGHT OF THE WEEK TO GO OVER THERE?
PIYO

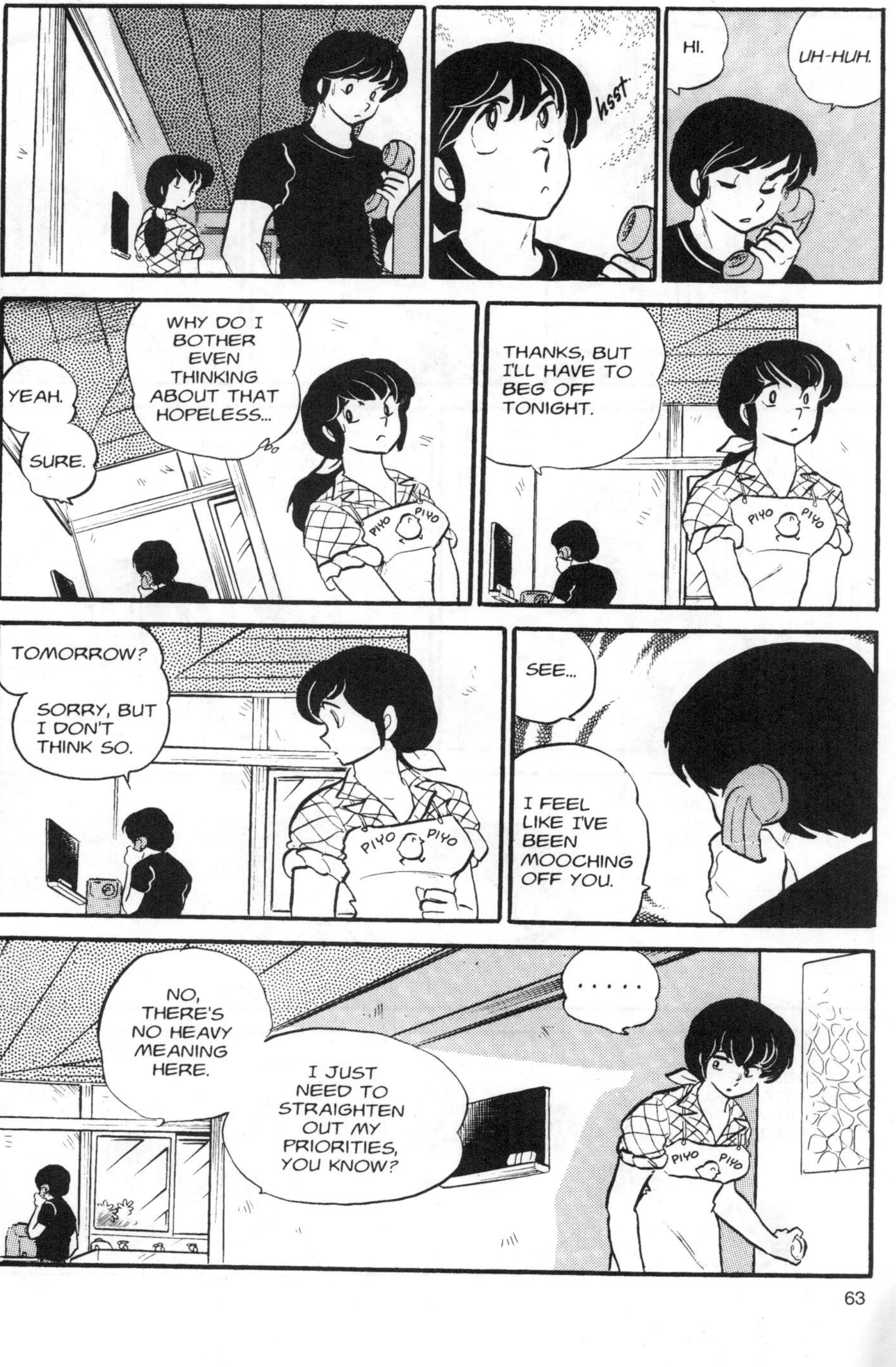
hsst
HI.
UH-HUH.
YEAH.
SURE.
WHY DO I BOTHER EVEN THINKING ABOUT THAT HOPELESS...
PIYO PIYO
THANKS, BUT I'LL HAVE TO BEG OFF TONIGHT.
PIYO PIYO
TOMORROW?
SORRY, BUT I DON'T THINK SO.
PIYO PIYO
SEE...
I FEEL LIKE I'VE BEEN MOOCHING OFF YOU.
NO, THERE'S NO HEAVY MEANING HERE.
I JUST NEED TO STRAIGHTEN OUT MY PRIORITIES, YOU KNOW?
.....
PIYO PIYO

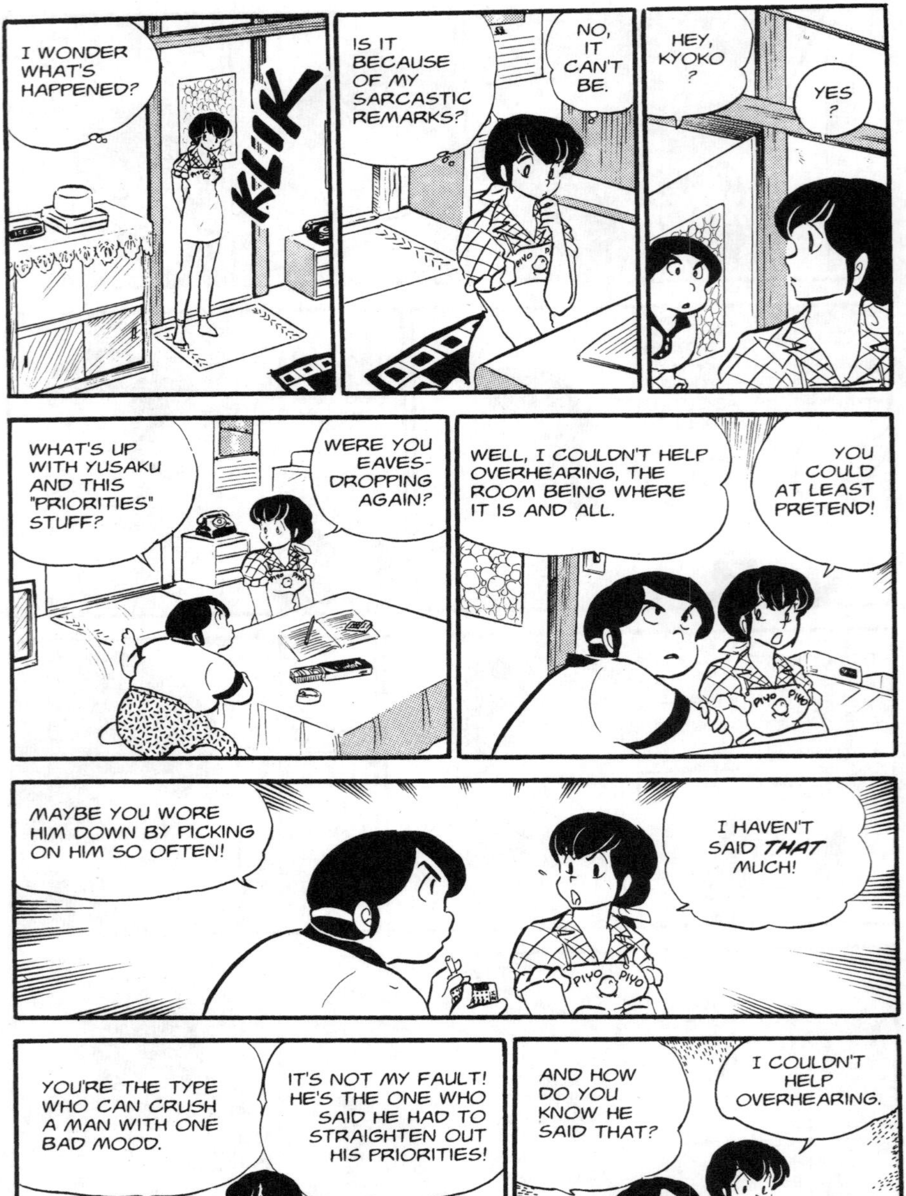
I WONDER WHAT'S HAPPENED?
KLIK
IS IT BECAUSE OF MY SARCASTIC REMARKS?
NO, IT CAN'T BE.
HEY, KYOKO?
YES?
WHAT'S UP WITH YUSAKU AND THIS "PRIORITIES" STUFF?
WERE YOU EAVES-DROPPING AGAIN?
WELL, I COULDN'T HELP OVERHEARING, THE ROOM BEING WHERE IT IS AND ALL.
YOU COULD AT LEAST PRETEND!
MAYBE YOU WORE HIM DOWN BY PICKING ON HIM SO OFTEN!
I HAVEN'T SAID *THAT* MUCH!
YOU'RE THE TYPE WHO CAN CRUSH A MAN WITH ONE BAD MOOD.
IT'S NOT MY FAULT! HE'S THE ONE WHO SAID HE HAD TO STRAIGHTEN OUT HIS PRIORITIES!
CHK.
AND HOW DO YOU KNOW HE SAID THAT?
I COULDN'T HELP OVERHEARING.

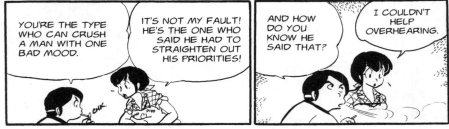

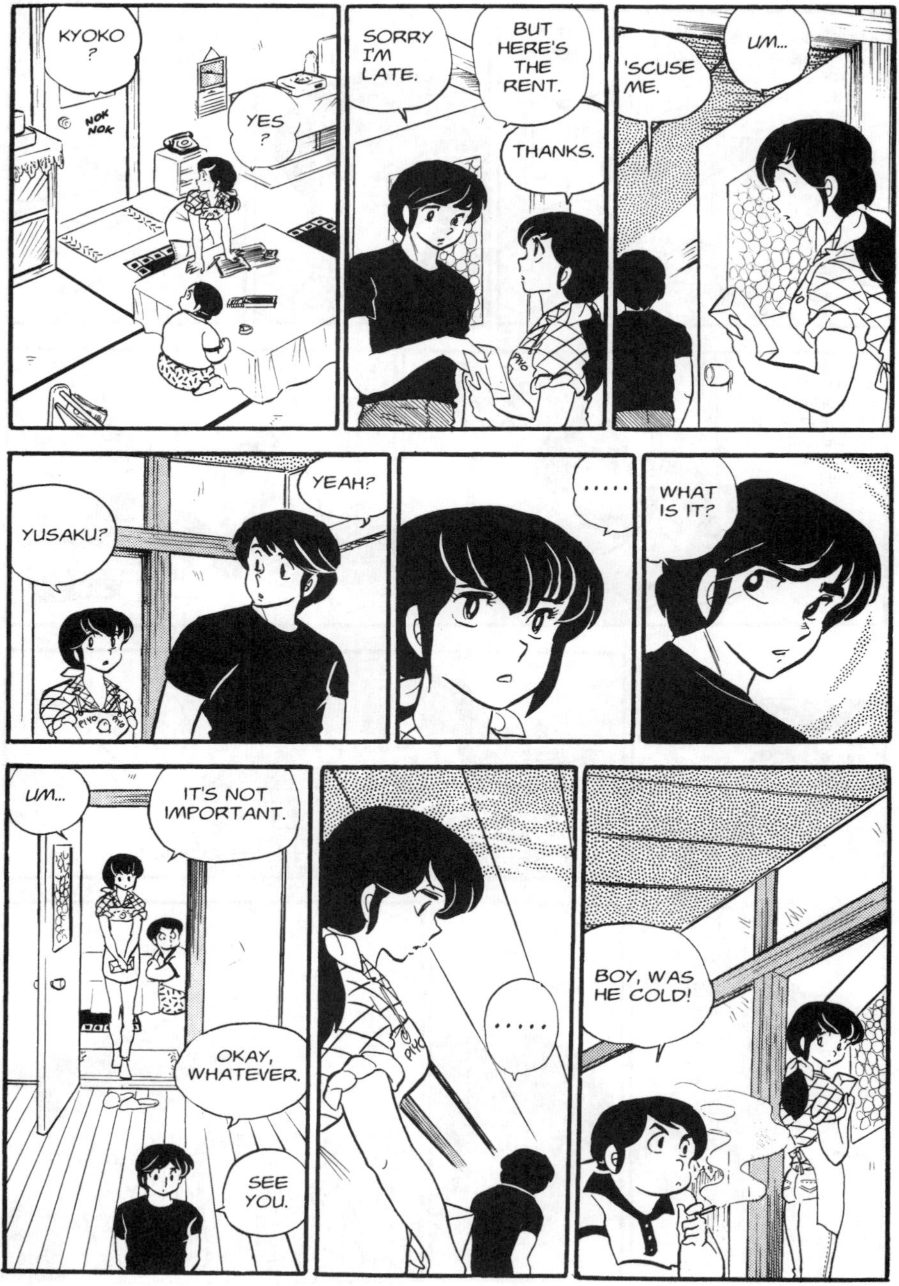
KYOKO ?
NOK NOK
YES ?
SORRY I'M LATE.
BUT HERE'S THE RENT.
THANKS.
PIYO
'SCUSE ME.
UM...
YUSAKU?
YEAH?
PIYO
.....
WHAT IS IT?
UM...
IT'S NOT IMPORTANT.
OKAY, WHATEVER.
SEE YOU.
.....
PIYO
BOY, WAS HE COLD!

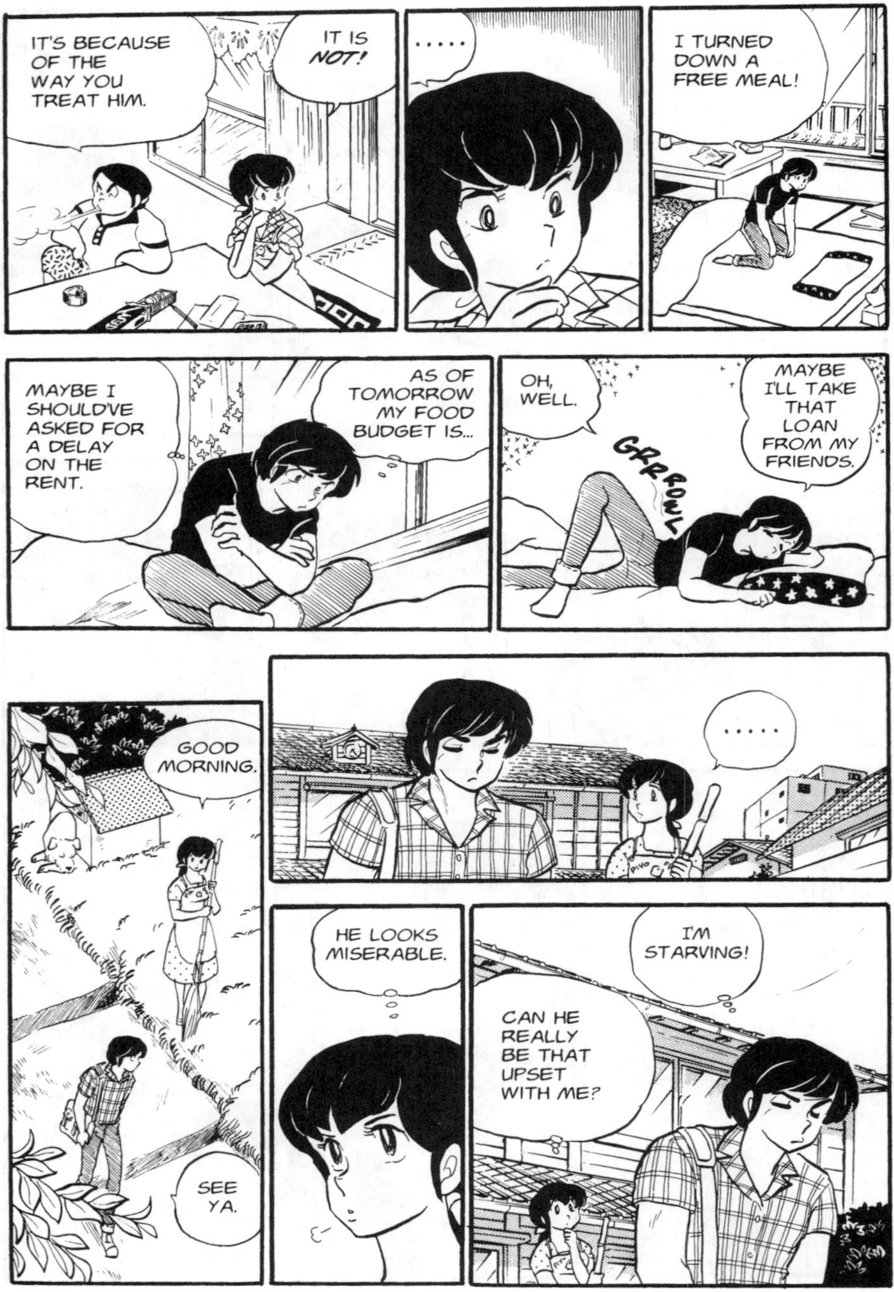
IT'S BECAUSE OF THE WAY YOU TREAT HIM.
IT IS NOT!
.....
I TURNED DOWN A FREE MEAL!
MAYBE I SHOULD'VE ASKED FOR A DELAY ON THE RENT.
AS OF TOMORROW MY FOOD BUDGET IS...
OH, WELL.
GRRROWL
MAYBE I'LL TAKE THAT LOAN FROM MY FRIENDS.
GOOD MORNING.
SEE YA.
.....
HE LOOKS MISERABLE.
I'M STARVING!
CAN HE REALLY BE THAT UPSET WITH ME?

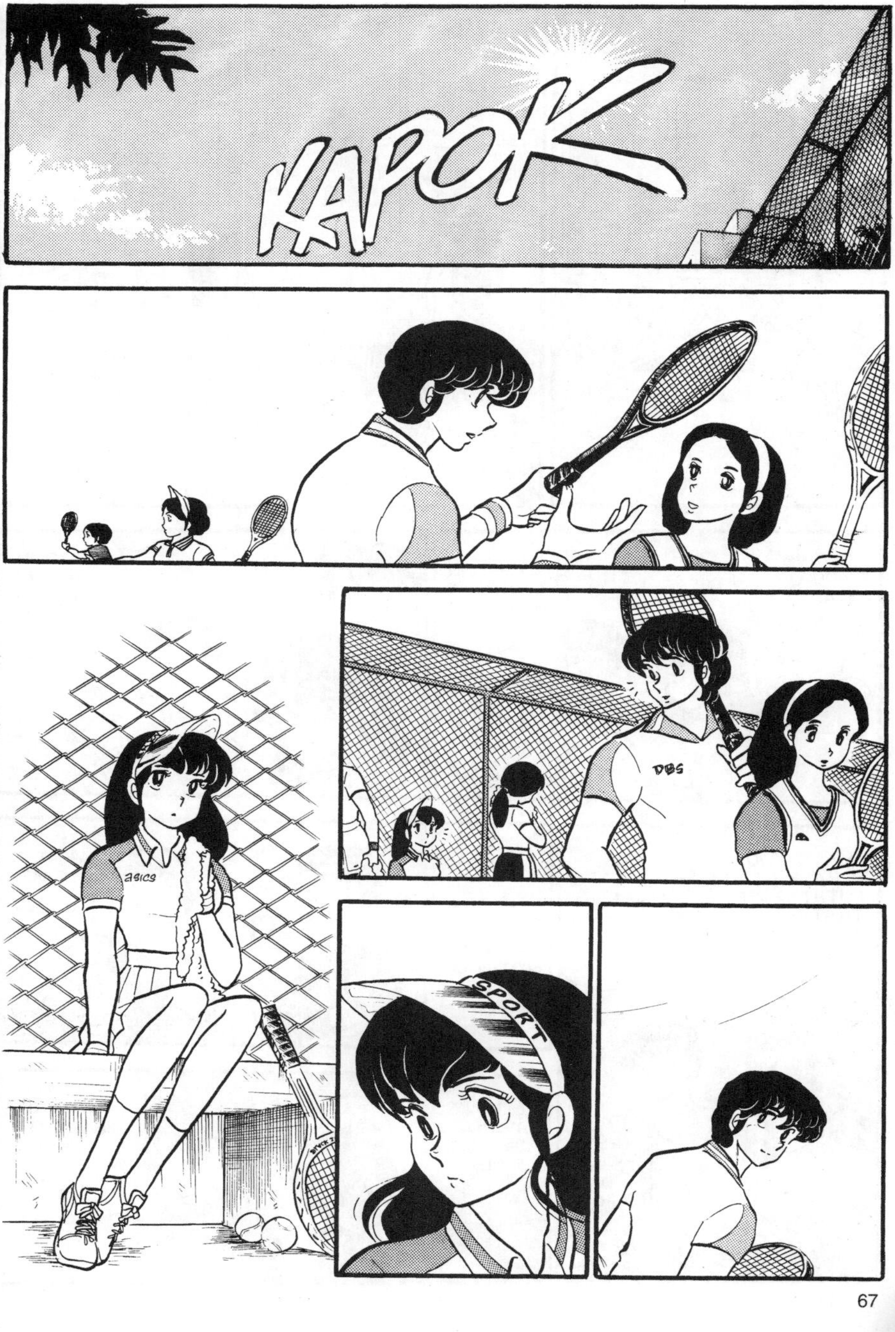
KAPOK
asics
DBS
SPORT

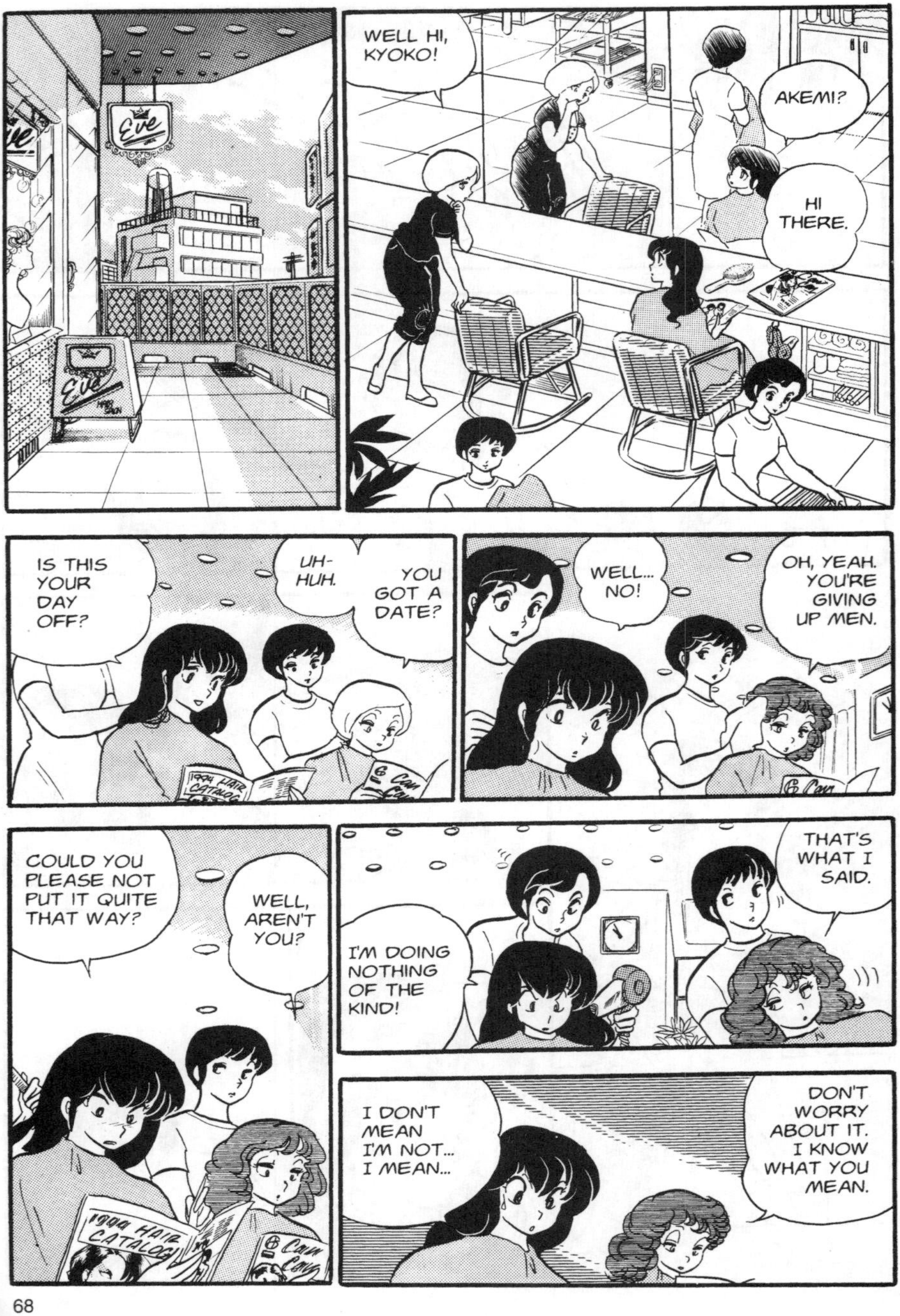
Eve
Eve
WELL HI, KYOKO!
AKEMI?
HI THERE.
IS THIS YOUR DAY OFF?
UH-HUH.
YOU GOT A DATE?
1994 HAIR CATALOG
WELL... NO!
OH, YEAH. YOU'RE GIVING UP MEN.
COULD YOU PLEASE NOT PUT IT QUITE THAT WAY?
WELL, AREN'T YOU?
1994 HAIR CATALOG
I'M DOING NOTHING OF THE KIND!
THAT'S WHAT I SAID.
I DON'T MEAN I'M NOT... I MEAN...
DON'T WORRY ABOUT IT. I KNOW WHAT YOU MEAN.

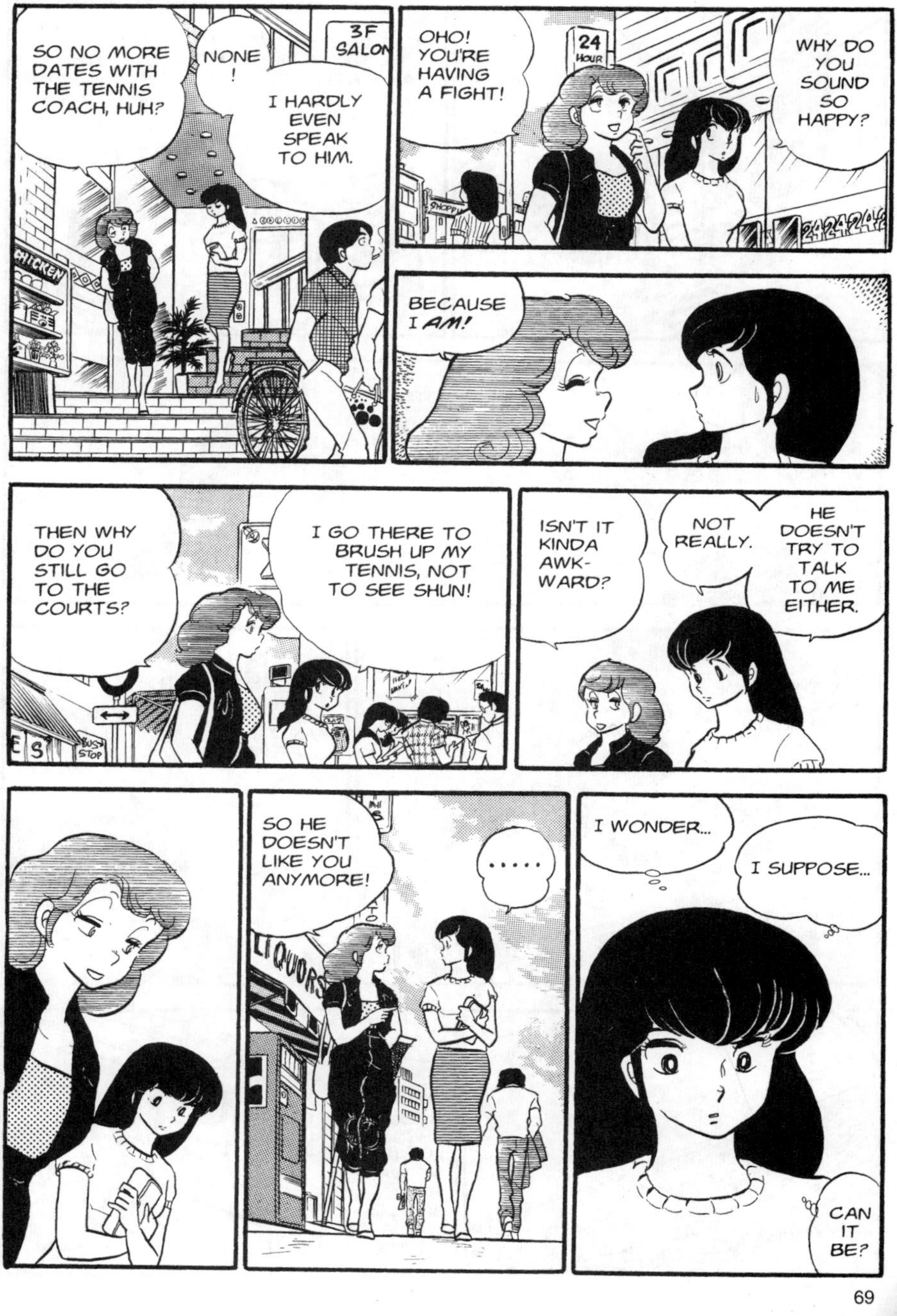
SO NO MORE DATES WITH THE TENNIS COACH, HUH?
NONE!
3F SALON
I HARDLY EVEN SPEAK TO HIM.
CHICKEN
OHO! YOU'RE HAVING A FIGHT!
24 HOUR
WHY DO YOU SOUND SO HAPPY?
BECAUSE I *AM!*
THEN WHY DO YOU STILL GO TO THE COURTS?
I GO THERE TO BRUSH UP MY TENNIS, NOT TO SEE SHUN!
BUS STOP
ISN'T IT KINDA AWK-WARD?
NOT REALLY.
HE DOESN'T TRY TO TALK TO ME EITHER.
SO HE DOESN'T LIKE YOU ANYMORE!
.....
LIQUORS
I WONDER...
I SUPPOSE...
CAN IT BE?

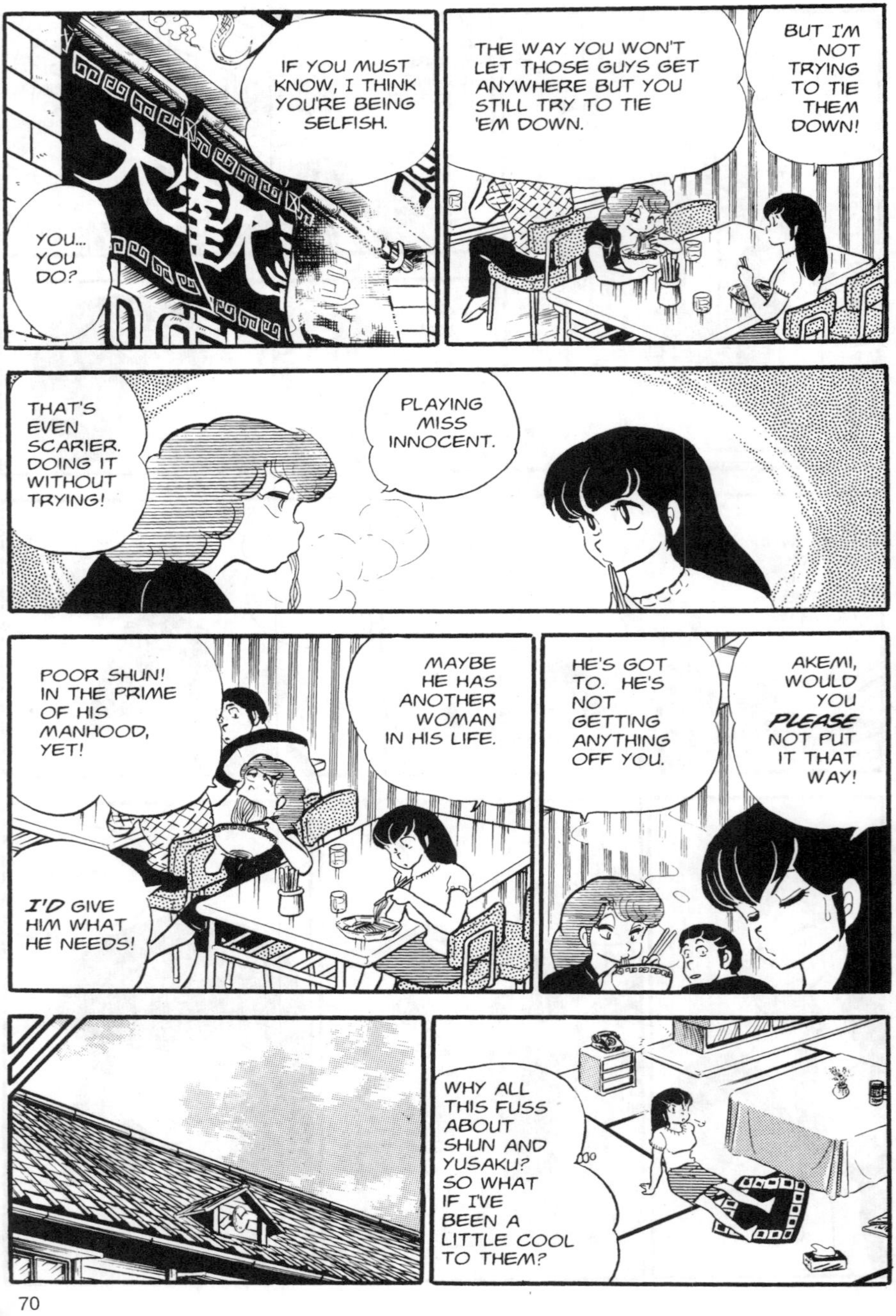
IF YOU MUST KNOW, I THINK YOU'RE BEING SELFISH.
YOU... YOU DO?
THE WAY YOU WON'T LET THOSE GUYS GET ANYWHERE BUT YOU STILL TRY TO TIE 'EM DOWN.
BUT I'M NOT TRYING TO TIE THEM DOWN!
THAT'S EVEN SCARIER. DOING IT WITHOUT TRYING!
PLAYING MISS INNOCENT.
POOR SHUN! IN THE PRIME OF HIS MANHOOD, YET!
MAYBE HE HAS ANOTHER WOMAN IN HIS LIFE.
I'D GIVE HIM WHAT HE NEEDS!
HE'S GOT TO. HE'S NOT GETTING ANYTHING OFF YOU.
AKEMI, WOULD YOU ***PLEASE*** NOT PUT IT THAT WAY!
WHY ALL THIS FUSS ABOUT SHUN AND YUSAKU? SO WHAT IF I'VE BEEN A LITTLE COOL TO THEM?

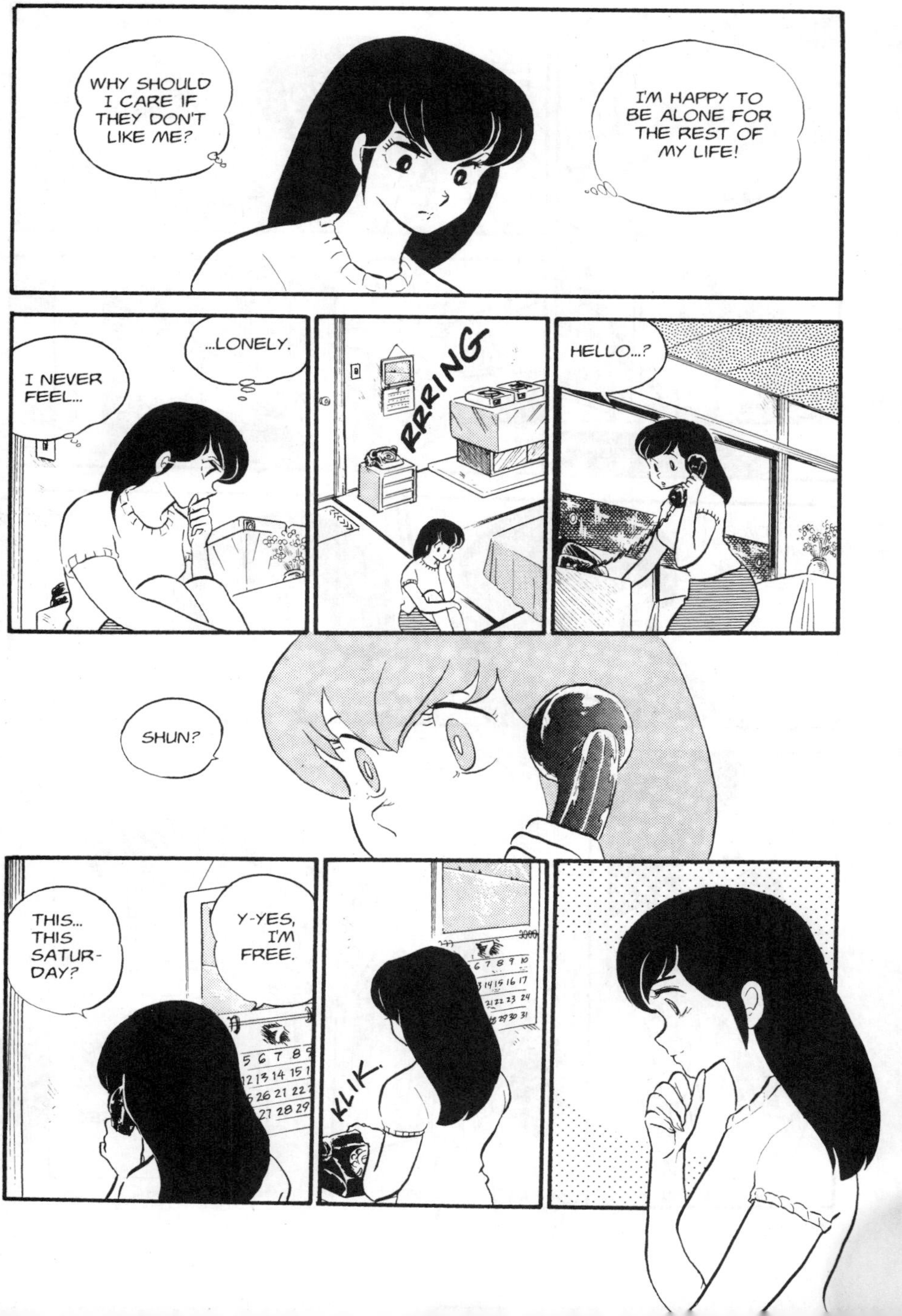
WHY SHOULD I CARE IF THEY DON'T LIKE ME?
I'M HAPPY TO BE ALONE FOR THE REST OF MY LIFE!
I NEVER FEEL...
...LONELY.
RRRING
HELLO...?
SHUN?
THIS... THIS SATUR-DAY?
Y-YES, I'M FREE.
KLIK.

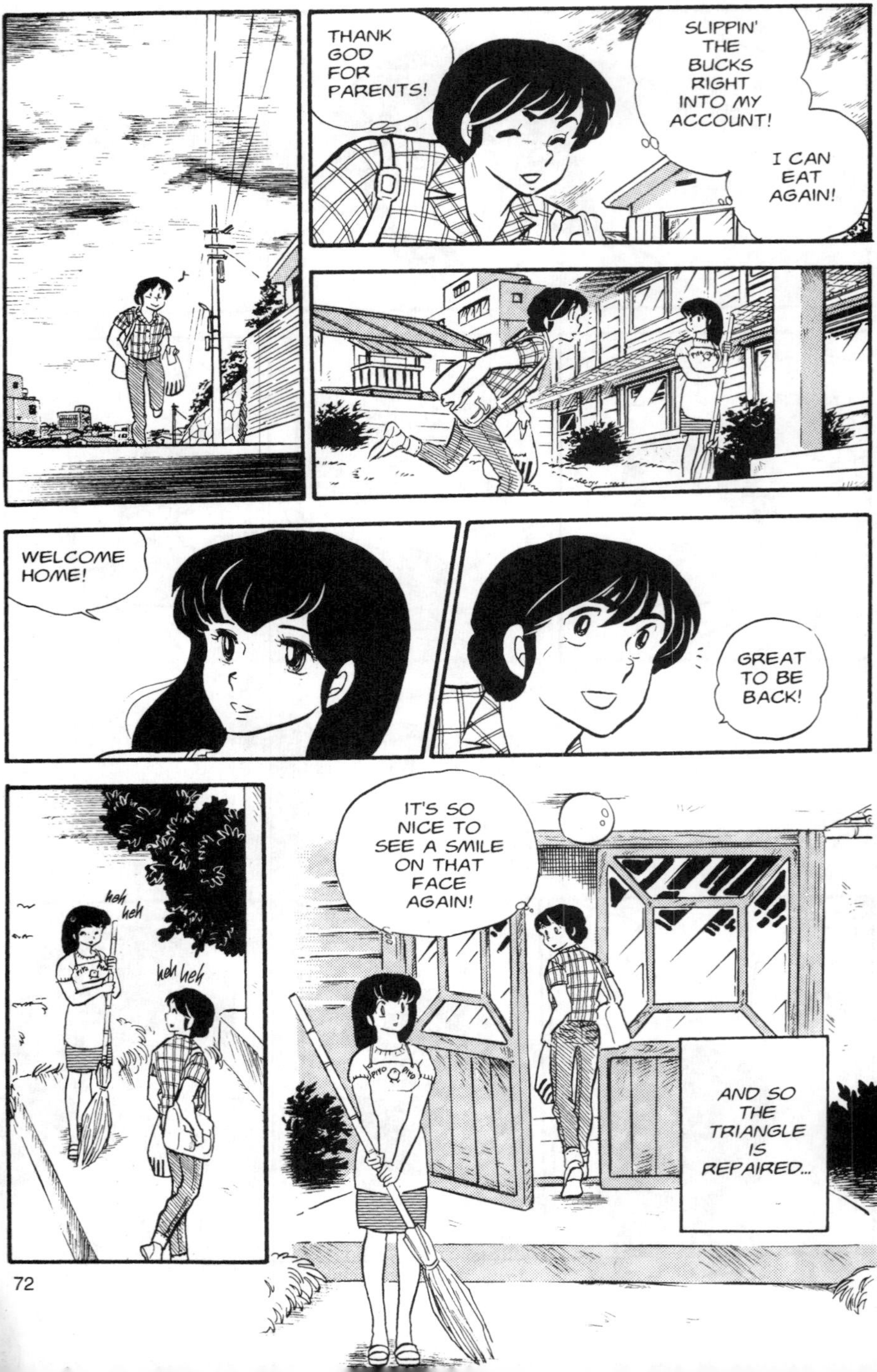
THANK GOD FOR PARENTS!
SLIPPIN' THE BUCKS RIGHT INTO MY ACCOUNT!
I CAN EAT AGAIN!
WELCOME HOME!
GREAT TO BE BACK!
heh heh
heh heh
IT'S SO NICE TO SEE A SMILE ON THAT FACE AGAIN!
AND SO THE TRIANGLE IS REPAIRED...

Part Four

Soichiro Turns Around

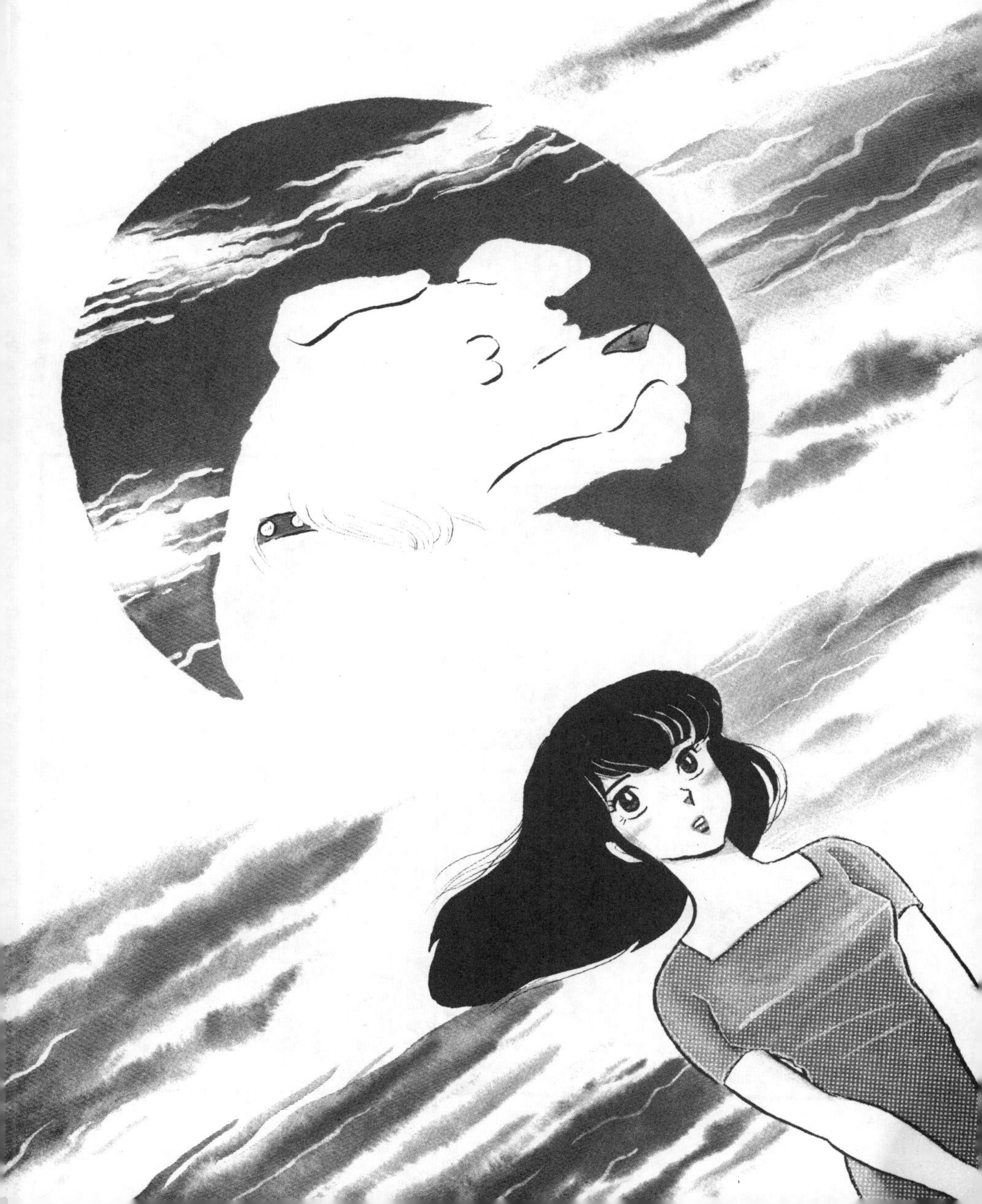

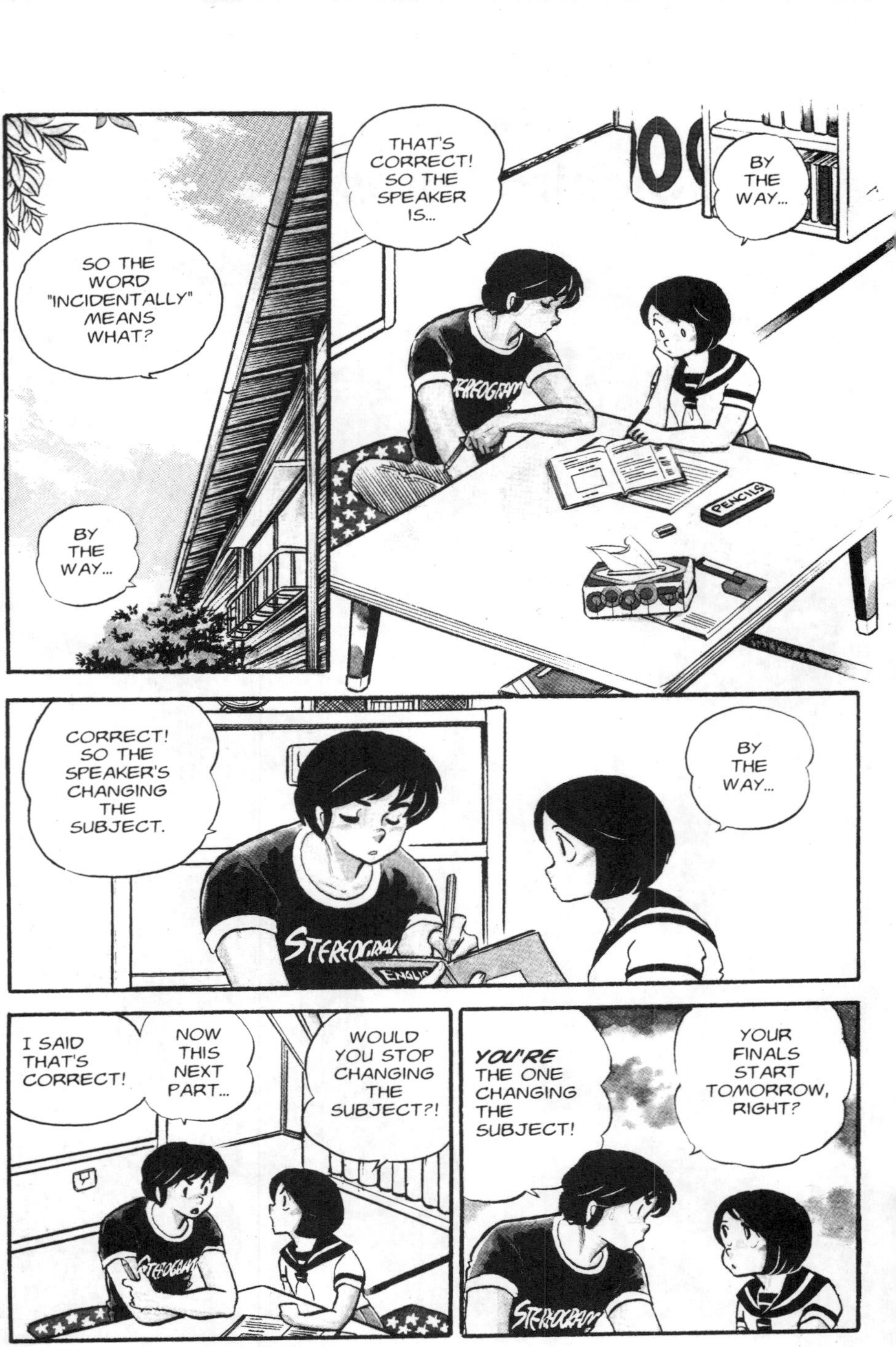
SO THE WORD "INCIDENTALLY" MEANS WHAT?
BY THE WAY...
THAT'S CORRECT! SO THE SPEAKER IS...
BY THE WAY...
PENCILS
CORRECT! SO THE SPEAKER'S CHANGING THE SUBJECT.
BY THE WAY...
I SAID THAT'S CORRECT!
NOW THIS NEXT PART...
WOULD YOU STOP CHANGING THE SUBJECT?!
YOU'RE THE ONE CHANGING THE SUBJECT!
YOUR FINALS START TOMORROW, RIGHT?

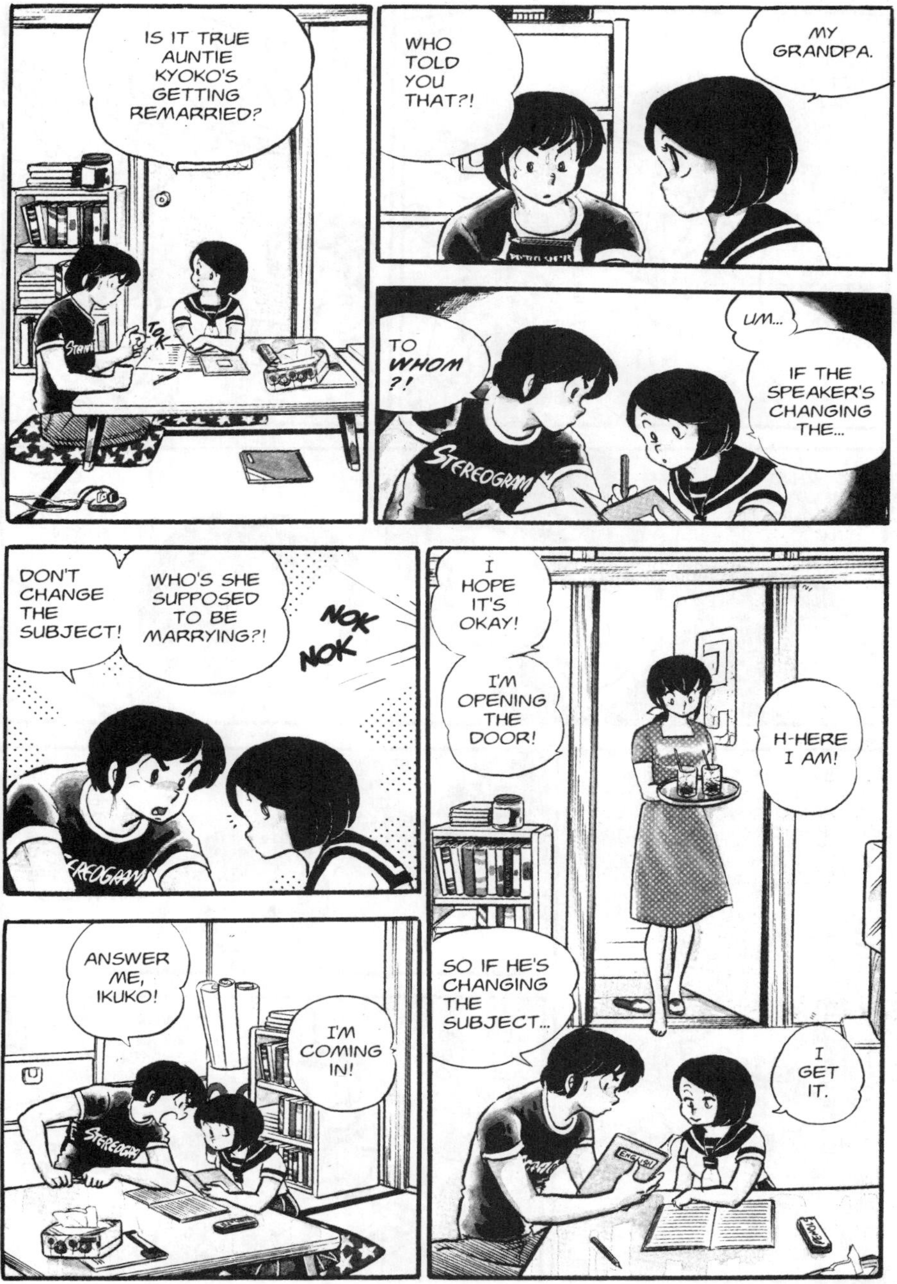
IS IT TRUE AUNTIE KYOKO'S GETTING REMARRIED?
TOK
WHO TOLD YOU THAT?!
MY GRANDPA.
TO WHOM?!
UM...
IF THE SPEAKER'S CHANGING THE...
DON'T CHANGE THE SUBJECT!
WHO'S SHE SUPPOSED TO BE MARRYING?!
NOK
NOK
ANSWER ME, IKUKO!
I'M COMING IN!
I HOPE IT'S OKAY!
I'M OPENING THE DOOR!
H-HERE I AM!
SO IF HE'S CHANGING THE SUBJECT...
I GET IT.

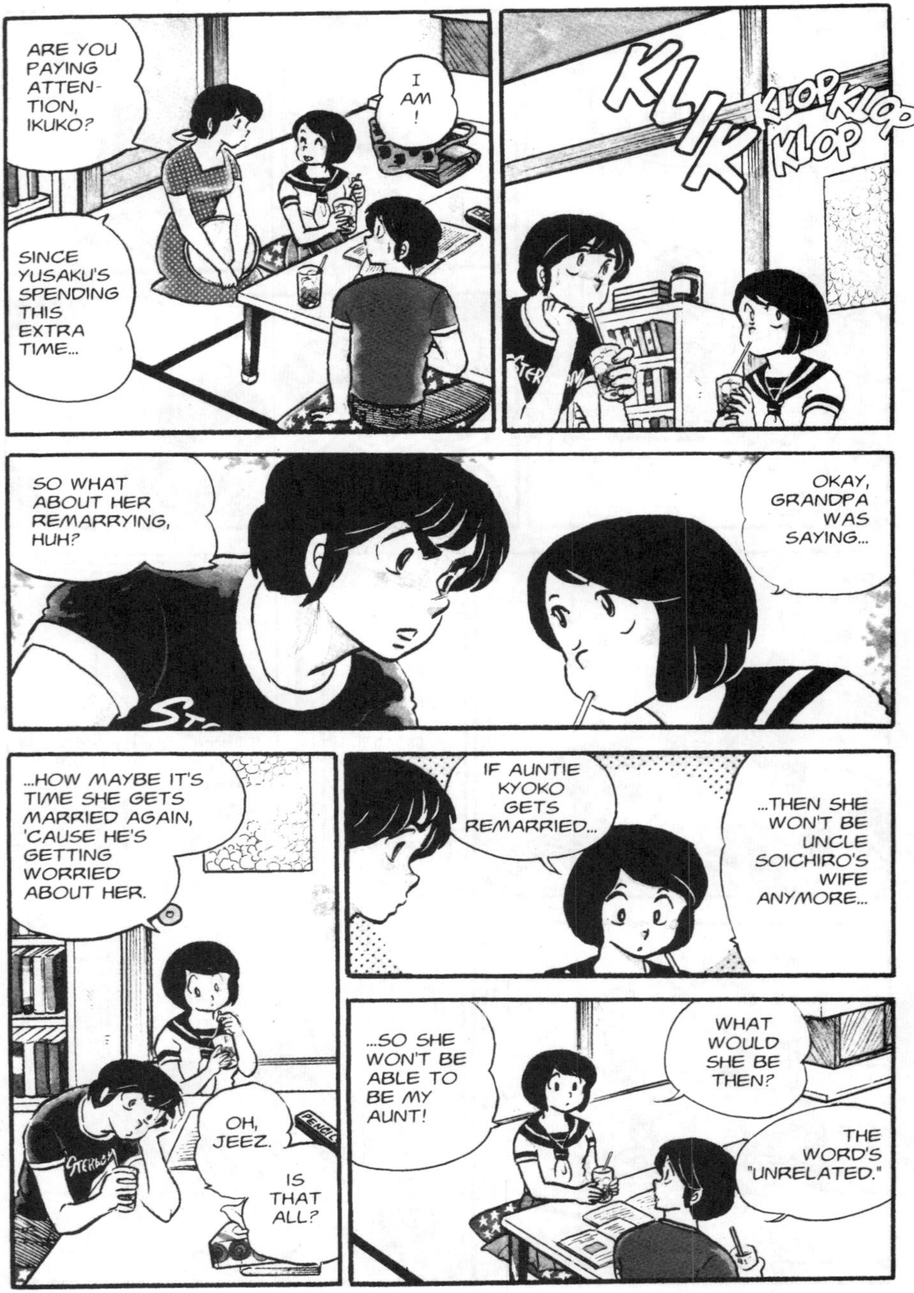
ARE YOU PAYING ATTEN- TION, IKUKO?
I AM!
SINCE YUSAKU'S SPENDING THIS EXTRA TIME...
KLIK
KLOP KLOP
KLOP
SO WHAT ABOUT HER REMARRYING, HUH?
OKAY, GRANDPA WAS SAYING...
...HOW MAYBE IT'S TIME SHE GETS MARRIED AGAIN, 'CAUSE HE'S GETTING WORRIED ABOUT HER.
OH, JEEZ.
IS THAT ALL?
IF AUNTIE KYOKO GETS REMARRIED...
...THEN SHE WON'T BE UNCLE SOICHIRO'S WIFE ANYMORE...
...SO SHE WON'T BE ABLE TO BE MY AUNT!
WHAT WOULD SHE BE THEN?
THE WORD'S "UNRELATED."

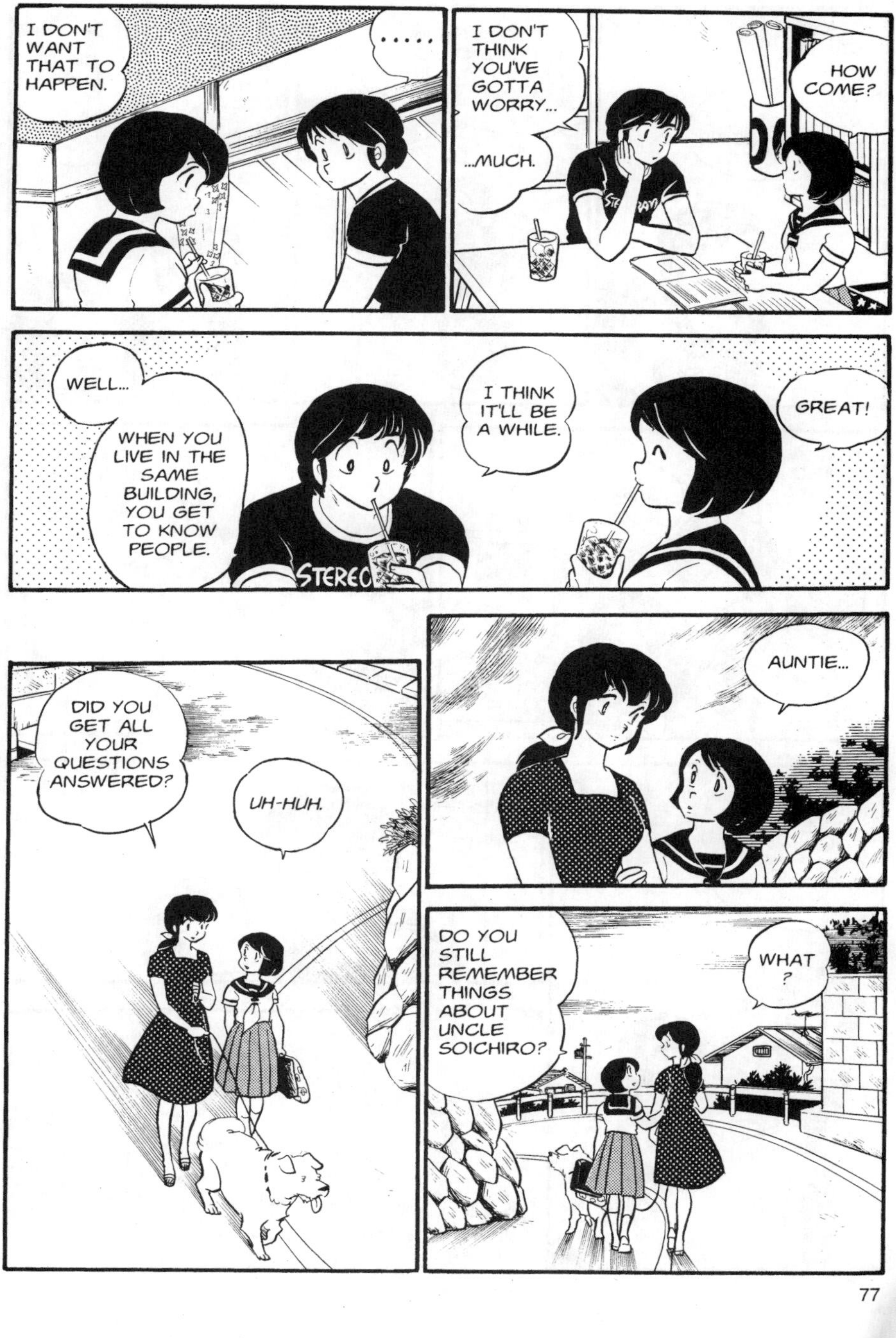
I DON'T WANT THAT TO HAPPEN.
.....
I DON'T THINK YOU'VE GOTTA WORRY...
...MUCH.
HOW COME?
WELL...
WHEN YOU LIVE IN THE SAME BUILDING, YOU GET TO KNOW PEOPLE.
I THINK IT'LL BE A WHILE.
GREAT!
DID YOU GET ALL YOUR QUESTIONS ANSWERED?
UH-HUH.
AUNTIE...
DO YOU STILL REMEMBER THINGS ABOUT UNCLE SOICHIRO?
WHAT?

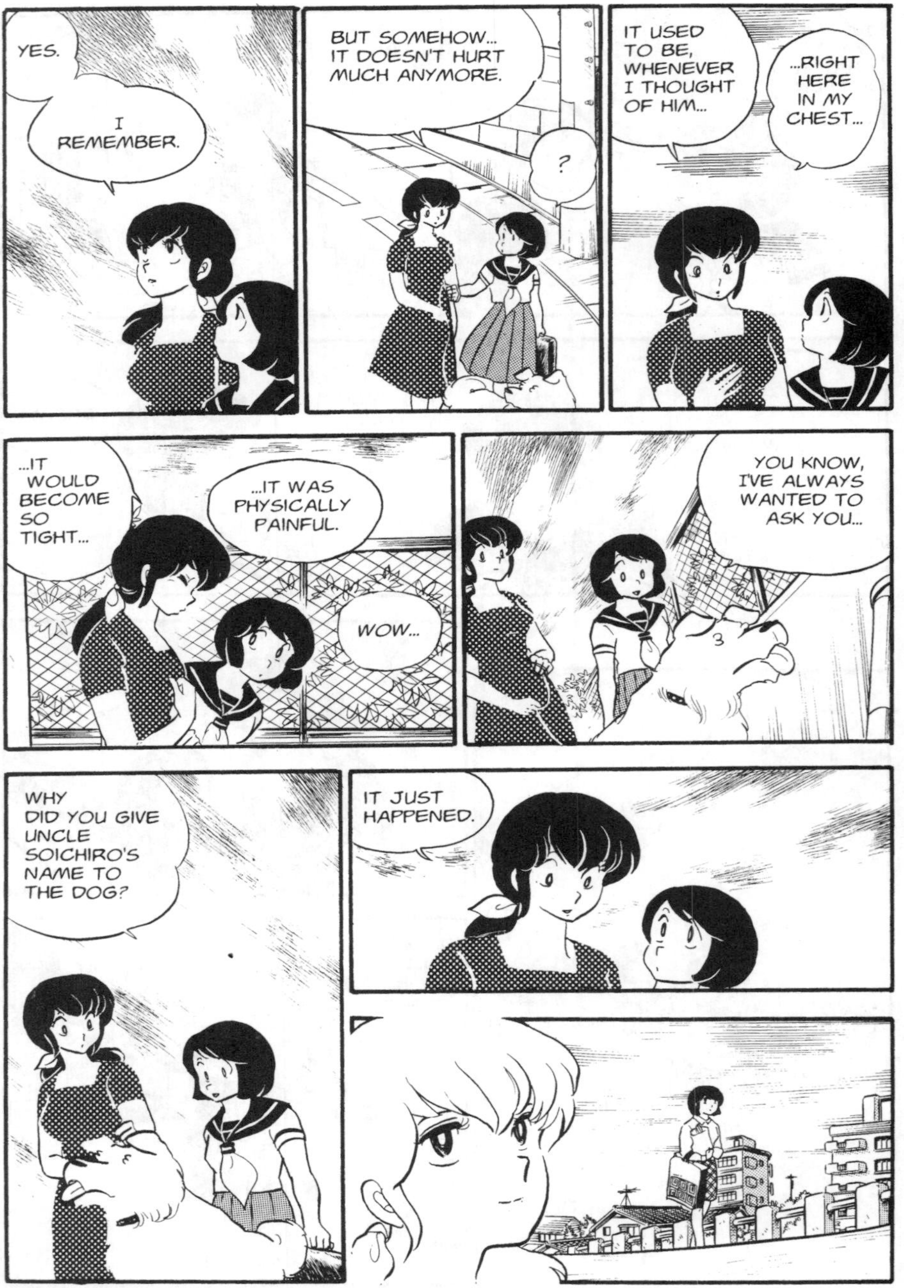
YES.
I REMEMBER.
BUT SOMEHOW... IT DOESN'T HURT MUCH ANYMORE.
?
IT USED TO BE, WHENEVER I THOUGHT OF HIM...
...RIGHT HERE IN MY CHEST...
...IT WOULD BECOME SO TIGHT...
...IT WAS PHYSICALLY PAINFUL.
WOW...
YOU KNOW, I'VE ALWAYS WANTED TO ASK YOU...
WHY DID YOU GIVE UNCLE SOICHIRO'S NAME TO THE DOG?
IT JUST HAPPENED.

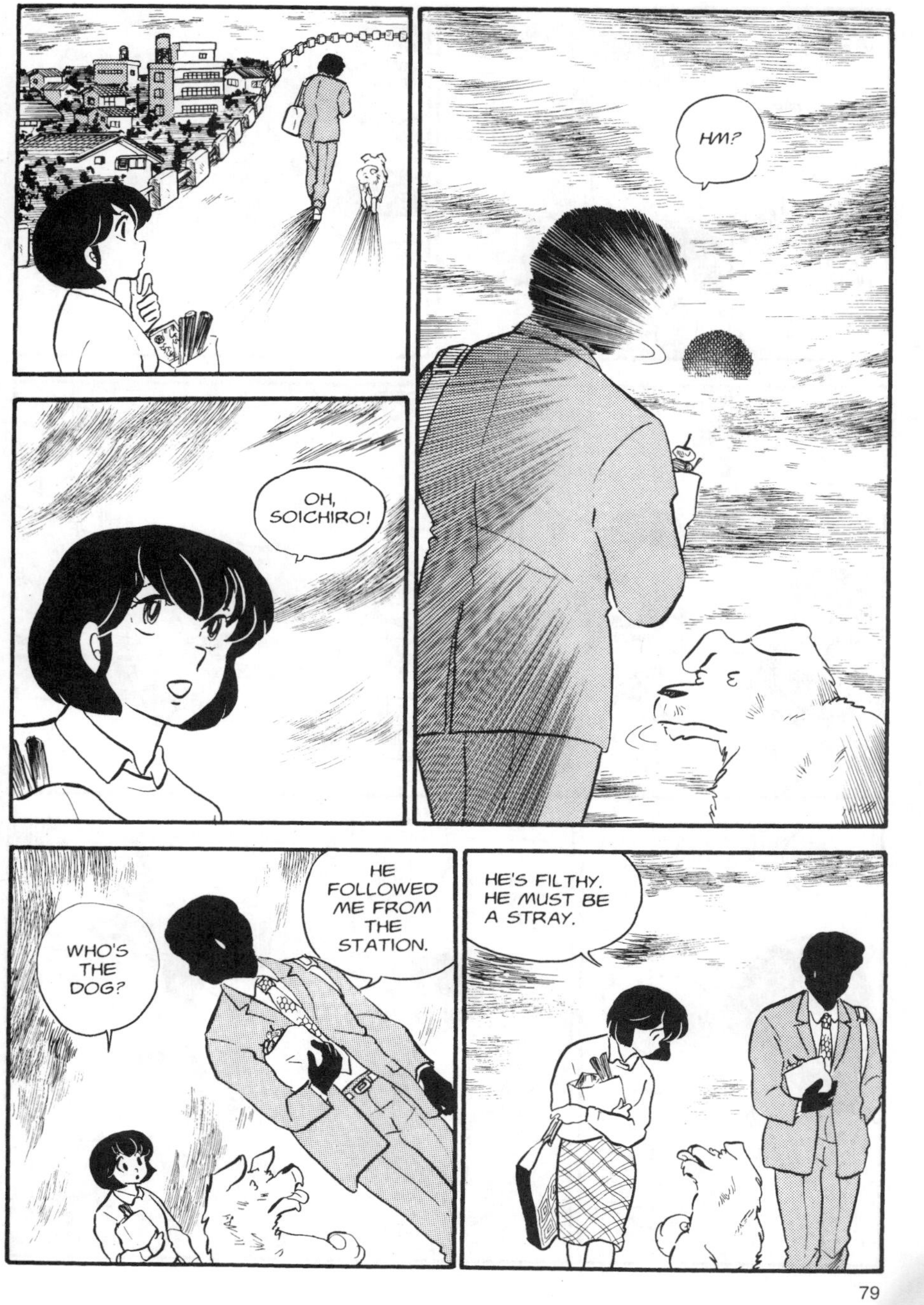
OH, SOICHIRO!
HM?
WHO'S THE DOG?
HE FOLLOWED ME FROM THE STATION.
HE'S FILTHY. HE MUST BE A STRAY.

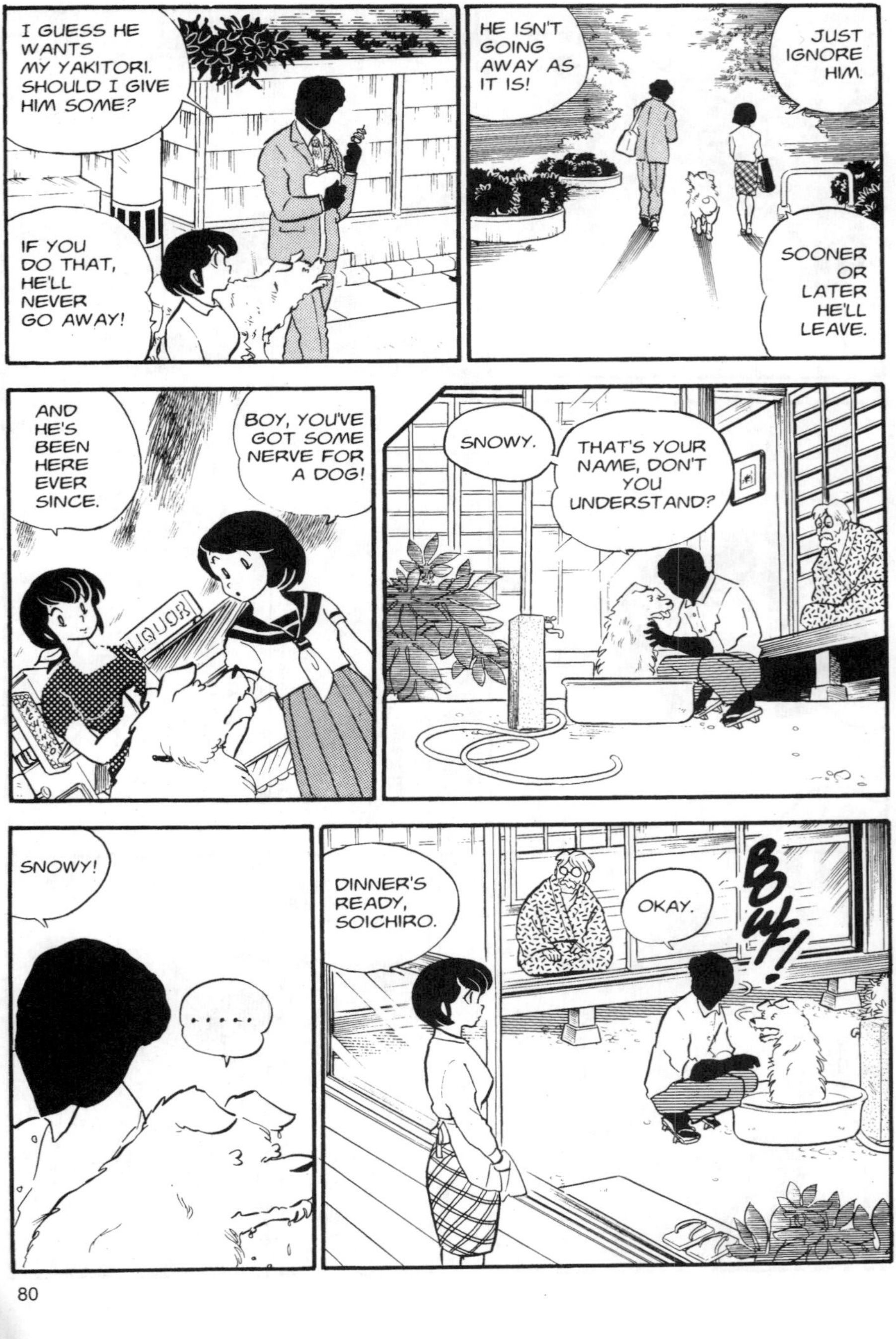

I GUESS HE WANTS MY YAKITORI. SHOULD I GIVE HIM SOME?
IF YOU DO THAT, HE'LL NEVER GO AWAY!
HE ISN'T GOING AWAY AS IT IS!
JUST IGNORE HIM.
SOONER OR LATER HE'LL LEAVE.
AND HE'S BEEN HERE EVER SINCE.
BOY, YOU'VE GOT SOME NERVE FOR A DOG!
LIQUOR
SNOWY.
THAT'S YOUR NAME, DON'T YOU UNDERSTAND?
SNOWY!
.....
DINNER'S READY, SOICHIRO.
OKAY.
BOWF!

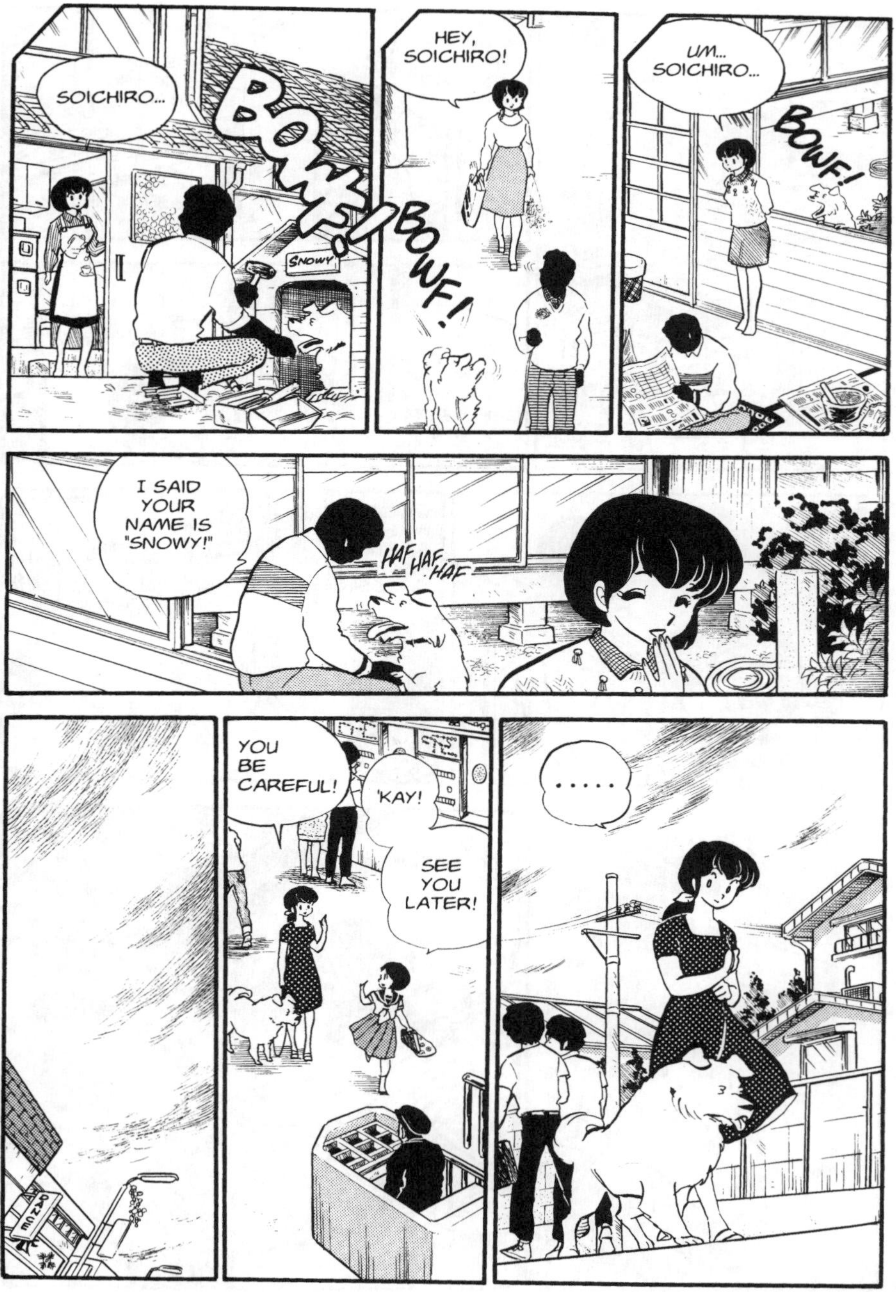
SOICHIRO...
BOWF!
SNOWY
BOWF!
HEY, SOICHIRO!
UM... SOICHIRO...
BOWF!
I SAID YOUR NAME IS "SNOWY!"
HAF HAF HAF
YOU BE CAREFUL!
'KAY!
SEE YOU LATER!
.....

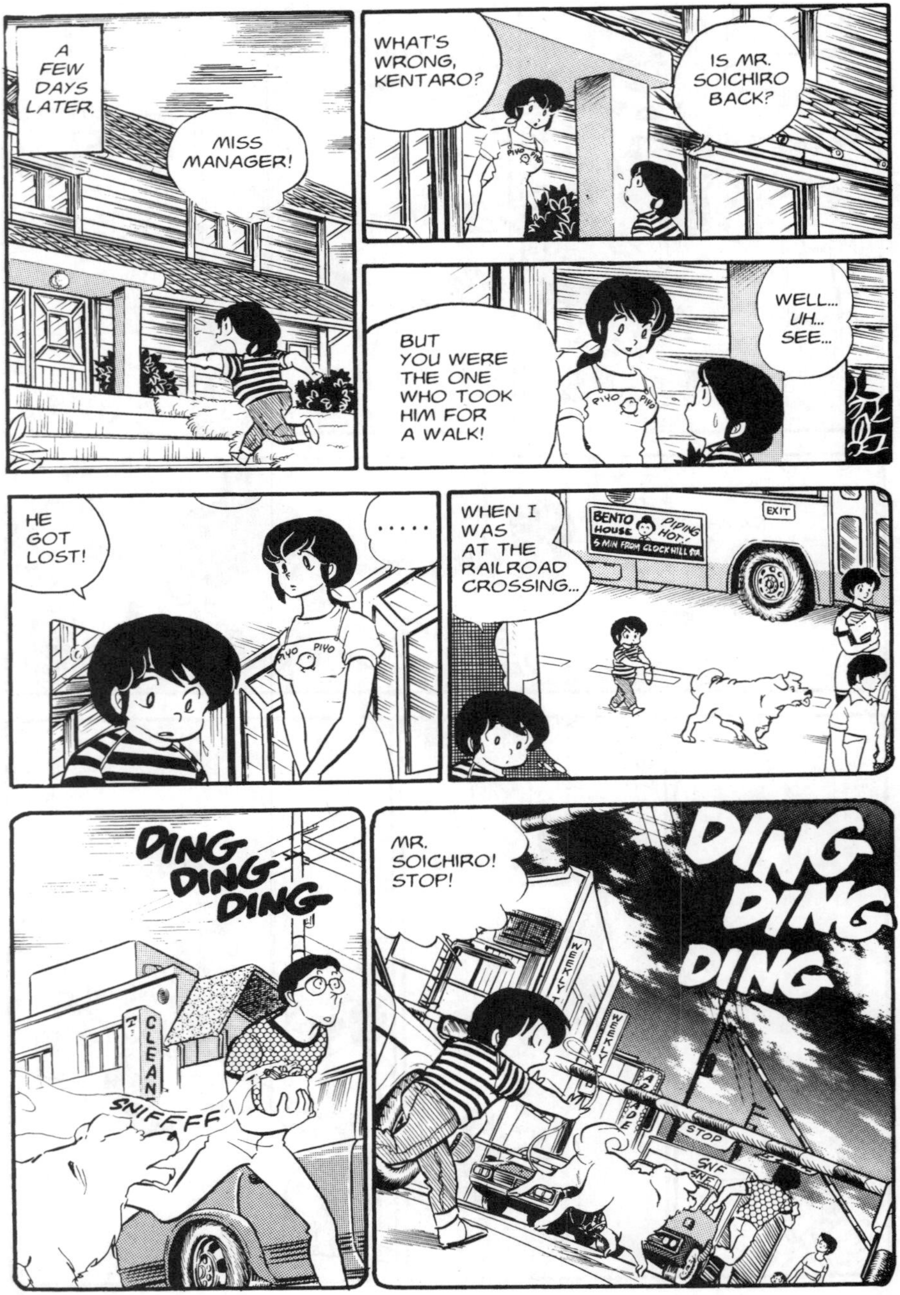
A FEW DAYS LATER.
MISS MANAGER!
WHAT'S WRONG, KENTARO?
IS MR. SOICHIRO BACK?
PIYO PIYO
BUT YOU WERE THE ONE WHO TOOK HIM FOR A WALK!
WELL... UH... SEE...
PIYO PIYO
HE GOT LOST!
.....
PIYO PIYO
WHEN I WAS AT THE RAILROAD CROSSING...
BENTO HOUSE PIPING HOT! 5 MIN FROM CLOCK HILL STA.
EXIT
DING DING DING
CLEANE
SNIFFFFF
MR. SOICHIRO! STOP!
DING DING DING
WEEKLY
WEEKLY
STOP
SNF SNF

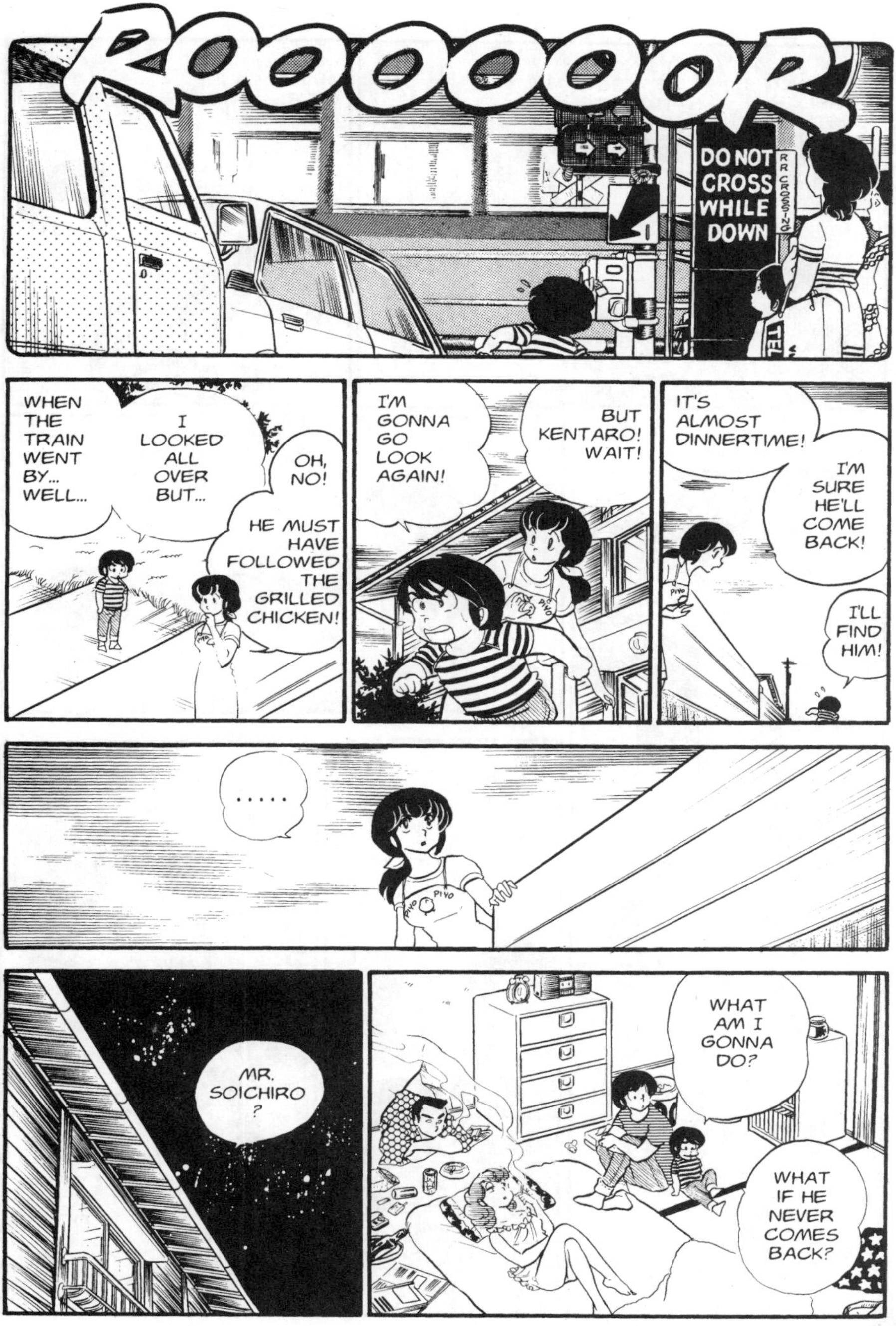
ROOOOOR
DO NOT CROSS WHILE DOWN
RR CROSSING
TEL
WHEN THE TRAIN WENT BY... WELL...
I LOOKED ALL OVER BUT...
OH, NO!
HE MUST HAVE FOLLOWED THE GRILLED CHICKEN!
I'M GONNA GO LOOK AGAIN!
BUT KENTARO! WAIT!
IT'S ALMOST DINNERTIME!
I'M SURE HE'LL COME BACK!
I'LL FIND HIM!
......
MR. SOICHIRO?
WHAT AM I GONNA DO?
WHAT IF HE NEVER COMES BACK?

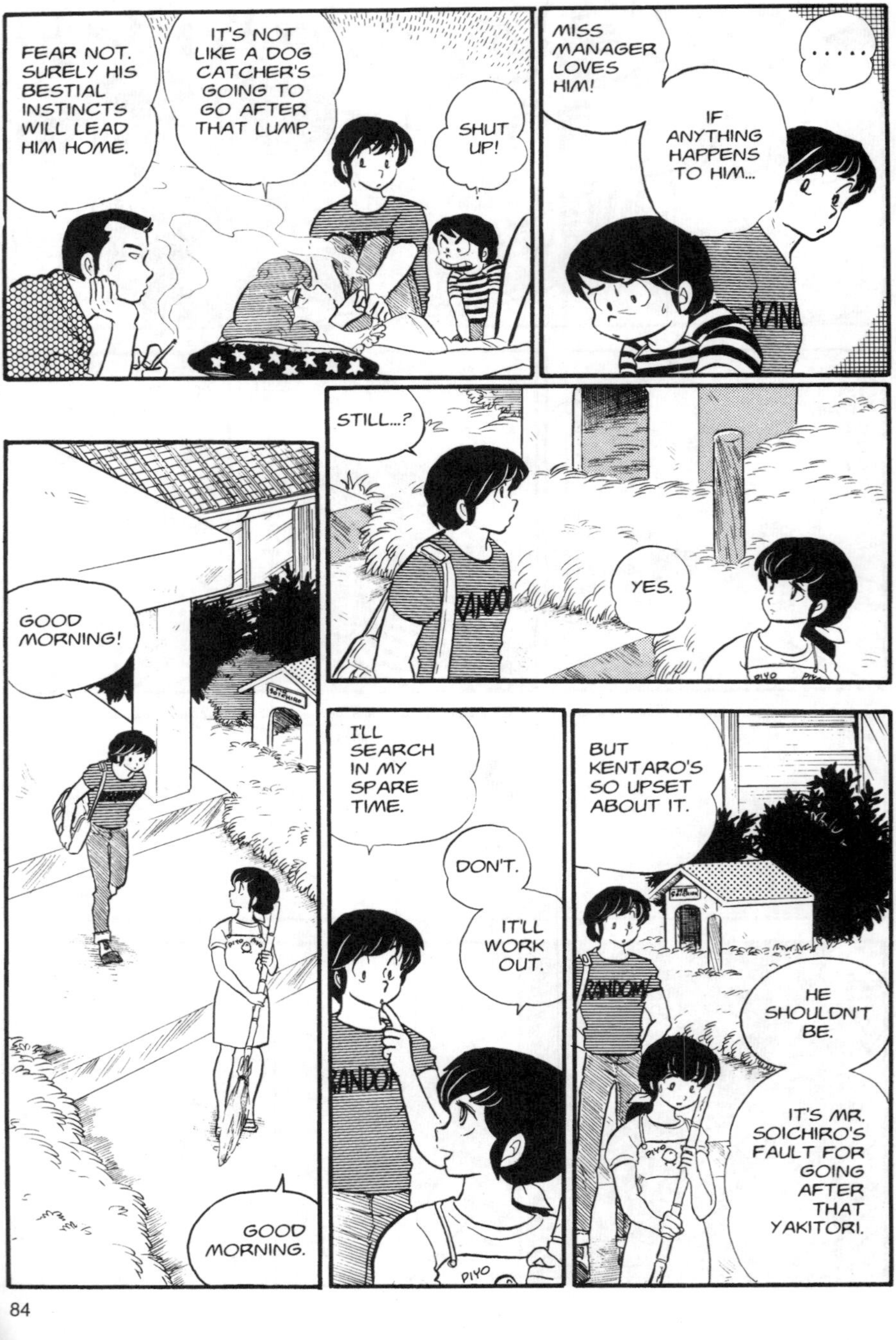
FEAR NOT. SURELY HIS BESTIAL INSTINCTS WILL LEAD HIM HOME.
IT'S NOT LIKE A DOG CATCHER'S GOING TO GO AFTER THAT LUMP.
SHUT UP!
MISS MANAGER LOVES HIM!
......
IF ANYTHING HAPPENS TO HIM...
GOOD MORNING!
GOOD MORNING.
STILL...?
YES.
I'LL SEARCH IN MY SPARE TIME.
DON'T.
IT'LL WORK OUT.
BUT KENTARO'S SO UPSET ABOUT IT.
HE SHOULDN'T BE.
IT'S MR. SOICHIRO'S FAULT FOR GOING AFTER THAT YAKITORI.

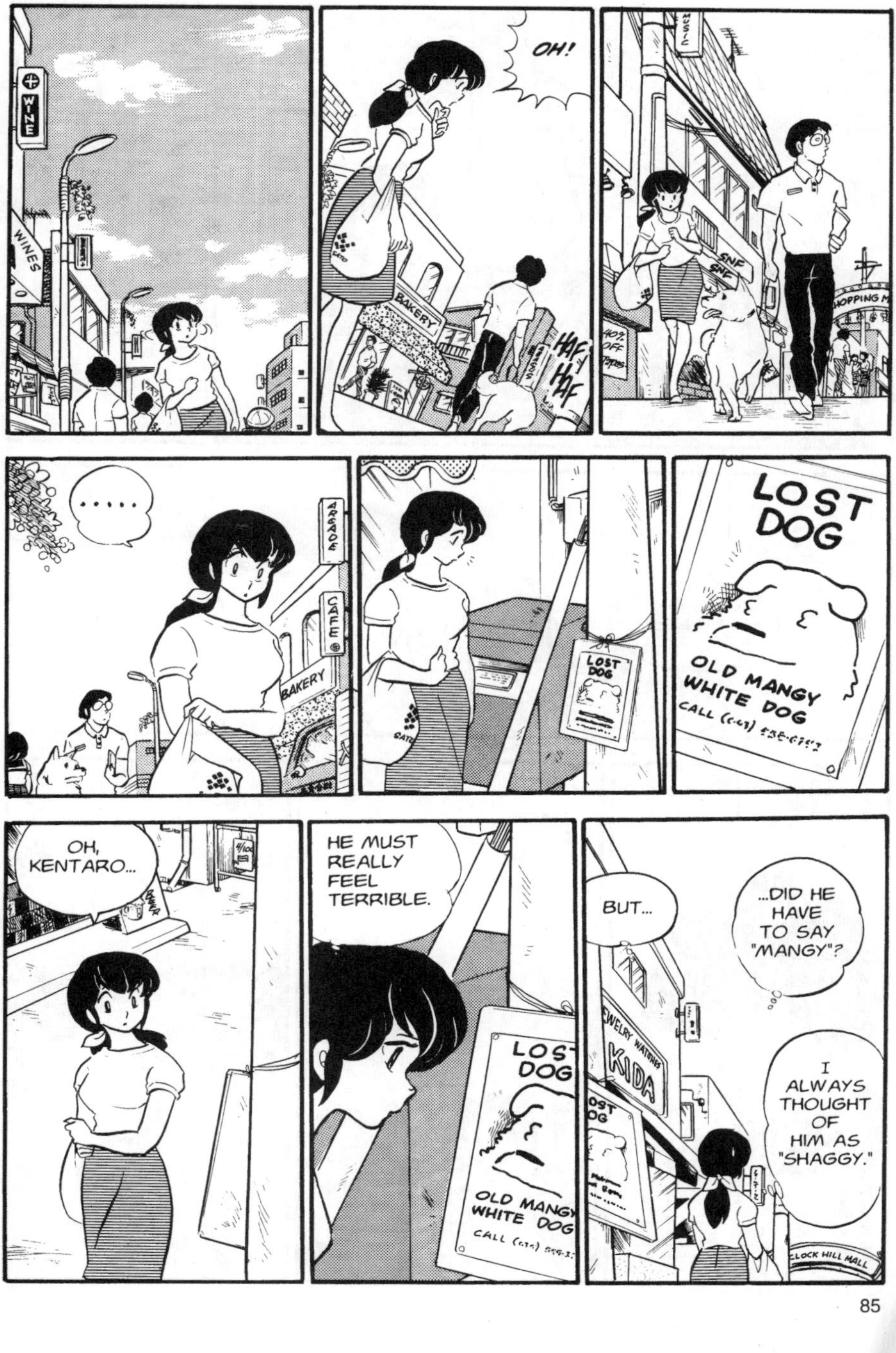
WINE
WINES
OH!
BAKERY
HAF HAF HAF
MUSIC
SNF SNF
.....
ARCADE
CAFE
BAKERY
LOST DOG
LOST DOG
OLD MANGY WHITE DOG
OH, KENTARO...
HE MUST REALLY FEEL TERRIBLE.
LOST DOG
OLD MANGY WHITE DOG
BUT...
...DID HE HAVE TO SAY "MANGY"?
I ALWAYS THOUGHT OF HIM AS "SHAGGY."
KIDA
CLOCK HILL MALL

HEY, KIDS, HAVE YOU SEEN A STRAY DOG AROUND?

A BIG OLD WHITE MANGY ONE?

UH-UH! SORRY!

ALWAYS THOUGHT THIS WAS A SMALL TOWN.

SUDDENLY IT FEELS HUGE.

A WEEK PASSES.

I'M REALLY SORRY.

MY KID'S SO DAMN CARELESS.

IT'S ALL RIGHT, REALLY.

PLEASE TELL POOR KENTARO NOT TO FEEL BAD.

. . . . .

GUESS I'LL CHECK THE POUND AGAIN.

BUT I'M RUNNING OUT OF HOPE.

WHERE CAN YOU BE?

WE'RE ALL SO WORRIED...

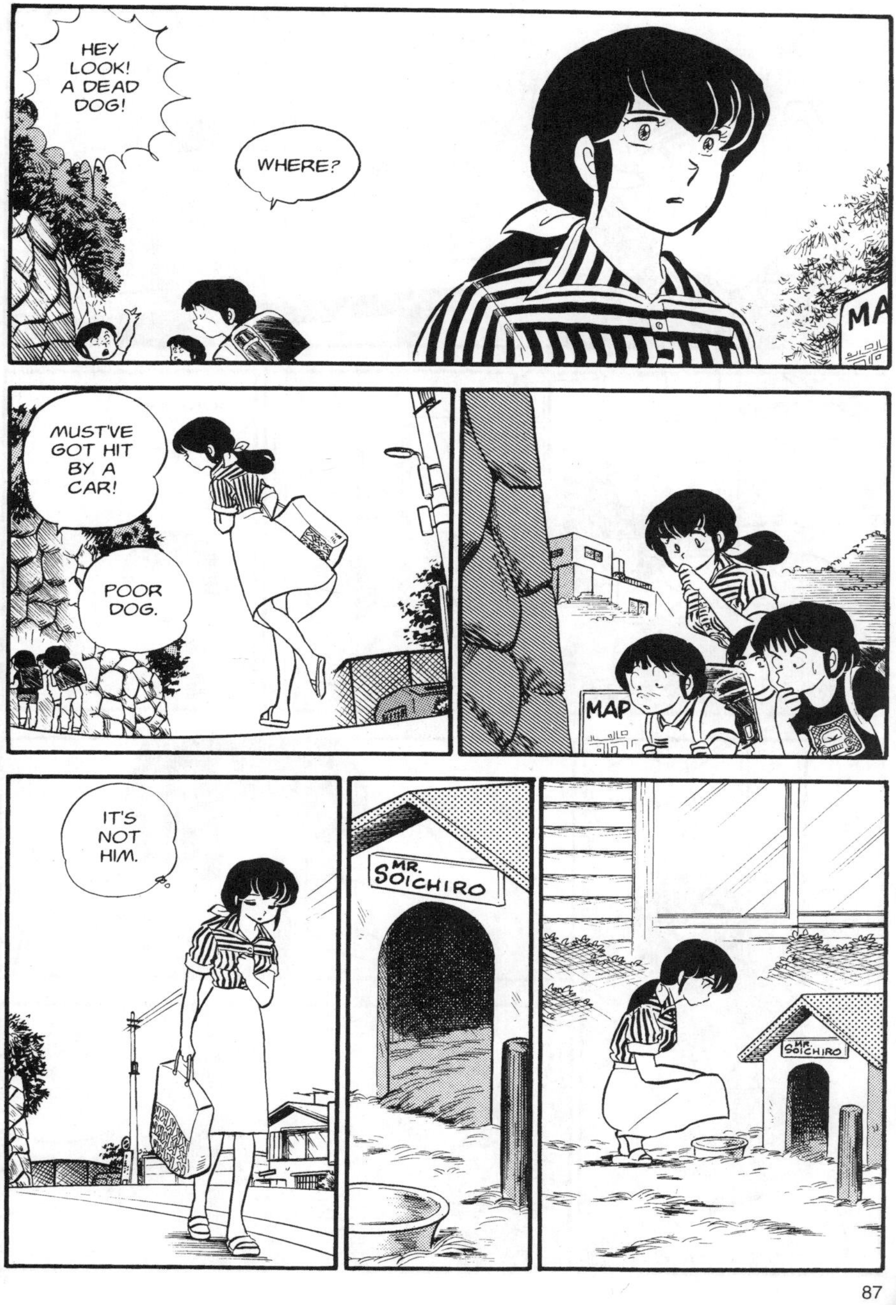
HEY LOOK! A DEAD DOG!
WHERE?
MA
MUST'VE GOT HIT BY A CAR!
POOR DOG.
MAP
IT'S NOT HIM.
MR. SOICHIRO
MR. SOICHIRO

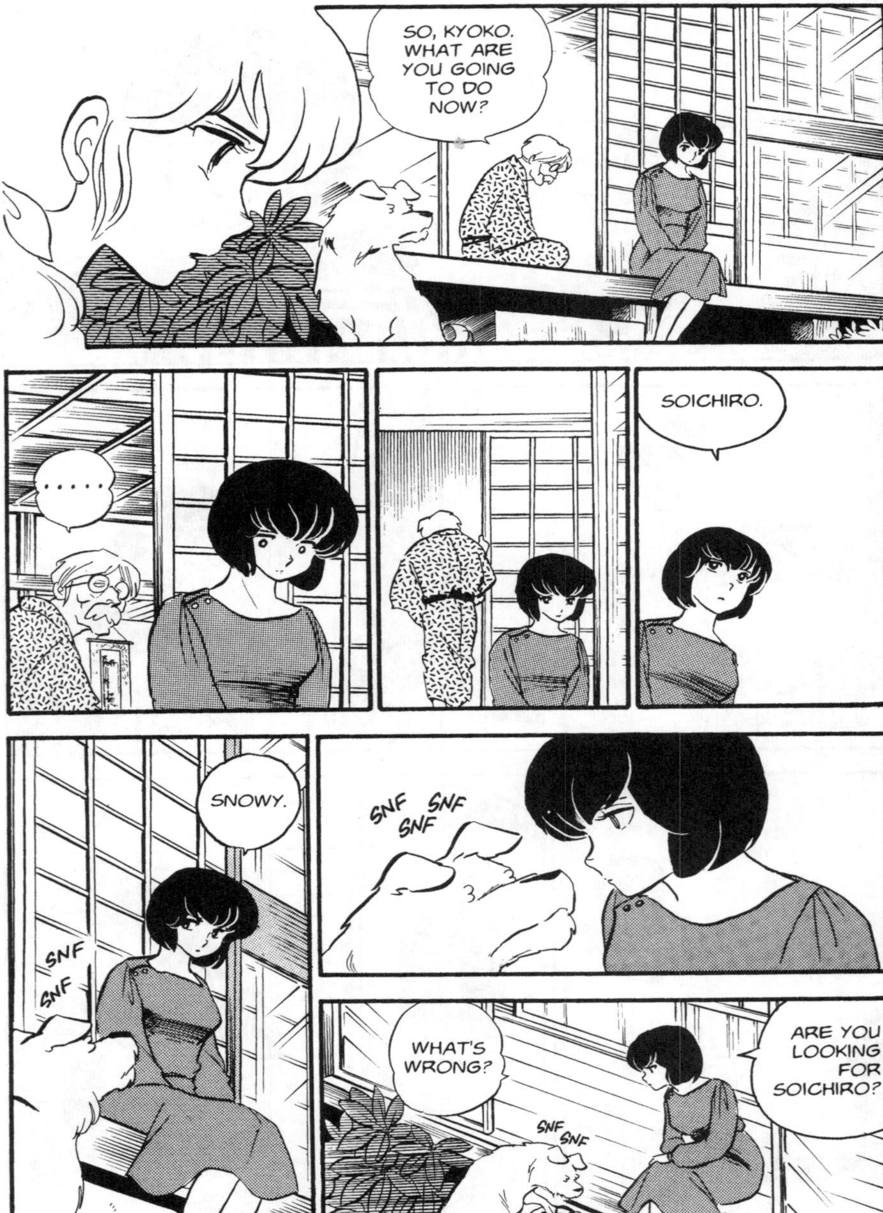
SO, KYOKO. WHAT ARE YOU GOING TO DO NOW?
......
SOICHIRO.
SNOWY.
SNF
SNF
SNF SNF SNF
WHAT'S WRONG?
SNF SNF
ARE YOU LOOKING FOR SOICHIRO?

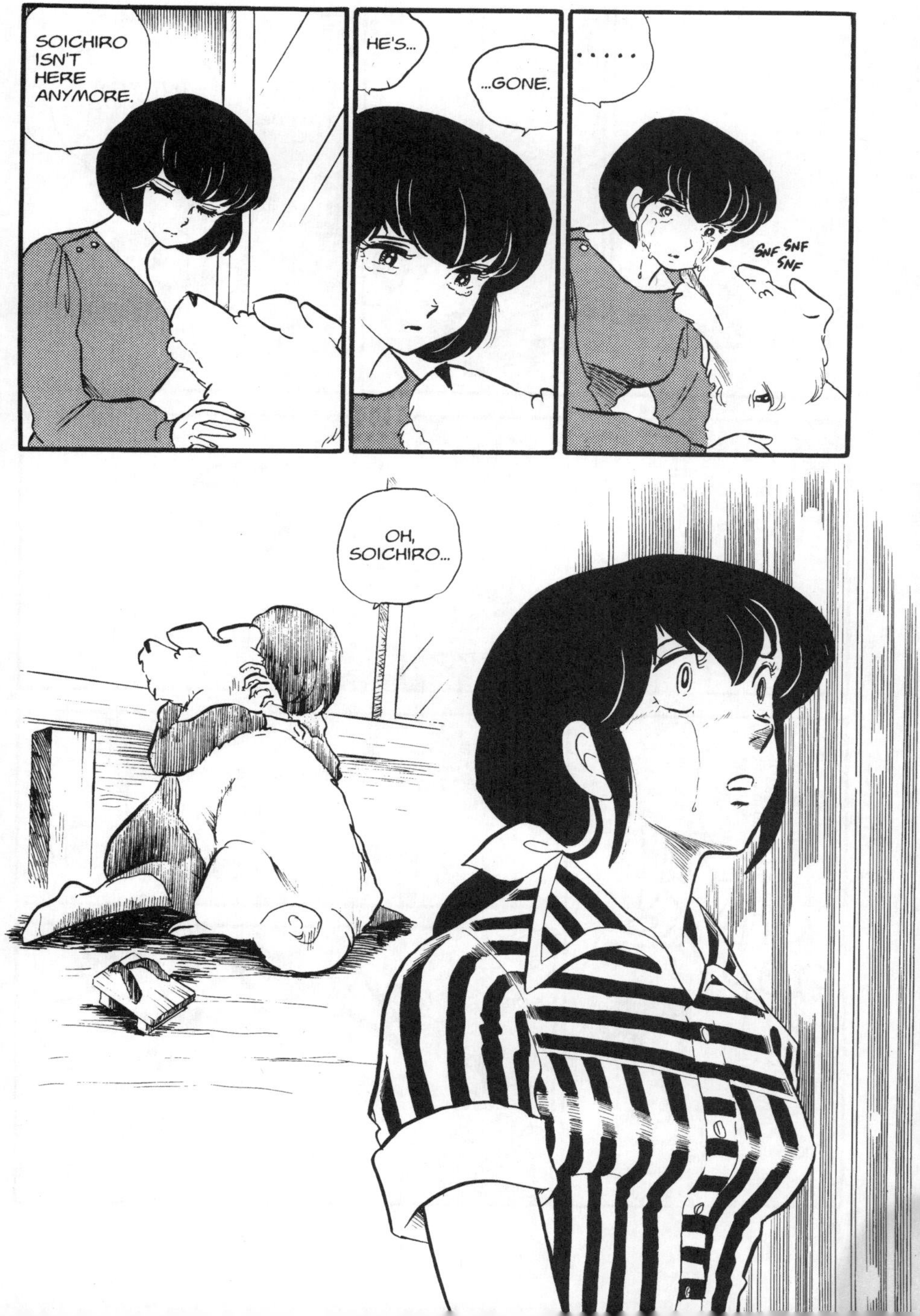
SOICHIRO ISN'T HERE ANYMORE.
HE'S...
...GONE.
.....
SNF SNF SNF
OH, SOICHIRO...

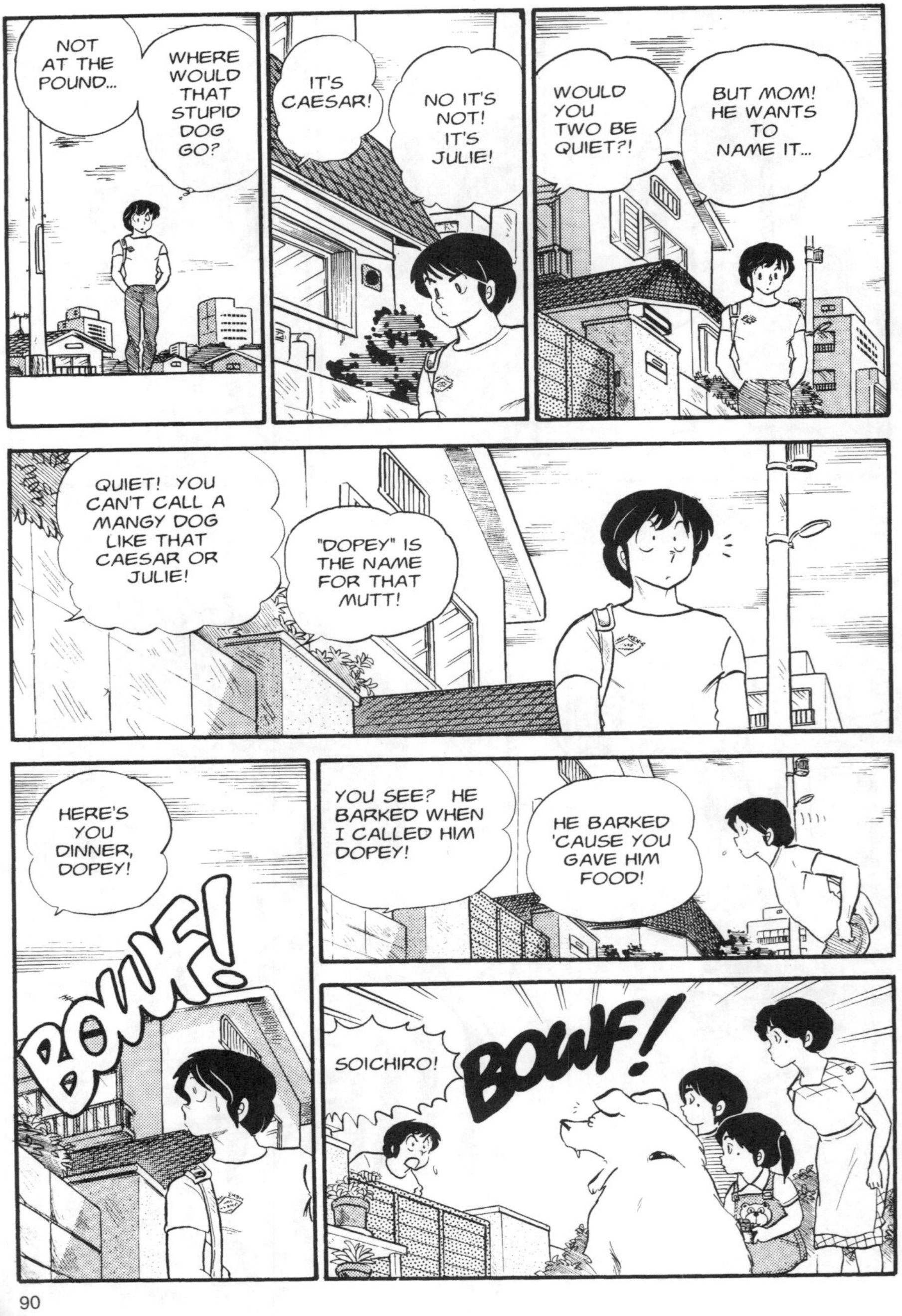
NOT AT THE POUND...
WHERE WOULD THAT STUPID DOG GO?
IT'S CAESAR!
NO IT'S NOT! IT'S JULIE!
WOULD YOU TWO BE QUIET?!
BUT MOM! HE WANTS TO NAME IT...
QUIET! YOU CAN'T CALL A MANGY DOG LIKE THAT CAESAR OR JULIE!
"DOPEY" IS THE NAME FOR THAT MUTT!
HERE'S YOU DINNER, DOPEY!
BOWF!
YOU SEE? HE BARKED WHEN I CALLED HIM DOPEY!
HE BARKED 'CAUSE YOU GAVE HIM FOOD!
SOICHIRO!
BOWF!

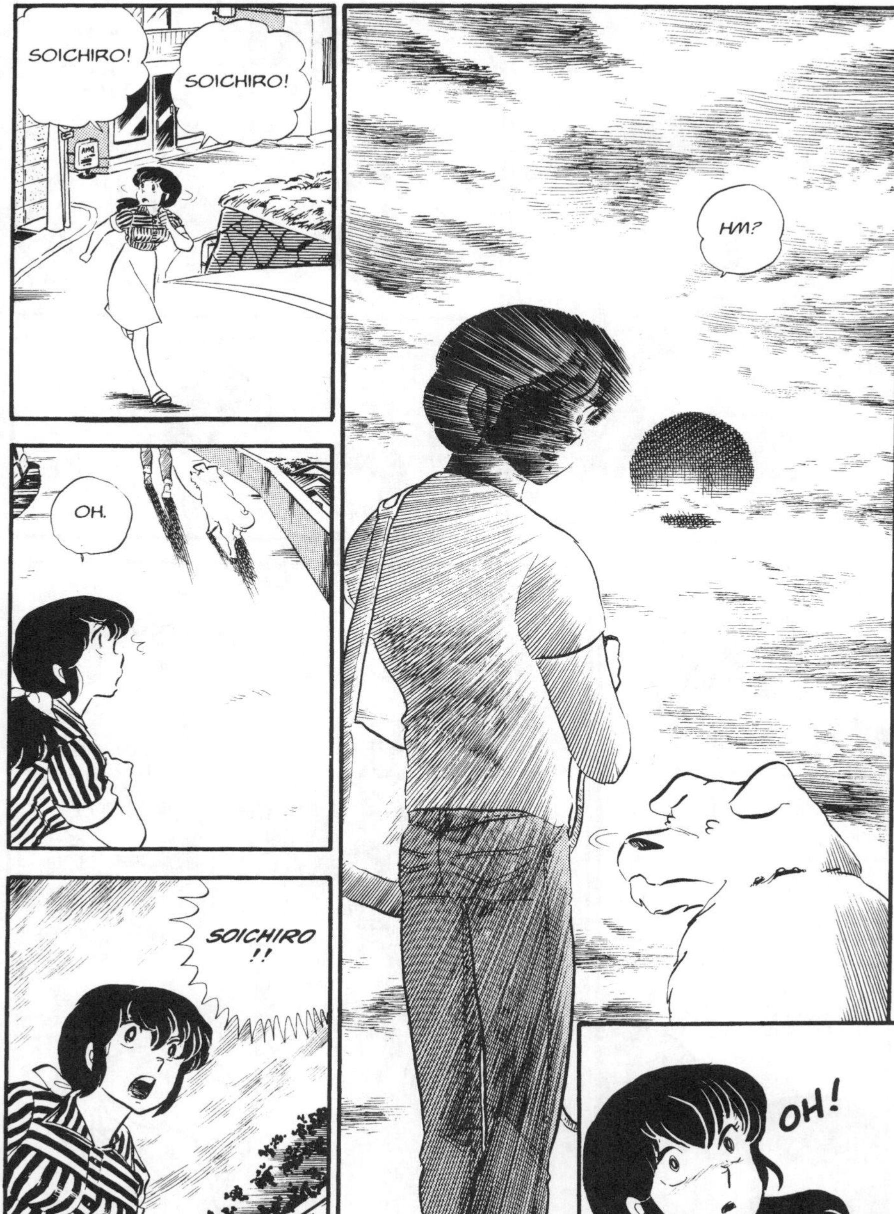
SOICHIRO!
SOICHIRO!
OH.
SOICHIRO !!
HM?
OH!

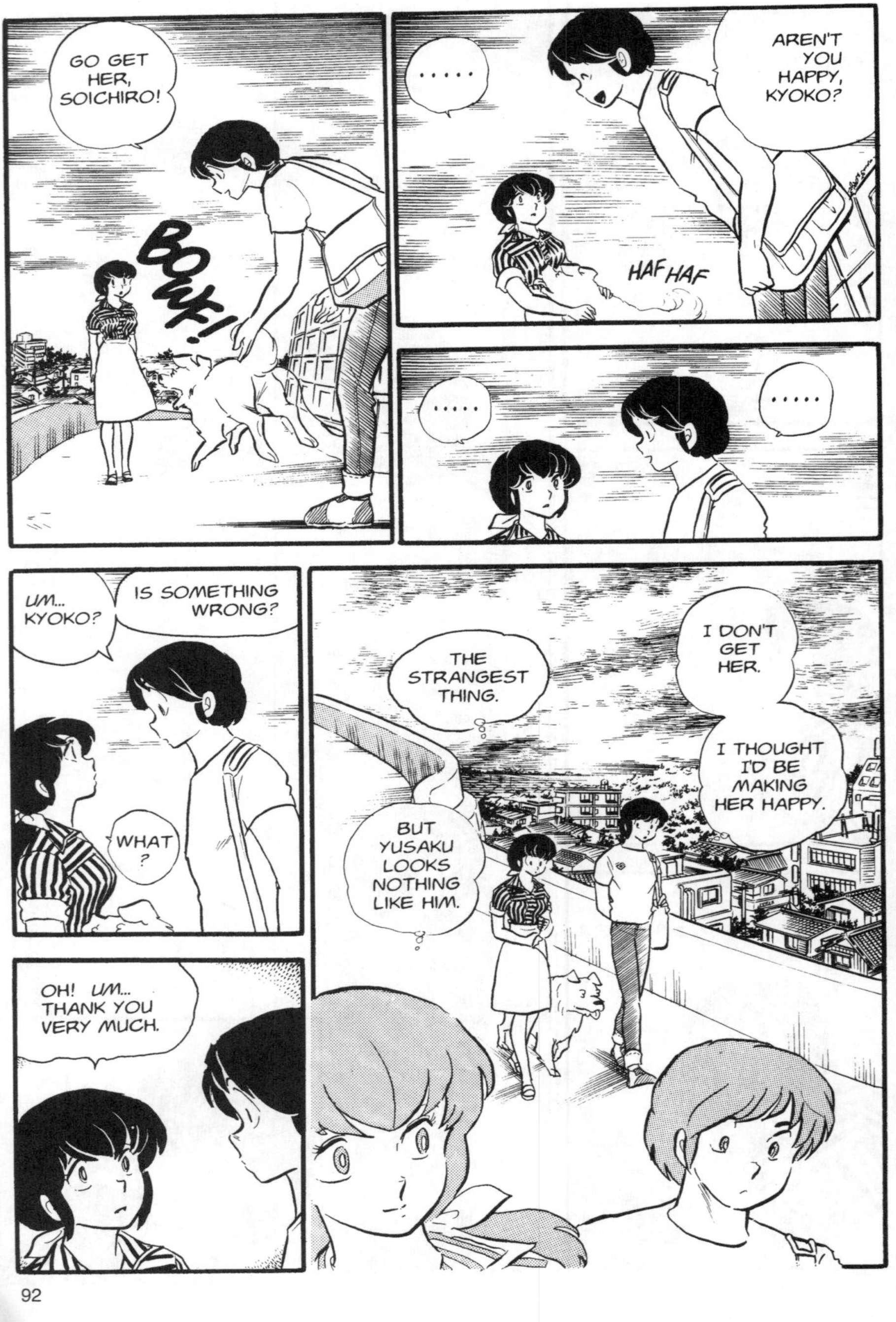

GO GET HER, SOICHIRO!
BOWF!
......
AREN'T YOU HAPPY, KYOKO?
HAF HAF
......
......
UM... KYOKO?
IS SOMETHING WRONG?
WHAT?
OH! UM... THANK YOU VERY MUCH.
THE STRANGEST THING.
BUT YUSAKU LOOKS NOTHING LIKE HIM.
I DON'T GET HER.
I THOUGHT I'D BE MAKING HER HAPPY.

Part Five

A Bunch of Mugs

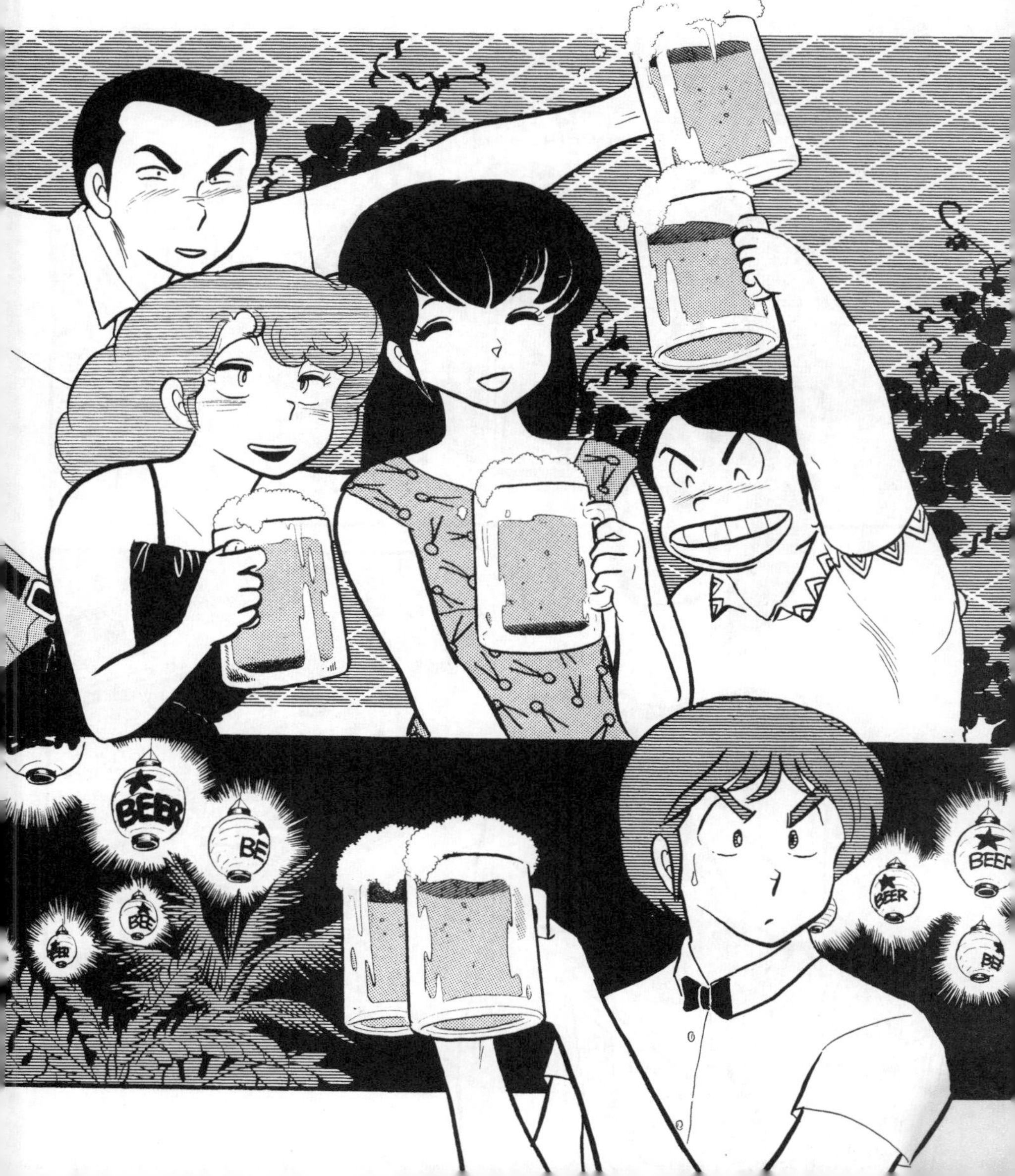
BEER
BE
BEER
BEER

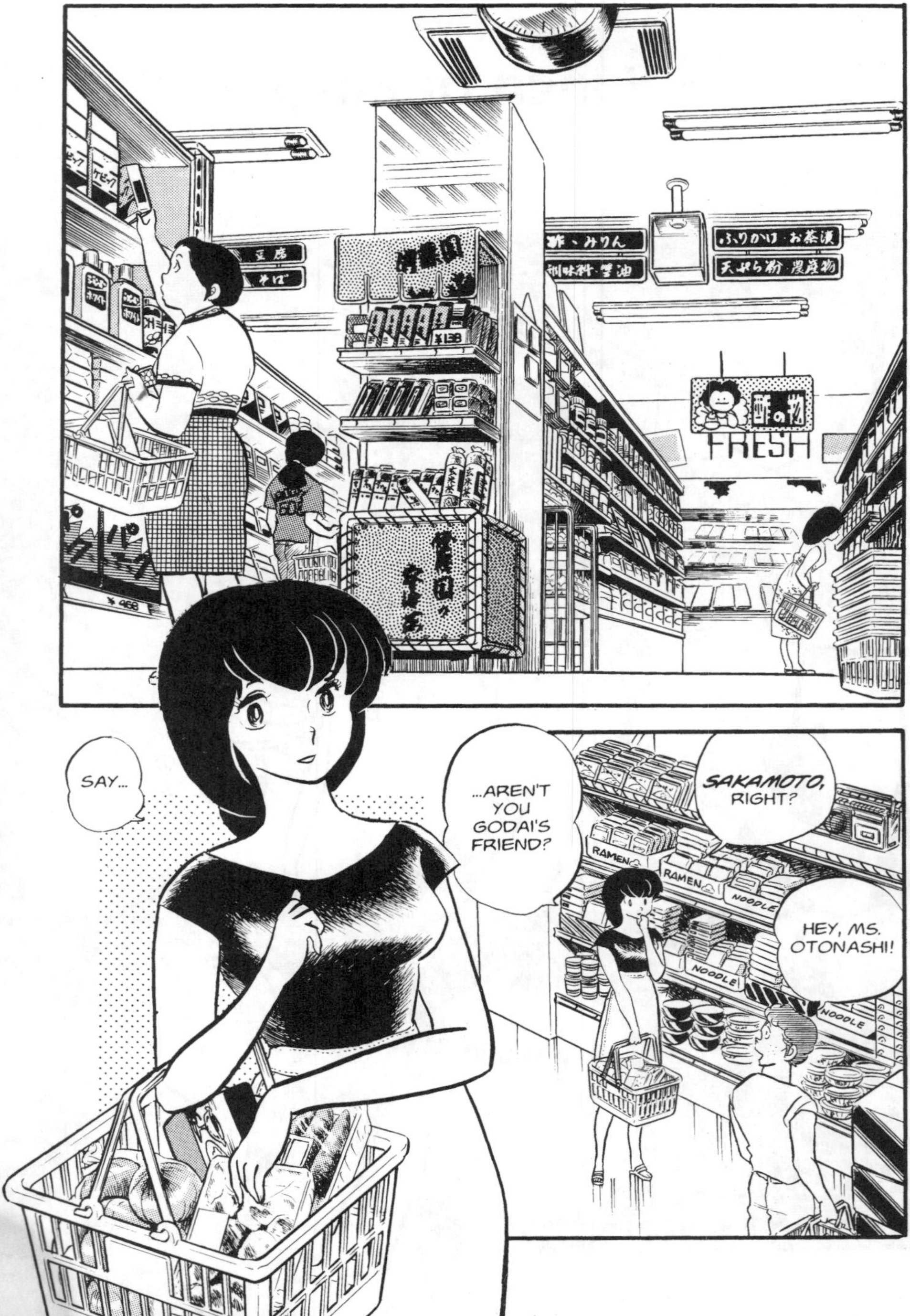

豆腐
そば
酢・みりん
ふりかけ・お茶漬
天ぷら粉・農産物
FRESH
SAY...
...AREN'T YOU GODAI'S FRIEND?
RAMEN
RAMEN
NOODLE
NOODLE
NOODLE
SAKAMOTO, RIGHT?
HEY, MS. OTONASHI!

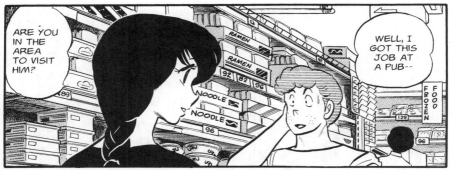

ARE YOU IN THE AREA TO VISIT HIM?
RAMEN
RAMEN
NOODLE
NOODLE
WELL, I GOT THIS JOB AT A PUB--
FROZEN FOOD
THE ONE YUSAKU'S WORKING AT?
YEAH...THE BIG ONE ACROSS FROM THE STATION.
IT'S ONLY FOR A WEEK OR SO, SO I FIGURED I'D JUST CAMP OUT AT HIS PLACE.
GOOD IDEA.
RESH
FROZEN FOOD
BUYING DINNER?
SALE
YUP.
YOU MUST BE HUNGRY...
NOODLE
NAW, IT'S THE WHOLE WEEK'S WORTH.
THAT'S NOT MUCH, THEN.
WELL, I FIGURED I'D GRAB A BITE OUT, EVERY ONCE IN A WHILE.

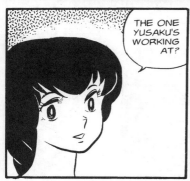

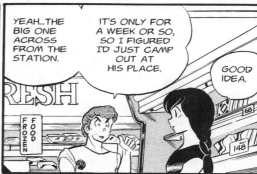

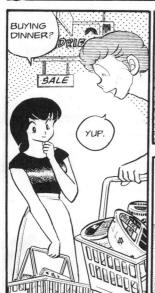

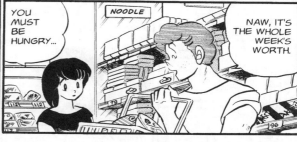

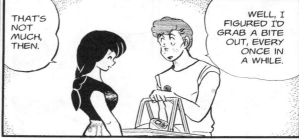

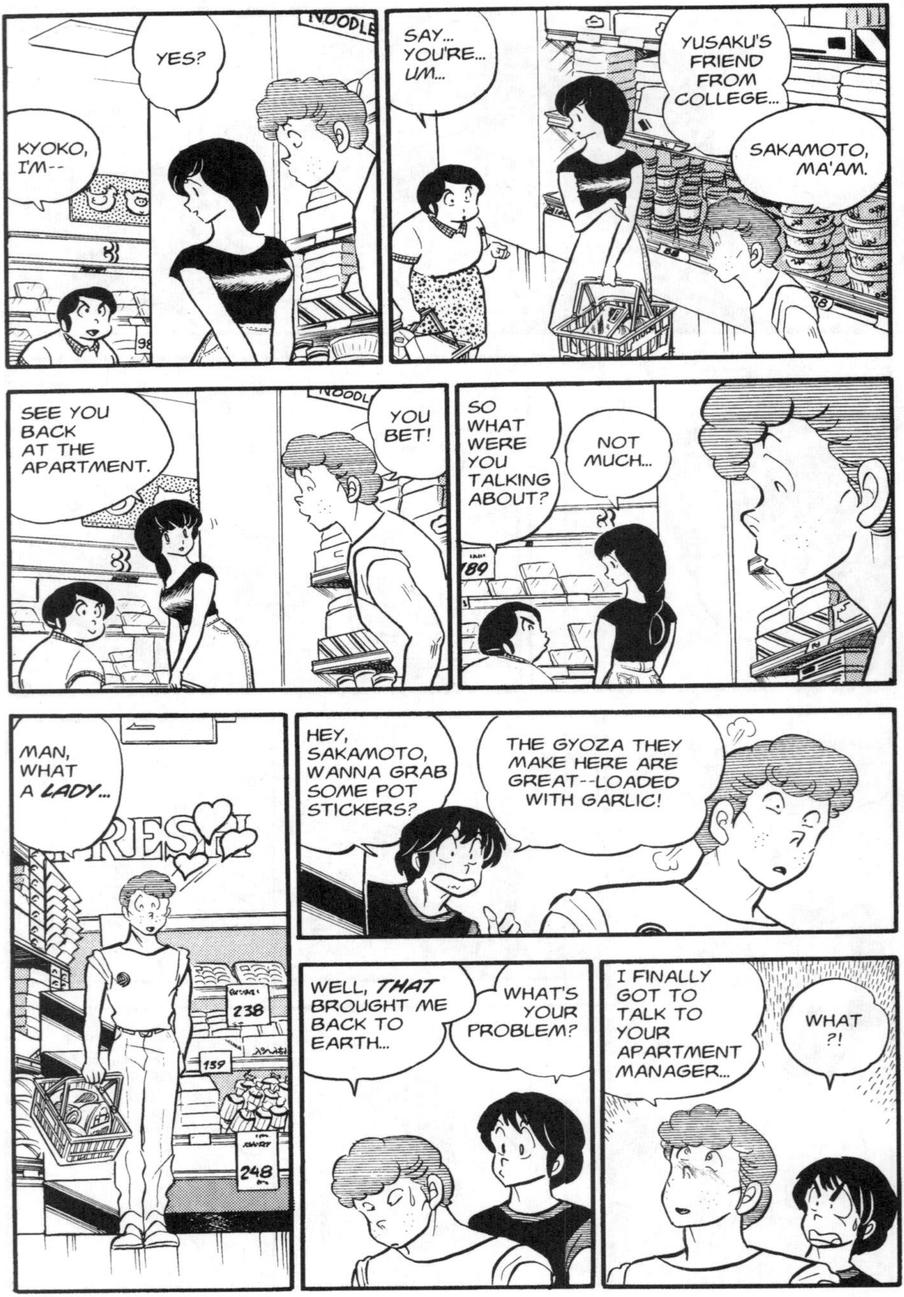
NOODLE
YES?
KYOKO, I'M--
SAY... YOU'RE... UM...
YUSAKU'S FRIEND FROM COLLEGE...
SAKAMOTO, MA'AM.
NOODLE
SEE YOU BACK AT THE APARTMENT.
YOU BET!
SO WHAT WERE YOU TALKING ABOUT?
NOT MUCH...
189
MAN, WHAT A *LADY*...
FRESH
238
139
248
HEY, SAKAMOTO, WANNA GRAB SOME POT STICKERS?
THE GYOZA THEY MAKE HERE ARE GREAT--LOADED WITH GARLIC!
WELL, *THAT* BROUGHT ME BACK TO EARTH...
WHAT'S YOUR PROBLEM?
I FINALLY GOT TO TALK TO YOUR APARTMENT MANAGER...
WHAT ?!

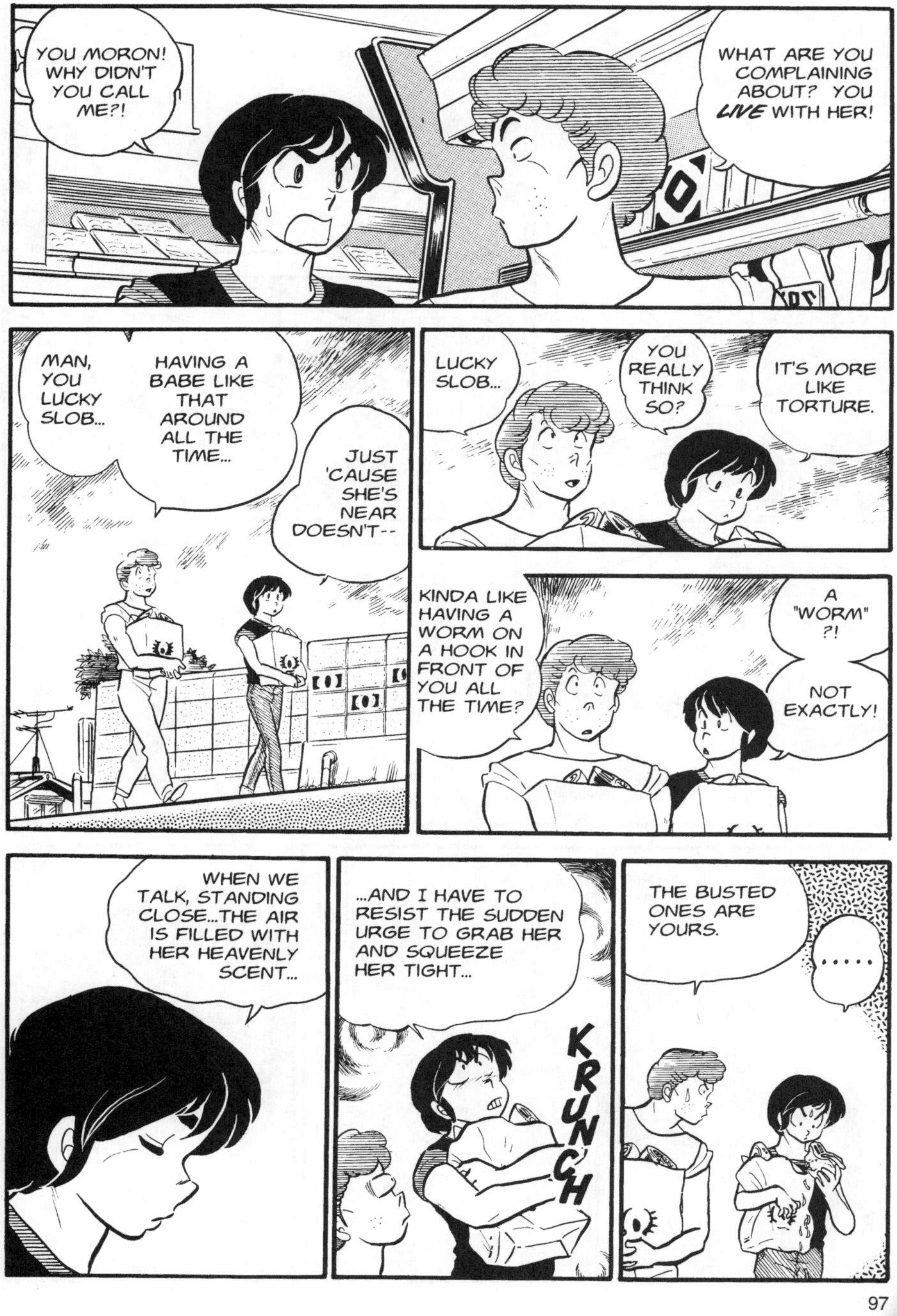
YOU MORON! WHY DIDN'T YOU CALL ME?!
WHAT ARE YOU COMPLAINING ABOUT? YOU *LIVE* WITH HER!
MAN, YOU LUCKY SLOB...
HAVING A BABE LIKE THAT AROUND ALL THE TIME...
JUST 'CAUSE SHE'S NEAR DOESN'T--
LUCKY SLOB...
YOU REALLY THINK SO?
IT'S MORE LIKE TORTURE.
KINDA LIKE HAVING A WORM ON A HOOK IN FRONT OF YOU ALL THE TIME?
A "WORM" ?!
NOT EXACTLY!
WHEN WE TALK, STANDING CLOSE...THE AIR IS FILLED WITH HER HEAVENLY SCENT...
...AND I HAVE TO RESIST THE SUDDEN URGE TO GRAB HER AND SQUEEZE HER TIGHT...
KRUNCH
THE BUSTED ONES ARE YOURS.
.....

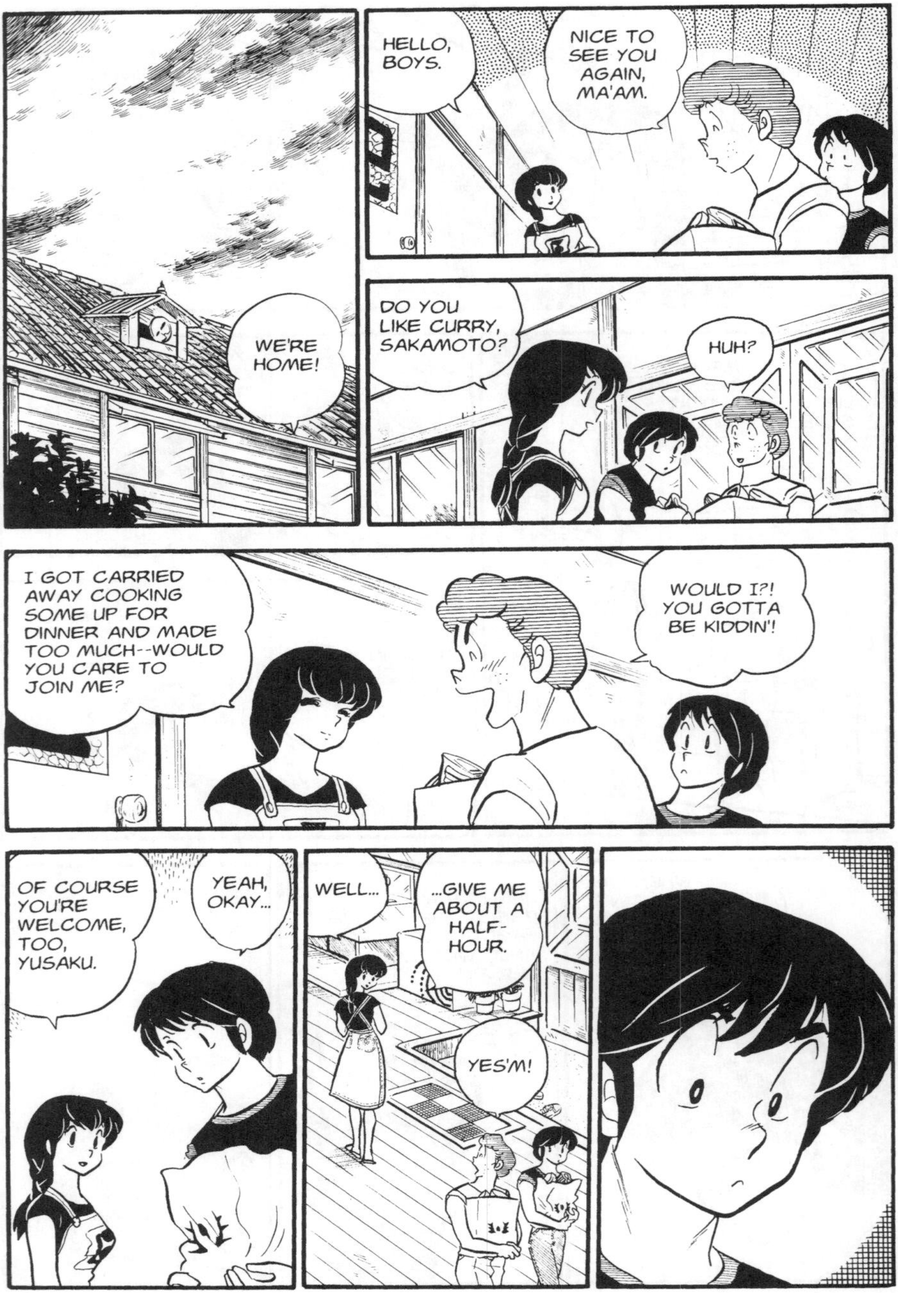
WE'RE HOME!
HELLO, BOYS.
NICE TO SEE YOU AGAIN, MA'AM.
DO YOU LIKE CURRY, SAKAMOTO?
HUH?
I GOT CARRIED AWAY COOKING SOME UP FOR DINNER AND MADE TOO MUCH--WOULD YOU CARE TO JOIN ME?
WOULD I?! YOU GOTTA BE KIDDIN'!
OF COURSE YOU'RE WELCOME, TOO, YUSAKU.
YEAH, OKAY...
WELL...
...GIVE ME ABOUT A HALF-HOUR.
YES'M!

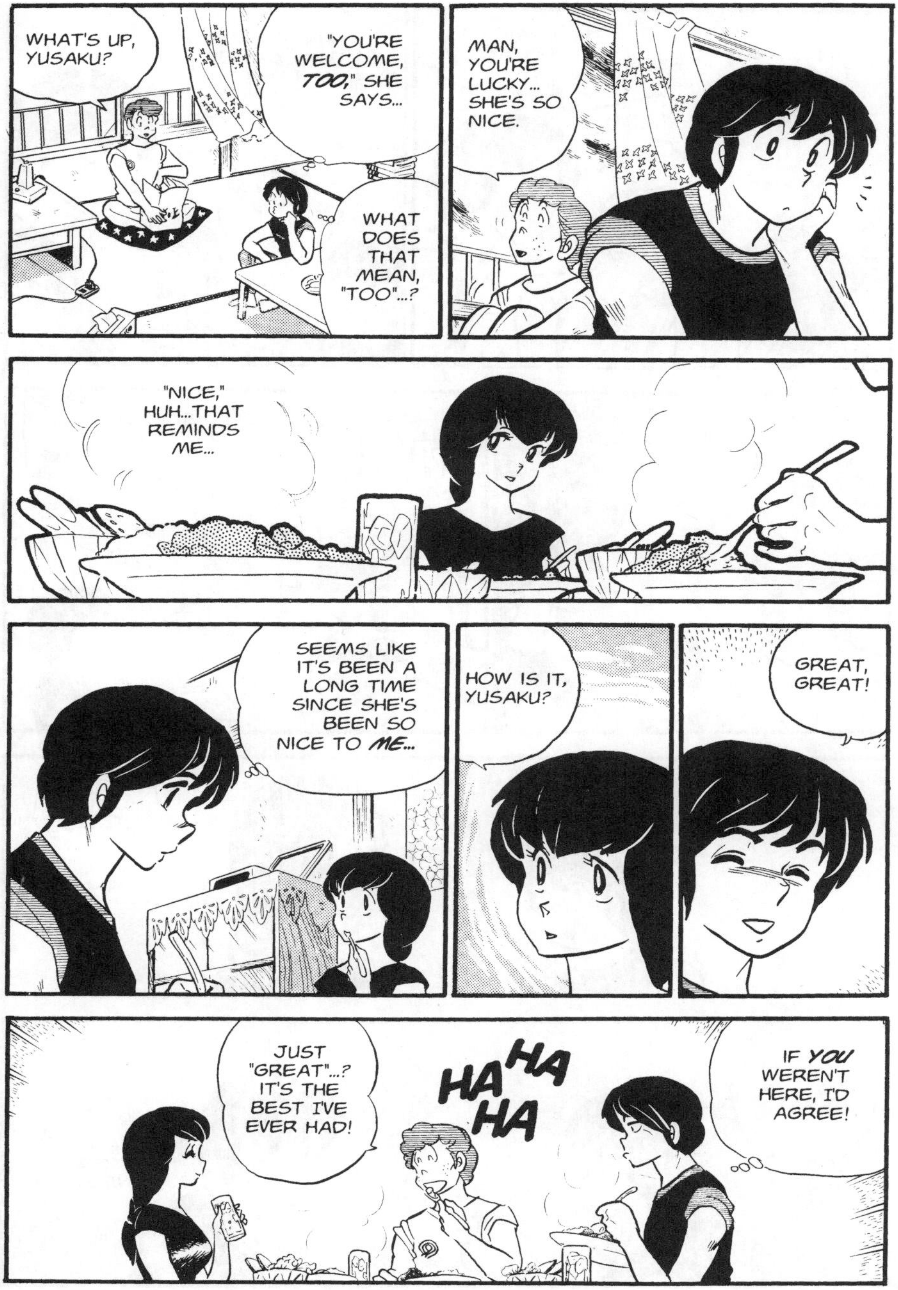
WHAT'S UP, YUSAKU?
"YOU'RE WELCOME, *TOO,*" SHE SAYS...
WHAT DOES THAT MEAN, "TOO"...?
MAN, YOU'RE LUCKY... SHE'S SO NICE.
"NICE," HUH...THAT REMINDS ME...
SEEMS LIKE IT'S BEEN A LONG TIME SINCE SHE'S BEEN SO NICE TO *ME*...
HOW IS IT, YUSAKU?
GREAT, GREAT!
JUST "GREAT"...? IT'S THE BEST I'VE EVER HAD!
HA HA HA HA
IF *YOU* WEREN'T HERE, I'D AGREE!

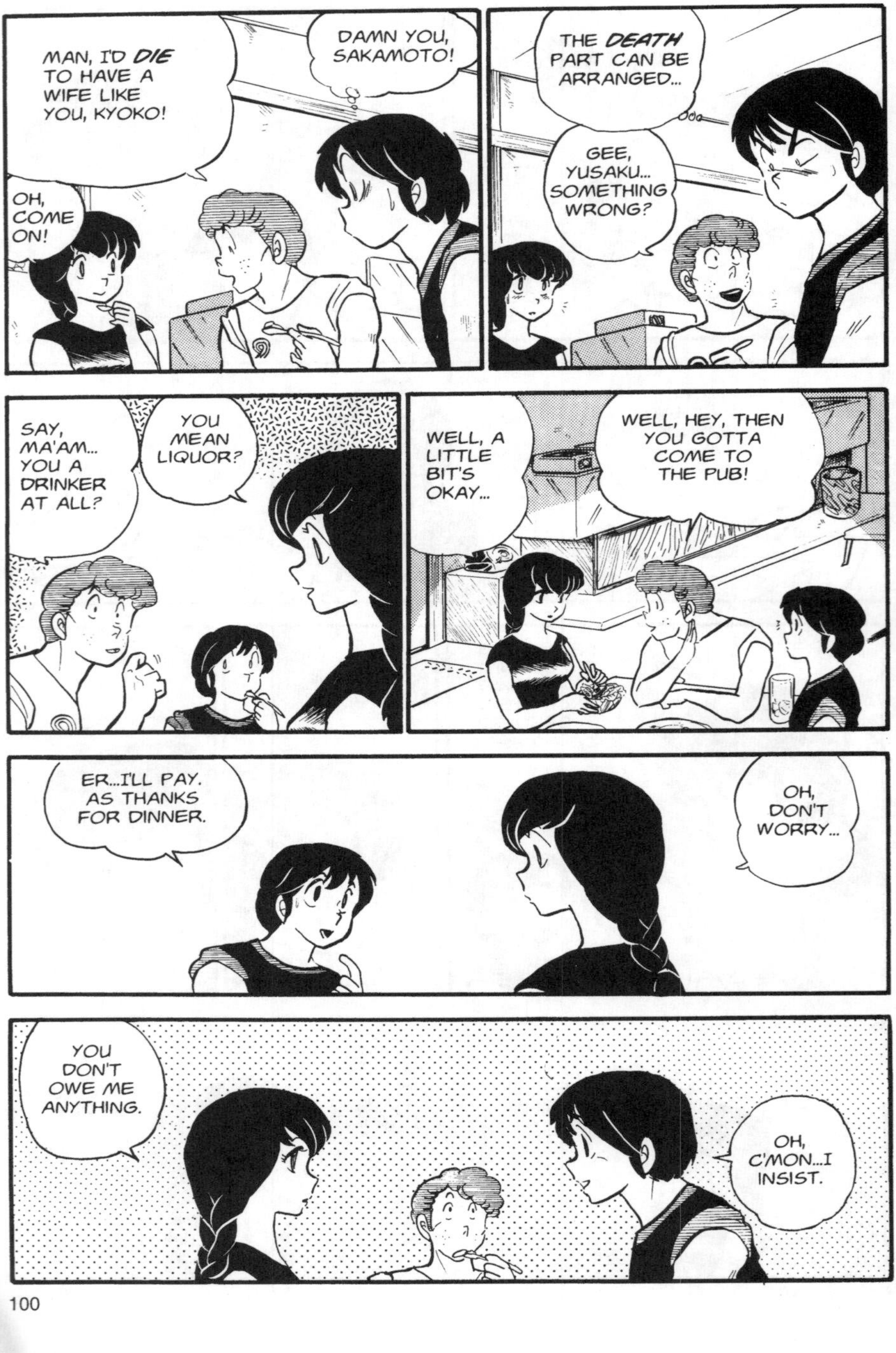
MAN, I'D DIE TO HAVE A WIFE LIKE YOU, KYOKO!
DAMN YOU, SAKAMOTO!
OH, COME ON!
THE DEATH PART CAN BE ARRANGED...
GEE, YUSAKU... SOMETHING WRONG?
SAY, MA'AM... YOU A DRINKER AT ALL?
YOU MEAN LIQUOR?
WELL, A LITTLE BIT'S OKAY...
WELL, HEY, THEN YOU GOTTA COME TO THE PUB!
ER...I'LL PAY. AS THANKS FOR DINNER.
OH, DON'T WORRY...
YOU DON'T OWE ME ANYTHING.
OH, C'MON...I INSIST.

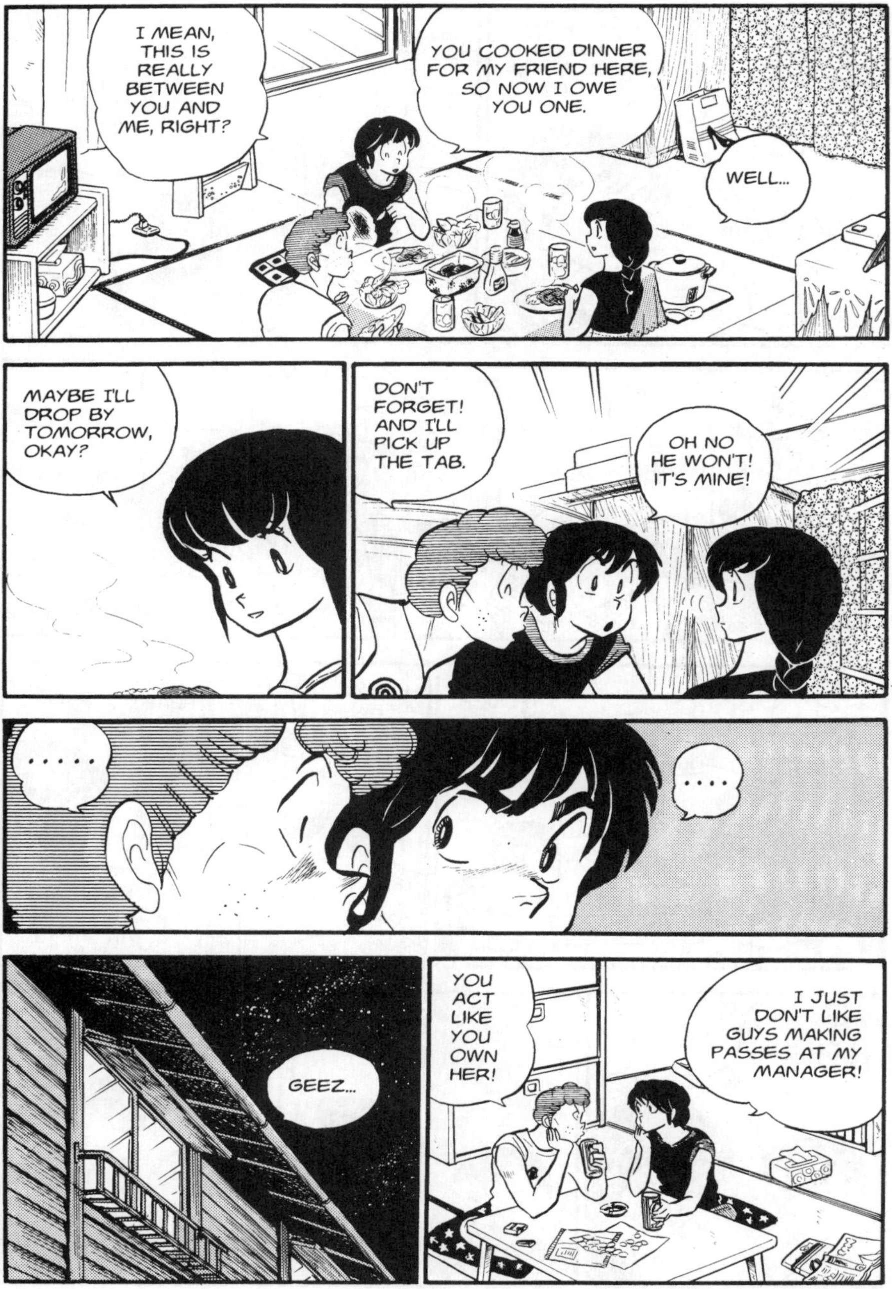
I MEAN, THIS IS REALLY BETWEEN YOU AND ME, RIGHT?
YOU COOKED DINNER FOR MY FRIEND HERE, SO NOW I OWE YOU ONE.
WELL...
MAYBE I'LL DROP BY TOMORROW, OKAY?
DON'T FORGET! AND I'LL PICK UP THE TAB.
OH NO HE WON'T! IT'S MINE!
.....
....
GEEZ...
YOU ACT LIKE YOU OWN HER!
I JUST DON'T LIKE GUYS MAKING PASSES AT MY MANAGER!

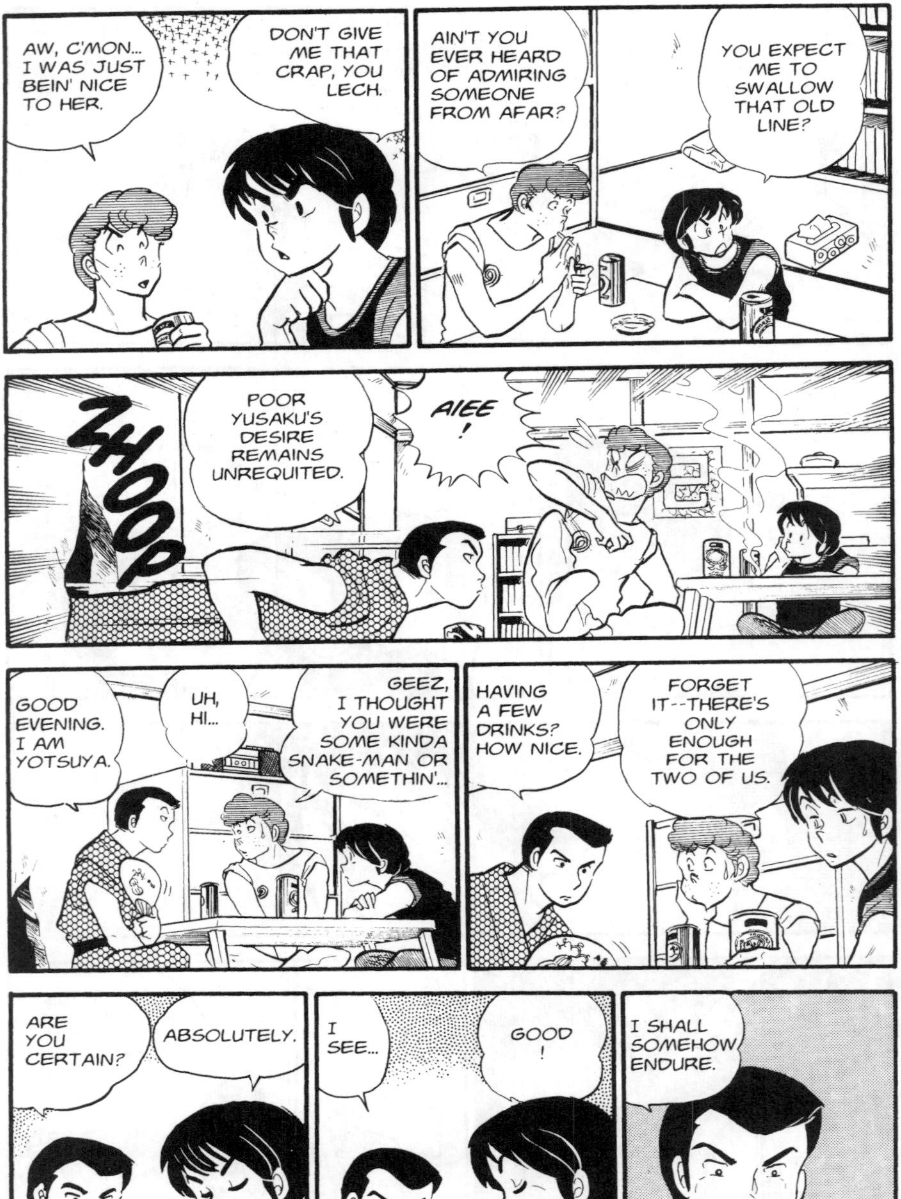
AW, C'MON... I WAS JUST BEIN' NICE TO HER.
DON'T GIVE ME THAT CRAP, YOU LECH.
AIN'T YOU EVER HEARD OF ADMIRING SOMEONE FROM AFAR?
YOU EXPECT ME TO SWALLOW THAT OLD LINE?
ZHOOP
POOR YUSAKU'S DESIRE REMAINS UNREQUITED.
AIEE!
GOOD EVENING. I AM YOTSUYA.
UH, HI...
GEEZ, I THOUGHT YOU WERE SOME KINDA SNAKE-MAN OR SOMETHIN'...
HAVING A FEW DRINKS? HOW NICE.
FORGET IT--THERE'S ONLY ENOUGH FOR THE TWO OF US.
ARE YOU CERTAIN?
ABSOLUTELY.
I SEE...
GOOD!
I SHALL SOMEHOW ENDURE.

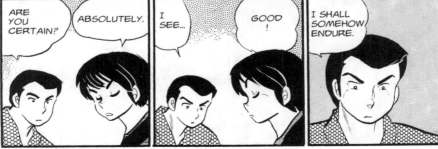

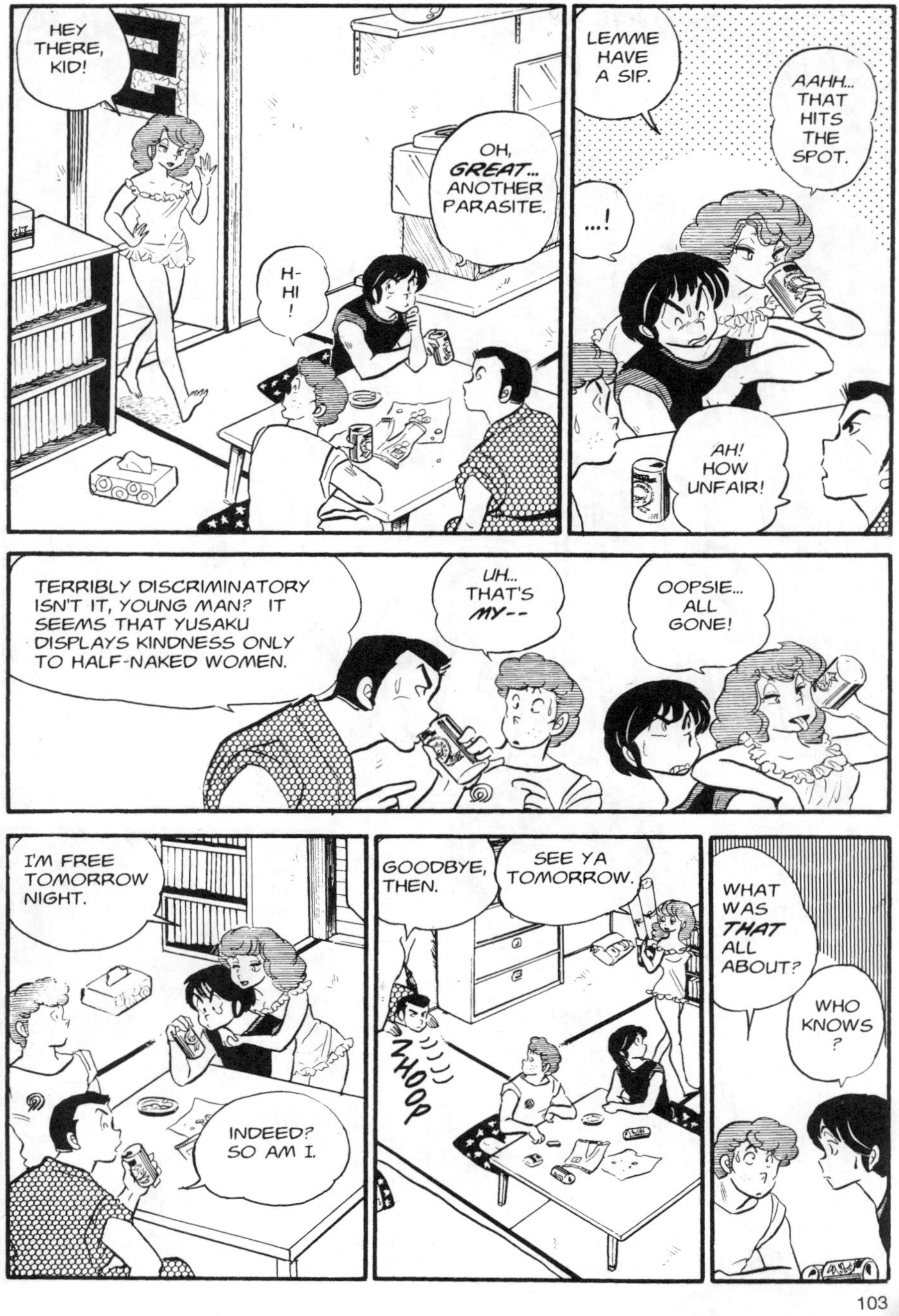
HEY THERE, KID!
OH, GREAT... ANOTHER PARASITE.
H-HI!
LEMME HAVE A SIP.
AAHH... THAT HITS THE SPOT.
...!
AH! HOW UNFAIR!
TERRIBLY DISCRIMINATORY ISN'T IT, YOUNG MAN? IT SEEMS THAT YUSAKU DISPLAYS KINDNESS ONLY TO HALF-NAKED WOMEN.
UH... THAT'S MY--
OOPSIE... ALL GONE!
I'M FREE TOMORROW NIGHT.
INDEED? SO AM I.
GOODBYE, THEN.
SEE YA TOMORROW.
WHOOP
WHAT WAS THAT ALL ABOUT?
WHO KNOWS?

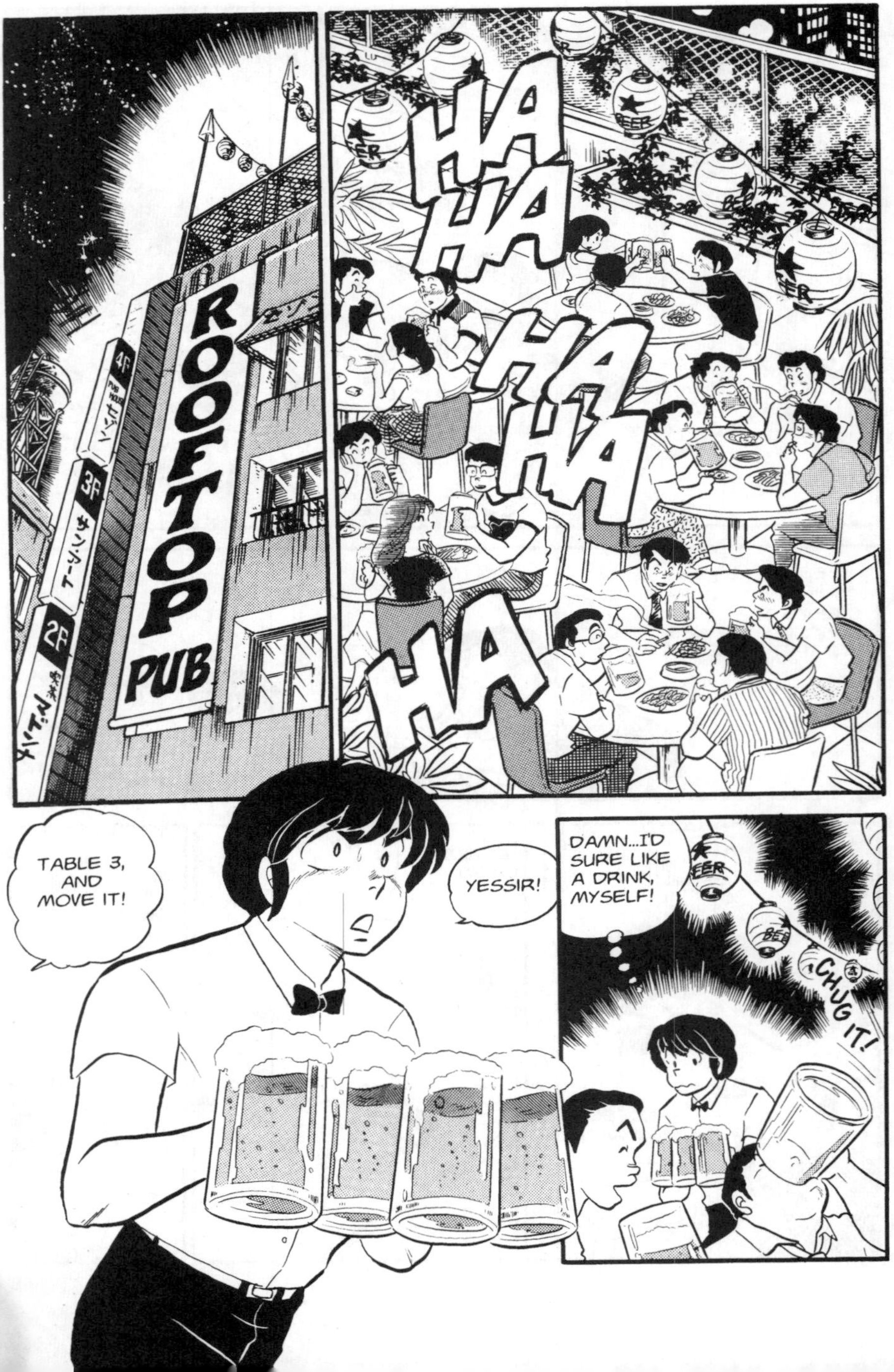
ROOFTOP PUB
4F
3F
2F
HA HA HA
HA HA HA
HA
TABLE 3, AND MOVE IT!
YESSIR!
DAMN...I'D SURE LIKE A DRINK, MYSELF!
CHUG IT!

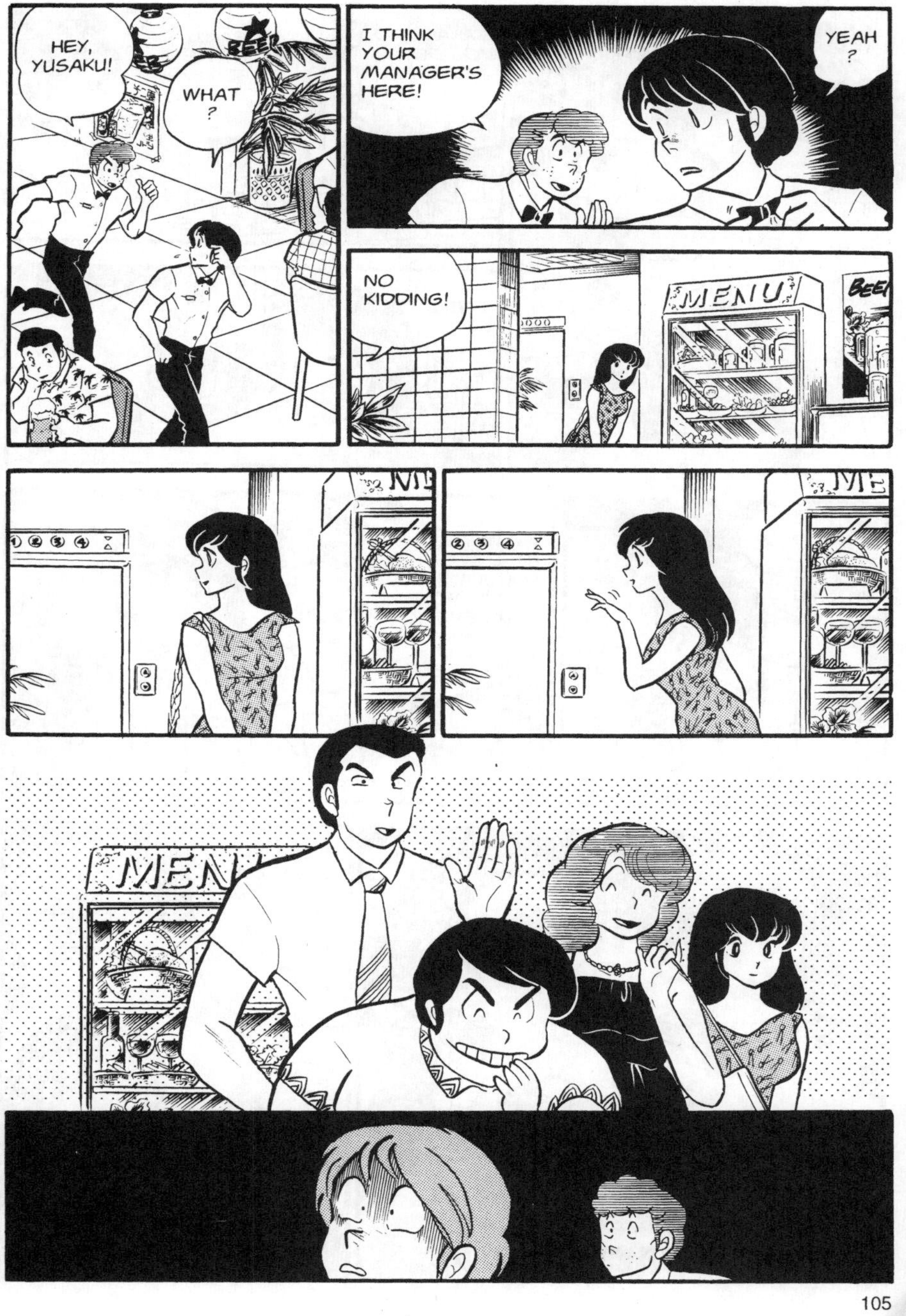
HEY, YUSAKU!
WHAT ?
BEER
I THINK YOUR MANAGER'S HERE!
YEAH ?
NO KIDDING!
MENU
BEER
MENU

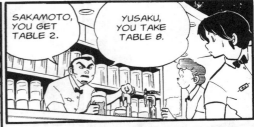

OH MAN, WHAT ARE *THEY* DOING HERE?!
YOU'RE KIDDING... YOU'VE NEVER BEEN TO ONE OF THESE ROOFTOP PUBS BEFORE?
NEVER.
SAKAMOTO, YOU GET TABLE 2.
YUSAKU, YOU TAKE TABLE 8.
TABLE 8...
BWA HA HA HA
HEY, SAKAMOTO-- SWAP TABLES WITH ME!
WHAT THE HELL ARE YOU WAITING FOR?! MOVE YOUR BUTT!
YESSIR!
YESSIR!
HERE Y'GO, FOLKS...
FAST WORK, KIDDO.
WHUD
YOU SHOULDA GOT A BIG MUG LIKE EVERYONE ELSE, KYOKO.
THIS IS BIG ENOUGH FOR *ME!*

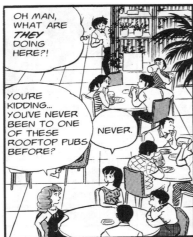

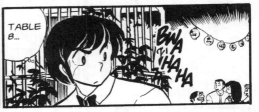

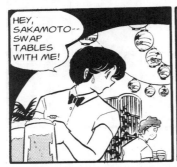

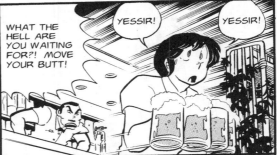

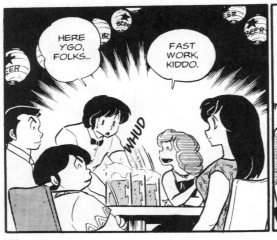

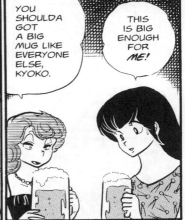

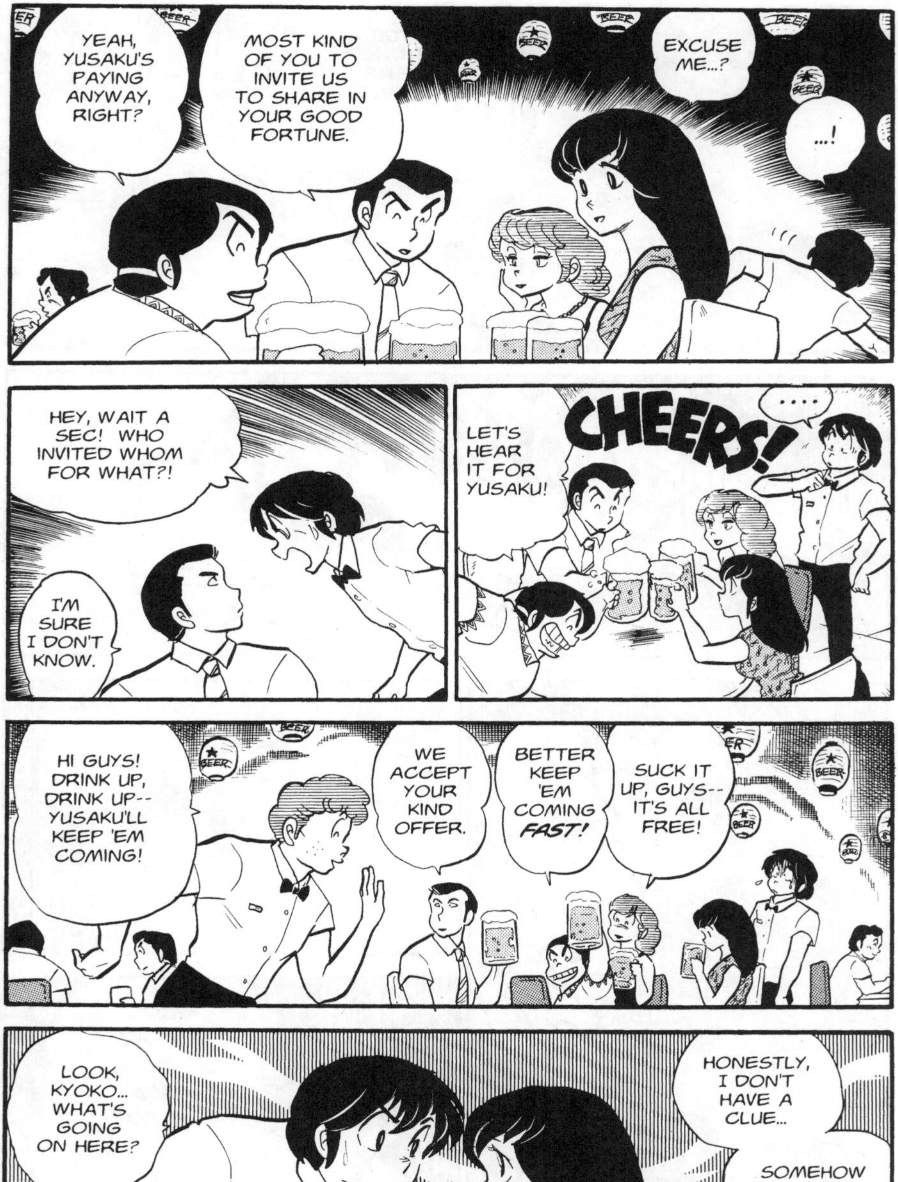
YEAH, YUSAKU'S PAYING ANYWAY, RIGHT?
MOST KIND OF YOU TO INVITE US TO SHARE IN YOUR GOOD FORTUNE.
EXCUSE ME...?
...!
HEY, WAIT A SEC! WHO INVITED WHOM FOR WHAT?!
I'M SURE I DON'T KNOW.
LET'S HEAR IT FOR YUSAKU!
CHEERS!
....
HI GUYS! DRINK UP, DRINK UP-- YUSAKU'LL KEEP 'EM COMING!
WE ACCEPT YOUR KIND OFFER.
BETTER KEEP 'EM COMING *FAST!*
SUCK IT UP, GUYS-- IT'S ALL FREE!
LOOK, KYOKO... WHAT'S GOING ON HERE?
HONESTLY, I DON'T HAVE A CLUE...
SOMEHOW THINGS JUST GOT ALL MIXED UP.

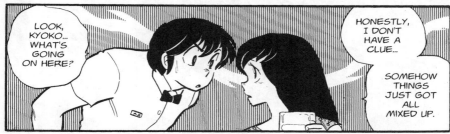

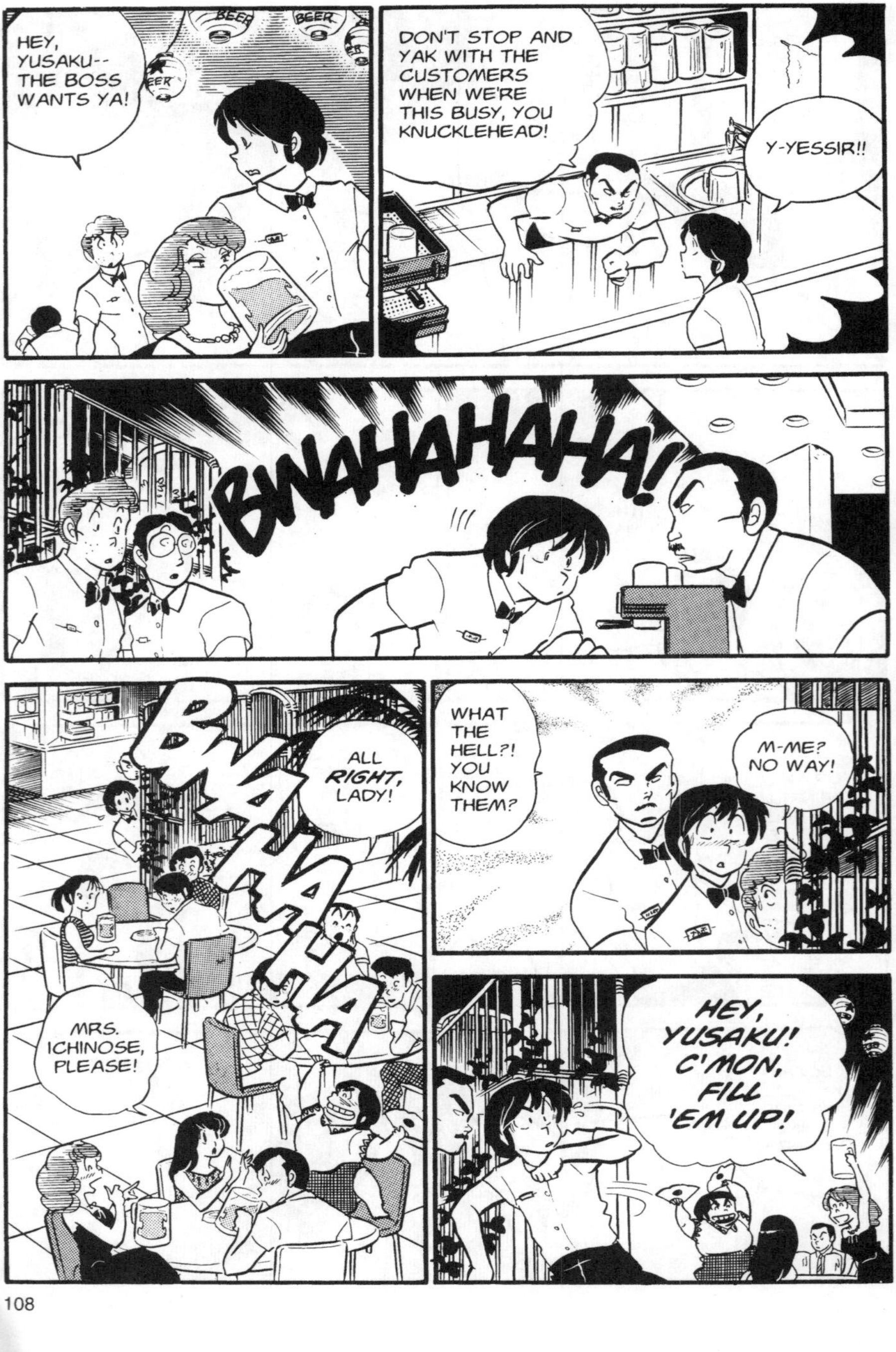
BEER
BEER
HEY, YUSAKU-- THE BOSS WANTS YA!
DON'T STOP AND YAK WITH THE CUSTOMERS WHEN WE'RE THIS BUSY, YOU KNUCKLEHEAD!
Y-YESSIR!!
BWAHAHAHAHA!
BWAHAHAHA
ALL RIGHT, LADY!
MRS. ICHINOSE, PLEASE!
WHAT THE HELL?! YOU KNOW THEM?
M-ME? NO WAY!
HEY, YUSAKU! C'MON, FILL 'EM UP!

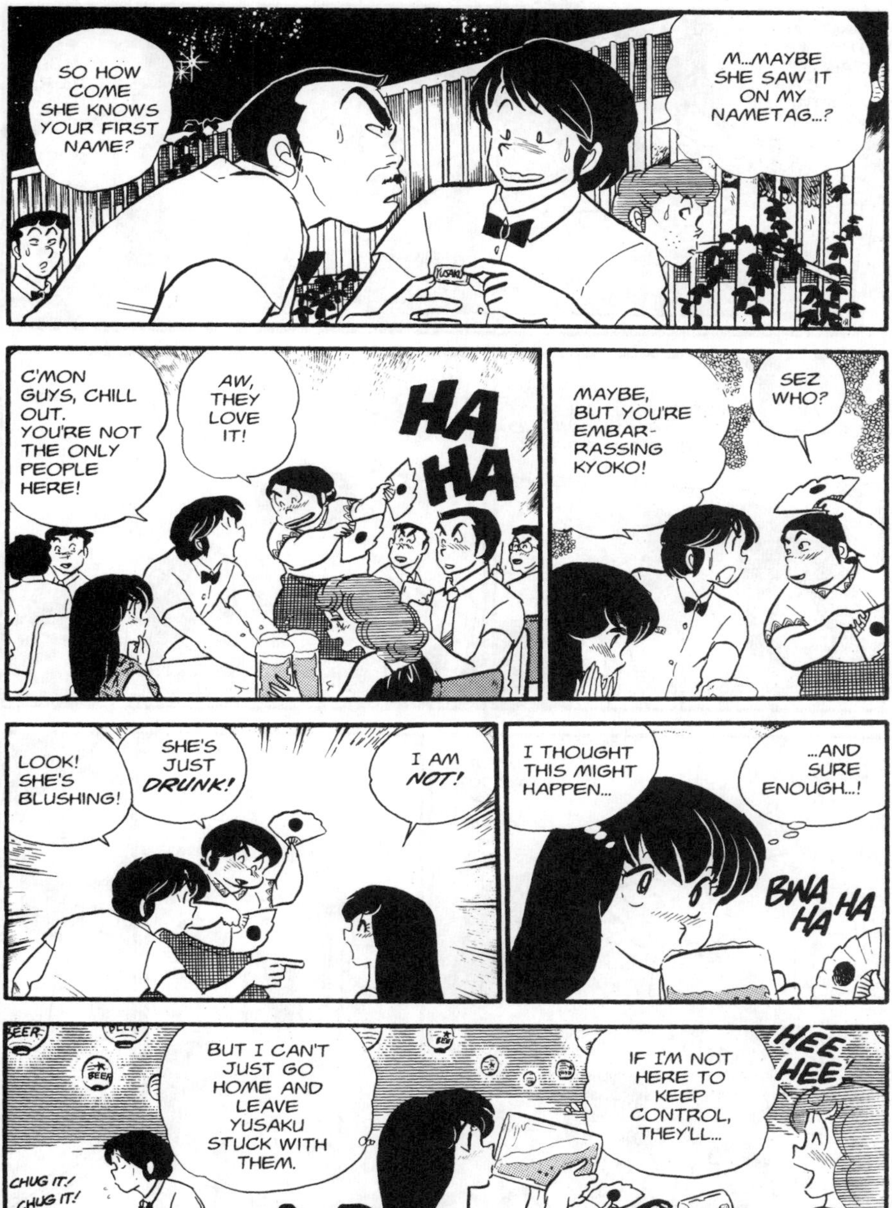
SO HOW COME SHE KNOWS YOUR FIRST NAME?
M...MAYBE SHE SAW IT ON MY NAMETAG...?
YUSAKU
C'MON GUYS, CHILL OUT. YOU'RE NOT THE ONLY PEOPLE HERE!
AW, THEY LOVE IT!
HA HA
MAYBE, BUT YOU'RE EMBAR-RASSING KYOKO!
SEZ WHO?
LOOK! SHE'S BLUSHING!
SHE'S JUST DRUNK!
I AM NOT!
I THOUGHT THIS MIGHT HAPPEN...
...AND SURE ENOUGH...!
BWA HA HA HA
BEER
BUT I CAN'T JUST GO HOME AND LEAVE YUSAKU STUCK WITH THEM.
IF I'M NOT HERE TO KEEP CONTROL, THEY'LL...
HEE HEE
CHUG IT! CHUG IT!

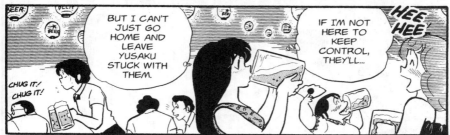

BROTHER, THAT WHOLE TABLE'S OUT OF CONTROL, EH?
HEY, KID! MORE BEER!
IF IT'S FREE, I HAVE NO LIMIT.
C'MON! FOUR MORE PITCHERS!
NONE FOR ME, PLEASH...
C'MON, WHY QUIT NOW? YOU'VE BEEN CHOKING THEM DOWN NO PROBLEM SO FAR...
UMM... ARE YOU ALL RIGHT, KYOKO?
WHAT ARE YOU TALKIN' ABOUT?
WHAT ABOUT YOU, HUH?
WHAT DO YOU MEAN, ME?
EH?
I MEAN, ABOUT THE BILL.
LOOK, JUSHT COME WITH ME.
I'M OKAY, JUSHT C'MON, 'KAY?
B-BETTER NOT STAND--
DID Y'SHEE THEIR EYES, HUH?
THEY'RE JUSHT TAKIN' ADVANTAGE OF YA, LIKE PARASHITES OR SOMETHIN'.
I...I SEE...
BEER
WOBBLE
WOBBLE
WOBBLE

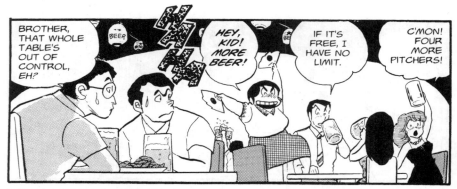

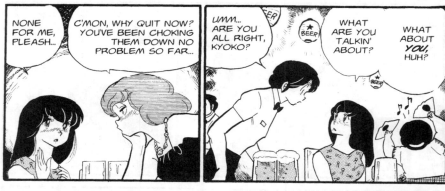

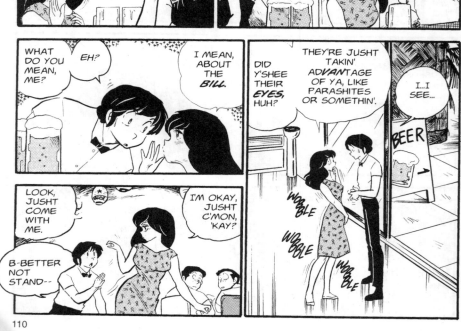

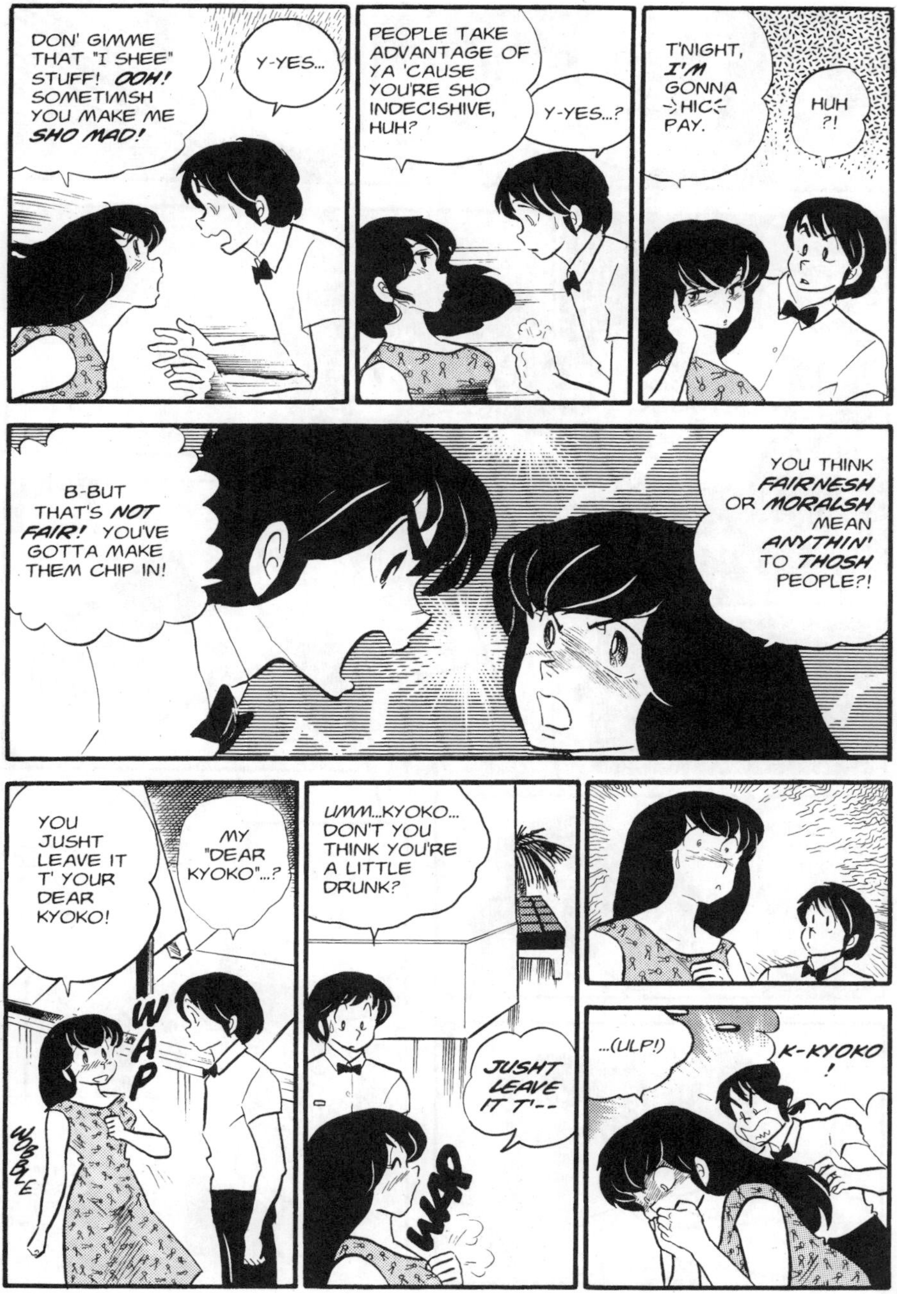
DON' GIMME THAT "I SHEE" STUFF! OOH! SOMETIMSH YOU MAKE ME SHO MAD!
Y-YES...
PEOPLE TAKE ADVANTAGE OF YA 'CAUSE YOU'RE SHO INDECISHIVE, HUH?
Y-YES...?
T'NIGHT, I'M GONNA -HIC- PAY.
HUH ?!
B-BUT THAT'S NOT FAIR! YOU'VE GOTTA MAKE THEM CHIP IN!
YOU THINK FAIRNESH OR MORALSH MEAN ANYTHIN' TO THOSH PEOPLE?!
YOU JUSHT LEAVE IT T' YOUR DEAR KYOKO!
MY "DEAR KYOKO"...?
WAP
WOBBLE
UMM...KYOKO... DON'T YOU THINK YOU'RE A LITTLE DRUNK?
JUSHT LEAVE IT T'--
WAP
...(ULP!)
K-KYOKO!

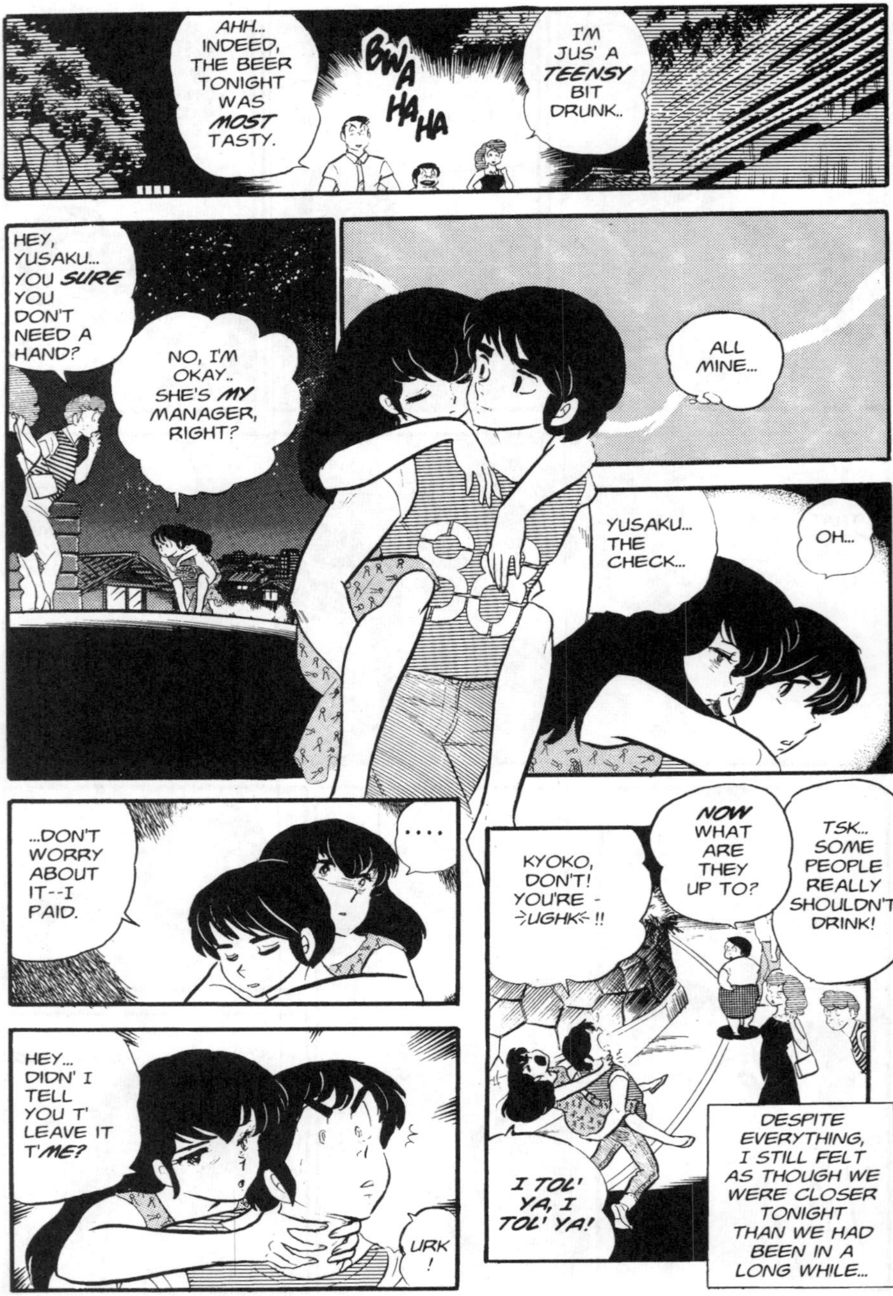
AHH... INDEED, THE BEER TONIGHT WAS MOST TASTY.
BWA HA HA
I'M JUS' A TEENSY BIT DRUNK..
HEY, YUSAKU... YOU SURE YOU DON'T NEED A HAND?
NO, I'M OKAY.. SHE'S MY MANAGER, RIGHT?
ALL MINE...
YUSAKU... THE CHECK...
OH...
...DON'T WORRY ABOUT IT--I PAID.
....
KYOKO, DON'T! YOU'RE - →UGHK← !!
NOW WHAT ARE THEY UP TO?
TSK... SOME PEOPLE REALLY SHOULDN'T DRINK!
HEY... DIDN' I TELL YOU T' LEAVE IT T'ME?
URK !
I TOL' YA, I TOL' YA!
DESPITE EVERYTHING, I STILL FELT AS THOUGH WE WERE CLOSER TONIGHT THAN WE HAD BEEN IN A LONG WHILE...

Part Six

The One That Got Away

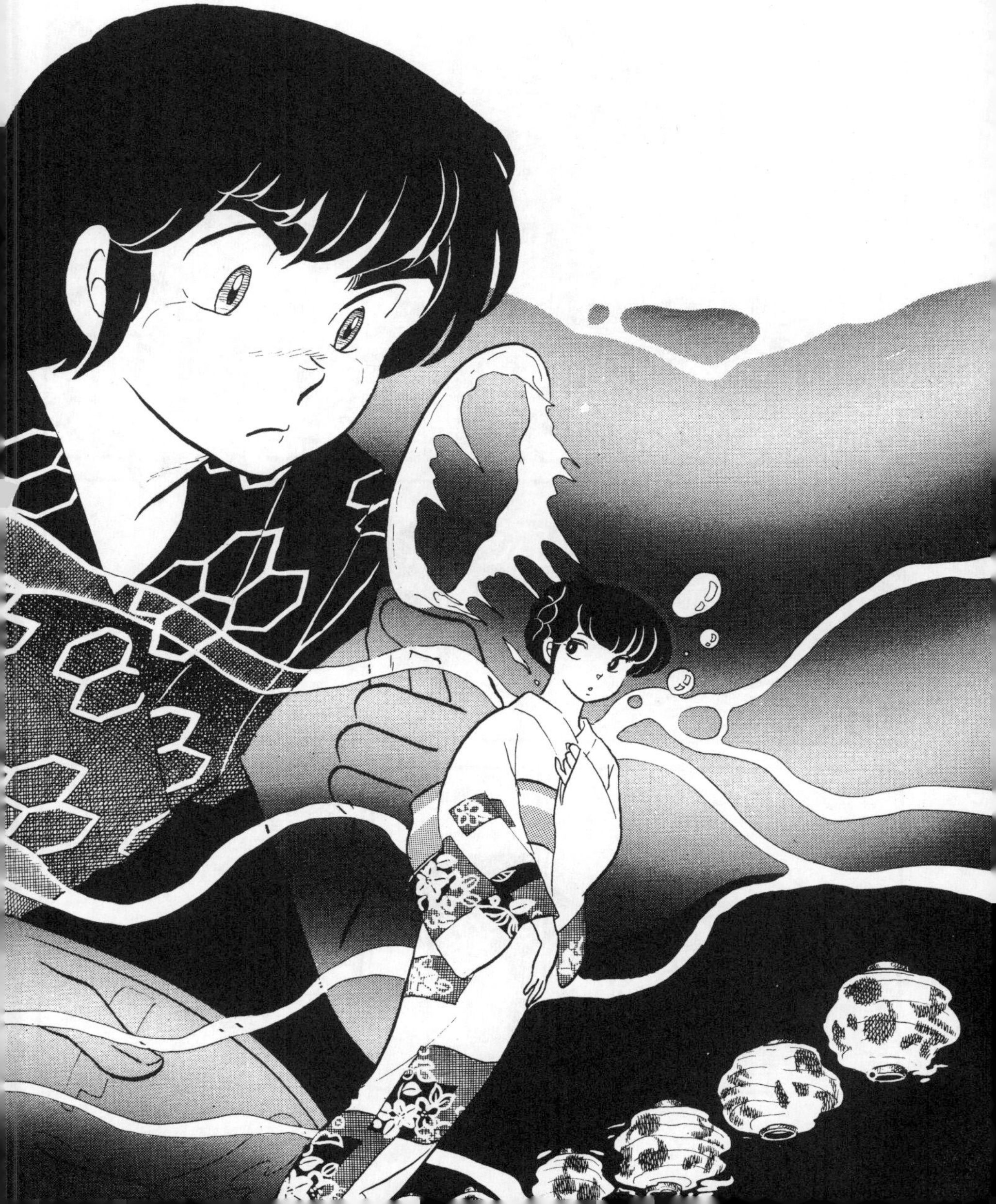

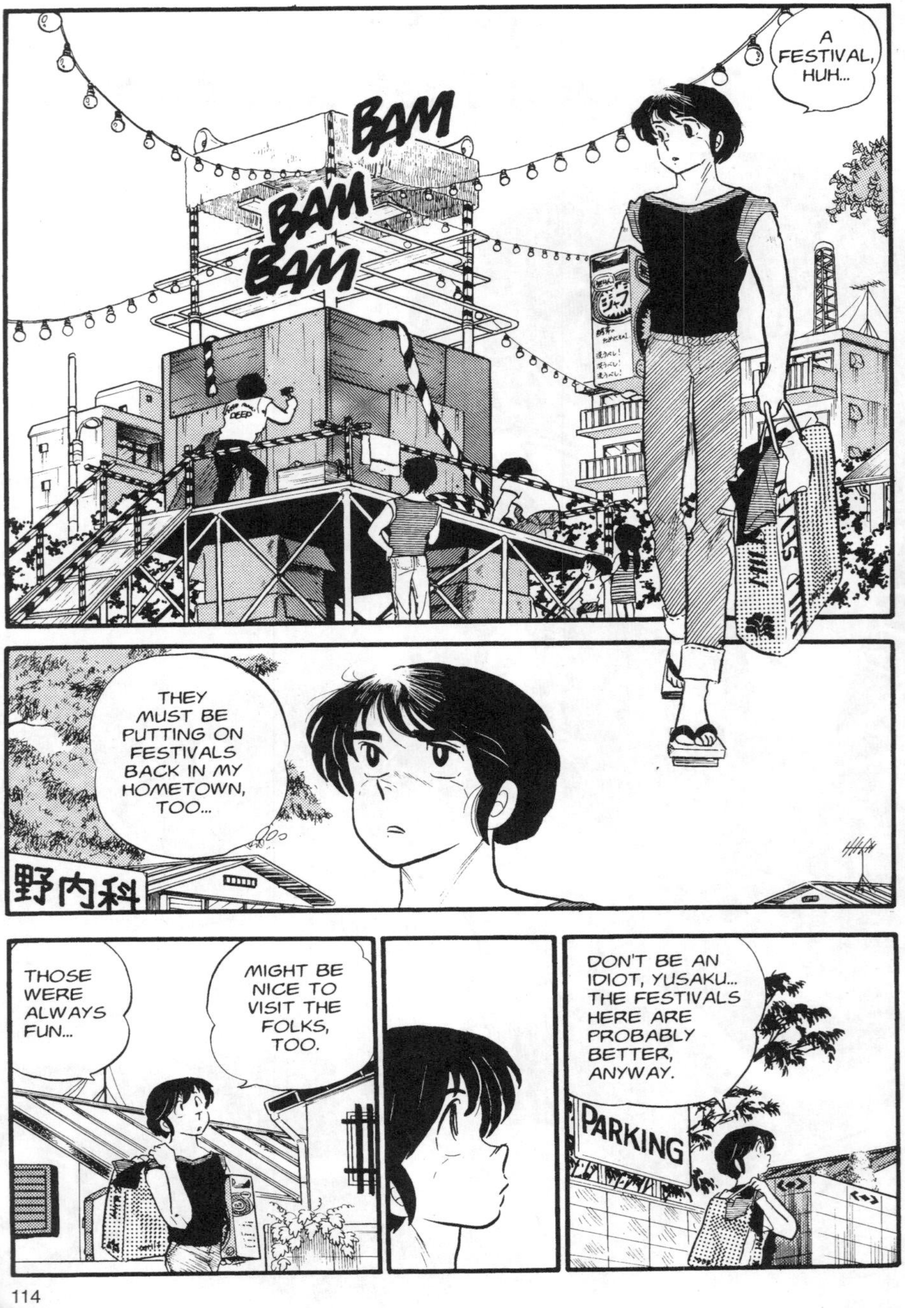
BAM
BAM
BAM
A FESTIVAL, HUH...
THEY MUST BE PUTTING ON FESTIVALS BACK IN MY HOMETOWN, TOO...
野内科
THOSE WERE ALWAYS FUN...
MIGHT BE NICE TO VISIT THE FOLKS, TOO.
DON'T BE AN IDIOT, YUSAKU... THE FESTIVALS HERE ARE PROBABLY BETTER, ANYWAY.
PARKING

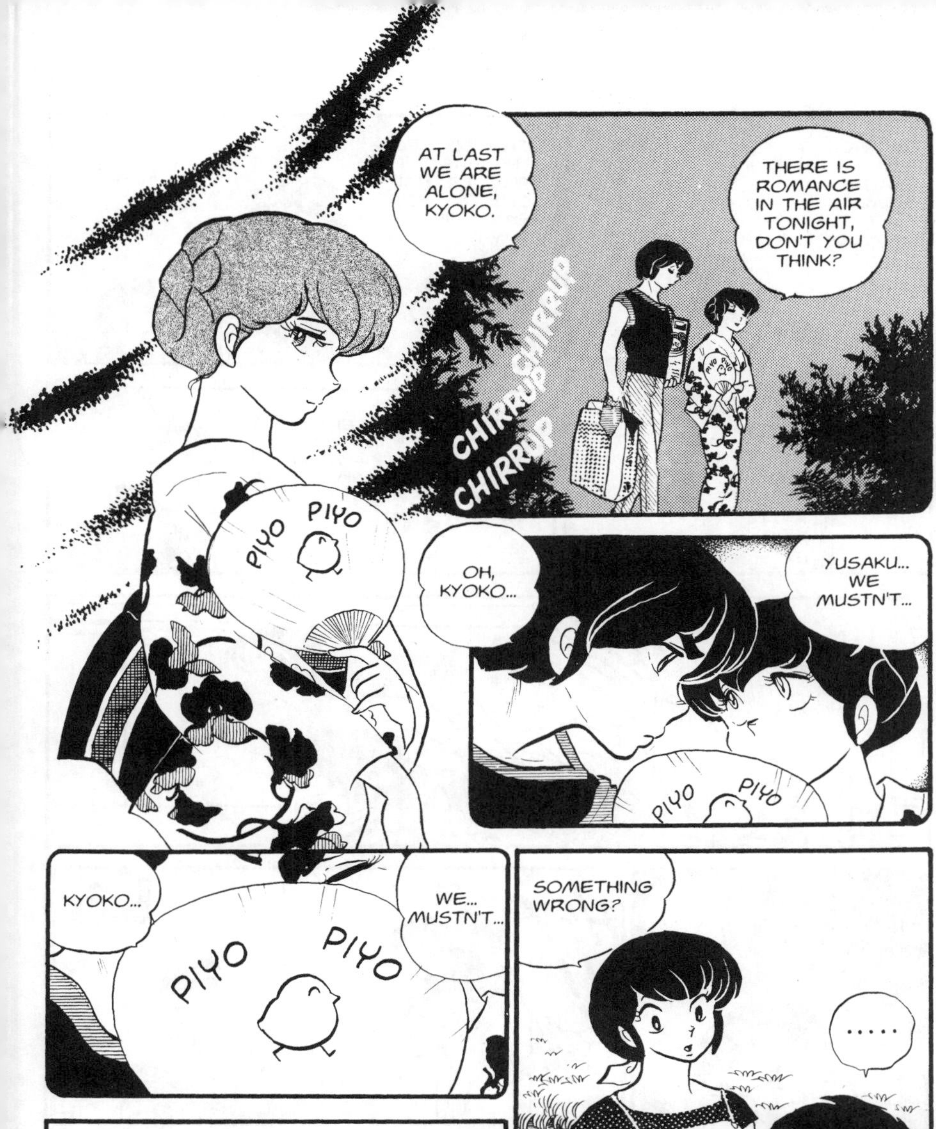

AT LAST WE ARE ALONE, KYOKO.
CHIRRUP CHIRRUP
CHIRRUP CHIRRUP
PIYO PIYO
THERE IS ROMANCE IN THE AIR TONIGHT, DON'T YOU THINK?
OH, KYOKO...
YUSAKU... WE MUSTN'T...
PIYO PIYO
KYOKO...
WE... MUSTN'T...
PIYO PIYO
KYOKO...
PIYO PIYO
YES...?
SOMETHING WRONG?
.....
PIYO PIYO

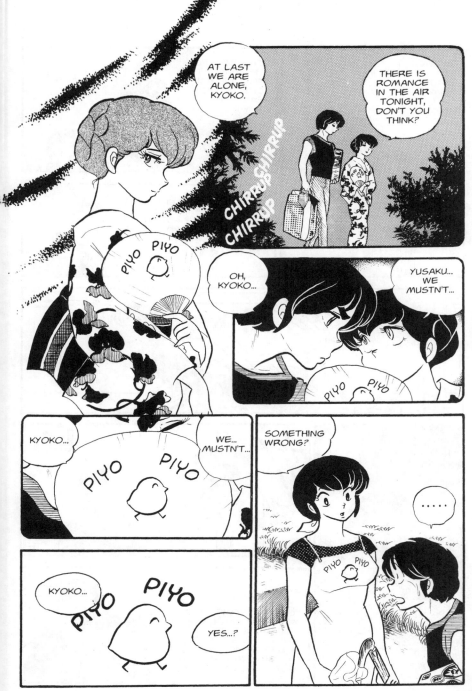

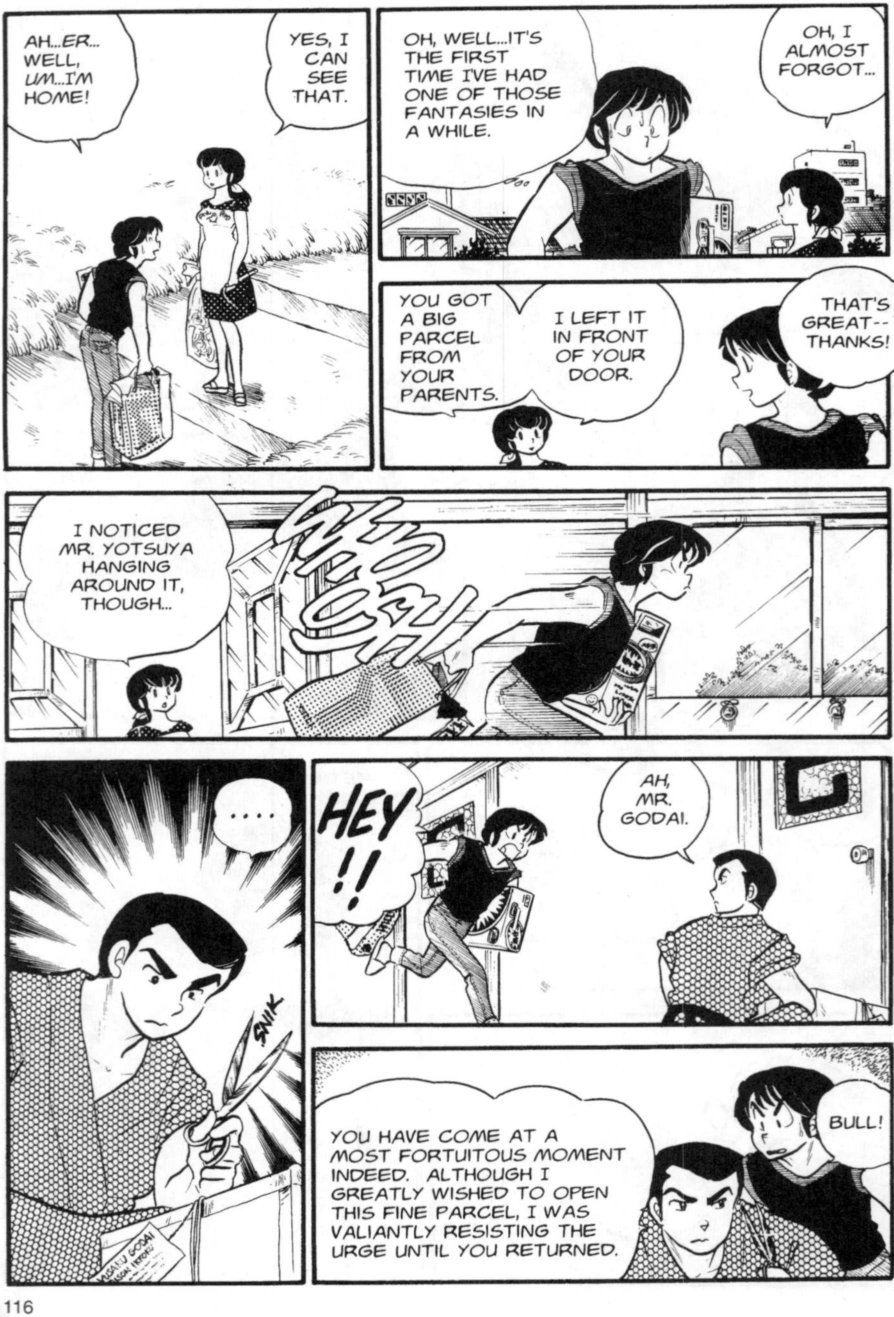
AH...ER... WELL, UM...I'M HOME!
YES, I CAN SEE THAT.
OH, WELL...IT'S THE FIRST TIME I'VE HAD ONE OF THOSE FANTASIES IN A WHILE.
OH, I ALMOST FORGOT...
YOU GOT A BIG PARCEL FROM YOUR PARENTS.
I LEFT IT IN FRONT OF YOUR DOOR.
THAT'S GREAT--THANKS!
I NOTICED MR. YOTSUYA HANGING AROUND IT, THOUGH...
WHOOSH!
AH, MR. GODAI.
HEY!!
....
SNIK
YOU HAVE COME AT A MOST FORTUITOUS MOMENT INDEED. ALTHOUGH I GREATLY WISHED TO OPEN THIS FINE PARCEL, I WAS VALIANTLY RESISTING THE URGE UNTIL YOU RETURNED.
BULL!

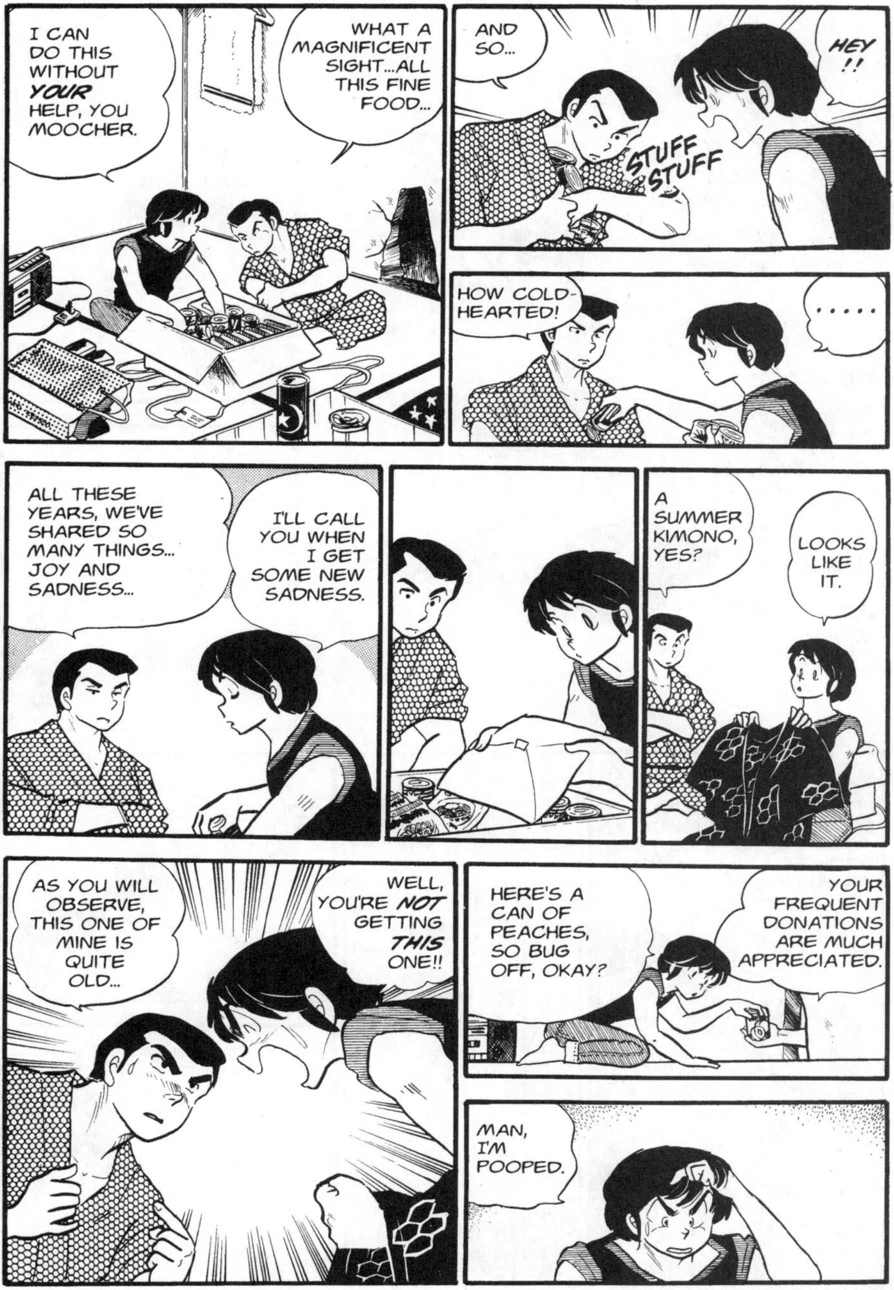
I CAN DO THIS WITHOUT YOUR HELP, YOU MOOCHER.
WHAT A MAGNIFICENT SIGHT...ALL THIS FINE FOOD...
AND SO...
HEY!!
STUFF STUFF
HOW COLD-HEARTED!
.....
ALL THESE YEARS, WE'VE SHARED SO MANY THINGS... JOY AND SADNESS...
I'LL CALL YOU WHEN I GET SOME NEW SADNESS.
A SUMMER KIMONO, YES?
LOOKS LIKE IT.
AS YOU WILL OBSERVE, THIS ONE OF MINE IS QUITE OLD...
WELL, YOU'RE NOT GETTING THIS ONE!!
HERE'S A CAN OF PEACHES, SO BUG OFF, OKAY?
YOUR FREQUENT DONATIONS ARE MUCH APPRECIATED.
MAN, I'M POOPED.

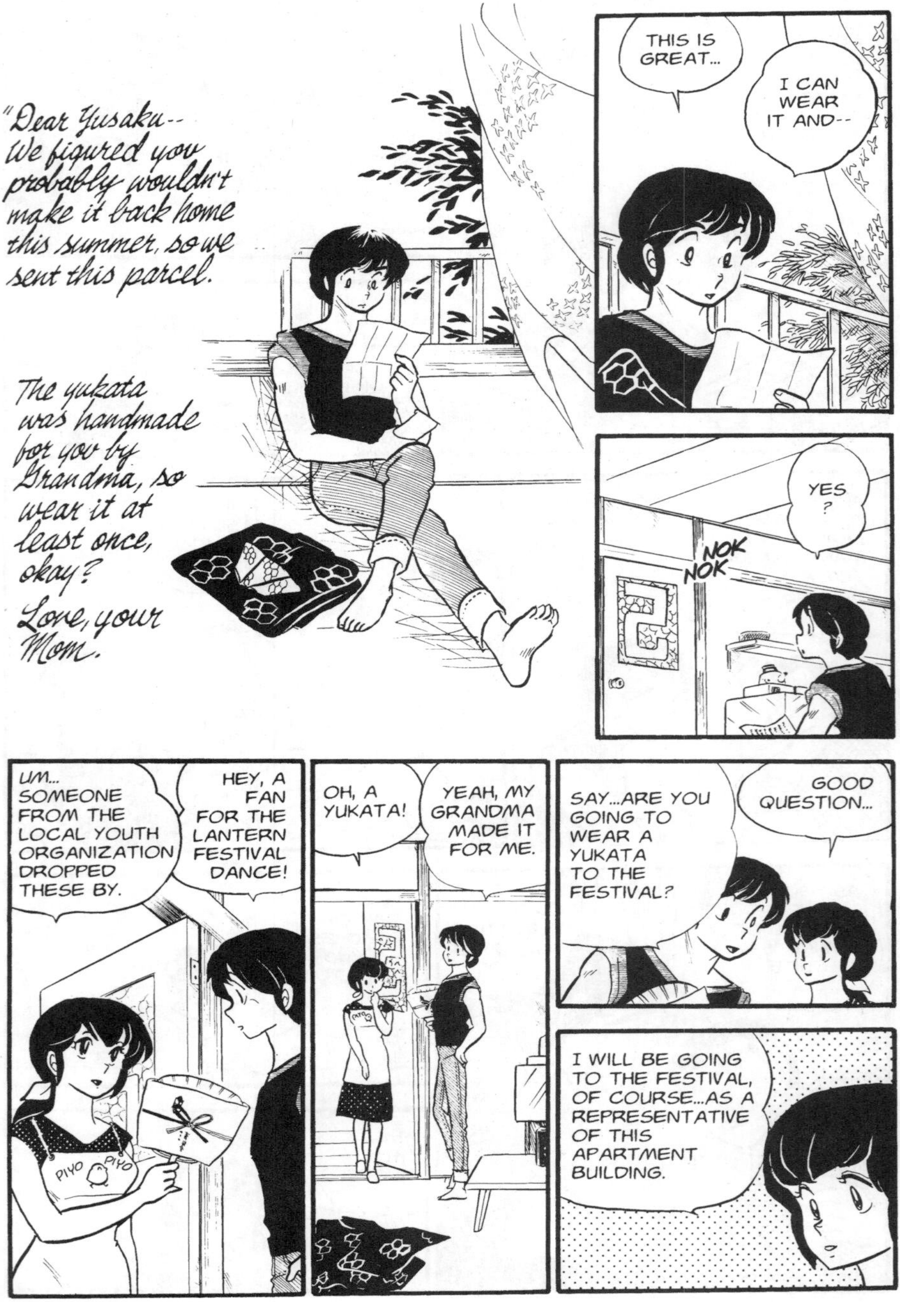
"Dear Yusaku--
We figured you probably wouldn't make it back home this summer, so we sent this parcel.
The yukata was handmade for you by Grandma, so wear it at least once, okay?
Love, your Mom.
THIS IS GREAT...
I CAN WEAR IT AND--
YES ?
NOK NOK
UM... SOMEONE FROM THE LOCAL YOUTH ORGANIZATION DROPPED THESE BY.
HEY, A FAN FOR THE LANTERN FESTIVAL DANCE!
PIYO PIYO
OH, A YUKATA!
YEAH, MY GRANDMA MADE IT FOR ME.
SAY...ARE YOU GOING TO WEAR A YUKATA TO THE FESTIVAL?
GOOD QUESTION...
I WILL BE GOING TO THE FESTIVAL, OF COURSE...AS A REPRESENTATIVE OF THIS APARTMENT BUILDING.

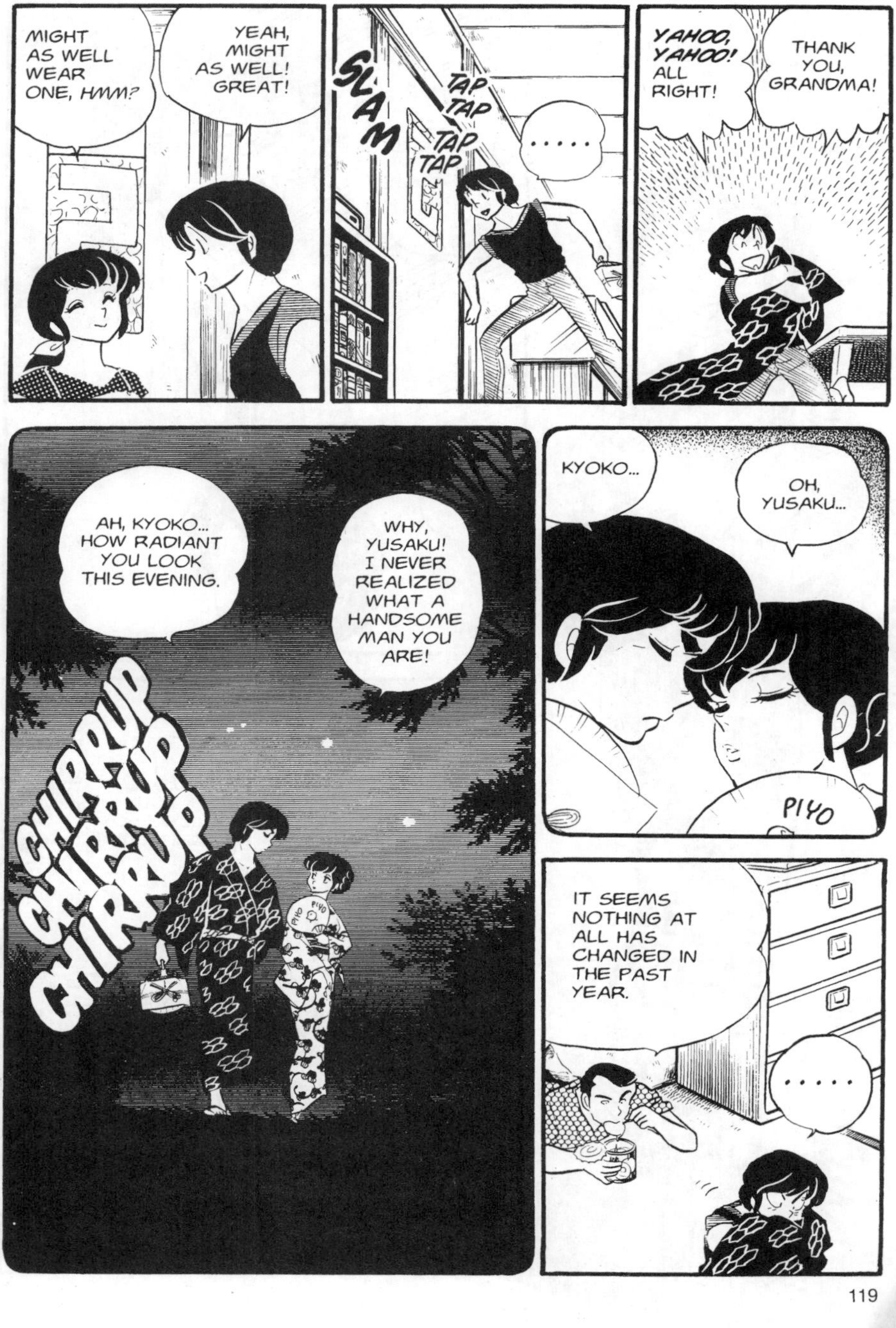
MIGHT AS WELL WEAR ONE, HMM?
YEAH, MIGHT AS WELL! GREAT!
SLAM
TAP TAP
TAP TAP
.....
YAHOO, YAHOO! ALL RIGHT!
THANK YOU, GRANDMA!
AH, KYOKO... HOW RADIANT YOU LOOK THIS EVENING.
WHY, YUSAKU! I NEVER REALIZED WHAT A HANDSOME MAN YOU ARE!
CHIRRUP CHIRRUP CHIRRUP
KYOKO...
OH, YUSAKU...
PIYO
IT SEEMS NOTHING AT ALL HAS CHANGED IN THE PAST YEAR.
.....

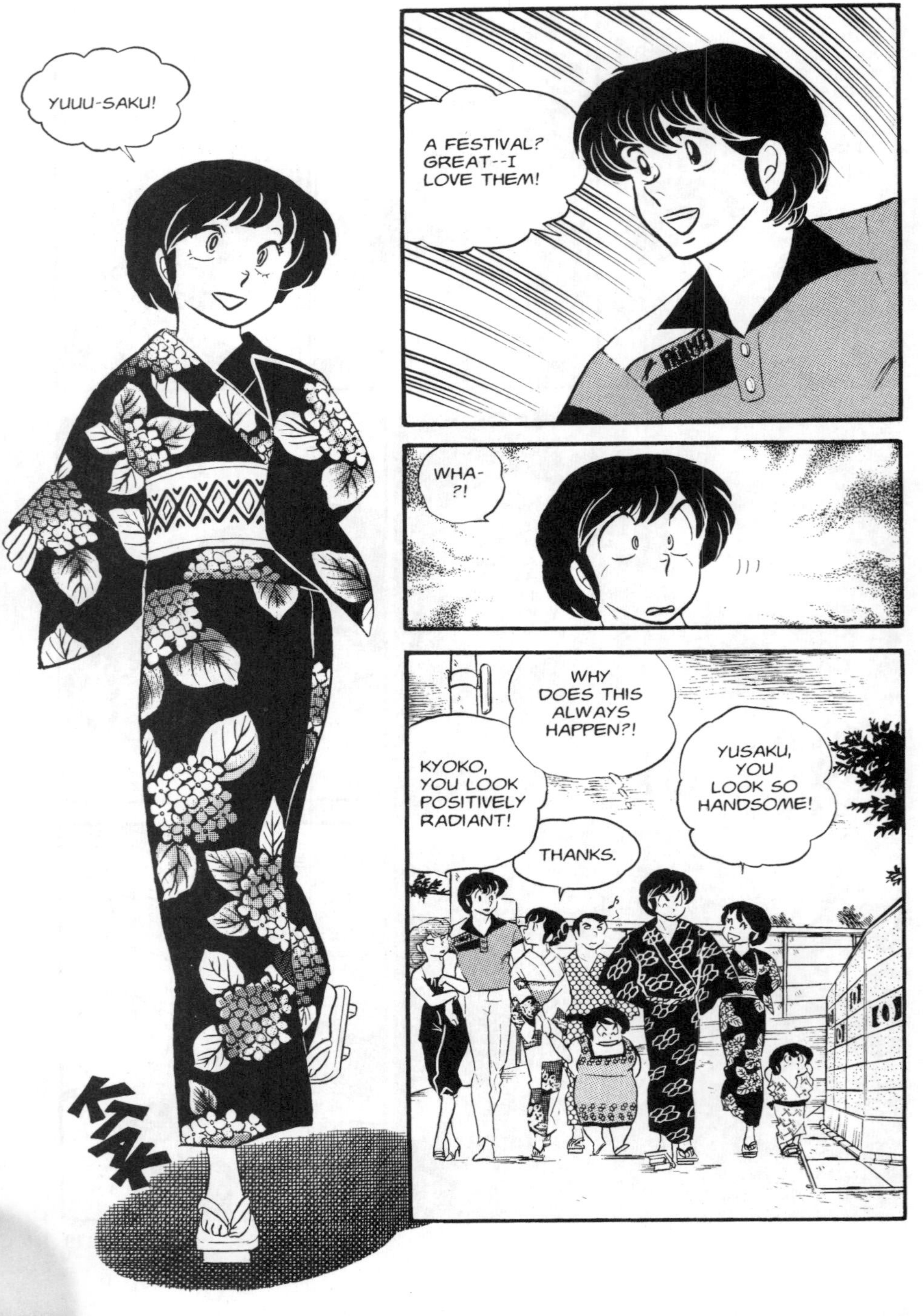
YUUU-SAKU!
KTAK
A FESTIVAL? GREAT--I LOVE THEM!
WHA- ?!
WHY DOES THIS ALWAYS HAPPEN?!
KYOKO, YOU LOOK POSITIVELY RADIANT!
YUSAKU, YOU LOOK SO HANDSOME!
THANKS.

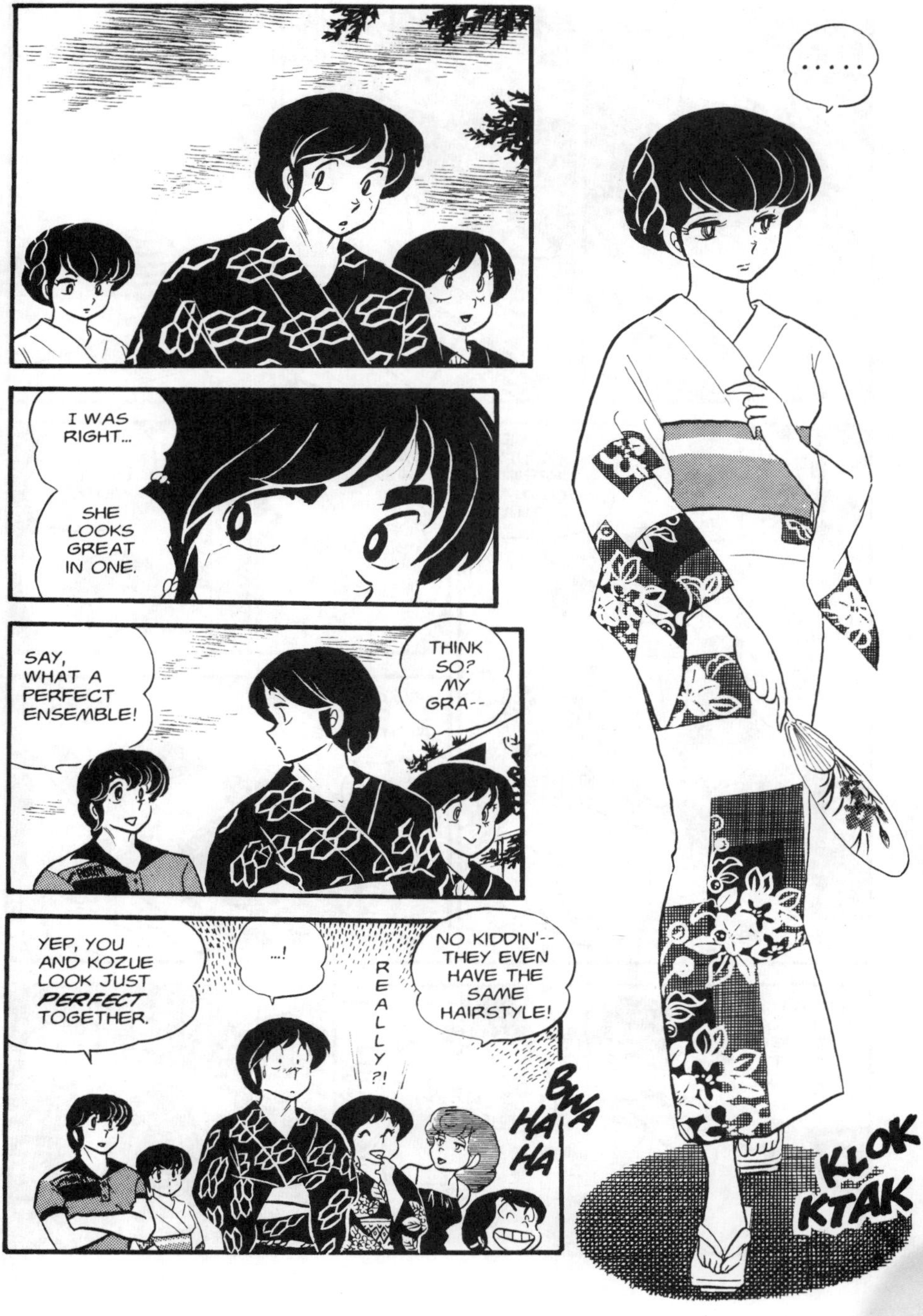
I WAS RIGHT...
SHE LOOKS GREAT IN ONE.
SAY, WHAT A PERFECT ENSEMBLE!
THINK SO? MY GRA--
YEP, YOU AND KOZUE LOOK JUST *PERFECT* TOGETHER.
...!
REALLY?!
NO KIDDIN'-- THEY EVEN HAVE THE SAME HAIRSTYLE!
BWA HA HA
......
KLOK KTAK

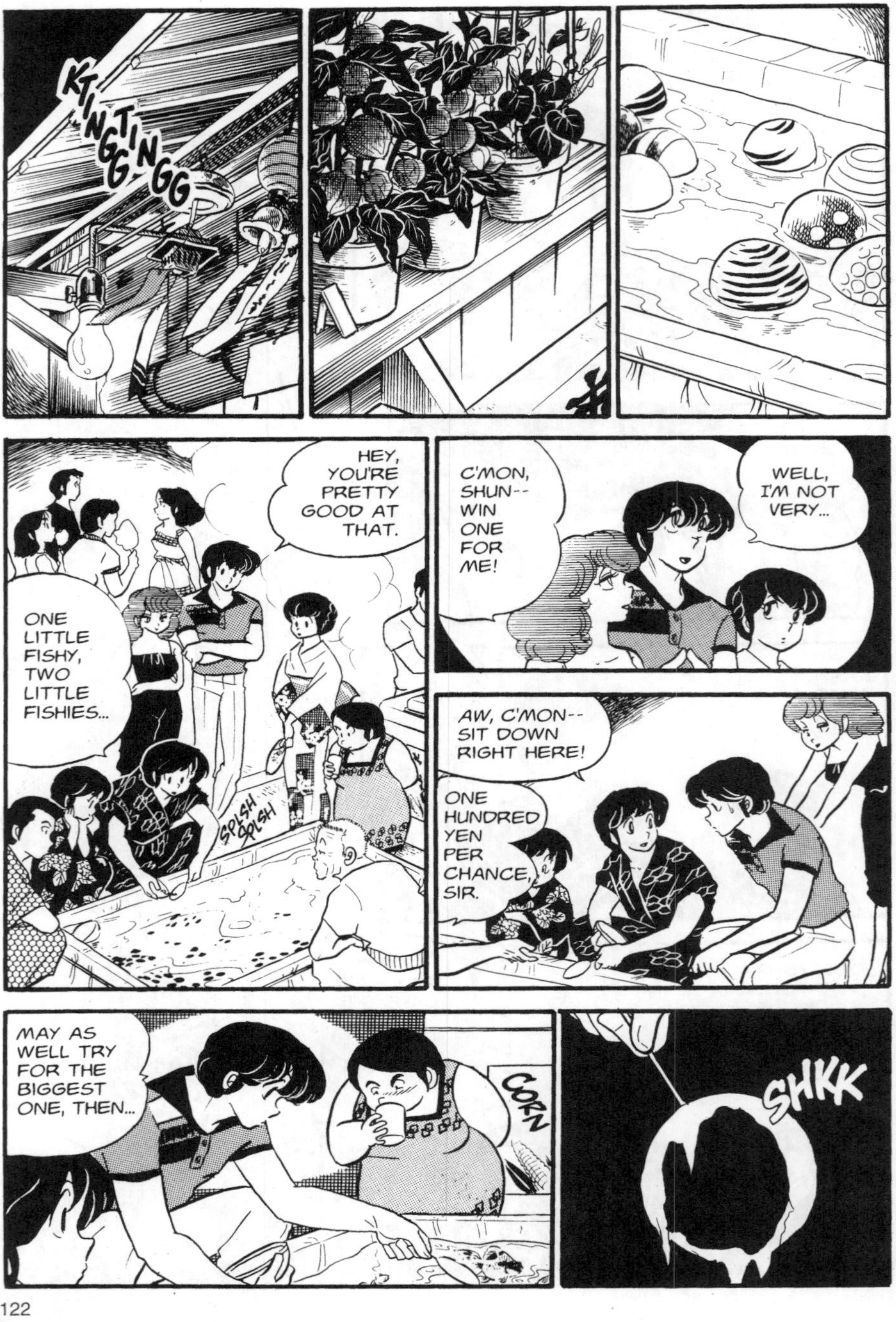
KTINGG TINGG
HEY, YOU'RE PRETTY GOOD AT THAT.
ONE LITTLE FISHY, TWO LITTLE FISHIES...
SPLSH SPLSH
C'MON, SHUN--WIN ONE FOR ME!
WELL, I'M NOT VERY...
AW, C'MON--SIT DOWN RIGHT HERE!
ONE HUNDRED YEN PER CHANCE, SIR.
MAY AS WELL TRY FOR THE BIGGEST ONE, THEN...
CORN
SHKK

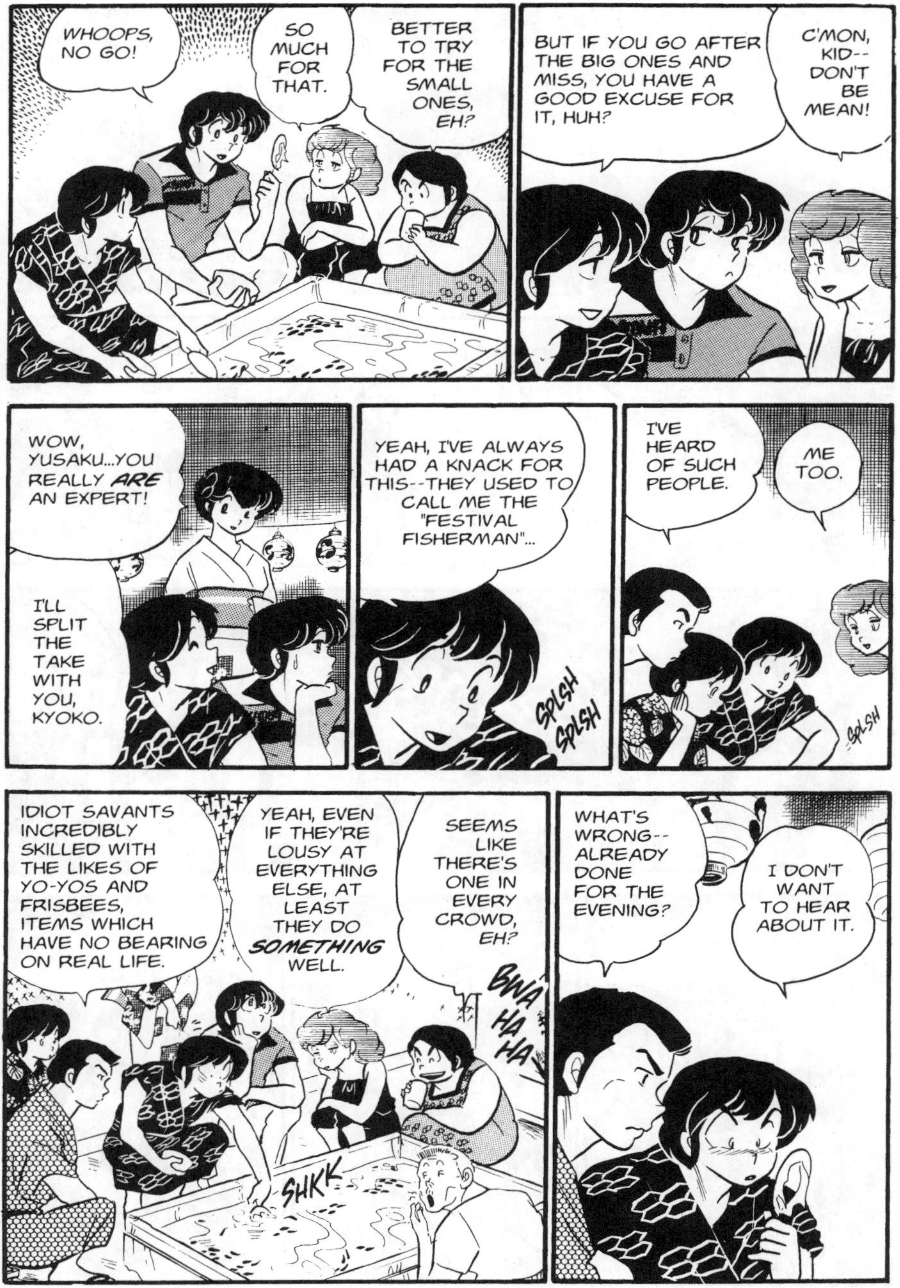
WHOOPS, NO GO!
SO MUCH FOR THAT.
BETTER TO TRY FOR THE SMALL ONES, EH?
BUT IF YOU GO AFTER THE BIG ONES AND MISS, YOU HAVE A GOOD EXCUSE FOR IT, HUH?
C'MON, KID-- DON'T BE MEAN!
WOW, YUSAKU...YOU REALLY ARE AN EXPERT!
I'LL SPLIT THE TAKE WITH YOU, KYOKO.
YEAH, I'VE ALWAYS HAD A KNACK FOR THIS--THEY USED TO CALL ME THE "FESTIVAL FISHERMAN"...
SPLSH SPLSH
I'VE HEARD OF SUCH PEOPLE.
ME TOO.
SPLSH
IDIOT SAVANTS INCREDIBLY SKILLED WITH THE LIKES OF YO-YOS AND FRISBEES, ITEMS WHICH HAVE NO BEARING ON REAL LIFE.
YEAH, EVEN IF THEY'RE LOUSY AT EVERYTHING ELSE, AT LEAST THEY DO SOMETHING WELL.
SEEMS LIKE THERE'S ONE IN EVERY CROWD, EH?
BWA HA HA
SHKK
WHAT'S WRONG-- ALREADY DONE FOR THE EVENING?
I DON'T WANT TO HEAR ABOUT IT.

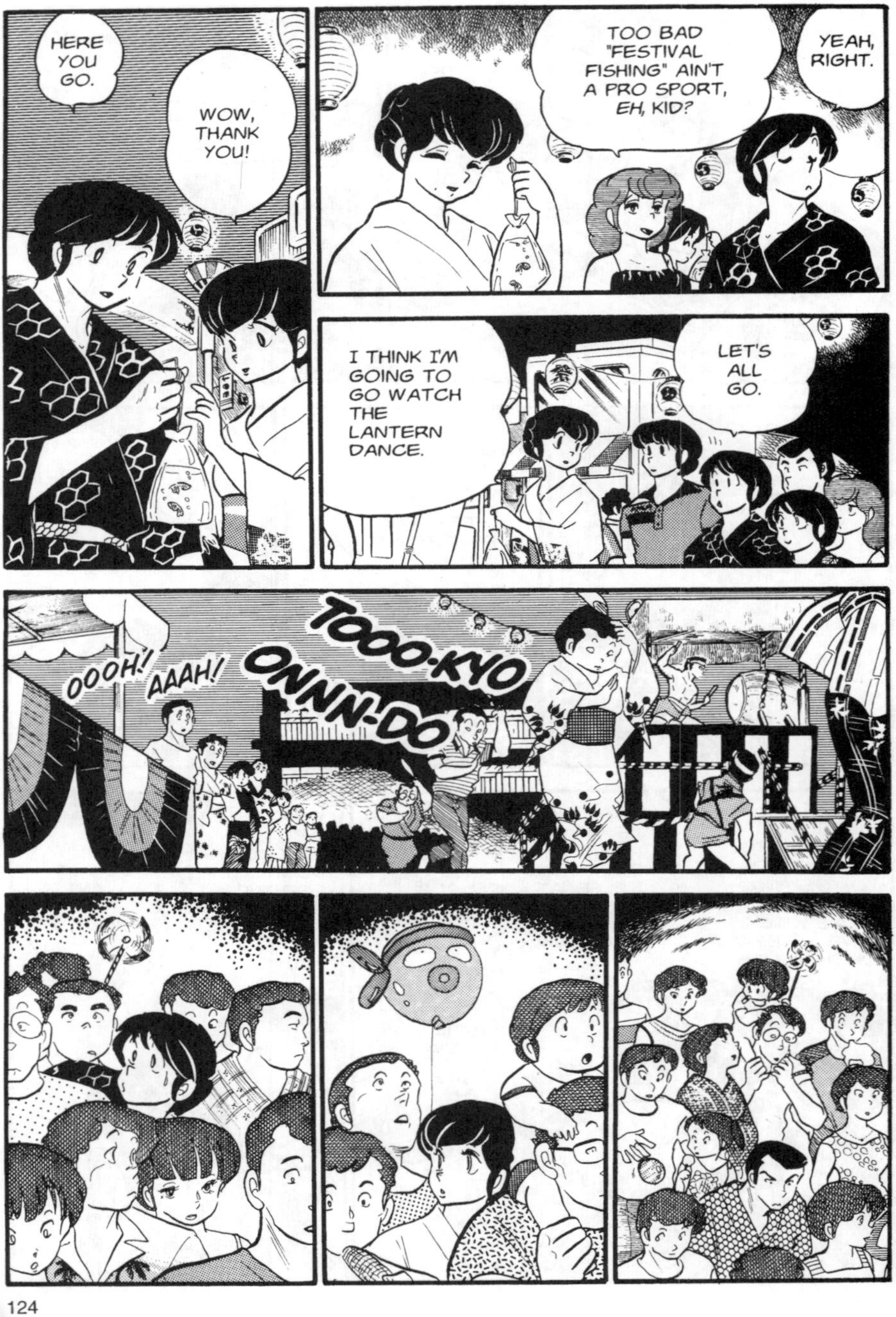
HERE YOU GO.
WOW, THANK YOU!
TOO BAD "FESTIVAL FISHING" AIN'T A PRO SPORT, EH, KID?
YEAH, RIGHT.
I THINK I'M GOING TO GO WATCH THE LANTERN DANCE.
LET'S ALL GO.
OOOH!
AAAH!
TOOO-KYO
ONNN-DO

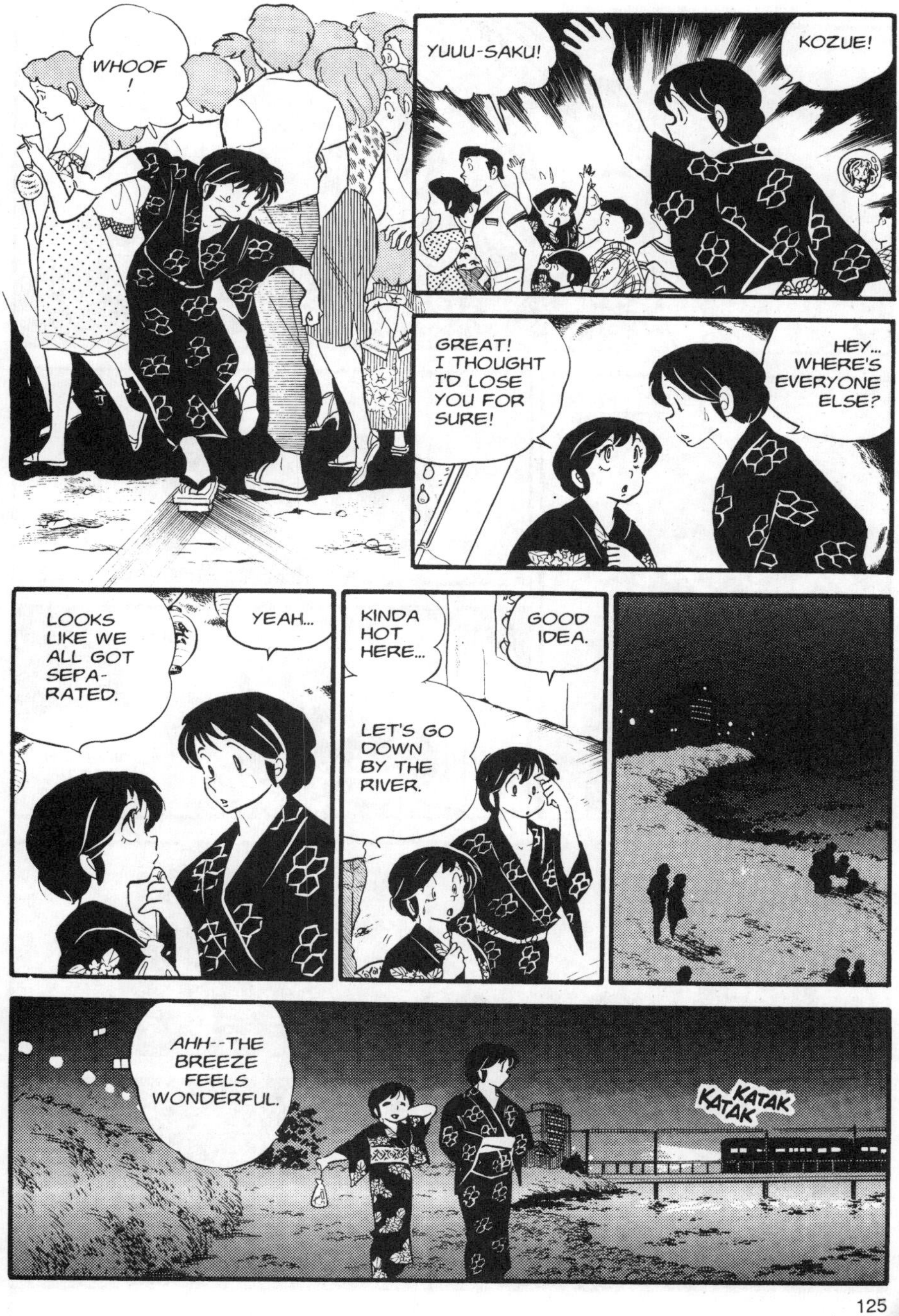
WHOOF!
YUUU-SAKU!
KOZUE!
GREAT! I THOUGHT I'D LOSE YOU FOR SURE!
HEY... WHERE'S EVERYONE ELSE?
LOOKS LIKE WE ALL GOT SEPA-RATED.
YEAH...
KINDA HOT HERE...
LET'S GO DOWN BY THE RIVER.
GOOD IDEA.
AHH--THE BREEZE FEELS WONDERFUL.
KATAK KATAK

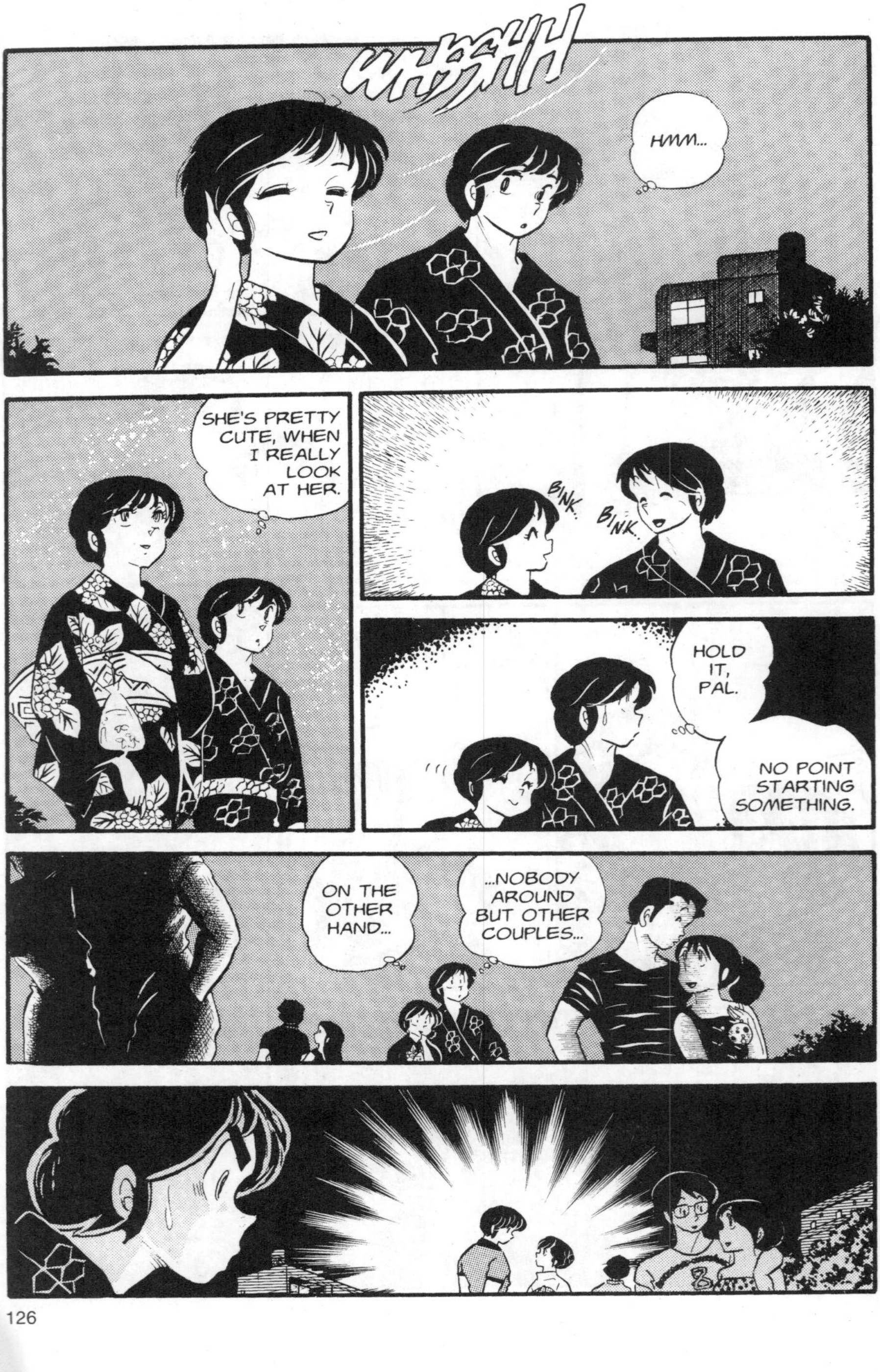
WHOSHH
HMM...
SHE'S PRETTY CUTE, WHEN I REALLY LOOK AT HER.
BINK.
BINK.
HOLD IT, PAL.
NO POINT STARTING SOMETHING.
ON THE OTHER HAND...
...NOBODY AROUND BUT OTHER COUPLES...

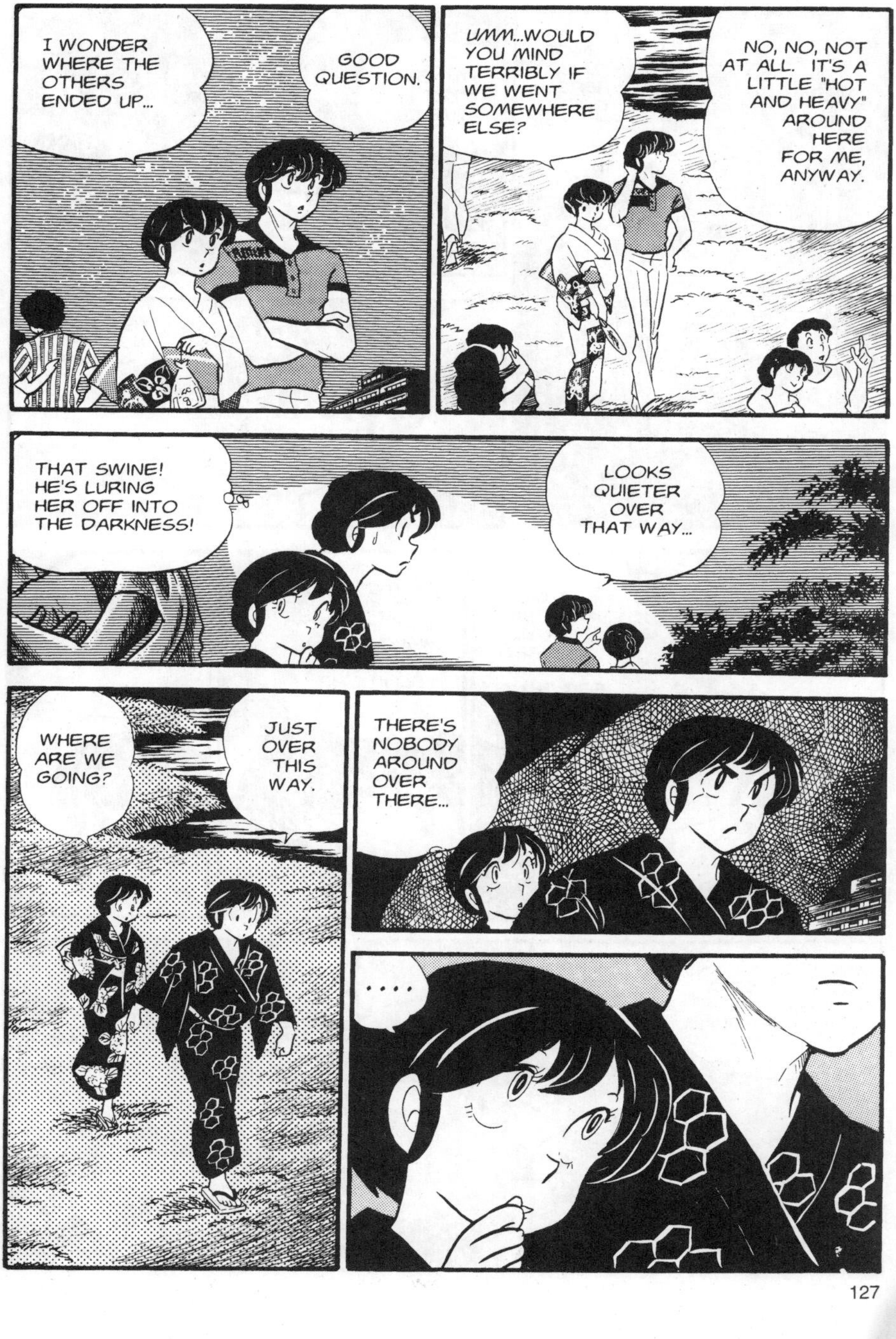
I WONDER WHERE THE OTHERS ENDED UP...
GOOD QUESTION.
UMM...WOULD YOU MIND TERRIBLY IF WE WENT SOMEWHERE ELSE?
NO, NO, NOT AT ALL. IT'S A LITTLE "HOT AND HEAVY" AROUND HERE FOR ME, ANYWAY.
THAT SWINE! HE'S LURING HER OFF INTO THE DARKNESS!
LOOKS QUIETER OVER THAT WAY...
WHERE ARE WE GOING?
JUST OVER THIS WAY.
THERE'S NOBODY AROUND OVER THERE...
....

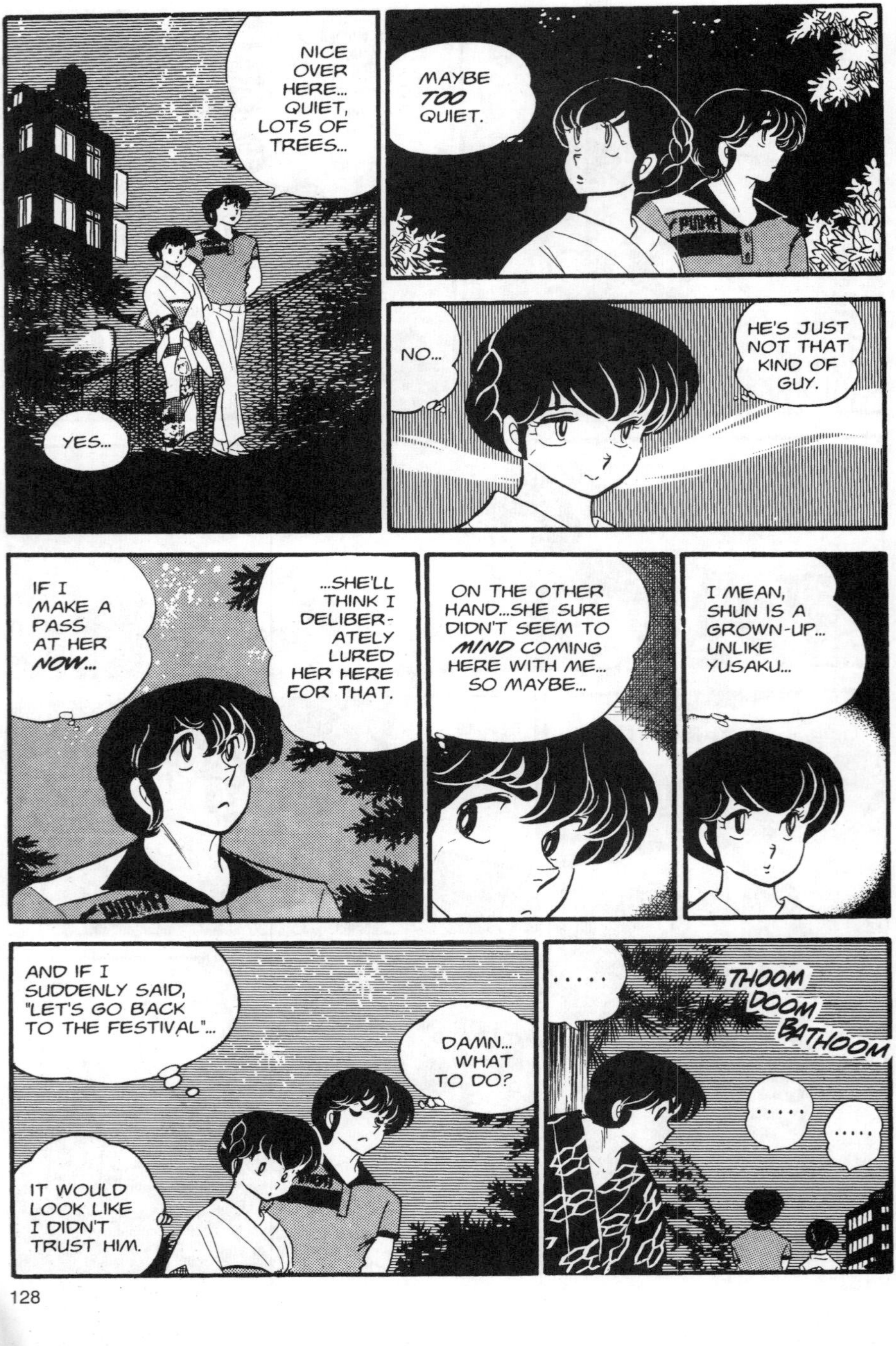
NICE OVER HERE... QUIET, LOTS OF TREES...
YES...
MAYBE TOO QUIET.
NO...
HE'S JUST NOT THAT KIND OF GUY.
IF I MAKE A PASS AT HER NOW...
...SHE'LL THINK I DELIBER-ATELY LURED HER HERE FOR THAT.
ON THE OTHER HAND...SHE SURE DIDN'T SEEM TO MIND COMING HERE WITH ME... SO MAYBE...
I MEAN, SHUN IS A GROWN-UP... UNLIKE YUSAKU...
AND IF I SUDDENLY SAID, "LET'S GO BACK TO THE FESTIVAL"...
DAMN... WHAT TO DO?
IT WOULD LOOK LIKE I DIDN'T TRUST HIM.
.....
THOOM DOOM BATHOOM
......
.....

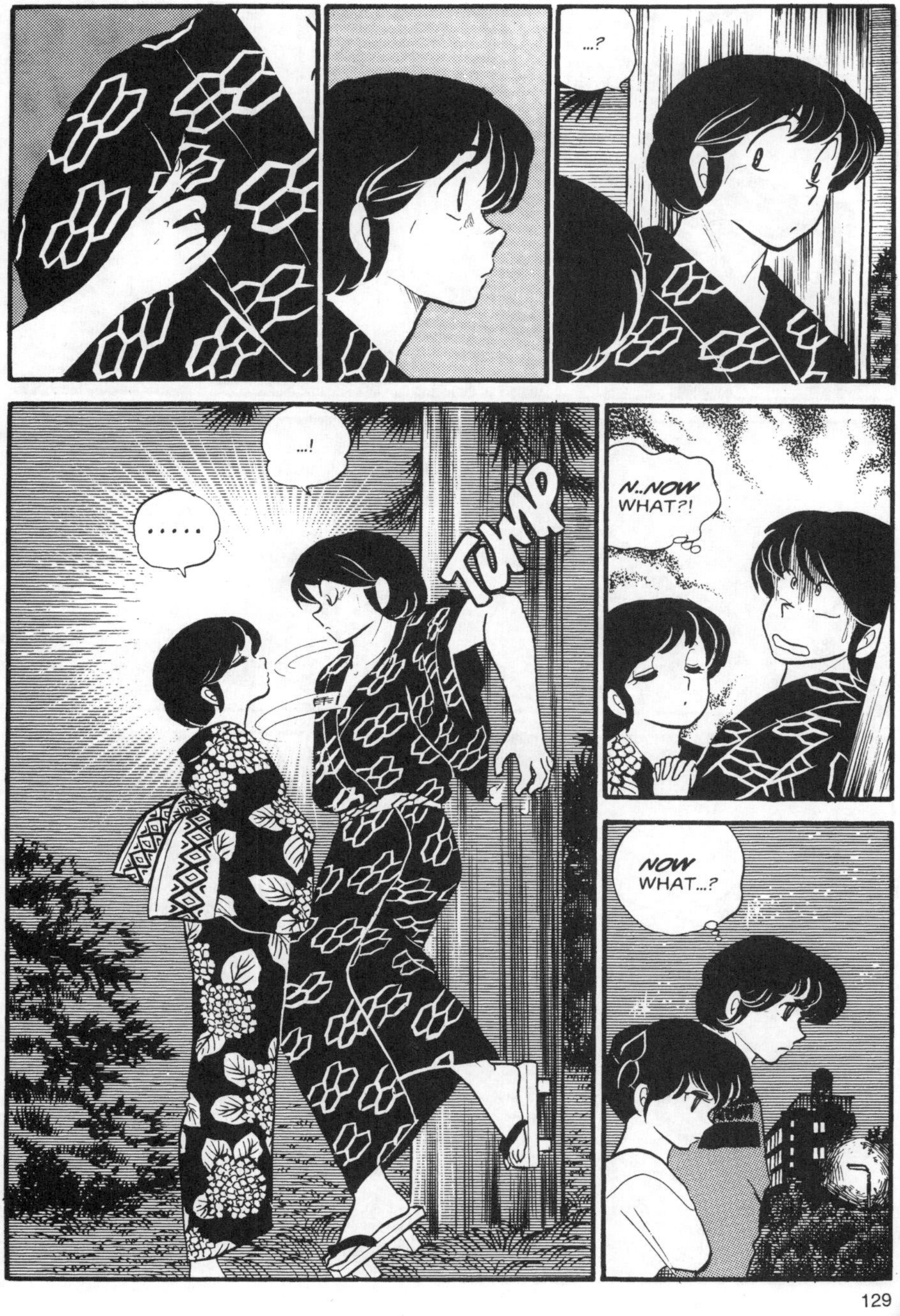
...?
.....
...!
TUMP
N..NOW WHAT?!
NOW WHAT...?

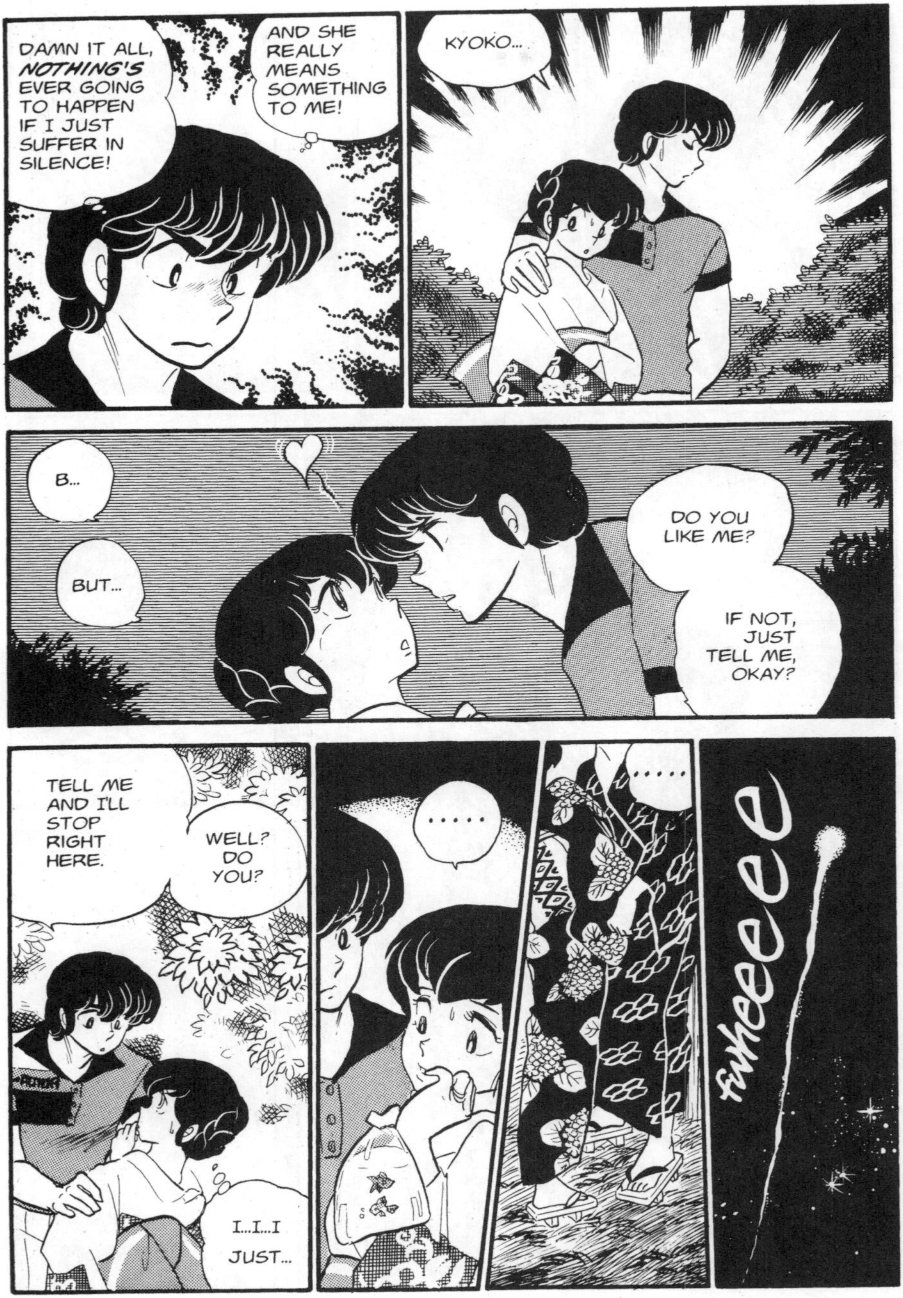
DAMN IT ALL, *NOTHING'S* EVER GOING TO HAPPEN IF I JUST SUFFER IN SILENCE!
AND SHE REALLY MEANS SOMETHING TO ME!
KYOKO...
B...
BUT...
DO YOU LIKE ME?
IF NOT, JUST TELL ME, OKAY?
TELL ME AND I'LL STOP RIGHT HERE.
WELL? DO YOU?
I...I...I JUST...
......
......
fwheeeee

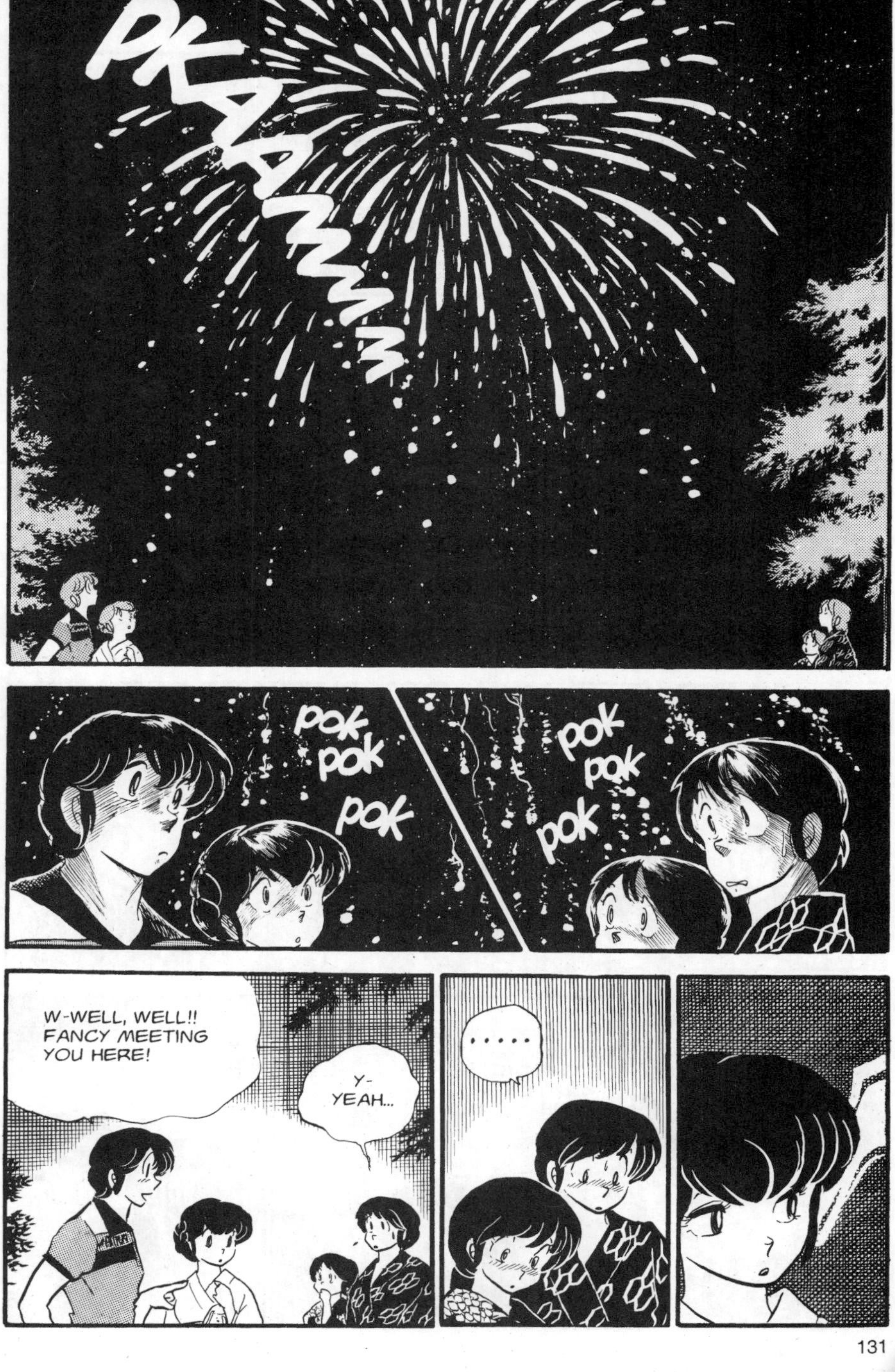
PKAAMMM
pok pok pok
pok pok pok
W-WELL, WELL!! FANCY MEETING YOU HERE!
Y- YEAH...
.....

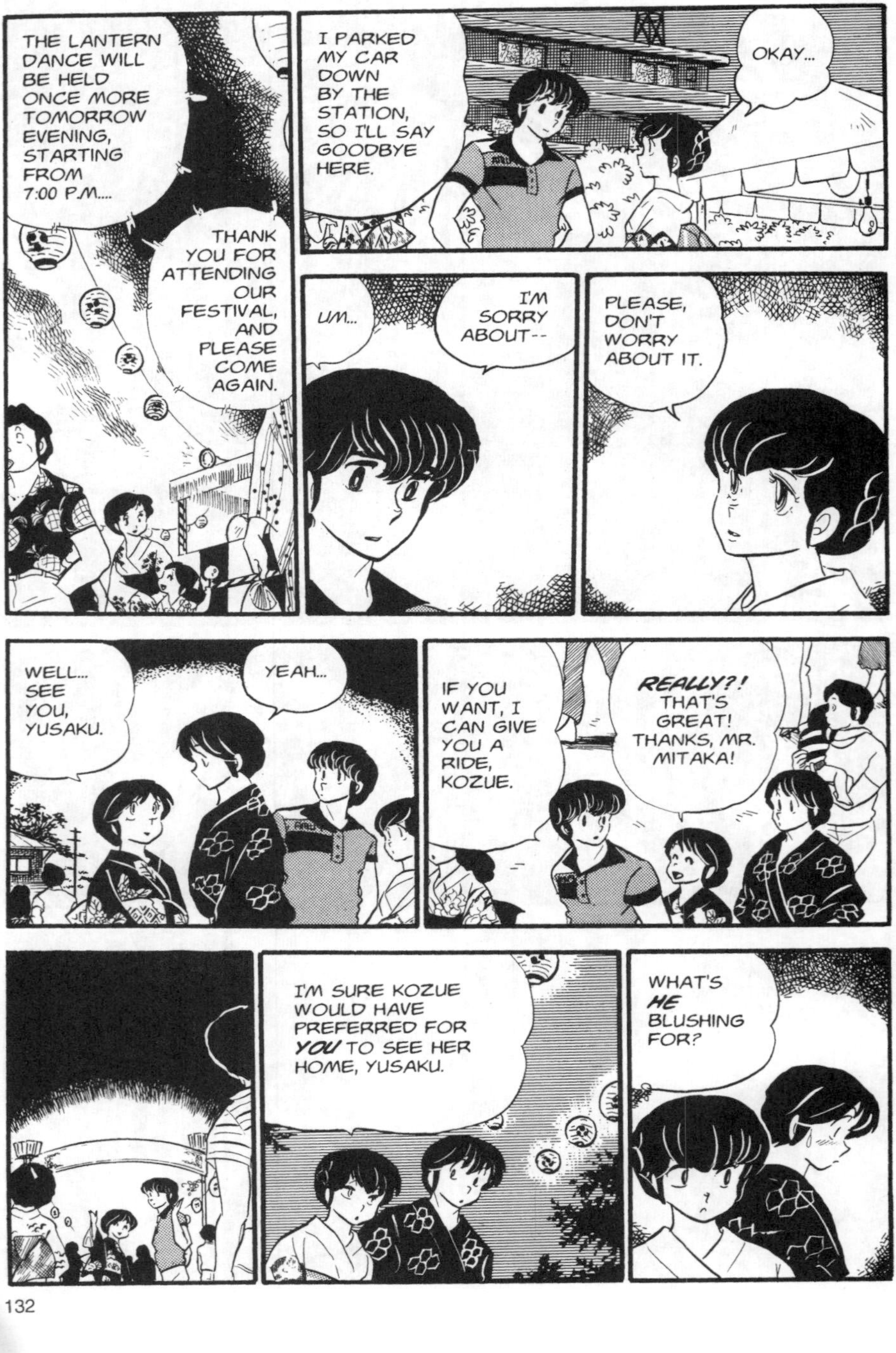
THE LANTERN DANCE WILL BE HELD ONCE MORE TOMORROW EVENING, STARTING FROM 7:00 P.M....
THANK YOU FOR ATTENDING OUR FESTIVAL, AND PLEASE COME AGAIN.
I PARKED MY CAR DOWN BY THE STATION, SO I'LL SAY GOODBYE HERE.
OKAY...
UM...
I'M SORRY ABOUT--
PLEASE, DON'T WORRY ABOUT IT.
WELL... SEE YOU, YUSAKU.
YEAH...
IF YOU WANT, I CAN GIVE YOU A RIDE, KOZUE.
REALLY?! THAT'S GREAT! THANKS, MR. MITAKA!
I'M SURE KOZUE WOULD HAVE PREFERRED FOR YOU TO SEE HER HOME, YUSAKU.
WHAT'S HE BLUSHING FOR?

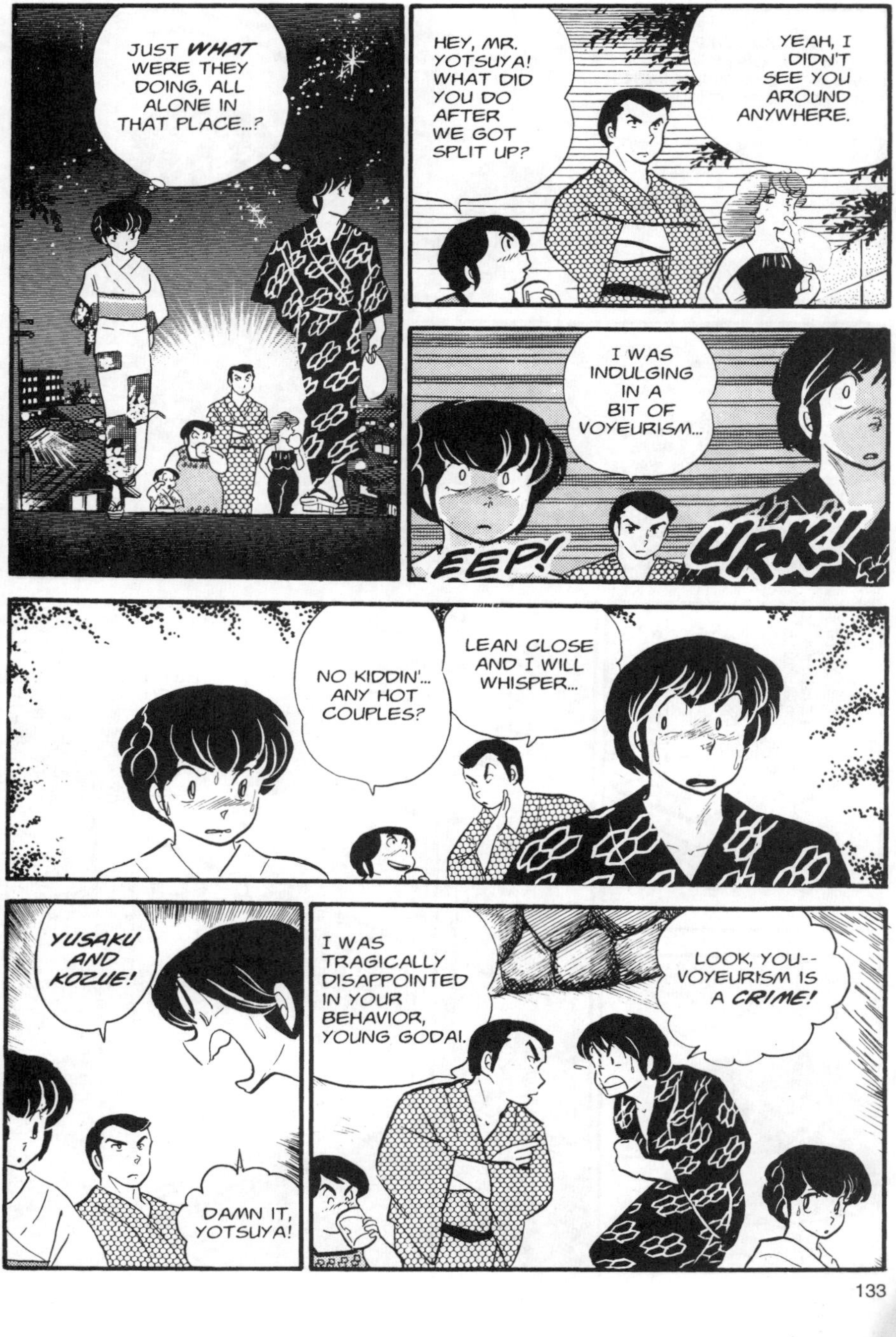
JUST WHAT WERE THEY DOING, ALL ALONE IN THAT PLACE...?
HEY, MR. YOTSUYA! WHAT DID YOU DO AFTER WE GOT SPLIT UP?
YEAH, I DIDN'T SEE YOU AROUND ANYWHERE.
I WAS INDULGING IN A BIT OF VOYEURISM...
EEP!
URK!
NO KIDDIN'... ANY HOT COUPLES?
LEAN CLOSE AND I WILL WHISPER...
YUSAKU AND KOZUE!
DAMN IT, YOTSUYA!
I WAS TRAGICALLY DISAPPOINTED IN YOUR BEHAVIOR, YOUNG GODAI.
LOOK, YOU-- VOYEURISM IS A CRIME!

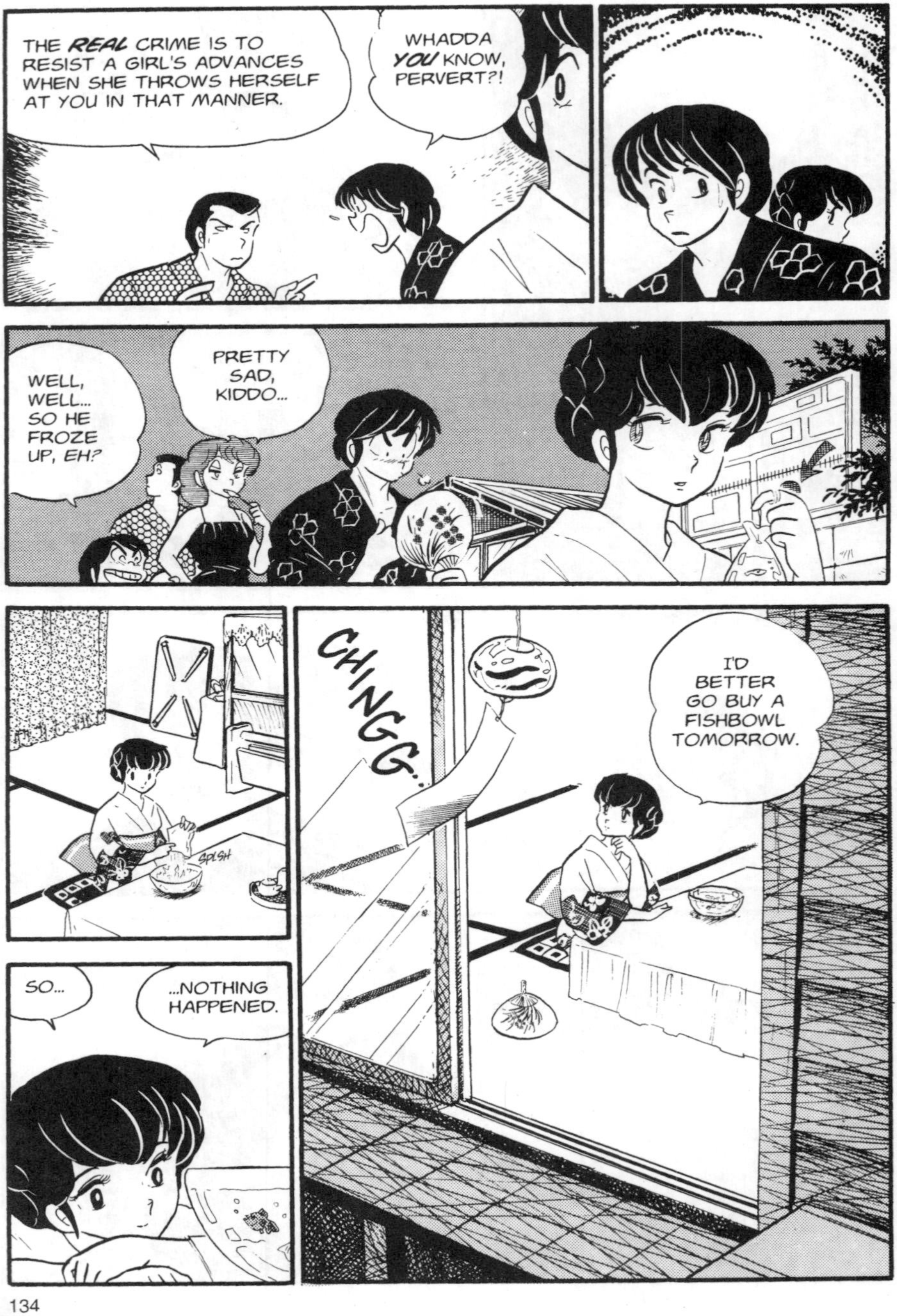
THE REAL CRIME IS TO RESIST A GIRL'S ADVANCES WHEN SHE THROWS HERSELF AT YOU IN THAT MANNER.
WHADDA YOU KNOW, PERVERT?!
WELL, WELL... SO HE FROZE UP, EH?
PRETTY SAD, KIDDO...
SPLSH
SO...
...NOTHING HAPPENED.
CHINGG...
I'D BETTER GO BUY A FISHBOWL TOMORROW.

Part Seven
Memories of You

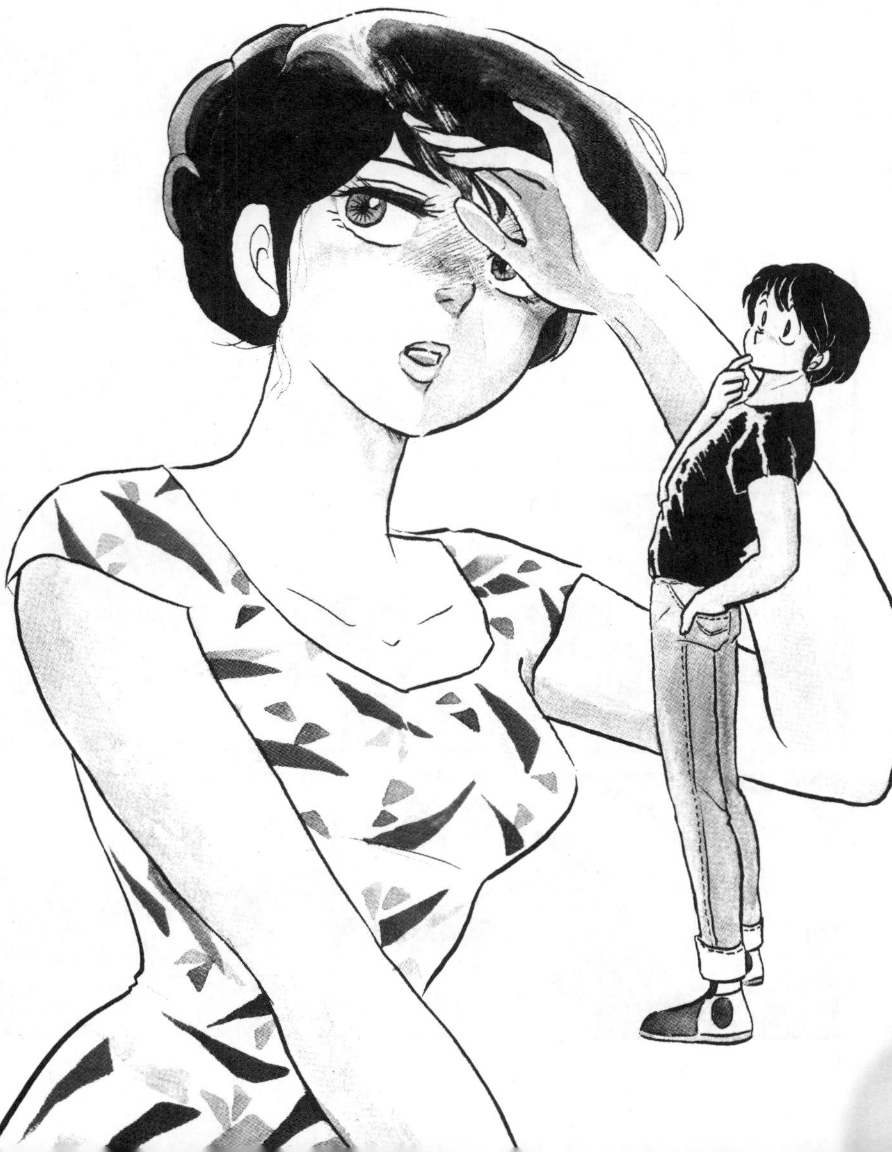

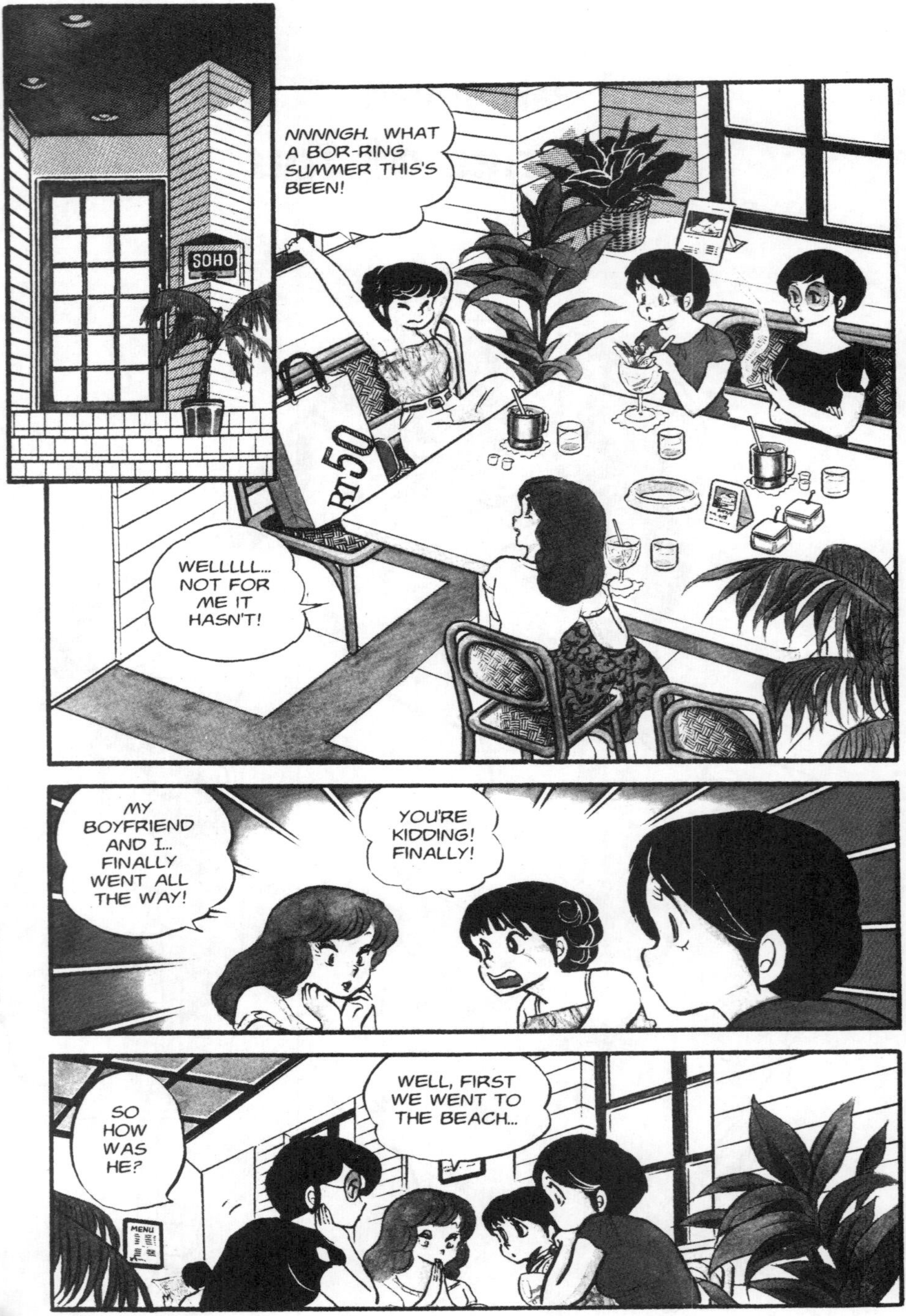
SOHO
NNNNGH. WHAT A BOR-RING SUMMER THIS'S BEEN!
RT50
WELLLLL... NOT FOR ME IT HASN'T!
MY BOYFRIEND AND I... FINALLY WENT ALL THE WAY!
YOU'RE KIDDING! FINALLY!
SO HOW WAS HE?
WELL, FIRST WE WENT TO THE BEACH...
MENU

...SO, LIKE, Y'KNOW, HE...
...I WAS KINDA NERVOUS, BUT...
...AND THEN...
...THEN WE...
...AND LIKE THAT.
WOW... OOOO
SO HOW ABOUT YOU, KOZUE?
YEAH, YOU'VE GOT A BOYFRIEND, RIGHT?
YUSAKU GODAI, ISN'T IT?
WELL, WE HAVEN'T REALLY... Y'KNOW.
AH, KOZUE. YOU'RE STILL SUCH A KID.
YOU THINK?
YOU GUYS HAVE BEEN DATING FOR ABOUT A YEAR, RIGHT?
AND YOU'RE TELLING US YOU HAVEN'T DONE *ANYTHING?*
THAT'S PRETTY WEIRD.

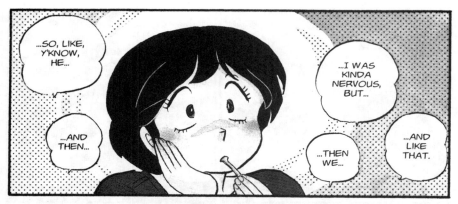

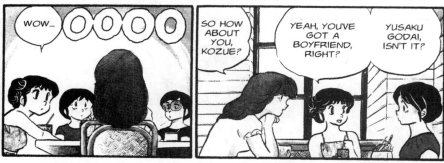

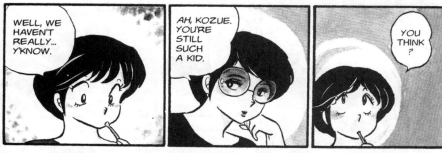

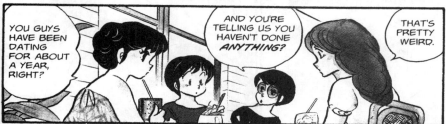

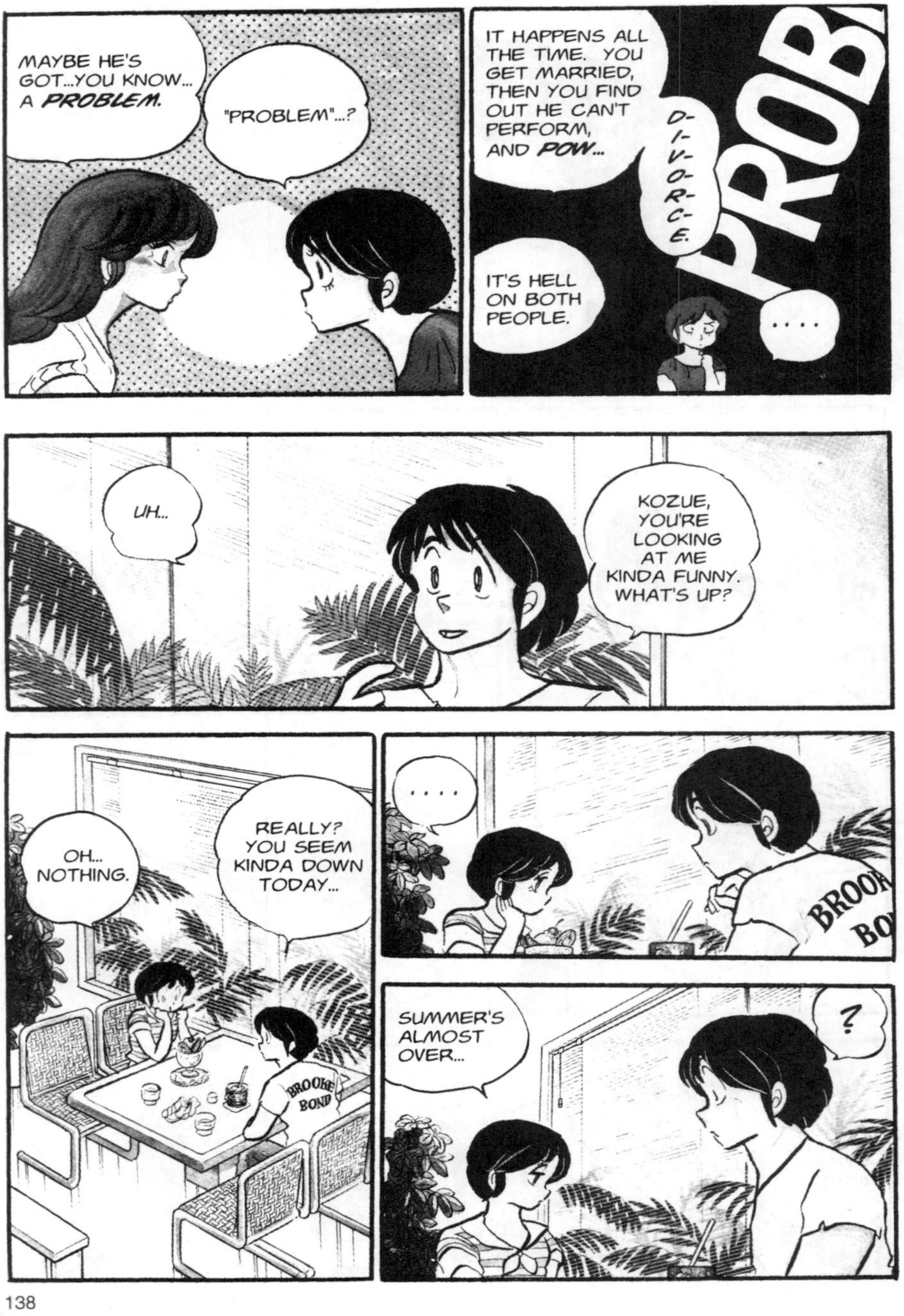
MAYBE HE'S GOT...YOU KNOW... A PROBLEM.
"PROBLEM"...?
IT HAPPENS ALL THE TIME. YOU GET MARRIED, THEN YOU FIND OUT HE CAN'T PERFORM, AND POW...
D-I-V-O-R-C-E.
PROB
IT'S HELL ON BOTH PEOPLE.
....
UH...
KOZUE, YOU'RE LOOKING AT ME KINDA FUNNY. WHAT'S UP?
OH... NOTHING.
REALLY? YOU SEEM KINDA DOWN TODAY...
BROOKE BOND
....
SUMMER'S ALMOST OVER...
?

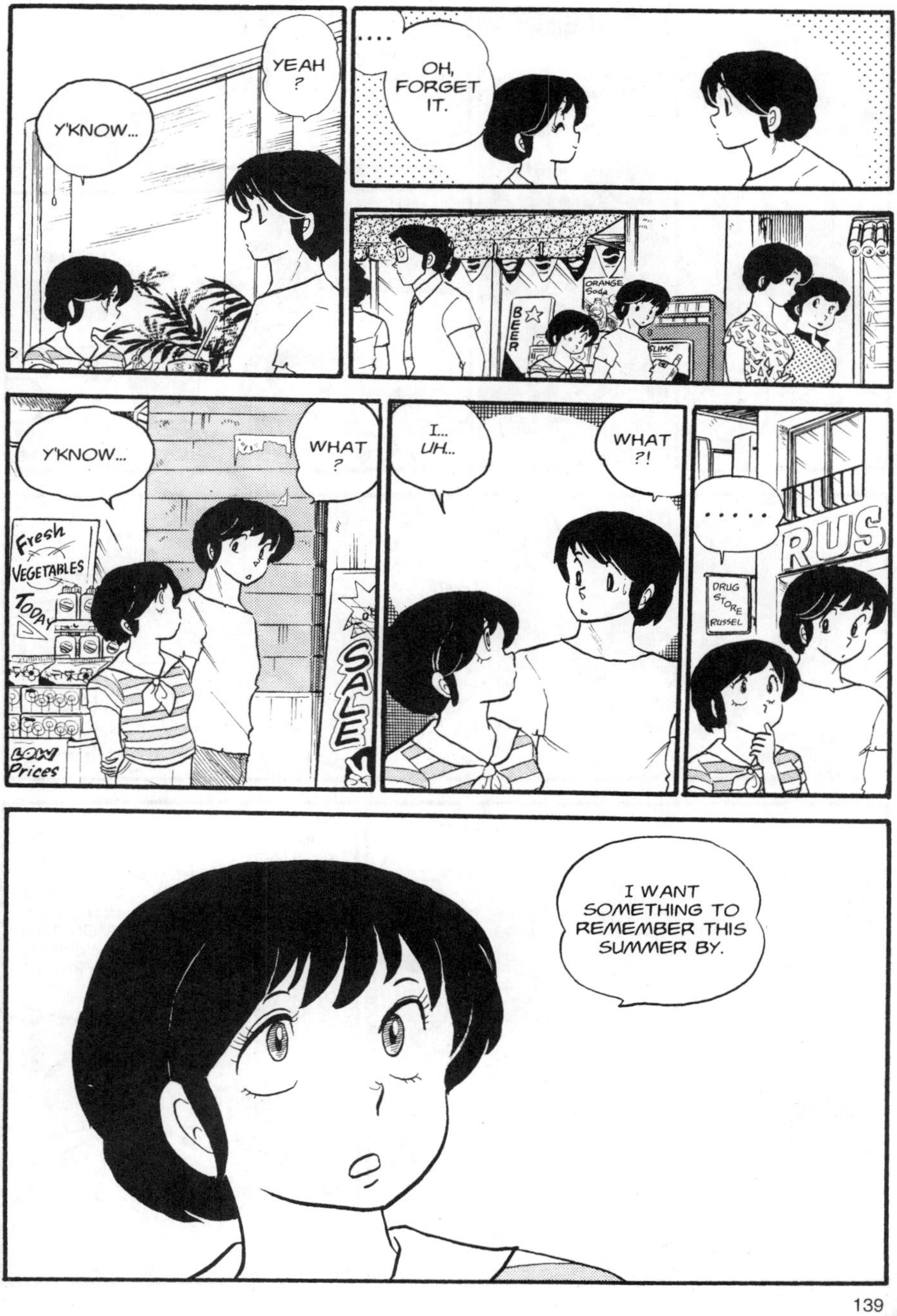
Y'KNOW...
YEAH ?
....
OH, FORGET IT.
ORANGE Soda
BEER
SLIMS
Y'KNOW...
WHAT ?
Fresh VEGETABLES TODAY
SALE
LOW Prices
I... UH...
WHAT ?!
.....
RUS
DRUG STORE RUSSEL
I WANT SOMETHING TO REMEMBER THIS SUMMER BY.

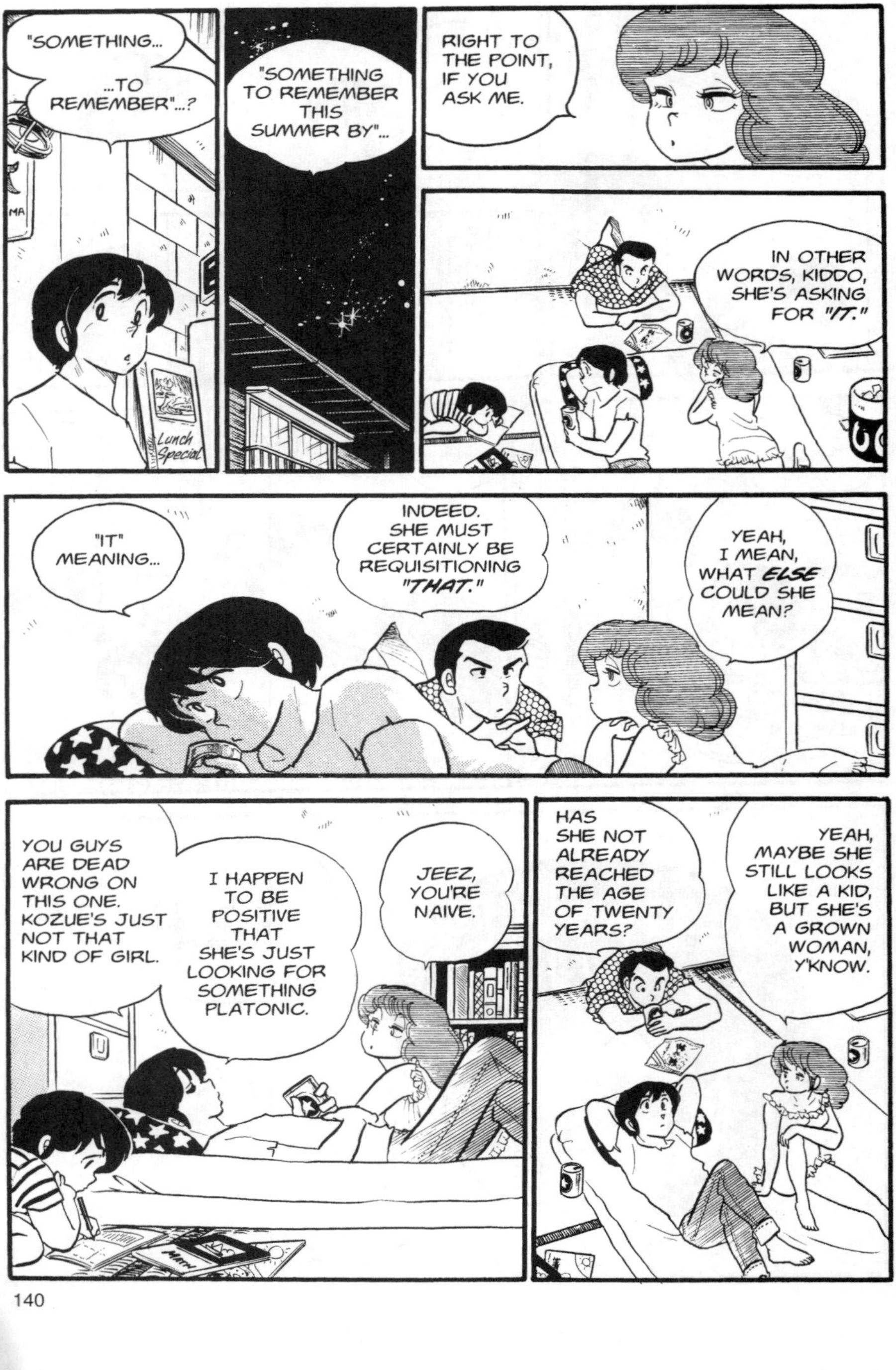
"SOMETHING...
...TO REMEMBER"...?
Lunch Special
"SOMETHING TO REMEMBER THIS SUMMER BY"...
RIGHT TO THE POINT, IF YOU ASK ME.
IN OTHER WORDS, KIDDO, SHE'S ASKING FOR "IT."
"IT" MEANING...
INDEED. SHE MUST CERTAINLY BE REQUISITIONING "THAT."
YEAH, I MEAN, WHAT ELSE COULD SHE MEAN?
YOU GUYS ARE DEAD WRONG ON THIS ONE. KOZUE'S JUST NOT THAT KIND OF GIRL.
I HAPPEN TO BE POSITIVE THAT SHE'S JUST LOOKING FOR SOMETHING PLATONIC.
JEEZ, YOU'RE NAIVE.
HAS SHE NOT ALREADY REACHED THE AGE OF TWENTY YEARS?
YEAH, MAYBE SHE STILL LOOKS LIKE A KID, BUT SHE'S A GROWN WOMAN, Y'KNOW.

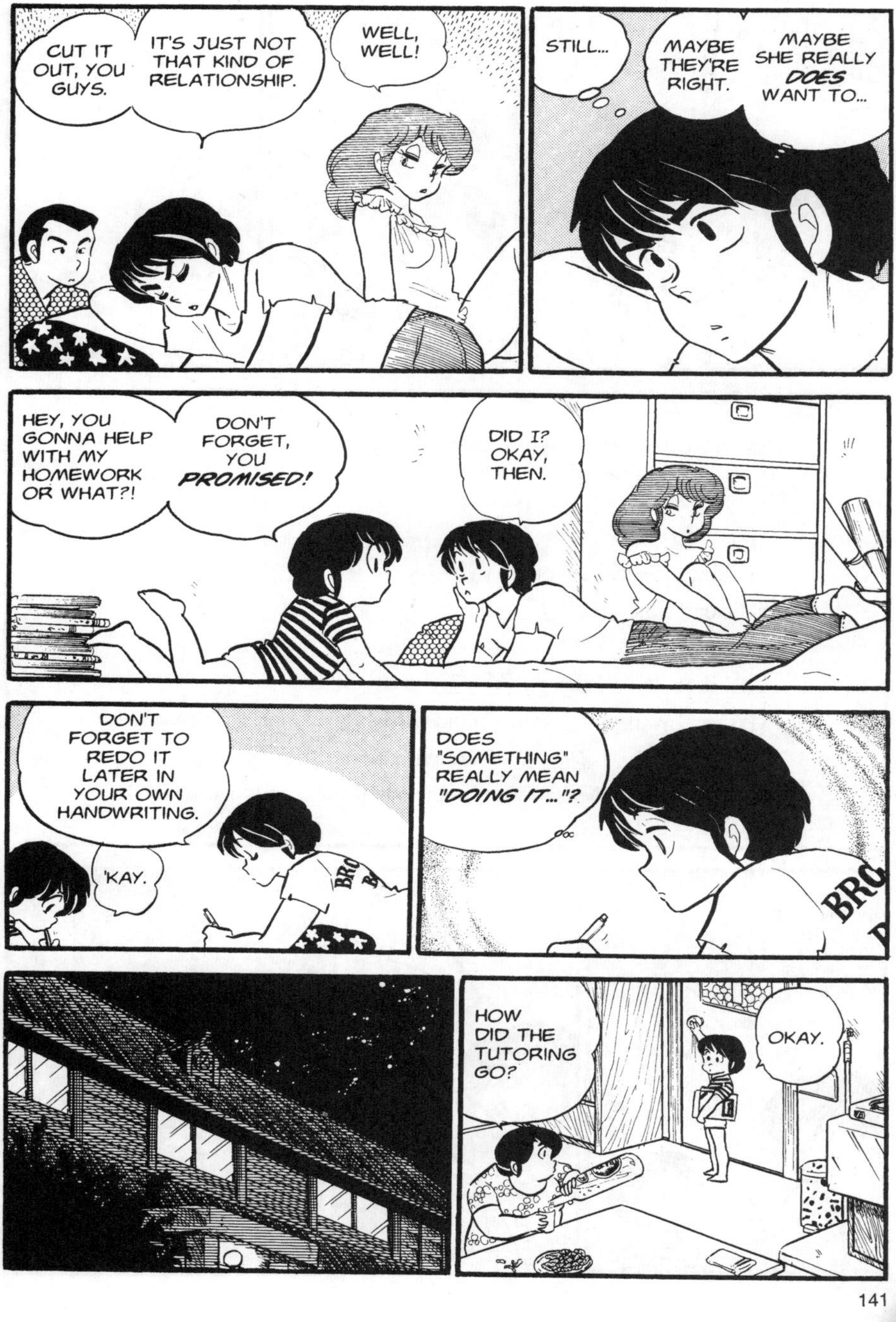
CUT IT OUT, YOU GUYS.
IT'S JUST NOT THAT KIND OF RELATIONSHIP.
WELL, WELL!
STILL...
MAYBE THEY'RE RIGHT.
MAYBE SHE REALLY DOES WANT TO...
HEY, YOU GONNA HELP WITH MY HOMEWORK OR WHAT?!
DON'T FORGET, YOU PROMISED!
DID I? OKAY, THEN.
DON'T FORGET TO REDO IT LATER IN YOUR OWN HANDWRITING.
'KAY.
DOES "SOMETHING" REALLY MEAN "DOING IT..."?
HOW DID THE TUTORING GO?
OKAY.

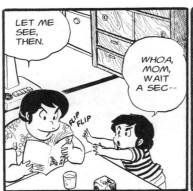

LET ME SEE, THEN.
WHOA, MOM, WAIT A SEC--
FLIP FLIP
WHAT'S THIS?!
LOOKS LIKE YUSAKU'S WRITING TO ME!
KONK
.....

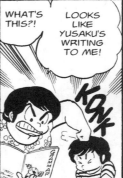

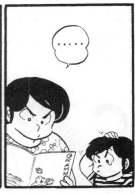

Exercise 3: Verbs: ***Words that describe actions***

Fill in the blank in each sentence with a verb (examples: run, play, etc.)

Yoshiko: "Masao, wouldn't you like to do it ?"

Masao: "Can we do it there?" Masao points to a grassy meadow.

Yoshiko: "No. Let's go do it at my place."

Masao: "Will your parents mind if we do it at your place?"

Yoshiko: "No, I do it there with all my friends."

So Yoshiko and Masao went over to her house and had fun.

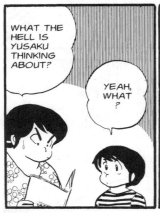

WHAT THE HELL IS YUSAKU THINKING ABOUT?
YEAH, WHAT ?
KONK
.....
.....

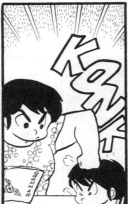

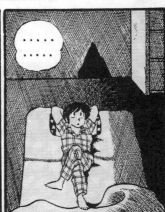

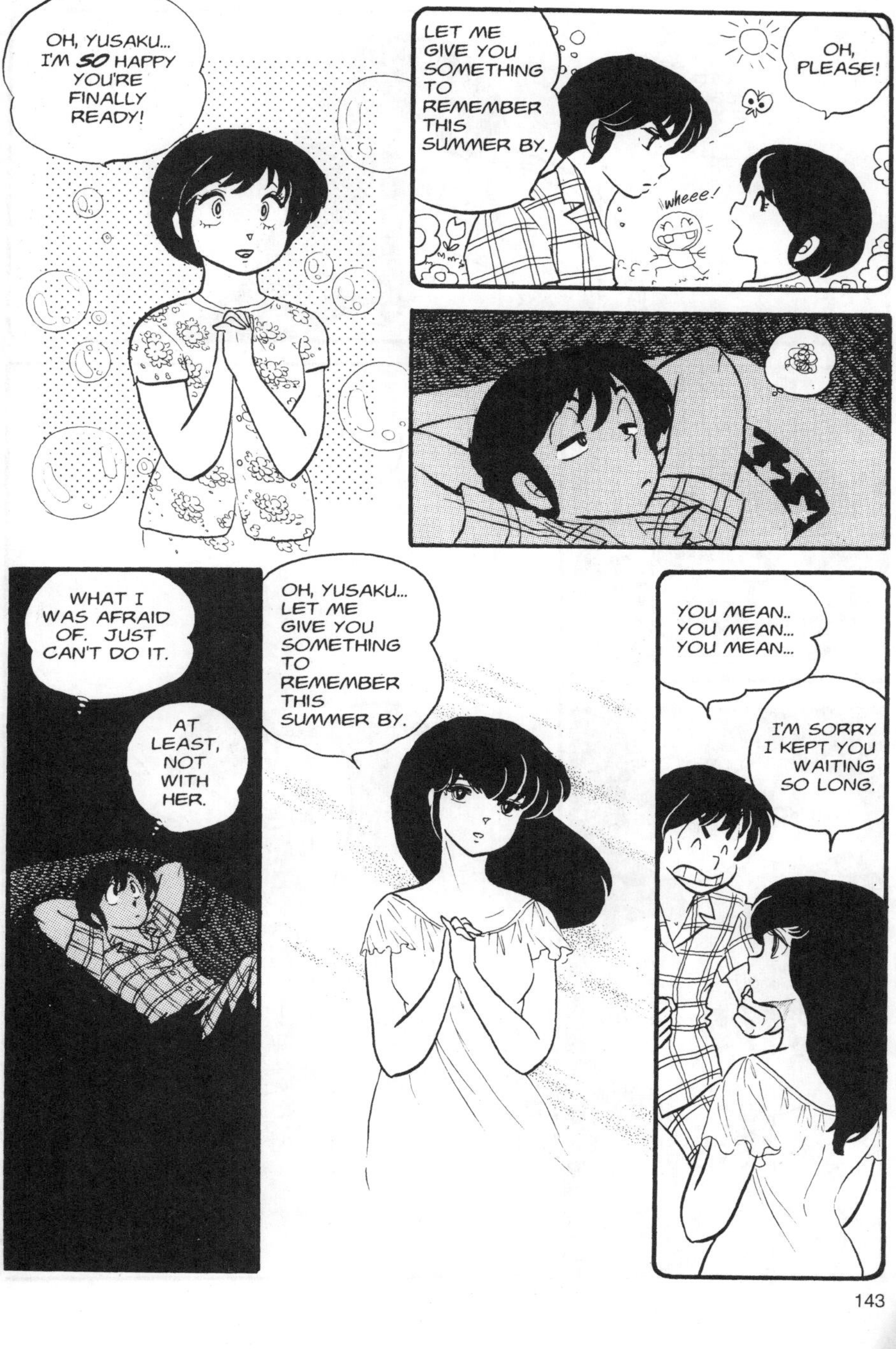
OH, YUSAKU... I'M SO HAPPY YOU'RE FINALLY READY!
LET ME GIVE YOU SOMETHING TO REMEMBER THIS SUMMER BY.
OH, PLEASE!
wheee!
WHAT I WAS AFRAID OF. JUST CAN'T DO IT.
AT LEAST, NOT WITH HER.
OH, YUSAKU... LET ME GIVE YOU SOMETHING TO REMEMBER THIS SUMMER BY.
YOU MEAN.. YOU MEAN... YOU MEAN...
I'M SORRY I KEPT YOU WAITING SO LONG.

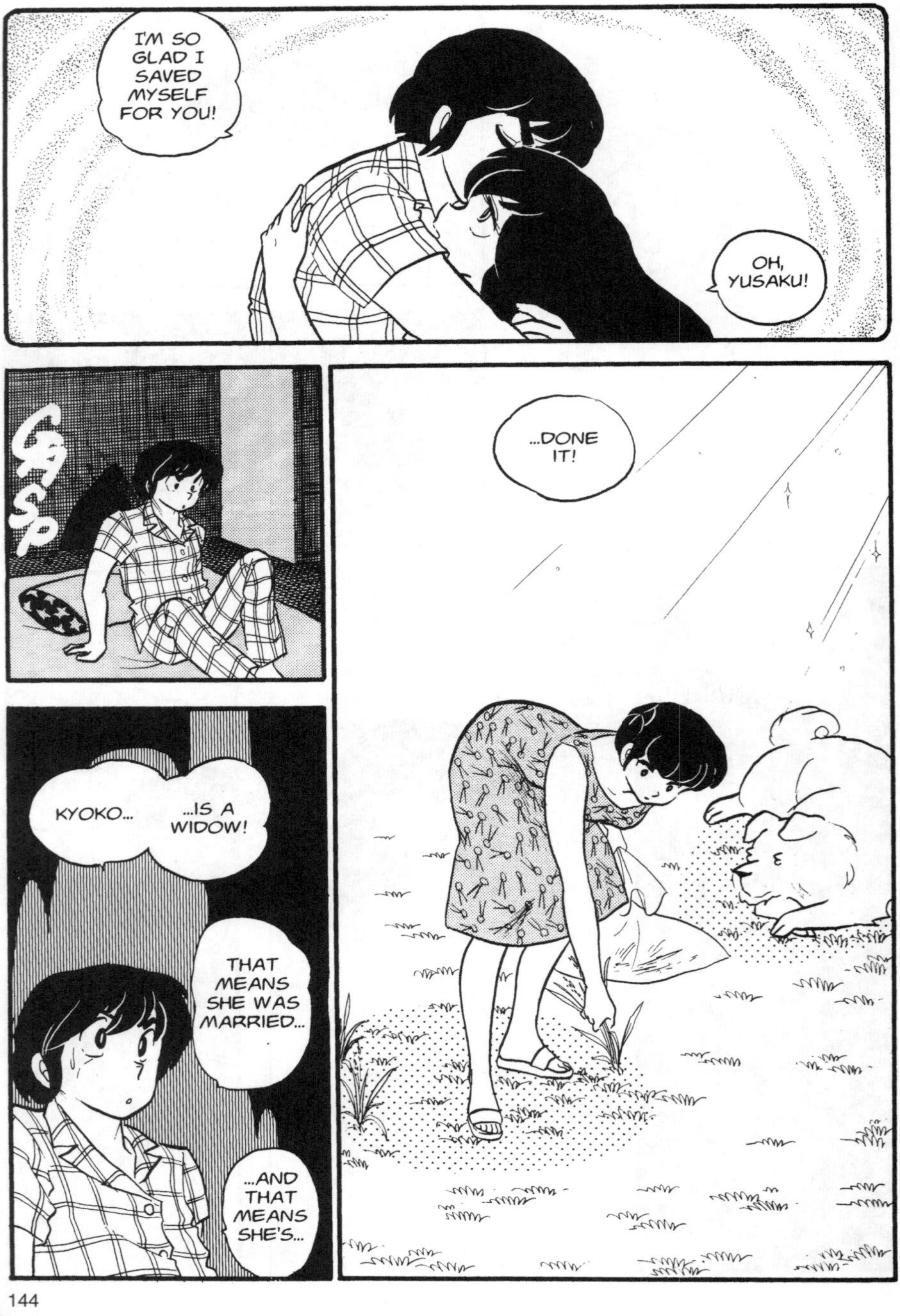
I'M SO GLAD I SAVED MYSELF FOR YOU!
OH, YUSAKU!
GASP
KYOKO...
...IS A WIDOW!
THAT MEANS SHE WAS MARRIED...
...AND THAT MEANS SHE'S...
...DONE IT!

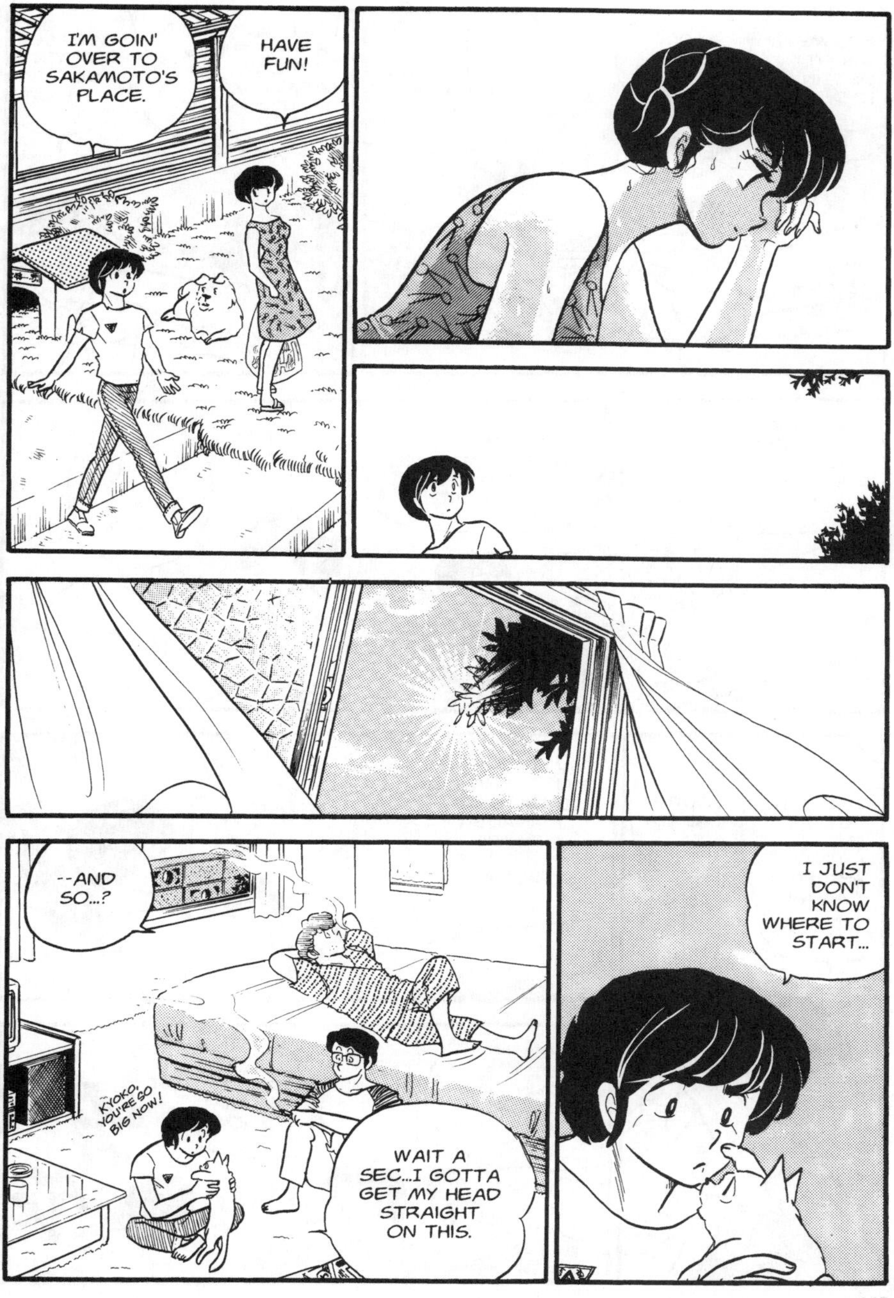
I'M GOIN' OVER TO SAKAMOTO'S PLACE.
HAVE FUN!
--AND SO...?
KYOKO, YOU'RE SO BIG NOW!
WAIT A SEC...I GOTTA GET MY HEAD STRAIGHT ON THIS.
I JUST DON'T KNOW WHERE TO START...

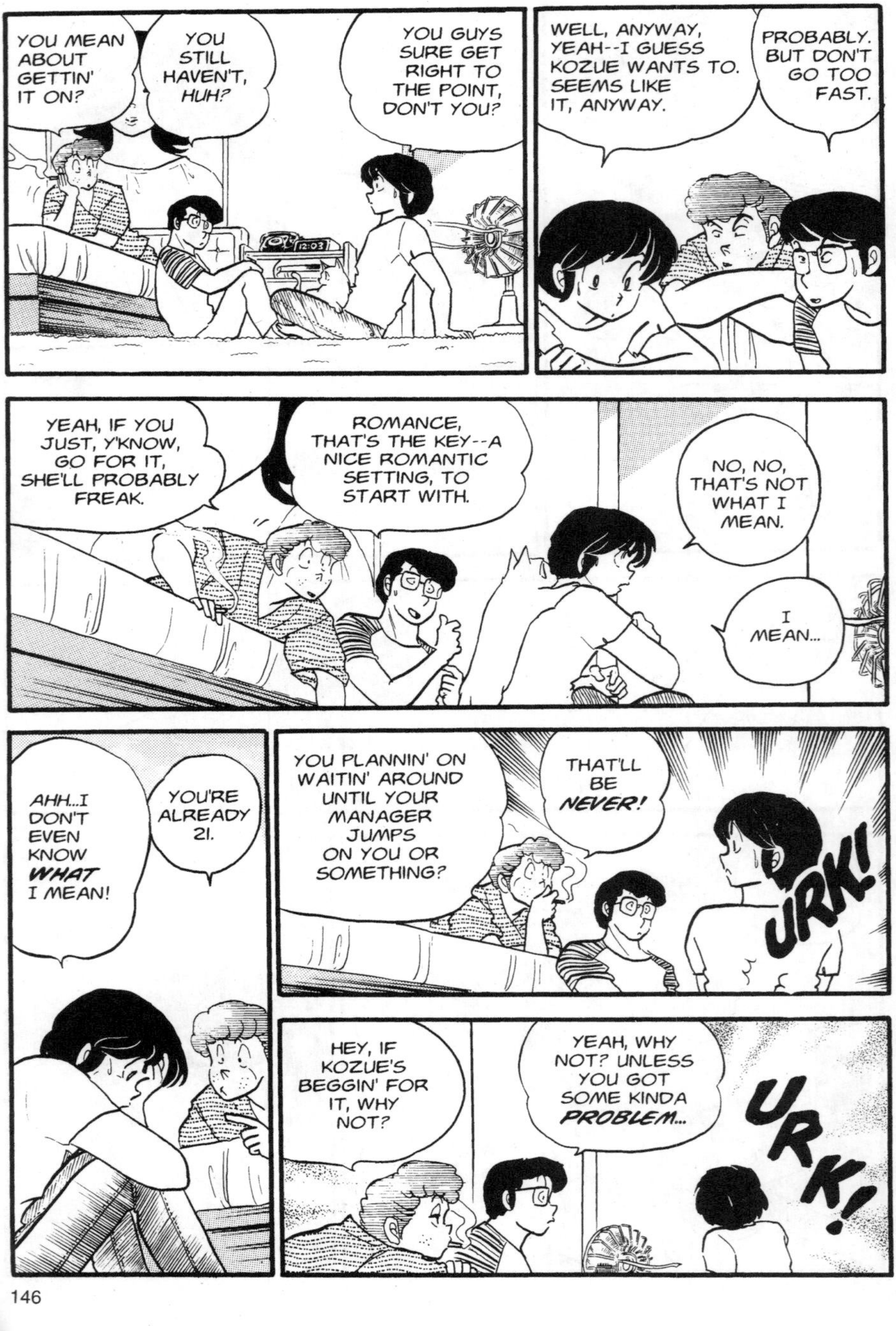
YOU MEAN ABOUT GETTIN' IT ON?
YOU STILL HAVEN'T, HUH?
YOU GUYS SURE GET RIGHT TO THE POINT, DON'T YOU?
12:03
WELL, ANYWAY, YEAH--I GUESS KOZUE WANTS TO. SEEMS LIKE IT, ANYWAY.
PROBABLY. BUT DON'T GO TOO FAST.
YEAH, IF YOU JUST, Y'KNOW, GO FOR IT, SHE'LL PROBABLY FREAK.
ROMANCE, THAT'S THE KEY--A NICE ROMANTIC SETTING, TO START WITH.
NO, NO, THAT'S NOT WHAT I MEAN.
I MEAN...
AHH...I DON'T EVEN KNOW *WHAT* I MEAN!
YOU'RE ALREADY 21.
YOU PLANNIN' ON WAITIN' AROUND UNTIL YOUR MANAGER JUMPS ON YOU OR SOMETHING?
THAT'LL BE *NEVER!*
URK!
HEY, IF KOZUE'S BEGGIN' FOR IT, WHY NOT?
YEAH, WHY NOT? UNLESS YOU GOT SOME KINDA *PROBLEM*...
URK!

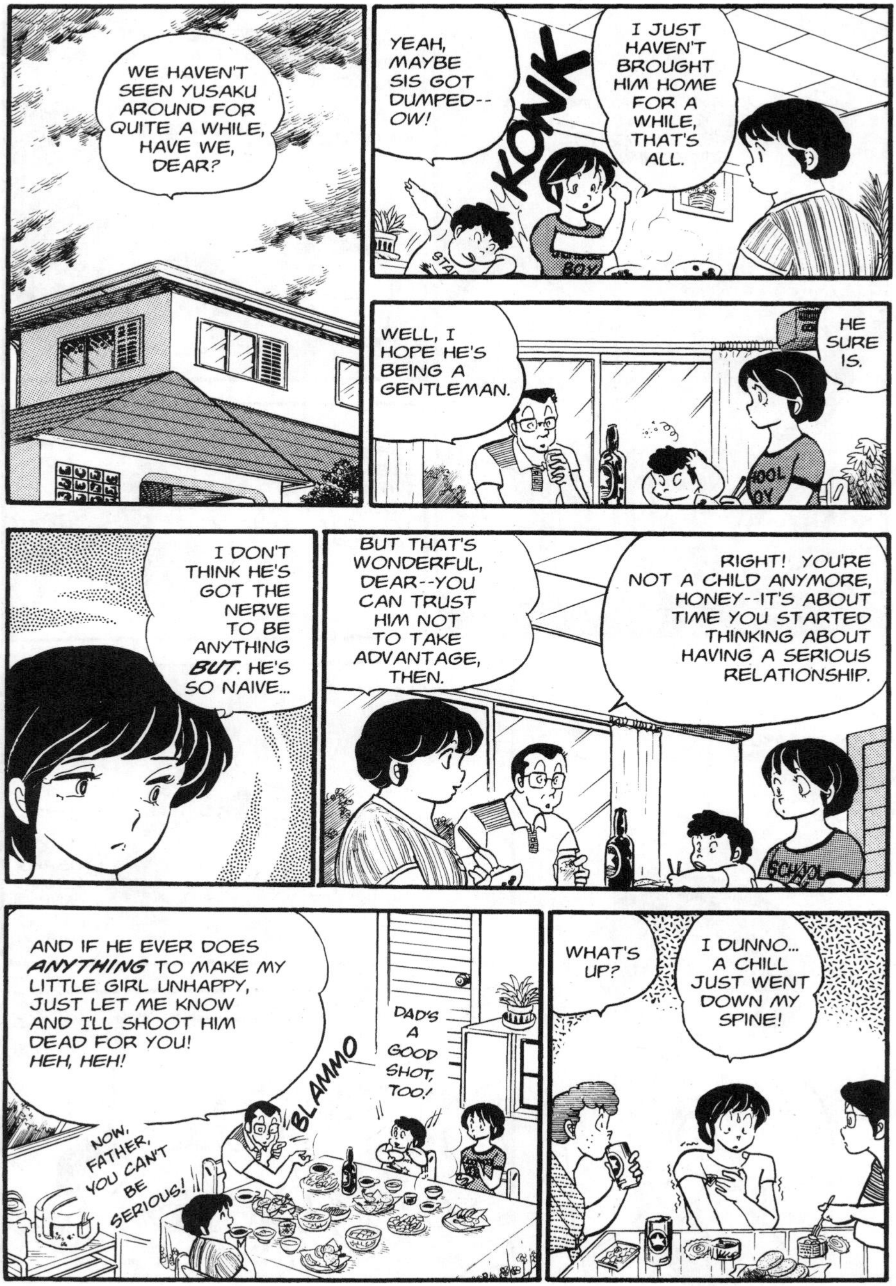
WE HAVEN'T SEEN YUSAKU AROUND FOR QUITE A WHILE, HAVE WE, DEAR?
YEAH, MAYBE SIS GOT DUMPED-- OW!
KONK
I JUST HAVEN'T BROUGHT HIM HOME FOR A WHILE, THAT'S ALL.
WELL, I HOPE HE'S BEING A GENTLEMAN.
HE SURE IS.
I DON'T THINK HE'S GOT THE NERVE TO BE ANYTHING *BUT*. HE'S SO NAIVE...
BUT THAT'S WONDERFUL, DEAR--YOU CAN TRUST HIM NOT TO TAKE ADVANTAGE, THEN.
RIGHT! YOU'RE NOT A CHILD ANYMORE, HONEY--IT'S ABOUT TIME YOU STARTED THINKING ABOUT HAVING A SERIOUS RELATIONSHIP.
AND IF HE EVER DOES *ANYTHING* TO MAKE MY LITTLE GIRL UNHAPPY, JUST LET ME KNOW AND I'LL SHOOT HIM DEAD FOR YOU! HEH, HEH!
BLAMMO
DAD'S A GOOD SHOT, TOO!
NOW, FATHER, YOU CAN'T BE SERIOUS!
WHAT'S UP?
I DUNNO... A CHILL JUST WENT DOWN MY SPINE!

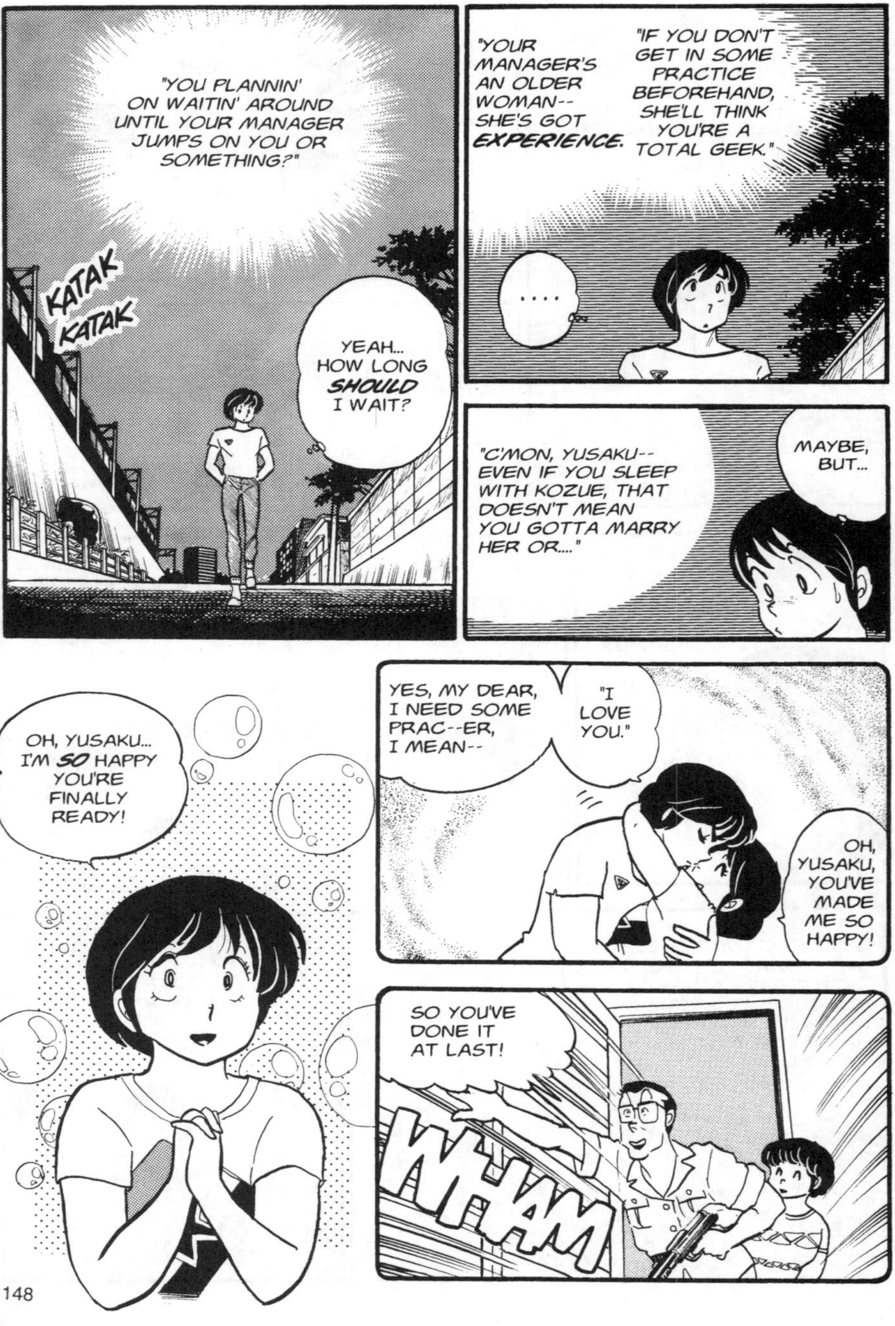
"YOU PLANNIN' ON WAITIN' AROUND UNTIL YOUR MANAGER JUMPS ON YOU OR SOMETHING?"
KATAK KATAK
YEAH... HOW LONG SHOULD I WAIT?
"YOUR MANAGER'S AN OLDER WOMAN-- SHE'S GOT EXPERIENCE.
"IF YOU DON'T GET IN SOME PRACTICE BEFOREHAND, SHE'LL THINK YOU'RE A TOTAL GEEK."
....
"C'MON, YUSAKU-- EVEN IF YOU SLEEP WITH KOZUE, THAT DOESN'T MEAN YOU GOTTA MARRY HER OR...."
MAYBE, BUT...
OH, YUSAKU... I'M SO HAPPY YOU'RE FINALLY READY!
YES, MY DEAR, I NEED SOME PRAC--ER, I MEAN--
"I LOVE YOU."
OH, YUSAKU, YOU'VE MADE ME SO HAPPY!
SO YOU'VE DONE IT AT LAST!
WHAM

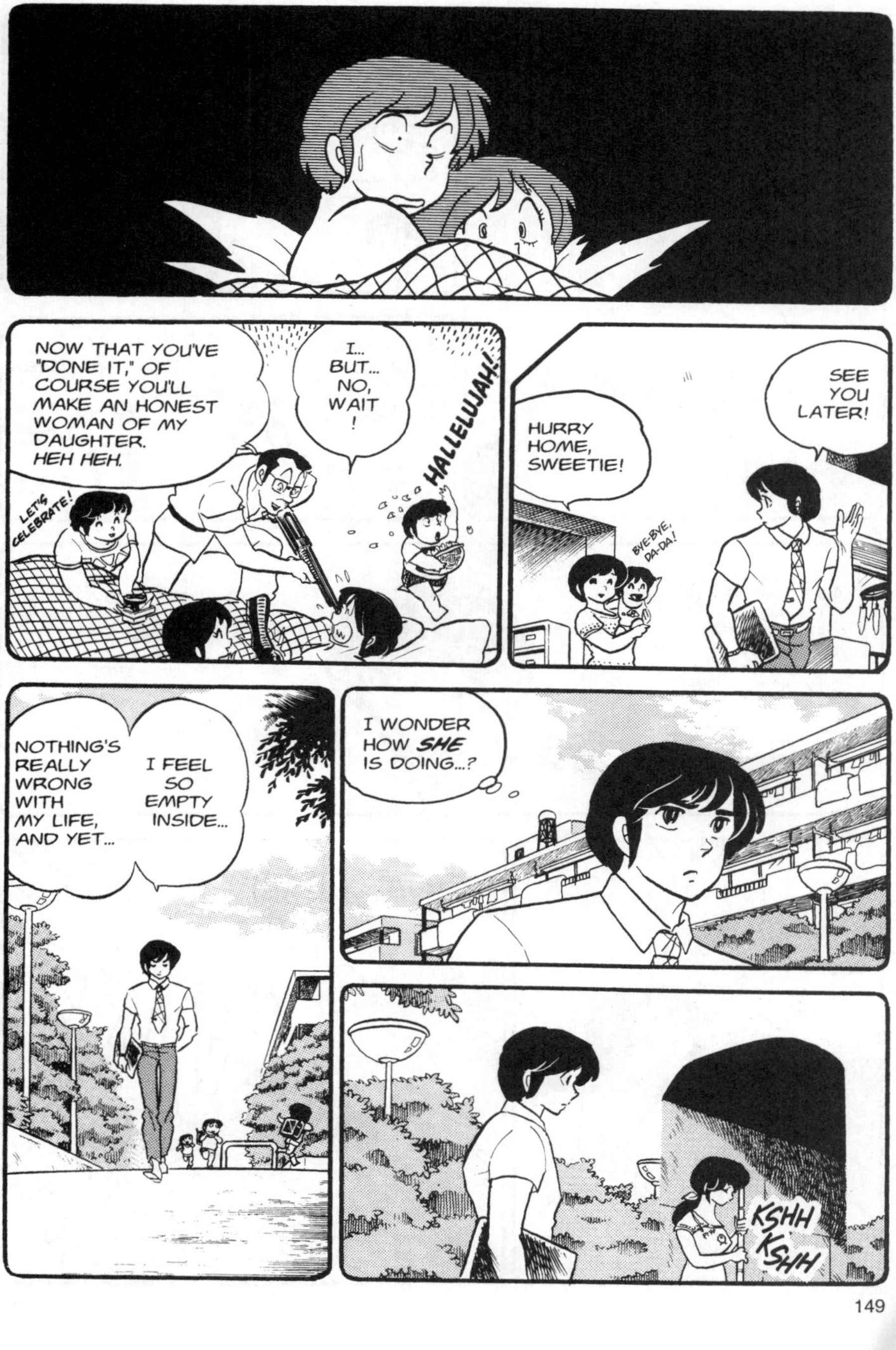
NOW THAT YOU'VE "DONE IT," OF COURSE YOU'LL MAKE AN HONEST WOMAN OF MY DAUGHTER. HEH HEH.
I... BUT... NO, WAIT!
HALLELUJAH!
LET'S CELEBRATE!
HURRY HOME, SWEETIE!
SEE YOU LATER!
BYE-BYE, DA-DA!
NOTHING'S REALLY WRONG WITH MY LIFE, AND YET...
I FEEL SO EMPTY INSIDE...
I WONDER HOW SHE IS DOING...?
KSHH KSHH

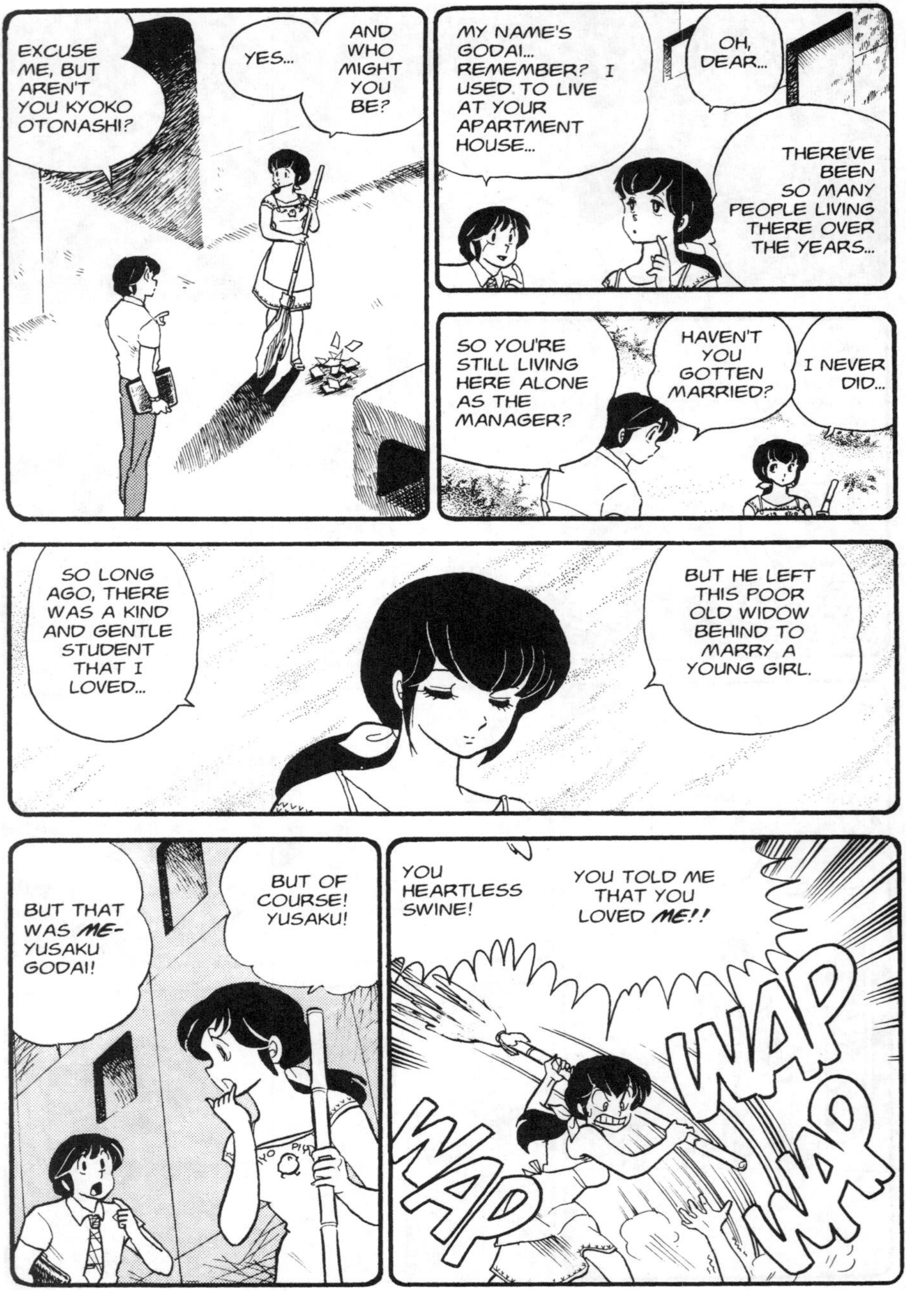
EXCUSE ME, BUT AREN'T YOU KYOKO OTONASHI?
YES...
AND WHO MIGHT YOU BE?
MY NAME'S GODAI... REMEMBER? I USED TO LIVE AT YOUR APARTMENT HOUSE...
OH, DEAR...
THERE'VE BEEN SO MANY PEOPLE LIVING THERE OVER THE YEARS...
SO YOU'RE STILL LIVING HERE ALONE AS THE MANAGER?
HAVEN'T YOU GOTTEN MARRIED?
I NEVER DID...
SO LONG AGO, THERE WAS A KIND AND GENTLE STUDENT THAT I LOVED...
BUT HE LEFT THIS POOR OLD WIDOW BEHIND TO MARRY A YOUNG GIRL.
BUT THAT WAS ME- YUSAKU GODAI!
BUT OF COURSE! YUSAKU!
YOU HEARTLESS SWINE!
YOU TOLD ME THAT YOU LOVED ME!!
WAP
WAP
WAP

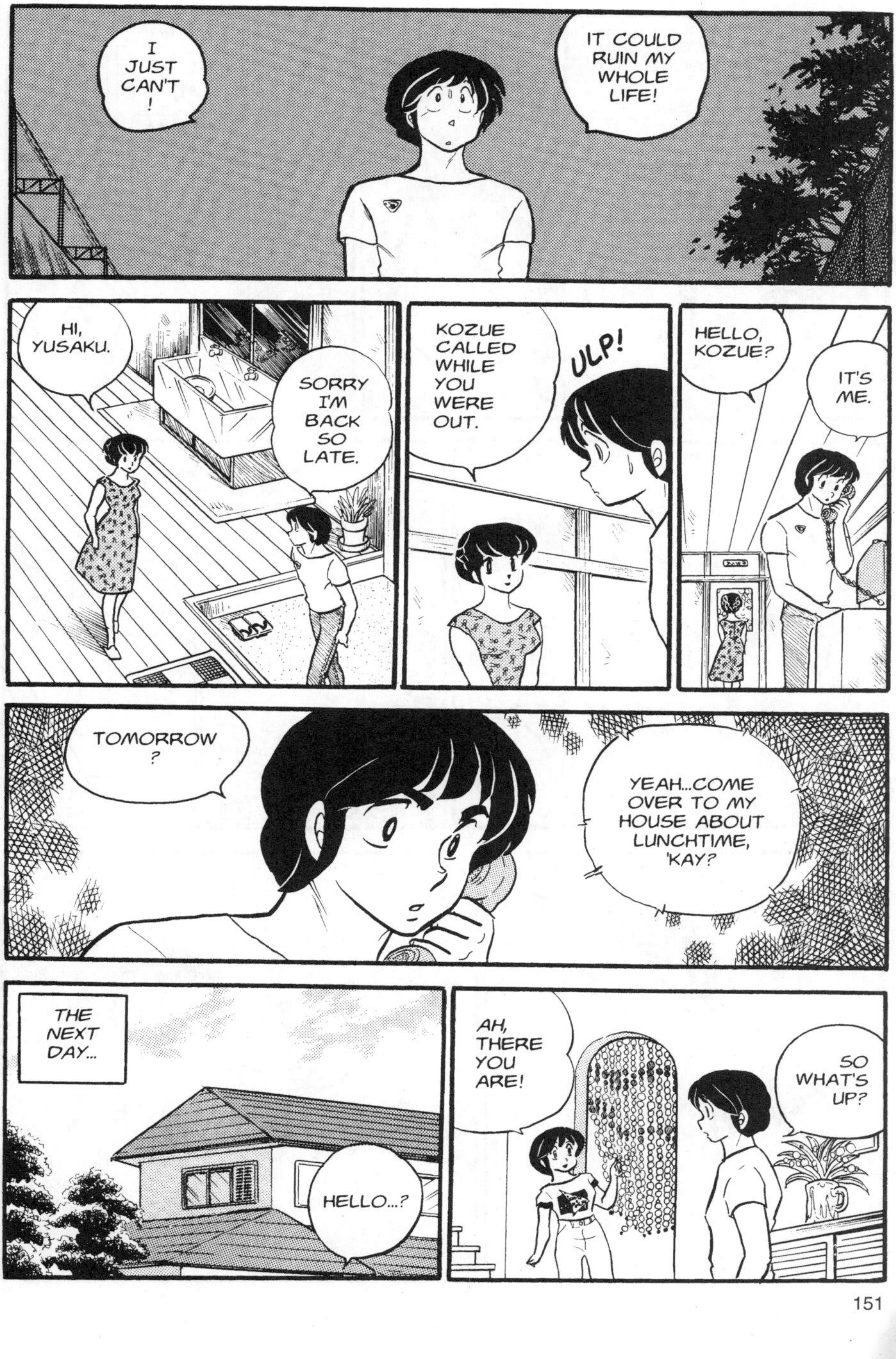
I JUST CAN'T!
IT COULD RUIN MY WHOLE LIFE!
HI, YUSAKU.
SORRY I'M BACK SO LATE.
KOZUE CALLED WHILE YOU WERE OUT.
ULP!
HELLO, KOZUE?
IT'S ME.
TOMORROW?
YEAH...COME OVER TO MY HOUSE ABOUT LUNCHTIME, 'KAY?
THE NEXT DAY...
HELLO...?
AH, THERE YOU ARE!
SO WHAT'S UP?

SO WHERE ARE YOUR FOLKS?

EVERYBODY'S GONE OUT.

"SOMETHING TO REMEMBER..."

TAKE OFF YOUR SHIRT.

...!

LOOK, KOZUE!

I CAN'T, I COULDN'T...

WELL, MAYBE A LITTLE KISS...

OH, SORRY.

I'LL GO OUT, THEN.

PUT ON THE SHIRT IN THAT BAG, OKAY?

HUH?

JIROBE

?

GREAT! LET'S GO...

...AND DO SOMETHING TO REMEMBER!

BUT...

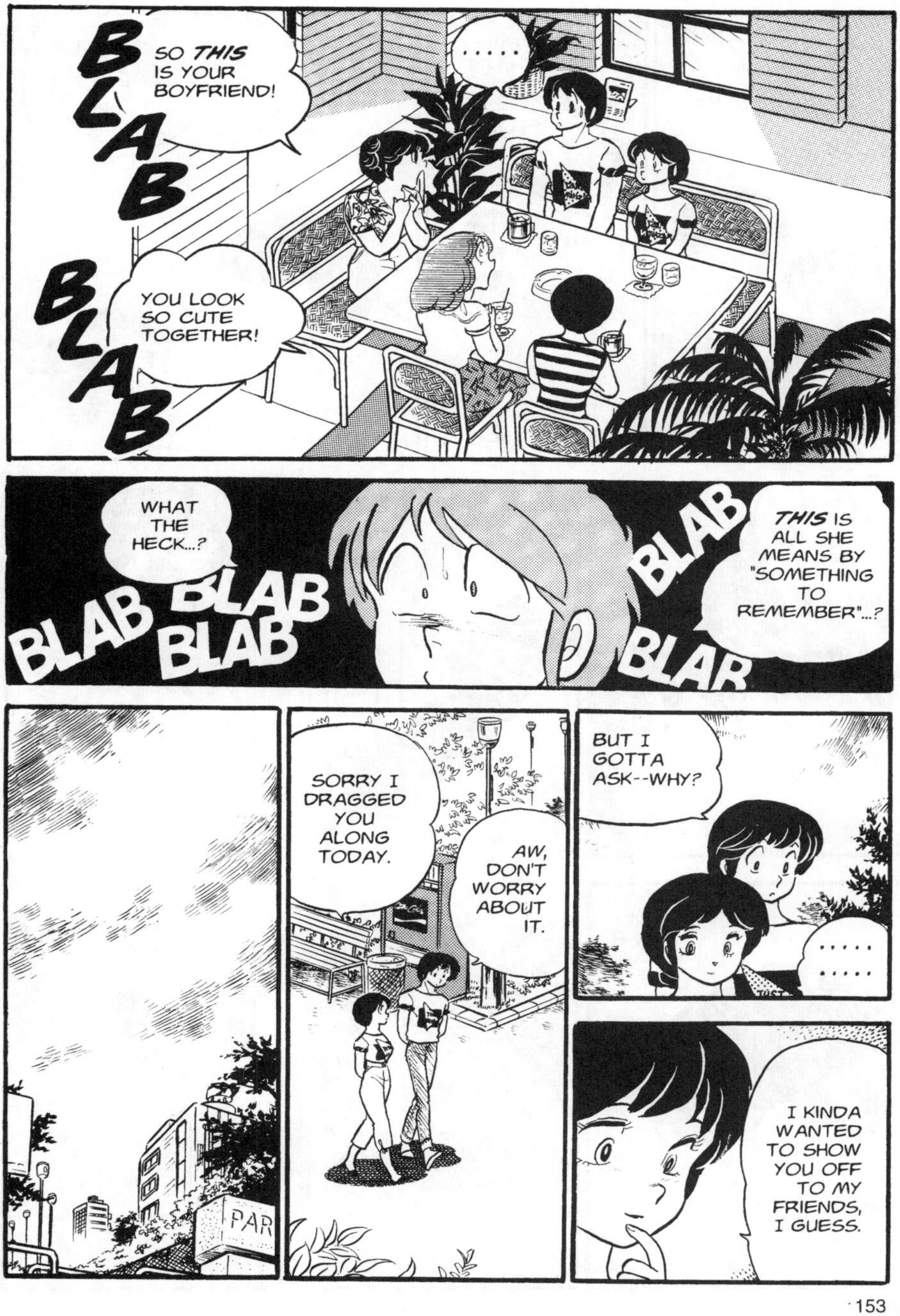
BLAB
SO THIS IS YOUR BOYFRIEND!
......
BLAB
YOU LOOK SO CUTE TOGETHER!
WHAT THE HECK...?
BLAB BLAB BLAB
BLAB BLAR
THIS IS ALL SHE MEANS BY "SOMETHING TO REMEMBER"...?
PAR
SORRY I DRAGGED YOU ALONG TODAY.
AW, DON'T WORRY ABOUT IT.
BUT I GOTTA ASK--WHY?
....
I KINDA WANTED TO SHOW YOU OFF TO MY FRIENDS, I GUESS.

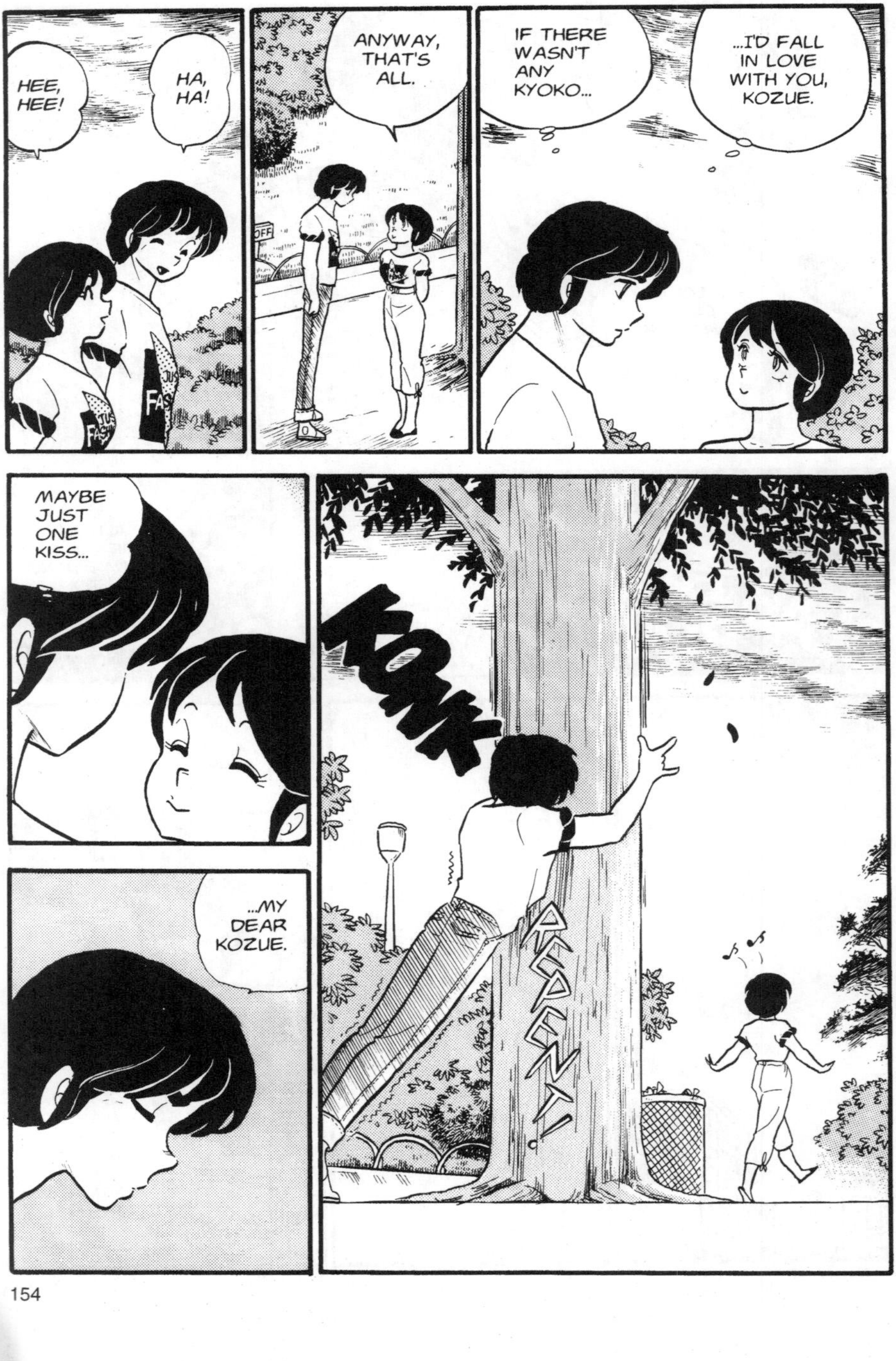
HEE, HEE!
HA, HA!
ANYWAY, THAT'S ALL.
IF THERE WASN'T ANY KYOKO...
...I'D FALL IN LOVE WITH YOU, KOZUE.
MAYBE JUST ONE KISS...
...MY DEAR KOZUE.
KONK
REPENT!

Part Eight
The Incident

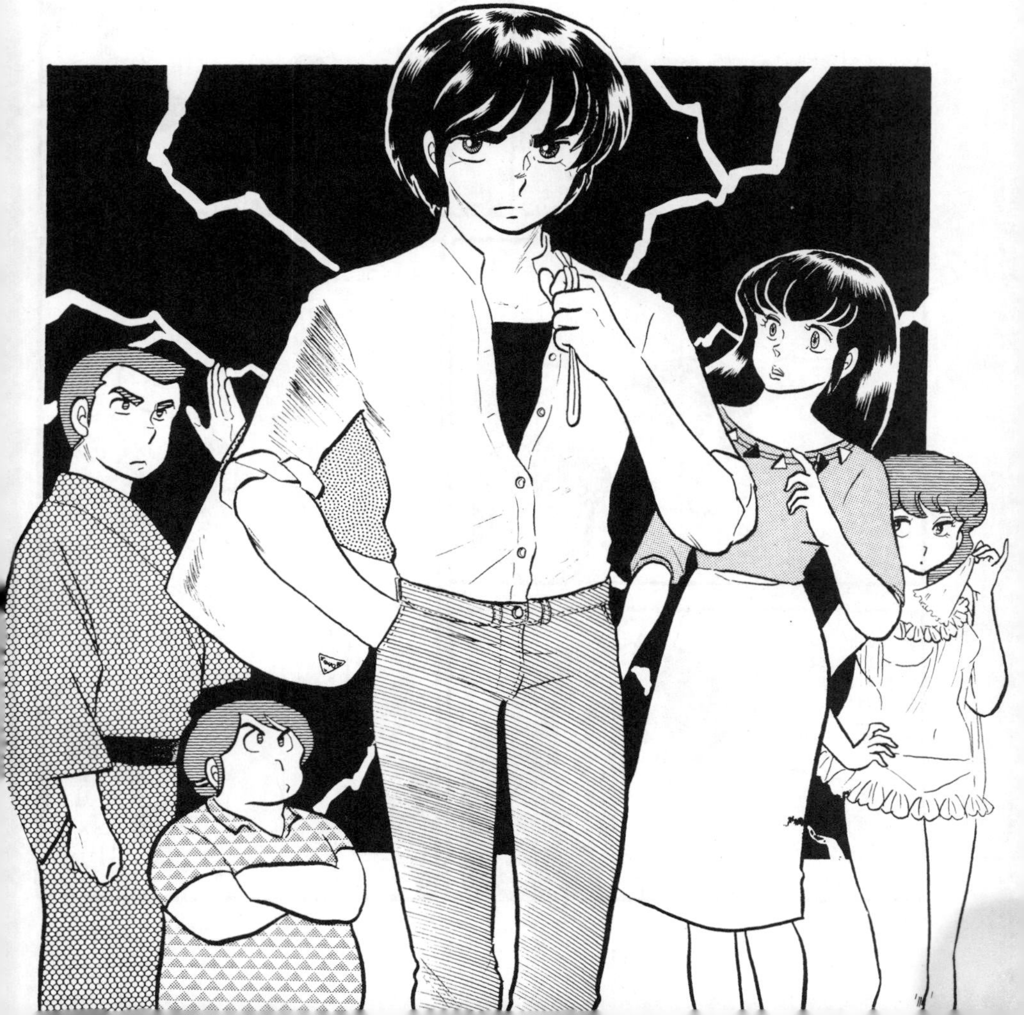

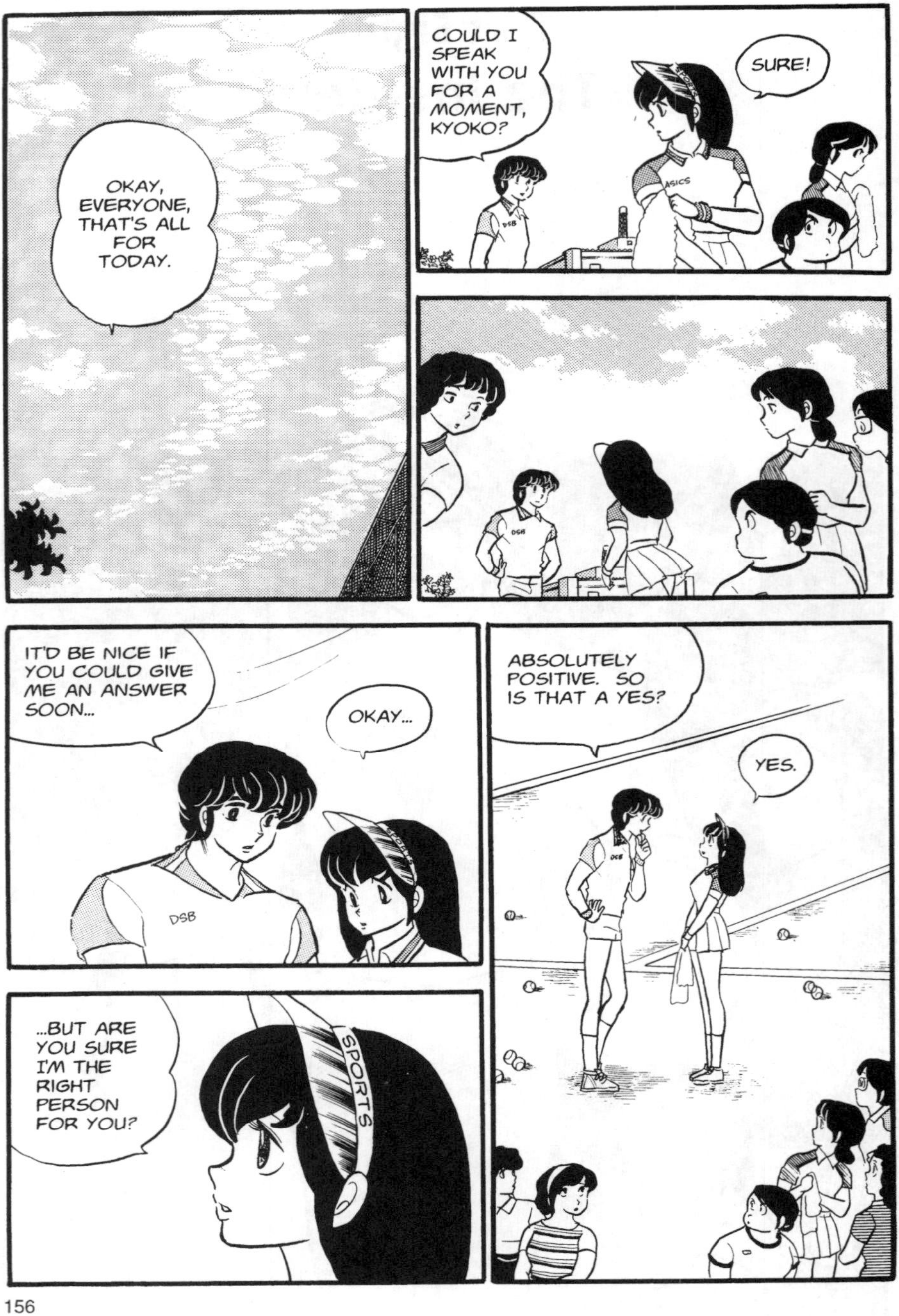
OKAY, EVERYONE, THAT'S ALL FOR TODAY.
COULD I SPEAK WITH YOU FOR A MOMENT, KYOKO?
SURE!
IT'D BE NICE IF YOU COULD GIVE ME AN ANSWER SOON...
OKAY...
...BUT ARE YOU SURE I'M THE RIGHT PERSON FOR YOU?
SPORTS
ABSOLUTELY POSITIVE. SO IS THAT A YES?
YES.

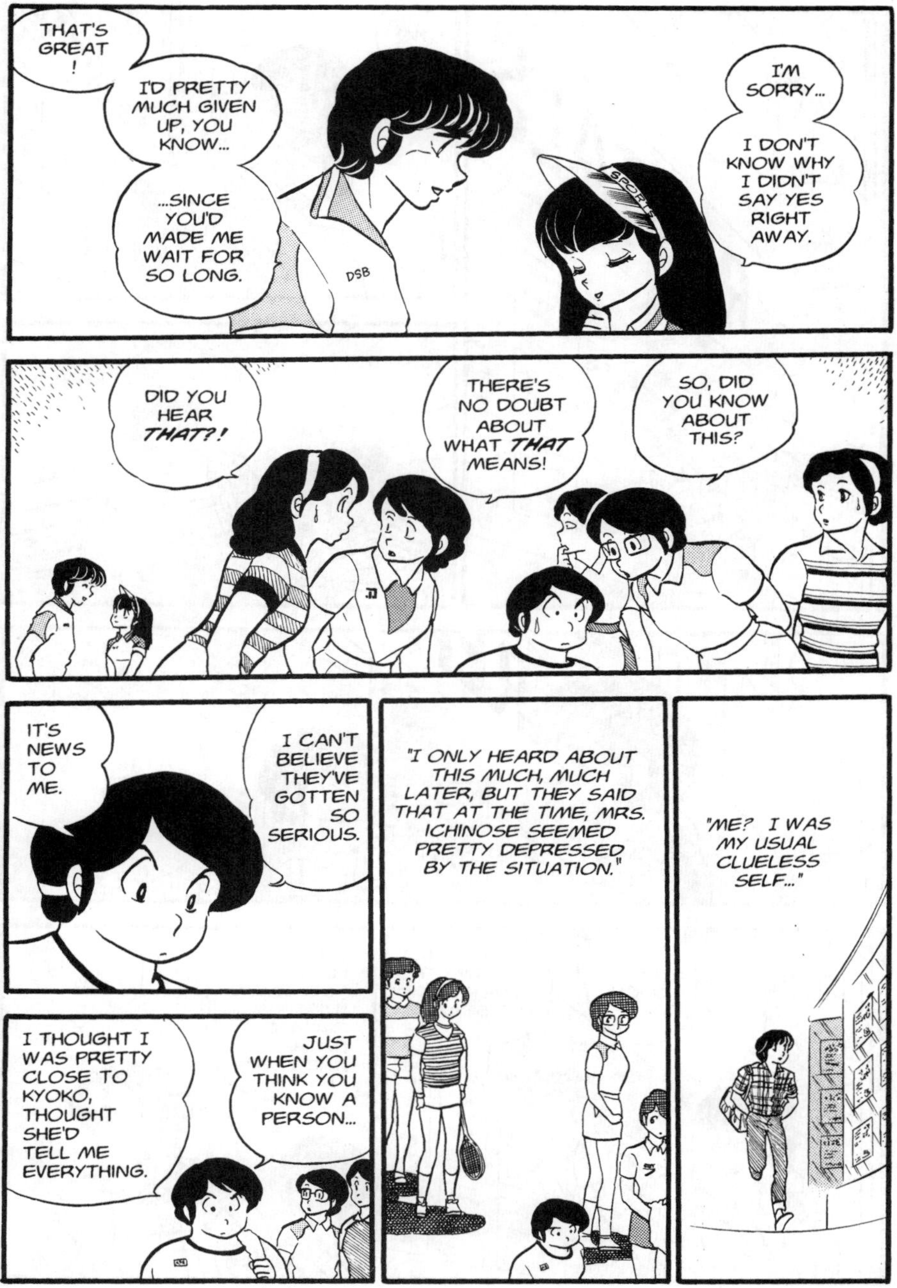

THAT'S GREAT !
I'D PRETTY MUCH GIVEN UP, YOU KNOW...
...SINCE YOU'D MADE ME WAIT FOR SO LONG.
DSB
SPORTS
I'M SORRY...
I DON'T KNOW WHY I DIDN'T SAY YES RIGHT AWAY.
DID YOU HEAR *THAT?!*
THERE'S NO DOUBT ABOUT WHAT *THAT* MEANS!
SO, DID YOU KNOW ABOUT THIS?
IT'S NEWS TO ME.
I CAN'T BELIEVE THEY'VE GOTTEN SO SERIOUS.
I THOUGHT I WAS PRETTY CLOSE TO KYOKO, THOUGHT SHE'D TELL ME EVERYTHING.
JUST WHEN YOU THINK YOU KNOW A PERSON...
"I ONLY HEARD ABOUT THIS MUCH, MUCH LATER, BUT THEY SAID THAT AT THE TIME, MRS. ICHINOSE SEEMED PRETTY DEPRESSED BY THE SITUATION."
"ME? I WAS MY USUAL CLUELESS SELF..."

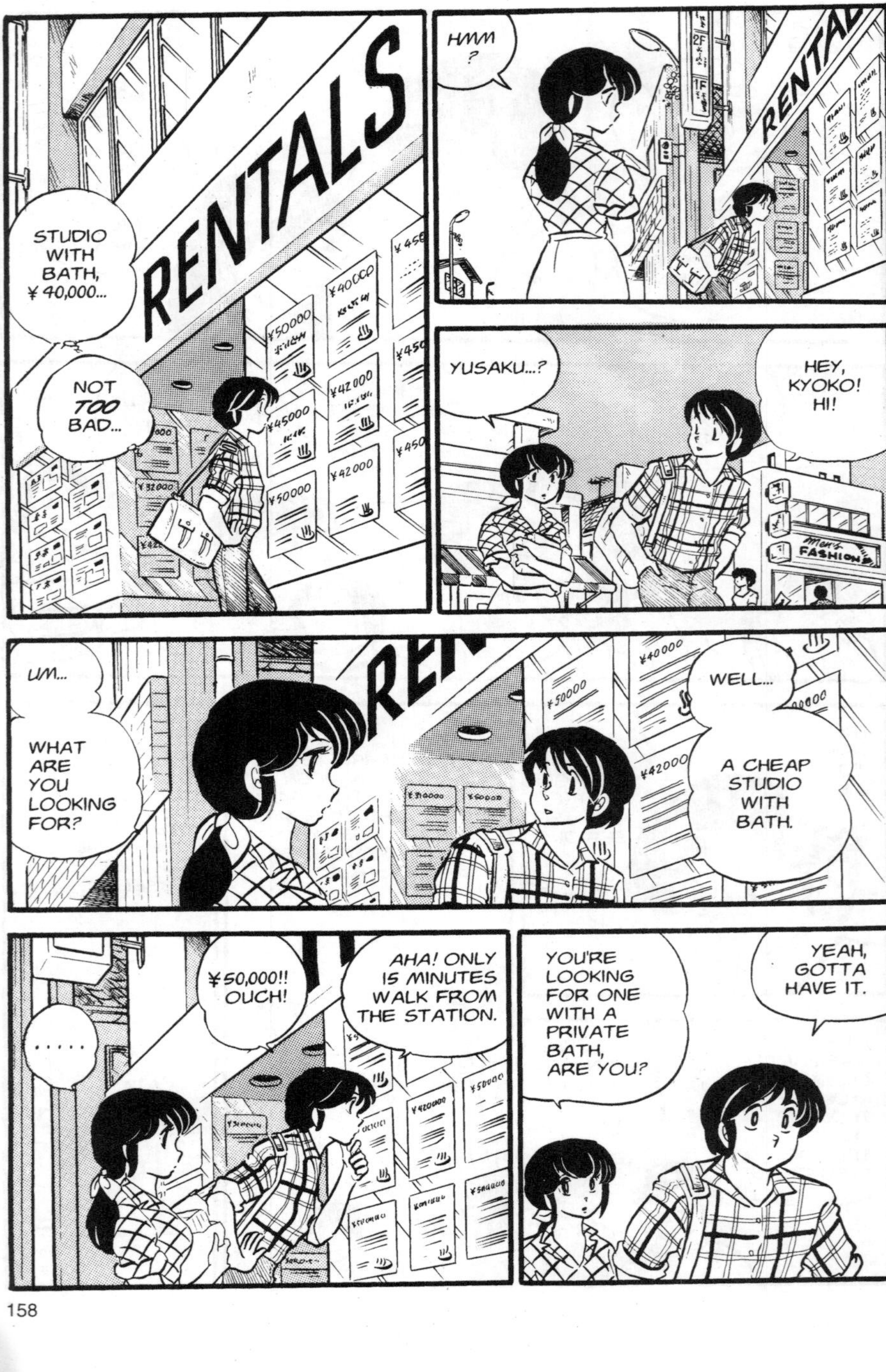
RENTALS
STUDIO WITH BATH, ¥40,000...
NOT *TOO* BAD...
HMM ?
RENTALS
YUSAKU...?
HEY, KYOKO! HI!
UM...
WHAT ARE YOU LOOKING FOR?
WELL...
A CHEAP STUDIO WITH BATH.
.....
¥50,000!! OUCH!
AHA! ONLY 15 MINUTES WALK FROM THE STATION.
YOU'RE LOOKING FOR ONE WITH A PRIVATE BATH, ARE YOU?
YEAH, GOTTA HAVE IT.

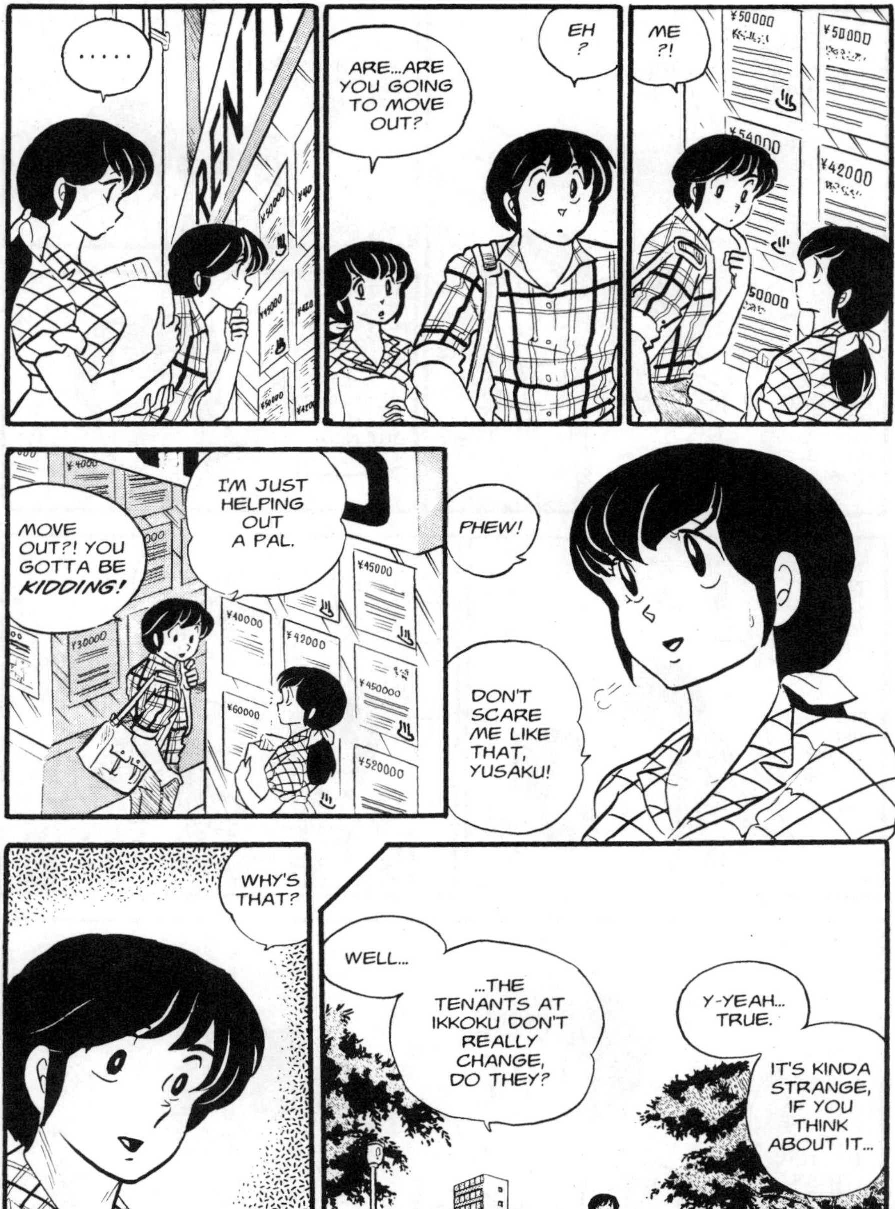

.....
ARE...ARE YOU GOING TO MOVE OUT?
EH?
ME?!
MOVE OUT?! YOU GOTTA BE **KIDDING!**
I'M JUST HELPING OUT A PAL.
PHEW!
DON'T SCARE ME LIKE THAT, YUSAKU!
WHY'S THAT?
WELL...
...THE TENANTS AT IKKOKU DON'T REALLY CHANGE, DO THEY?
Y-YEAH... TRUE.
IT'S KINDA STRANGE, IF YOU THINK ABOUT IT...

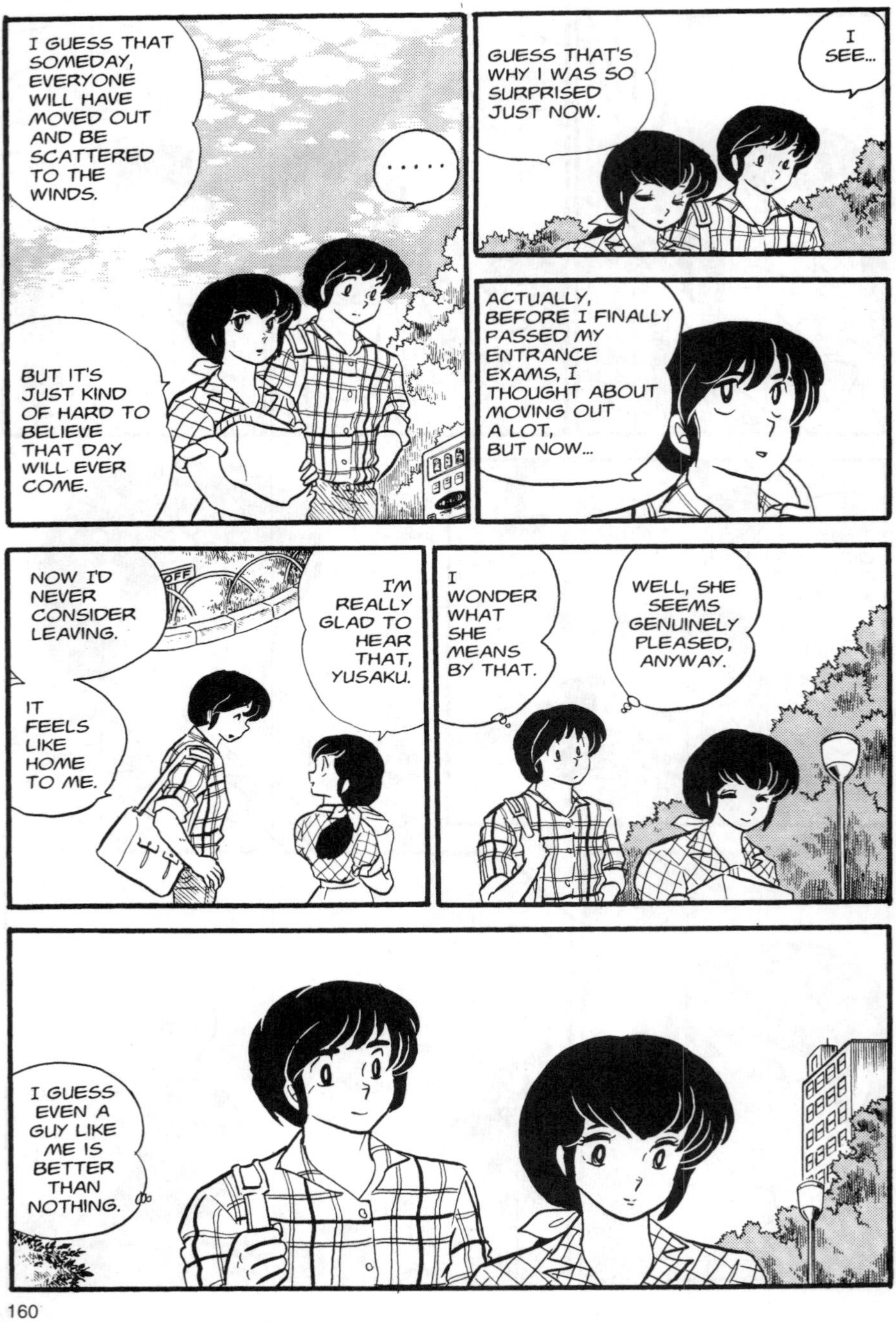
I GUESS THAT SOMEDAY, EVERYONE WILL HAVE MOVED OUT AND BE SCATTERED TO THE WINDS.
......
BUT IT'S JUST KIND OF HARD TO BELIEVE THAT DAY WILL EVER COME.
GUESS THAT'S WHY I WAS SO SURPRISED JUST NOW.
I SEE...
ACTUALLY, BEFORE I FINALLY PASSED MY ENTRANCE EXAMS, I THOUGHT ABOUT MOVING OUT A LOT, BUT NOW...
NOW I'D NEVER CONSIDER LEAVING.
IT FEELS LIKE HOME TO ME.
OFF
I'M REALLY GLAD TO HEAR THAT, YUSAKU.
I WONDER WHAT SHE MEANS BY THAT.
WELL, SHE SEEMS GENUINELY PLEASED, ANYWAY.
I GUESS EVEN A GUY LIKE ME IS BETTER THAN NOTHING.

SHE'S A WICKED WOMAN.

ONCE IN A WHILE SHE'LL SAY SOMETHING LIKE THAT...

...SOMETHING TO MAKE ME THINK SHE MIGHT REALLY CARE...

...AND SO SHE KEEPS ME HANGING ONTO MY DREAMS.

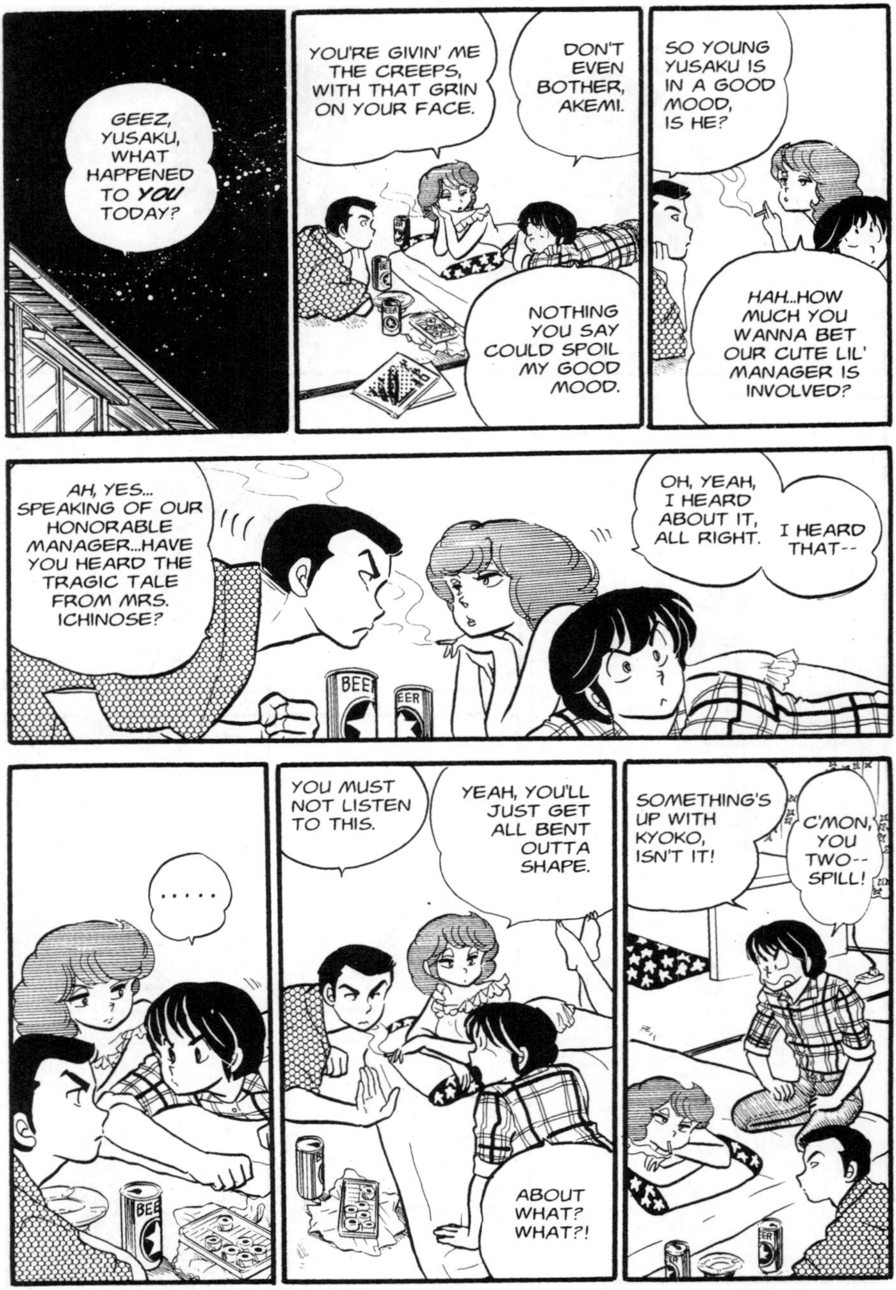
GEEZ, YUSAKU, WHAT HAPPENED TO YOU TODAY?
YOU'RE GIVIN' ME THE CREEPS, WITH THAT GRIN ON YOUR FACE.
DON'T EVEN BOTHER, AKEMI.
NOTHING YOU SAY COULD SPOIL MY GOOD MOOD.
SO YOUNG YUSAKU IS IN A GOOD MOOD, IS HE?
HAH...HOW MUCH YOU WANNA BET OUR CUTE LIL' MANAGER IS INVOLVED?
AH, YES... SPEAKING OF OUR HONORABLE MANAGER...HAVE YOU HEARD THE TRAGIC TALE FROM MRS. ICHINOSE?
OH, YEAH, I HEARD ABOUT IT, ALL RIGHT.
I HEARD THAT--
.....
YOU MUST NOT LISTEN TO THIS.
YEAH, YOU'LL JUST GET ALL BENT OUTTA SHAPE.
ABOUT WHAT? WHAT?!
SOMETHING'S UP WITH KYOKO, ISN'T IT!
C'MON, YOU TWO-- SPILL!

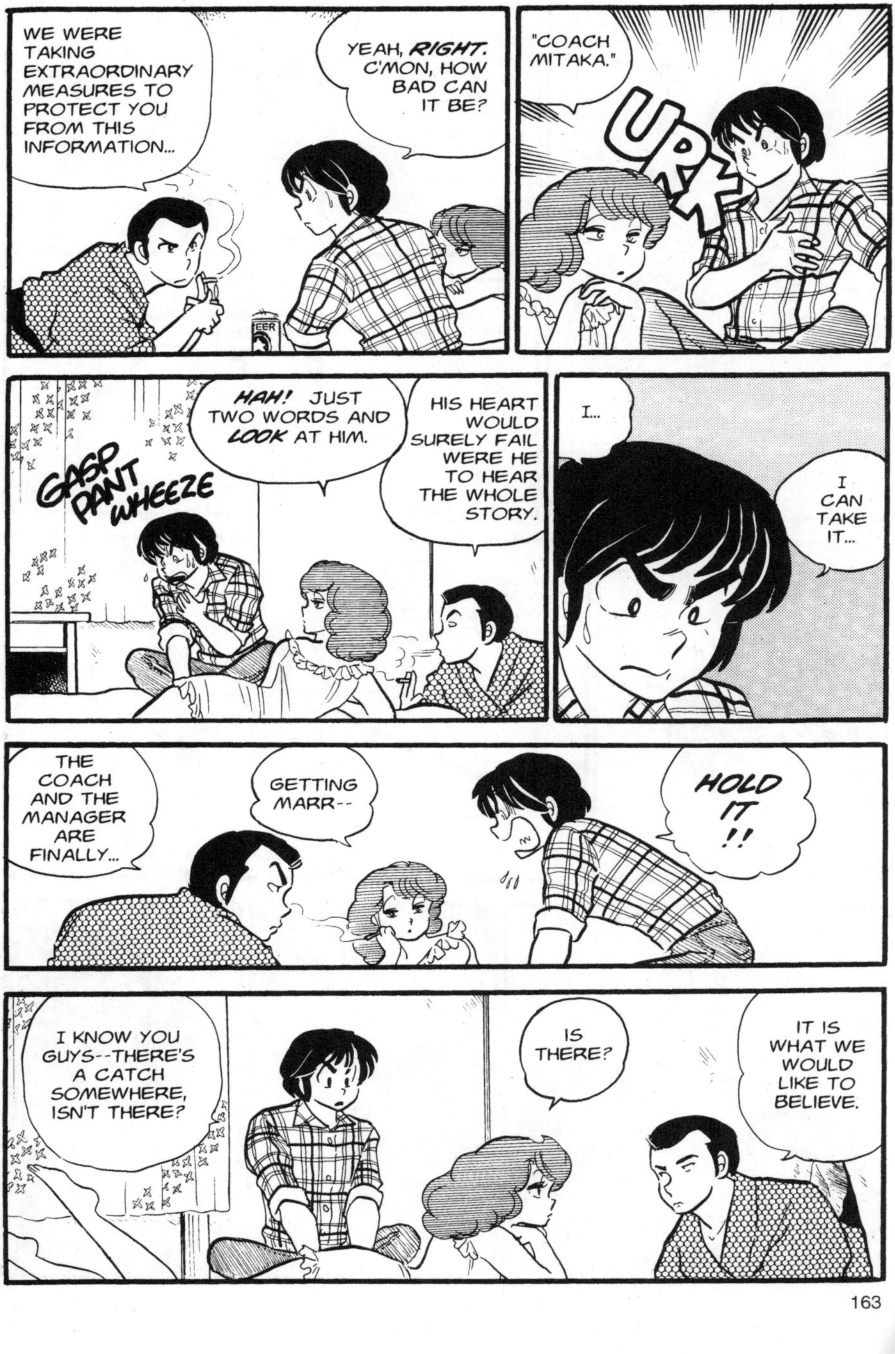
WE WERE TAKING EXTRAORDINARY MEASURES TO PROTECT YOU FROM THIS INFORMATION...
YEAH, RIGHT. C'MON, HOW BAD CAN IT BE?
"COACH MITAKA."
URK
GASP PANT WHEEZE
HAH! JUST TWO WORDS AND LOOK AT HIM.
HIS HEART WOULD SURELY FAIL WERE HE TO HEAR THE WHOLE STORY.
I...
I CAN TAKE IT...
THE COACH AND THE MANAGER ARE FINALLY...
GETTING MARR--
HOLD IT !!
I KNOW YOU GUYS--THERE'S A CATCH SOMEWHERE, ISN'T THERE?
IS THERE?
IT IS WHAT WE WOULD LIKE TO BELIEVE.

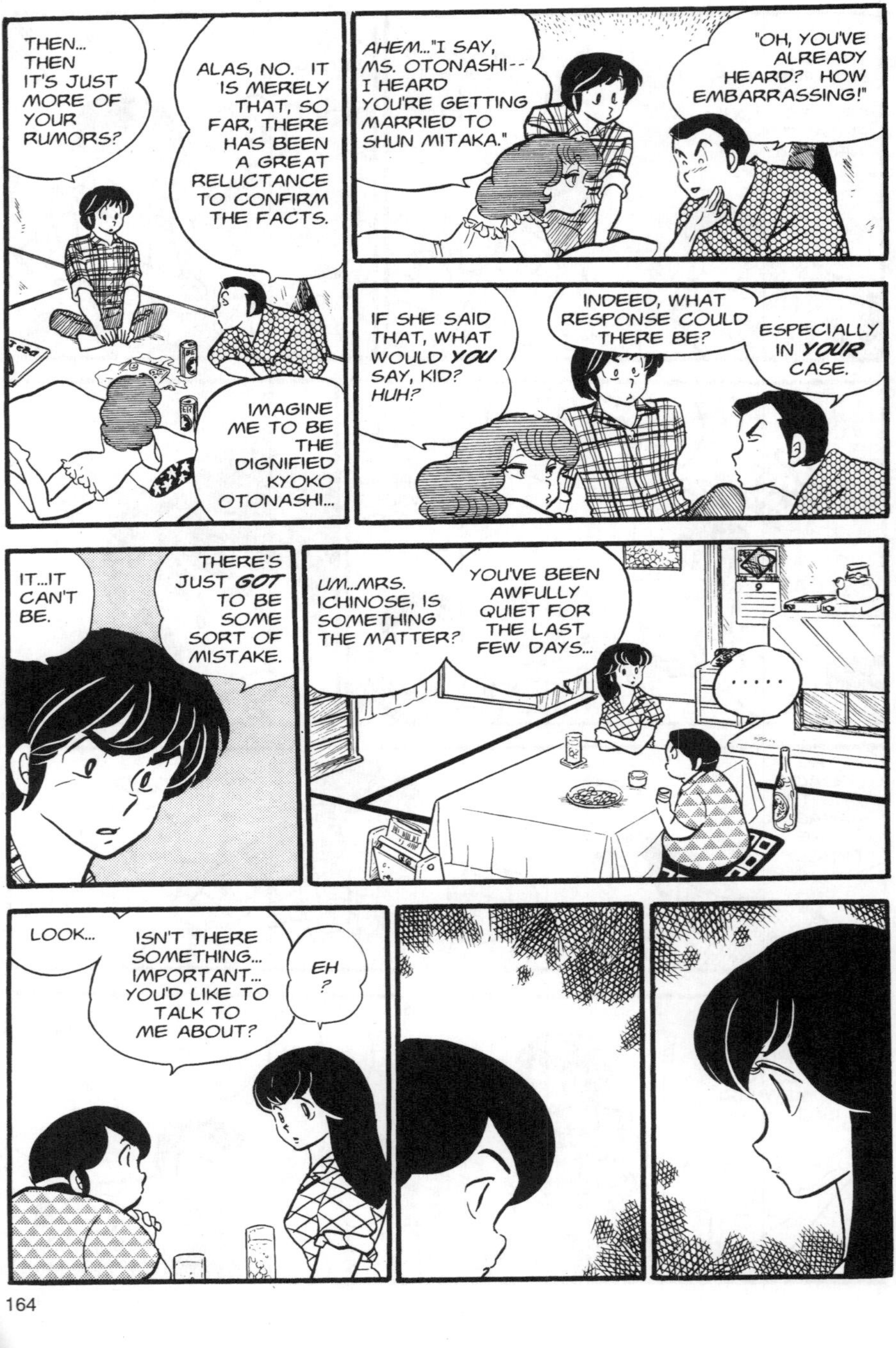
THEN... THEN IT'S JUST MORE OF YOUR RUMORS?
ALAS, NO. IT IS MERELY THAT, SO FAR, THERE HAS BEEN A GREAT RELUCTANCE TO CONFIRM THE FACTS.
IMAGINE ME TO BE THE DIGNIFIED KYOKO OTONASHI...
AHEM..."I SAY, MS. OTONASHI-- I HEARD YOU'RE GETTING MARRIED TO SHUN MITAKA."
"OH, YOU'VE ALREADY HEARD? HOW EMBARRASSING!"
IF SHE SAID THAT, WHAT WOULD YOU SAY, KID? HUH?
INDEED, WHAT RESPONSE COULD THERE BE?
ESPECIALLY IN YOUR CASE.
IT...IT CAN'T BE.
THERE'S JUST GOT TO BE SOME SORT OF MISTAKE.
UM...MRS. ICHINOSE, IS SOMETHING THE MATTER?
YOU'VE BEEN AWFULLY QUIET FOR THE LAST FEW DAYS...
.....
LOOK...
ISN'T THERE SOMETHING... IMPORTANT... YOU'D LIKE TO TALK TO ME ABOUT?
EH ?

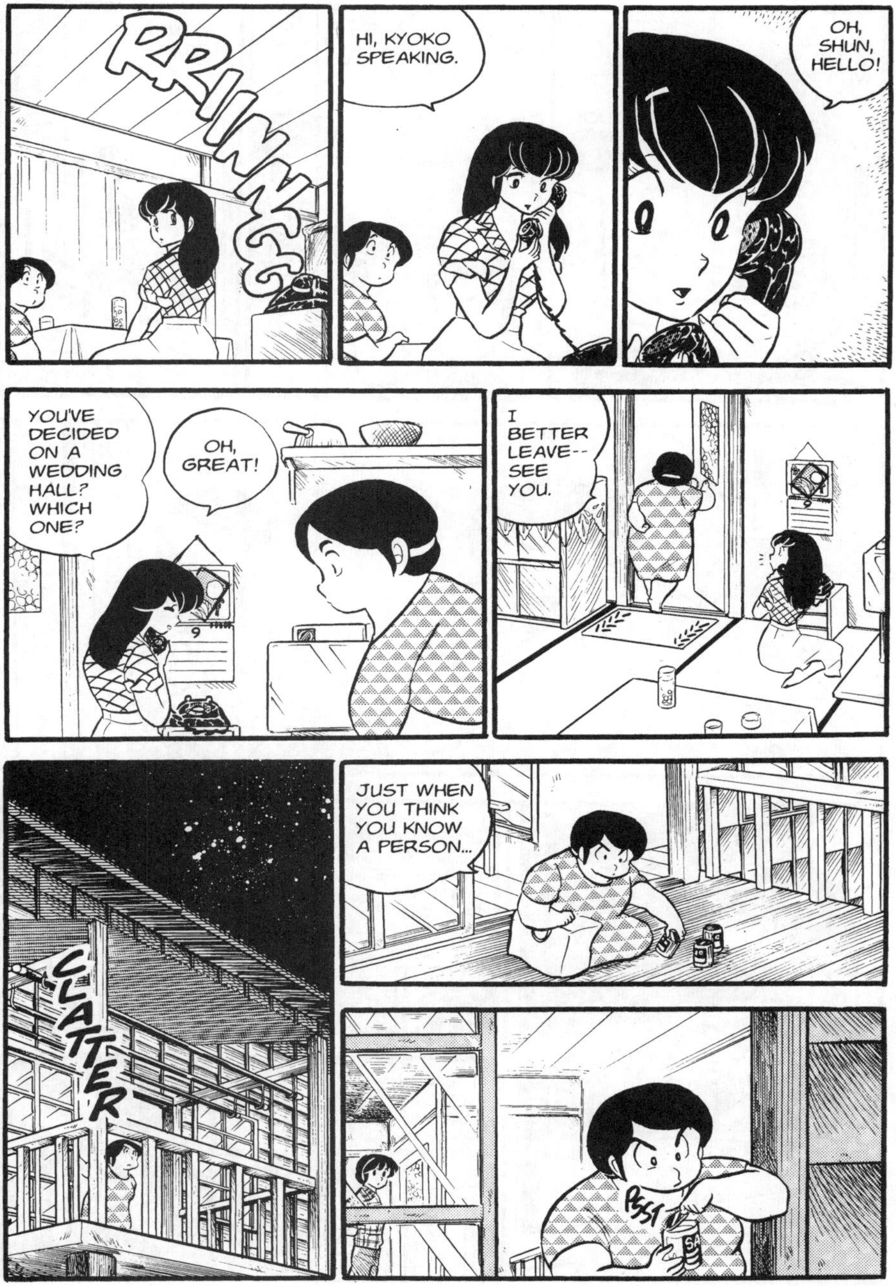
RRIINNGG
HI, KYOKO SPEAKING.
OH, SHUN, HELLO!
YOU'VE DECIDED ON A WEDDING HALL? WHICH ONE?
OH, GREAT!
I BETTER LEAVE-- SEE YOU.
CLATTER
JUST WHEN YOU THINK YOU KNOW A PERSON...
PSSST

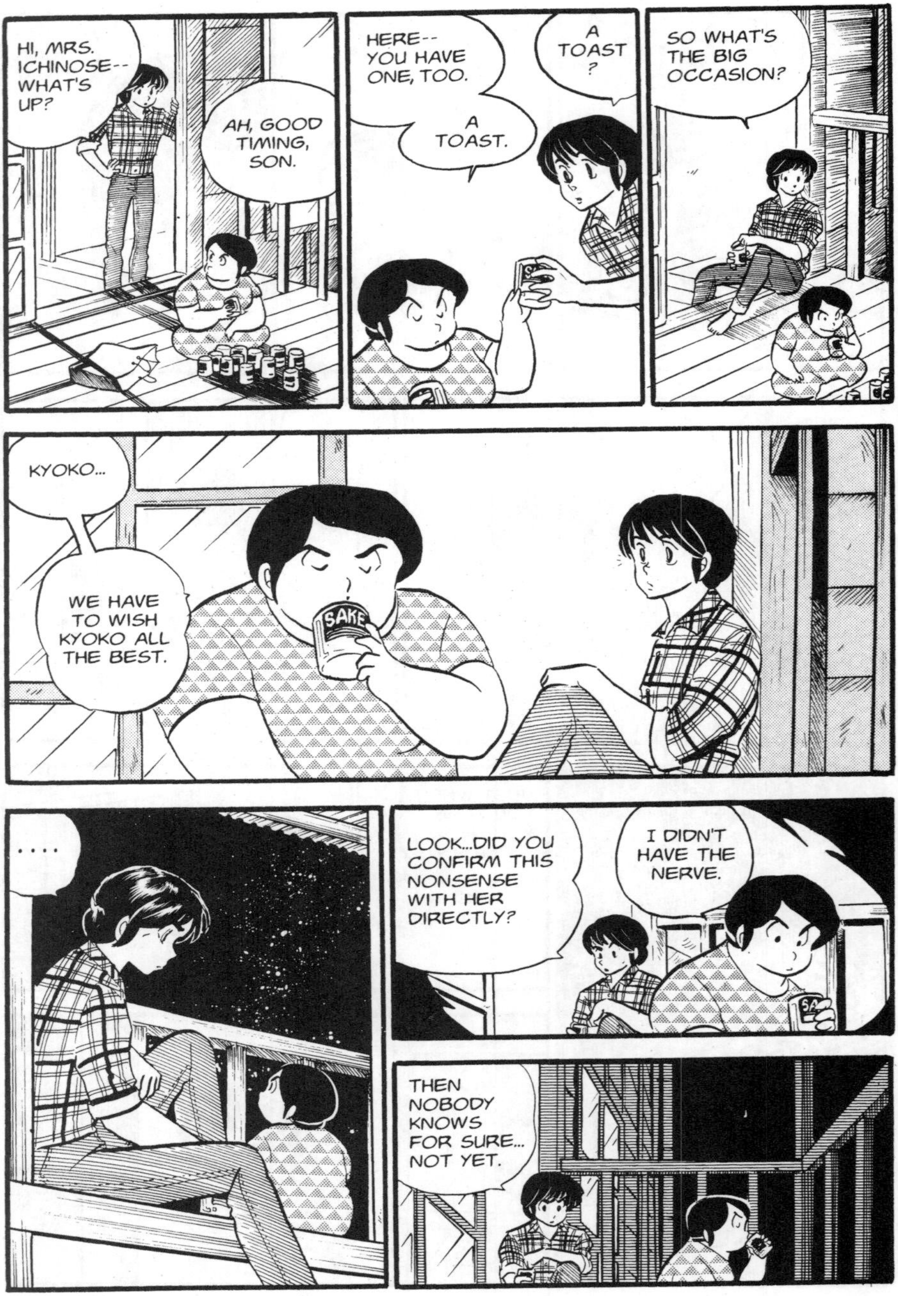
HI, MRS. ICHINOSE-- WHAT'S UP?
AH, GOOD TIMING, SON.
HERE-- YOU HAVE ONE, TOO.
A TOAST.
A TOAST?
SO WHAT'S THE BIG OCCASION?
KYOKO...
WE HAVE TO WISH KYOKO ALL THE BEST.
SAKE
....
LOOK...DID YOU CONFIRM THIS NONSENSE WITH HER DIRECTLY?
I DIDN'T HAVE THE NERVE.
THEN NOBODY KNOWS FOR SURE... NOT YET.

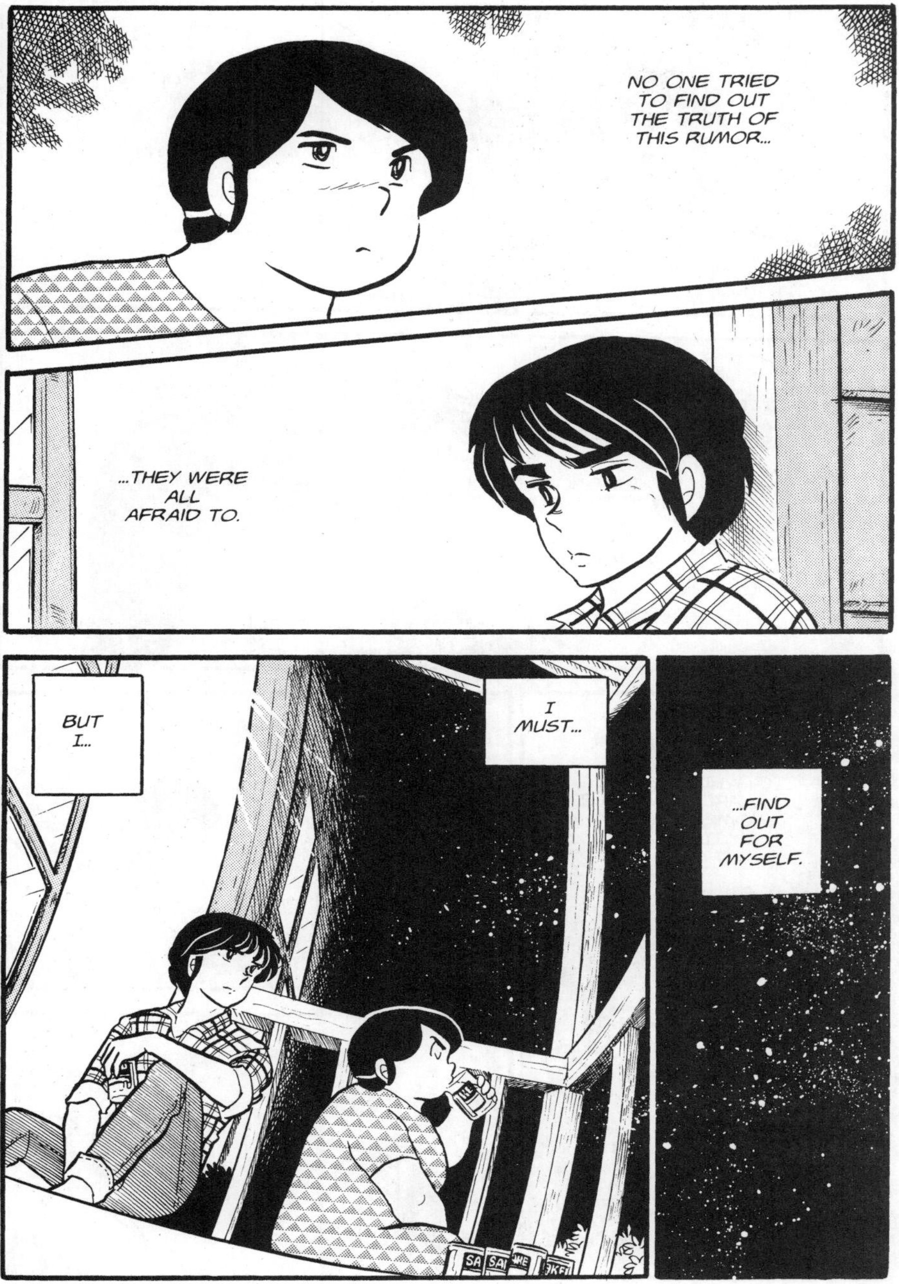
NO ONE TRIED TO FIND OUT THE TRUTH OF THIS RUMOR...
...THEY WERE ALL AFRAID TO.
BUT I...
I MUST...
...FIND OUT FOR MYSELF.

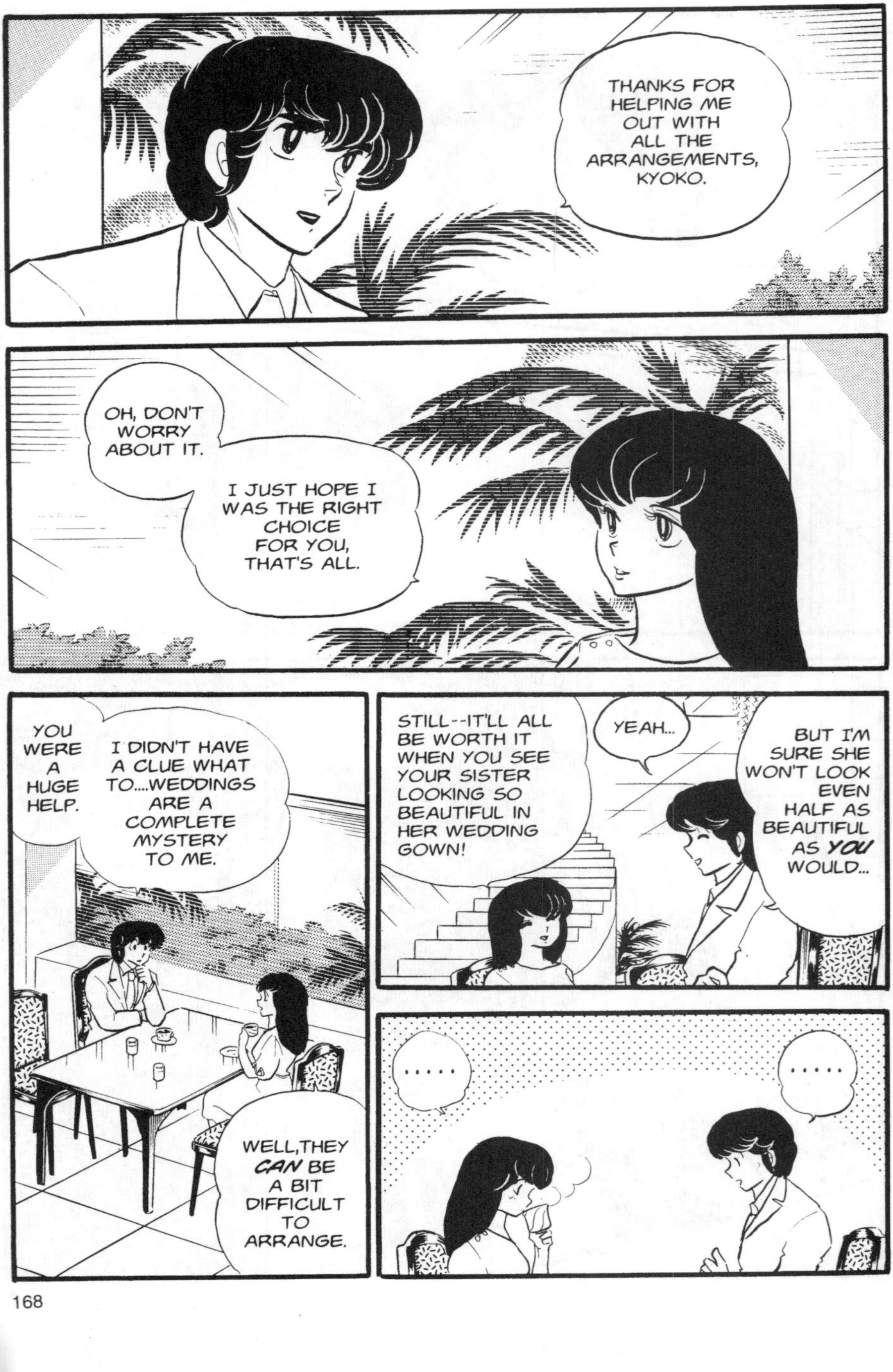
THANKS FOR HELPING ME OUT WITH ALL THE ARRANGEMENTS, KYOKO.
OH, DON'T WORRY ABOUT IT.
I JUST HOPE I WAS THE RIGHT CHOICE FOR YOU, THAT'S ALL.
YOU WERE A HUGE HELP.
I DIDN'T HAVE A CLUE WHAT TO....WEDDINGS ARE A COMPLETE MYSTERY TO ME.
WELL, THEY *CAN* BE A BIT DIFFICULT TO ARRANGE.
STILL--IT'LL ALL BE WORTH IT WHEN YOU SEE YOUR SISTER LOOKING SO BEAUTIFUL IN HER WEDDING GOWN!
YEAH...
BUT I'M SURE SHE WON'T LOOK EVEN HALF AS BEAUTIFUL AS *YOU* WOULD...
.....
.....

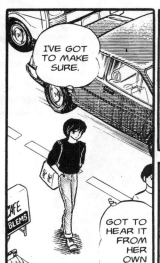

I'VE GOT TO MAKE SURE.
CAFE
GOT TO HEAR IT FROM HER OWN LIPS.
AND IF IT *IS* TRUE...
THEN... THEN WHAT?
KANG KANG KANG KANG
YUSAKU...?
BEEN OUT SOMEWHERE?
BOOKS
Piping HOT
of MOTHER
WELL, YES... I WAS WITH SHUN.
BOOK
Gulp...
I-IS THERE...
...GOING TO BE A... W-WED-DING?
OH...
...YOU'VE ALREADY HEARD?

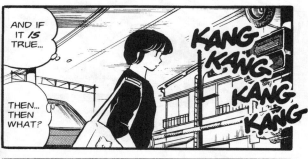

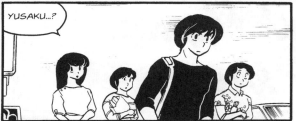

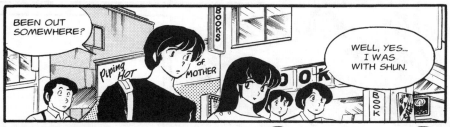

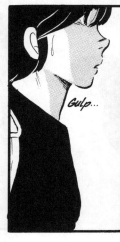

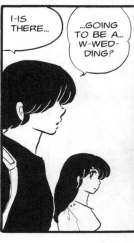

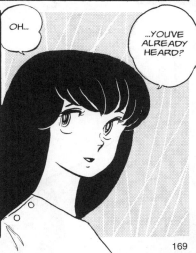

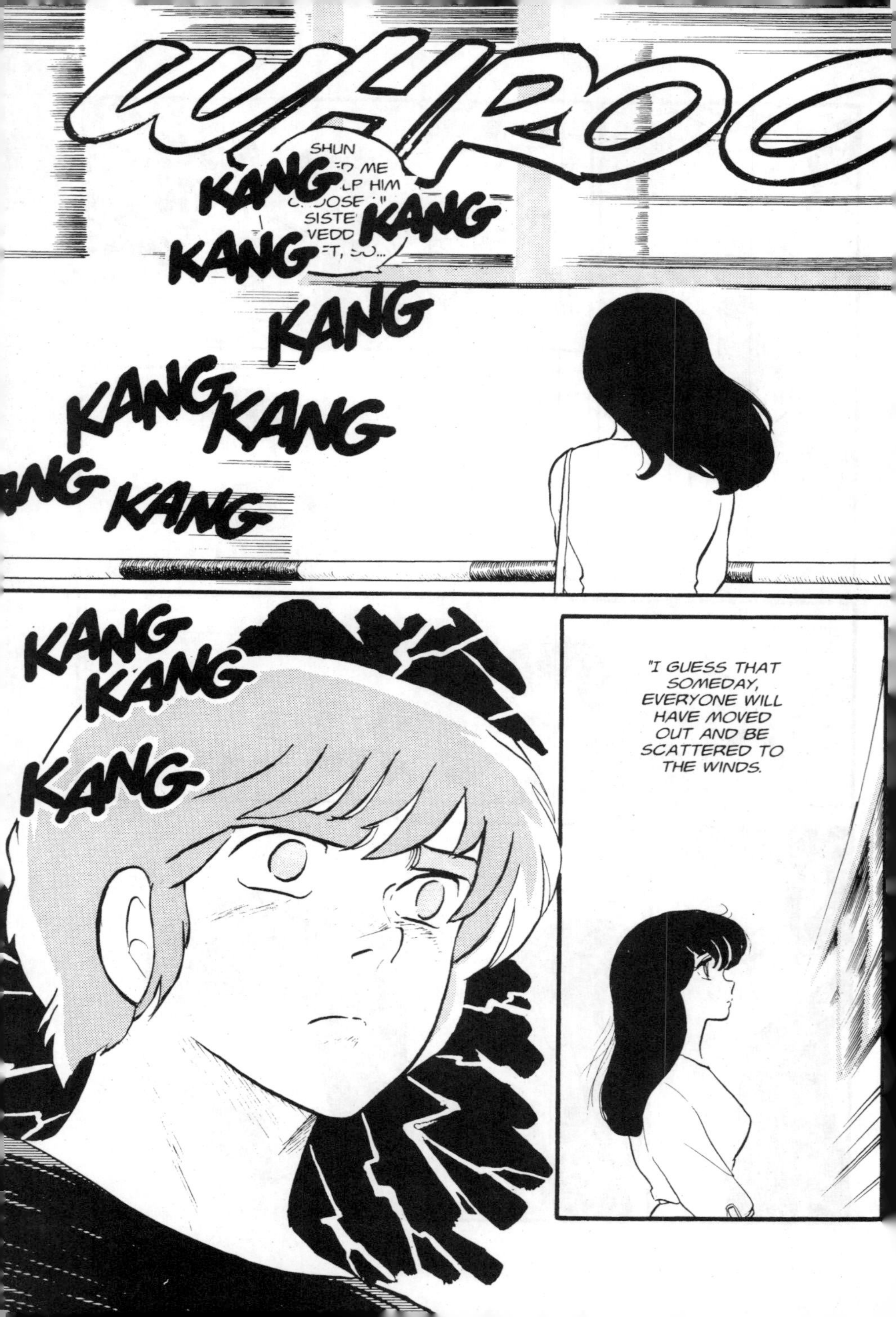
WHROO
SHUN ED ME LP HIM OOSE SISTE VEDD FT, SO...
KANG KANG KANG KANG KANG KANG KANG KANG
KANG KANG KANG
"I GUESS THAT SOMEDAY, EVERYONE WILL HAVE MOVED OUT AND BE SCATTERED TO THE WINDS.

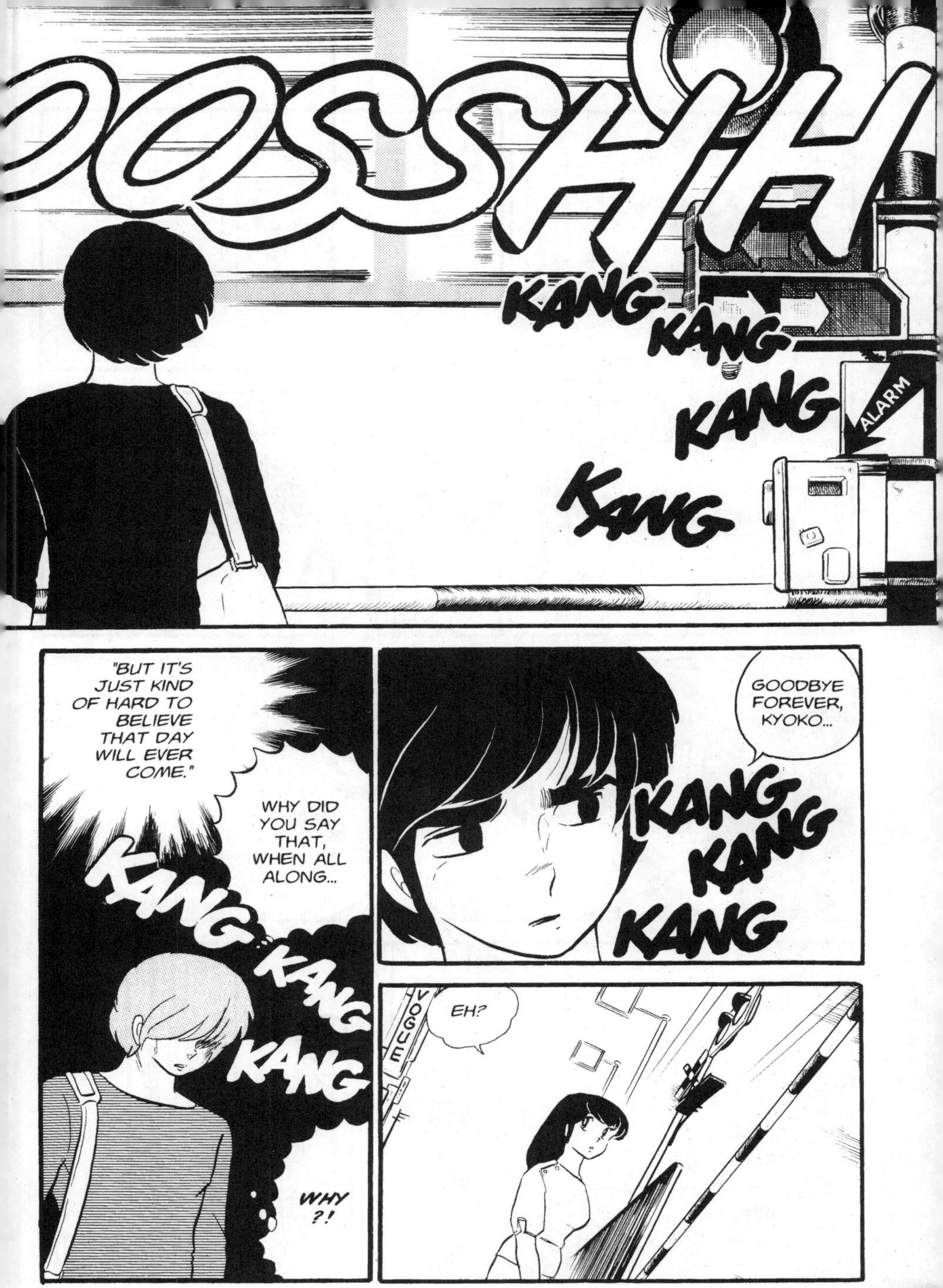
OOSHH
KANG
KANG
KANG
KANG
ALARM
"BUT IT'S JUST KIND OF HARD TO BELIEVE THAT DAY WILL EVER COME."
WHY DID YOU SAY THAT, WHEN ALL ALONG...
KANG KANG KANG KANG
WHY ?!
GOODBYE FOREVER, KYOKO...
KANG KANG KANG
VOGUE
EH?

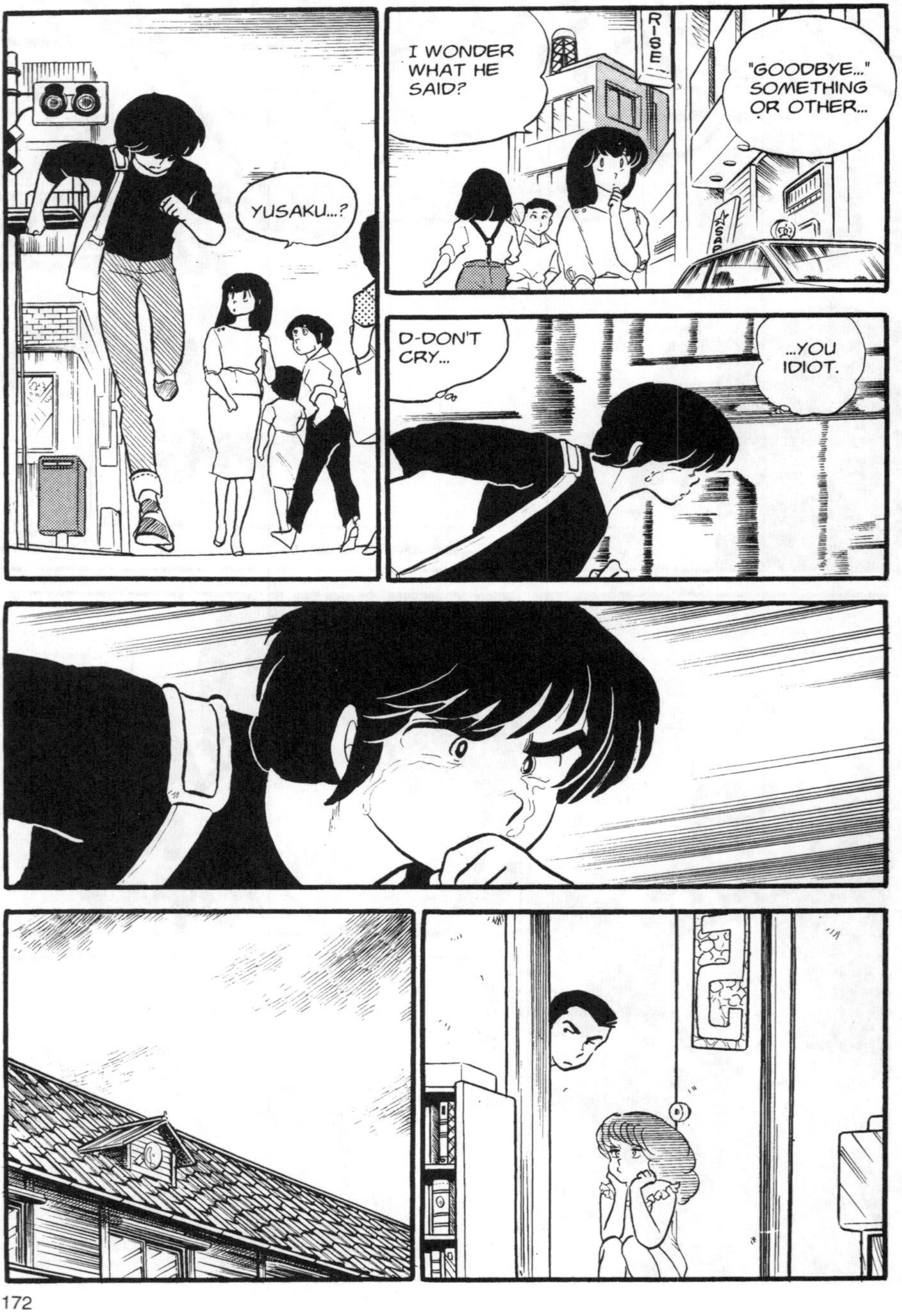
YUSAKU...?
I WONDER WHAT HE SAID?
"GOODBYE..." SOMETHING OR OTHER...
D-DON'T CRY...
...YOU IDIOT.

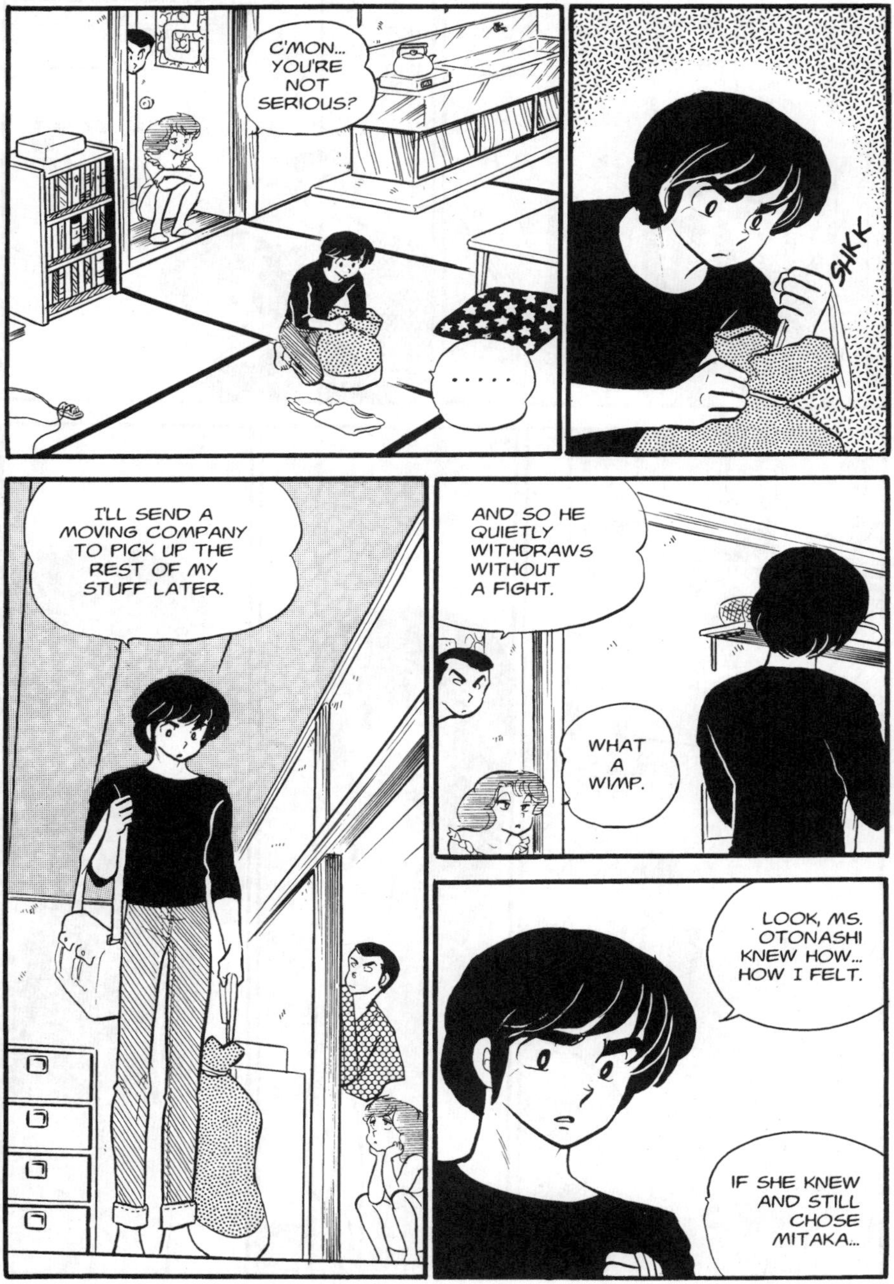
C'MON... YOU'RE NOT SERIOUS?
.....
SHKK
I'LL SEND A MOVING COMPANY TO PICK UP THE REST OF MY STUFF LATER.
AND SO HE QUIETLY WITHDRAWS WITHOUT A FIGHT.
WHAT A WIMP.
LOOK, MS. OTONASHI KNEW HOW... HOW I FELT.
IF SHE KNEW AND STILL CHOSE MITAKA...

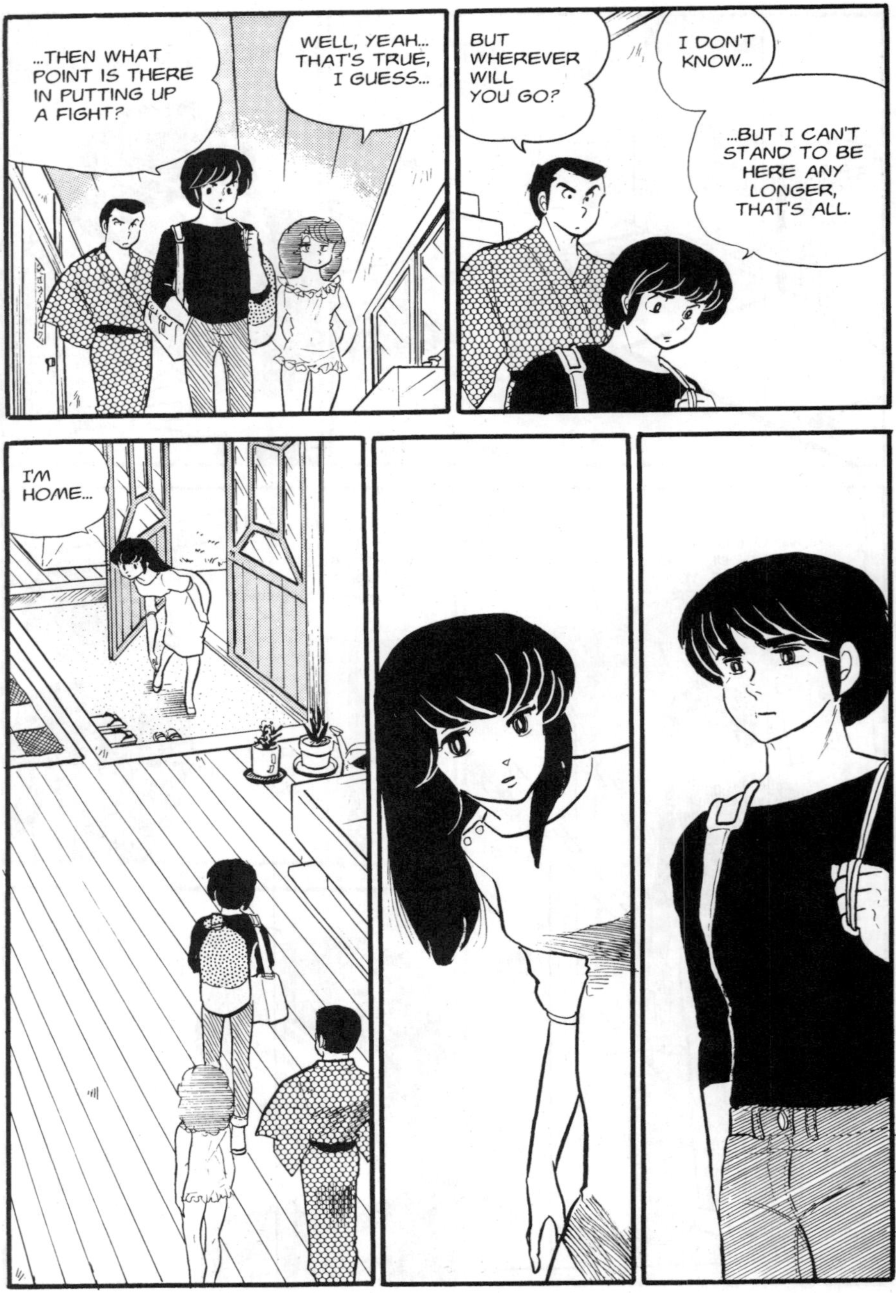
...THEN WHAT POINT IS THERE IN PUTTING UP A FIGHT?
WELL, YEAH... THAT'S TRUE, I GUESS...
BUT WHEREVER WILL YOU GO?
I DON'T KNOW...
...BUT I CAN'T STAND TO BE HERE ANY LONGER, THAT'S ALL.
I'M HOME...

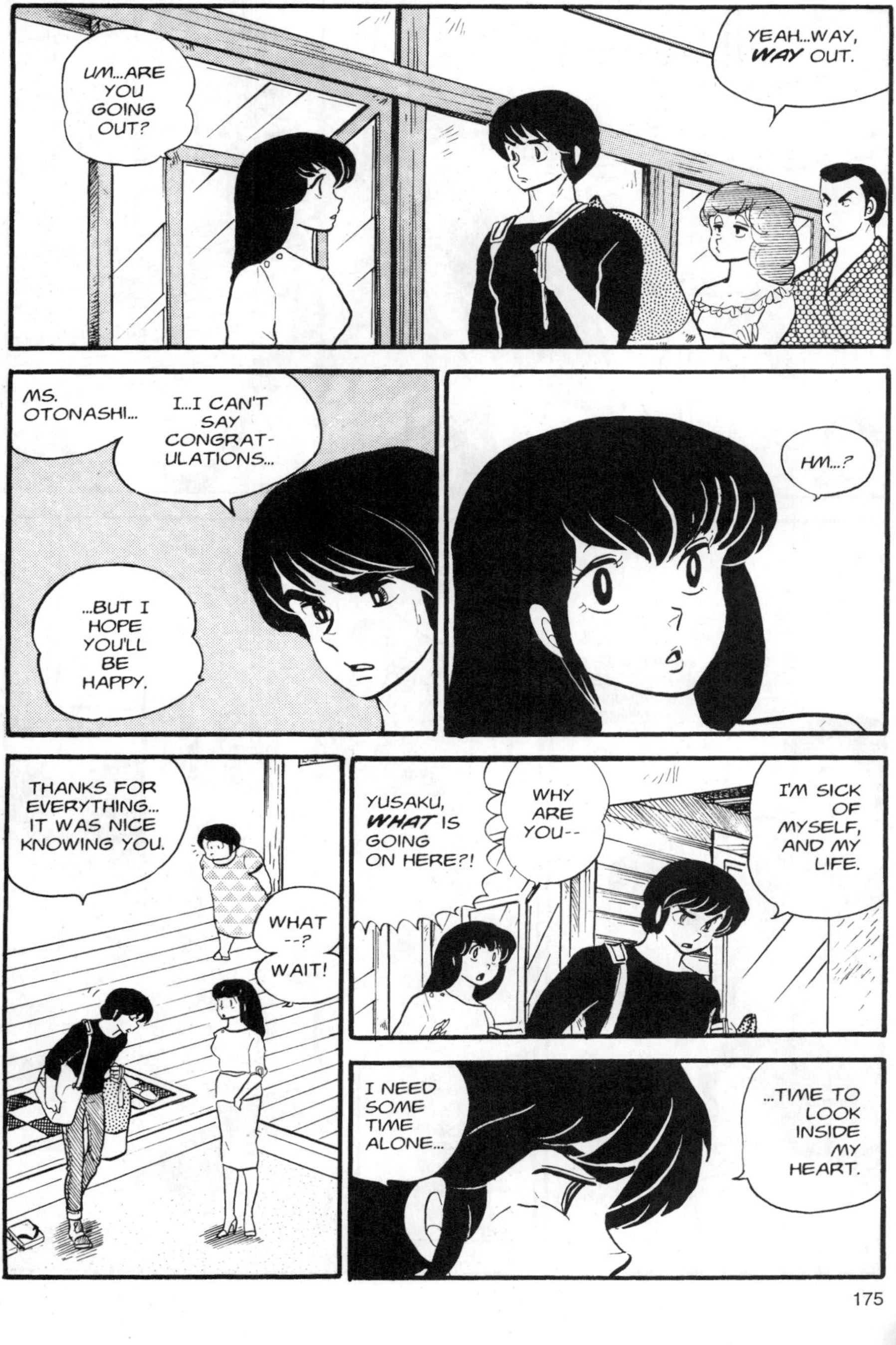
UM...ARE YOU GOING OUT?
YEAH...WAY, WAY OUT.
MS. OTONASHI...
I...I CAN'T SAY CONGRAT-ULATIONS...
...BUT I HOPE YOU'LL BE HAPPY.
HM...?
THANKS FOR EVERYTHING... IT WAS NICE KNOWING YOU.
WHAT --?
WAIT!
YUSAKU, WHAT IS GOING ON HERE?!
WHY ARE YOU--
I'M SICK OF MYSELF, AND MY LIFE.
I NEED SOME TIME ALONE...
...TIME TO LOOK INSIDE MY HEART.

GOODBYE!

HE HAS SURELY DONE IT, THIS TIME.

WHAT DO YOU S'POSE HE'S GONNA DO NOW?

WHO KNOWS? BUT FOR STARTERS...

...WHEN DO YOU THINK HE'S GOING TO GET UP?

HIS BIG EXIT KINDA FELL FLAT, HUH?

AND SO I "KISSED" MAISON IKKOKU GOODBYE...

Part Nine

A Small Space

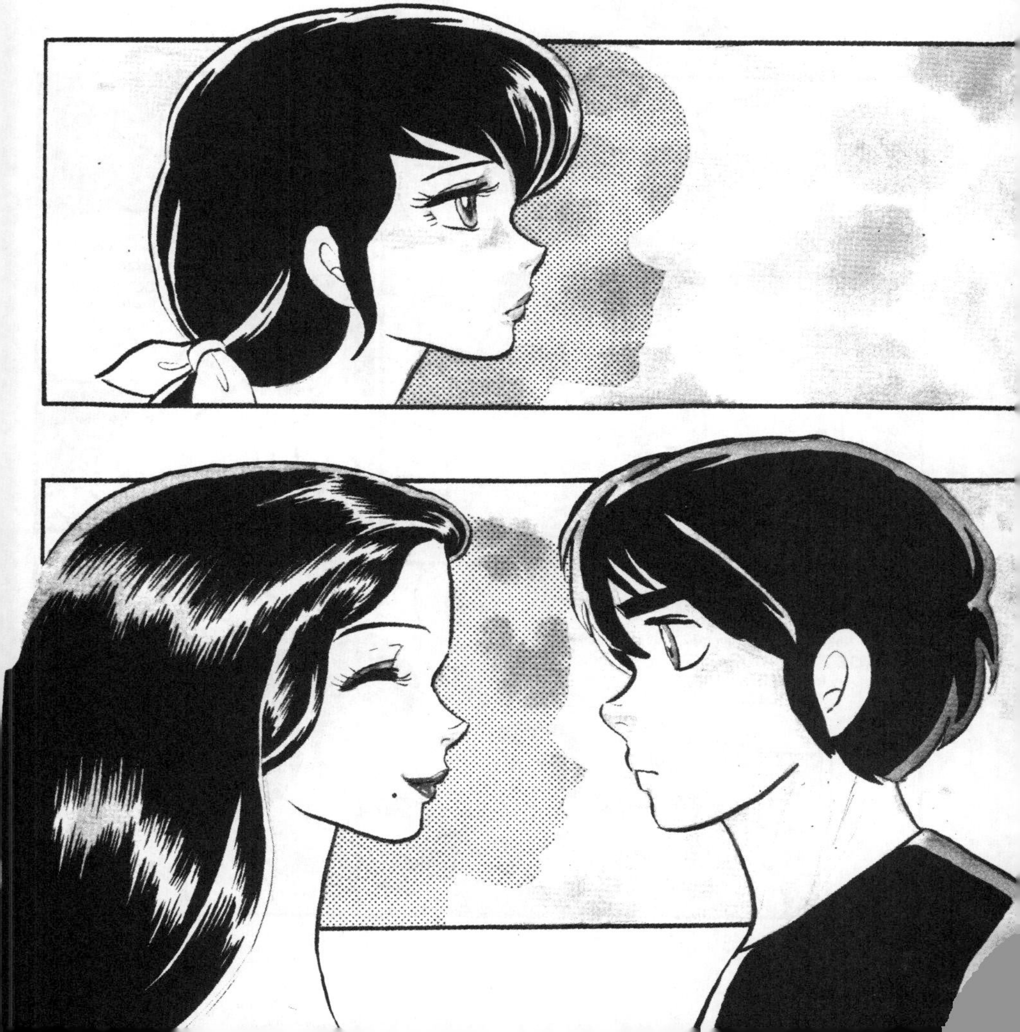

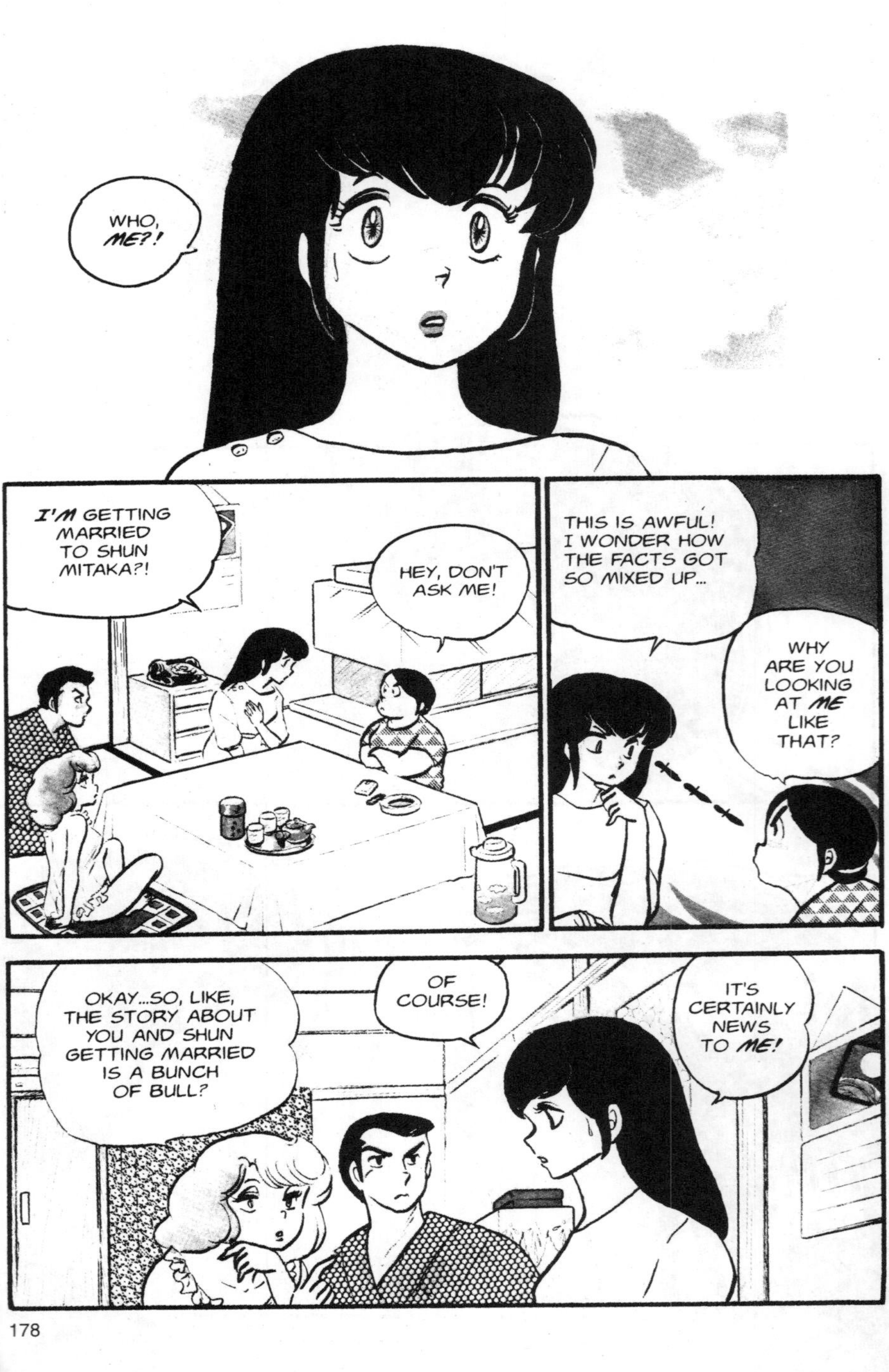
WHO, ME?!
I'M GETTING MARRIED TO SHUN MITAKA?!
HEY, DON'T ASK ME!
THIS IS AWFUL! I WONDER HOW THE FACTS GOT SO MIXED UP...
WHY ARE YOU LOOKING AT ME LIKE THAT?
OKAY...SO, LIKE, THE STORY ABOUT YOU AND SHUN GETTING MARRIED IS A BUNCH OF BULL?
OF COURSE!
IT'S CERTAINLY NEWS TO ME!

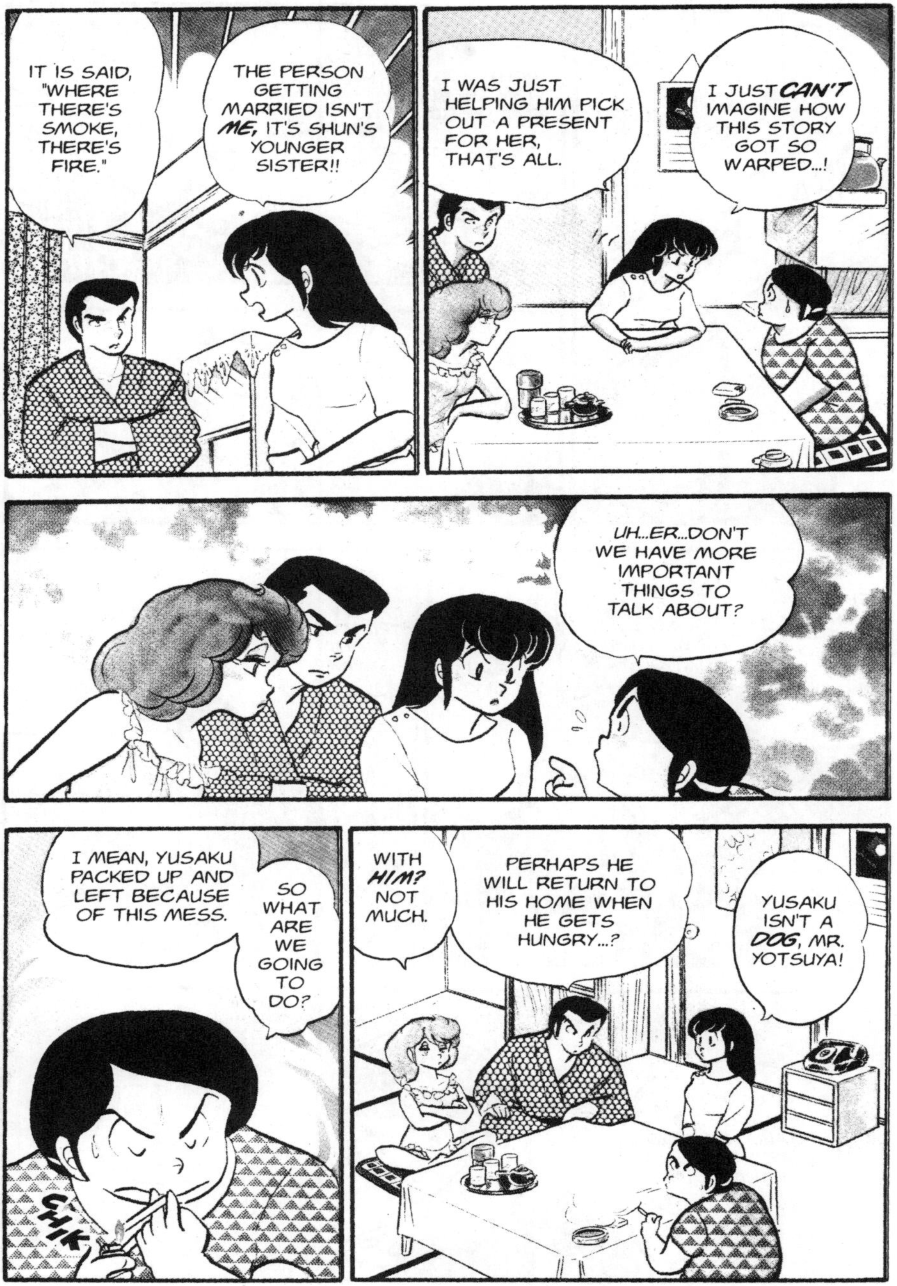
IT IS SAID, "WHERE THERE'S SMOKE, THERE'S FIRE."
THE PERSON GETTING MARRIED ISN'T ME, IT'S SHUN'S YOUNGER SISTER!!
I WAS JUST HELPING HIM PICK OUT A PRESENT FOR HER, THAT'S ALL.
I JUST CAN'T IMAGINE HOW THIS STORY GOT SO WARPED...!
UH...ER...DON'T WE HAVE MORE IMPORTANT THINGS TO TALK ABOUT?
I MEAN, YUSAKU PACKED UP AND LEFT BECAUSE OF THIS MESS.
SO WHAT ARE WE GOING TO DO?
CHIK
WITH HIM? NOT MUCH.
PERHAPS HE WILL RETURN TO HIS HOME WHEN HE GETS HUNGRY...?
YUSAKU ISN'T A DOG, MR. YOTSUYA!

THE NEXT DAY...

REAL ESTATE

RIGHT, JUST SIGN THERE, AND THERE.

I'VE GOTTA SAY, YOU'RE ONE LUCKY YOUNG MAN.

CH/NGG

THIS APARTMENT WAS JUST LISTED THIS MORNING.

YOU HARDLY EVER SEE ONE SO NEAR THE STATION FOR ONLY ¥20,000.

YEAH...

I TELL YA, KID-- YOU'RE DAMN LUCKY.

SO I FOUND A NEW PLACE RIGHT AWAY.

ROCK HILL ATION WI

BY SIGNING, I TRULY SEVERED MY TIES TO MAISON IKKOKU.

THIS IS MY CHANCE TO REALLY CHANGE MY LIFE...TO FIND MYSELF.

FOR ONE THING, I'M THROUGH WITH WOMEN!

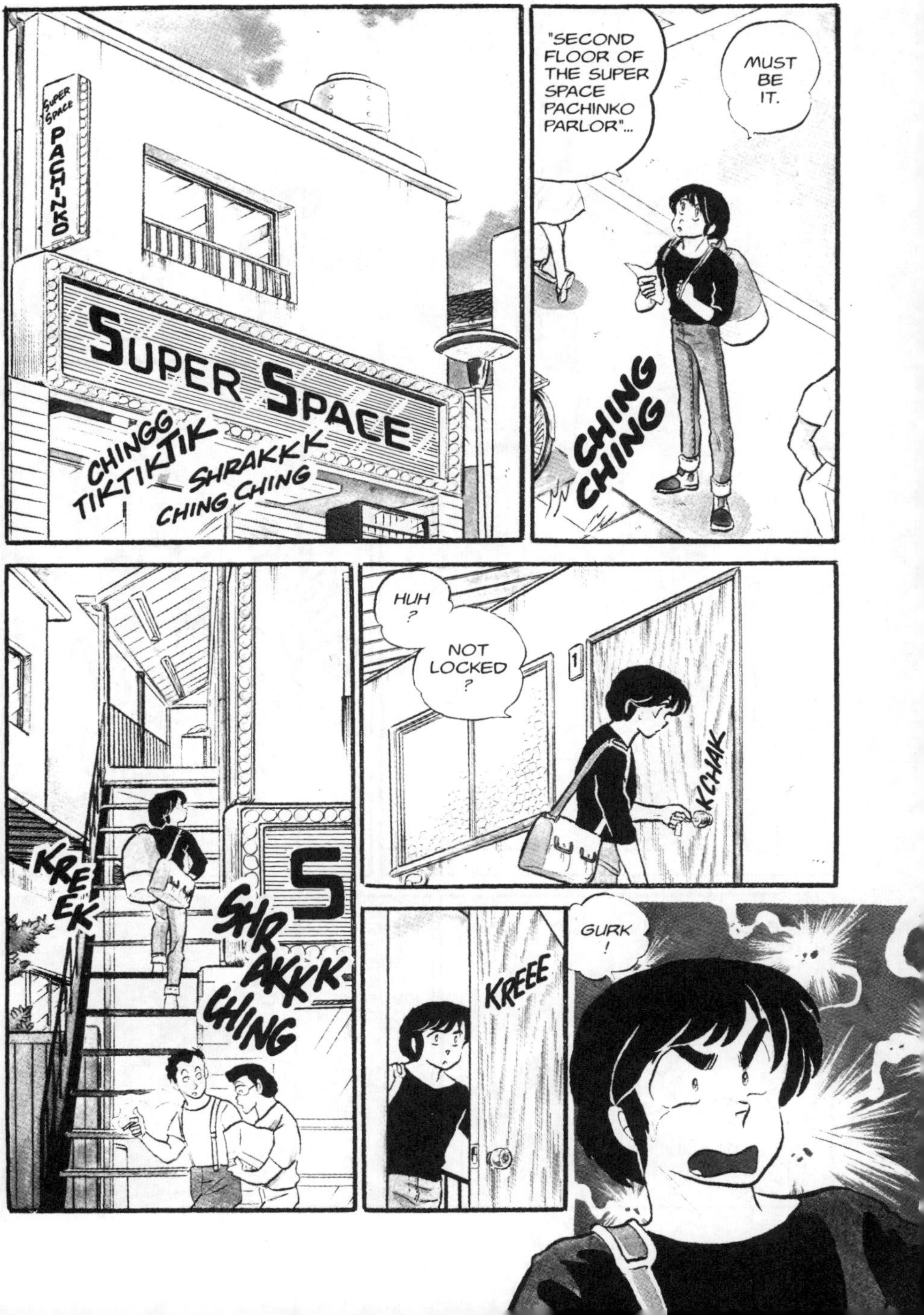
SUPER SPACE PACHINKO
SUPER SPACE
CHINGG TIKTIKTIK SHRAKKK CHING CHING
"SECOND FLOOR OF THE SUPER SPACE PACHINKO PARLOR"...
MUST BE IT.
CHING CHING
KREEEK
SHRAKKK CHING
HUH?
NOT LOCKED?
KCHAK
KREEE
GURK!

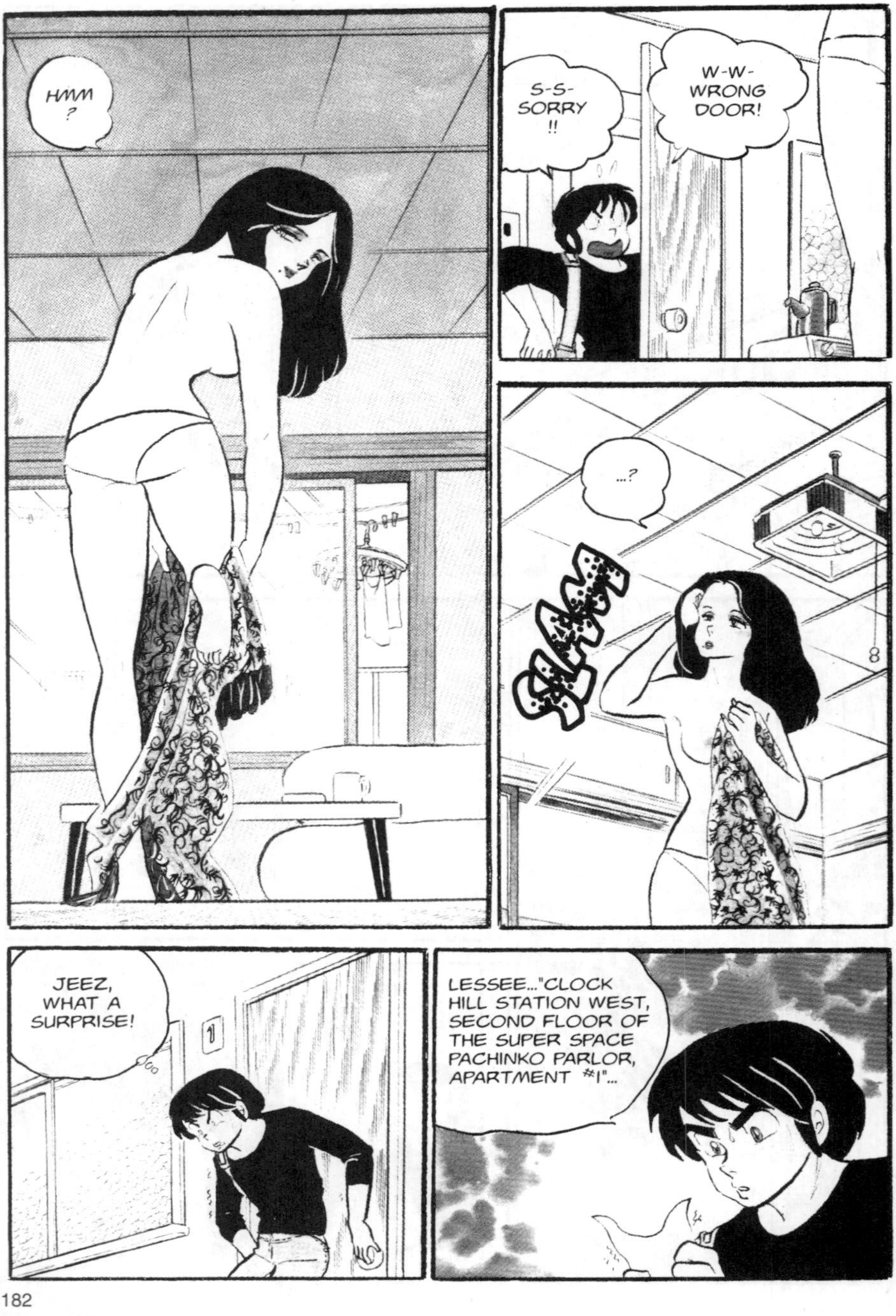

HMM ?
S-S-SORRY !!
W-W-WRONG DOOR!
...?
SLAM
JEEZ, WHAT A SURPRISE!
LESSEE..."CLOCK HILL STATION WEST, SECOND FLOOR OF THE SUPER SPACE PACHINKO PARLOR, APARTMENT #1"...

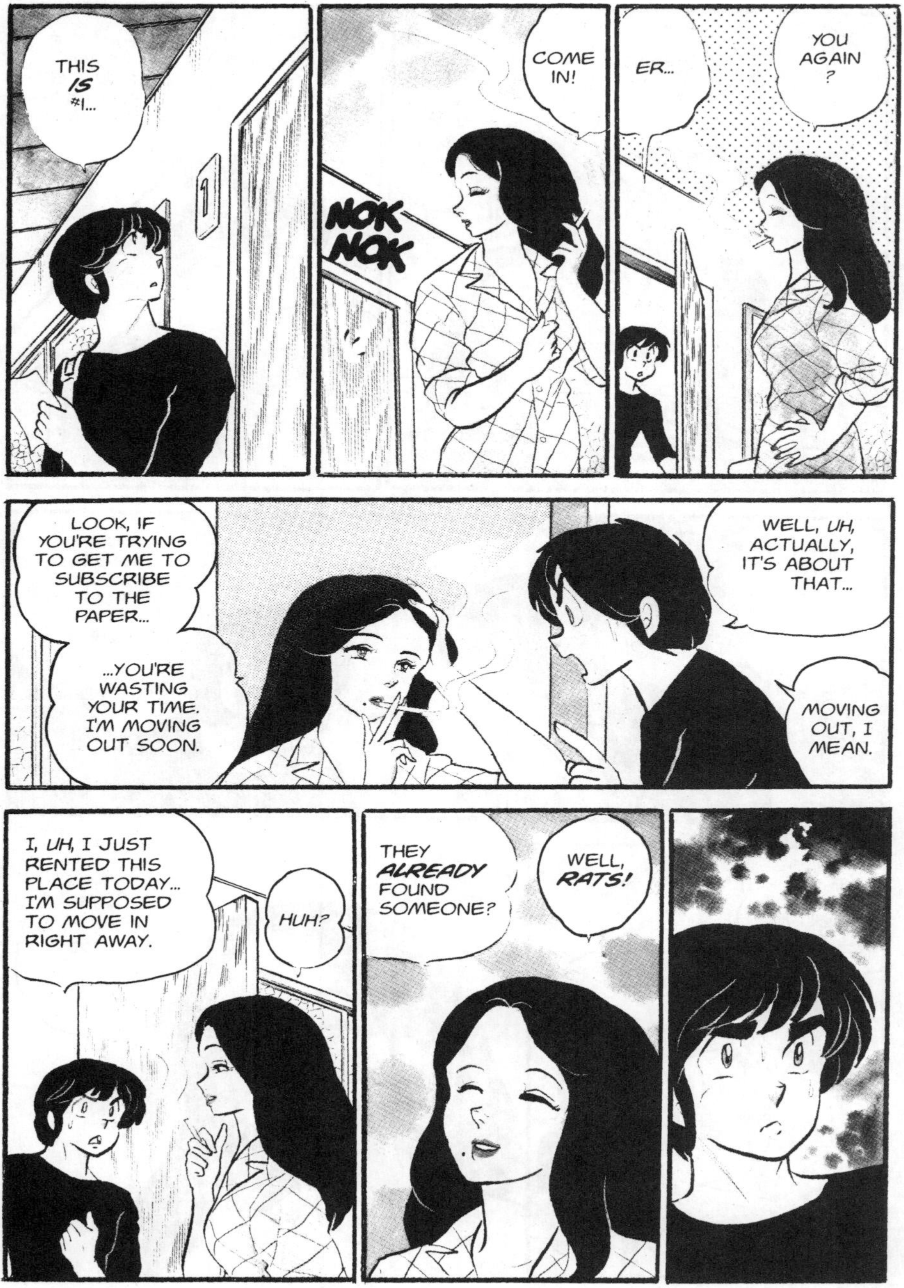

THIS *IS* #1...
COME IN!
NOK NOK
ER...
YOU AGAIN ?
LOOK, IF YOU'RE TRYING TO GET ME TO SUBSCRIBE TO THE PAPER...
...YOU'RE WASTING YOUR TIME. I'M MOVING OUT SOON.
WELL, *UH*, ACTUALLY, IT'S ABOUT THAT...
MOVING OUT, I MEAN.
I, *UH*, I JUST RENTED THIS PLACE TODAY... I'M SUPPOSED TO MOVE IN RIGHT AWAY.
HUH?
THEY *ALREADY* FOUND SOMEONE?
WELL, *RATS!*

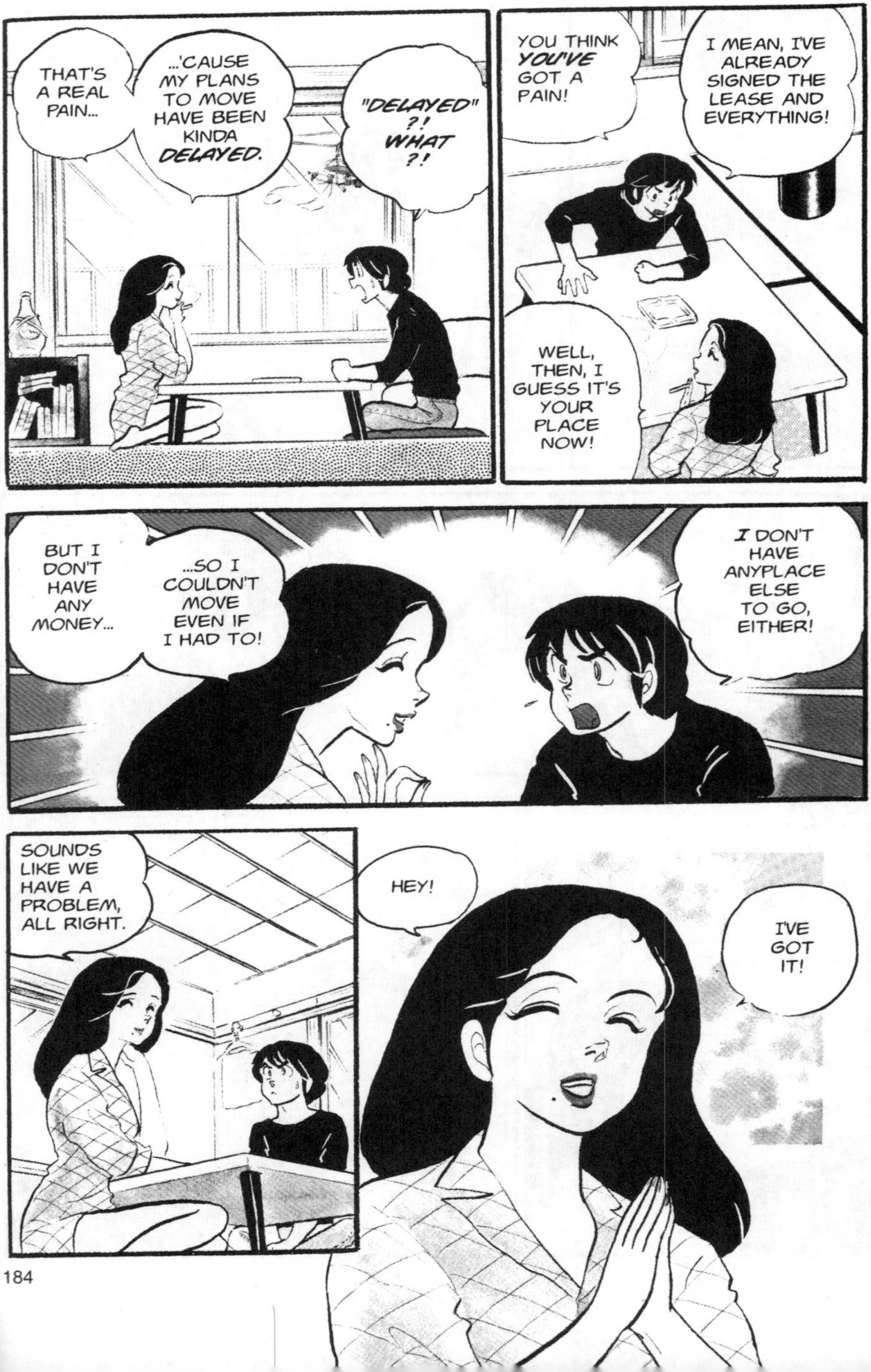
THAT'S A REAL PAIN...
...'CAUSE MY PLANS TO MOVE HAVE BEEN KINDA DELAYED.
"DELAYED" ?! WHAT ?!
YOU THINK YOU'VE GOT A PAIN!
I MEAN, I'VE ALREADY SIGNED THE LEASE AND EVERYTHING!
WELL, THEN, I GUESS IT'S YOUR PLACE NOW!
BUT I DON'T HAVE ANY MONEY...
...SO I COULDN'T MOVE EVEN IF I HAD TO!
I DON'T HAVE ANYPLACE ELSE TO GO, EITHER!
SOUNDS LIKE WE HAVE A PROBLEM, ALL RIGHT.
HEY!
I'VE GOT IT!

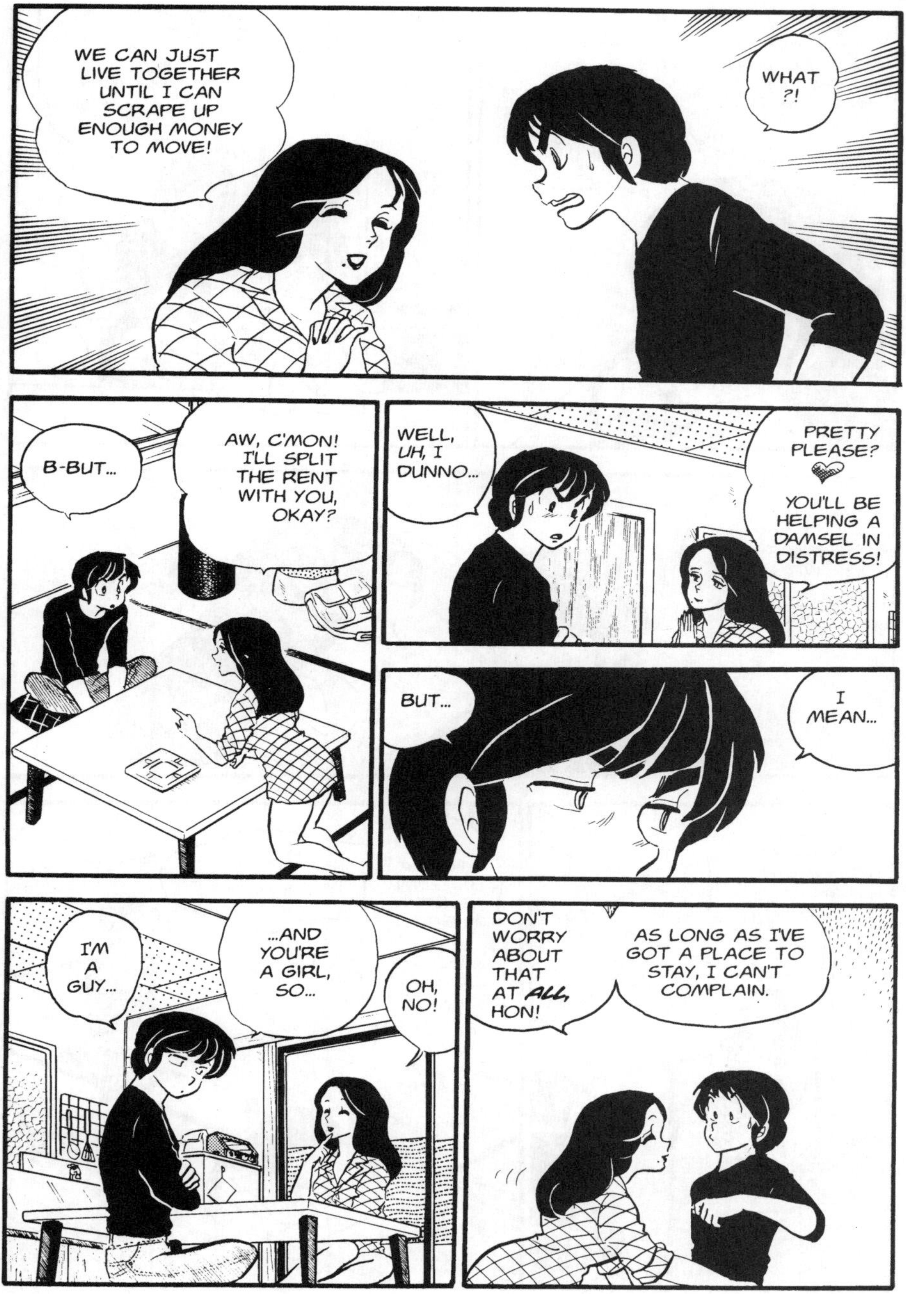
WE CAN JUST LIVE TOGETHER UNTIL I CAN SCRAPE UP ENOUGH MONEY TO MOVE!
WHAT ?!
B-BUT...
AW, C'MON! I'LL SPLIT THE RENT WITH YOU, OKAY?
WELL, UH, I DUNNO...
PRETTY PLEASE?
YOU'LL BE HELPING A DAMSEL IN DISTRESS!
BUT...
I MEAN...
I'M A GUY...
...AND YOU'RE A GIRL, SO...
OH, NO!
DON'T WORRY ABOUT THAT AT ALL, HON!
AS LONG AS I'VE GOT A PLACE TO STAY, I CAN'T COMPLAIN.

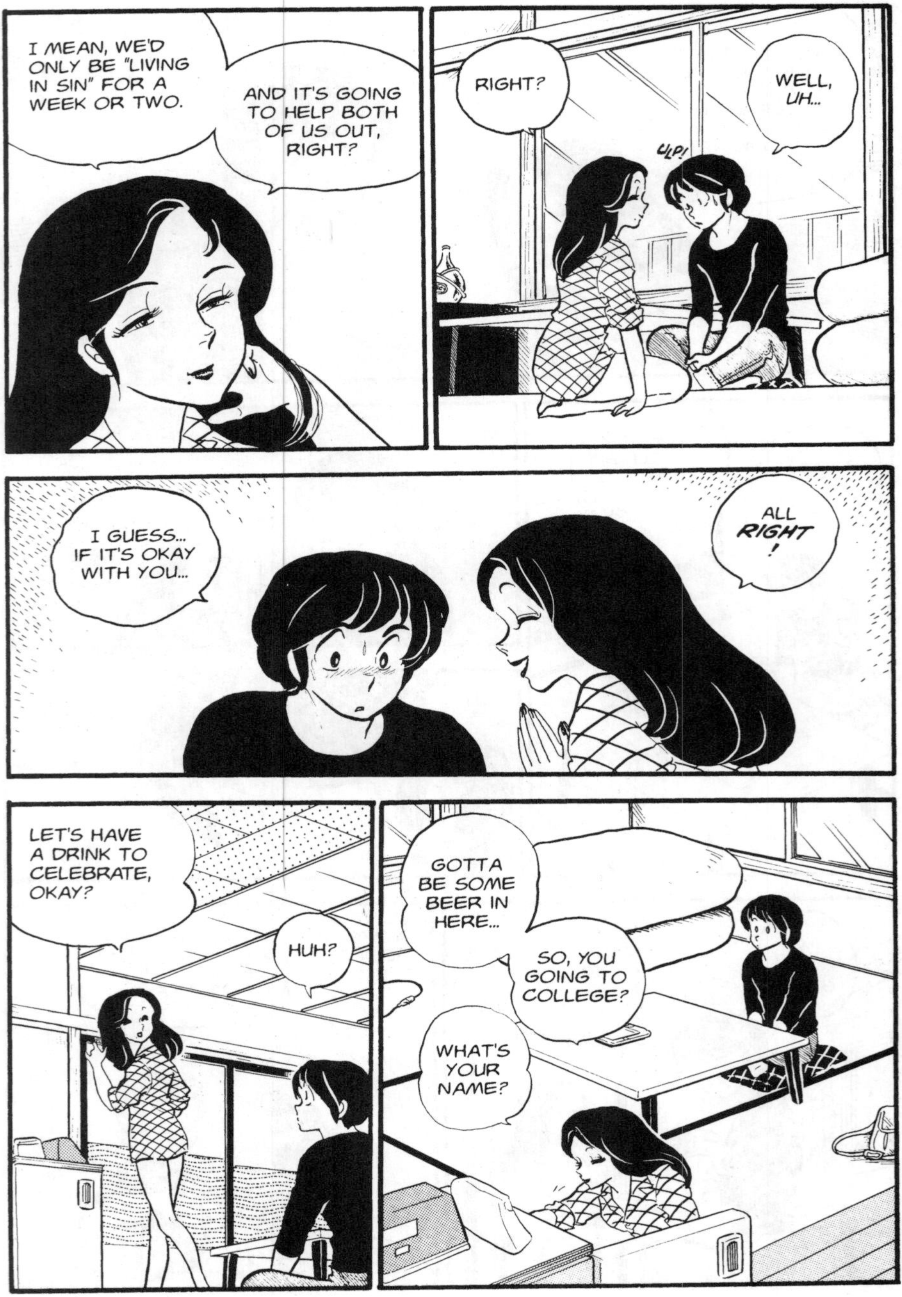
I MEAN, WE'D ONLY BE "LIVING IN SIN" FOR A WEEK OR TWO.
AND IT'S GOING TO HELP BOTH OF US OUT, RIGHT?
RIGHT?
WELL, UH...
ULP!
I GUESS... IF IT'S OKAY WITH YOU...
ALL RIGHT!
LET'S HAVE A DRINK TO CELEBRATE, OKAY?
HUH?
GOTTA BE SOME BEER IN HERE...
SO, YOU GOING TO COLLEGE?
WHAT'S YOUR NAME?

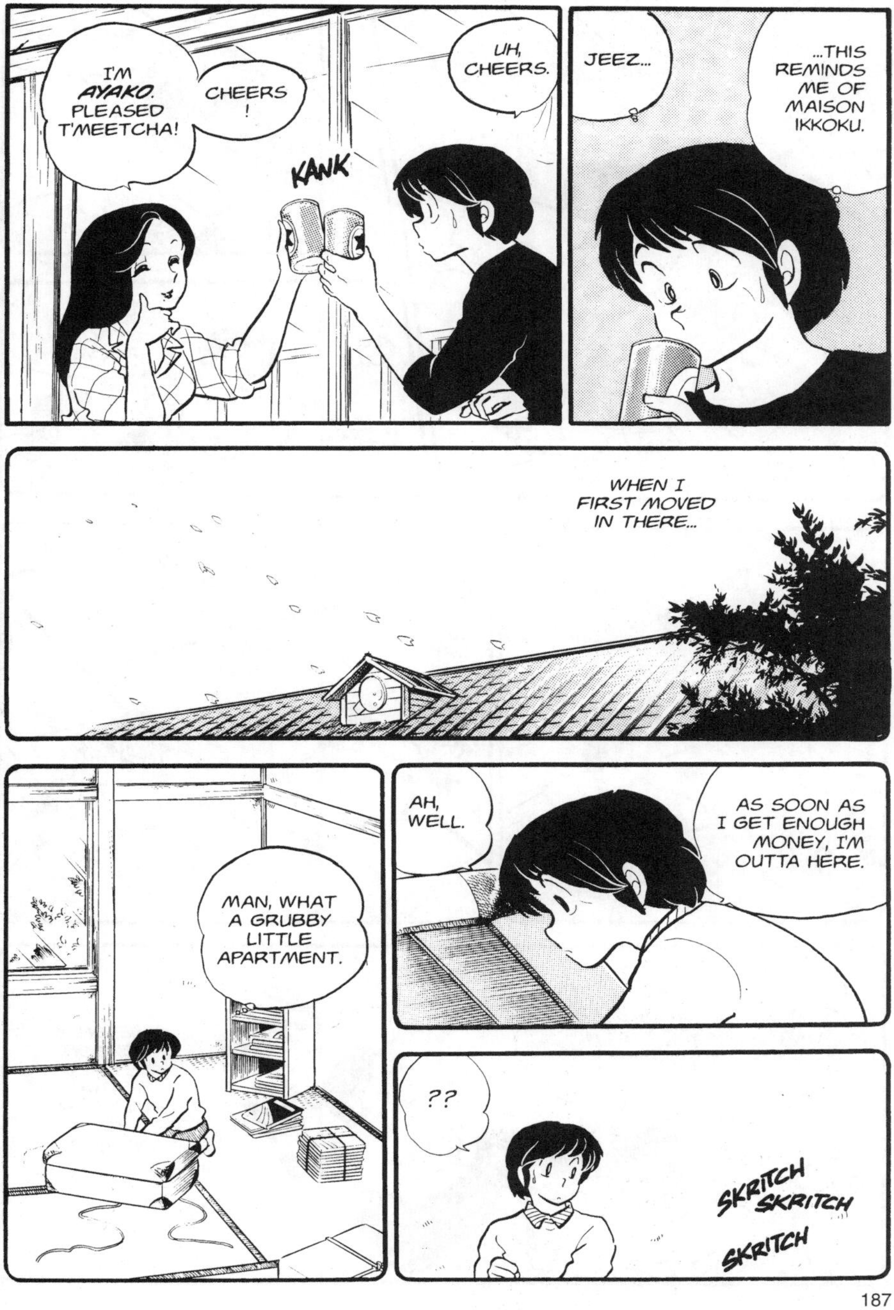
I'M AYAKO. PLEASED T'MEETCHA!
CHEERS!
UH, CHEERS.
KANK
JEEZ...
...THIS REMINDS ME OF MAISON IKKOKU.
WHEN I FIRST MOVED IN THERE...
MAN, WHAT A GRUBBY LITTLE APARTMENT.
AH, WELL.
AS SOON AS I GET ENOUGH MONEY, I'M OUTTA HERE.
??
SKRITCH SKRITCH
SKRITCH

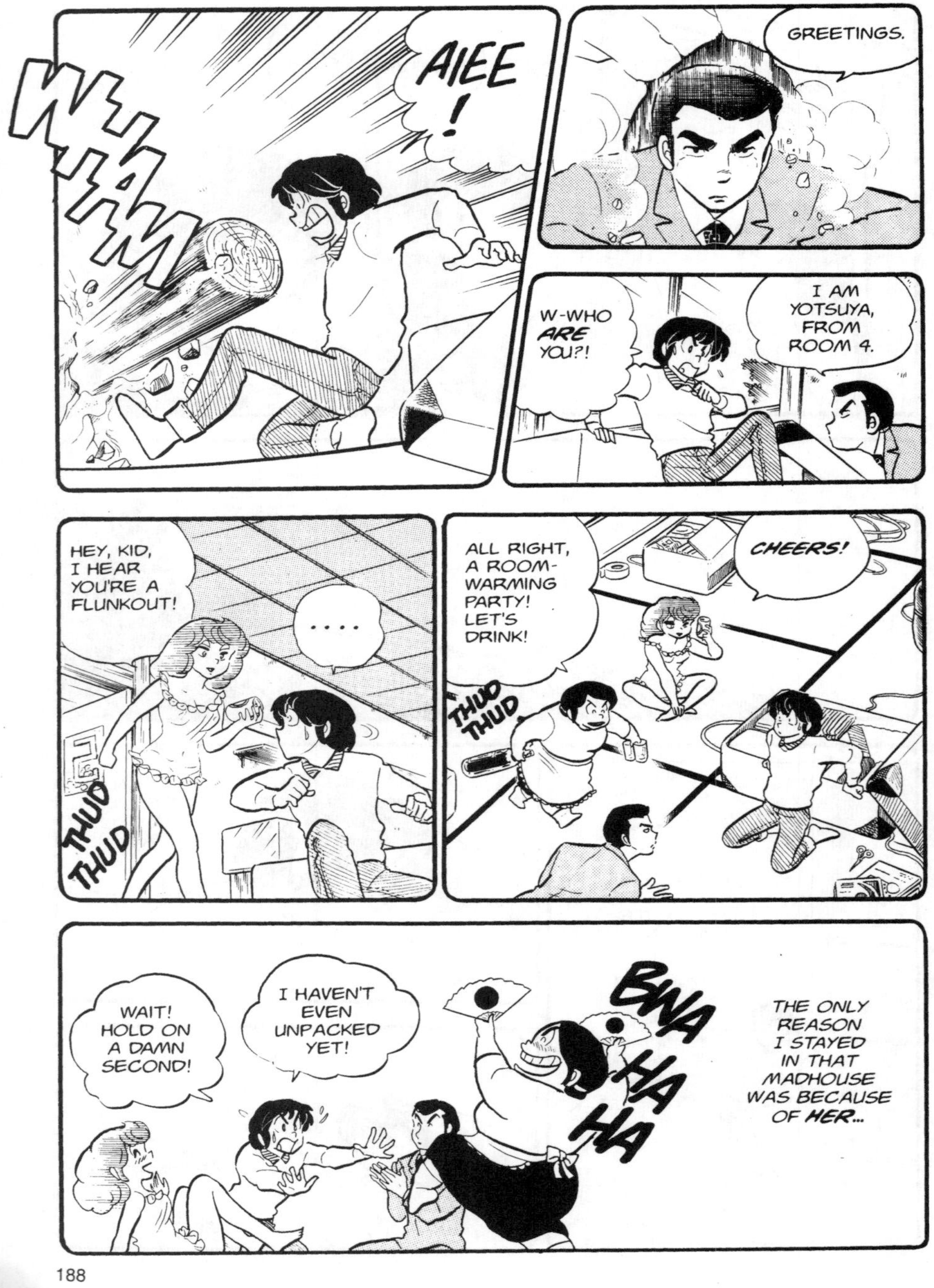
WHAM
AIEE!
GREETINGS.
W-WHO ARE YOU?!
I AM YOTSUYA, FROM ROOM 4.
HEY, KID, I HEAR YOU'RE A FLUNKOUT!
....
THUD THUD
ALL RIGHT, A ROOM-WARMING PARTY! LET'S DRINK!
CHEERS!
THUD THUD
WAIT! HOLD ON A DAMN SECOND!
I HAVEN'T EVEN UNPACKED YET!
BWA HA HA HA
THE ONLY REASON I STAYED IN THAT MADHOUSE WAS BECAUSE OF HER...

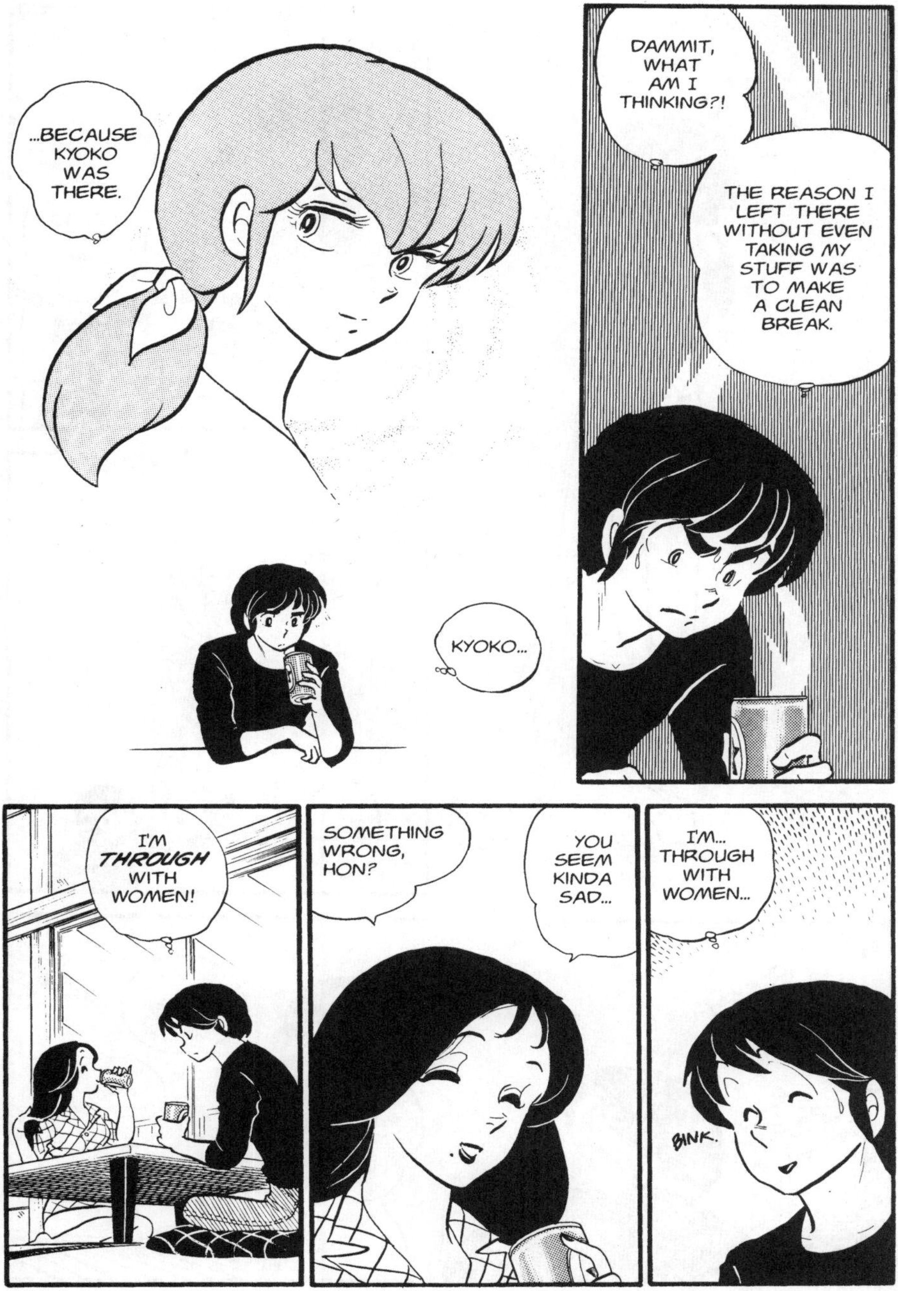
...BECAUSE KYOKO WAS THERE.
KYOKO...
DAMMIT, WHAT AM I THINKING?!
THE REASON I LEFT THERE WITHOUT EVEN TAKING MY STUFF WAS TO MAKE A CLEAN BREAK.
I'M ***THROUGH*** WITH WOMEN!
SOMETHING WRONG, HON?
YOU SEEM KINDA SAD...
I'M... THROUGH WITH WOMEN...
BINK.

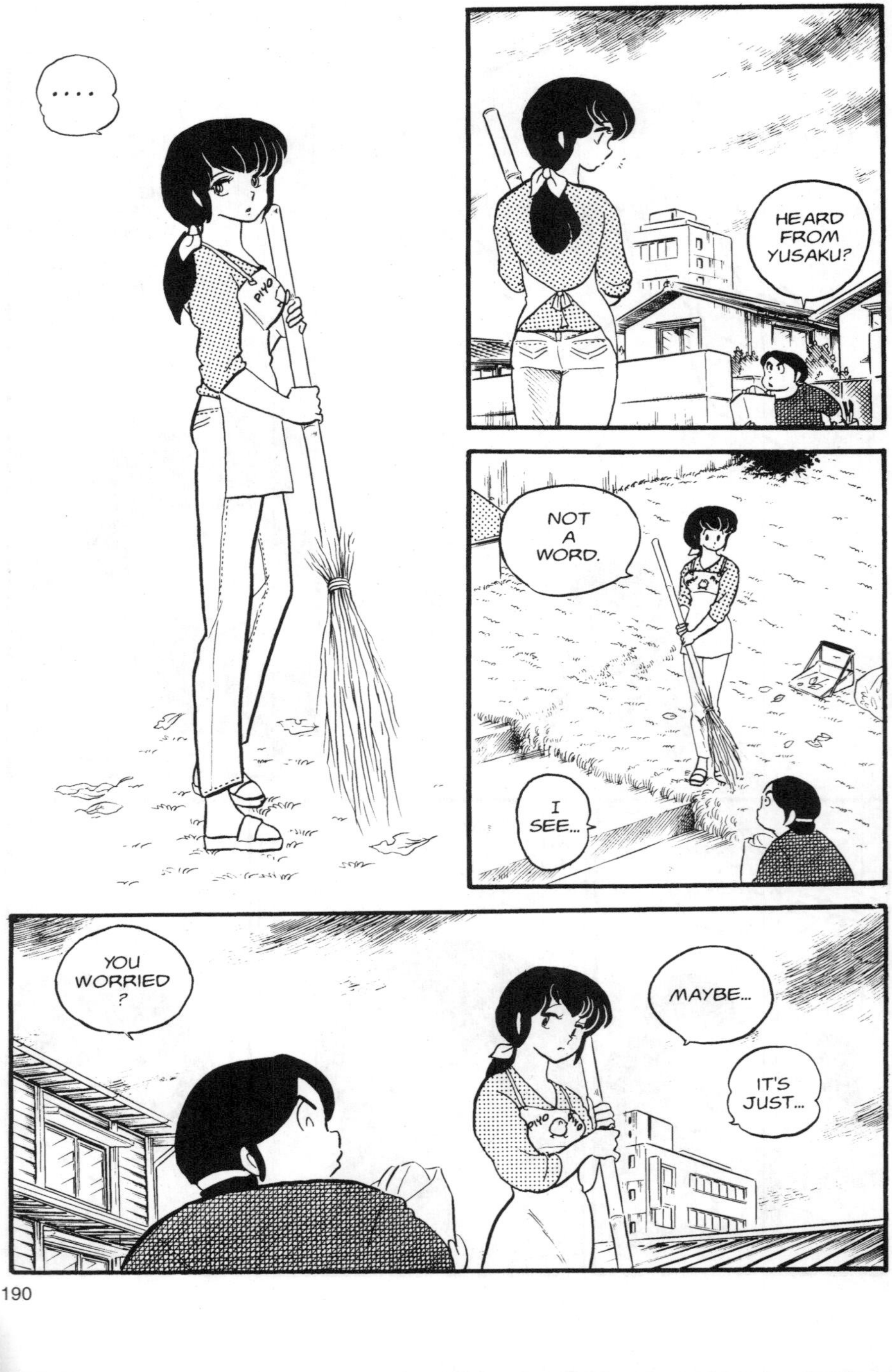
....
HEARD FROM YUSAKU?
NOT A WORD.
I SEE...
YOU WORRIED ?
MAYBE...
IT'S JUST...

...WELL, I JUST DON'T WANT THINGS TO END THIS WAY.

I WANT HIM TO KNOW THE TRUTH.

WELL, YOU CAN'T BLAME HIM.

THE IDEA OF YOU GETTING MARRIED HIT HIM PRETTY HARD.

BUT IF HE HADN'T FLOWN OFF THE HANDLE, WE WOULDN'T HAVE THIS PROBLEM!

WHAT ARE YOU COMPLAINING ABOUT? AT LEAST IT PROVES HOW STRONGLY HE CARES FOR YOU.

SO WHO'S COMPLAINING?

HE GIVES UP TOO EASILY!

THAT... THAT WIMP!

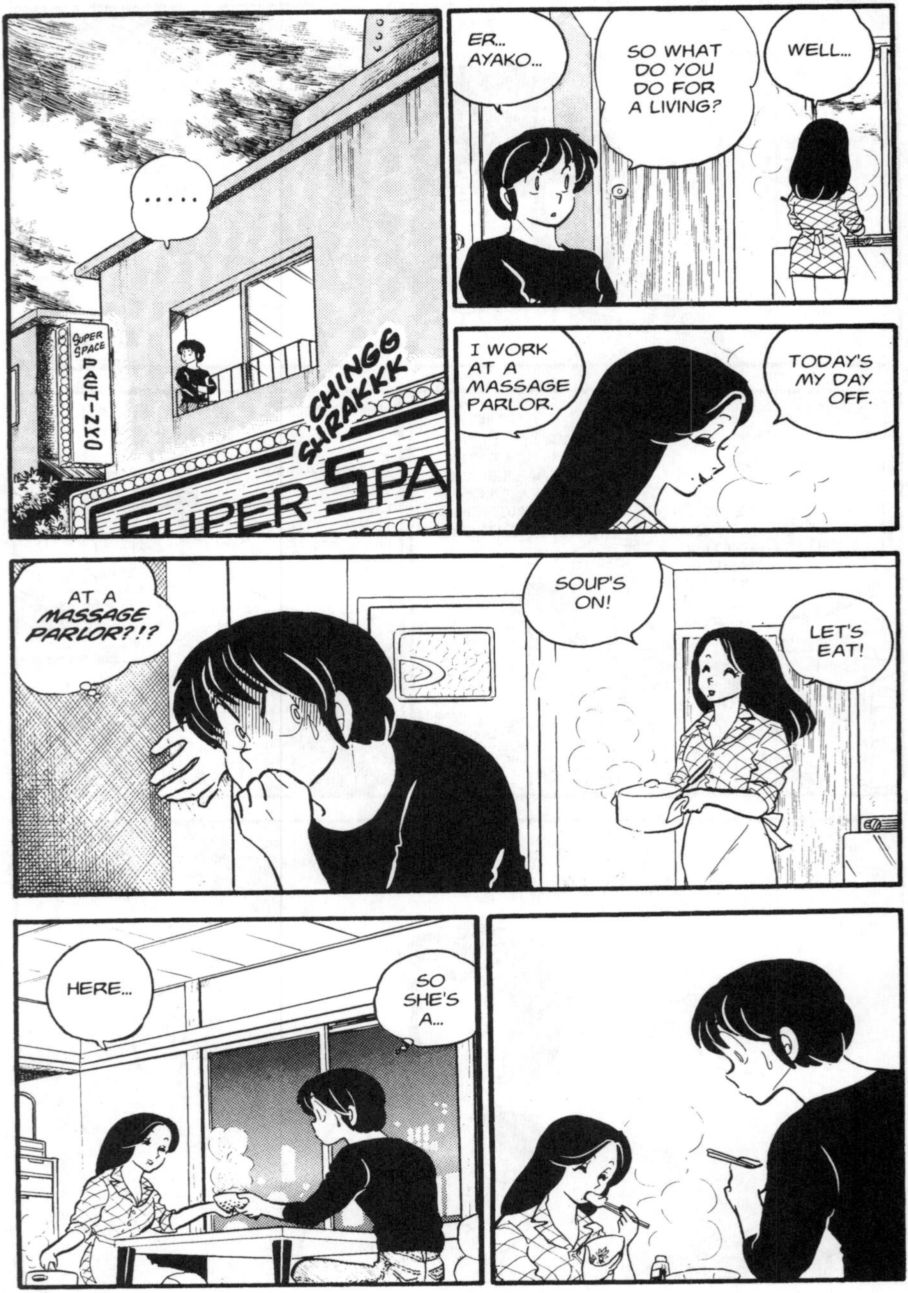
......
SUPER SPACE PACHI-NKO
CHINGG SHRAKKK
SUPER SPA
ER... AYAKO...
SO WHAT DO YOU DO FOR A LIVING?
WELL...
I WORK AT A MASSAGE PARLOR.
TODAY'S MY DAY OFF.
AT A *MASSAGE PARLOR?!?*
SOUP'S ON!
LET'S EAT!
HERE...
SO SHE'S A...

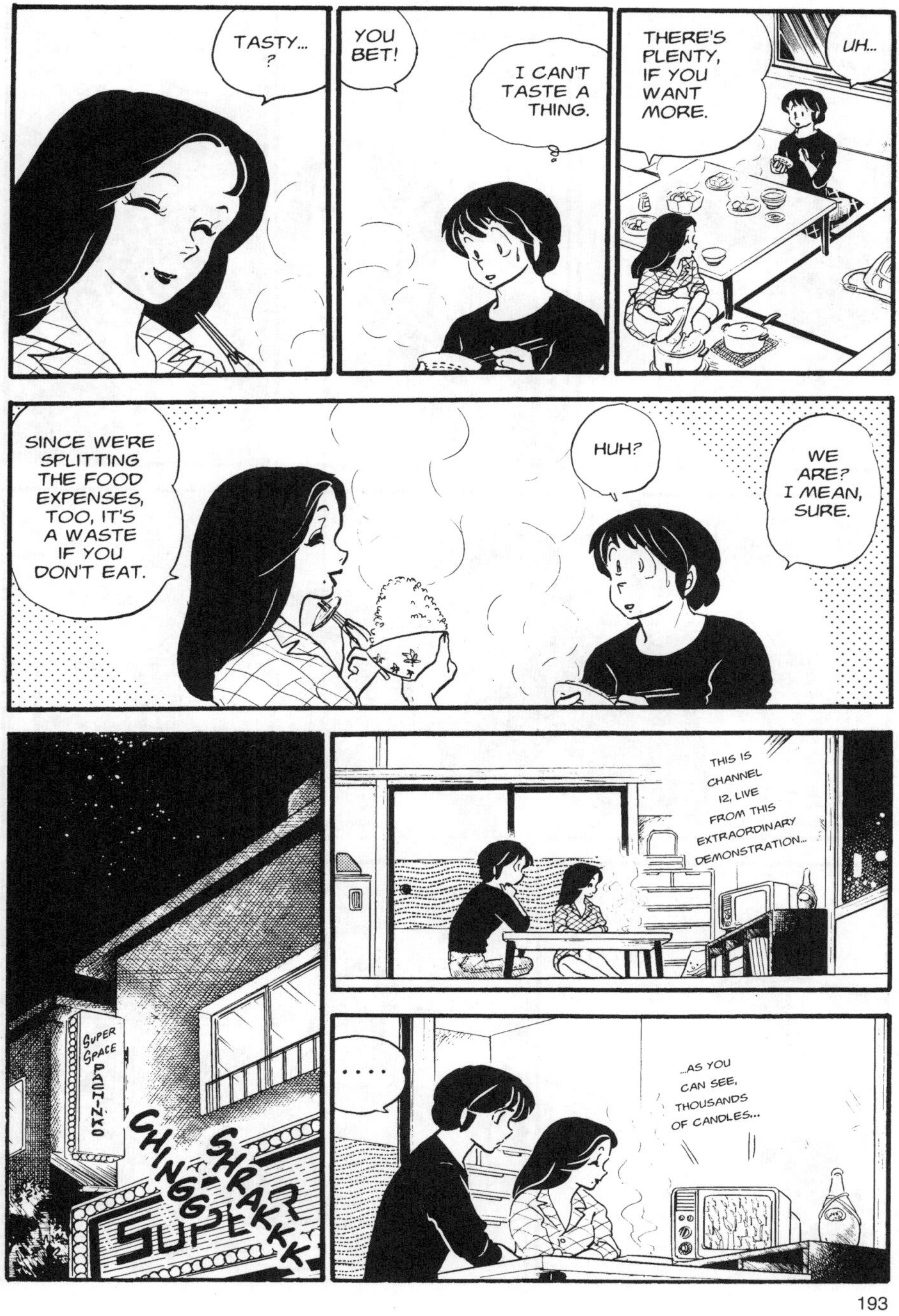

TASTY... ?
YOU BET!
I CAN'T TASTE A THING.
THERE'S PLENTY, IF YOU WANT MORE.
UH...
SINCE WE'RE SPLITTING THE FOOD EXPENSES, TOO, IT'S A WASTE IF YOU DON'T EAT.
HUH?
WE ARE? I MEAN, SURE.
SUPER SPACE PACHINKO
SUPER
CHINGG-
SHRAKKK
THIS IS CHANNEL 12, LIVE FROM THIS EXTRAORDINARY DEMONSTRATION...
....
...AS YOU CAN SEE, THOUSANDS OF CANDLES...

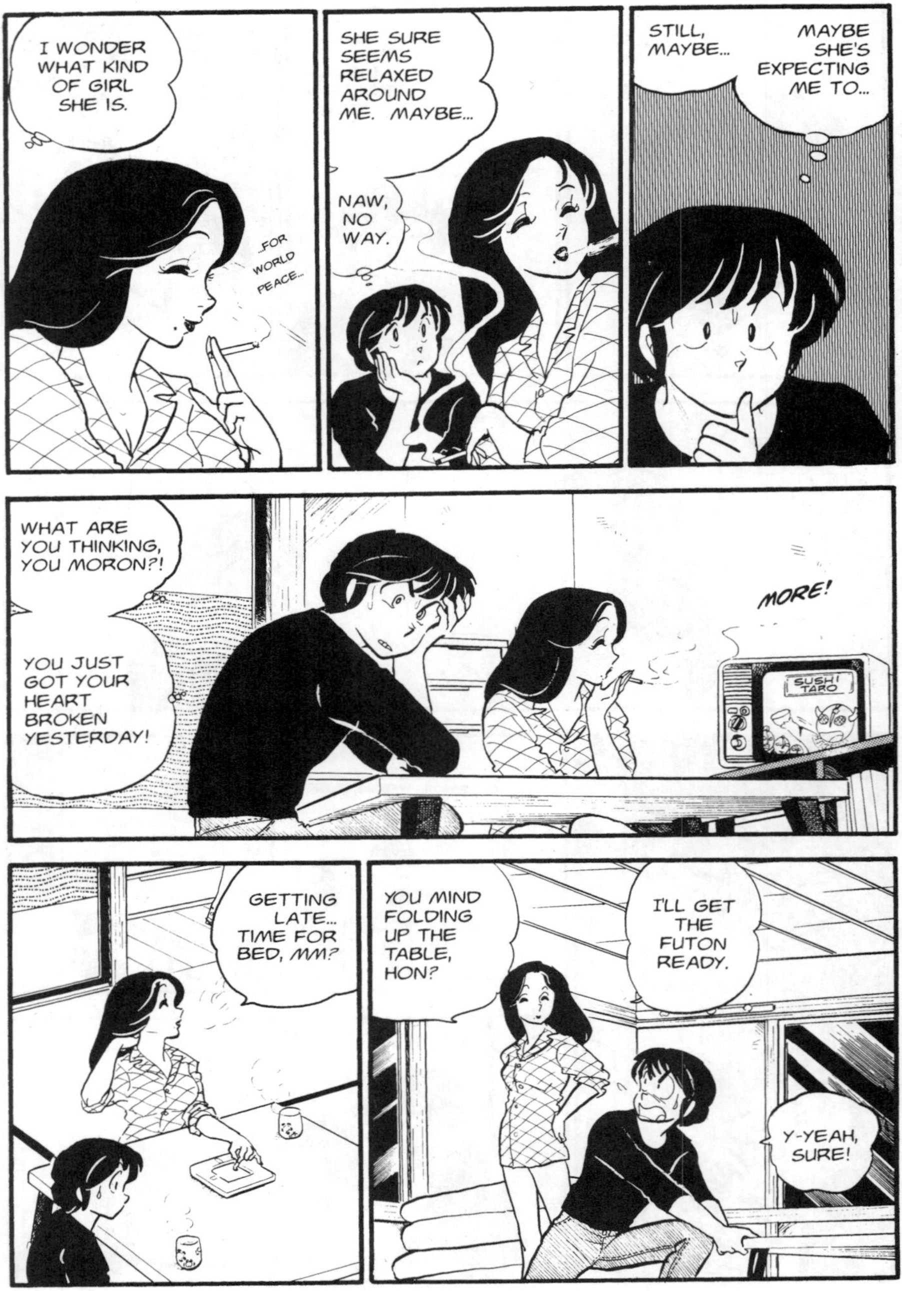
I WONDER WHAT KIND OF GIRL SHE IS.
...FOR WORLD PEACE...
SHE SURE SEEMS RELAXED AROUND ME. MAYBE...
NAW, NO WAY.
STILL, MAYBE...
MAYBE SHE'S EXPECTING ME TO...
WHAT ARE YOU THINKING, YOU MORON?!
YOU JUST GOT YOUR HEART BROKEN YESTERDAY!
MORE!
SUSHI TARO
GETTING LATE... TIME FOR BED, MM?
YOU MIND FOLDING UP THE TABLE, HON?
I'LL GET THE FUTON READY.
Y-YEAH, SURE!

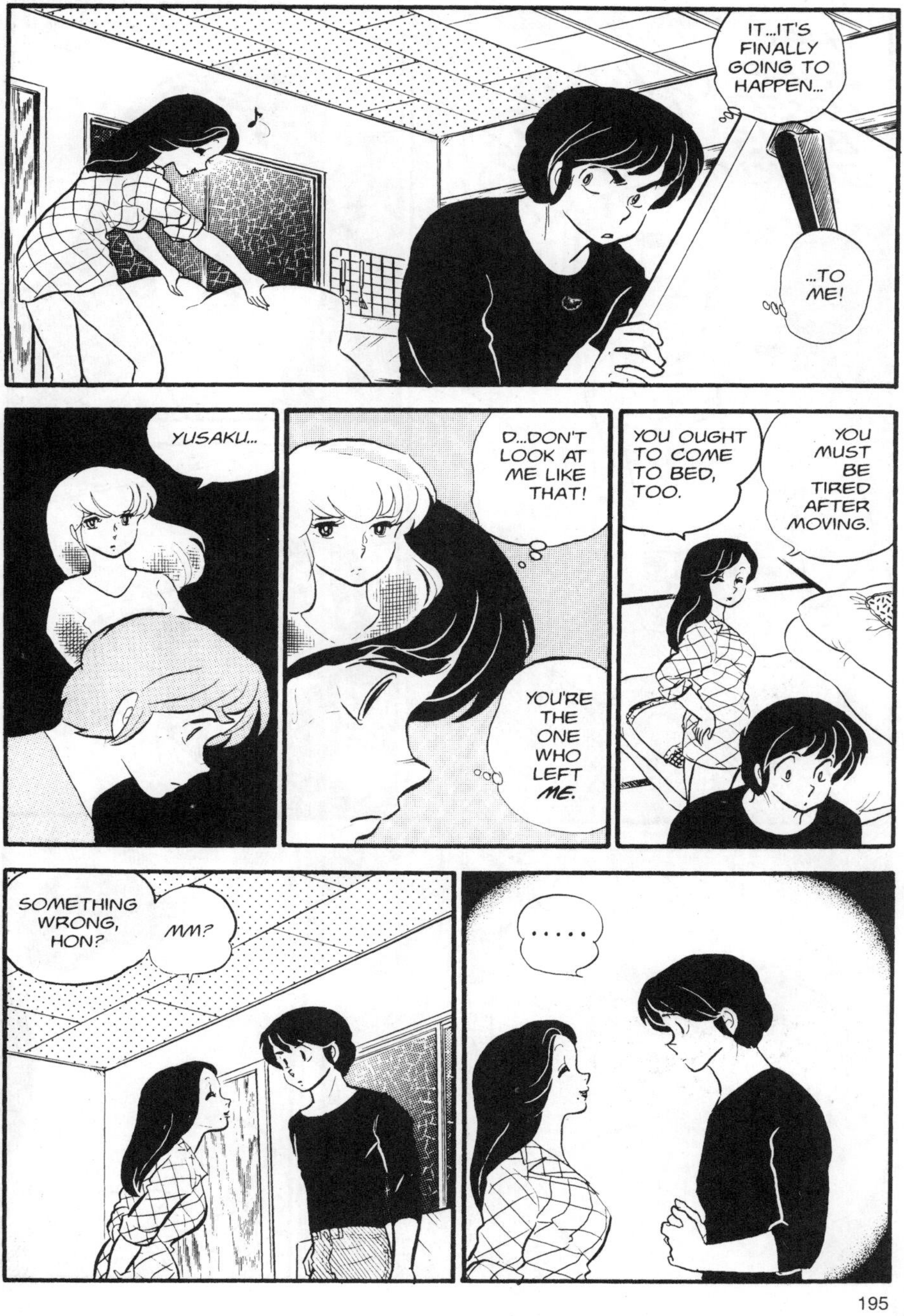
IT...IT'S FINALLY GOING TO HAPPEN...
...TO ME!
YUSAKU...
D...DON'T LOOK AT ME LIKE THAT!
YOU'RE THE ONE WHO LEFT *ME*.
YOU OUGHT TO COME TO BED, TOO.
YOU MUST BE TIRED AFTER MOVING.
SOMETHING WRONG, HON?
MM?
.....

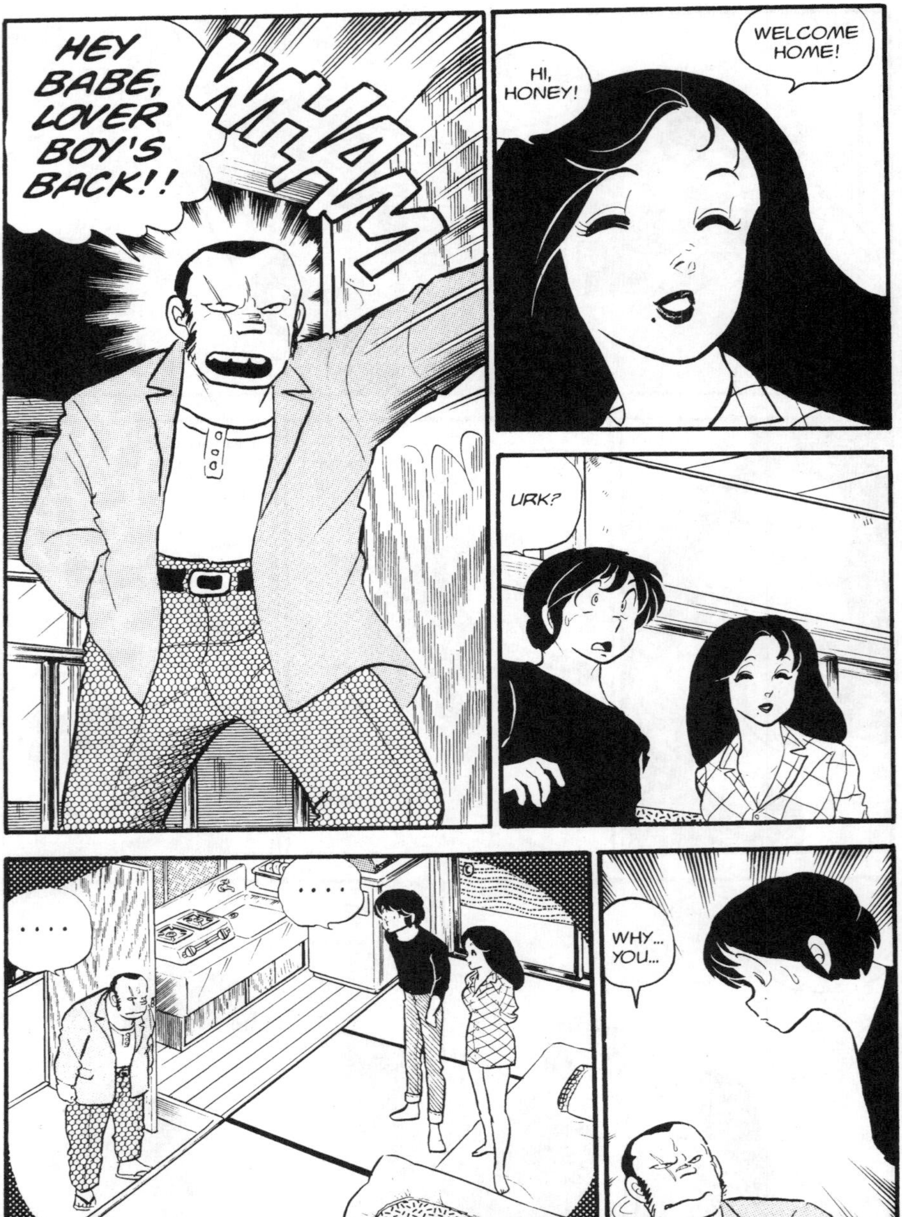
HEY BABE, LOVER BOY'S BACK!!
WHAM
HI, HONEY!
WELCOME HOME!
URK?
....
....
WHY... YOU...

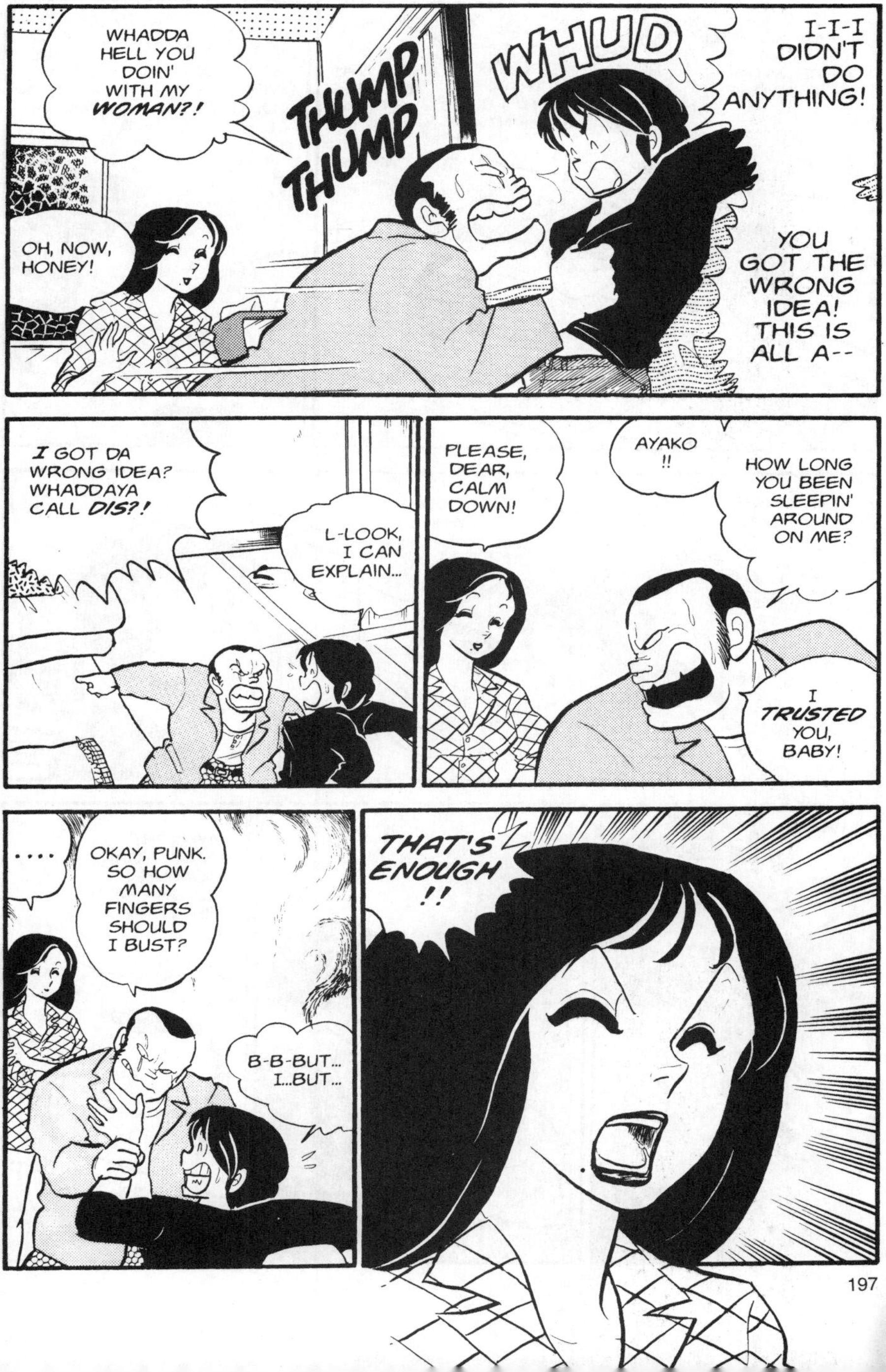
WHADDA HELL YOU DOIN' WITH MY WOMAN?!
THUMP THUMP
OH, NOW, HONEY!
WHUD
I-I-I DIDN'T DO ANYTHING!
YOU GOT THE WRONG IDEA! THIS IS ALL A--
I GOT DA WRONG IDEA? WHADDAYA CALL DIS?!
L-LOOK, I CAN EXPLAIN...
PLEASE, DEAR, CALM DOWN!
AYAKO !!
HOW LONG YOU BEEN SLEEPIN' AROUND ON ME?
I TRUSTED YOU, BABY!
....
OKAY, PUNK. SO HOW MANY FINGERS SHOULD I BUST?
B-B-BUT... I...BUT...
THAT'S ENOUGH !!

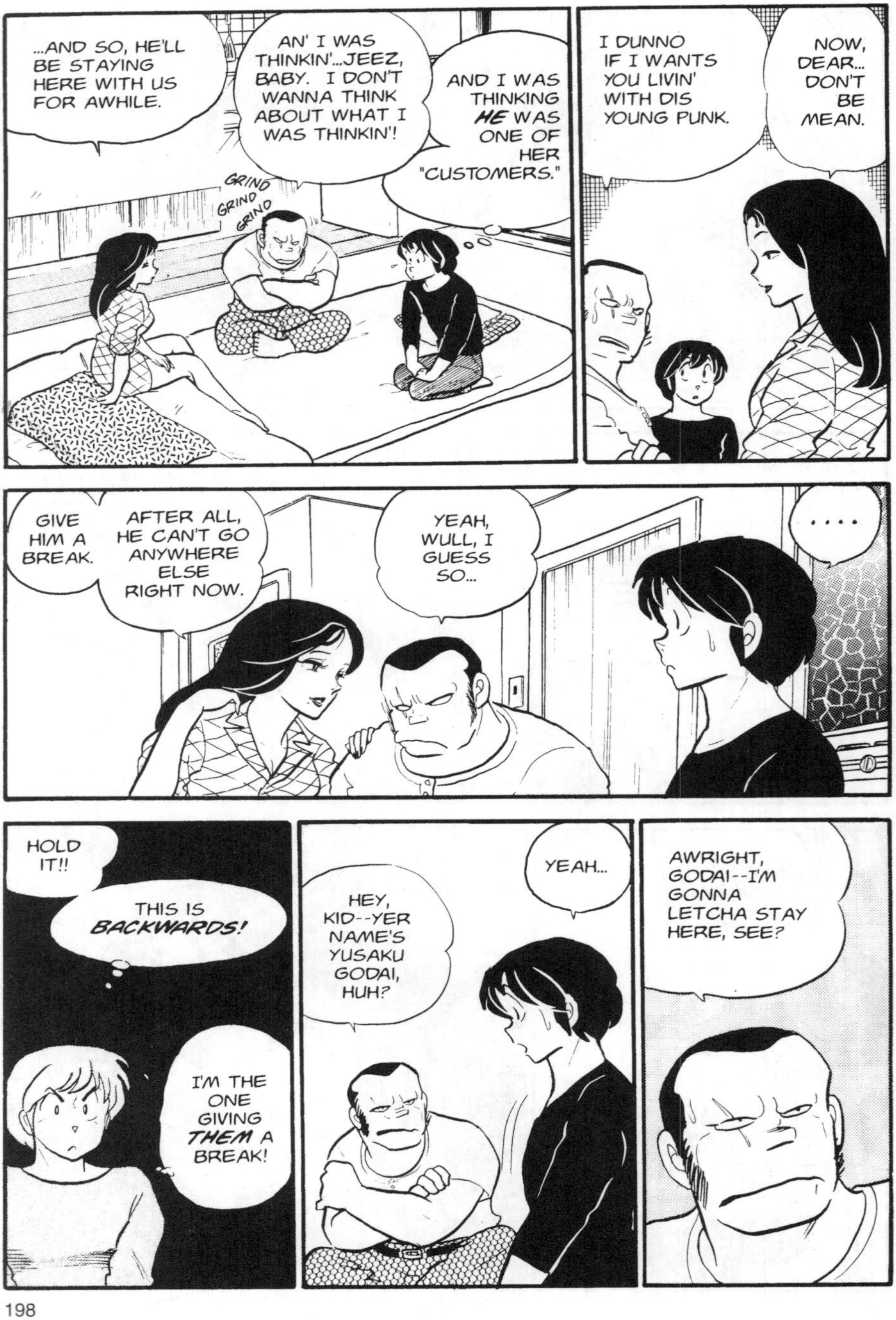
...AND SO, HE'LL BE STAYING HERE WITH US FOR AWHILE.
AN' I WAS THINKIN'...JEEZ, BABY. I DON'T WANNA THINK ABOUT WHAT I WAS THINKIN'!
GRIND GRIND GRIND
AND I WAS THINKING HE WAS ONE OF HER "CUSTOMERS."
I DUNNO IF I WANTS YOU LIVIN' WITH DIS YOUNG PUNK.
NOW, DEAR... DON'T BE MEAN.
GIVE HIM A BREAK.
AFTER ALL, HE CAN'T GO ANYWHERE ELSE RIGHT NOW.
YEAH, WULL, I GUESS SO...
....
HOLD IT!!
THIS IS BACKWARDS!
I'M THE ONE GIVING THEM A BREAK!
YEAH...
HEY, KID--YER NAME'S YUSAKU GODAI, HUH?
AWRIGHT, GODAI--I'M GONNA LETCHA STAY HERE, SEE?

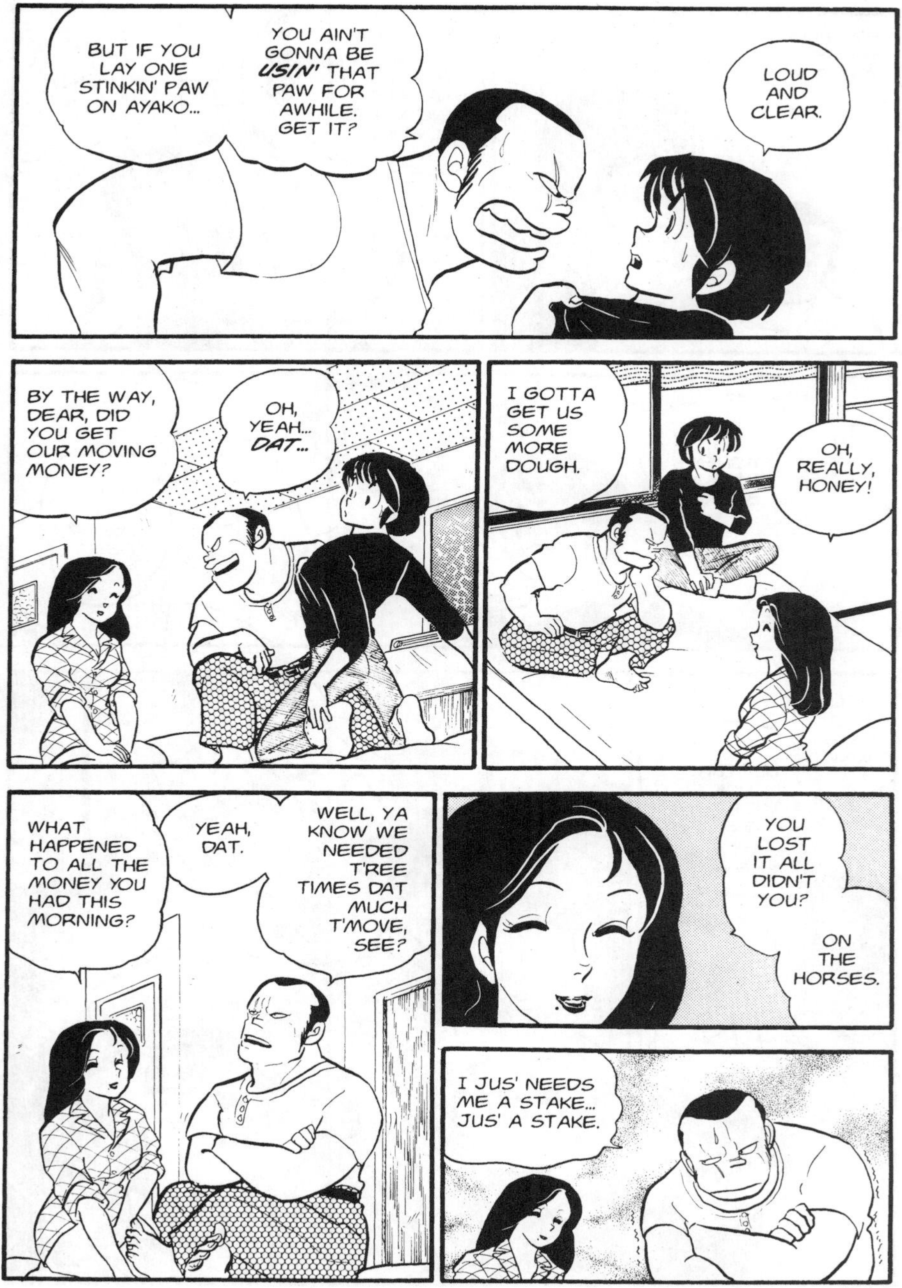

BUT IF YOU LAY ONE STINKIN' PAW ON AYAKO...
YOU AIN'T GONNA BE USIN' THAT PAW FOR AWHILE. GET IT?
LOUD AND CLEAR.
BY THE WAY, DEAR, DID YOU GET OUR MOVING MONEY?
OH, YEAH... DAT...
I GOTTA GET US SOME MORE DOUGH.
OH, REALLY, HONEY!
WHAT HAPPENED TO ALL THE MONEY YOU HAD THIS MORNING?
YEAH, DAT.
WELL, YA KNOW WE NEEDED T'REE TIMES DAT MUCH T'MOVE, SEE?
YOU LOST IT ALL DIDN'T YOU?
ON THE HORSES.
I JUS' NEEDS ME A STAKE... JUS' A STAKE.

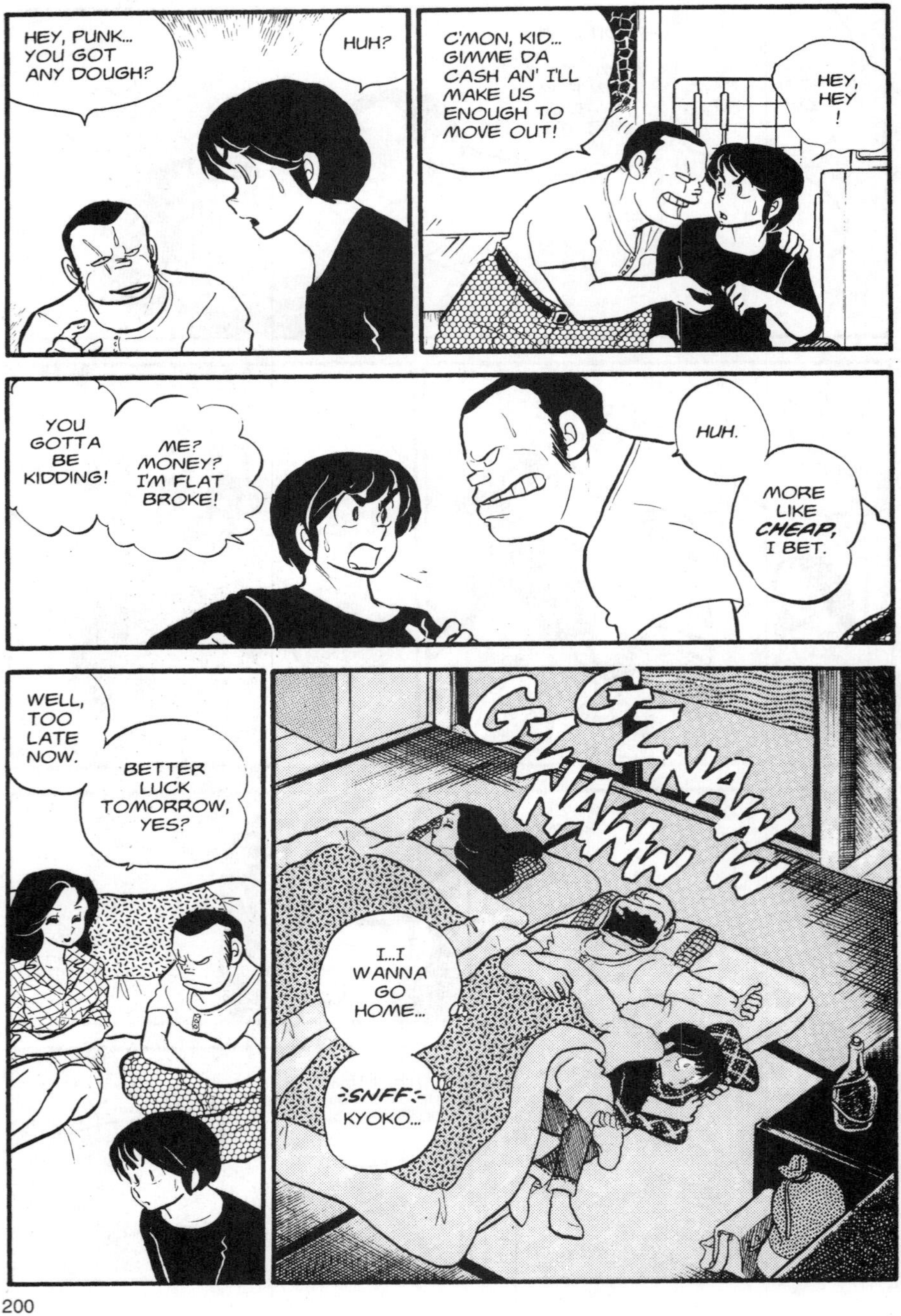
HEY, PUNK... YOU GOT ANY DOUGH?
HUH?
C'MON, KID... GIMME DA CASH AN' I'LL MAKE US ENOUGH TO MOVE OUT!
HEY, HEY!
YOU GOTTA BE KIDDING!
ME? MONEY? I'M FLAT BROKE!
HUH.
MORE LIKE *CHEAP,* I BET.
WELL, TOO LATE NOW.
BETTER LUCK TOMORROW, YES?
GZZ GNAW GNAW NAWW W
I...I WANNA GO HOME...
SNFF
KYOKO...

Part Ten
Recipe for Misunderstanding

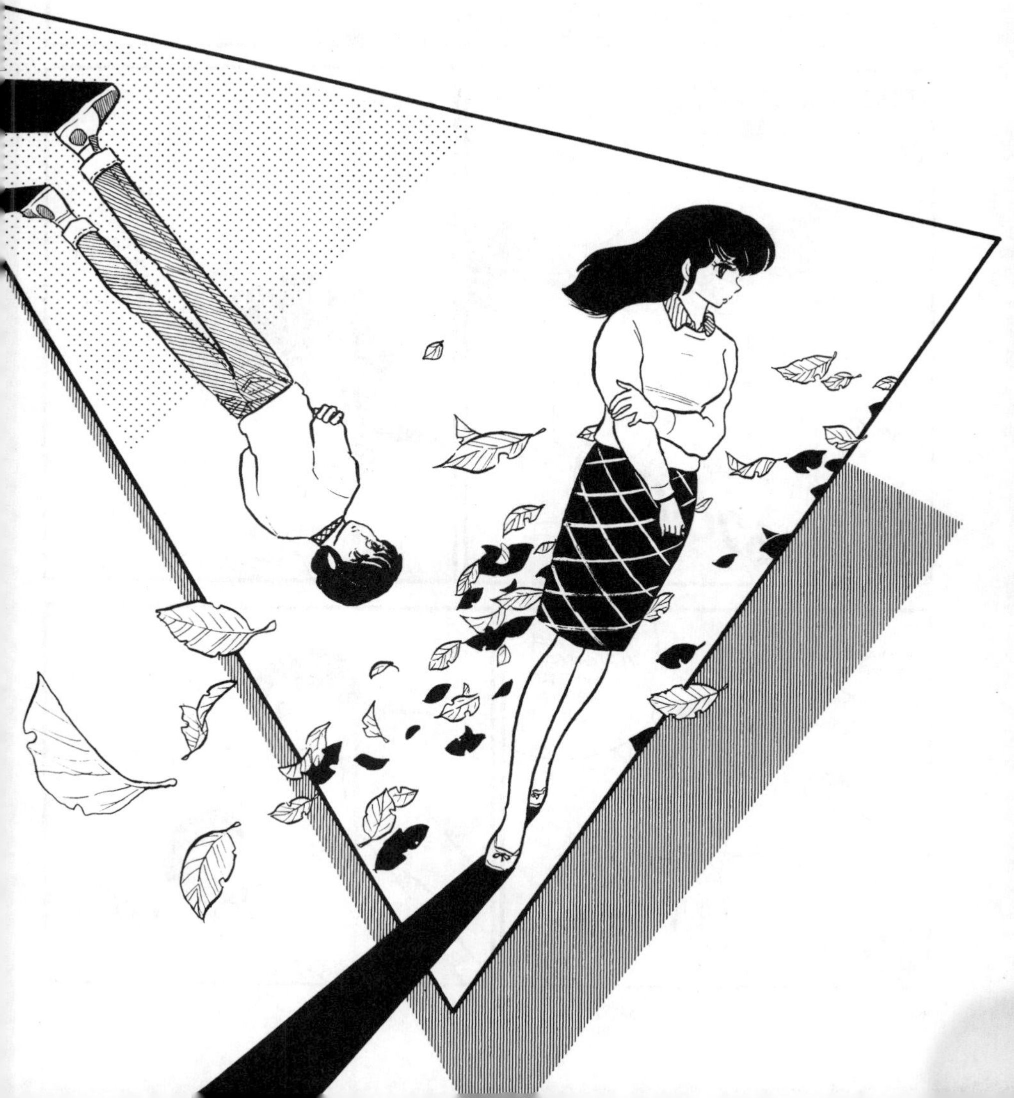

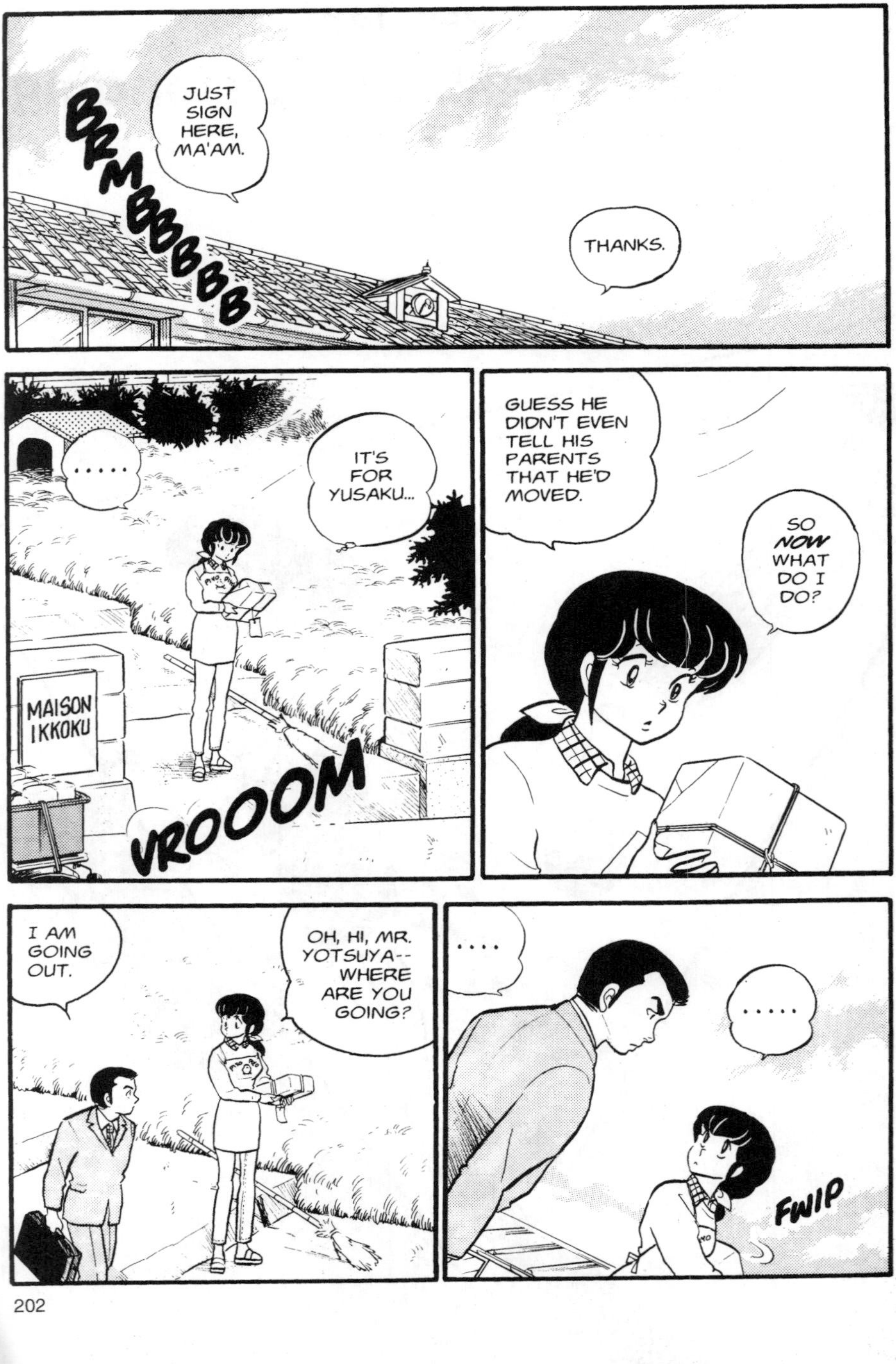
BRMBBBBB
JUST SIGN HERE, MA'AM.
THANKS.
.....
IT'S FOR YUSAKU...
MAISON IKKOKU
VROOOM
GUESS HE DIDN'T EVEN TELL HIS PARENTS THAT HE'D MOVED.
SO *NOW* WHAT DO I DO?
I AM GOING OUT.
OH, HI, MR. YOTSUYA-- WHERE ARE YOU GOING?
....
.....
FWIP

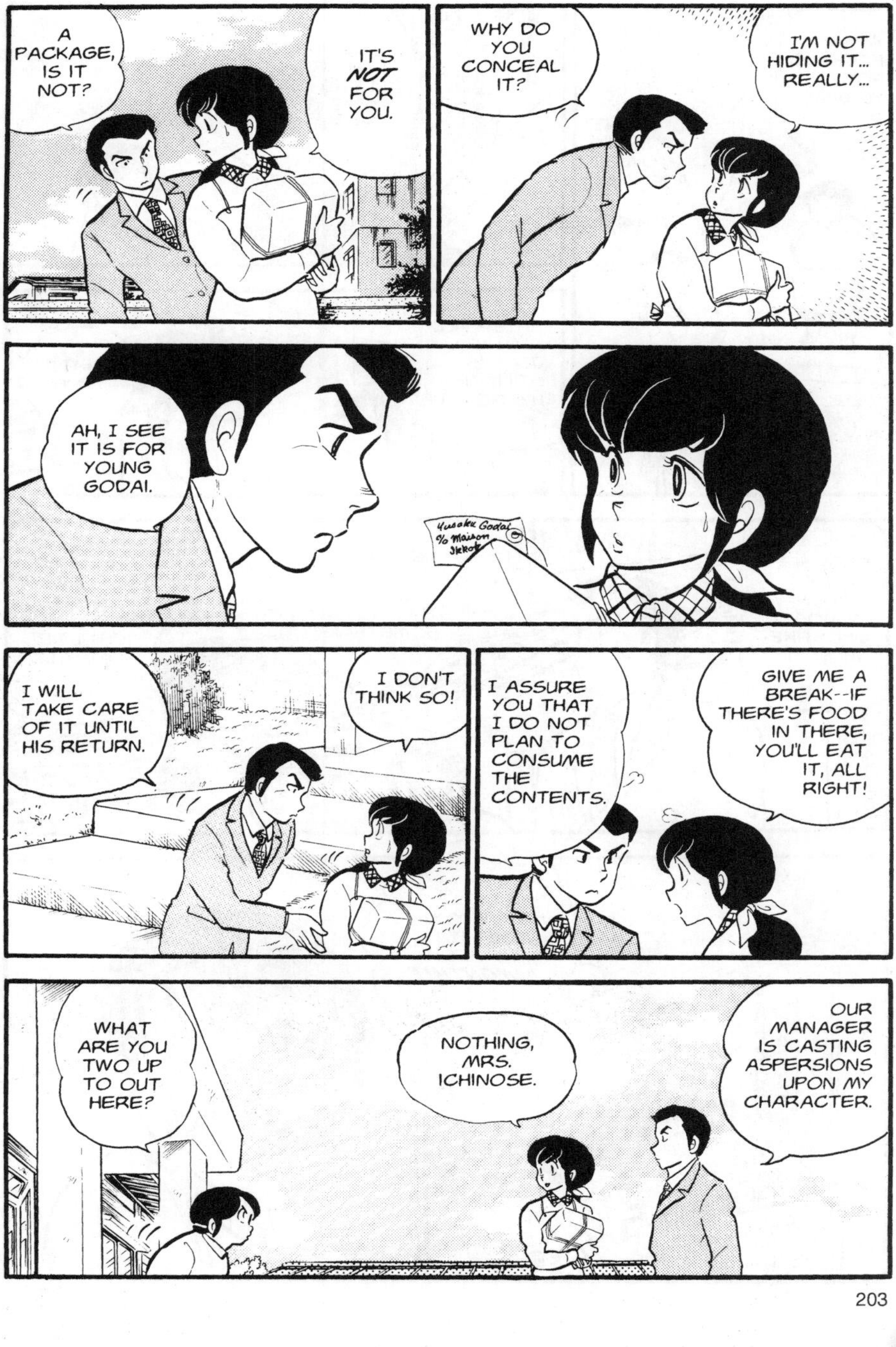
A PACKAGE, IS IT NOT?
IT'S *NOT* FOR YOU.
WHY DO YOU CONCEAL IT?
I'M NOT HIDING IT... REALLY...
AH, I SEE IT IS FOR YOUNG GODAI.
I WILL TAKE CARE OF IT UNTIL HIS RETURN.
I DON'T THINK SO!
I ASSURE YOU THAT I DO NOT PLAN TO CONSUME THE CONTENTS.
GIVE ME A BREAK--IF THERE'S FOOD IN THERE, YOU'LL EAT IT, ALL RIGHT!
WHAT ARE YOU TWO UP TO OUT HERE?
NOTHING, MRS. ICHINOSE.
OUR MANAGER IS CASTING ASPERSIONS UPON MY CHARACTER.

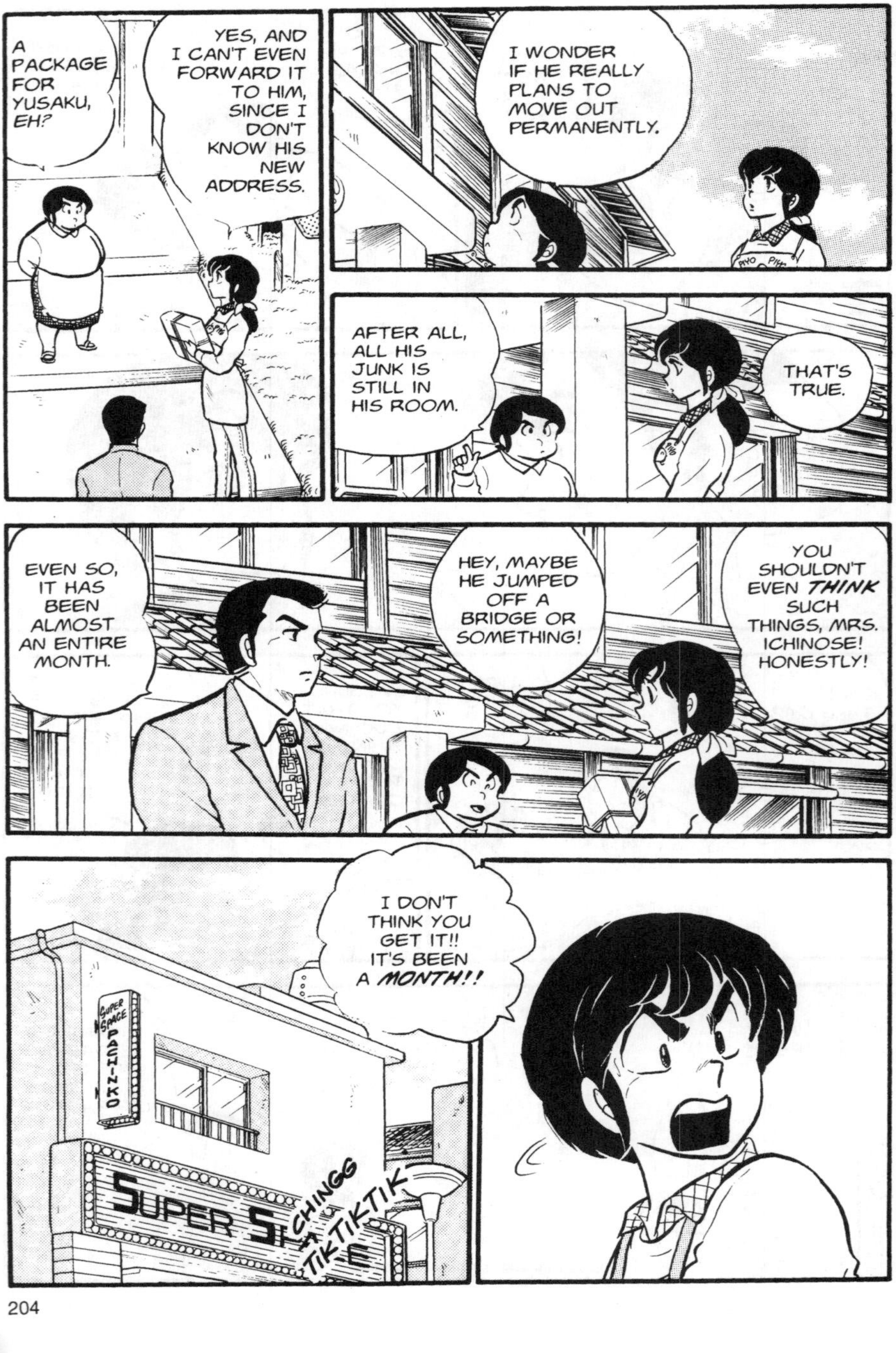
A PACKAGE FOR YUSAKU, EH?
YES, AND I CAN'T EVEN FORWARD IT TO HIM, SINCE I DON'T KNOW HIS NEW ADDRESS.
I WONDER IF HE REALLY PLANS TO MOVE OUT PERMANENTLY.
PIYO PIYO
AFTER ALL, ALL HIS JUNK IS STILL IN HIS ROOM.
THAT'S TRUE.
EVEN SO, IT HAS BEEN ALMOST AN ENTIRE MONTH.
HEY, MAYBE HE JUMPED OFF A BRIDGE OR SOMETHING!
YOU SHOULDN'T EVEN THINK SUCH THINGS, MRS. ICHINOSE! HONESTLY!
SUPER SPACE PACHINKO
SUPER SPACE
CHINGG
TIKTIKTIK
I DON'T THINK YOU GET IT!! IT'S BEEN A MONTH!!

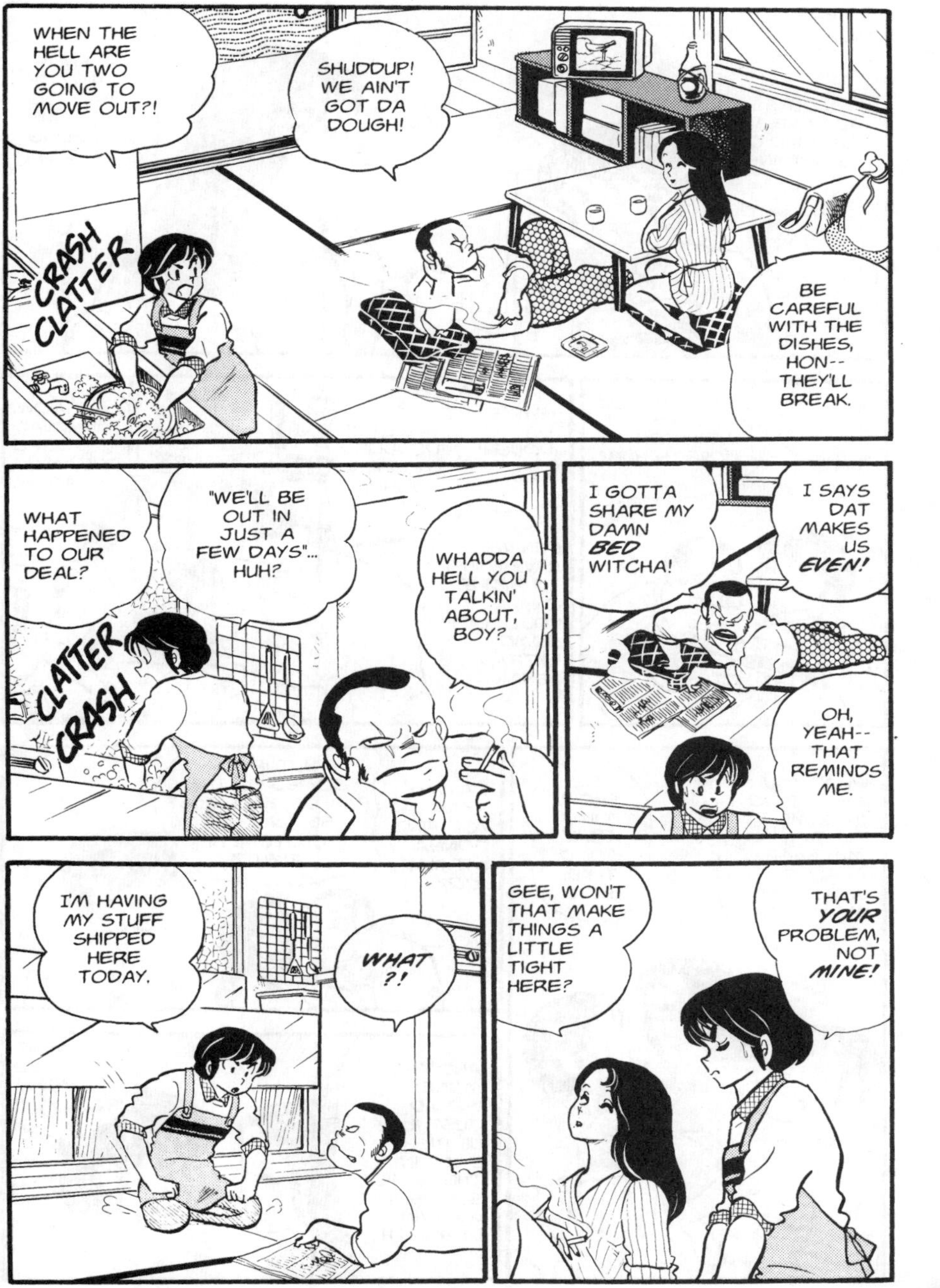
WHEN THE HELL ARE YOU TWO GOING TO MOVE OUT?!
SHUDDUP! WE AIN'T GOT DA DOUGH!
CRASH CLATTER
BE CAREFUL WITH THE DISHES, HON-- THEY'LL BREAK.
WHAT HAPPENED TO OUR DEAL?
"WE'LL BE OUT IN JUST A FEW DAYS"... HUH?
CLATTER CRASH
WHADDA HELL YOU TALKIN' ABOUT, BOY?
I GOTTA SHARE MY DAMN BED WITCHA!
I SAYS DAT MAKES US EVEN!
OH, YEAH-- THAT REMINDS ME.
I'M HAVING MY STUFF SHIPPED HERE TODAY.
WHAT ?!
GEE, WON'T THAT MAKE THINGS A LITTLE TIGHT HERE?
THAT'S YOUR PROBLEM, NOT MINE!

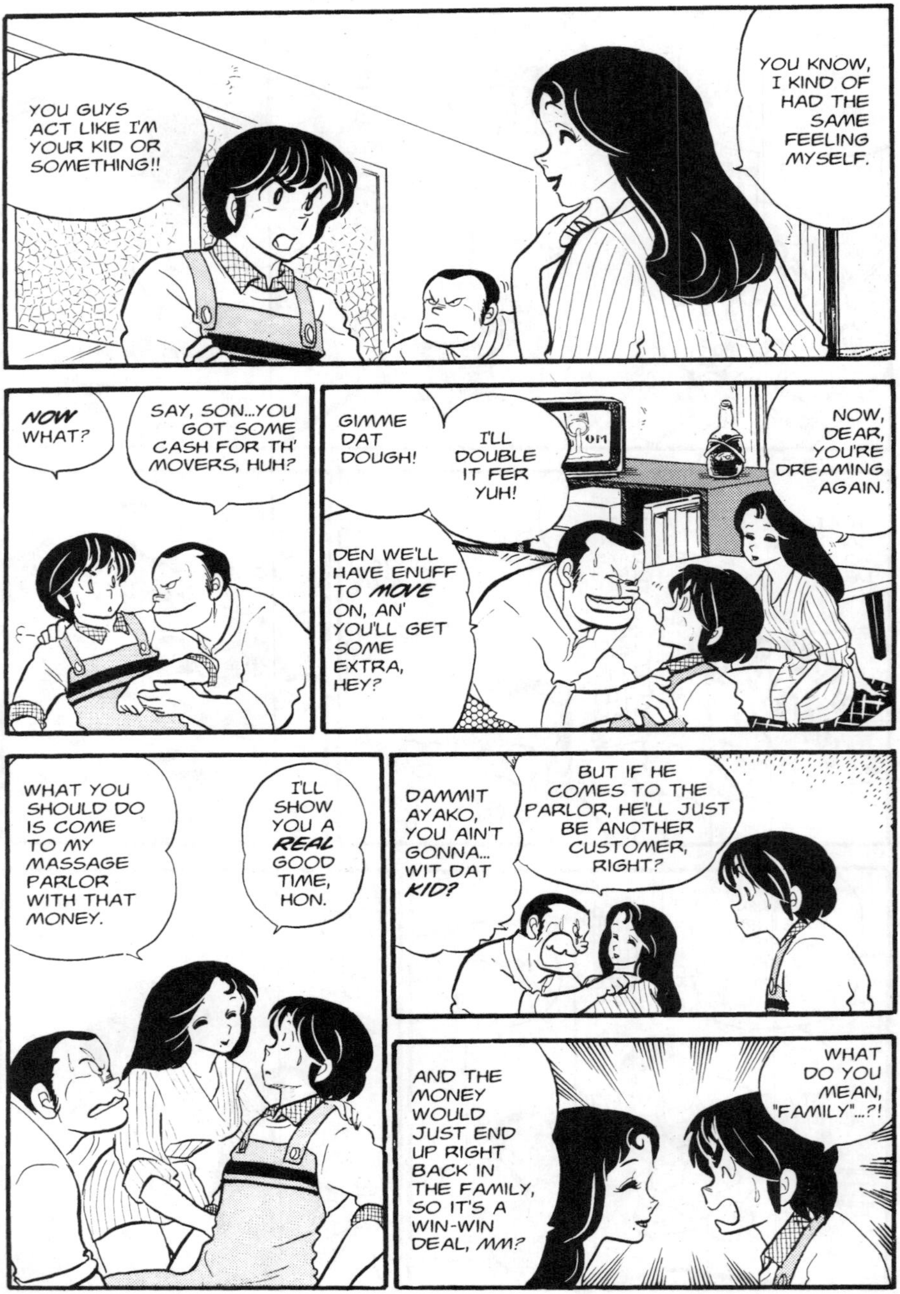
YOU GUYS ACT LIKE I'M YOUR KID OR SOMETHING!!
YOU KNOW, I KIND OF HAD THE SAME FEELING MYSELF.
NOW WHAT?
SAY, SON...YOU GOT SOME CASH FOR TH' MOVERS, HUH?
GIMME DAT DOUGH!
I'LL DOUBLE IT FER YUH!
DEN WE'LL HAVE ENUFF TO *MOVE* ON, AN' YOU'LL GET SOME EXTRA, HEY?
NOW, DEAR, YOU'RE DREAMING AGAIN.
WHAT YOU SHOULD DO IS COME TO MY MASSAGE PARLOR WITH THAT MONEY.
I'LL SHOW YOU A *REAL* GOOD TIME, HON.
DAMMIT AYAKO, YOU AIN'T GONNA... WIT DAT *KID?*
BUT IF HE COMES TO THE PARLOR, HE'LL JUST BE ANOTHER CUSTOMER, RIGHT?
AND THE MONEY WOULD JUST END UP RIGHT BACK IN THE FAMILY, SO IT'S A WIN-WIN DEAL, *MM?*
WHAT DO YOU MEAN, "FAMILY"...?!

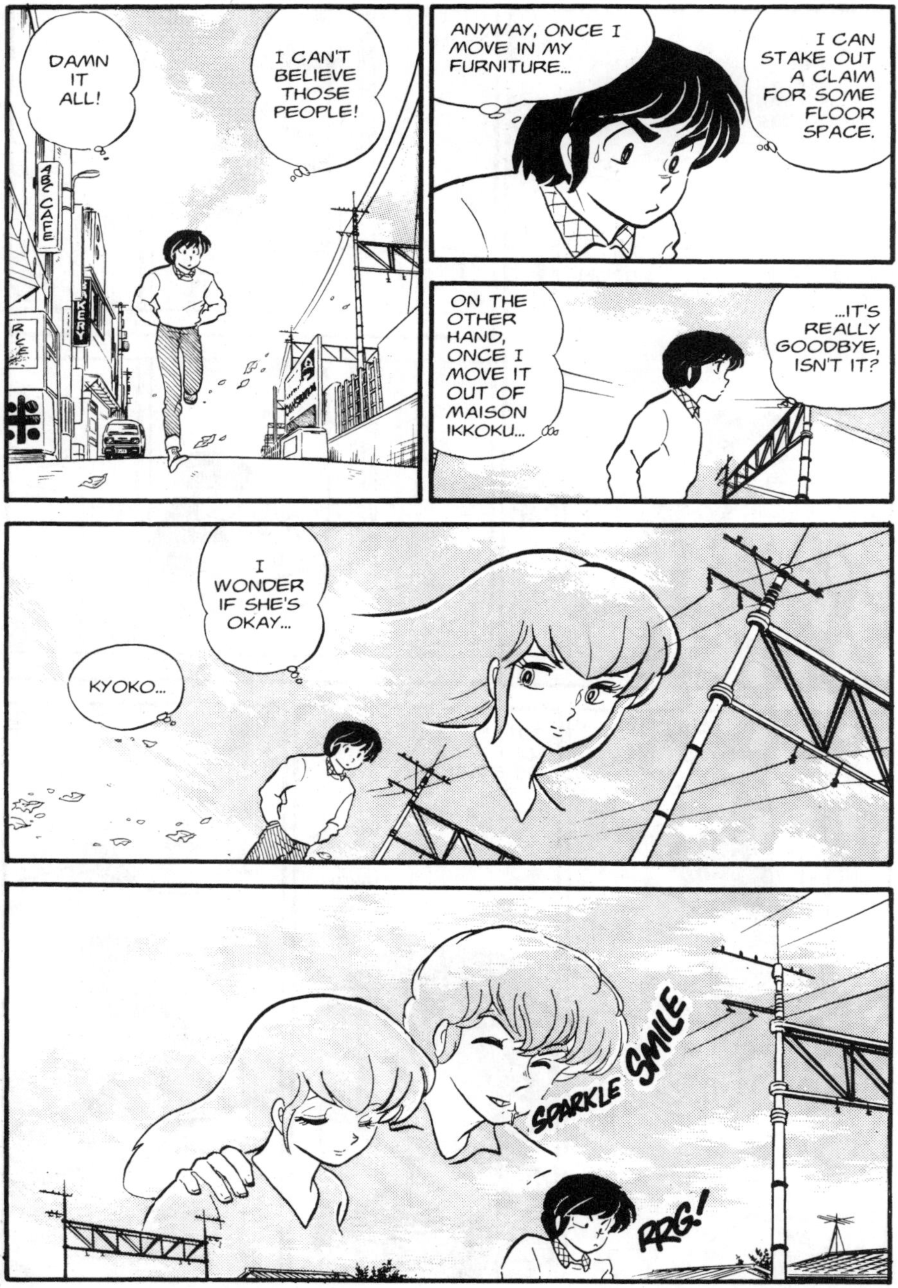
DAMN IT ALL!
I CAN'T BELIEVE THOSE PEOPLE!
ABC CAFE
ANYWAY, ONCE I MOVE IN MY FURNITURE...
I CAN STAKE OUT A CLAIM FOR SOME FLOOR SPACE.
ON THE OTHER HAND, ONCE I MOVE IT OUT OF MAISON IKKOKU...
...IT'S REALLY GOODBYE, ISN'T IT?
I WONDER IF SHE'S OKAY...
KYOKO...
SPARKLE SMILE
RRG!

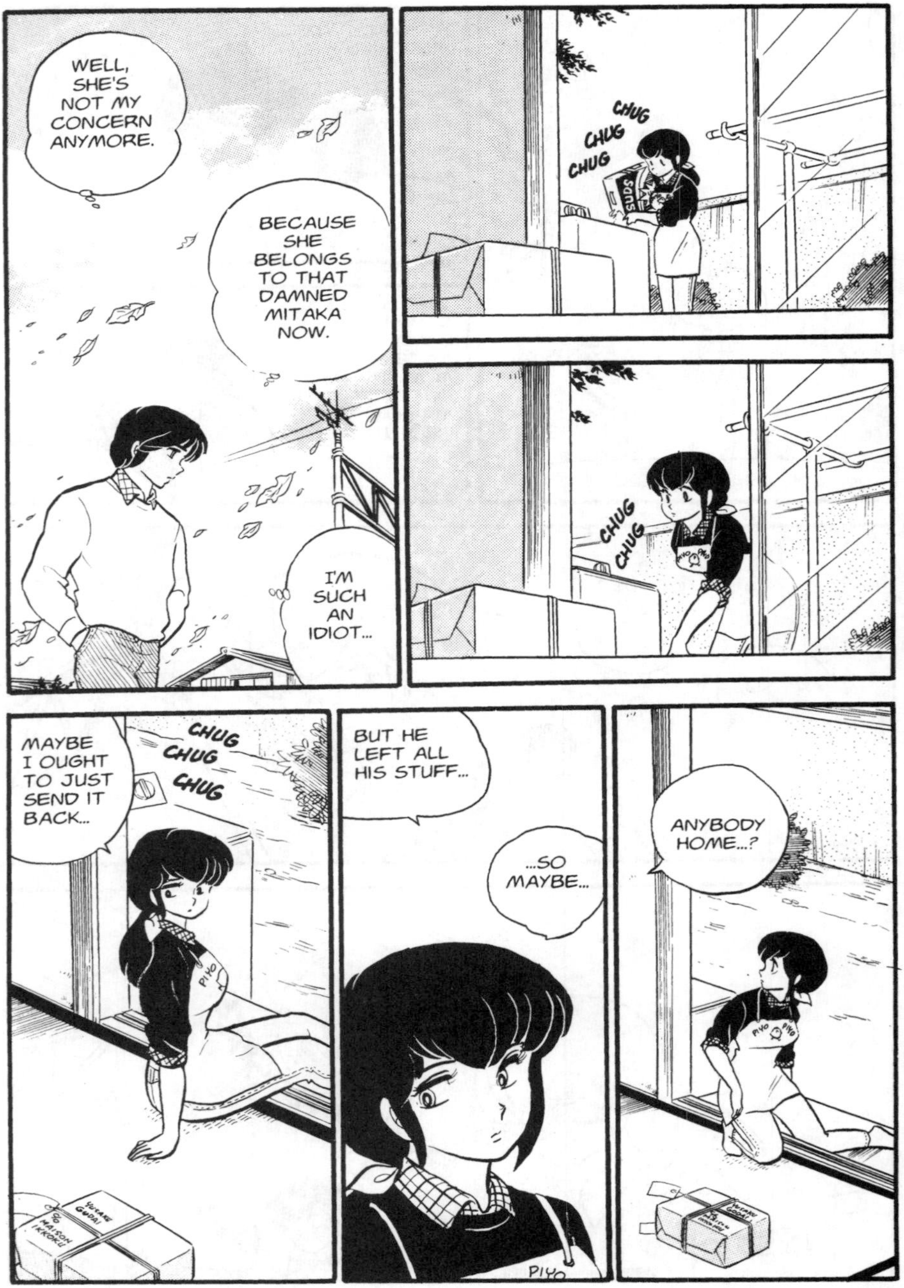
WELL, SHE'S NOT MY CONCERN ANYMORE.
BECAUSE SHE BELONGS TO THAT DAMNED MITAKA NOW.
I'M SUCH AN IDIOT...
CHUG
CHUG
CHUG
SUDS
CHUG
CHUG
MAYBE I OUGHT TO JUST SEND IT BACK...
CHUG
CHUG
CHUG
PIYO
BUT HE LEFT ALL HIS STUFF...
...SO MAYBE...
PIYO
ANYBODY HOME...?
PIYO PIYO

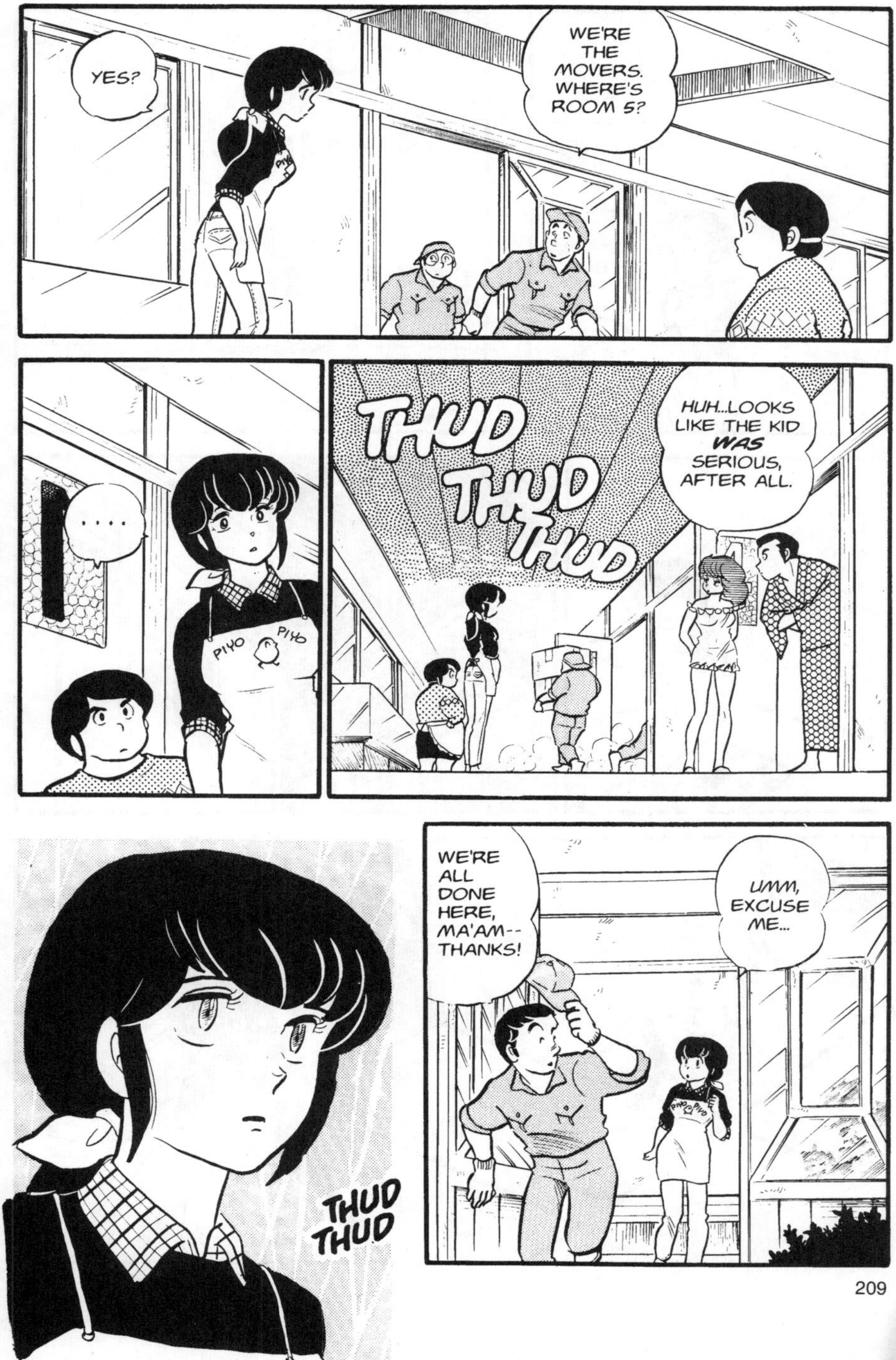
YES?
WE'RE THE MOVERS. WHERE'S ROOM 5?
. . . .
THUD THUD THUD
HUH...LOOKS LIKE THE KID WAS SERIOUS, AFTER ALL.
THUD THUD
WE'RE ALL DONE HERE, MA'AM-- THANKS!
UMM, EXCUSE ME...

COULD YOU GIVE ME HIS NEW ADDRESS?

I..UH... SORT OF MISPLACED IT.

SURE, NO PROBLEM.

CLOCK HILL WEST...

WHY, THAT'S JUST THE NEXT STATION OVER.

MAYBE... MAYBE I SHOULD HAVE JUST GIVEN IT TO THE MOVERS...

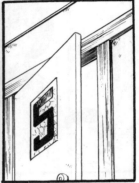

VROOOSH

VROOSH

KLIK

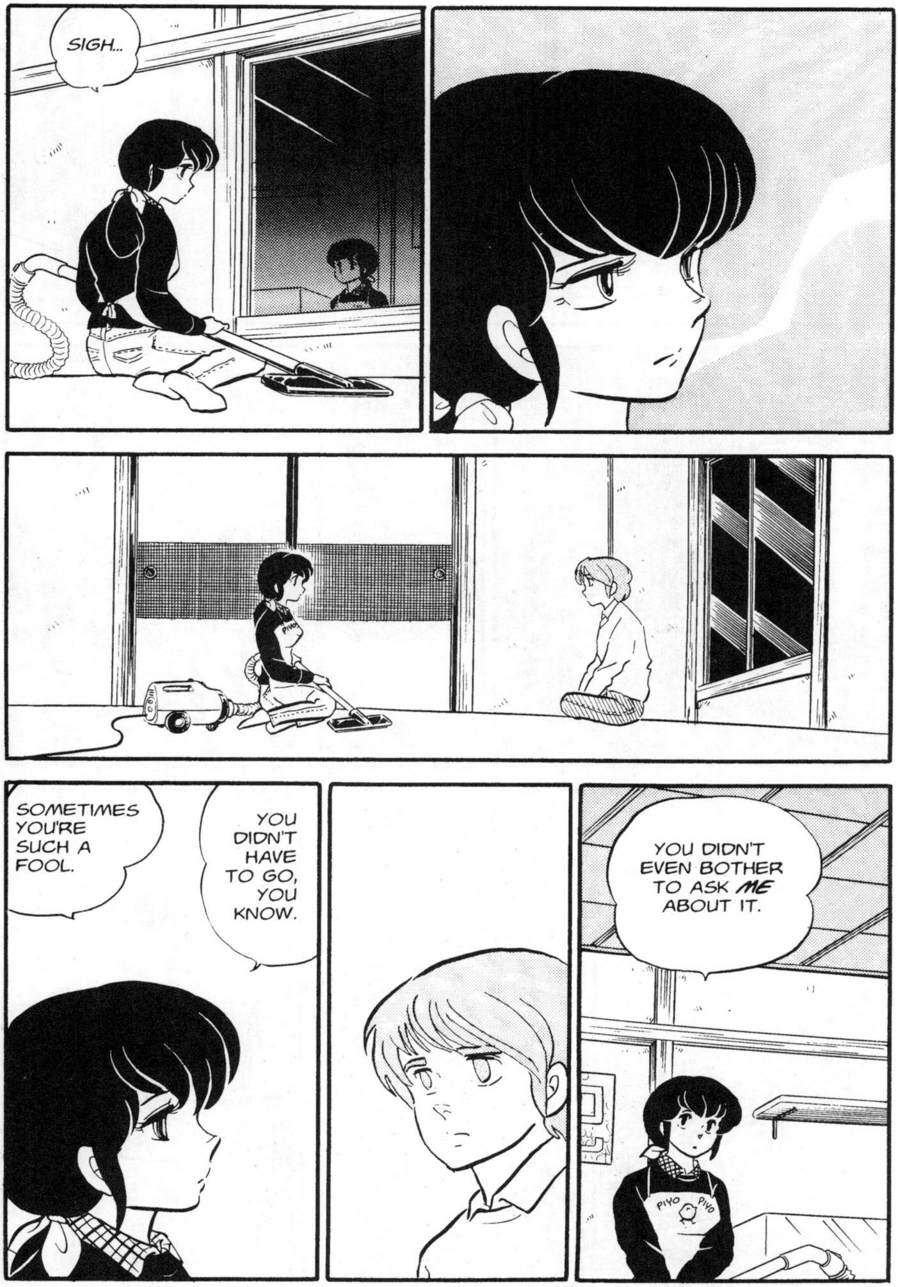
SIGH...
PIYO
SOMETIMES YOU'RE SUCH A FOOL.
YOU DIDN'T HAVE TO GO, YOU KNOW.
YOU DIDN'T EVEN BOTHER TO ASK ME ABOUT IT.
PIYO PIYO

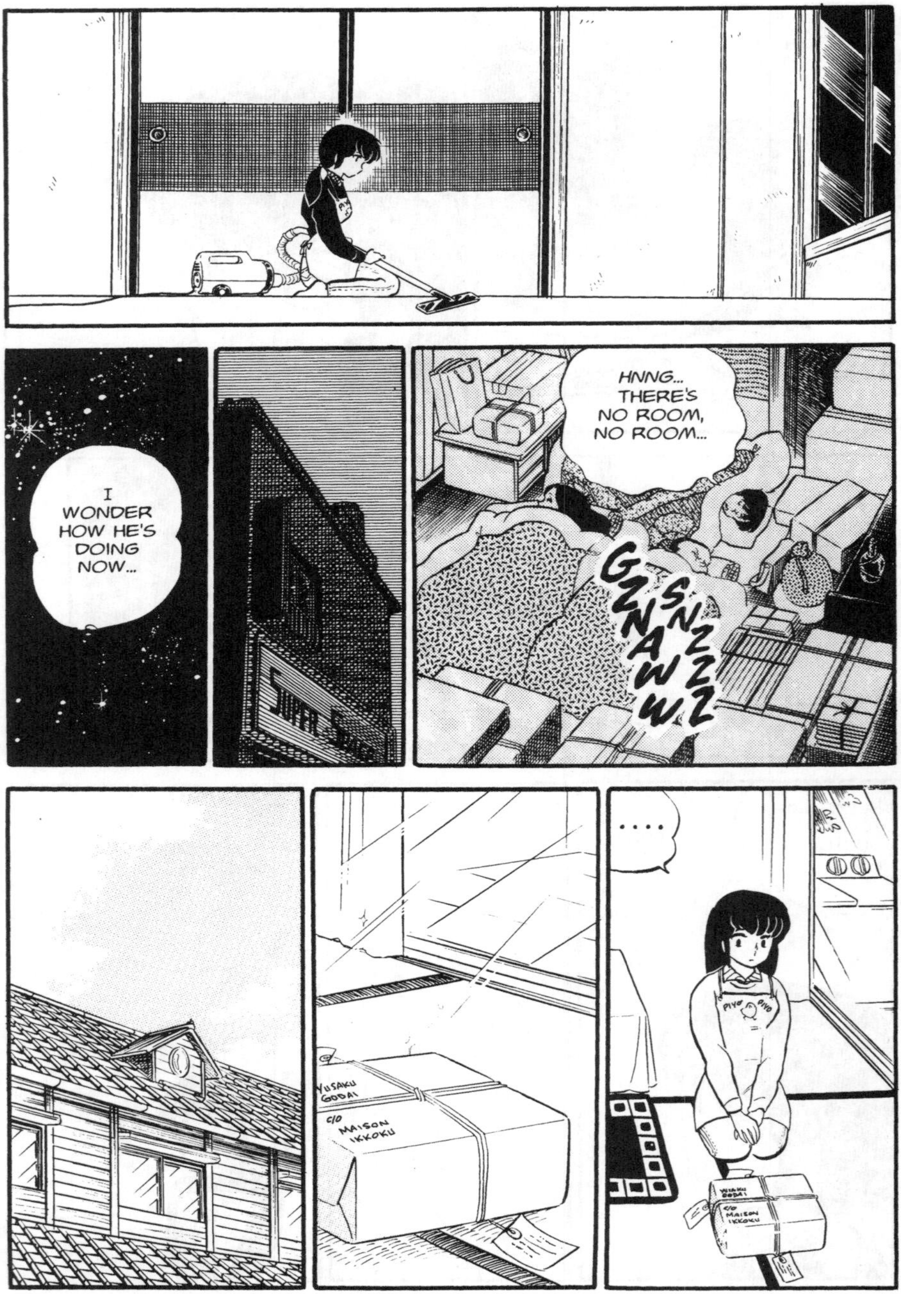
I WONDER HOW HE'S DOING NOW...
HNNG... THERE'S NO ROOM, NO ROOM...
GZNAWW
SNZZZ
YUSAKU GODAI
c/o MAISON IKKOKU
....
PIYO PIYO

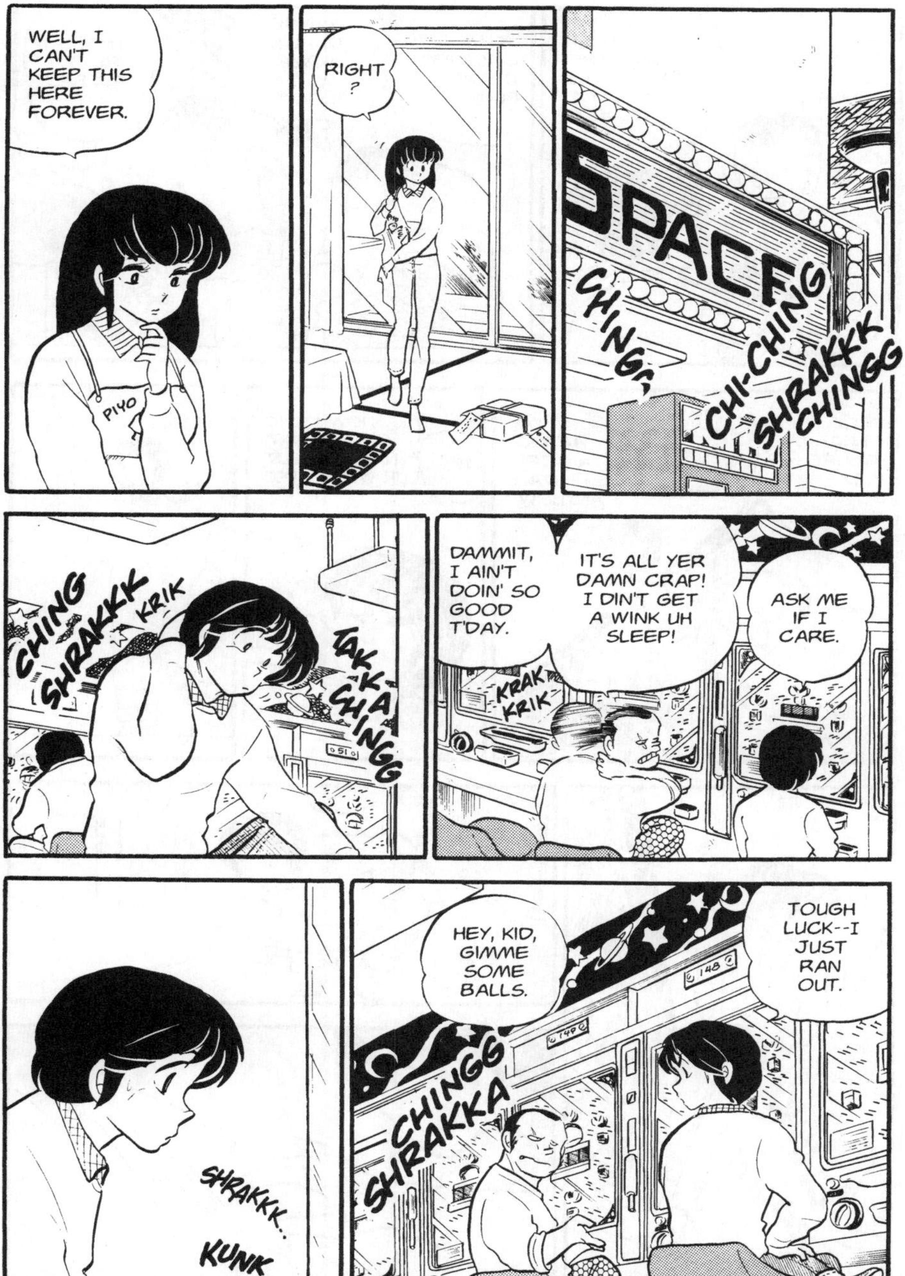
WELL, I CAN'T KEEP THIS HERE FOREVER.
PIYO
RIGHT?
SPACE
CHING
CHI-CHING
SHRAKKK CHINGG
CHING SHRAKKK
KRIK
TAK-KA-CHINGG
DAMMIT, I AIN'T DOIN' SO GOOD T'DAY.
IT'S ALL YER DAMN CRAP! I DIN'T GET A WINK UH SLEEP!
KRAK KRIK
ASK ME IF I CARE.
SHRAKKK..
KUNK
HEY, KID, GIMME SOME BALLS.
TOUGH LUCK--I JUST RAN OUT.
CHINGG SHRAKKA

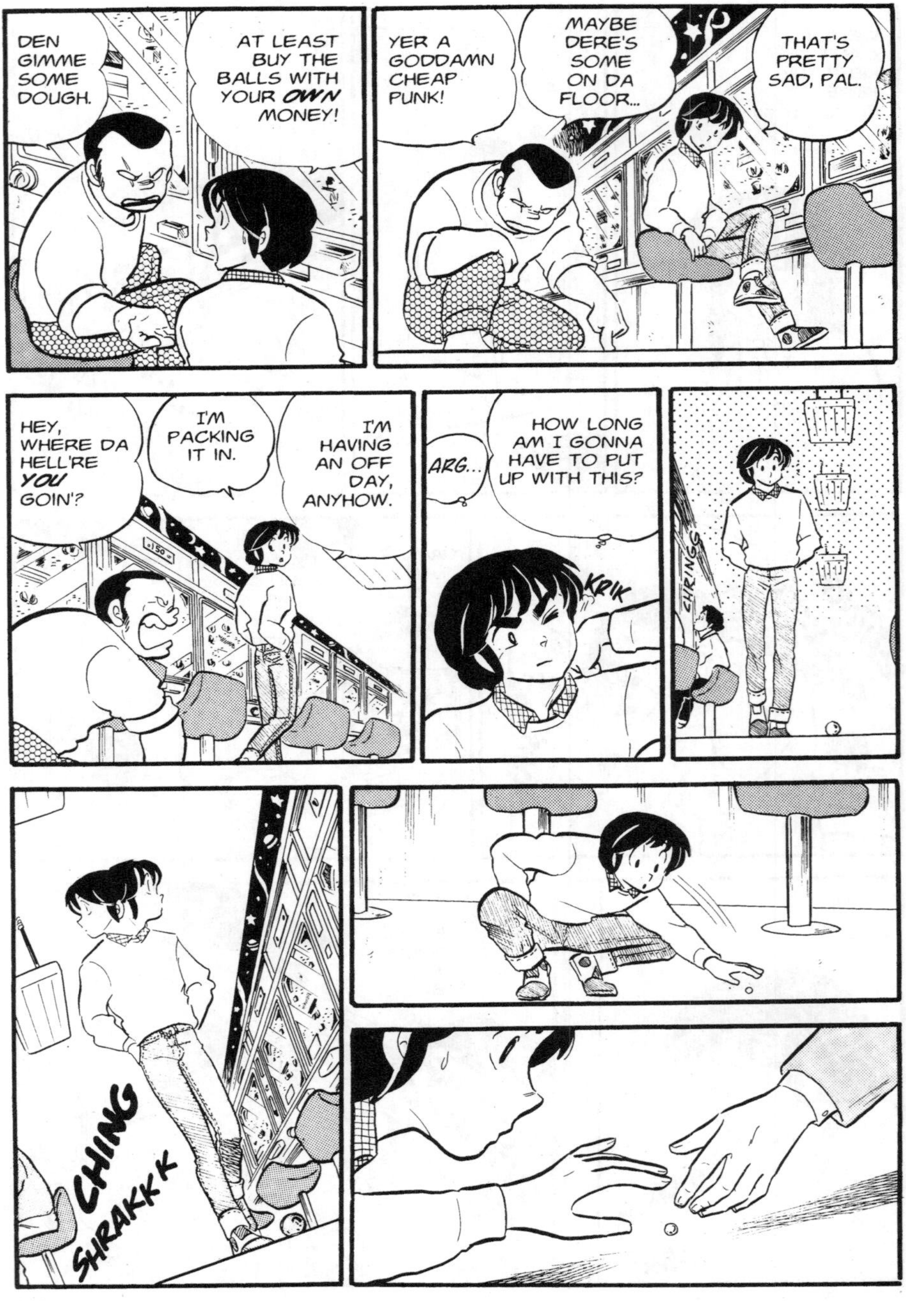

DEN GIMME SOME DOUGH.
AT LEAST BUY THE BALLS WITH YOUR OWN MONEY!
YER A GODDAMN CHEAP PUNK!
MAYBE DERE'S SOME ON DA FLOOR...
THAT'S PRETTY SAD, PAL.
HEY, WHERE DA HELL'RE YOU GOIN'?
I'M PACKING IT IN.
I'M HAVING AN OFF DAY, ANYHOW.
ARG...
HOW LONG AM I GONNA HAVE TO PUT UP WITH THIS?
KRIK
CHRINGG
CHING
SHRAKKK

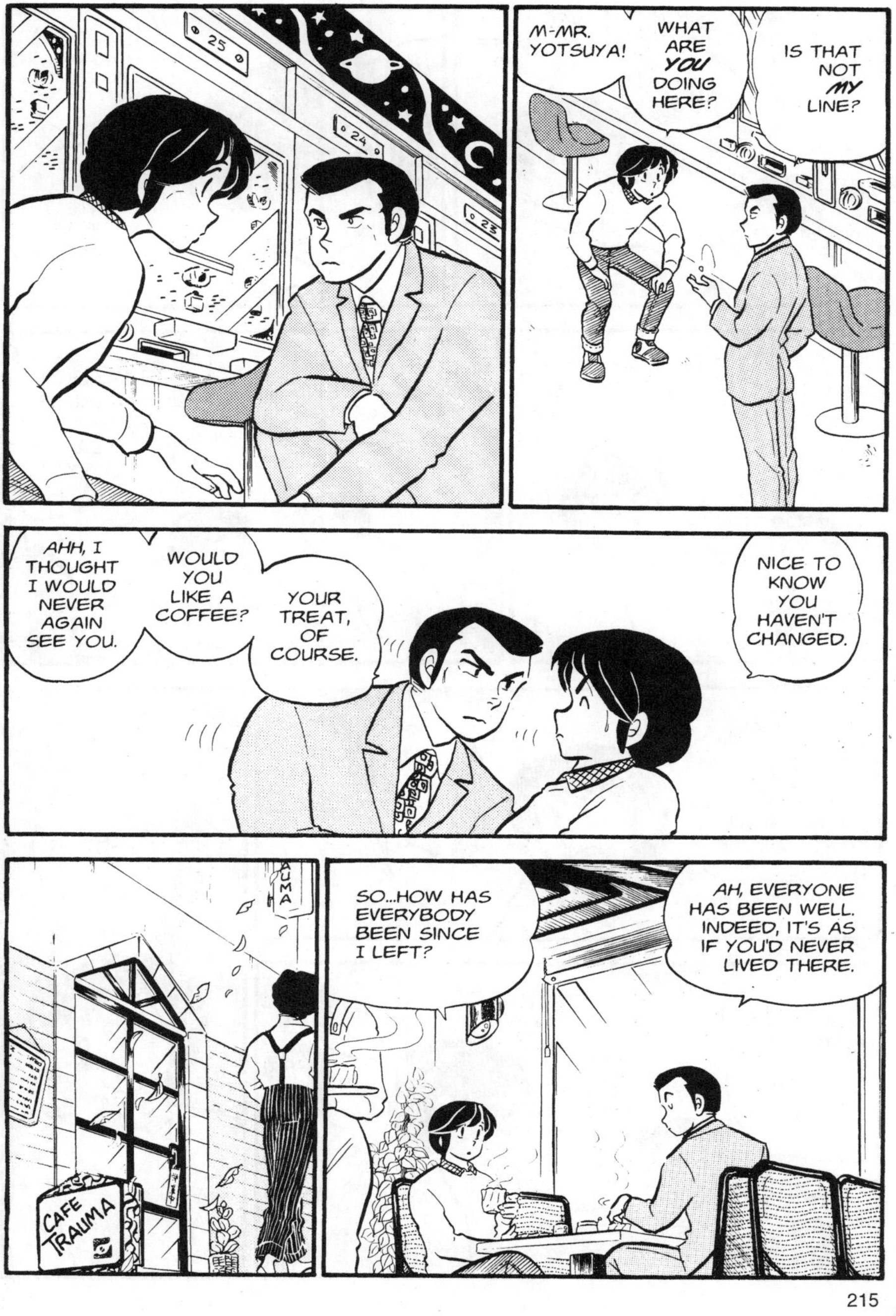
M-MR. YOTSUYA!
WHAT ARE YOU DOING HERE?
IS THAT NOT MY LINE?
AHH, I THOUGHT I WOULD NEVER AGAIN SEE YOU.
WOULD YOU LIKE A COFFEE?
YOUR TREAT, OF COURSE.
NICE TO KNOW YOU HAVEN'T CHANGED.
CAFE TRAUMA
SO...HOW HAS EVERYBODY BEEN SINCE I LEFT?
AH, EVERYONE HAS BEEN WELL. INDEED, IT'S AS IF YOU'D NEVER LIVED THERE.

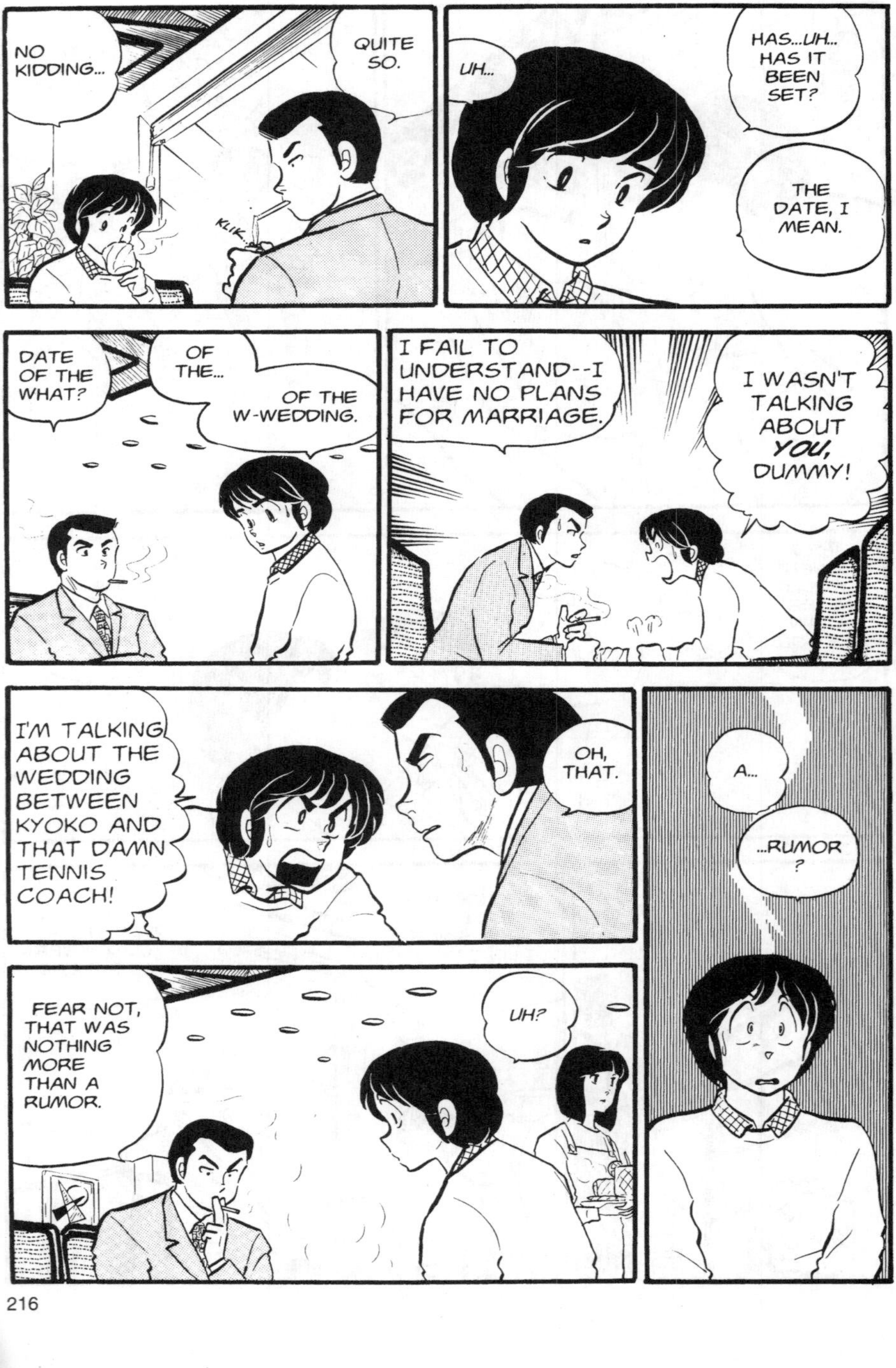
NO KIDDING...
QUITE SO.
KLIK...
UH...
HAS...UH... HAS IT BEEN SET?
THE DATE, I MEAN.
DATE OF THE WHAT?
OF THE...
OF THE W-WEDDING.
I FAIL TO UNDERSTAND--I HAVE NO PLANS FOR MARRIAGE.
I WASN'T TALKING ABOUT YOU, DUMMY!
I'M TALKING ABOUT THE WEDDING BETWEEN KYOKO AND THAT DAMN TENNIS COACH!
OH, THAT.
A...
...RUMOR?
FEAR NOT, THAT WAS NOTHING MORE THAN A RUMOR.
UH?

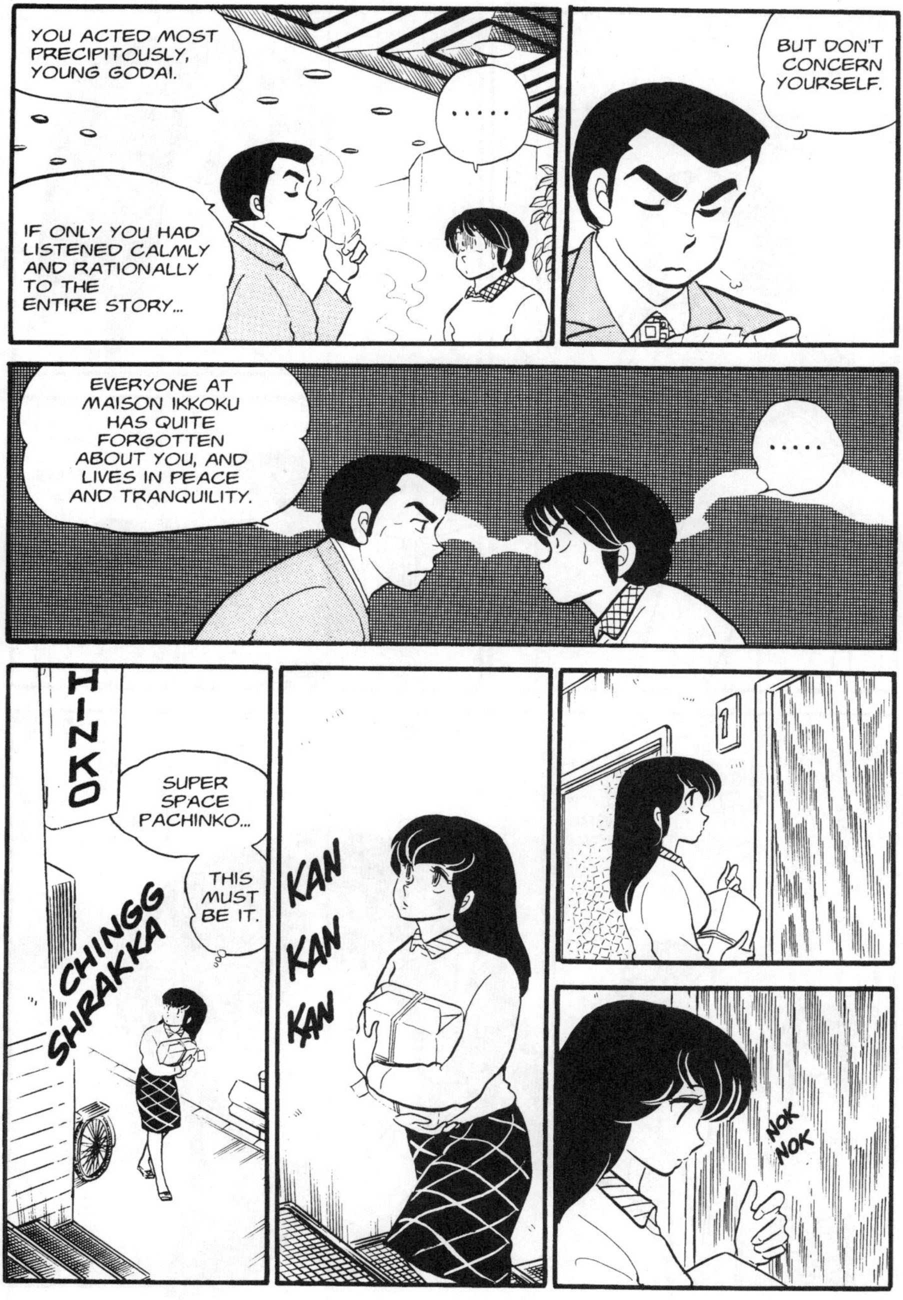
YOU ACTED MOST PRECIPITOUSLY, YOUNG GODAI.
.....
IF ONLY YOU HAD LISTENED CALMLY AND RATIONALLY TO THE ENTIRE STORY...
BUT DON'T CONCERN YOURSELF.
EVERYONE AT MAISON IKKOKU HAS QUITE FORGOTTEN ABOUT YOU, AND LIVES IN PEACE AND TRANQUILITY.
.....
HINKO
SUPER SPACE PACHINKO...
THIS MUST BE IT.
CHINGG SHRAKKA
KAN
KAN
KAN
NOK NOK

HELLO
?

ER...THIS ISN'T
YUSAKU
GODAI'S
ROOM, IS IT...?

SURE
IS!

UM, SORRY
TO PRY,
BUT JUST
WHO ARE
YOU?

AYAKO...I'M
LIVING HERE
WITH YUSAKU.

I...

I
SEE...

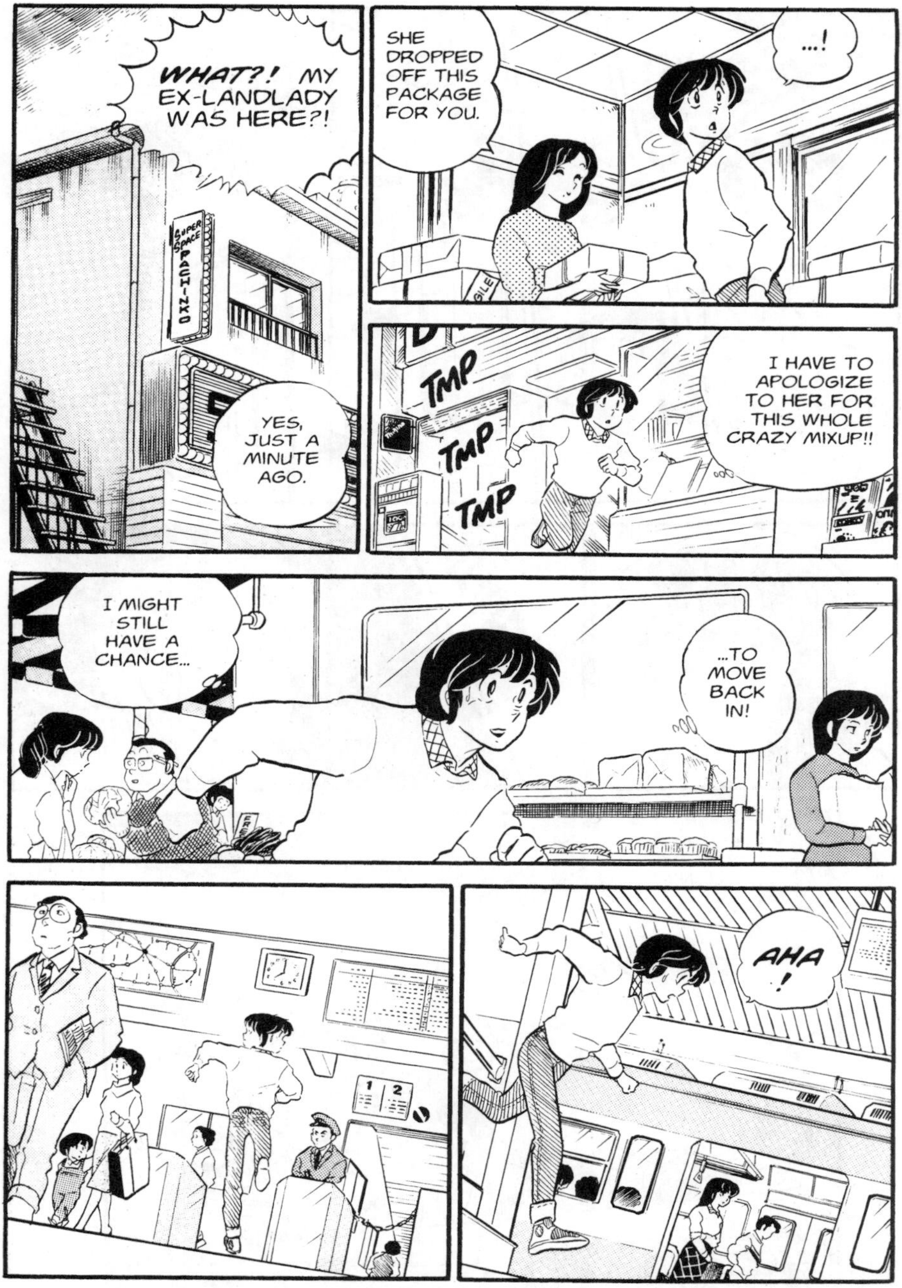
WHAT?! MY EX-LANDLADY WAS HERE?!
SUPER SPACE PACHINKO
YES, JUST A MINUTE AGO.
SHE DROPPED OFF THIS PACKAGE FOR YOU.
...!
TMP
TMP
TMP
I HAVE TO APOLOGIZE TO HER FOR THIS WHOLE CRAZY MIXUP!!
I MIGHT STILL HAVE A CHANCE...
...TO MOVE BACK IN!
AHA!

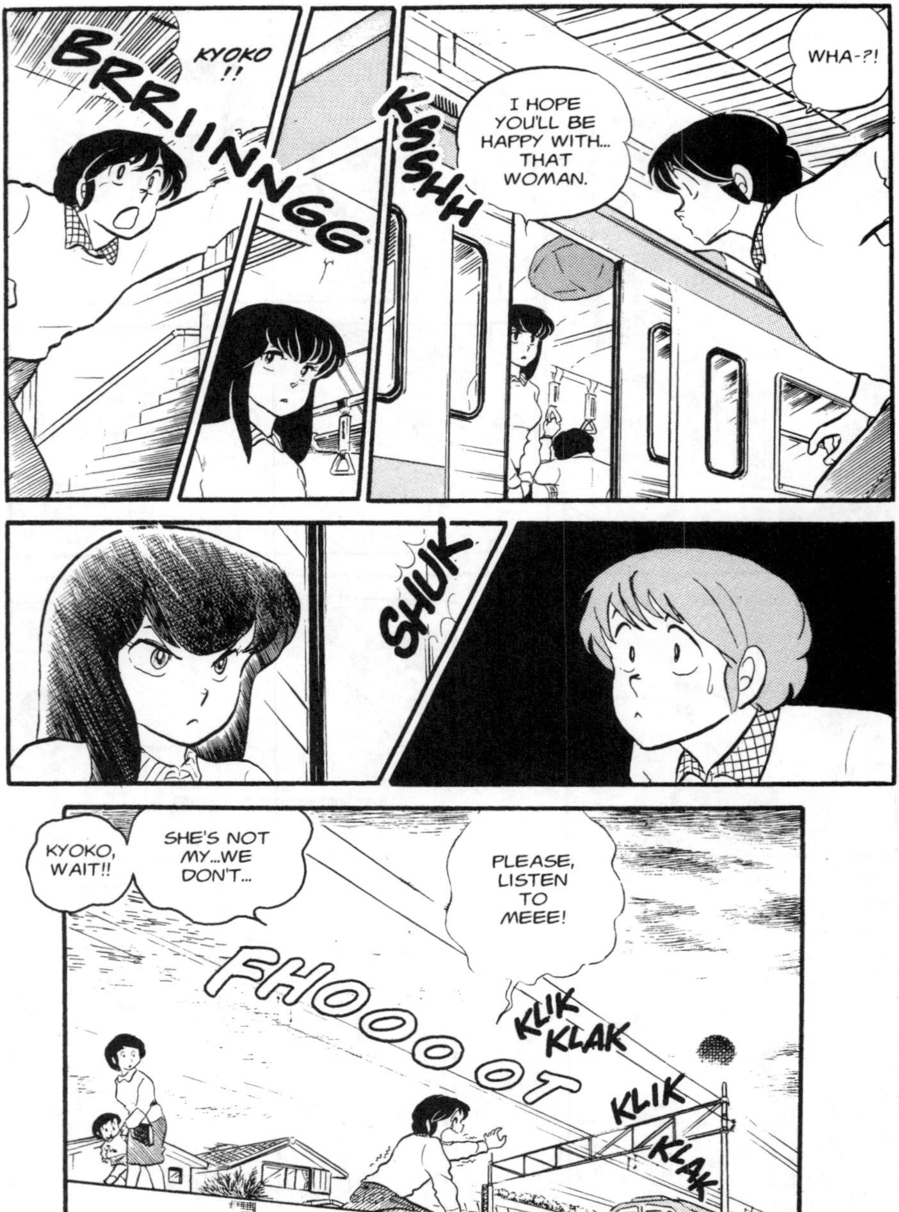
BRRIINNGG
KYOKO !!
KSSHH
I HOPE YOU'LL BE HAPPY WITH... THAT WOMAN.
WHA-?!
SHUK
KYOKO, WAIT!!
SHE'S NOT MY...WE DON'T...
PLEASE, LISTEN TO MEEE!
FHOOOOOT
KLIK KLAK
KLIK KLAK

Part Eleven
The Light in Room 5

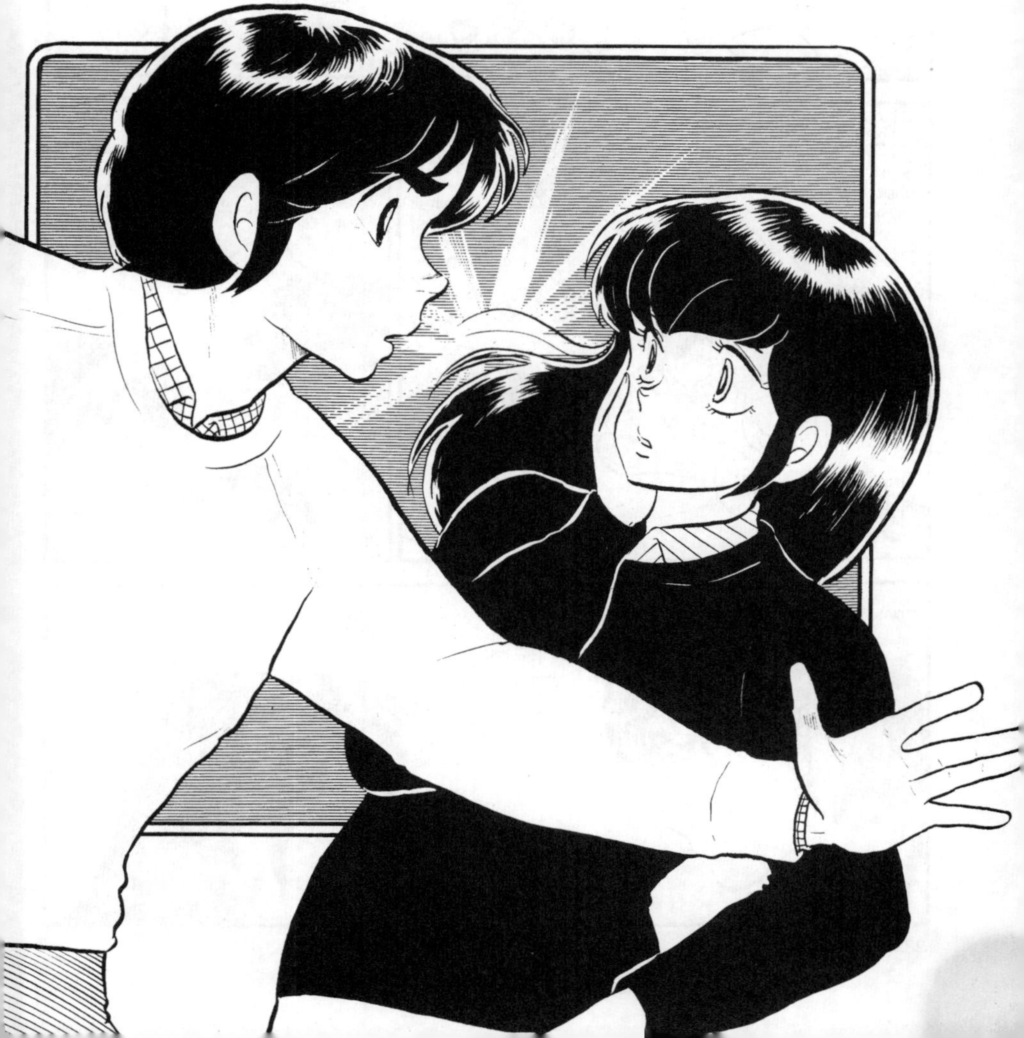

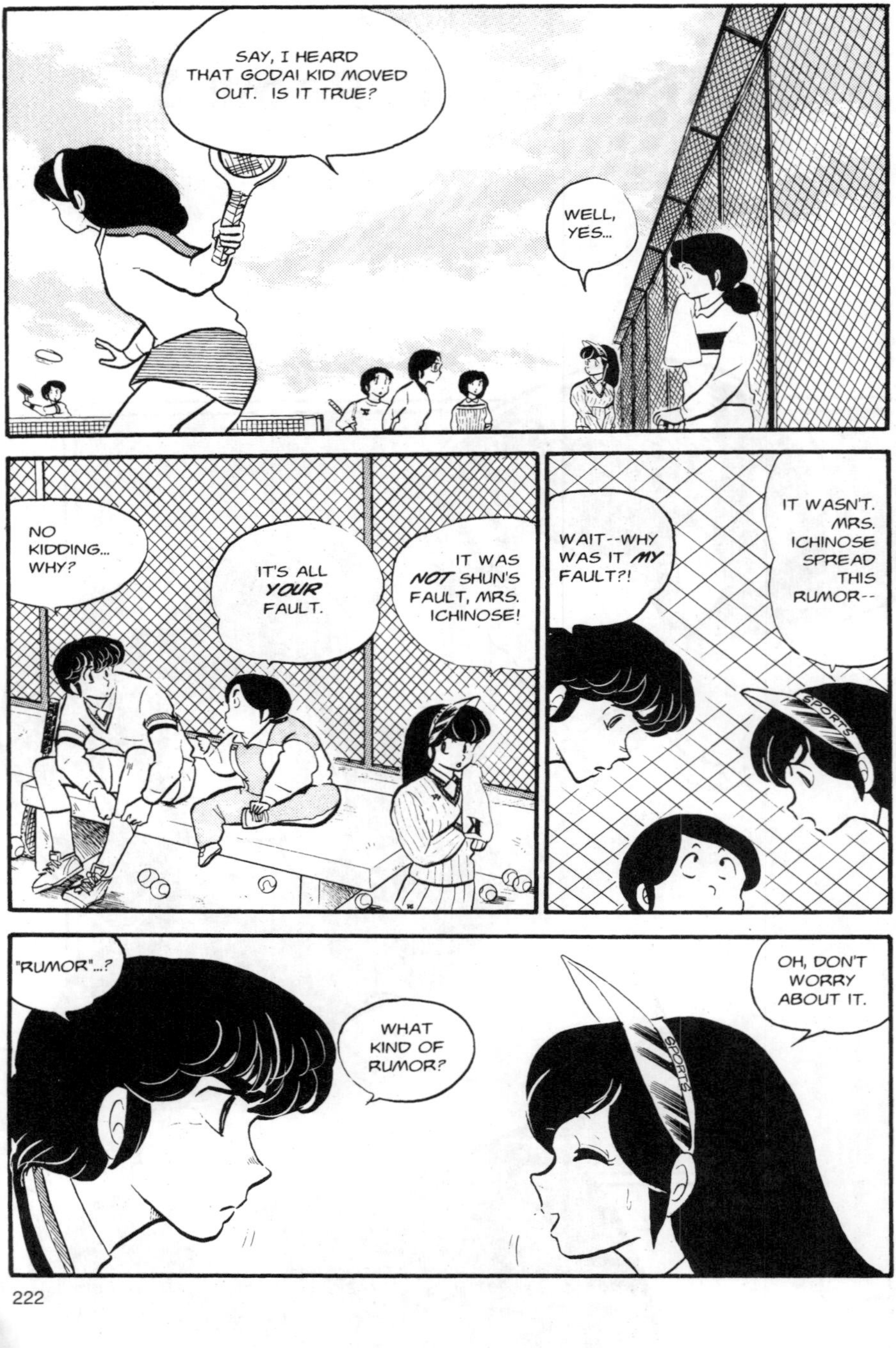
SAY, I HEARD THAT GODAI KID MOVED OUT. IS IT TRUE?
WELL, YES...
NO KIDDING... WHY?
IT'S ALL *YOUR* FAULT.
IT WAS *NOT* SHUN'S FAULT, MRS. ICHINOSE!
WAIT--WHY WAS IT *MY* FAULT?!
IT WASN'T. MRS. ICHINOSE SPREAD THIS RUMOR--
"RUMOR"...?
WHAT KIND OF RUMOR?
OH, DON'T WORRY ABOUT IT.

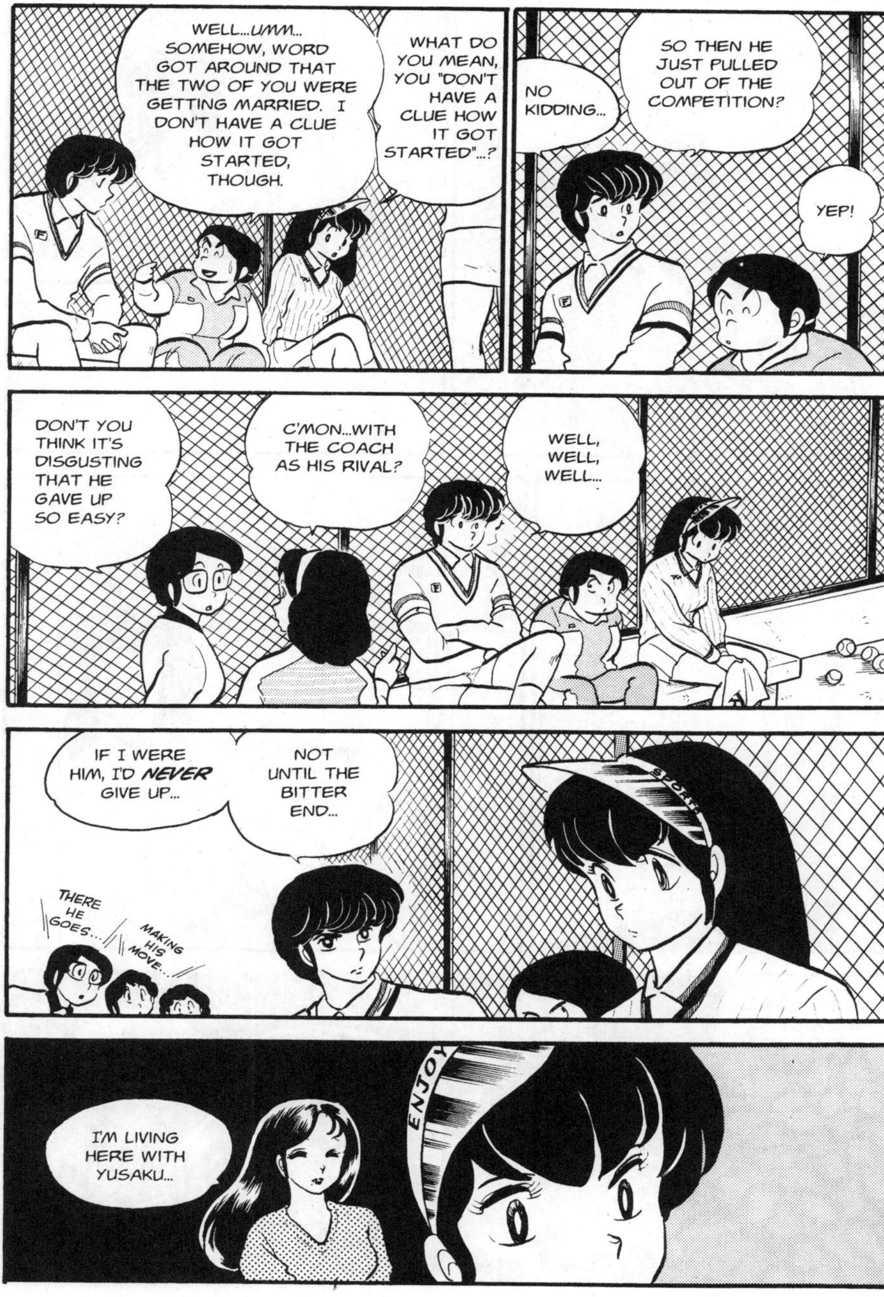
WELL...UMM... SOMEHOW, WORD GOT AROUND THAT THE TWO OF YOU WERE GETTING MARRIED. I DON'T HAVE A CLUE HOW IT GOT STARTED, THOUGH.
WHAT DO YOU MEAN, YOU "DON'T HAVE A CLUE HOW IT GOT STARTED"...?
NO KIDDING...
SO THEN HE JUST PULLED OUT OF THE COMPETITION?
YEP!
DON'T YOU THINK IT'S DISGUSTING THAT HE GAVE UP SO EASY?
C'MON...WITH THE COACH AS HIS RIVAL?
WELL, WELL, WELL...
IF I WERE HIM, I'D NEVER GIVE UP...
NOT UNTIL THE BITTER END...
THERE HE GOES...
MAKING HIS MOVE...
SPORT
ENJOY
I'M LIVING HERE WITH YUSAKU...

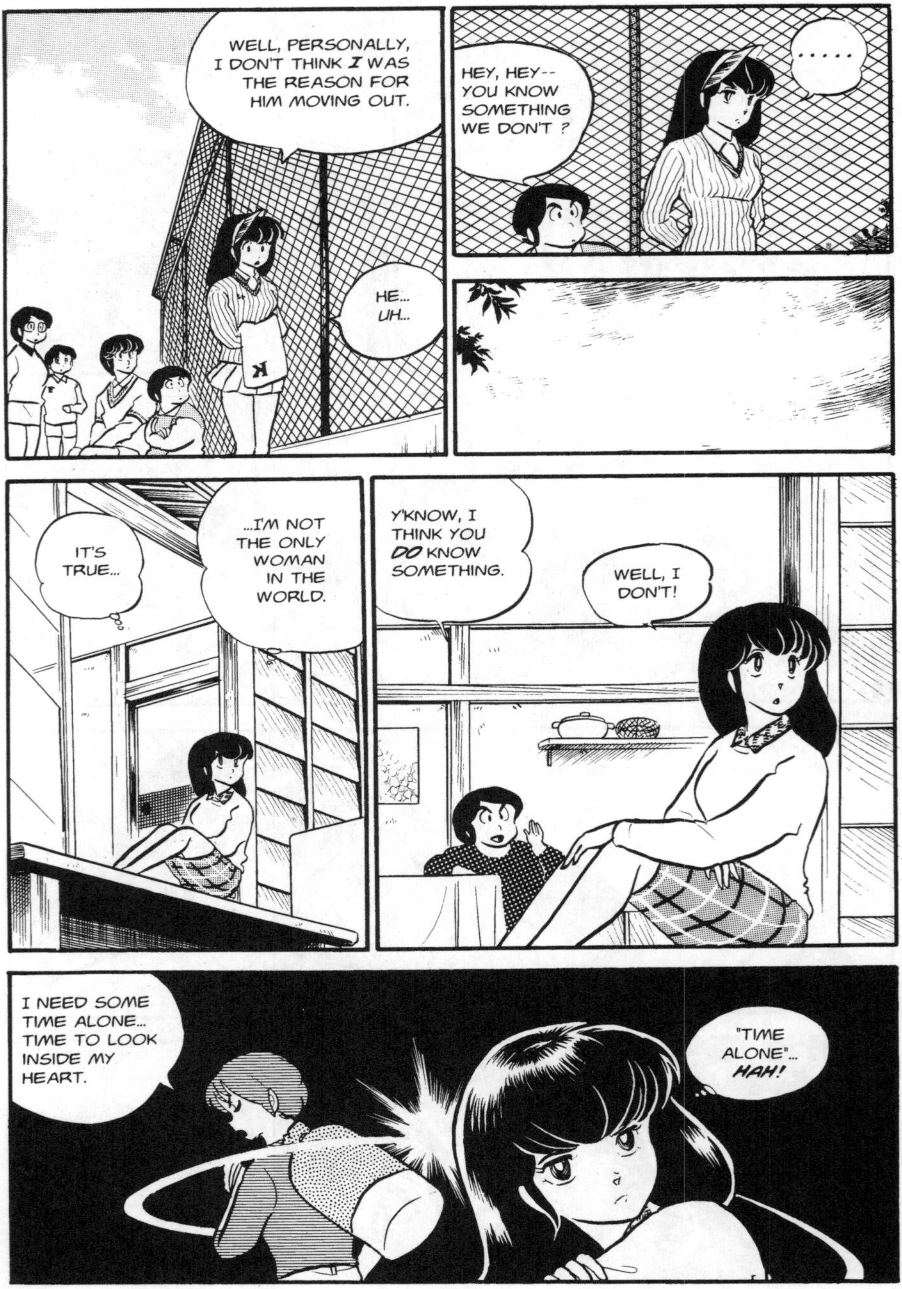
WELL, PERSONALLY, I DON'T THINK I WAS THE REASON FOR HIM MOVING OUT.
HE... UH...
HEY, HEY-- YOU KNOW SOMETHING WE DON'T ?
......
IT'S TRUE...
...I'M NOT THE ONLY WOMAN IN THE WORLD.
Y'KNOW, I THINK YOU DO KNOW SOMETHING.
WELL, I DON'T!
I NEED SOME TIME ALONE... TIME TO LOOK INSIDE MY HEART.
"TIME ALONE"... HAH!

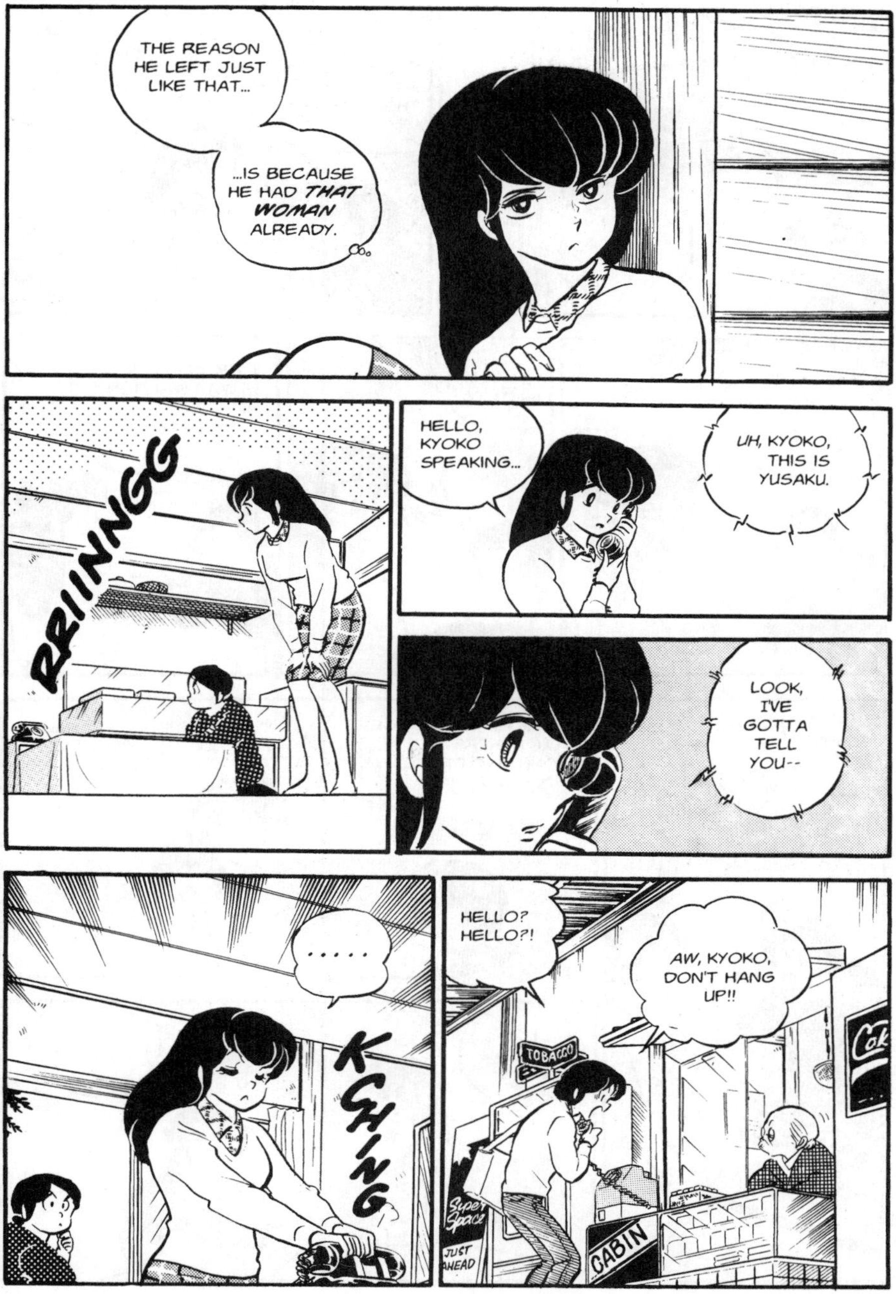
THE REASON HE LEFT JUST LIKE THAT...
...IS BECAUSE HE HAD *THAT WOMAN* ALREADY.
RRIINNGG
HELLO, KYOKO SPEAKING...
UH, KYOKO, THIS IS YUSAKU.
LOOK, I'VE GOTTA TELL YOU--
.....
KCHING
HELLO? HELLO?!
AW, KYOKO, DON'T HANG UP!!
TOBACCO
Super Space
JUST AHEAD
CABIN

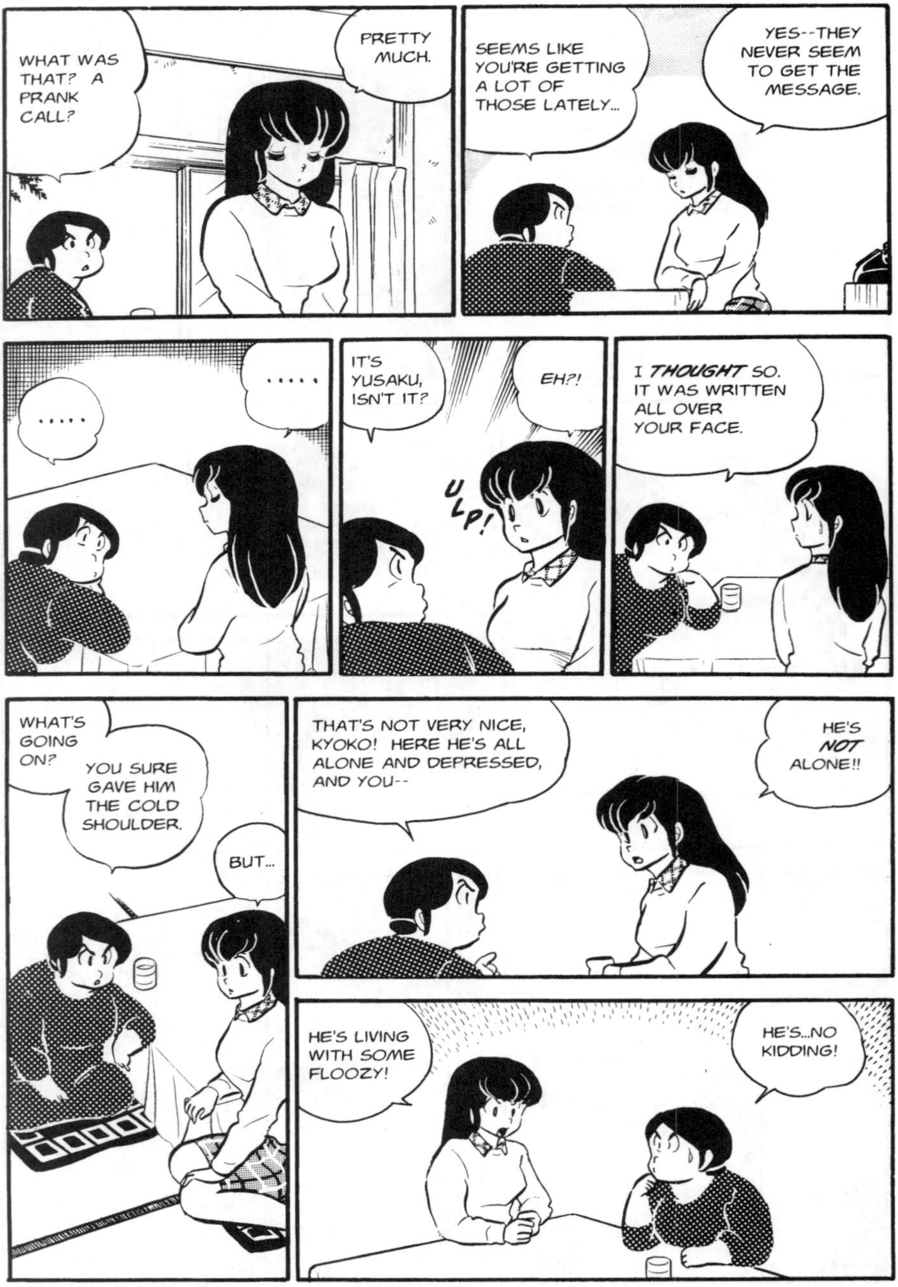
WHAT WAS THAT? A PRANK CALL?
PRETTY MUCH.
SEEMS LIKE YOU'RE GETTING A LOT OF THOSE LATELY...
YES--THEY NEVER SEEM TO GET THE MESSAGE.
.....
.....
IT'S YUSAKU, ISN'T IT?
EH?!
ULP!
I THOUGHT SO. IT WAS WRITTEN ALL OVER YOUR FACE.
WHAT'S GOING ON?
YOU SURE GAVE HIM THE COLD SHOULDER.
BUT...
THAT'S NOT VERY NICE, KYOKO! HERE HE'S ALL ALONE AND DEPRESSED, AND YOU--
HE'S NOT ALONE!!
HE'S LIVING WITH SOME FLOOZY!
HE'S...NO KIDDING!

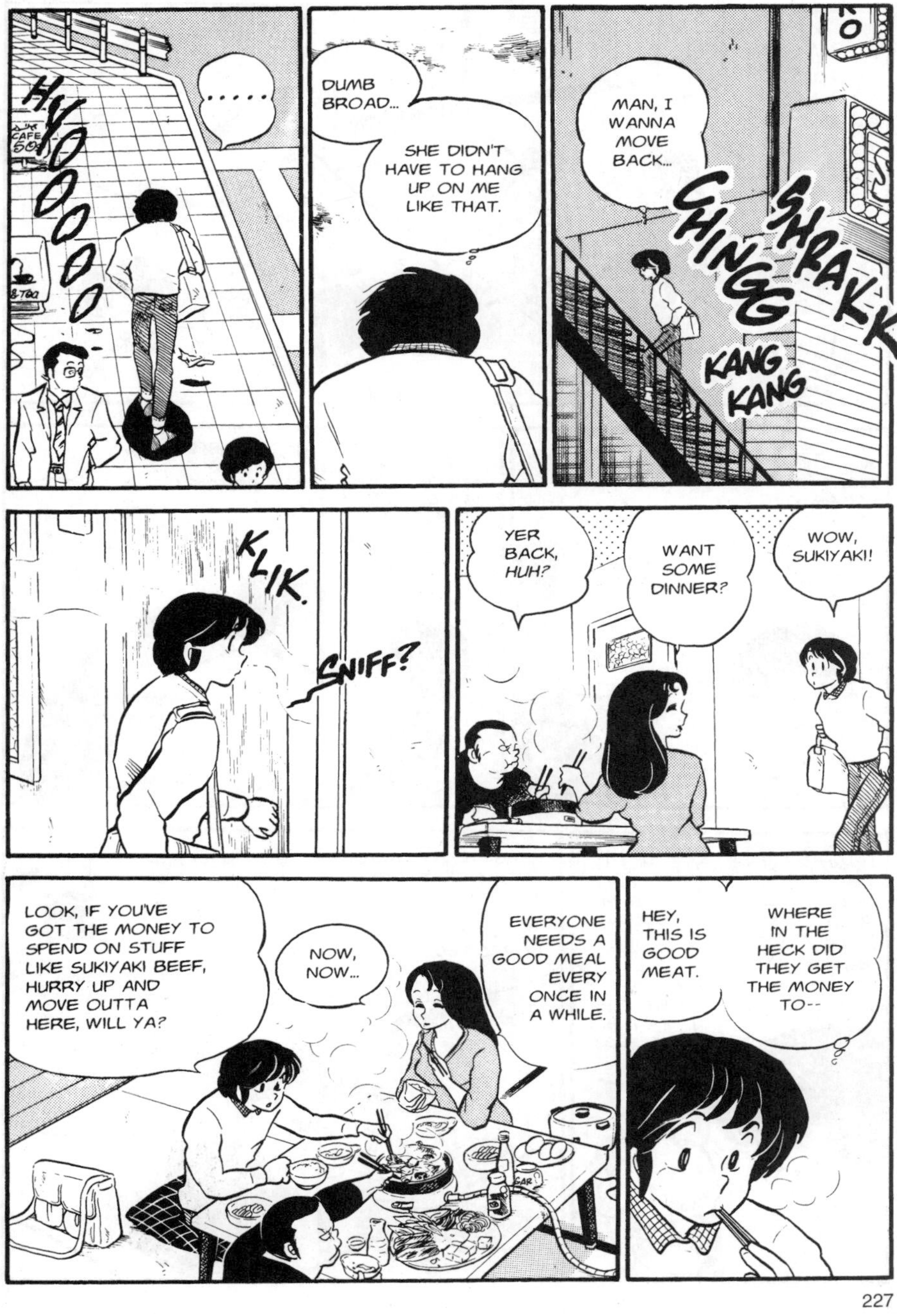
HYOOOOOOO
.....
DUMB BROAD...
SHE DIDN'T HAVE TO HANG UP ON ME LIKE THAT.
MAN, I WANNA MOVE BACK...
CHINGG
SHRAKKK
KANG KANG
KLIK.
SNIFF?
YER BACK, HUH?
WANT SOME DINNER?
WOW, SUKIYAKI!
LOOK, IF YOU'VE GOT THE MONEY TO SPEND ON STUFF LIKE SUKIYAKI BEEF, HURRY UP AND MOVE OUTTA HERE, WILL YA?
NOW, NOW...
EVERYONE NEEDS A GOOD MEAL EVERY ONCE IN A WHILE.
HEY, THIS IS GOOD MEAT.
WHERE IN THE HECK DID THEY GET THE MONEY TO--

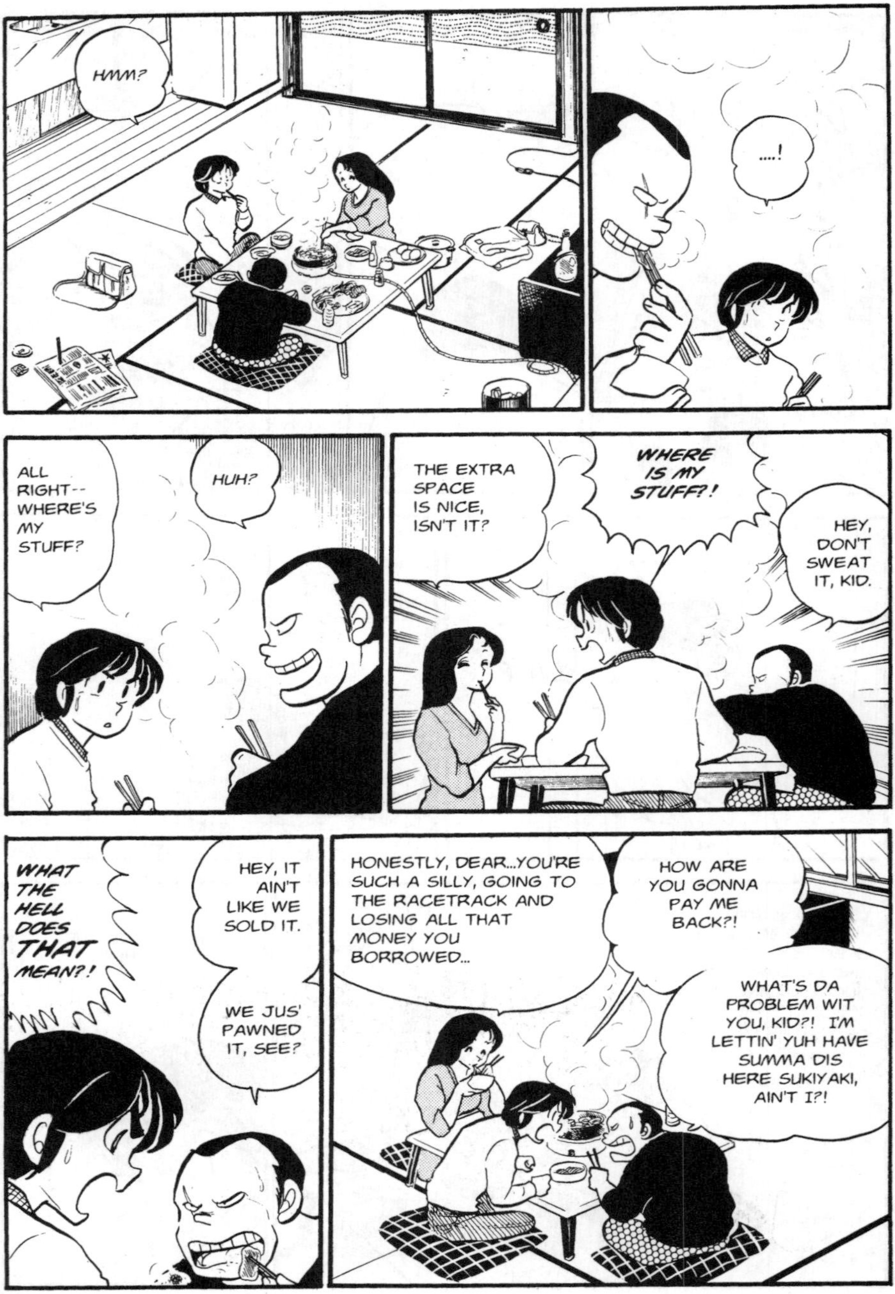
HMM?
....!
ALL RIGHT-- WHERE'S MY STUFF?
HUH?
THE EXTRA SPACE IS NICE, ISN'T IT?
WHERE IS MY STUFF?!
HEY, DON'T SWEAT IT, KID.
WHAT THE HELL DOES THAT MEAN?!
HEY, IT AIN'T LIKE WE SOLD IT.
WE JUS' PAWNED IT, SEE?
HONESTLY, DEAR...YOU'RE SUCH A SILLY, GOING TO THE RACETRACK AND LOSING ALL THAT MONEY YOU BORROWED...
HOW ARE YOU GONNA PAY ME BACK?!
WHAT'S DA PROBLEM WIT YOU, KID?! I'M LETTIN' YUH HAVE SUMMA DIS HERE SUKIYAKI, AIN'T I?!

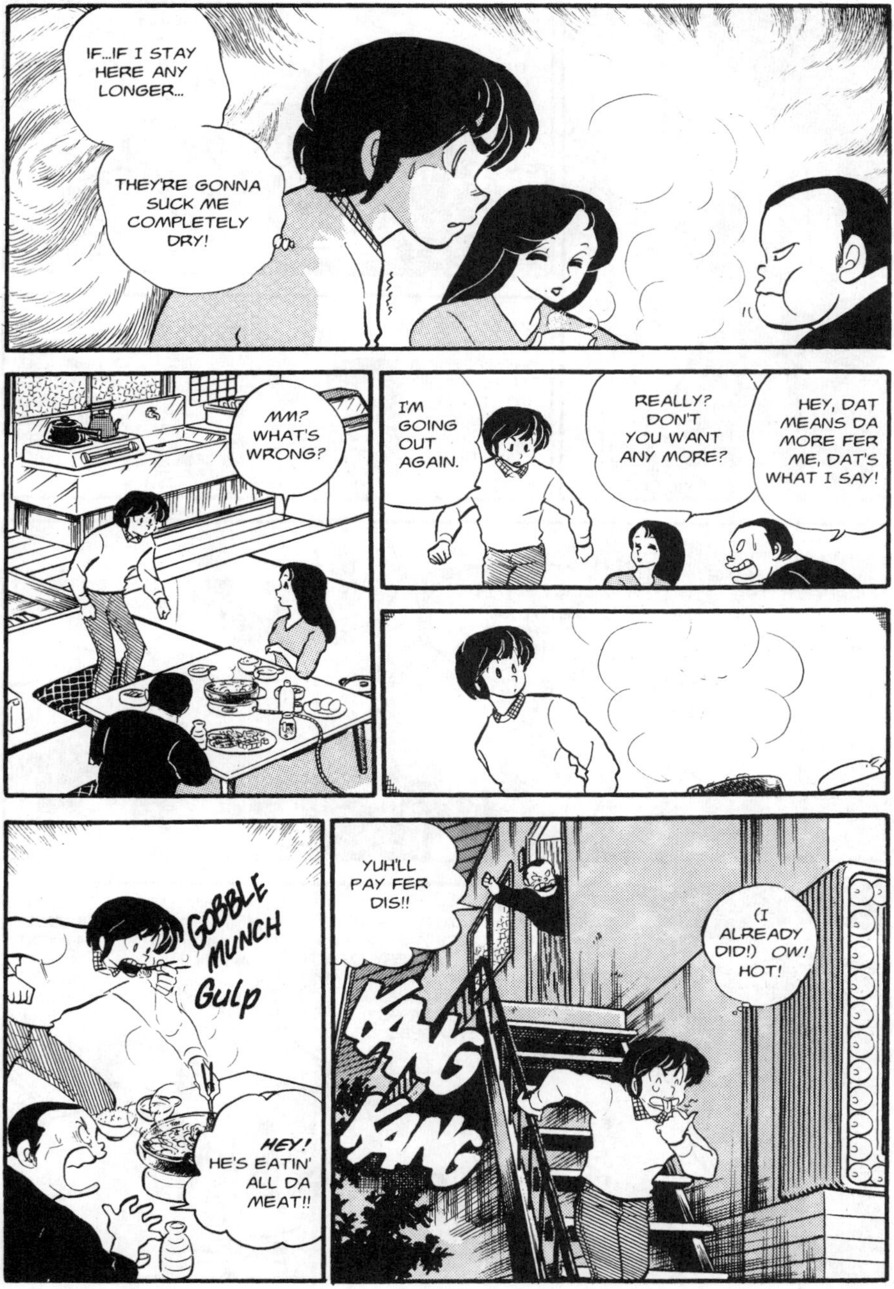

IF...IF I STAY HERE ANY LONGER...
THEY'RE GONNA SUCK ME COMPLETELY DRY!
MM? WHAT'S WRONG?
I'M GOING OUT AGAIN.
REALLY? DON'T YOU WANT ANY MORE?
HEY, DAT MEANS DA MORE FER ME, DAT'S WHAT I SAY!
GOBBLE MUNCH Gulp
HEY! HE'S EATIN' ALL DA MEAT!!
YUH'LL PAY FER DIS!!
KANG KANG
(I ALREADY DID!) OW! HOT!

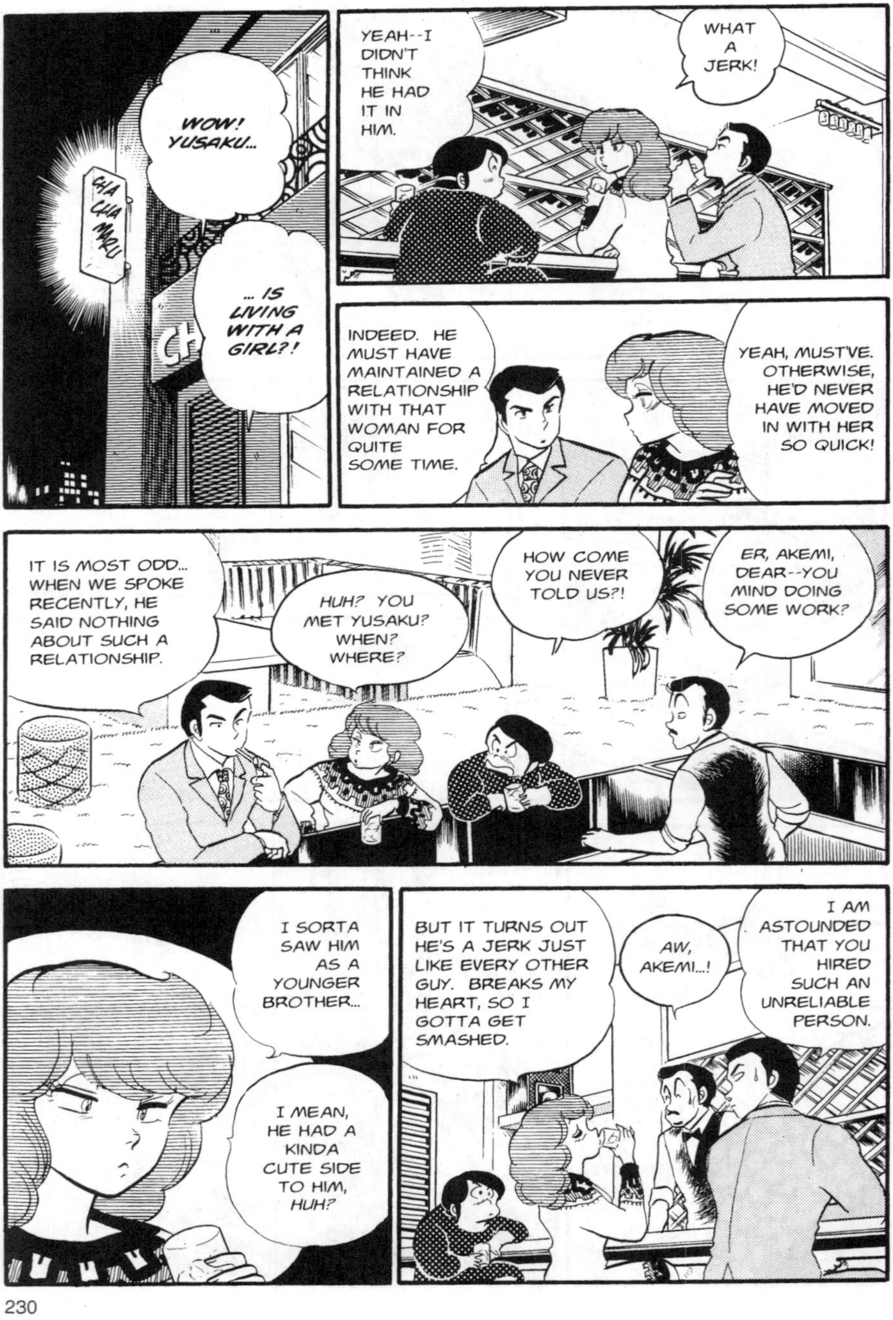
WOW! YUSAKU...
CHA CHA MARU
... IS LIVING WITH A GIRL?!
YEAH--I DIDN'T THINK HE HAD IT IN HIM.
WHAT A JERK!
INDEED. HE MUST HAVE MAINTAINED A RELATIONSHIP WITH THAT WOMAN FOR QUITE SOME TIME.
YEAH, MUST'VE. OTHERWISE, HE'D NEVER HAVE MOVED IN WITH HER SO QUICK!
IT IS MOST ODD... WHEN WE SPOKE RECENTLY, HE SAID NOTHING ABOUT SUCH A RELATIONSHIP.
HUH? YOU MET YUSAKU? WHEN? WHERE?
HOW COME YOU NEVER TOLD US?!
ER, AKEMI, DEAR--YOU MIND DOING SOME WORK?
I SORTA SAW HIM AS A YOUNGER BROTHER...
I MEAN, HE HAD A KINDA CUTE SIDE TO HIM, HUH?
BUT IT TURNS OUT HE'S A JERK JUST LIKE EVERY OTHER GUY. BREAKS MY HEART, SO I GOTTA GET SMASHED.
AW, AKEMI...!
I AM ASTOUNDED THAT YOU HIRED SUCH AN UNRELIABLE PERSON.

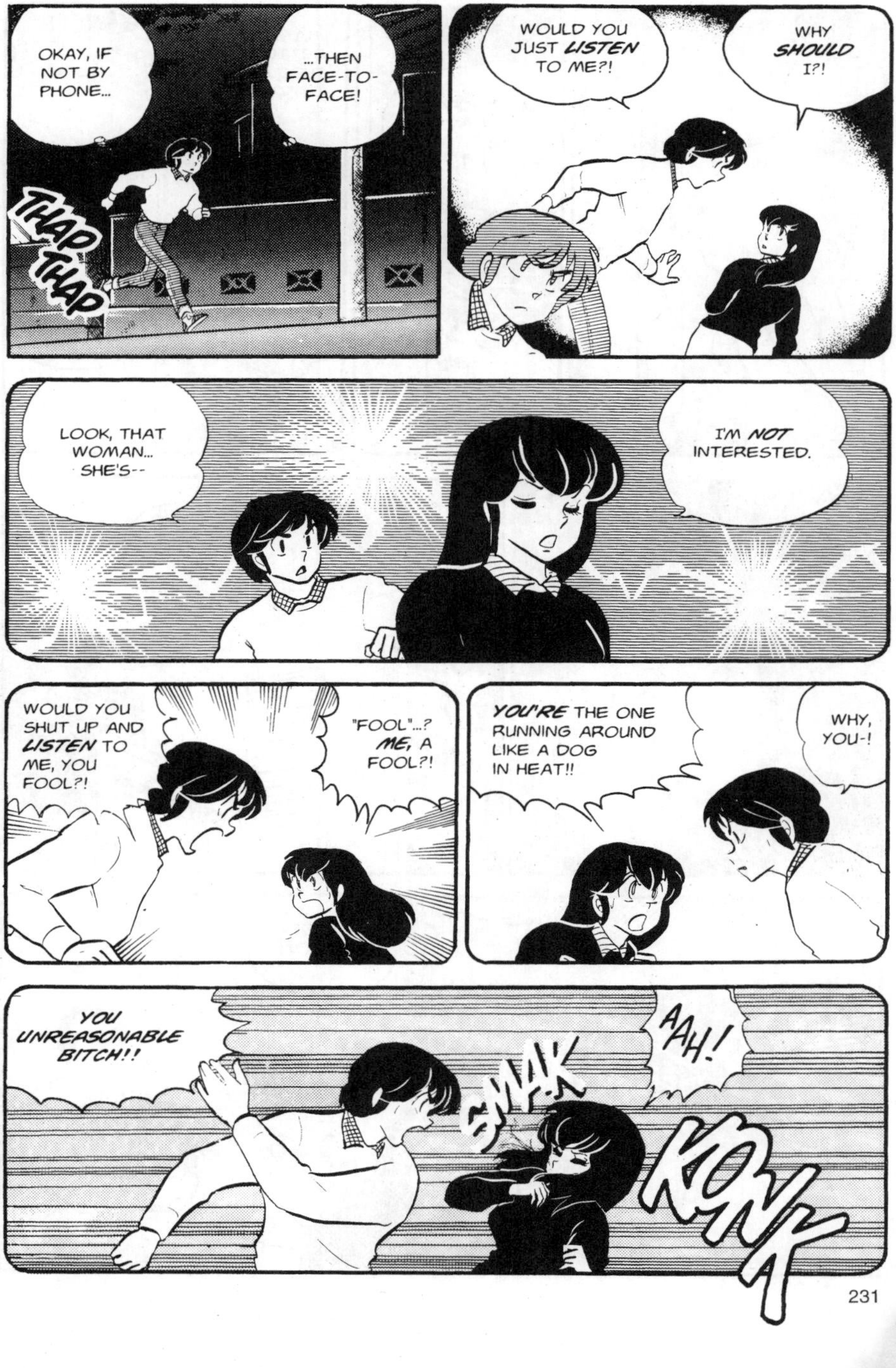
OKAY, IF NOT BY PHONE...
...THEN FACE-TO-FACE!
THAP THAP
WOULD YOU JUST LISTEN TO ME?!
WHY SHOULD I?!
LOOK, THAT WOMAN... SHE'S--
I'M NOT INTERESTED.
WOULD YOU SHUT UP AND LISTEN TO ME, YOU FOOL?!
"FOOL"...? ME, A FOOL?!
YOU'RE THE ONE RUNNING AROUND LIKE A DOG IN HEAT!!
WHY, YOU-!
YOU UNREASONABLE BITCH!!
SMAK
AAH!
KONK

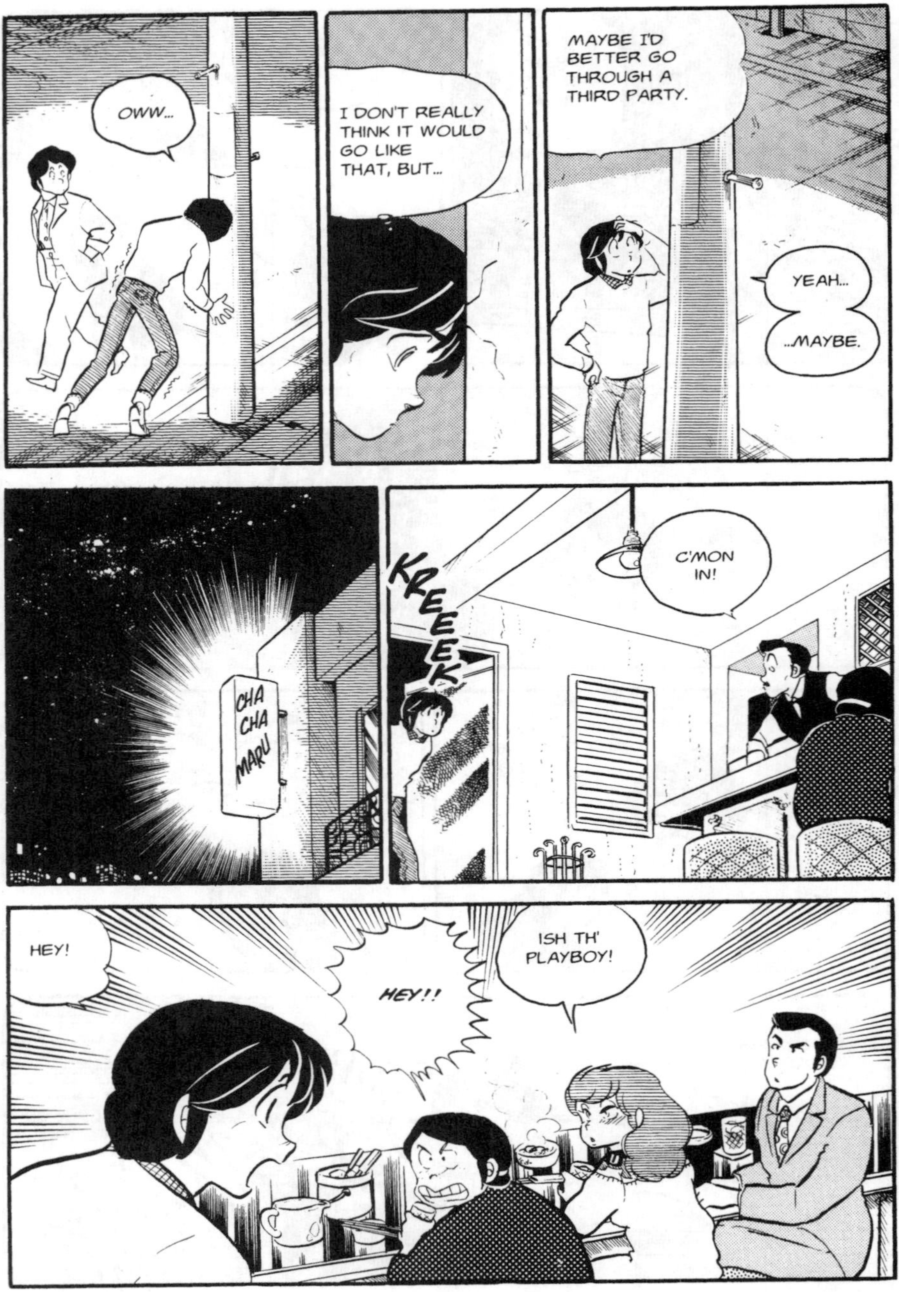
OWW...
I DON'T REALLY THINK IT WOULD GO LIKE THAT, BUT...
MAYBE I'D BETTER GO THROUGH A THIRD PARTY.
YEAH...
...MAYBE.
CHA CHA MARU
KREEEEK
C'MON IN!
HEY!
HEY!!
ISH TH' PLAYBOY!

"PLAYBOY"...? W-WHAT DO YOU MEAN BY *THAT?*

DON'T TRY T' ACT THE INNOSHENT WITH *ME,* SON!

FWAP

YEAH, YOU GOT A LOTTA *GUTSH* COMING 'ROUND HERE!

SAY...YOU'RE ALL PRETTY DRUNK!

FFT FFT

FORGET IT, THEN.

YOU GUYS ARE USELESS.

RUNNIN' AWAY, HUH?! COWARD!

HALT, YOUNG MAN.

I AM QUITE SOBER.

I WILL GLADLY HEAR YOUR TALE.

IF YOU WILL, IN RETURN, BUY ME A DRINK OR TWO.

. . . . .

--AND SO SHE WAS JUST LIVING THERE WHEN I ARRIVED. SHE'S GOT A HUSBAND, TOO!

SLAP

SHO SHE'S A *HIC* *MARRIED* WOMAN, HUH?

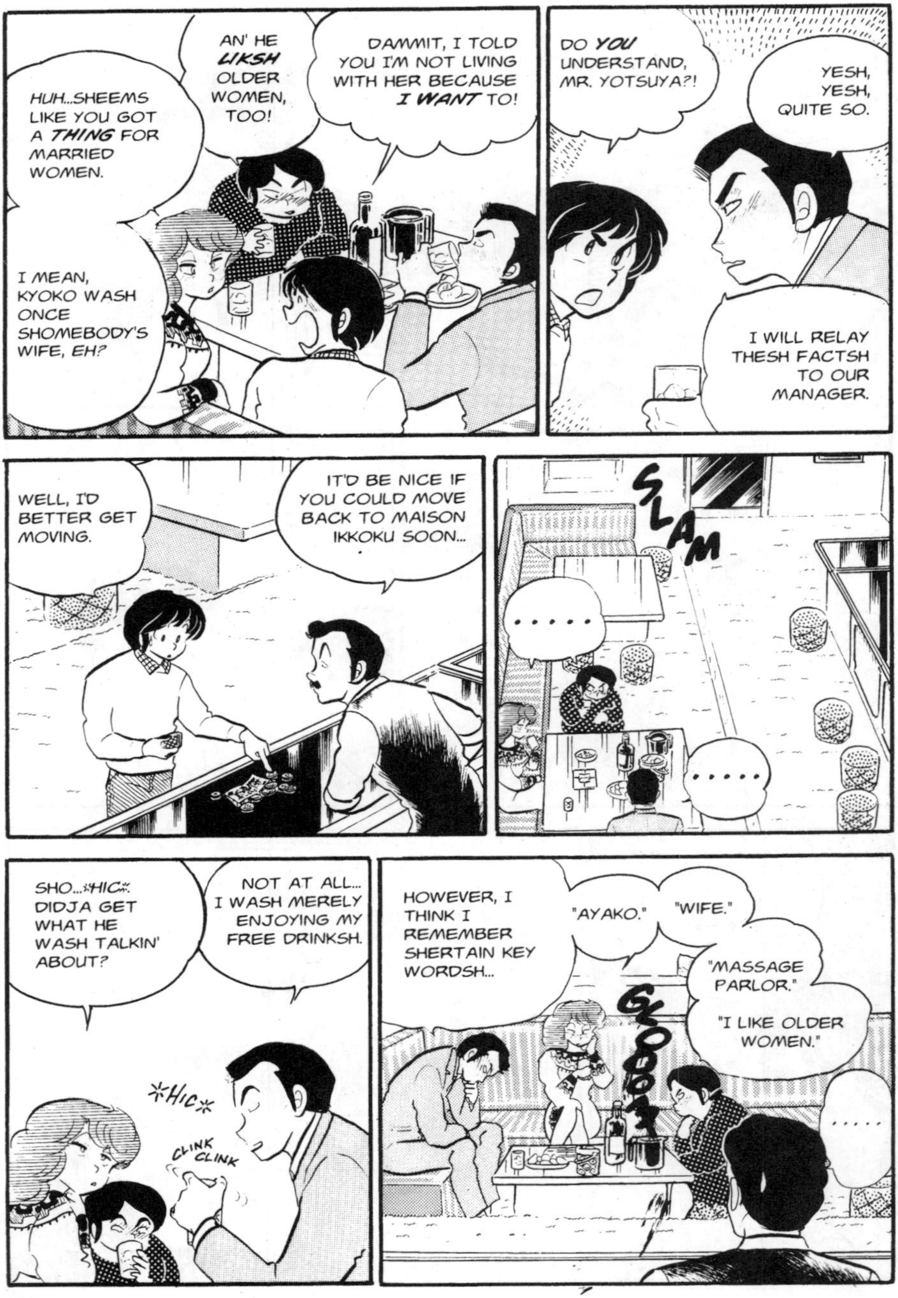
HUH...SHEEMS LIKE YOU GOT A THING FOR MARRIED WOMEN.
AN' HE LIKSH OLDER WOMEN, TOO!
DAMMIT, I TOLD YOU I'M NOT LIVING WITH HER BECAUSE I WANT TO!
I MEAN, KYOKO WASH ONCE SHOMEBODY'S WIFE, EH?
DO YOU UNDERSTAND, MR. YOTSUYA?!
YESH, YESH, QUITE SO.
I WILL RELAY THESH FACTSH TO OUR MANAGER.
WELL, I'D BETTER GET MOVING.
IT'D BE NICE IF YOU COULD MOVE BACK TO MAISON IKKOKU SOON...
SLAM
......
.....
SHO...*HIC* DIDJA GET WHAT HE WASH TALKIN' ABOUT?
NOT AT ALL... I WASH MERELY ENJOYING MY FREE DRINKSH.
HIC
CLINK CLINK
HOWEVER, I THINK I REMEMBER SHERTAIN KEY WORDSH...
"AYAKO."
"WIFE."
"MASSAGE PARLOR."
"I LIKE OLDER WOMEN."
.....

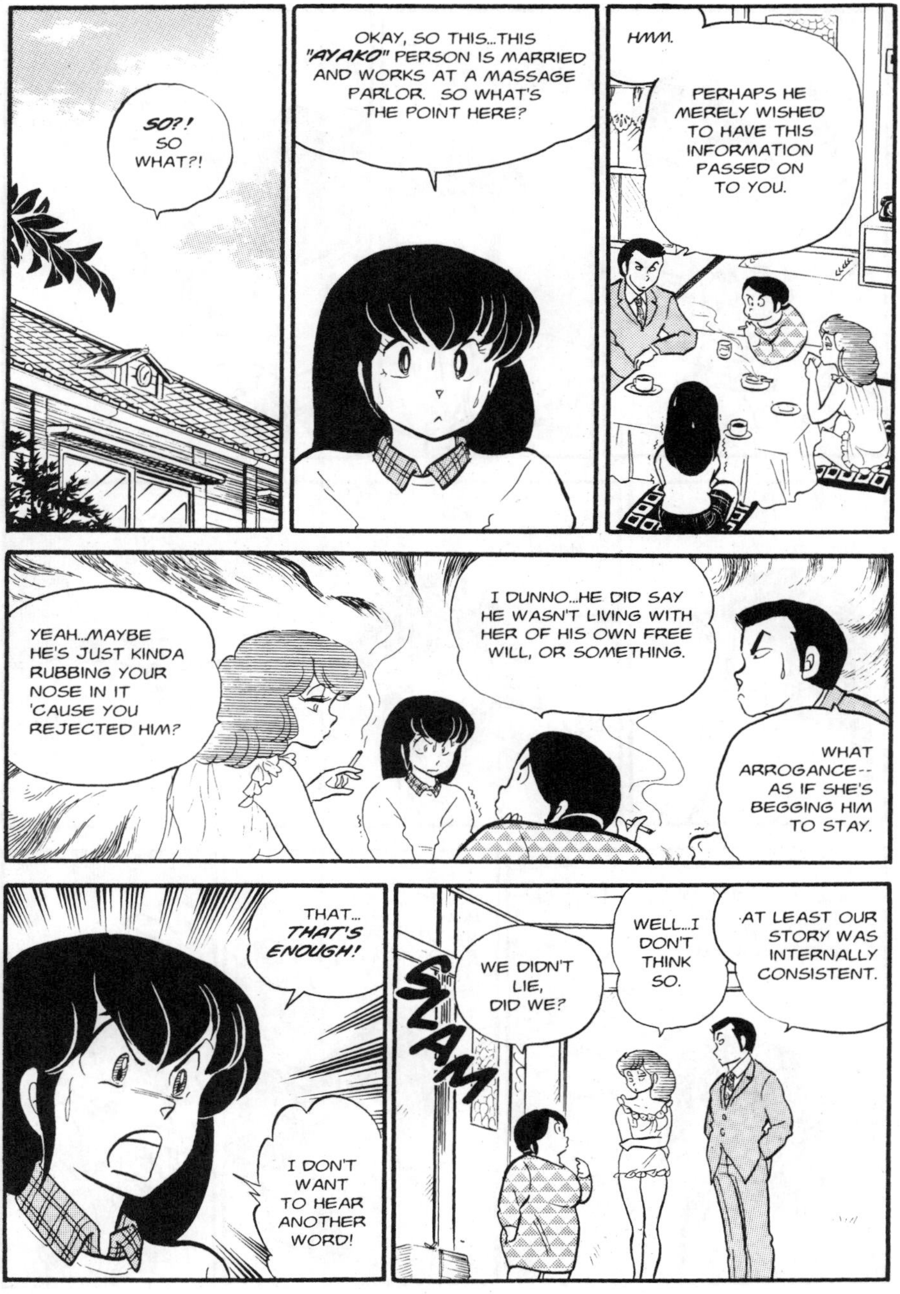
SO?! SO WHAT?!
OKAY, SO THIS...THIS "AYAKO" PERSON IS MARRIED AND WORKS AT A MASSAGE PARLOR. SO WHAT'S THE POINT HERE?
HMM.
PERHAPS HE MERELY WISHED TO HAVE THIS INFORMATION PASSED ON TO YOU.
YEAH...MAYBE HE'S JUST KINDA RUBBING YOUR NOSE IN IT 'CAUSE YOU REJECTED HIM?
I DUNNO...HE DID SAY HE WASN'T LIVING WITH HER OF HIS OWN FREE WILL, OR SOMETHING.
WHAT ARROGANCE-- AS IF SHE'S BEGGING HIM TO STAY.
THAT... THAT'S ENOUGH!
I DON'T WANT TO HEAR ANOTHER WORD!
SLAM
WE DIDN'T LIE, DID WE?
WELL...I DON'T THINK SO.
AT LEAST OUR STORY WAS INTERNALLY CONSISTENT.

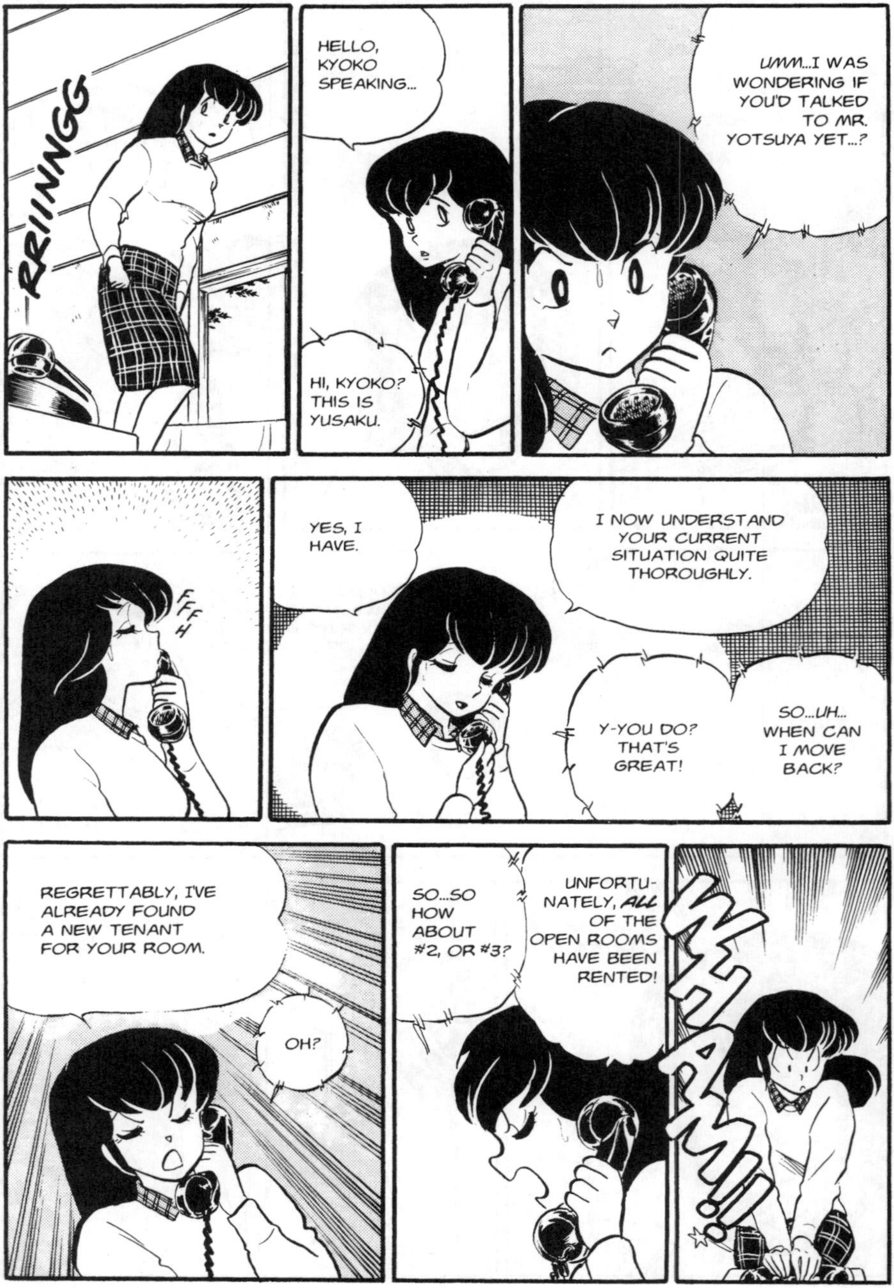
RRIINNGG
HELLO, KYOKO SPEAKING...
HI, KYOKO? THIS IS YUSAKU.
UMM...I WAS WONDERING IF YOU'D TALKED TO MR. YOTSUYA YET...?
FFFH
YES, I HAVE.
I NOW UNDERSTAND YOUR CURRENT SITUATION QUITE THOROUGHLY.
Y-YOU DO? THAT'S GREAT!
SO...UH... WHEN CAN I MOVE BACK?
REGRETTABLY, I'VE ALREADY FOUND A NEW TENANT FOR YOUR ROOM.
OH?
SO...SO HOW ABOUT #2, OR #3?
UNFORTU-NATELY, ALL OF THE OPEN ROOMS HAVE BEEN RENTED!
WHAM!!

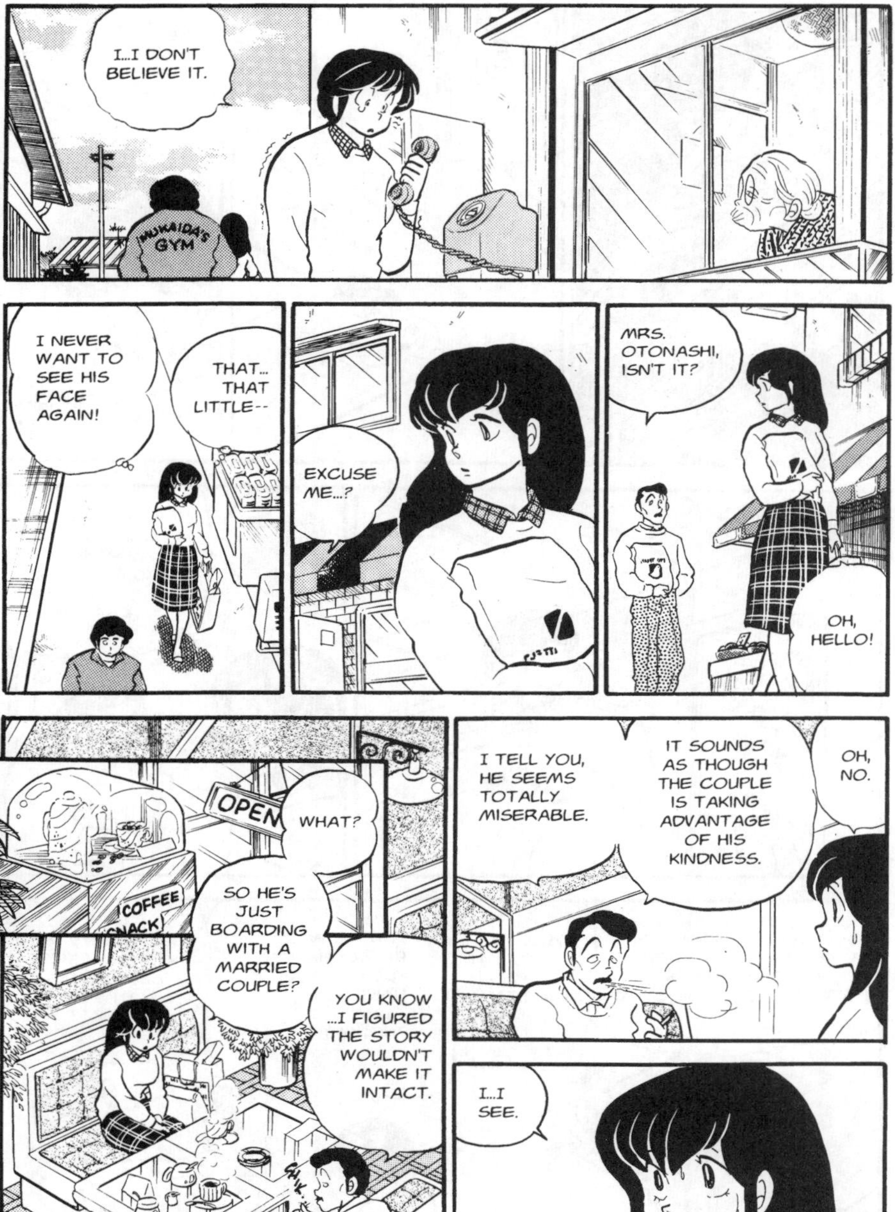
I...I DON'T BELIEVE IT.
MUKAIDA'S GYM
I NEVER WANT TO SEE HIS FACE AGAIN!
THAT... THAT LITTLE--
EXCUSE ME...?
MRS. OTONASHI, ISN'T IT?
OH, HELLO!
OPEN
COFFEE
SNACK
WHAT?
SO HE'S JUST BOARDING WITH A MARRIED COUPLE?
YOU KNOW ...I FIGURED THE STORY WOULDN'T MAKE IT INTACT.
I TELL YOU, HE SEEMS TOTALLY MISERABLE.
IT SOUNDS AS THOUGH THE COUPLE IS TAKING ADVANTAGE OF HIS KINDNESS.
OH, NO.
I...I SEE.

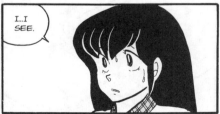

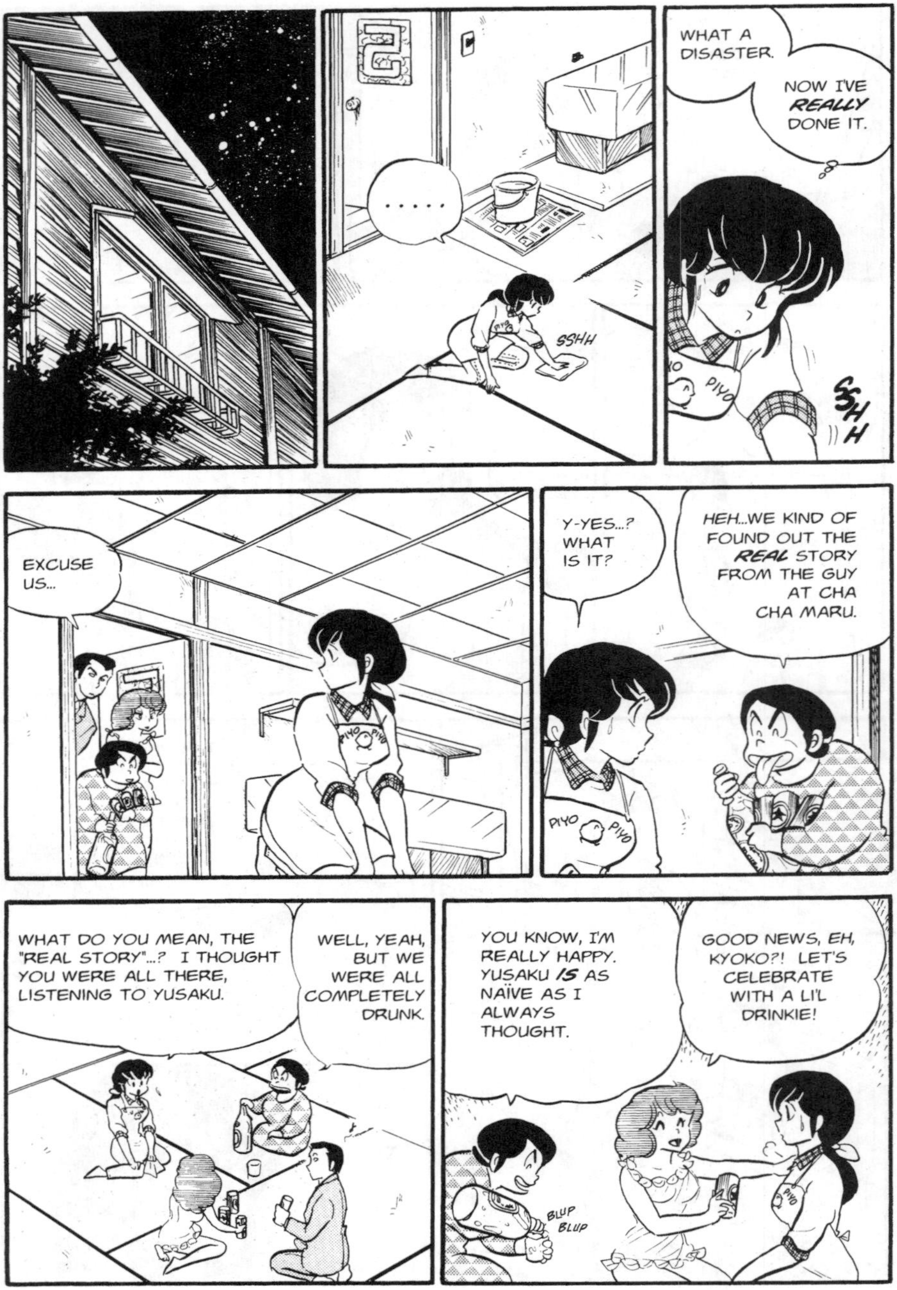
......
PIYO
SSHH
WHAT A DISASTER.
NOW I'VE *REALLY* DONE IT.
PIYO PIYO
SSHH
EXCUSE US...
PIYO PIYO
Y-YES...? WHAT IS IT?
HEH...WE KIND OF FOUND OUT THE *REAL* STORY FROM THE GUY AT CHA CHA MARU.
PIYO PIYO
WHAT DO YOU MEAN, THE "REAL STORY"...? I THOUGHT YOU WERE ALL THERE, LISTENING TO YUSAKU.
WELL, YEAH, BUT WE WERE ALL COMPLETELY DRUNK.
YOU KNOW, I'M REALLY HAPPY. YUSAKU *IS* AS NAÏVE AS I ALWAYS THOUGHT.
GOOD NEWS, EH, KYOKO?! LET'S CELEBRATE WITH A LI'L DRINKIE!
BLUP BLUP
PIYO

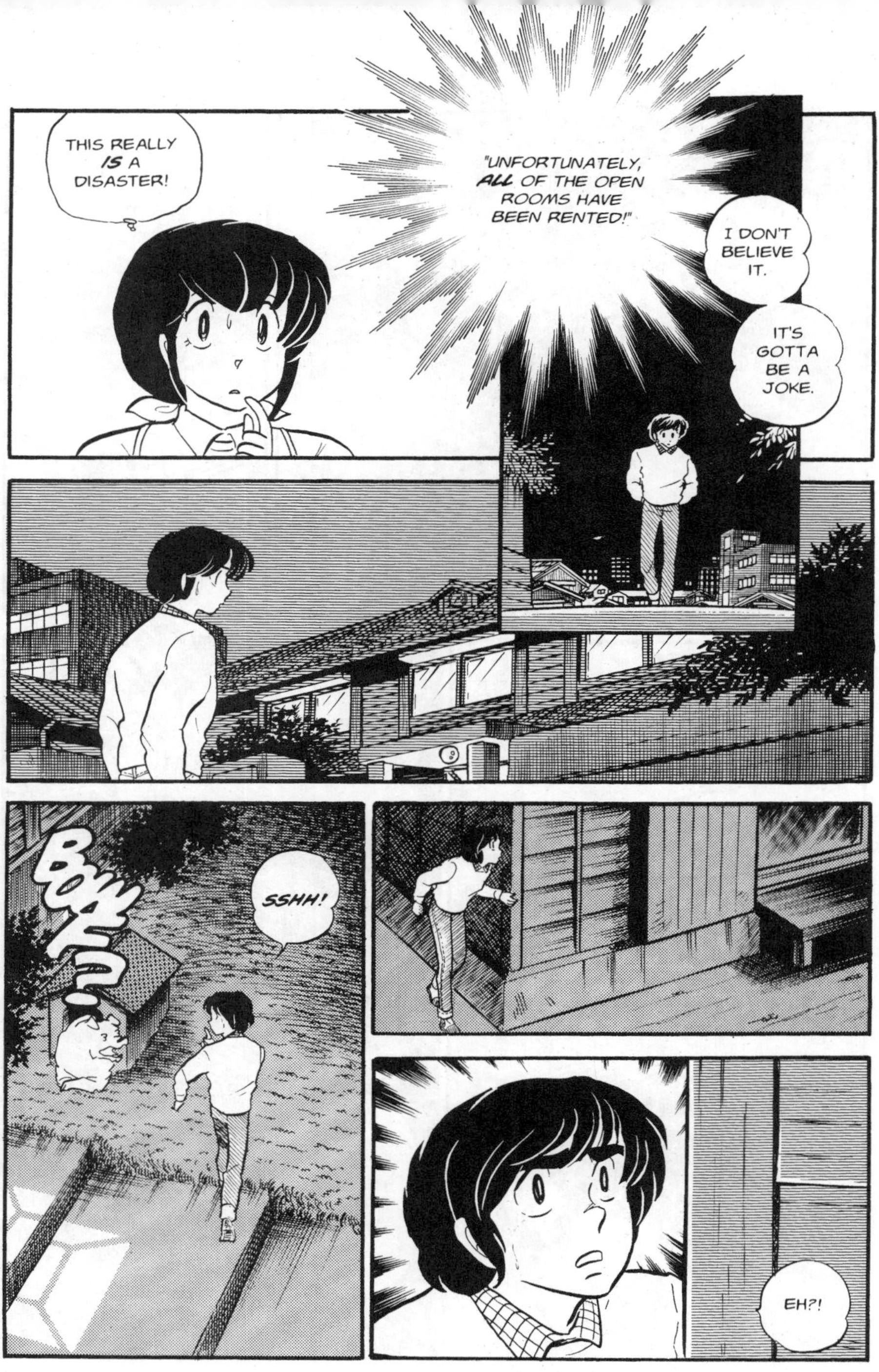
THIS REALLY IS A DISASTER!
"UNFORTUNATELY, ALL OF THE OPEN ROOMS HAVE BEEN RENTED!"
I DON'T BELIEVE IT.
IT'S GOTTA BE A JOKE.
SSHH!
EH?!

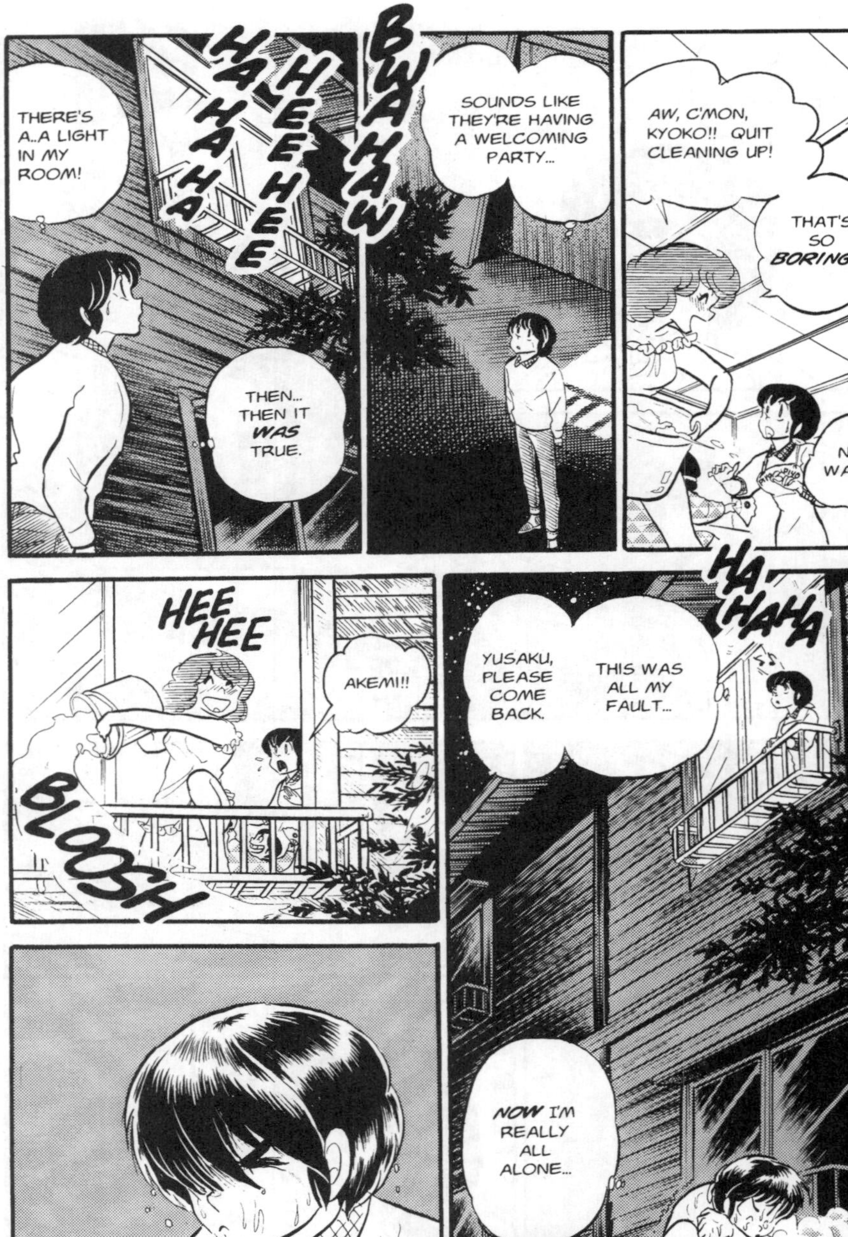

HA HA HA HA HA
THERE'S A..A LIGHT IN MY ROOM!
HEE HEE HEE HEE
THEN... THEN IT WAS TRUE.
BWAHAHAW
SOUNDS LIKE THEY'RE HAVING A WELCOMING PARTY...
AW, C'MON, KYOKO!! QUIT CLEANING UP!
THAT'S SO BORING!!
NO, WAIT-!
HEE HEE
AKEMI!!
BLOOSH
HA, HAHAHA
YUSAKU, PLEASE COME BACK.
THIS WAS ALL MY FAULT...
NOW I'M REALLY ALL ALONE...

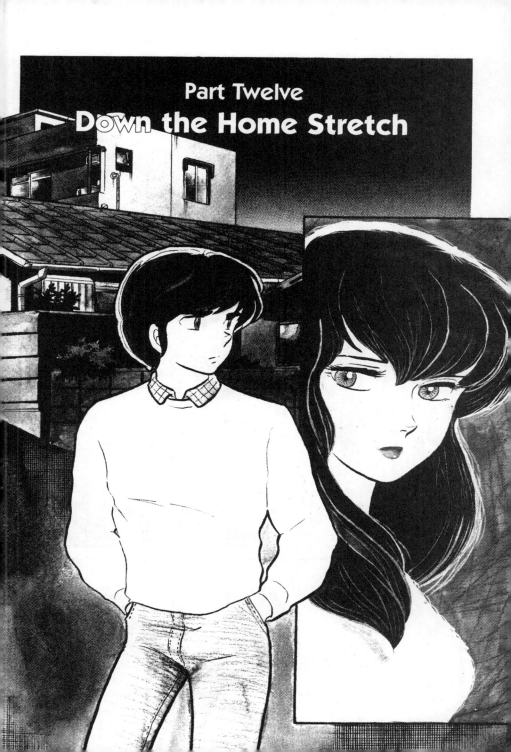

Part Twelve
Down the Home Stretch

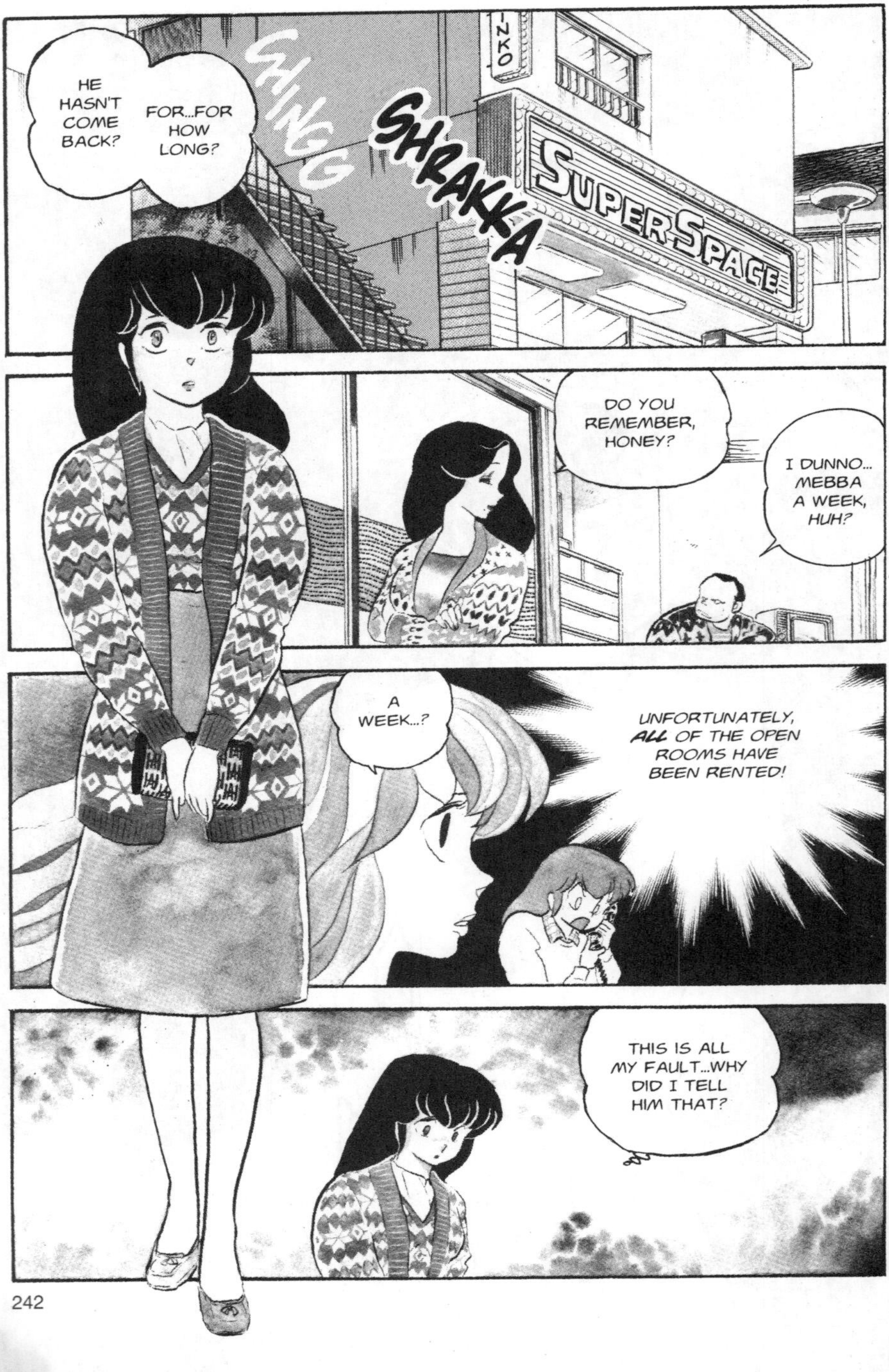
HE HASN'T COME BACK?
FOR...FOR HOW LONG?
SHINGG
SHRAKKA
SUPER SPACE
DO YOU REMEMBER, HONEY?
I DUNNO... MEBBA A WEEK, HUH?
A WEEK...?
UNFORTUNATELY, ALL OF THE OPEN ROOMS HAVE BEEN RENTED!
THIS IS ALL MY FAULT...WHY DID I TELL HIM THAT?

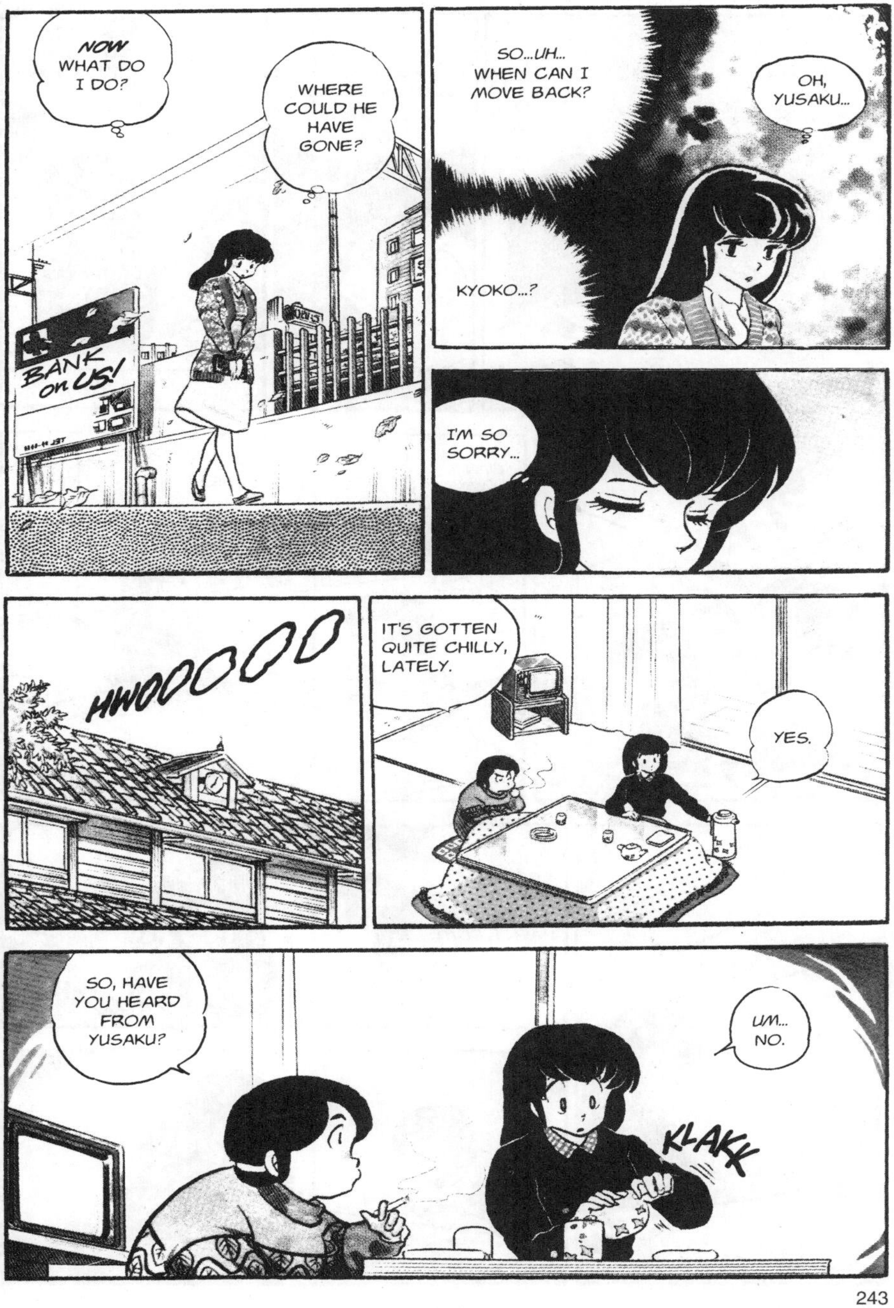
NOW WHAT DO I DO?
WHERE COULD HE HAVE GONE?
BANK on US!
SO...UH... WHEN CAN I MOVE BACK?
OH, YUSAKU...
KYOKO...?
I'M SO SORRY...
HWOOOOOO
IT'S GOTTEN QUITE CHILLY, LATELY.
YES.
SO, HAVE YOU HEARD FROM YUSAKU?
UM... NO.
KLAKK

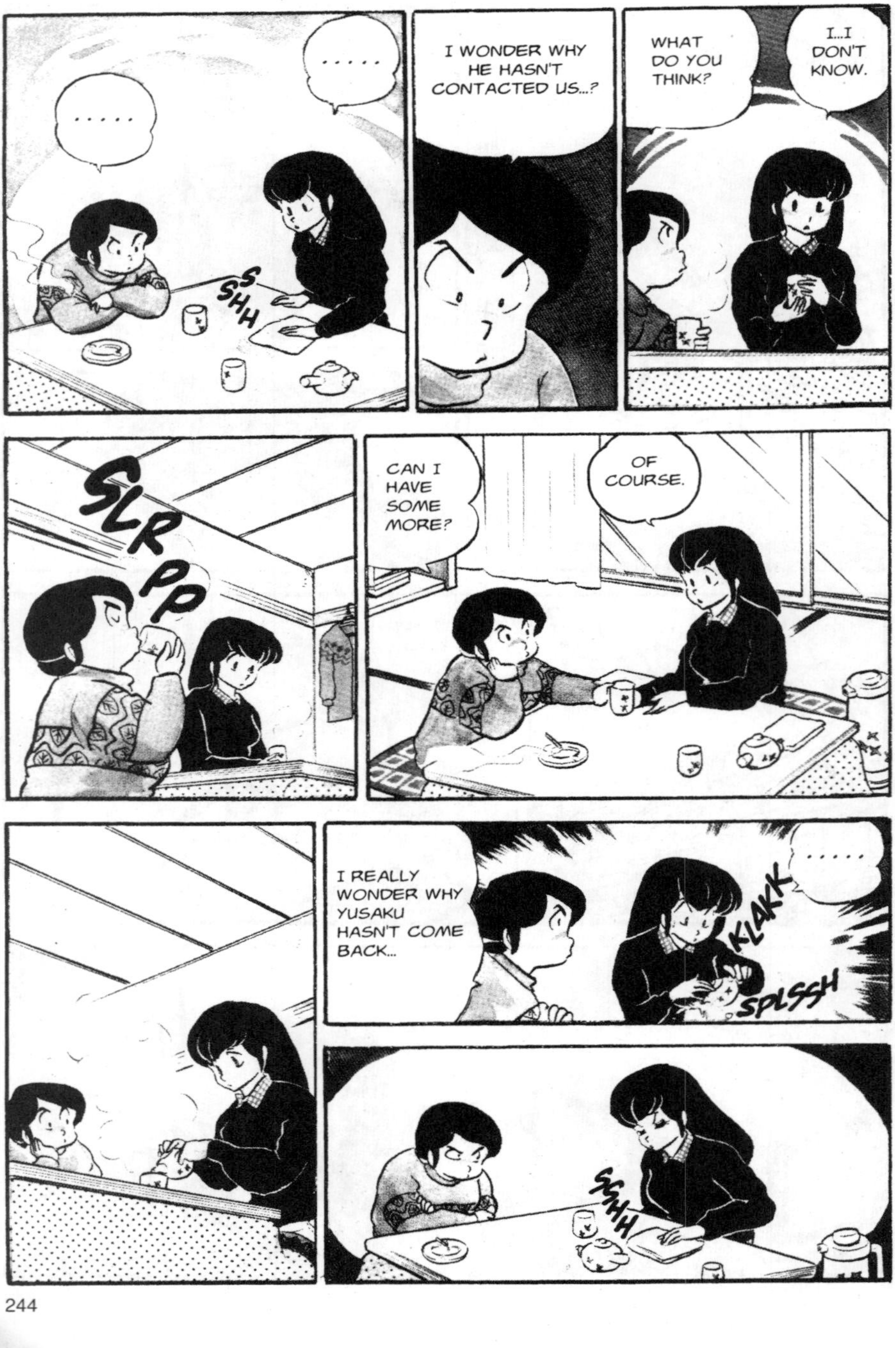
......
......
SSHH
I WONDER WHY HE HASN'T CONTACTED US...?
WHAT DO YOU THINK?
I...I DON'T KNOW.
SLRPP
CAN I HAVE SOME MORE?
OF COURSE.
I REALLY WONDER WHY YUSAKU HASN'T COME BACK...
......
KLAKK
SPLSSH
SSHH

HEY, YOU!

W-WHAT? WHAT?

ALL RIGHT, WHAT DID YOU DO?

W-WHAT DO YOU MEAN?

LOOK, MAYBE YOU CAN FOOL THE REST OF THE WORLD, BUT I KNOW YOU BETTER THAN THAT.

.....

SO WHAT HAPPENED?

C'MON, YOU CAN TELL ME.

B... BUT...

LOOK, IF I KNOW WHAT HAPPENED, MAYBE WE CAN DO SOMETHING ABOUT IT...

...IF WE PUT OUR HEADS TOGETHER.

YOU REALLY THINK SO?

WELL, THEN...

245

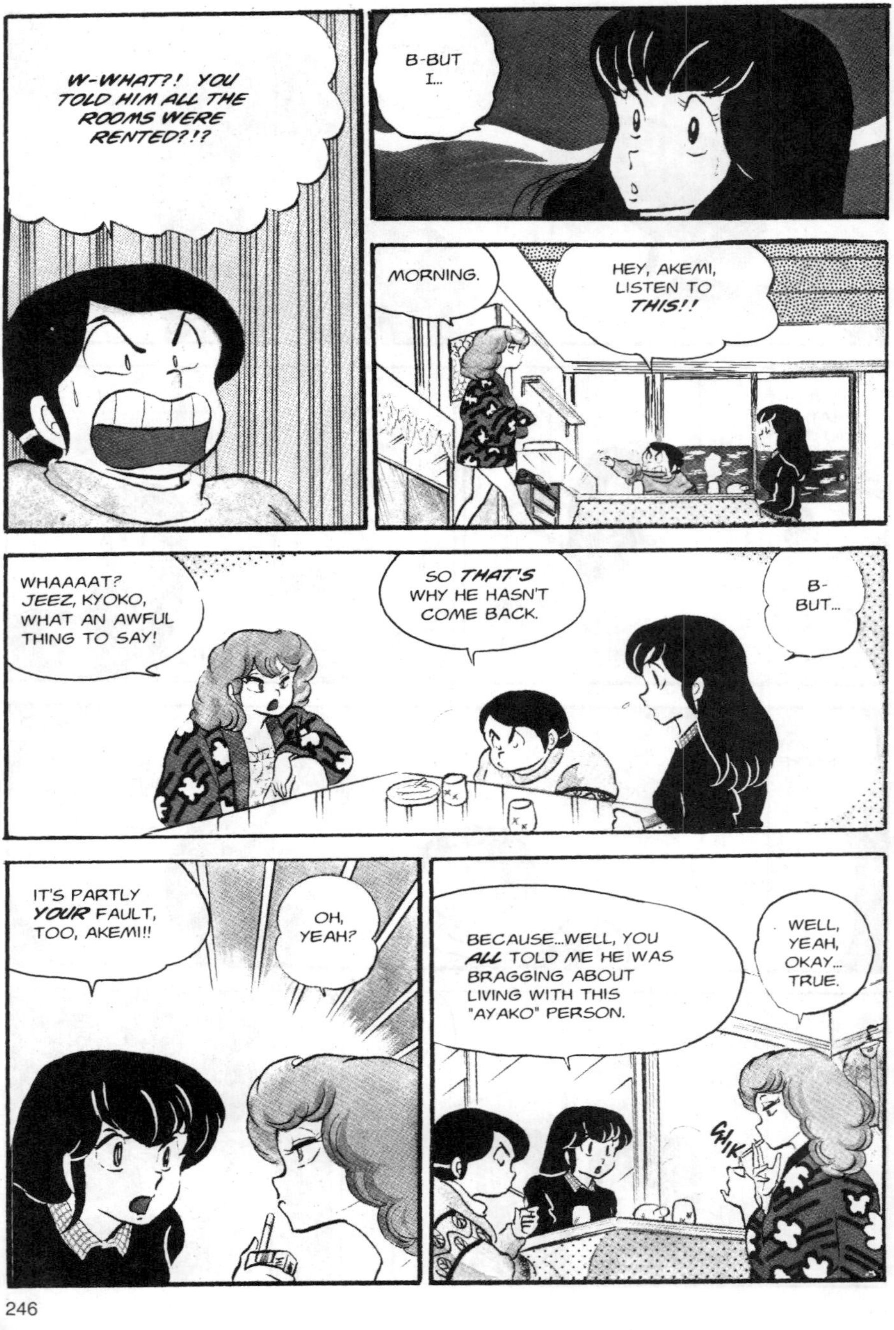
W-WHAT?! YOU TOLD HIM ALL THE ROOMS WERE RENTED?!?
B-BUT I...
MORNING.
HEY, AKEMI, LISTEN TO THIS!!
WHAAAAT? JEEZ, KYOKO, WHAT AN AWFUL THING TO SAY!
SO THAT'S WHY HE HASN'T COME BACK.
B-BUT...
IT'S PARTLY YOUR FAULT, TOO, AKEMI!!
OH, YEAH?
BECAUSE...WELL, YOU ALL TOLD ME HE WAS BRAGGING ABOUT LIVING WITH THIS "AYAKO" PERSON.
WELL, YEAH, OKAY... TRUE.
CHIK

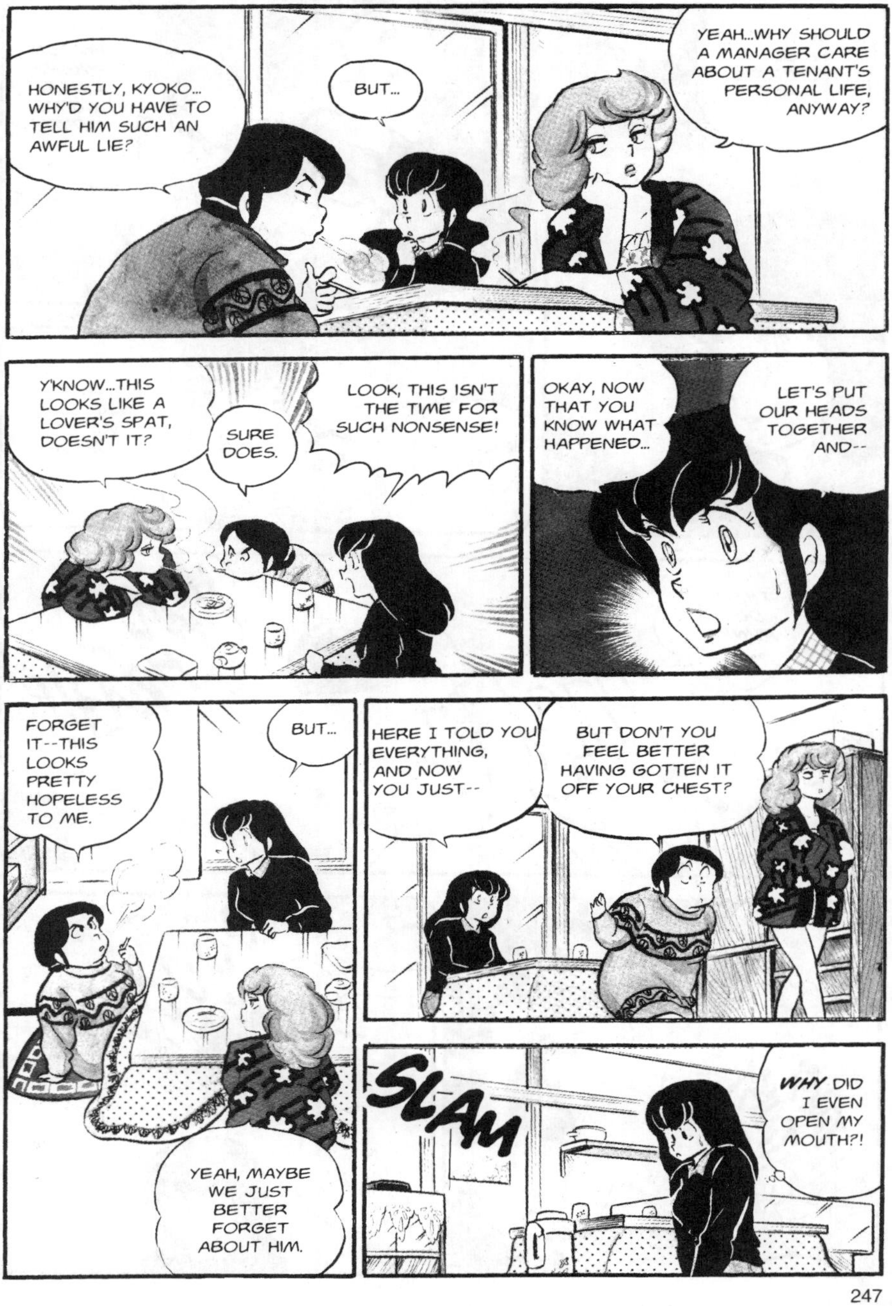
HONESTLY, KYOKO... WHY'D YOU HAVE TO TELL HIM SUCH AN AWFUL LIE?
BUT...
YEAH...WHY SHOULD A MANAGER CARE ABOUT A TENANT'S PERSONAL LIFE, ANYWAY?
Y'KNOW...THIS LOOKS LIKE A LOVER'S SPAT, DOESN'T IT?
SURE DOES.
LOOK, THIS ISN'T THE TIME FOR SUCH NONSENSE!
OKAY, NOW THAT YOU KNOW WHAT HAPPENED...
LET'S PUT OUR HEADS TOGETHER AND--
FORGET IT--THIS LOOKS PRETTY HOPELESS TO ME.
BUT...
YEAH, MAYBE WE JUST BETTER FORGET ABOUT HIM.
HERE I TOLD YOU EVERYTHING, AND NOW YOU JUST--
BUT DON'T YOU FEEL BETTER HAVING GOTTEN IT OFF YOUR CHEST?
SLAM
WHY DID I EVEN OPEN MY MOUTH?!

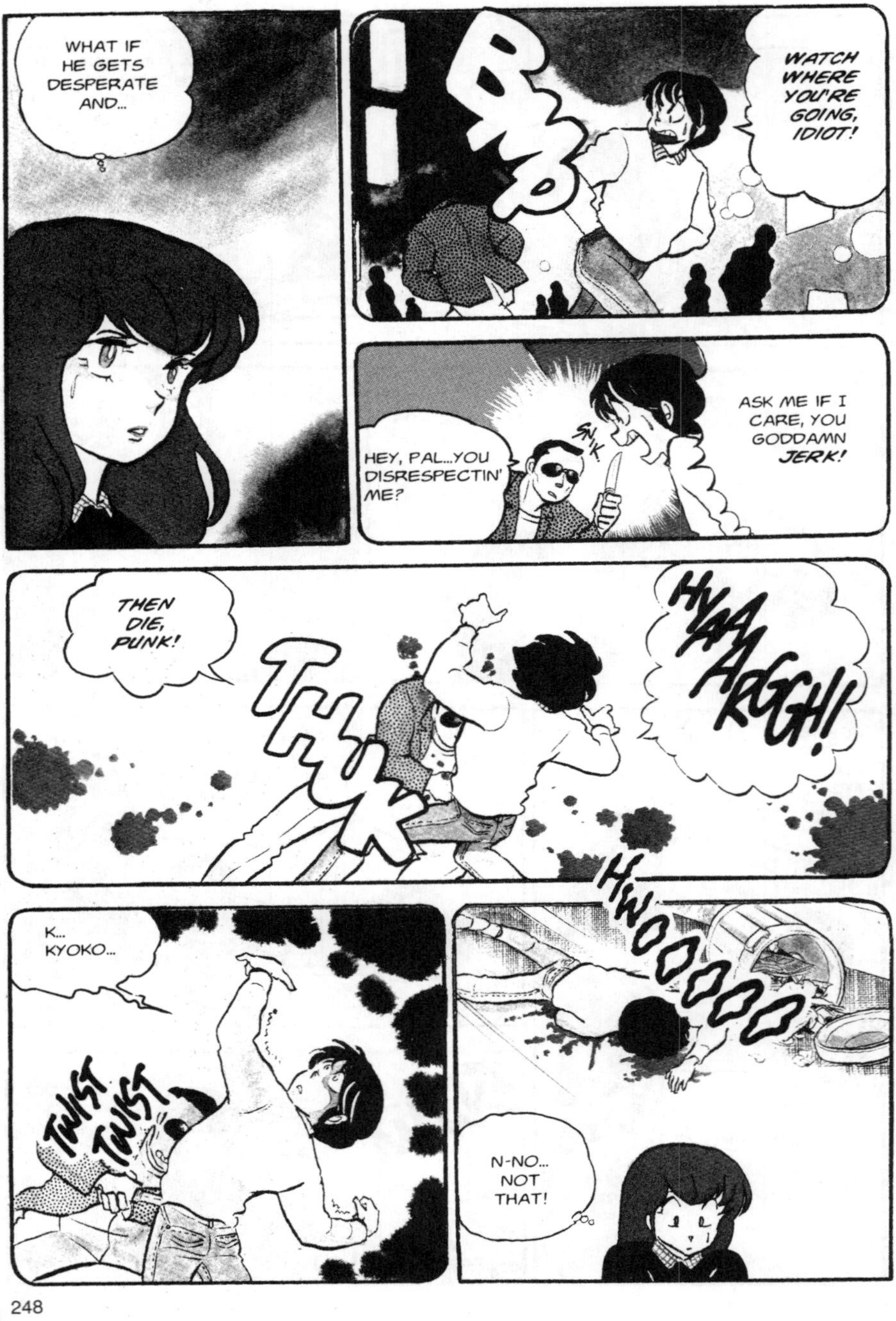
WHAT IF HE GETS DESPERATE AND...
BMP
WATCH WHERE YOU'RE GOING, IDIOT!
HEY, PAL...YOU DISRESPECTIN' ME?
SNIK
ASK ME IF I CARE, YOU GODDAMN JERK!
THEN DIE, PUNK!
THUK
HYAAARGGH!
K... KYOKO...
TWIST TWIST
HWOOOOOO
N-NO... NOT THAT!

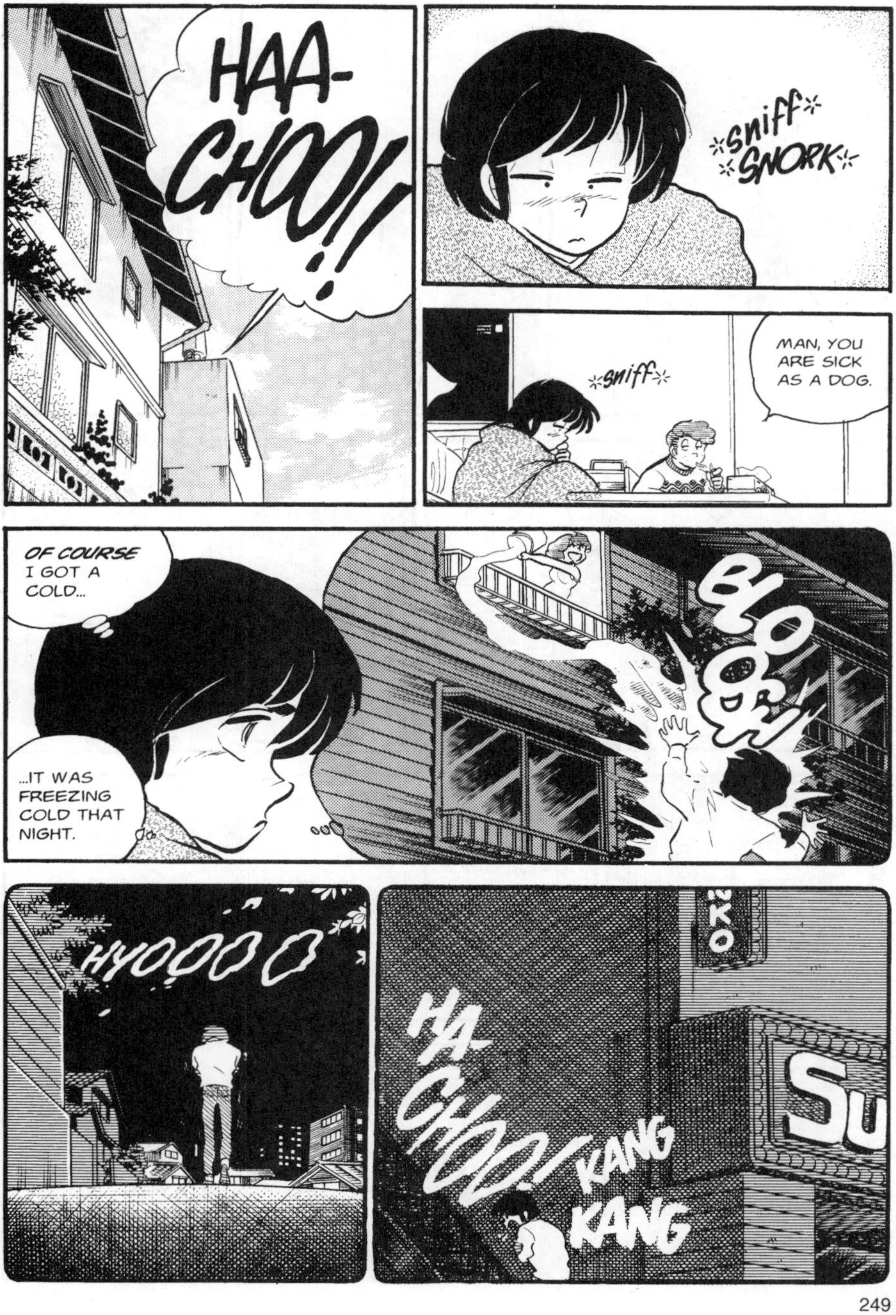
HAA-CHOO!!
sniff
SNORK
sniff
MAN, YOU ARE SICK AS A DOG.
OF COURSE I GOT A COLD...
...IT WAS FREEZING COLD THAT NIGHT.
BLOOSH!
HYOOOO
HA-CHOO!
KANG
KANG

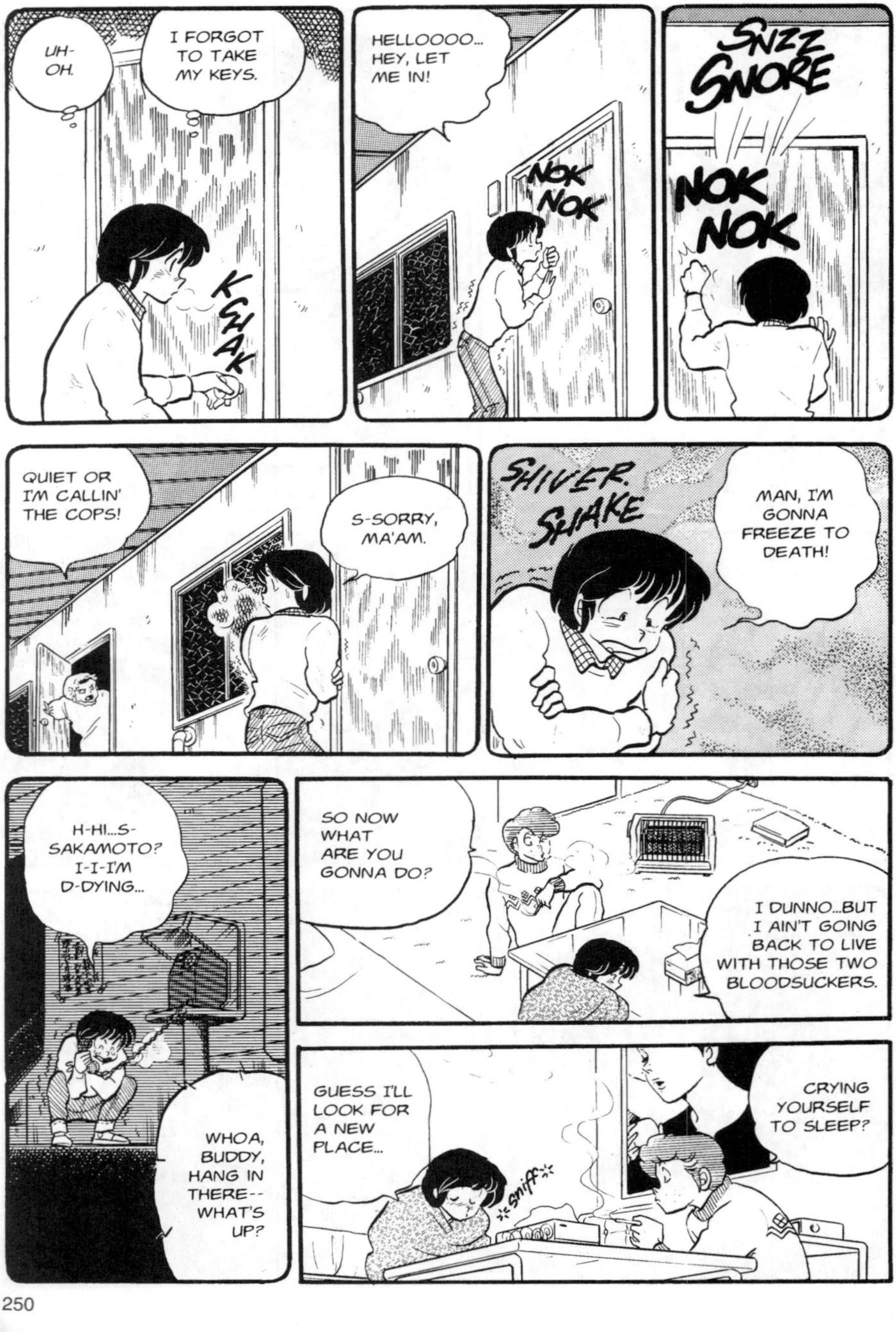
UH-OH.
I FORGOT TO TAKE MY KEYS.
KCHAK
HELLOOOO... HEY, LET ME IN!
NOK NOK
SNZZ SNORE
NOK NOK
QUIET OR I'M CALLIN' THE COPS!
S-SORRY, MA'AM.
SHIVER. SHAKE
MAN, I'M GONNA FREEZE TO DEATH!
H-HI...S-SAKAMOTO? I-I-I'M D-DYING...
WHOA, BUDDY, HANG IN THERE--WHAT'S UP?
SO NOW WHAT ARE YOU GONNA DO?
I DUNNO...BUT I AIN'T GOING BACK TO LIVE WITH THOSE TWO BLOODSUCKERS.
GUESS I'LL LOOK FOR A NEW PLACE...
sniff
CRYING YOURSELF TO SLEEP?

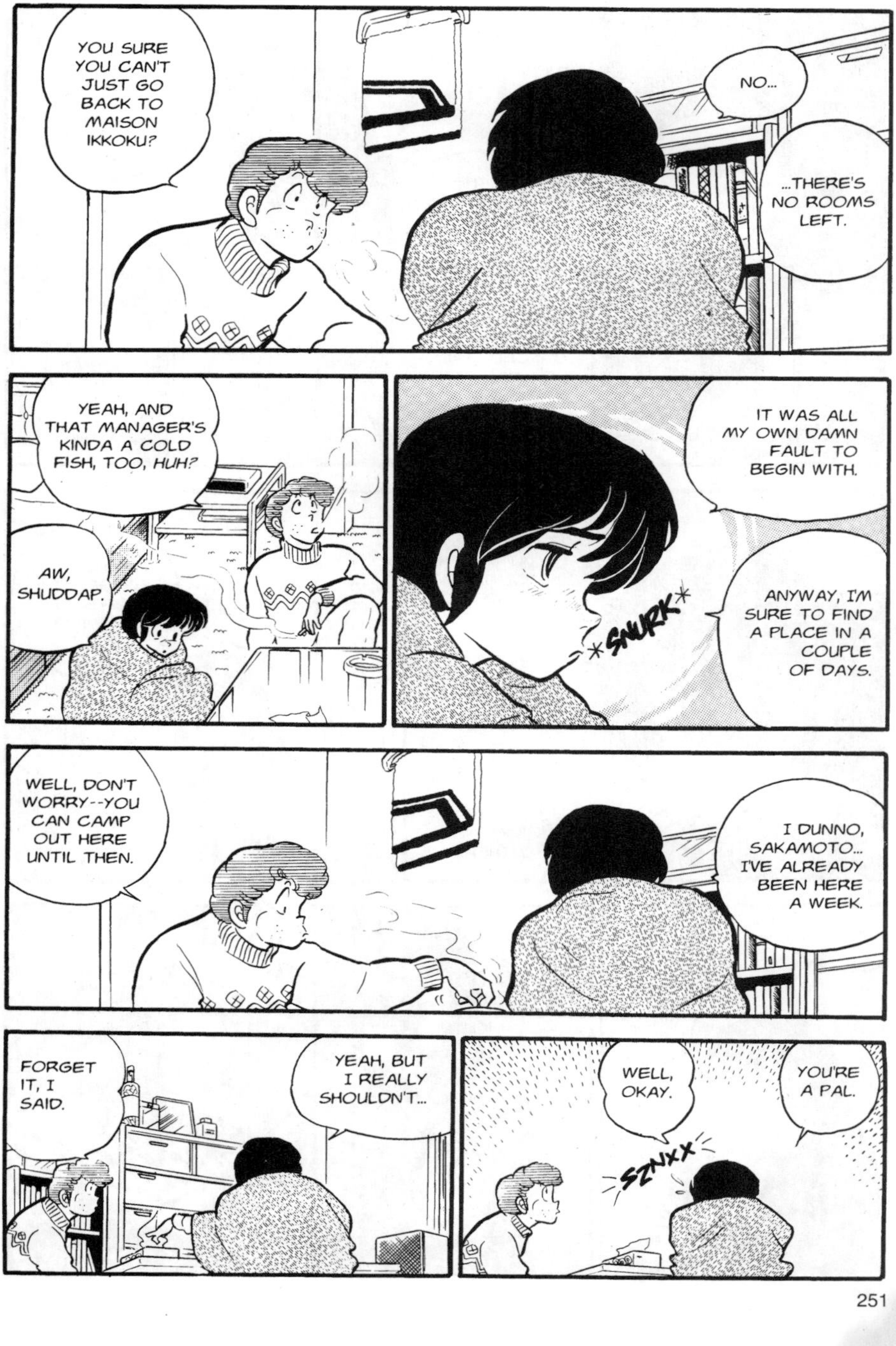
YOU SURE YOU CAN'T JUST GO BACK TO MAISON IKKOKU?
NO...
...THERE'S NO ROOMS LEFT.
YEAH, AND THAT MANAGER'S KINDA A COLD FISH, TOO, *HUH?*
AW, SHUDDAP.
IT WAS ALL MY OWN DAMN FAULT TO BEGIN WITH.
SNURK
ANYWAY, I'M SURE TO FIND A PLACE IN A COUPLE OF DAYS.
WELL, DON'T WORRY--YOU CAN CAMP OUT HERE UNTIL THEN.
I DUNNO, SAKAMOTO... I'VE ALREADY BEEN HERE A WEEK.
FORGET IT, I SAID.
YEAH, BUT I REALLY SHOULDN'T...
WELL, OKAY.
SZNXX
YOU'RE A PAL.

HELLO, MR. OTONASHI...?

KYOKO HERE. *UMM...IS YUSAKU THERE?*

TODAY'S THE DAY HE TUTORS IKUKO, RIGHT?

YUSAKU GODAI?

WELL, DEAR, HE CALLED IN TO CANCEL--SAID HE HAD A BAD COLD.

HIS VOICE SOUNDED TERRIBLE.

HE...HE'S REALLY SICK?

HE SOUNDED LIKE HE WAS AT DEATH'S DOOR, IN MY OPINION.

ISN'T HE THERE?

DID SOMETHING HAPPEN TO HIM?

N-NO... FORGET IT. THANKS, MR. OTONASHI.

SICK...

I WONDER WHY...?

KLIK

KOFF KOFF

HADDDD

KOFF
STAGGER...
WHDD

KOFF
KOFF KOFF

K...KYOKO...

KANGG

N-NO... NOT THAT!

HWOOOO

HOW COME THINGS HAD TO TURN OUT LIKE THIS?

WURF
BOWF

IF I COULD ONLY SEE HIM JUST ONCE MORE...

...SO I COULD APOLOGIZE.

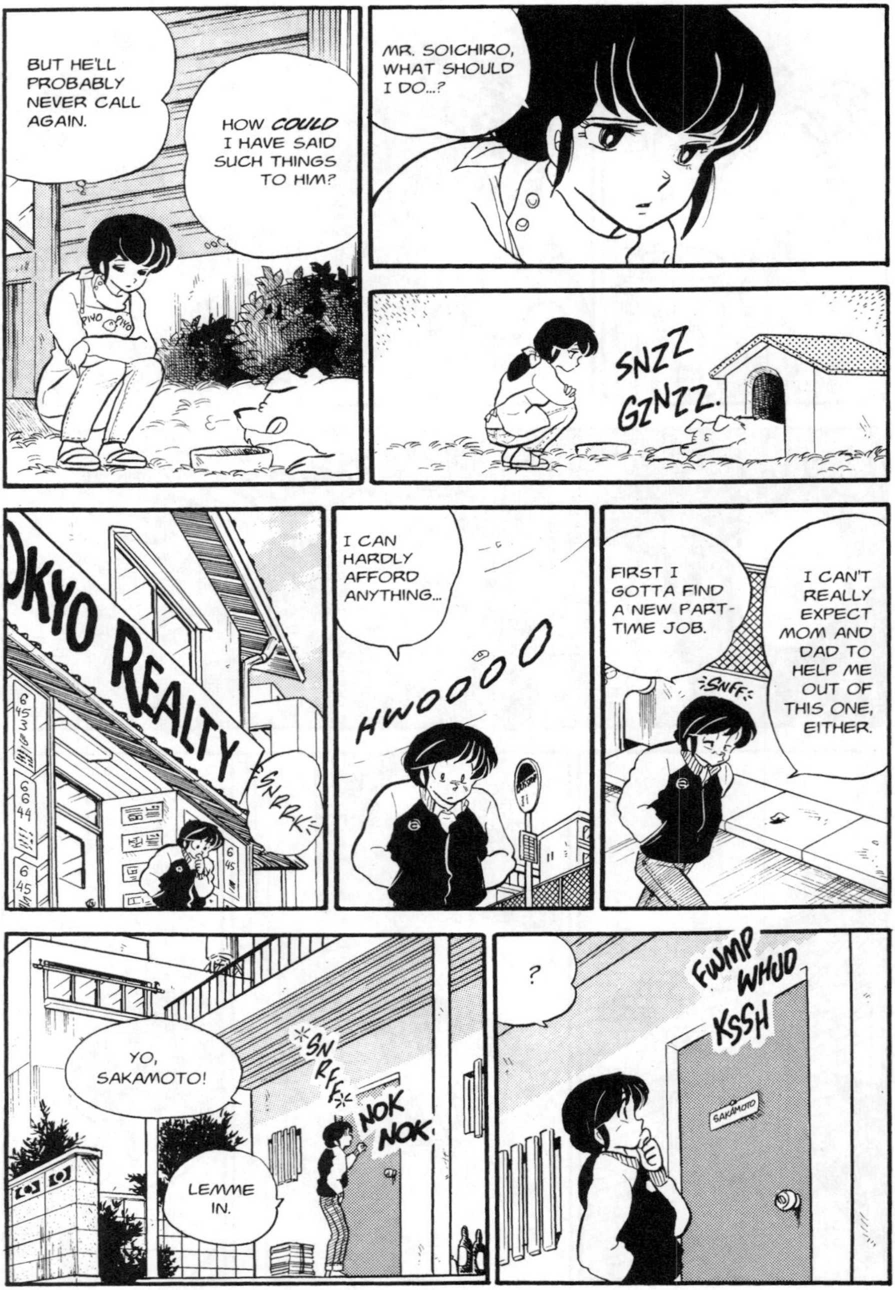
BUT HE'LL PROBABLY NEVER CALL AGAIN.
HOW COULD I HAVE SAID SUCH THINGS TO HIM?
MR. SOICHIRO, WHAT SHOULD I DO...?
SNZZ GZNZZ
OKYO REALTY
SNRRK
I CAN HARDLY AFFORD ANYTHING...
HWOOOOO
FIRST I GOTTA FIND A NEW PART-TIME JOB.
SNFF
I CAN'T REALLY EXPECT MOM AND DAD TO HELP ME OUT OF THIS ONE, EITHER.
YO, SAKAMOTO!
SNRFF
NOK NOK
LEMME IN.
?
FWUMP WHUD
KSSH
SAKAMOTO

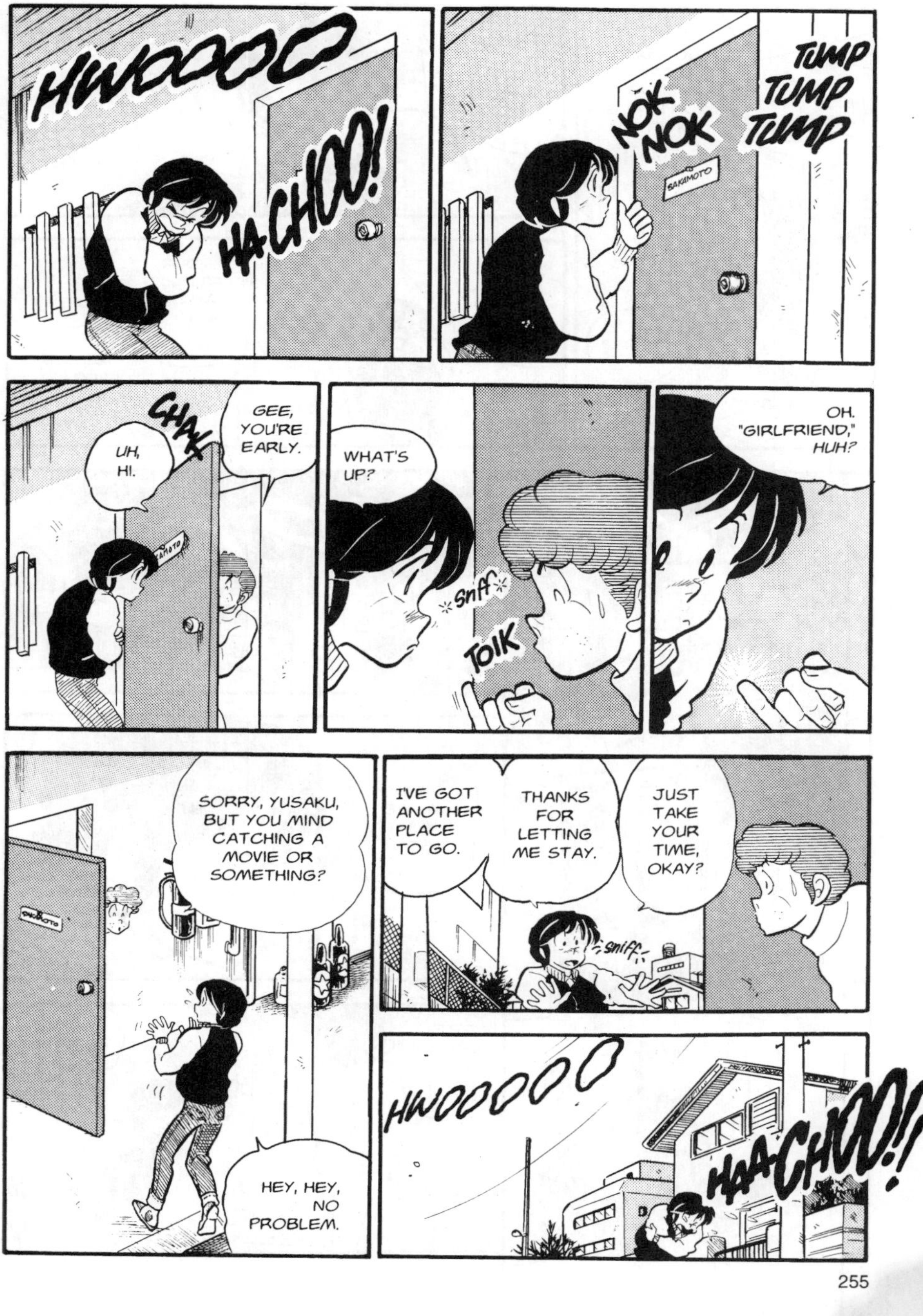
HWOOOOO
HACHOO!
NOK NOK
TUMP TUMP TUMP
SAKAMOTO
UH, HI.
CHAK
GEE, YOU'RE EARLY.
WHAT'S UP?
Sniff
TOIK
OH. "GIRLFRIEND," HUH?
SORRY, YUSAKU, BUT YOU MIND CATCHING A MOVIE OR SOMETHING?
HEY, HEY, NO PROBLEM.
I'VE GOT ANOTHER PLACE TO GO.
THANKS FOR LETTING ME STAY.
JUST TAKE YOUR TIME, OKAY?
sniff
HWOOOOOO
HAACHOO!!

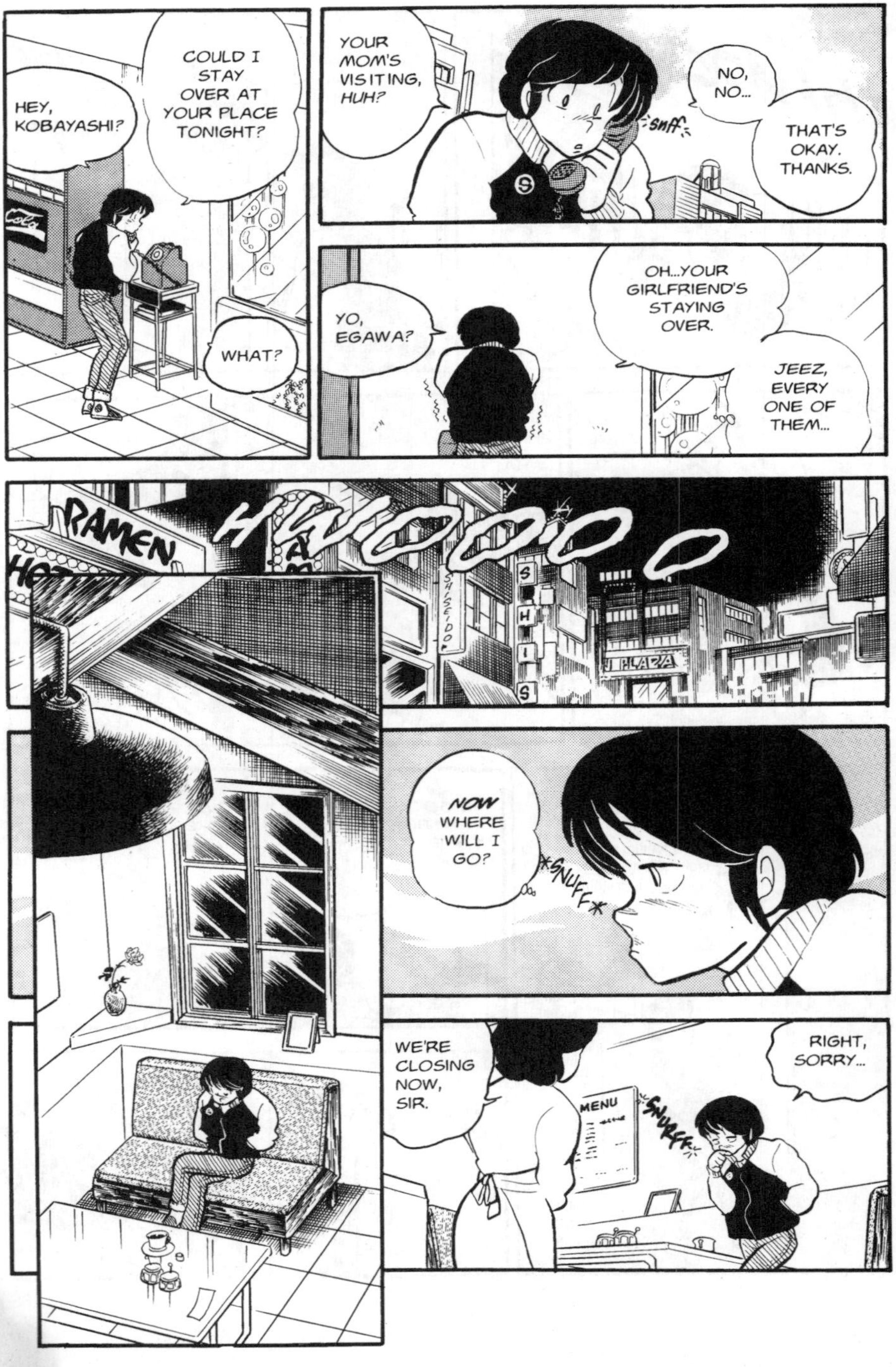
HEY, KOBAYASHI?
COULD I STAY OVER AT YOUR PLACE TONIGHT?
Cola
WHAT?
YOUR MOM'S VISITING, HUH?
NO, NO...
snff
THAT'S OKAY. THANKS.
YO, EGAWA?
OH...YOUR GIRLFRIEND'S STAYING OVER.
JEEZ, EVERY ONE OF THEM...
RAMEN
HWOOOOO
SHISEIDO
SHIS
PLAZA
NOW WHERE WILL I GO?
SNUFF
WE'RE CLOSING NOW, SIR.
MENU
SNUFF
RIGHT, SORRY...

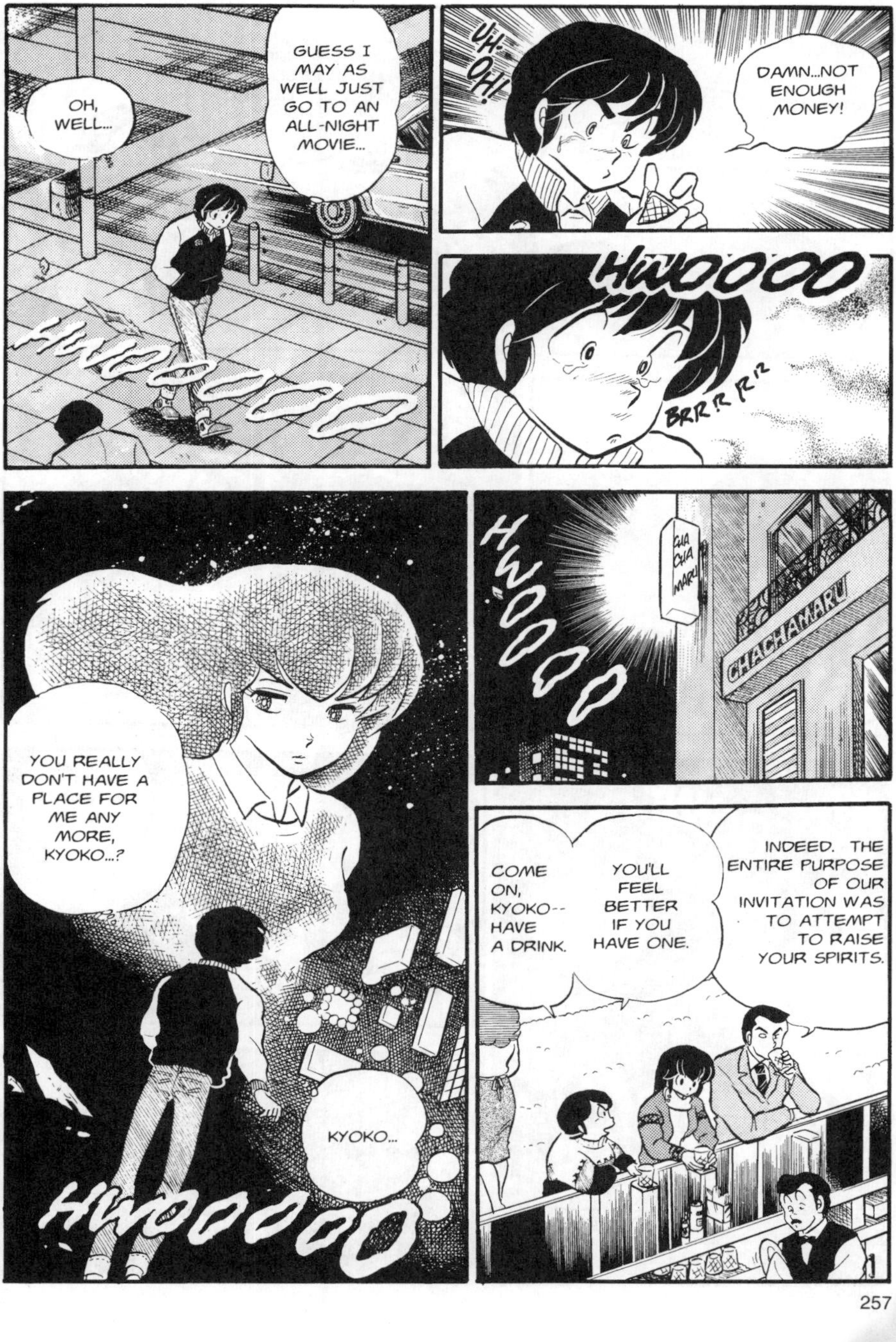
OH, WELL...
GUESS I MAY AS WELL JUST GO TO AN ALL-NIGHT MOVIE...
HWOOOOOOOO
UH-OH!
DAMN...NOT ENOUGH MONEY!
HWOOOOO
BRRRRR
YOU REALLY DON'T HAVE A PLACE FOR ME ANY MORE, KYOKO...?
KYOKO...
HWOOOOOO
HWOOOOO
CHA CHA MARU
CHACHAMARU
COME ON, KYOKO-- HAVE A DRINK.
YOU'LL FEEL BETTER IF YOU HAVE ONE.
INDEED. THE ENTIRE PURPOSE OF OUR INVITATION WAS TO ATTEMPT TO RAISE YOUR SPIRITS.

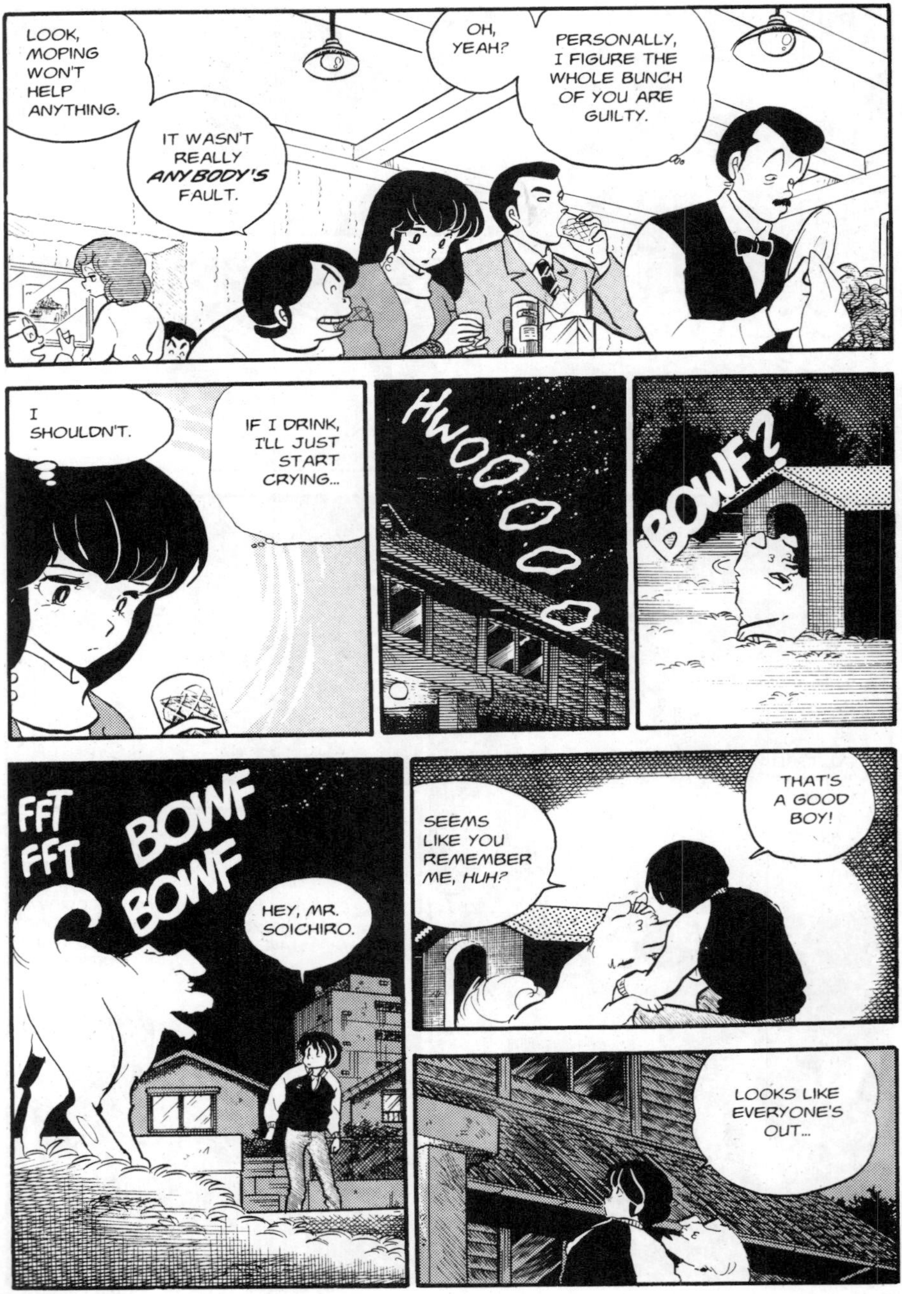
LOOK, MOPING WON'T HELP ANYTHING.
IT WASN'T REALLY ANYBODY'S FAULT.
OH, YEAH?
PERSONALLY, I FIGURE THE WHOLE BUNCH OF YOU ARE GUILTY.
I SHOULDN'T.
IF I DRINK, I'LL JUST START CRYING...
HWOOOOOOO
BOWF?
FFT FFT
BOWF BOWF
HEY, MR. SOICHIRO.
SEEMS LIKE YOU REMEMBER ME, HUH?
THAT'S A GOOD BOY!
LOOKS LIKE EVERYONE'S OUT...

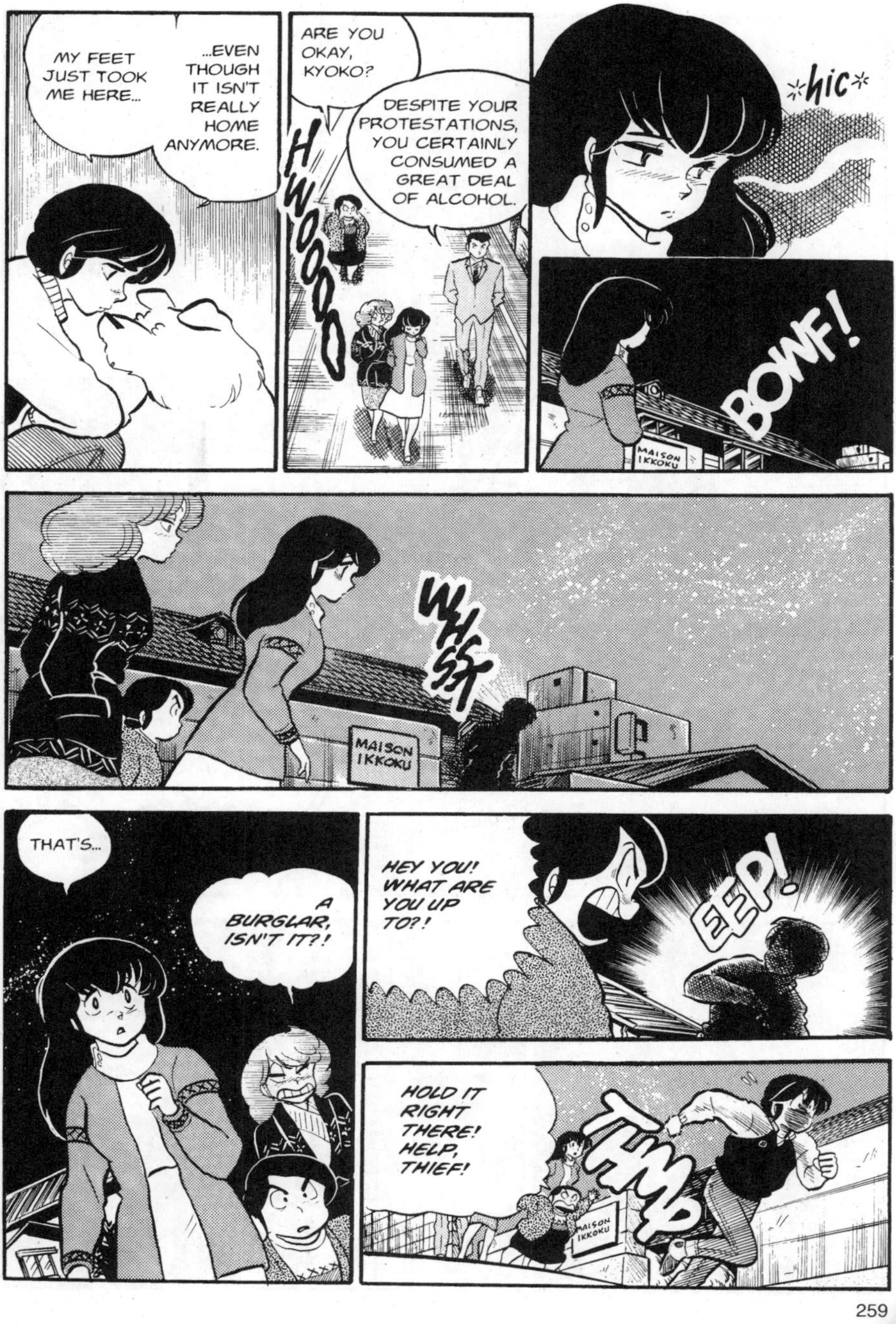
MY FEET JUST TOOK ME HERE...
...EVEN THOUGH IT ISN'T REALLY HOME ANYMORE.
ARE YOU OKAY, KYOKO?
HWOOOOO
DESPITE YOUR PROTESTATIONS, YOU CERTAINLY CONSUMED A GREAT DEAL OF ALCOHOL.
hic
BOWF!
MAISON IKKOKU
MAISON IKKOKU
WHSSST
THAT'S...
A BURGLAR, ISN'T IT?!
HEY YOU! WHAT ARE YOU UP TO?!
EEP!
HOLD IT RIGHT THERE! HELP, THIEF!
THMP
MAISON IKKOKU

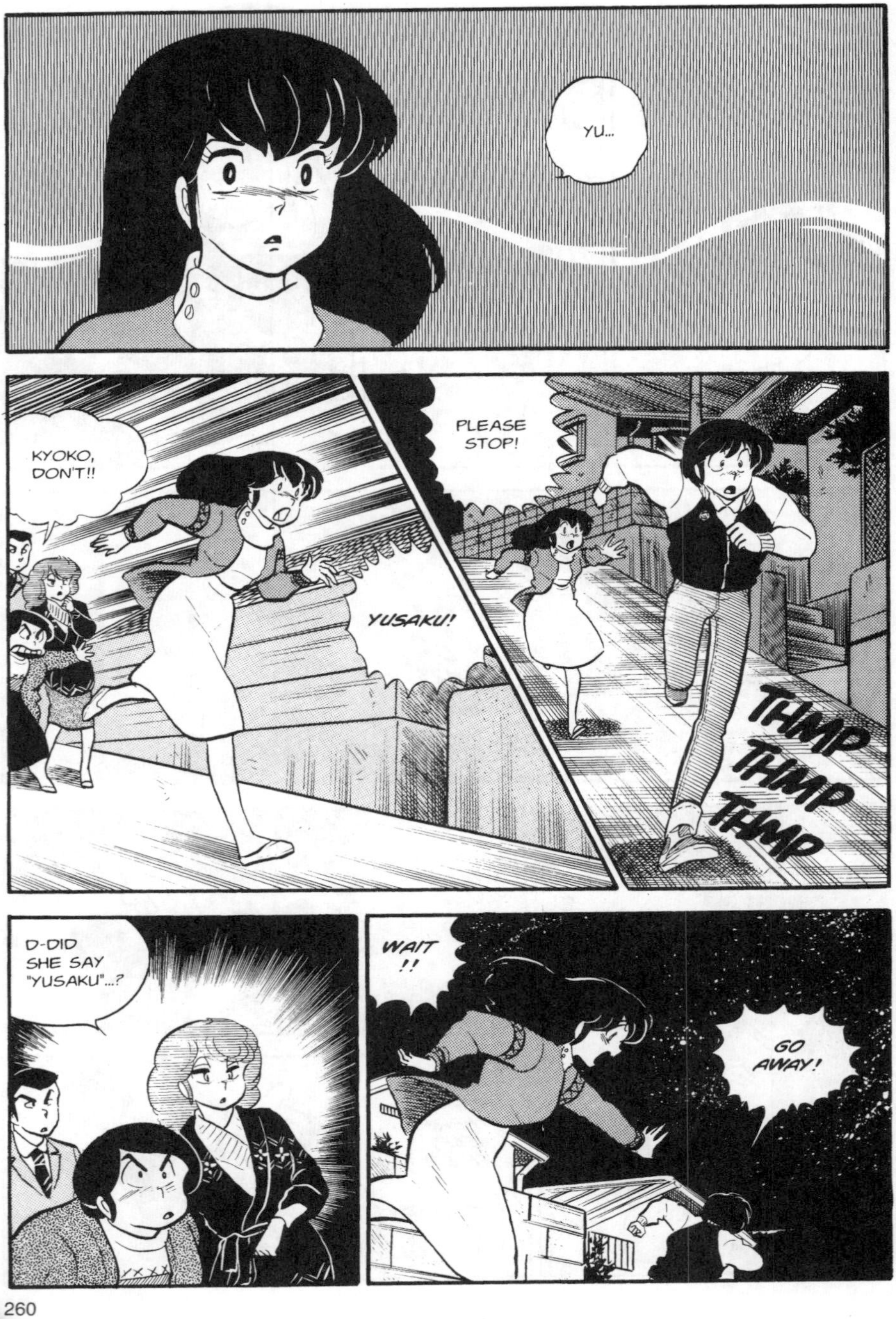
YU...
KYOKO, DON'T!!
YUSAKU!
PLEASE STOP!
THMP THMP THMP
D-DID SHE SAY "YUSAKU"...?
WAIT !!
GO AWAY!

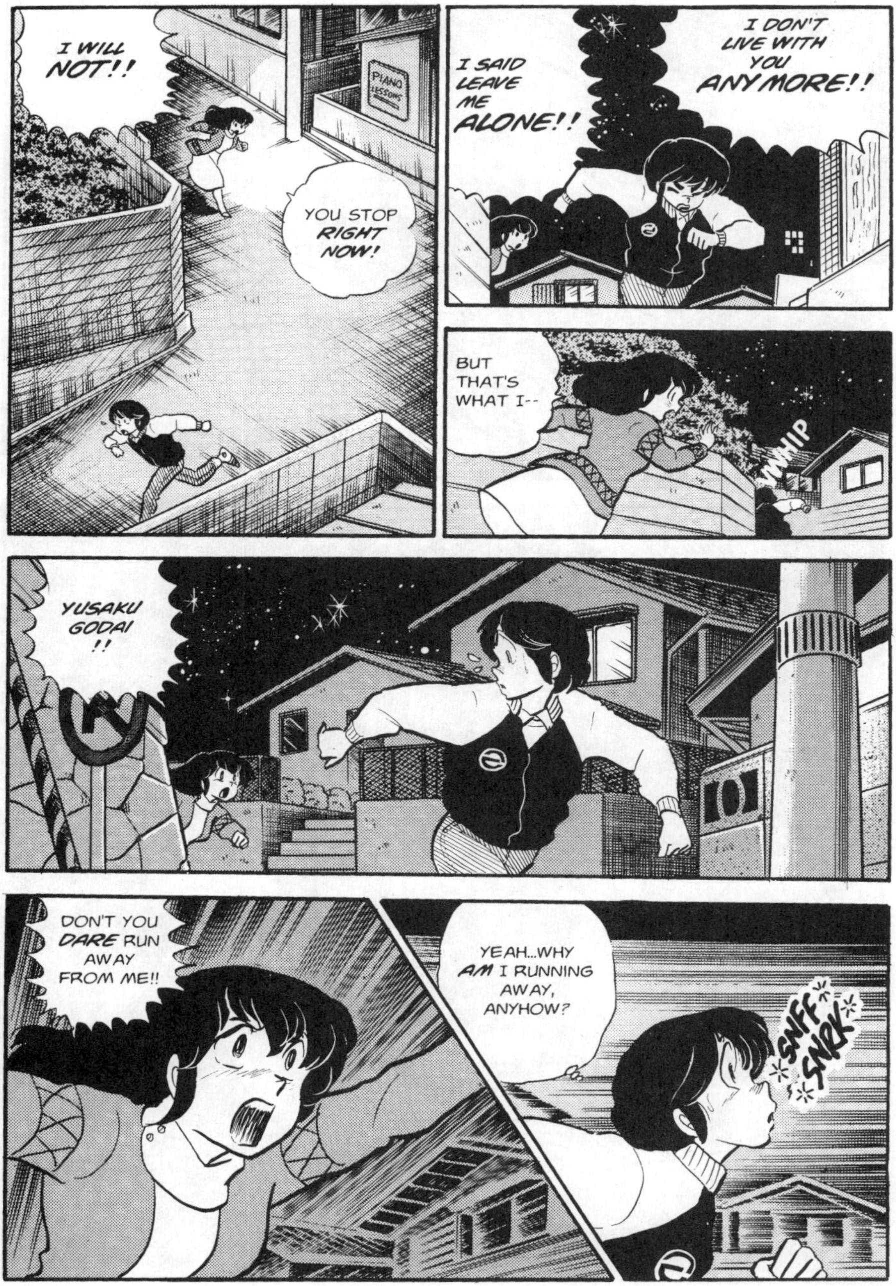
I WILL NOT!!
YOU STOP RIGHT NOW!
I SAID LEAVE ME ALONE!!
I DON'T LIVE WITH YOU ANYMORE!!
BUT THAT'S WHAT I--
WHIP
YUSAKU GODAI!!
DON'T YOU DARE RUN AWAY FROM ME!!
YEAH...WHY AM I RUNNING AWAY, ANYHOW?
SNFF SNRK

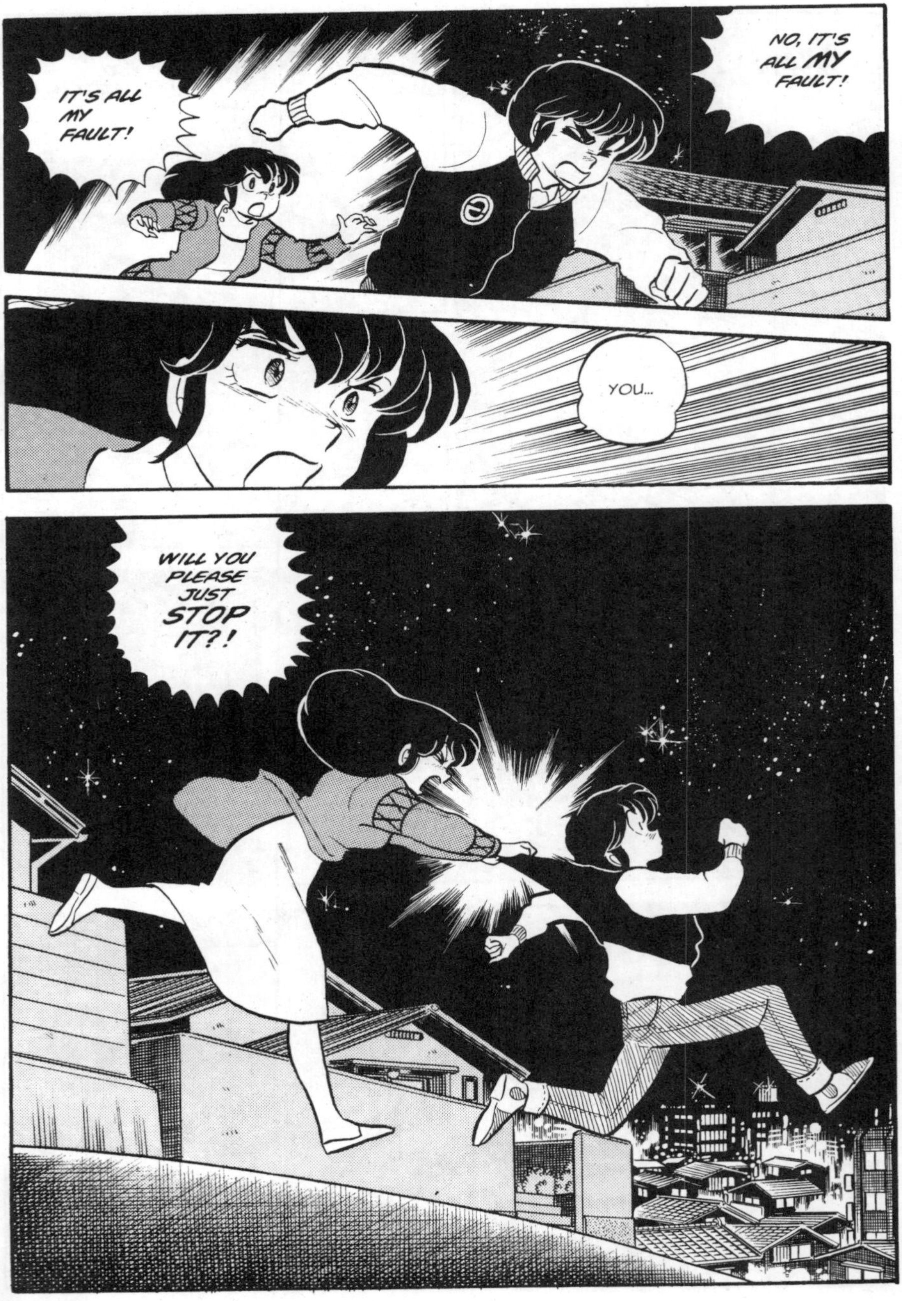
IT'S ALL MY FAULT!
NO, IT'S ALL MY FAULT!
YOU...
WILL YOU PLEASE JUST STOP IT?!

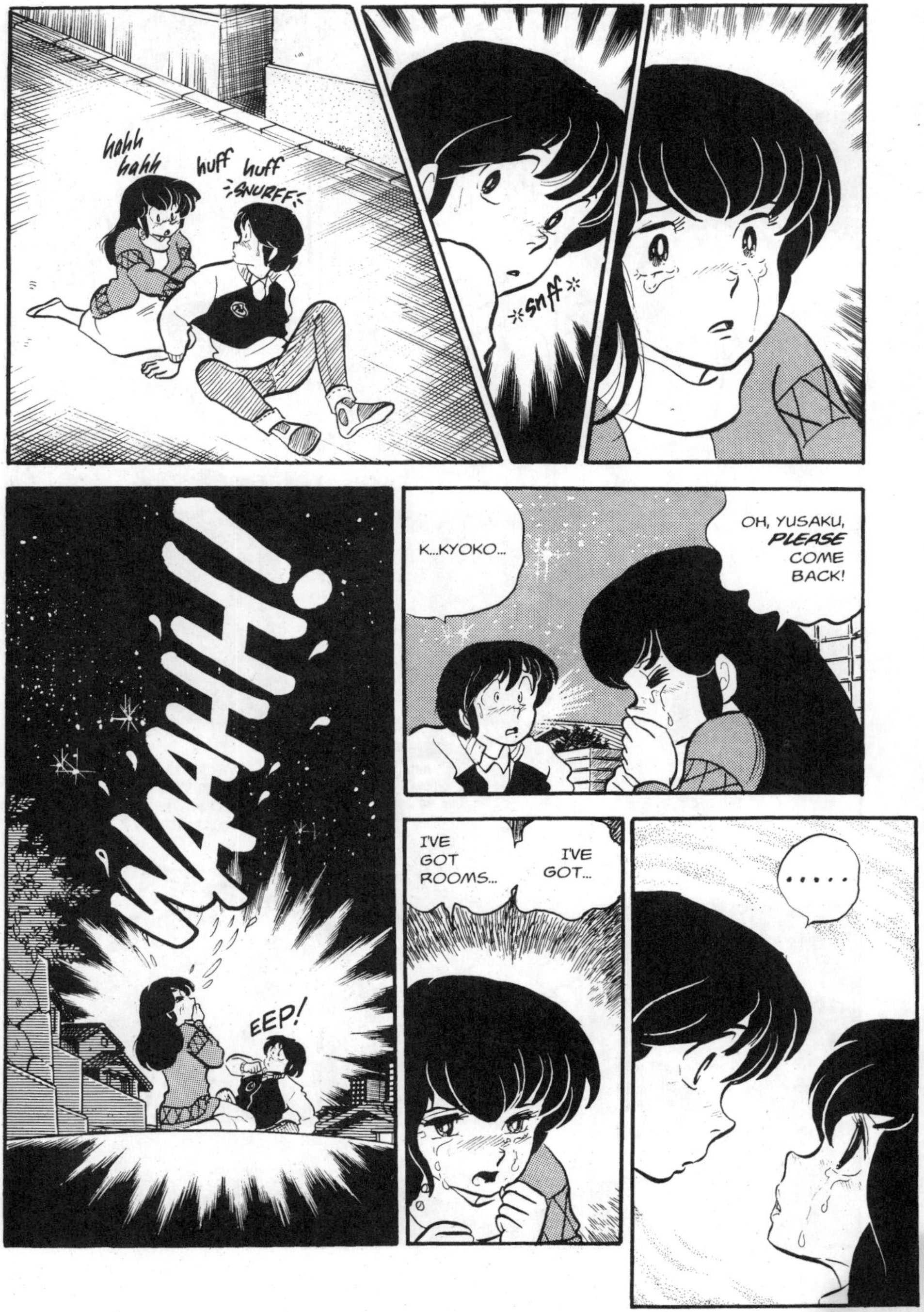
hahh hahh
huff huff
SNURFF
snff
WAAH!
EEP!
K...KYOKO...
OH, YUSAKU, PLEASE COME BACK!
I'VE GOT ROOMS...
I'VE GOT...
.....

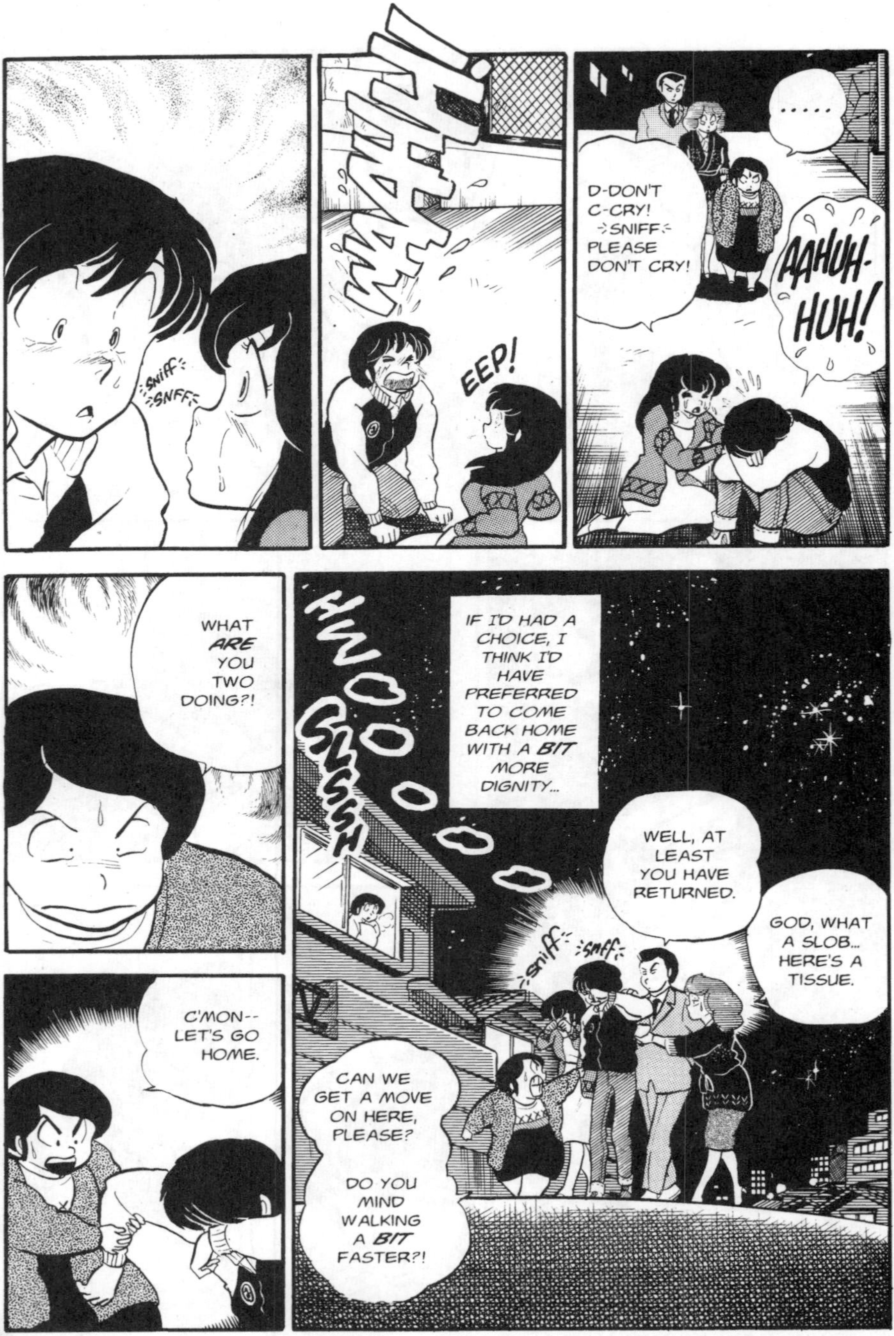
SNIFF
SNFF
WAAHH!
EEP!
D-DON'T C-CRY! SNIFF PLEASE DON'T CRY!
......
AAHUH-HUH!
WHAT ARE YOU TWO DOING?!
C'MON-- LET'S GO HOME.
HWOOOSH
SLSSH
IF I'D HAD A CHOICE, I THINK I'D HAVE PREFERRED TO COME BACK HOME WITH A BIT MORE DIGNITY...
WELL, AT LEAST YOU HAVE RETURNED.
GOD, WHAT A SLOB... HERE'S A TISSUE.
SNIFF
SNFF
CAN WE GET A MOVE ON HERE, PLEASE?
DO YOU MIND WALKING A BIT FASTER?!

END. MAISON IKOKU, "HOME SWEET HOME"